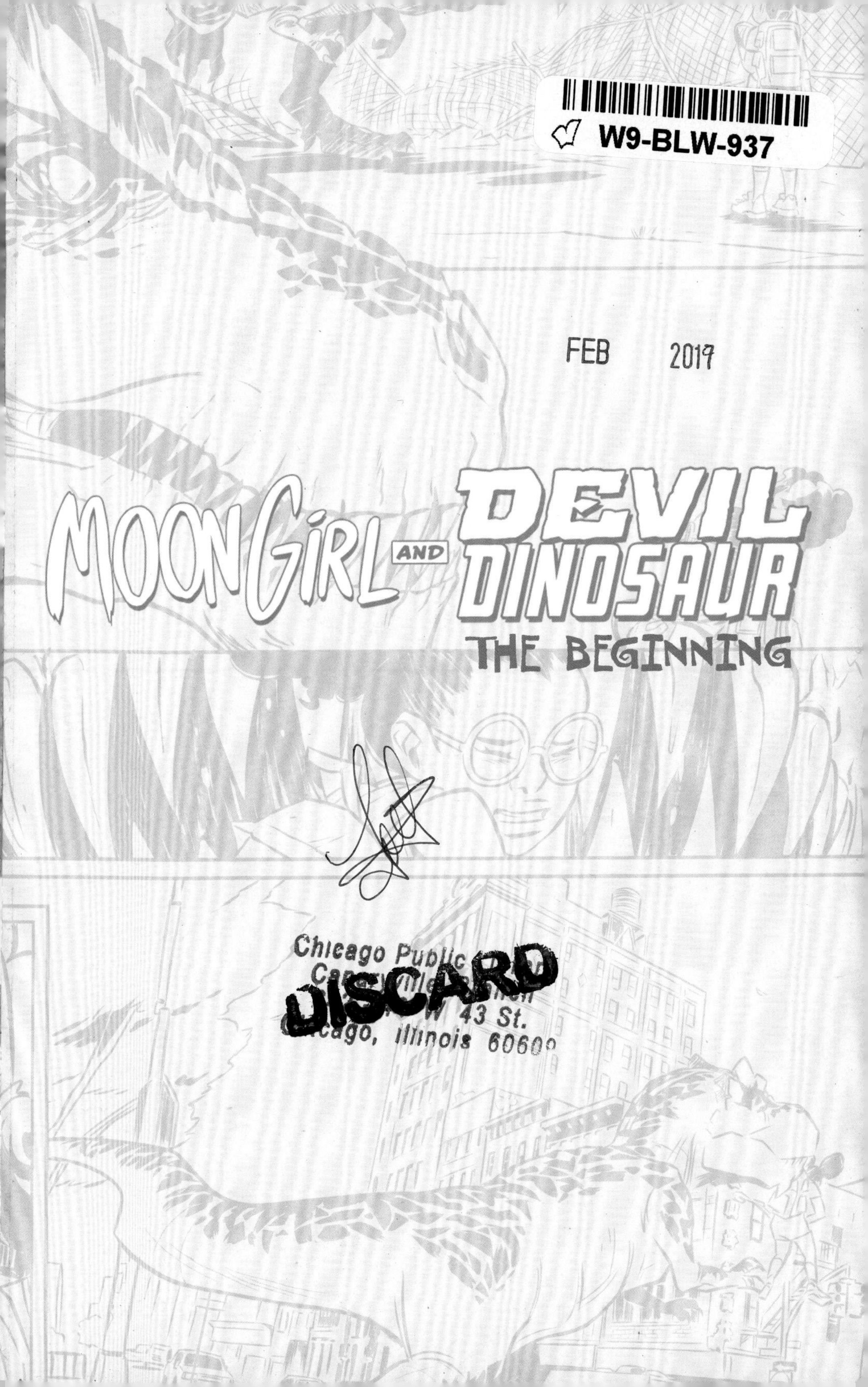

MOON GIRL AND DEVIL DINOSAUR
THE BEGINNING

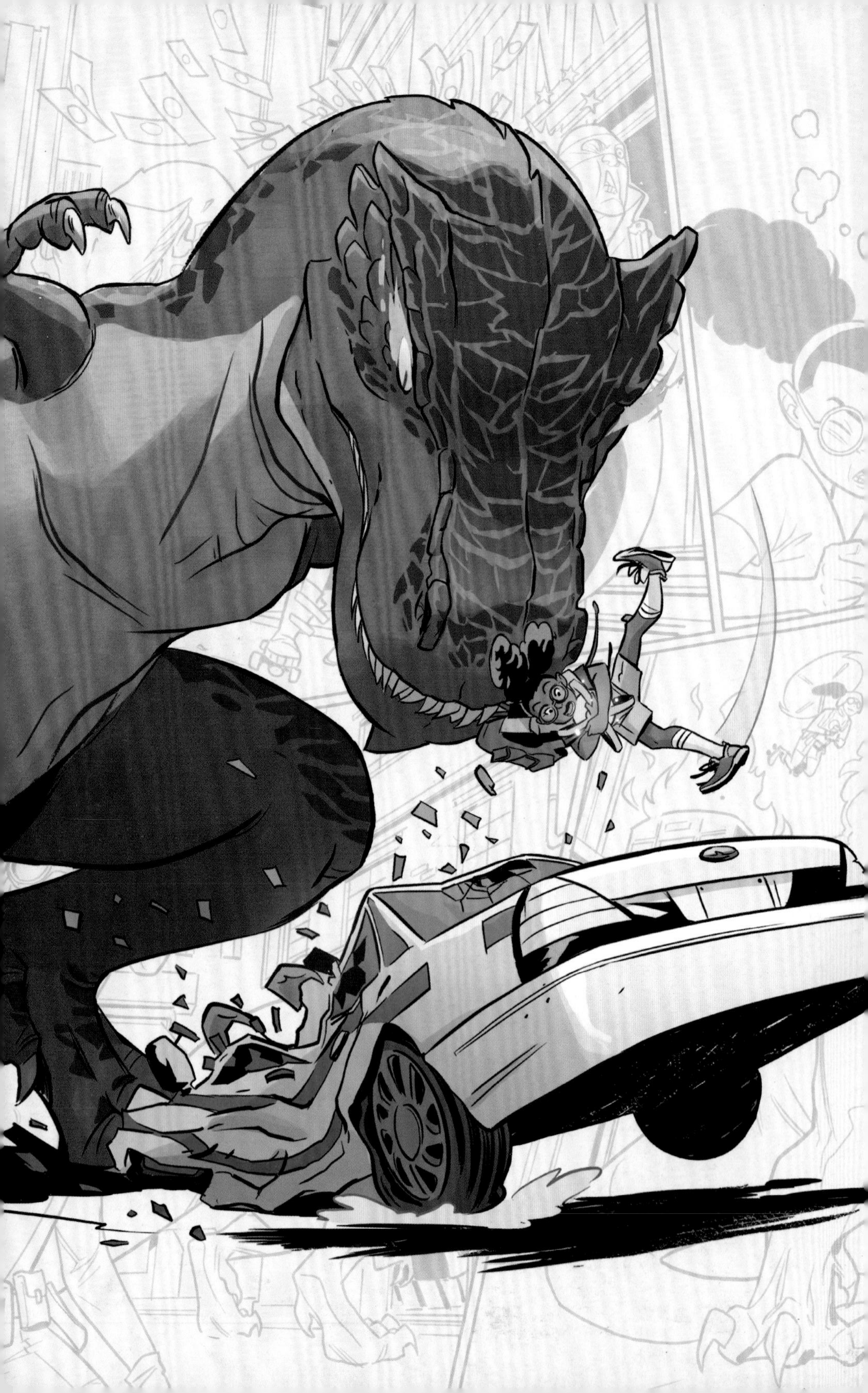

MOON GIRL AND DEVIL DINOSAUR

THE BEGINNING

writers
BRANDON MONTCLARE & AMY REEDER
artists
NATACHA BUSTOS (#1-6, #8-12)
& MARCO FAILLA (#7)
color artist
TAMRA BONVILLAIN
letterer
VC's TRAVIS LANHAM
cover art
AMY REEDER
assistant editor
CHRIS ROBINSON
editors
MARK PANICCIA & EMILY SHAW

Special thanks to Sana Amanat & David Gabriel

DEVIL DINOSAUR CREATED BY JACK KIRBY

collection editor JENNIFER GRÜNWALD
assistant editor CAITLIN O'CONNELL • associate managing editor KATERI WOODY
editor, special projects MARK D. BEAZLEY • vp production & special projects JEFF YOUNGQUIST
svp print, sales & marketing DAVID GABRIEL

editor in chief C.B. CEBULSKI • chief creative officer JOE QUESADA
president DAN BUCKLEY • executive producer ALAN FINE

MOON GIRL AND DEVIL DINOSAUR: THE BEGINNING. Contains material originally published in magazine form as MOON GIRL AND DEVIL DINOSAUR #1-12. First printing 2018. ISBN 978-1-302-91654-1. Published by MARVEL WORLDWIDE, INC., a subsidiary of MARVEL ENTERTAINMENT, LLC. OFFICE OF PUBLICATION: 135 West 50th Street, New York, NY 10020. Copyright © 2018 MARVEL No similarity between any of the names, characters, persons, and/or institutions in this magazine with those of any living or dead person or institution is intended, and any such similarity which may exist is purely coincidental. **Printed in Canada.** DAN BUCKLEY, President, Marvel Entertainment; JOHN NEE, Publisher; JOE QUESADA, Chief Creative Officer; TOM BREVOORT, SVP of Publishing; DAVID BOGART, SVP of Business Affairs & Operations, Publishing & Partnership; DAVID GABRIEL, SVP of Sales & Marketing, Publishing; JEFF YOUNGQUIST, VP of Production & Special Projects; DAN CARR, Executive Director of Publishing Technology; ALEX MORALES, Director of Publishing Operations; DAN EDINGTON, Managing Editor; SUSAN CRESPI, Production Manager; STAN LEE, Chairman Emeritus. For information regarding advertising in Marvel Comics or on Marvel.com, please contact Vit DeBellis, Custom Solutions & Integrated Advertising Manager, at vdebellis@marvel.com. For Marvel subscription inquiries, please call 888-511-5480. **Manufactured between 12/14/2018 and 1/15/2019 by SOLISCO PRINTERS, SCOTT, QC, CANADA.**

10 9 8 7 6 5 4 3 2 1

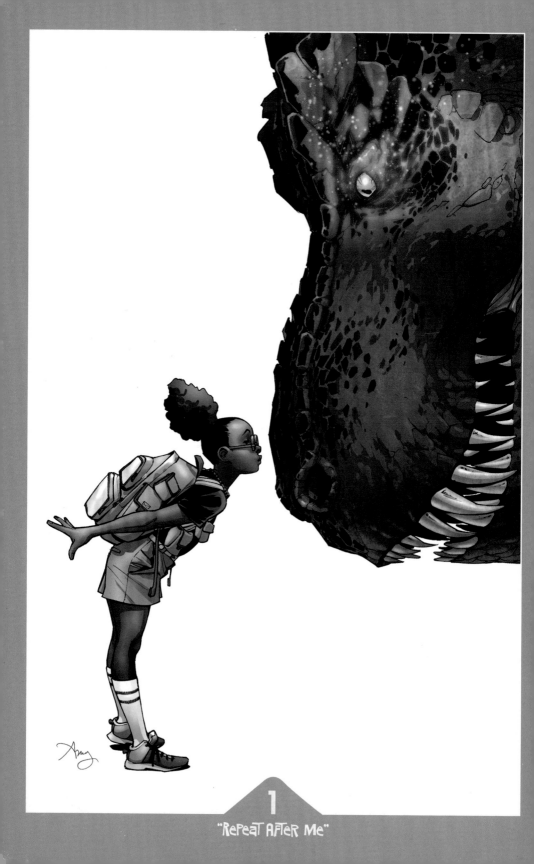

1

"Repeat After Me"

"Humanity is leaving its childhood and moving into its adolescence as its powers infuse into a realm hitherto beyond our reach." - Dr. Gregory Stock

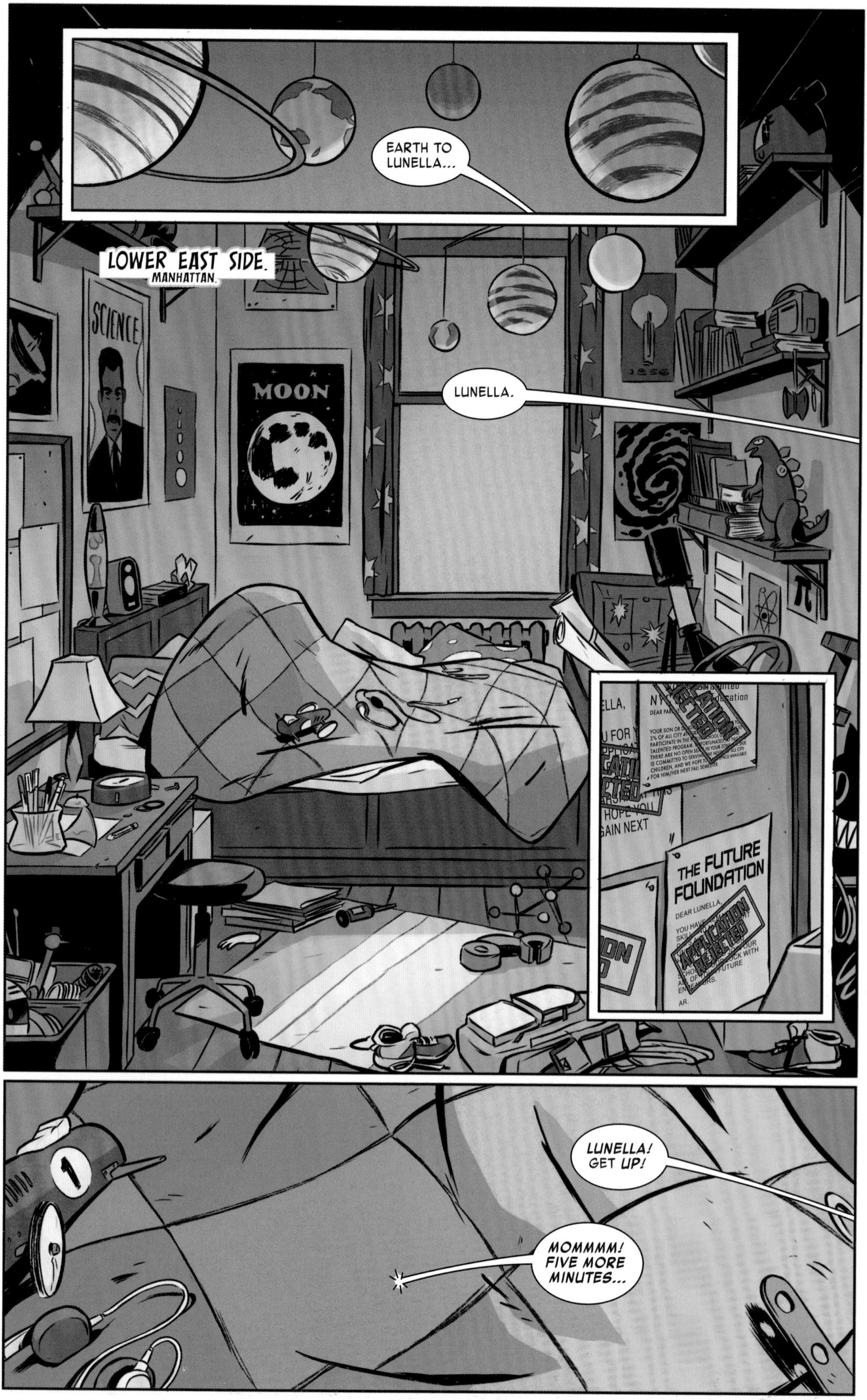
EARTH TO LUNELLA...
LOWER EAST SIDE. MANHATTAN.
SCIENCE
MOON
LUNELLA.
THE FUTURE FOUNDATION
DEAR LUNELLA,
APPLICATION REJECTED
LUNELLA! GET UP!
MOMMMM! FIVE MORE MINUTES...

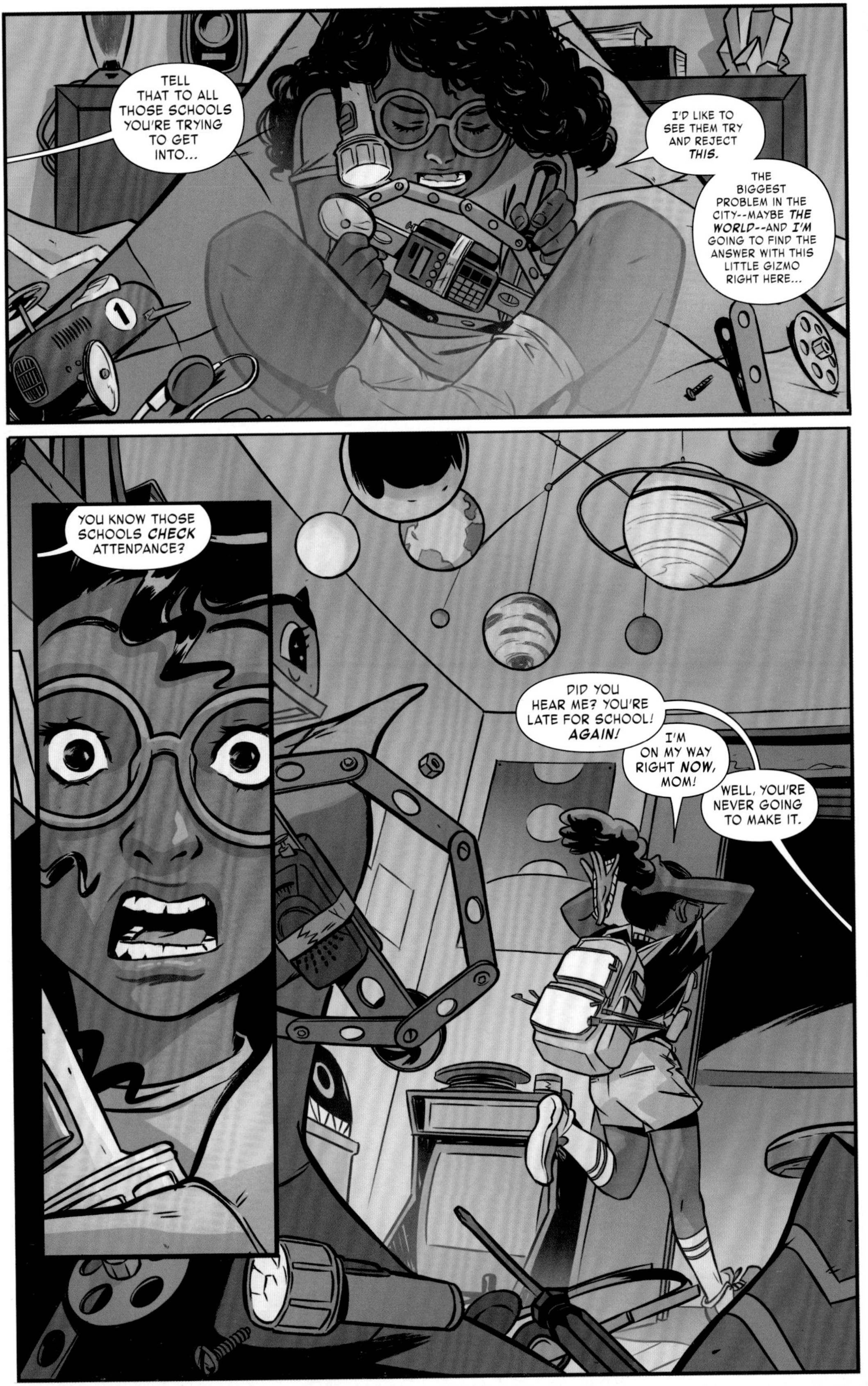
TELL THAT TO ALL THOSE SCHOOLS YOU'RE TRYING TO GET INTO...
I'D LIKE TO SEE THEM TRY AND REJECT *THIS.*
THE BIGGEST PROBLEM IN THE CITY--MAYBE *THE WORLD*--AND *I'M* GOING TO FIND THE ANSWER WITH THIS LITTLE GIZMO RIGHT HERE...
YOU KNOW THOSE SCHOOLS *CHECK* ATTENDANCE?
DID YOU HEAR ME? YOU'RE LATE FOR SCHOOL! *AGAIN!*
I'M ON MY WAY RIGHT *NOW,* MOM!
WELL, YOU'RE NEVER GOING TO MAKE IT.

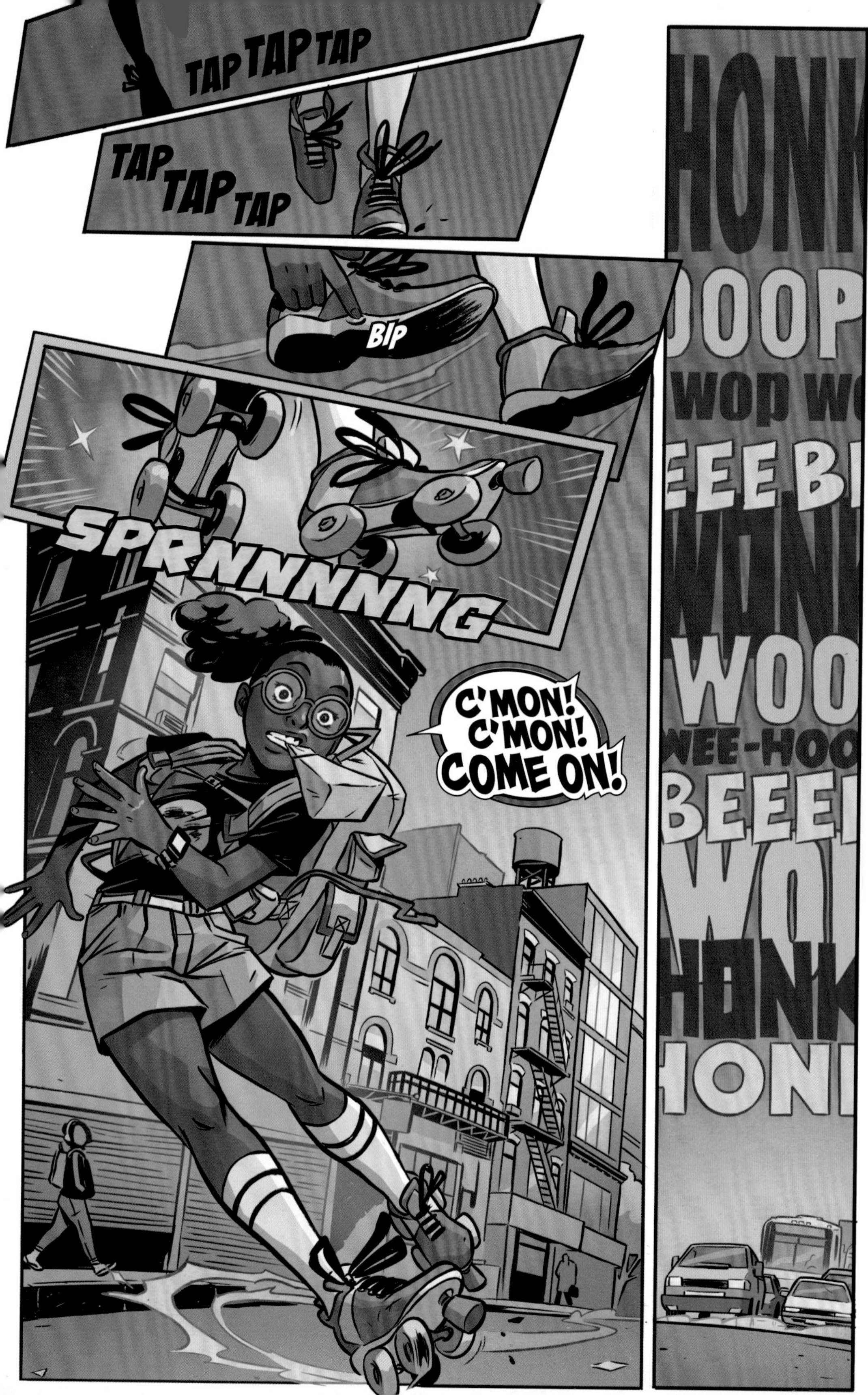
TAP TAP TAP
TAP TAP TAP
BIP
SPRNNNNNNG
C'MON! C'MON! COME ON!
HONK
OOOP
WOP WO
EEE B
WOO
WEE-HOO
BEEE
HONK
HON

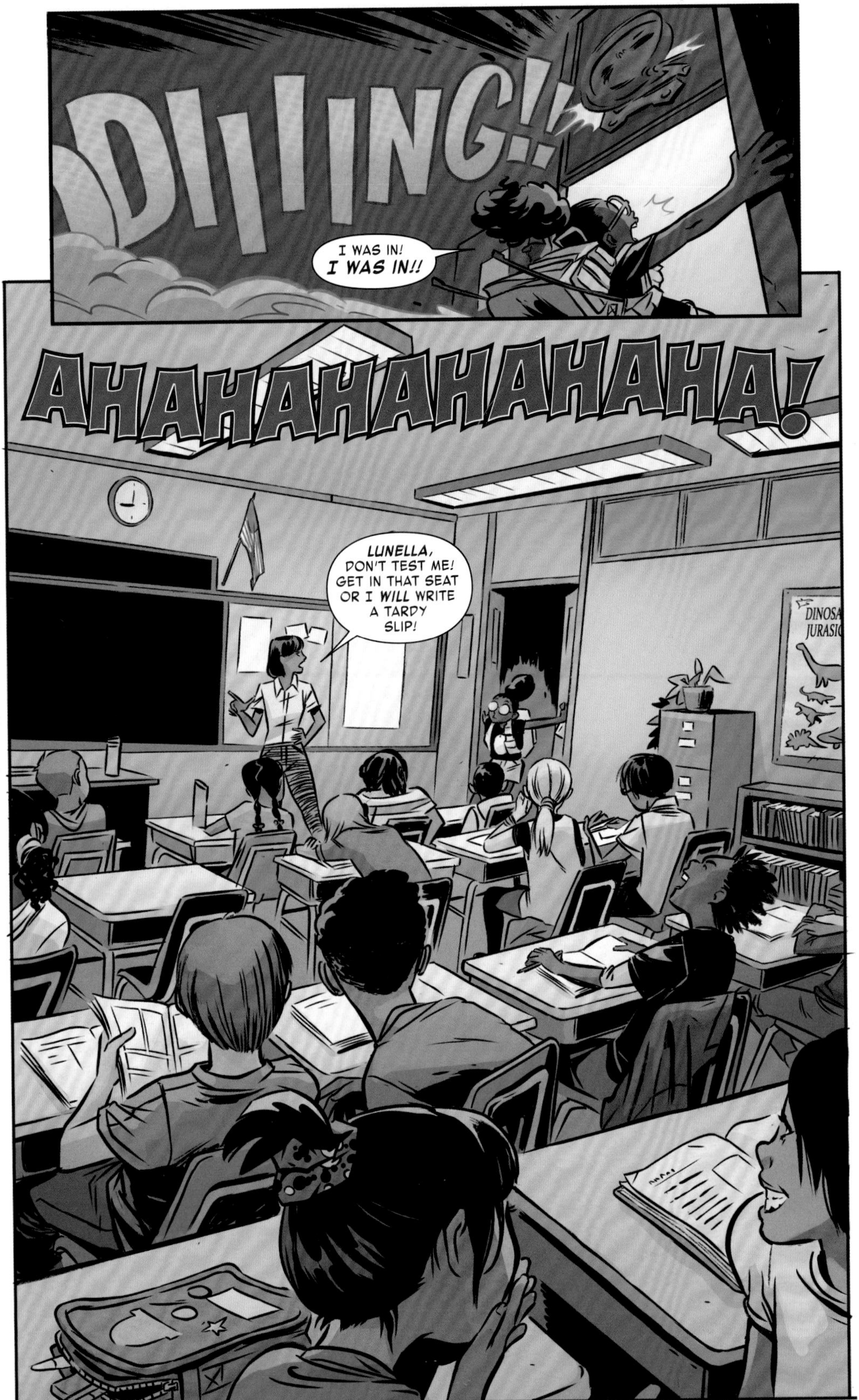
DIIIING!!
I WAS IN!
I WAS IN!!
AHAHAHAHAHAHAHA!
LUNELLA, DON'T TEST ME! GET IN THAT SEAT OR I WILL WRITE A TARDY SLIP!

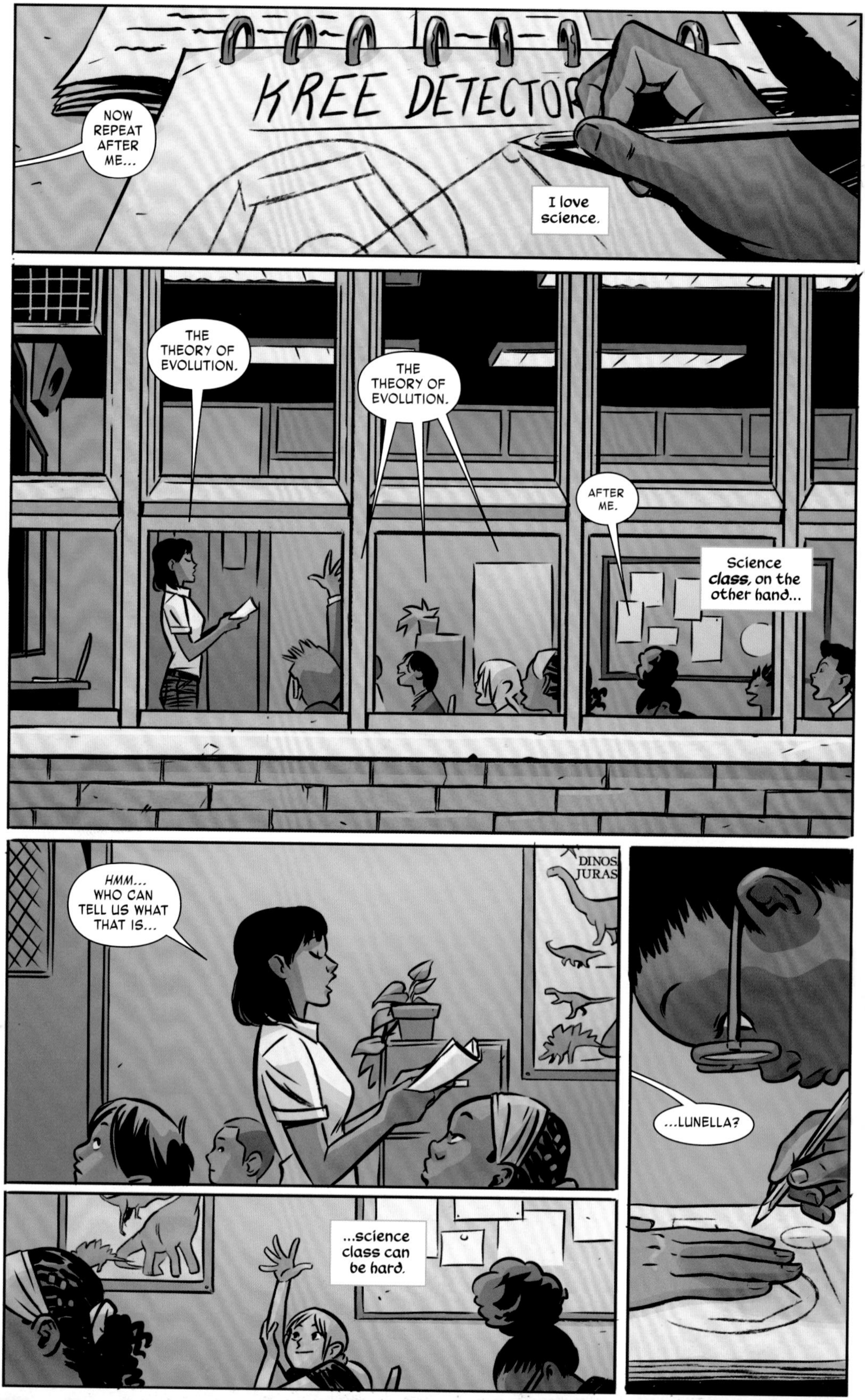
KREE DETECTOR
NOW REPEAT AFTER ME...
I love science.
THE THEORY OF EVOLUTION.
THE THEORY OF EVOLUTION.
AFTER ME.
Science class, on the other hand...
HMM... WHO CAN TELL US WHAT THAT IS...
...LUNELLA?
...science class can be hard.

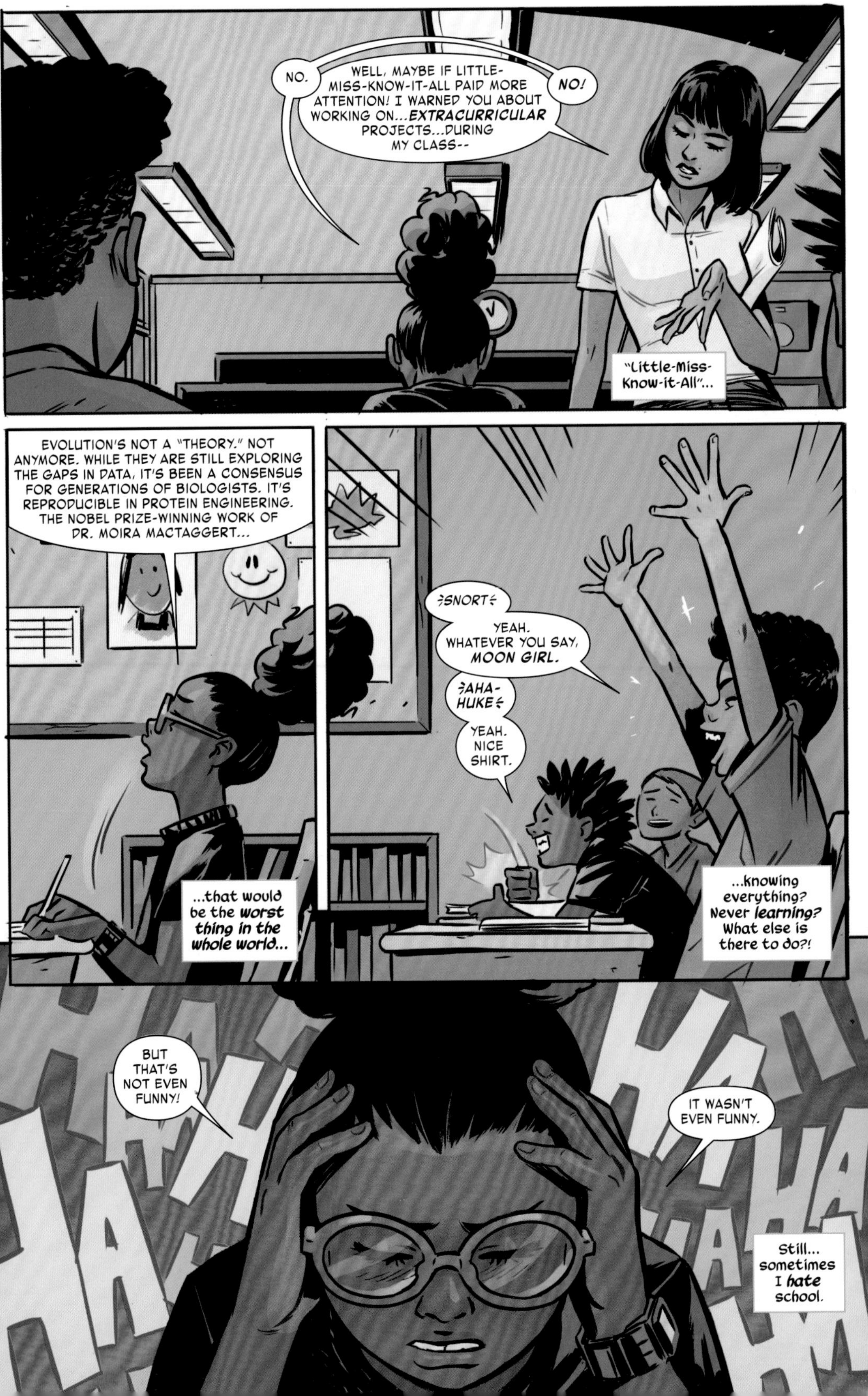
NO.
WELL, MAYBE IF LITTLE-MISS-KNOW-IT-ALL PAID MORE ATTENTION! I WARNED YOU ABOUT WORKING ON...EXTRACURRICULAR PROJECTS...DURING MY CLASS--
NO!
"Little-Miss-Know-it-All"...
EVOLUTION'S NOT A "THEORY." NOT ANYMORE. WHILE THEY ARE STILL EXPLORING THE GAPS IN DATA, IT'S BEEN A CONSENSUS FOR GENERATIONS OF BIOLOGISTS. IT'S REPRODUCIBLE IN PROTEIN ENGINEERING. THE NOBEL PRIZE-WINNING WORK OF DR. MOIRA MACTAGGERT...
...that would be the worst thing in the whole world...
SNORT
YEAH. WHATEVER YOU SAY, MOON GIRL.
AHA-HUKE
YEAH. NICE SHIRT.
...knowing everything? Never learning? What else is there to do?!
BUT THAT'S NOT EVEN FUNNY!
IT WASN'T EVEN FUNNY.
Still... sometimes I hate school.

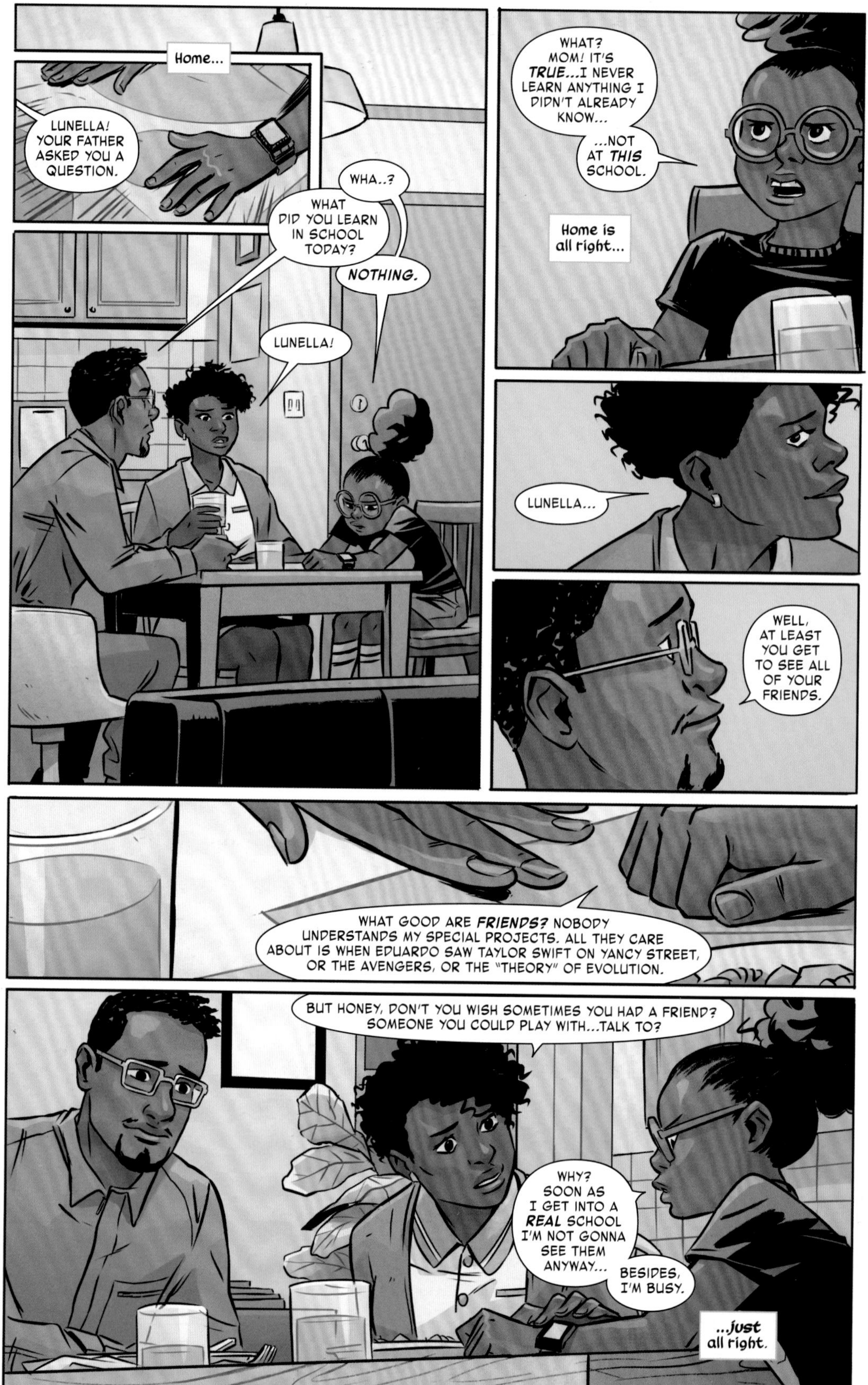
Home...
LUNELLA! YOUR FATHER ASKED YOU A QUESTION.
WHAT DID YOU LEARN IN SCHOOL TODAY?
WHA..?
NOTHING.
LUNELLA!
WHAT? MOM! IT'S TRUE...I NEVER LEARN ANYTHING I DIDN'T ALREADY KNOW...
...NOT AT THIS SCHOOL.
Home is all right...
LUNELLA...
WELL, AT LEAST YOU GET TO SEE ALL OF YOUR FRIENDS.
WHAT GOOD ARE FRIENDS? NOBODY UNDERSTANDS MY SPECIAL PROJECTS. ALL THEY CARE ABOUT IS WHEN EDUARDO SAW TAYLOR SWIFT ON YANCY STREET, OR THE AVENGERS, OR THE "THEORY" OF EVOLUTION.
BUT HONEY, DON'T YOU WISH SOMETIMES YOU HAD A FRIEND? SOMEONE YOU COULD PLAY WITH...TALK TO?
WHY? SOON AS I GET INTO A REAL SCHOOL I'M NOT GONNA SEE THEM ANYWAY...
BESIDES, I'M BUSY.
...just all right.

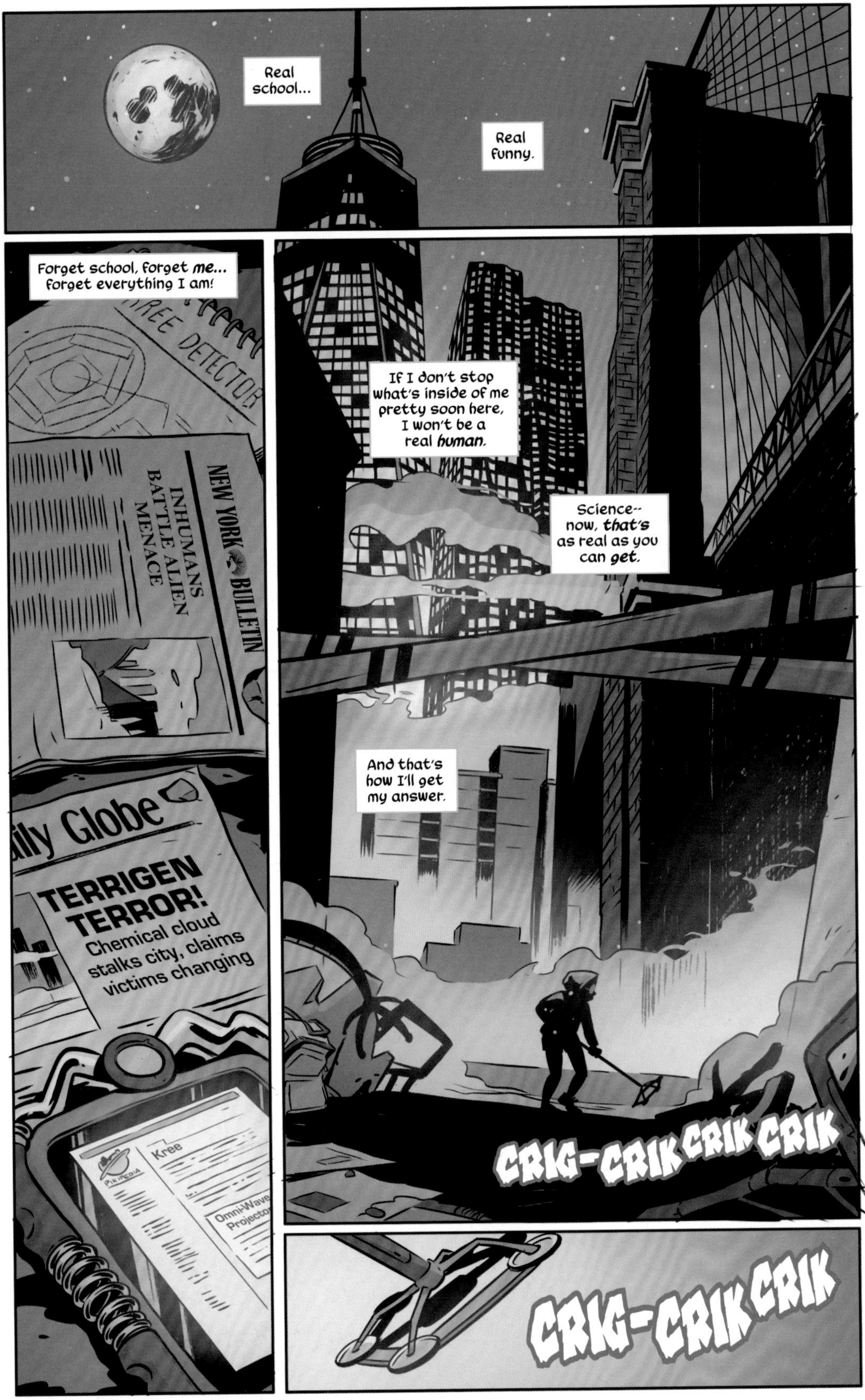
Real school...
Real funny.
Forget school, forget *me*... forget everything I am!
REE DETECTOR
NEW YORK BULLETIN
INHUMANS BATTLE ALIEN MENACE
ily Globe
TERRIGEN TERROR!
Chemical cloud stalks city, claims victims changing
Kree
Omni-Wave
If I don't stop what's inside of me pretty soon here, I won't be a real *human*.
Science-- now, *that's* as real as you can *get*.
And that's how I'll get my answer.
CRIG-CRIK CRIK CRIK
CRIG-CRIK CRIK

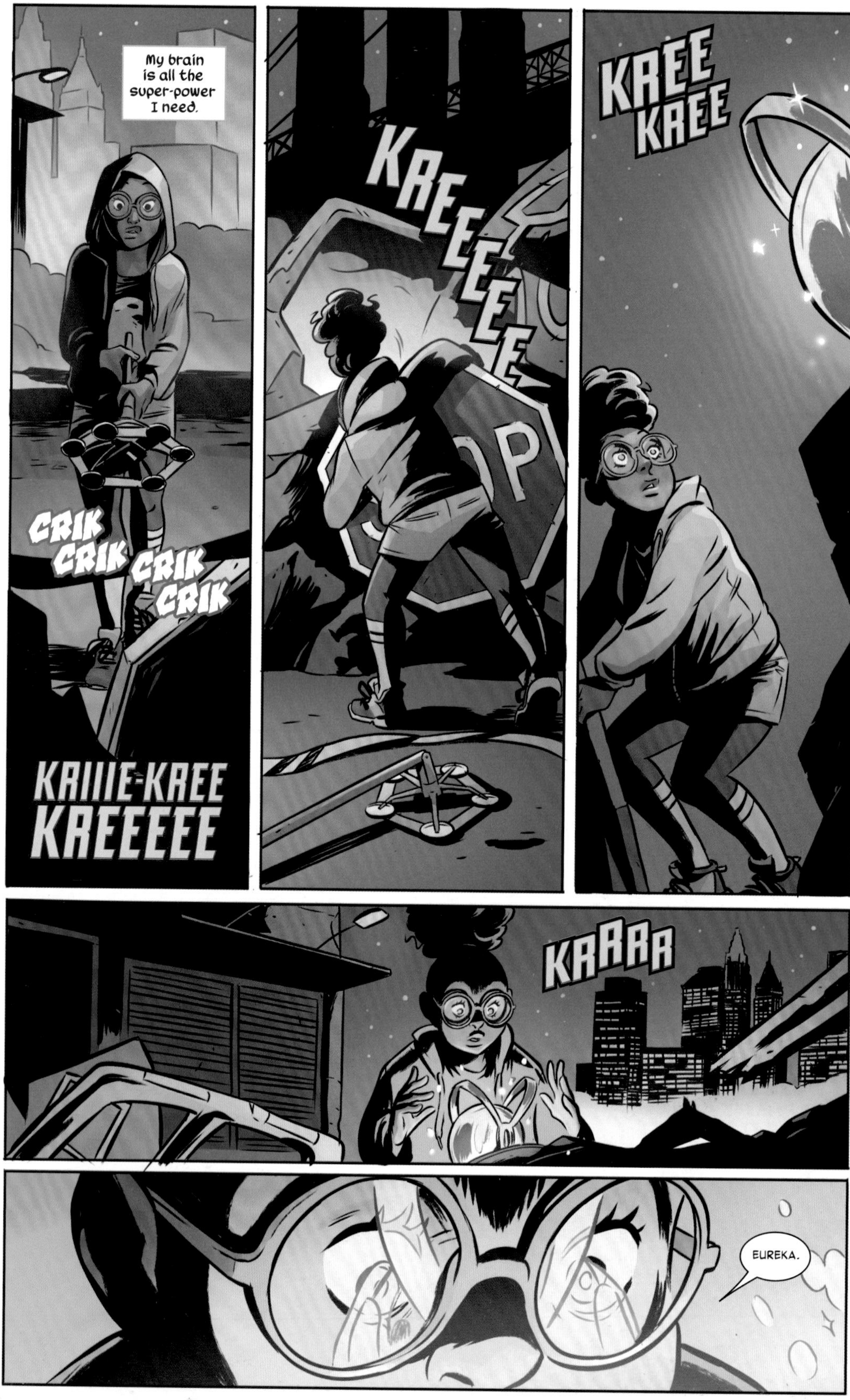
My brain is all the super-power I need.
CRIK CRIK
CRIK CRIK
KRIIIE-KREE KREEEEE
KREEEEEE
KREE KREE
KRRRR
EUREKA.

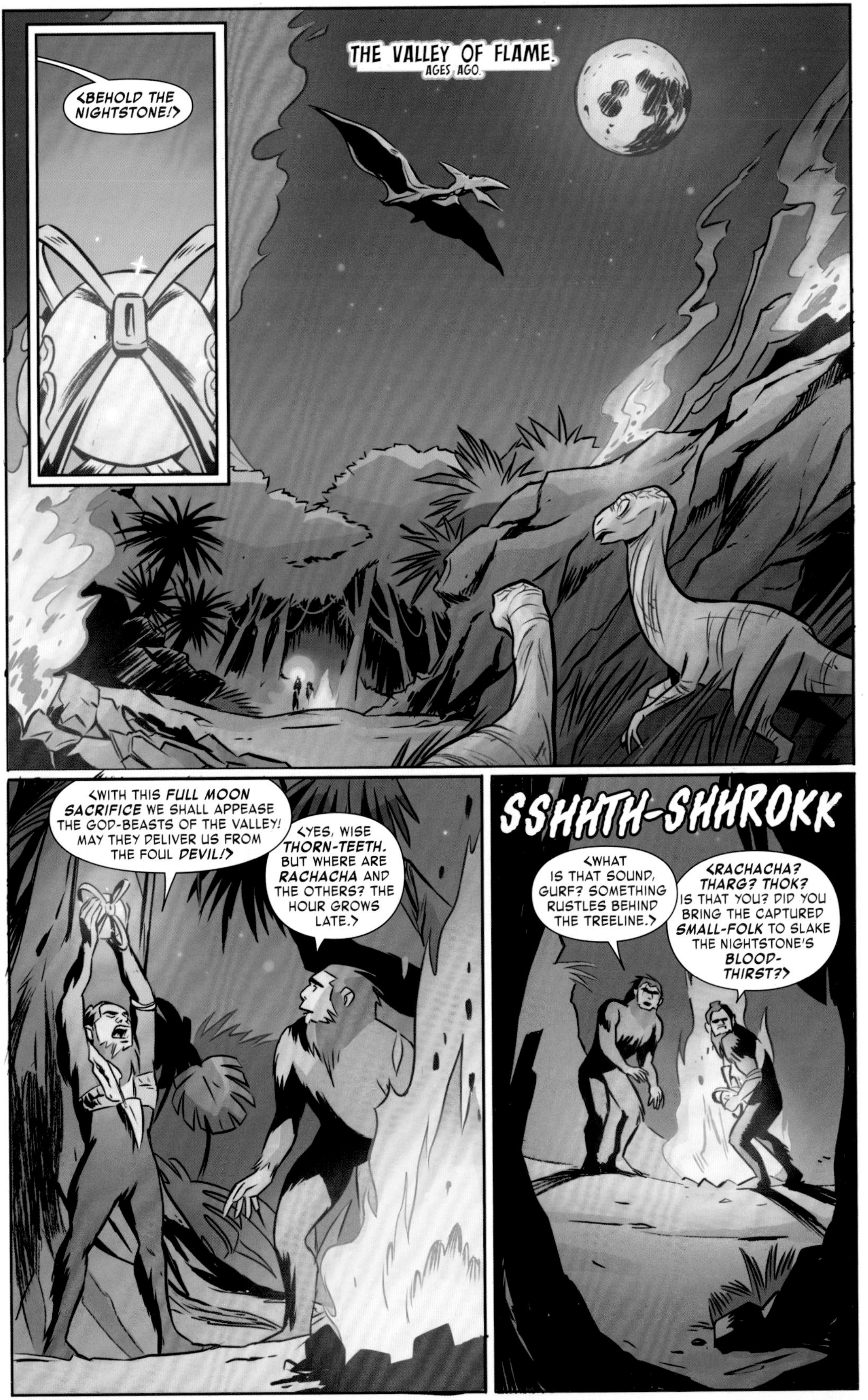
THE VALLEY OF FLAME. AGES AGO.
<BEHOLD THE NIGHTSTONE!>
<WITH THIS FULL MOON SACRIFICE WE SHALL APPEASE THE GOD-BEASTS OF THE VALLEY! MAY THEY DELIVER US FROM THE FOUL DEVIL!>
<YES, WISE THORN-TEETH. BUT WHERE ARE RACHACHA AND THE OTHERS? THE HOUR GROWS LATE.>
SSHHTH-SHHROKK
<WHAT IS THAT SOUND, GURF? SOMETHING RUSTLES BEHIND THE TREELINE.>
<RACHACHA? THARG? THOK? IS THAT YOU? DID YOU BRING THE CAPTURED SMALL-FOLK TO SLAKE THE NIGHTSTONE'S BLOOD-THIRST?>

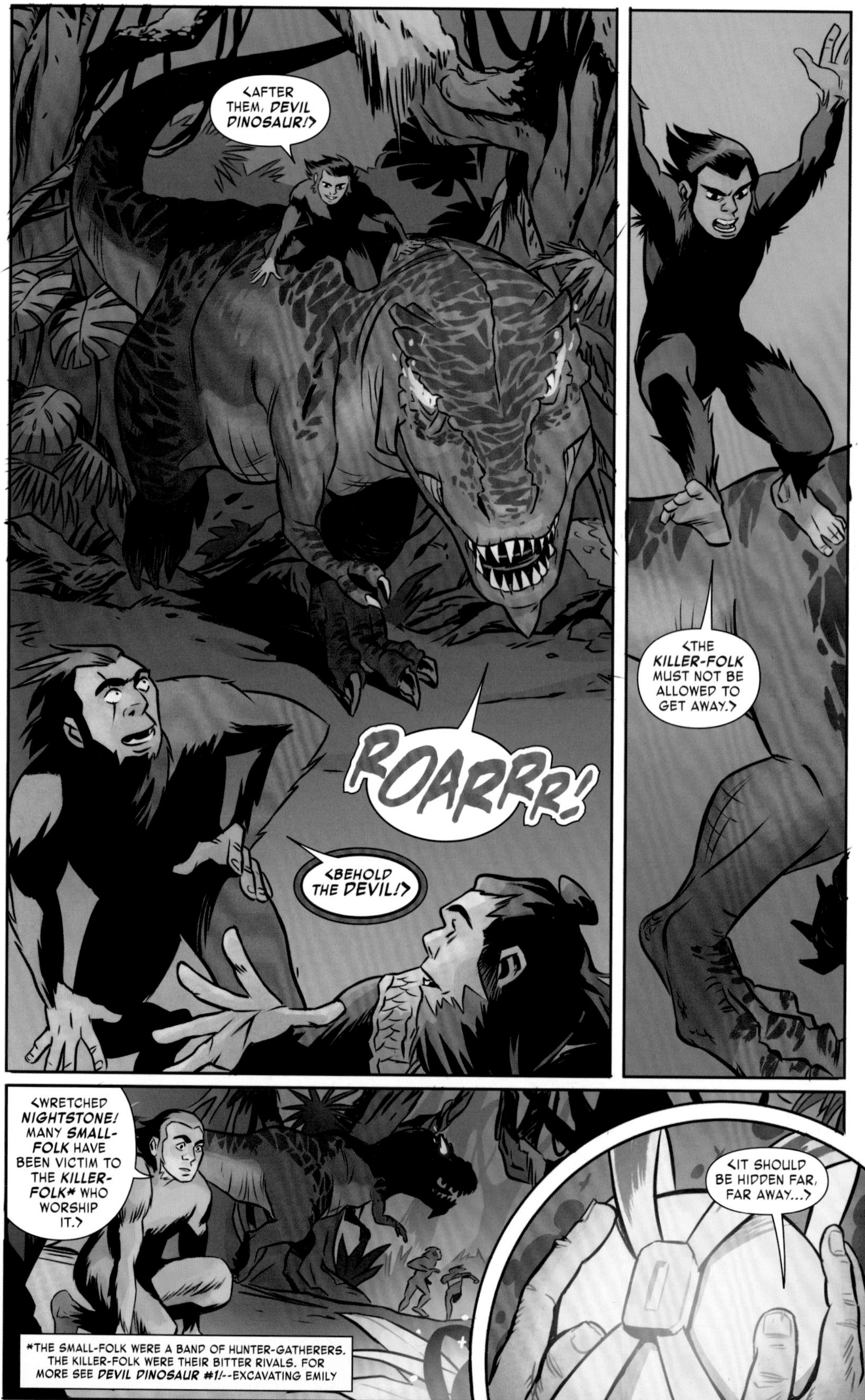
<AFTER THEM, DEVIL DINOSAUR!>
ROARRR!
<BEHOLD THE DEVIL!>
<THE KILLER-FOLK MUST NOT BE ALLOWED TO GET AWAY.>
<WRETCHED NIGHTSTONE! MANY SMALL-FOLK HAVE BEEN VICTIM TO THE KILLER-FOLK* WHO WORSHIP IT.>
*THE SMALL-FOLK WERE A BAND OF HUNTER-GATHERERS. THE KILLER-FOLK WERE THEIR BITTER RIVALS. FOR MORE SEE DEVIL DINOSAUR #1!--EXCAVATING EMILY
<IT SHOULD BE HIDDEN FAR, FAR AWAY...>

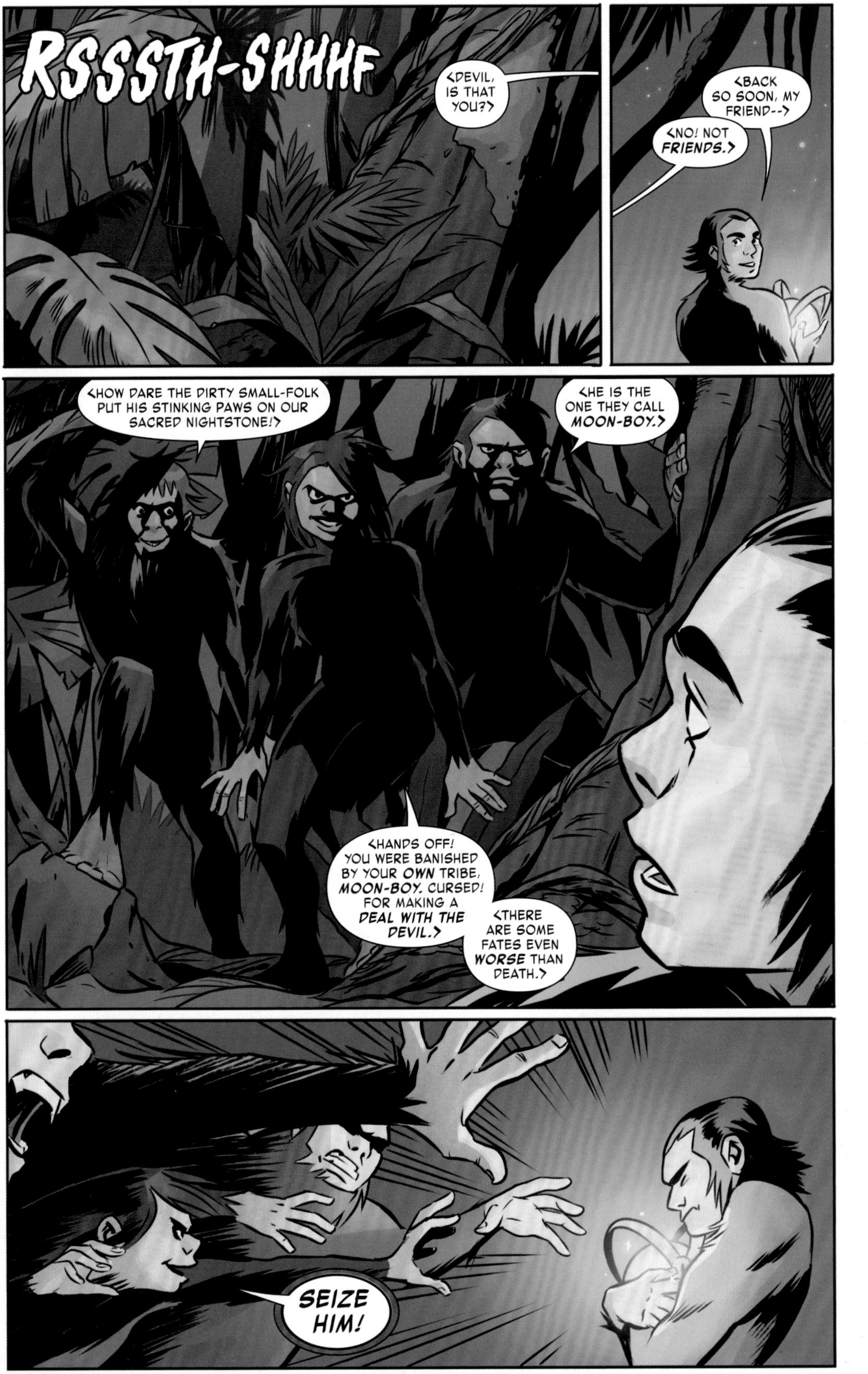
RSSSTH-SHHHF
<DEVIL, IS THAT YOU?>
<BACK SO SOON, MY FRIEND-->
<NO! NOT FRIENDS.>
<HOW DARE THE DIRTY SMALL-FOLK PUT HIS STINKING PAWS ON OUR SACRED NIGHTSTONE!>
<HE IS THE ONE THEY CALL MOON-BOY.>
<HANDS OFF! YOU WERE BANISHED BY YOUR OWN TRIBE, MOON-BOY. CURSED! FOR MAKING A DEAL WITH THE DEVIL.>
<THERE ARE SOME FATES EVEN WORSE THAN DEATH.>
SEIZE HIM!

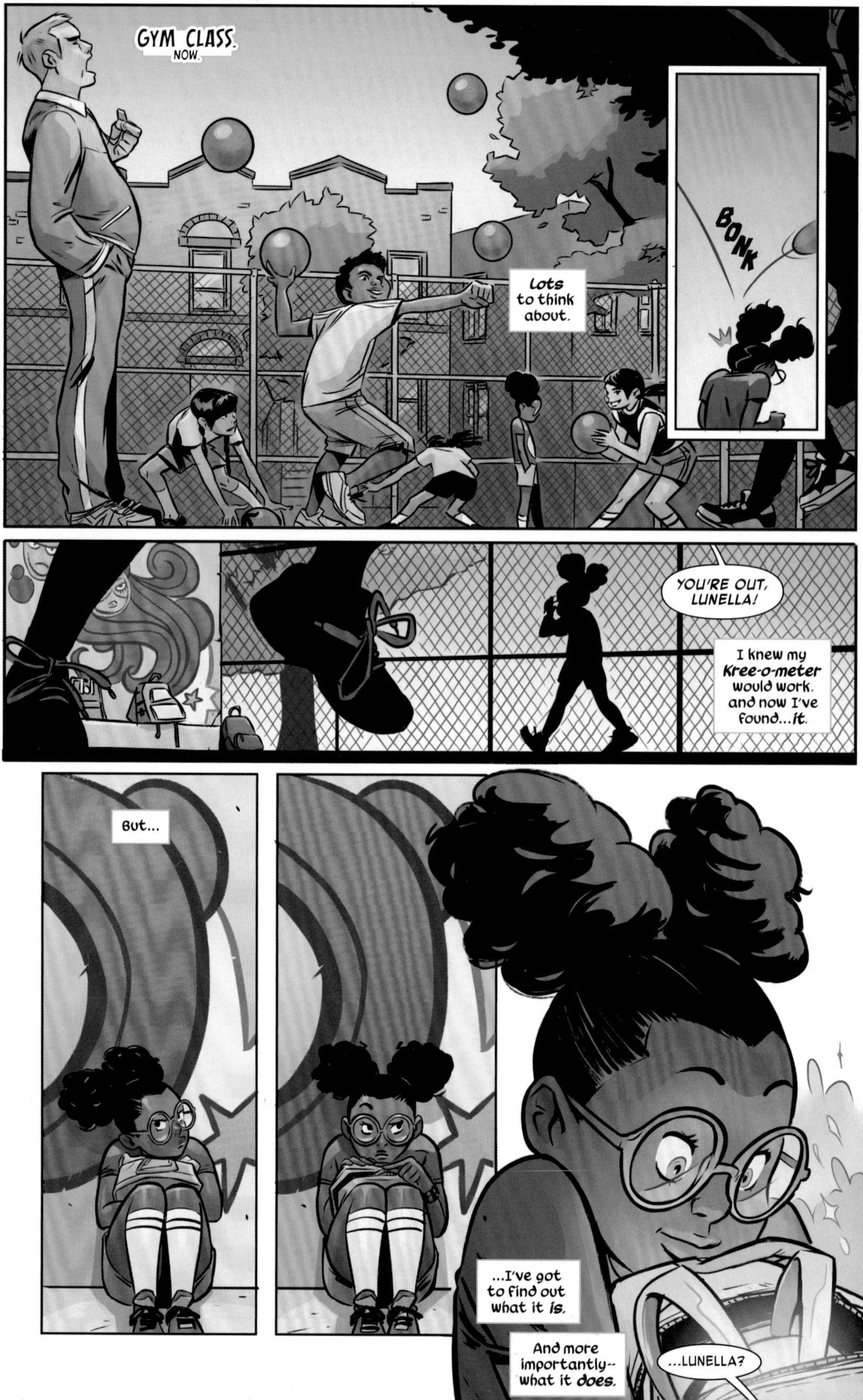
GYM CLASS.
NOW.
Lots to think about.
BONK
YOU'RE OUT, LUNELLA!
I knew my Kree-o-meter would work, and now I've found...it.
But...
...I've got to find out what it is.
And more importantly--what it does.
...LUNELLA?

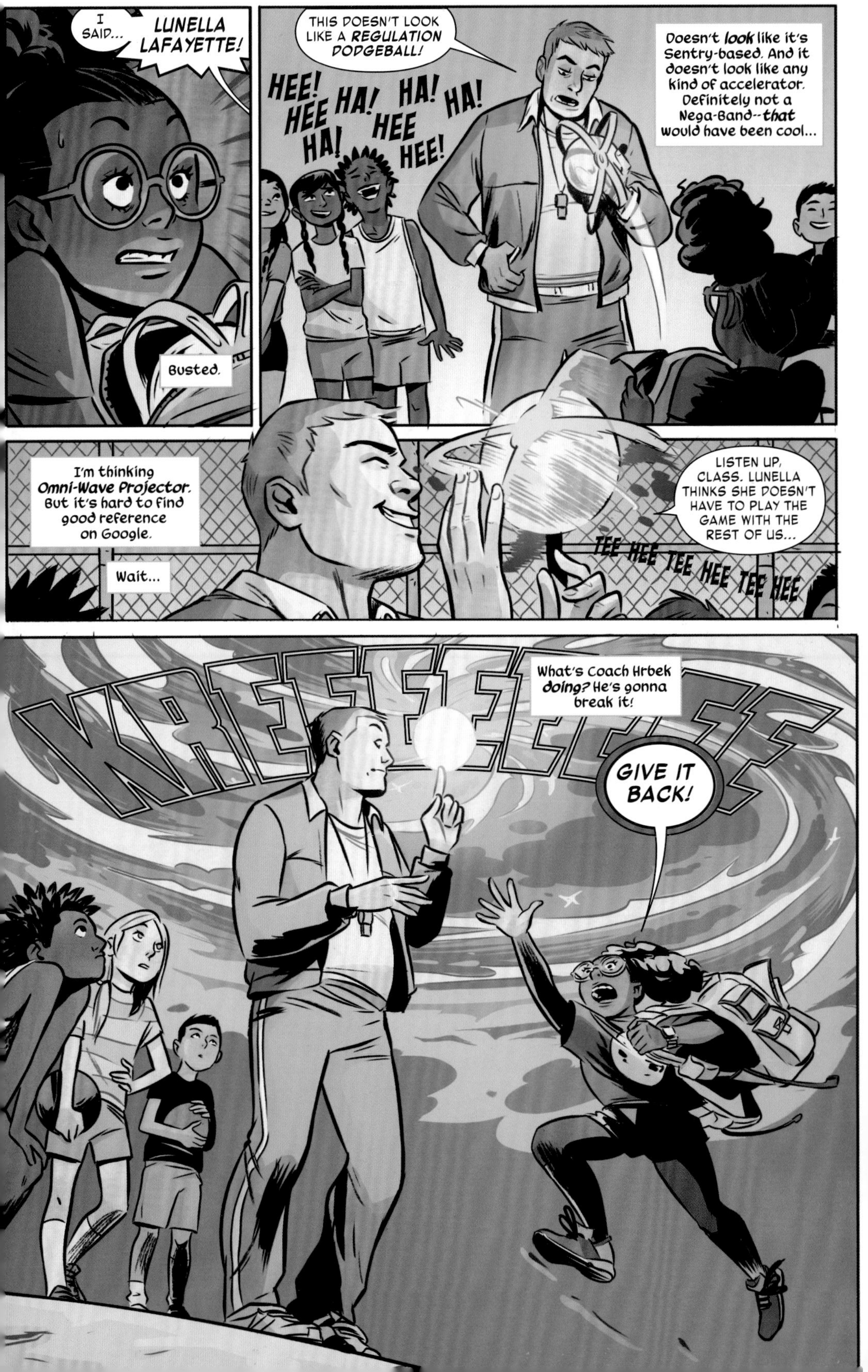
I SAID... LUNELLA LAFAYETTE!
Busted.
THIS DOESN'T LOOK LIKE A REGULATION DODGEBALL!
HEE! HEE HA! HA! HEE HEE! HA! HA! HEE HA!
Doesn't look like it's Sentry-based. And it doesn't look like any kind of accelerator. Definitely not a Nega-Band--that would have been cool...
I'm thinking Omni-Wave Projector. But it's hard to find good reference on Google.
Wait...
LISTEN UP, CLASS. LUNELLA THINKS SHE DOESN'T HAVE TO PLAY THE GAME WITH THE REST OF US...
TEE HEE TEE HEE TEE HEE
KREEEEEE
What's Coach Hrbek doing? He's gonna break it!
GIVE IT BACK!

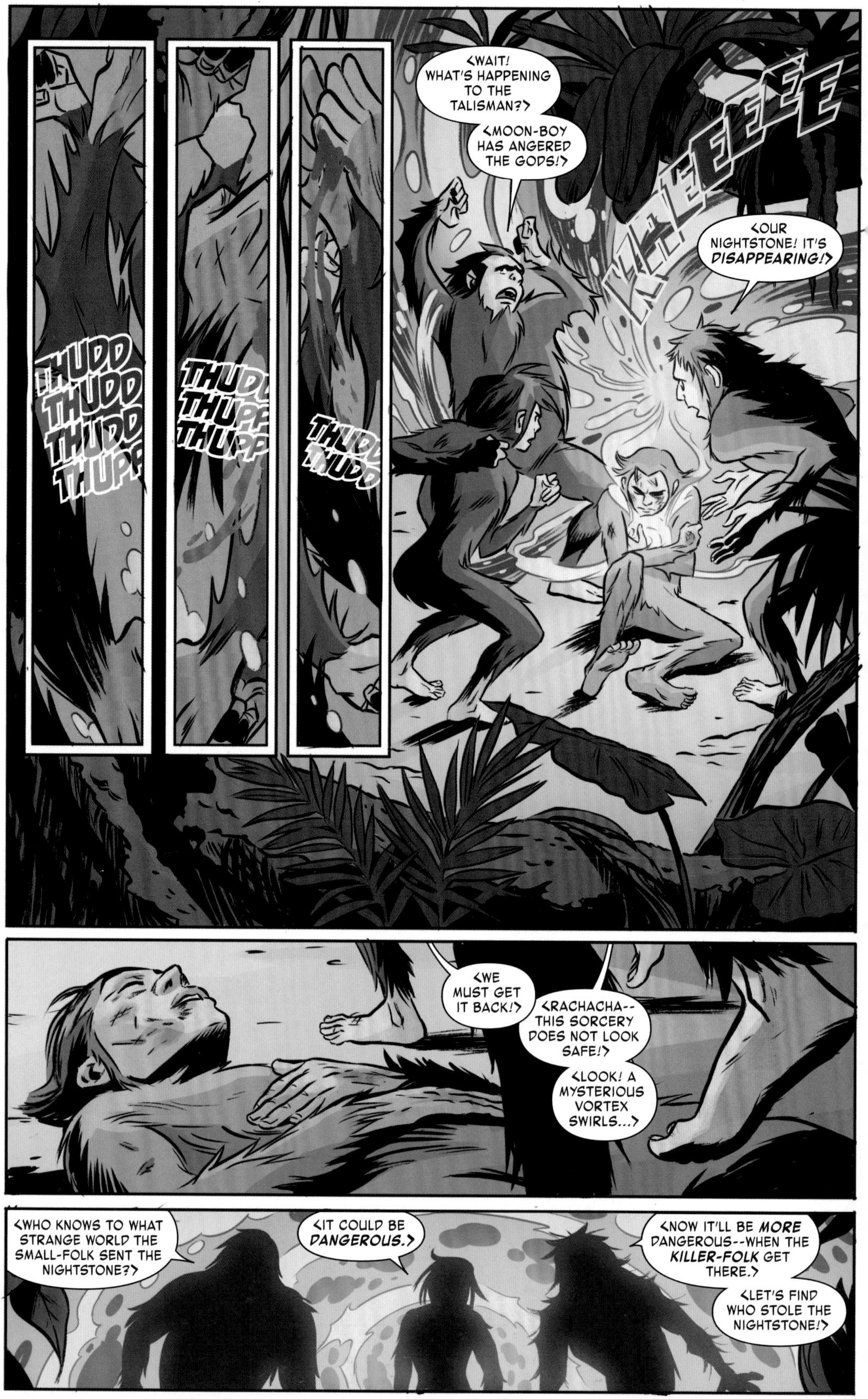
THUDD THUDD THUDD THUPP
THUDD THUPP THUPP
THUDD THUDD
<WAIT! WHAT'S HAPPENING TO THE TALISMAN?>
<MOON-BOY HAS ANGERED THE GODS!>
<OUR NIGHTSTONE! IT'S DISAPPEARING!>
<WE MUST GET IT BACK!>
<RACHACHA--THIS SORCERY DOES NOT LOOK SAFE!>
<LOOK! A MYSTERIOUS VORTEX SWIRLS...>
<WHO KNOWS TO WHAT STRANGE WORLD THE SMALL-FOLK SENT THE NIGHTSTONE?>
<IT COULD BE DANGEROUS.>
<NOW IT'LL BE MORE DANGEROUS--WHEN THE KILLER-FOLK GET THERE.>
<LET'S FIND WHO STOLE THE NIGHTSTONE!>

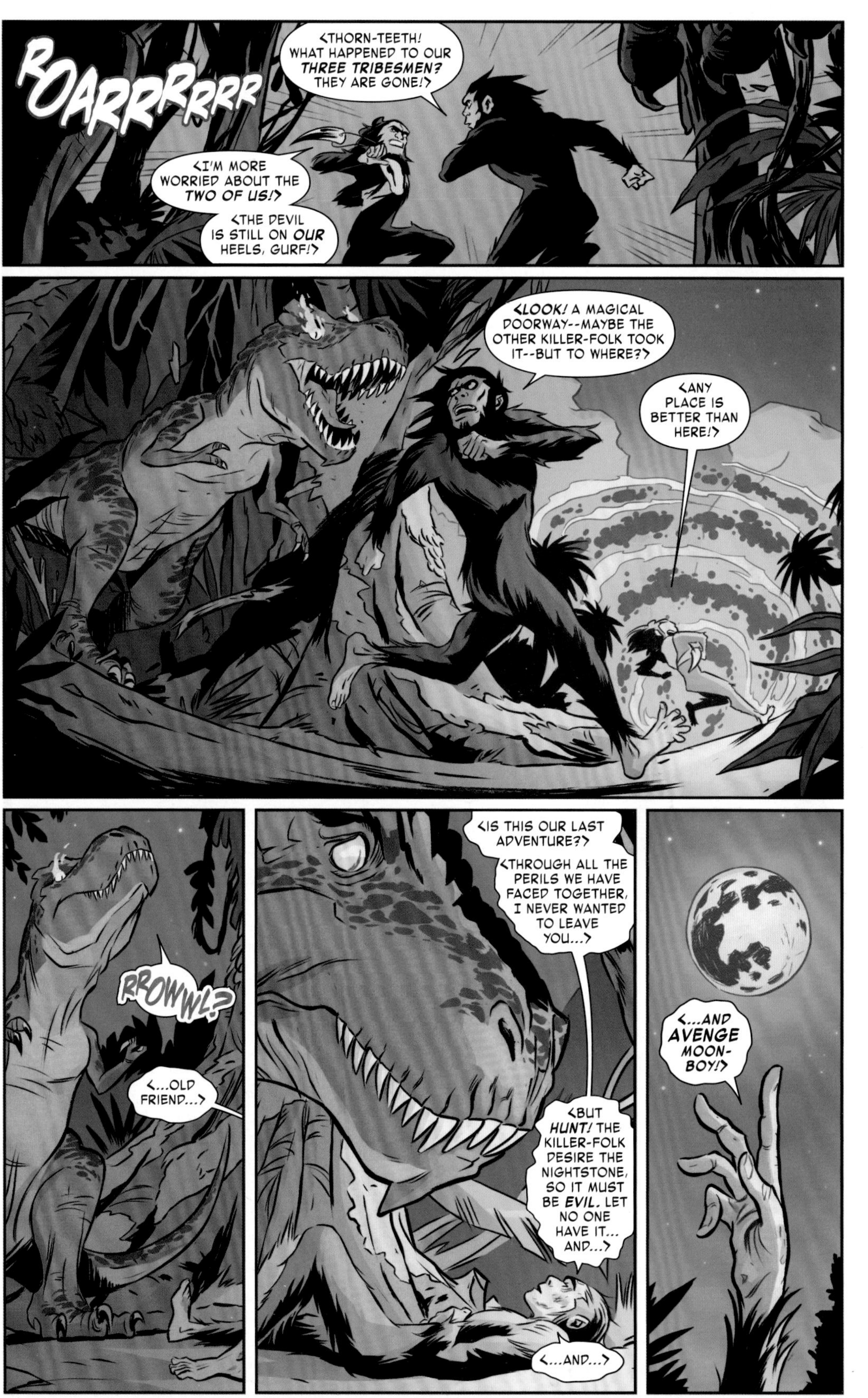
ROARRRRRR
<THORN-TEETH! WHAT HAPPENED TO OUR THREE TRIBESMEN? THEY ARE GONE!>
<I'M MORE WORRIED ABOUT THE TWO OF US!>
<THE DEVIL IS STILL ON OUR HEELS, GURF!>
<LOOK! A MAGICAL DOORWAY--MAYBE THE OTHER KILLER-FOLK TOOK IT--BUT TO WHERE?>
<ANY PLACE IS BETTER THAN HERE!>
RROWWL?
<...OLD FRIEND...>
<IS THIS OUR LAST ADVENTURE?>
<THROUGH ALL THE PERILS WE HAVE FACED TOGETHER, I NEVER WANTED TO LEAVE YOU...>
<BUT HUNT! THE KILLER-FOLK DESIRE THE NIGHTSTONE, SO IT MUST BE EVIL. LET NO ONE HAVE IT... AND...>
<...AND...>
<...AND AVENGE MOON-BOY!>

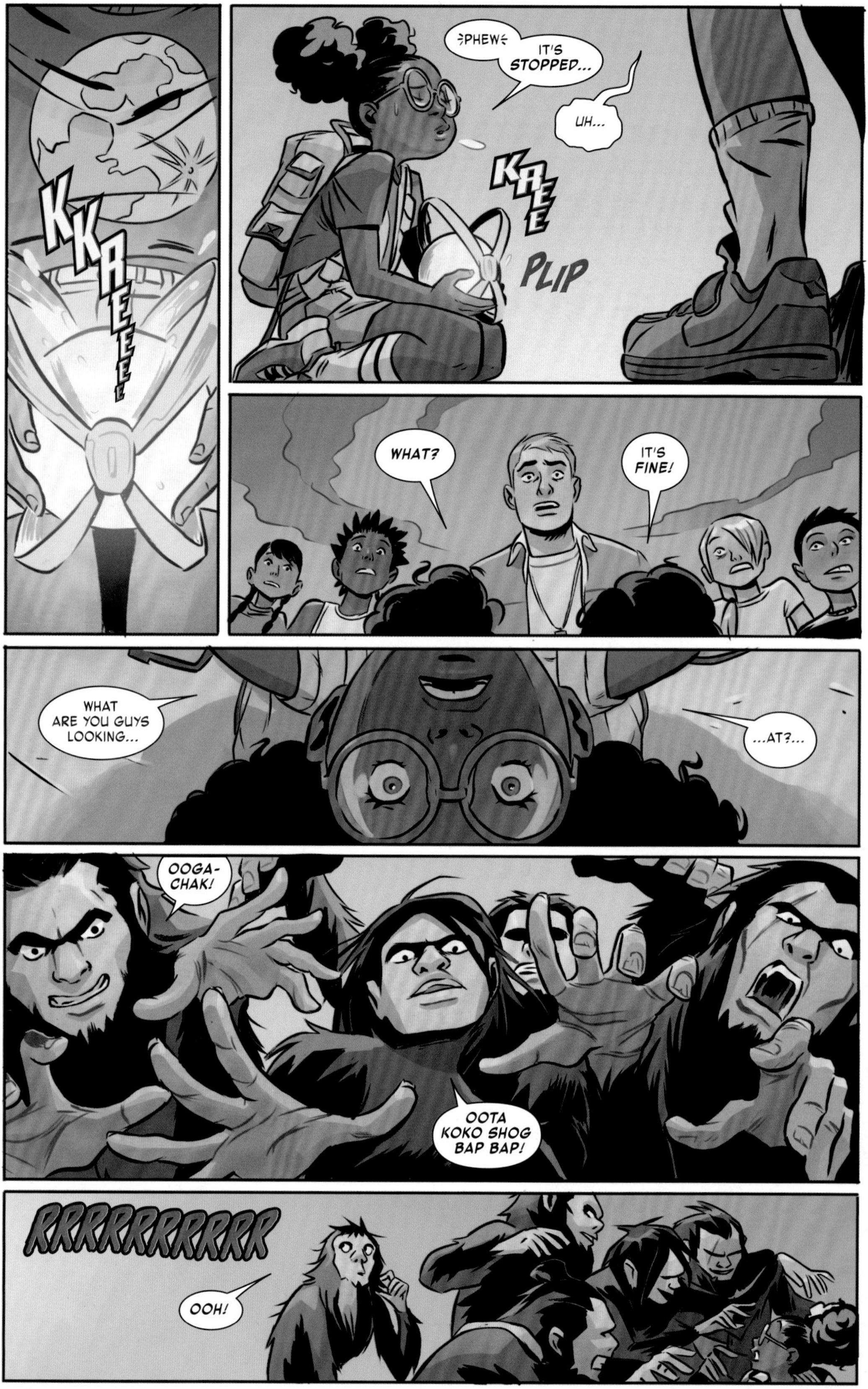
KKREEEEE
≠PHEW≠ IT'S STOPPED...
UH...
KREE
PLIP
WHAT?
IT'S FINE!
WHAT ARE YOU GUYS LOOKING...
...AT?...
OOGA-CHAK!
OOTA KOKO SHOG BAP BAP!
RRRRRRRRRRR
OOH!

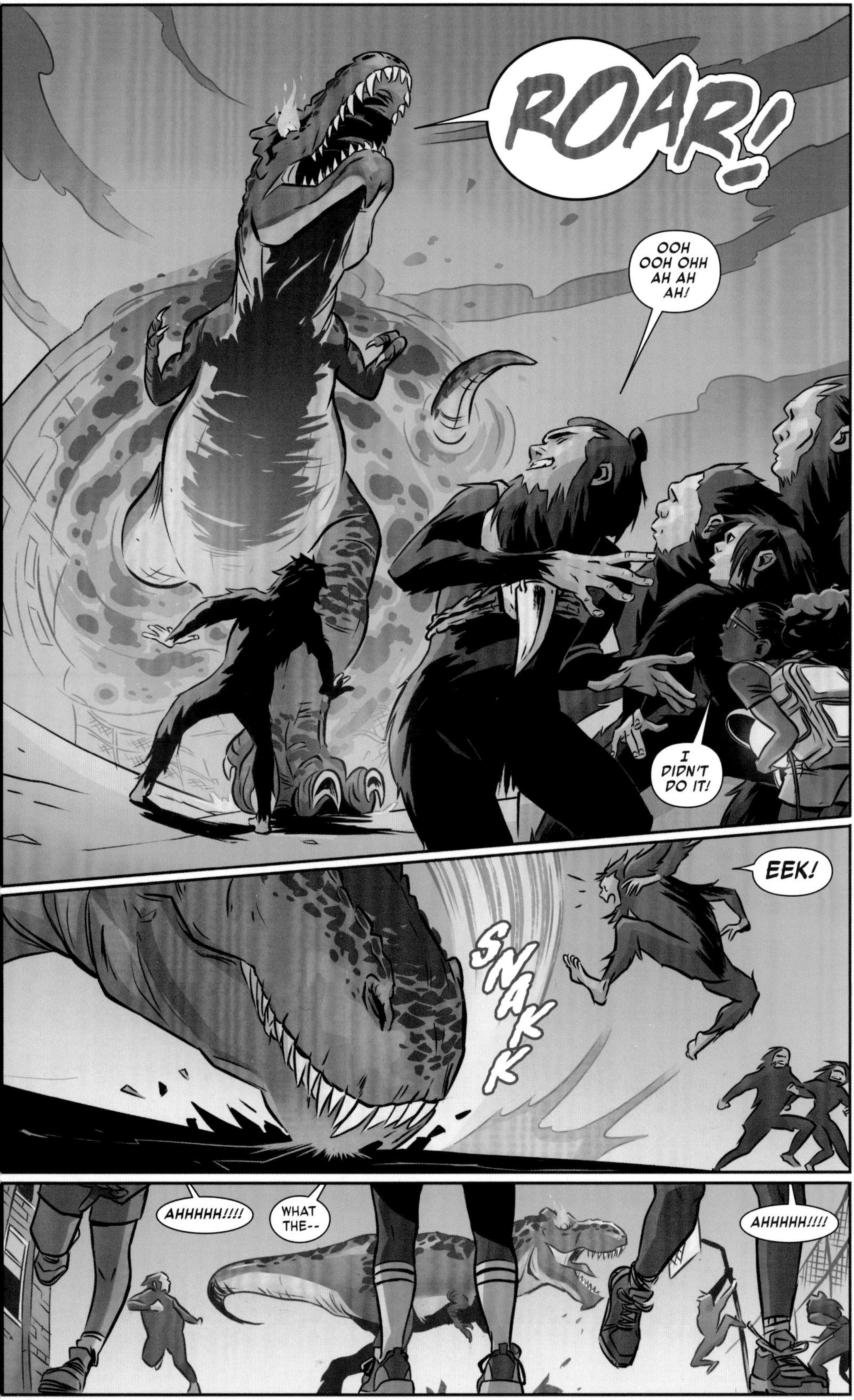
ROAR!
OOH OOH OHH AH AH AH!
I DIDN'T DO IT!
EEK!
SNAKK
AHHHHH!!!!
WHAT THE--
AHHHHH!!!!

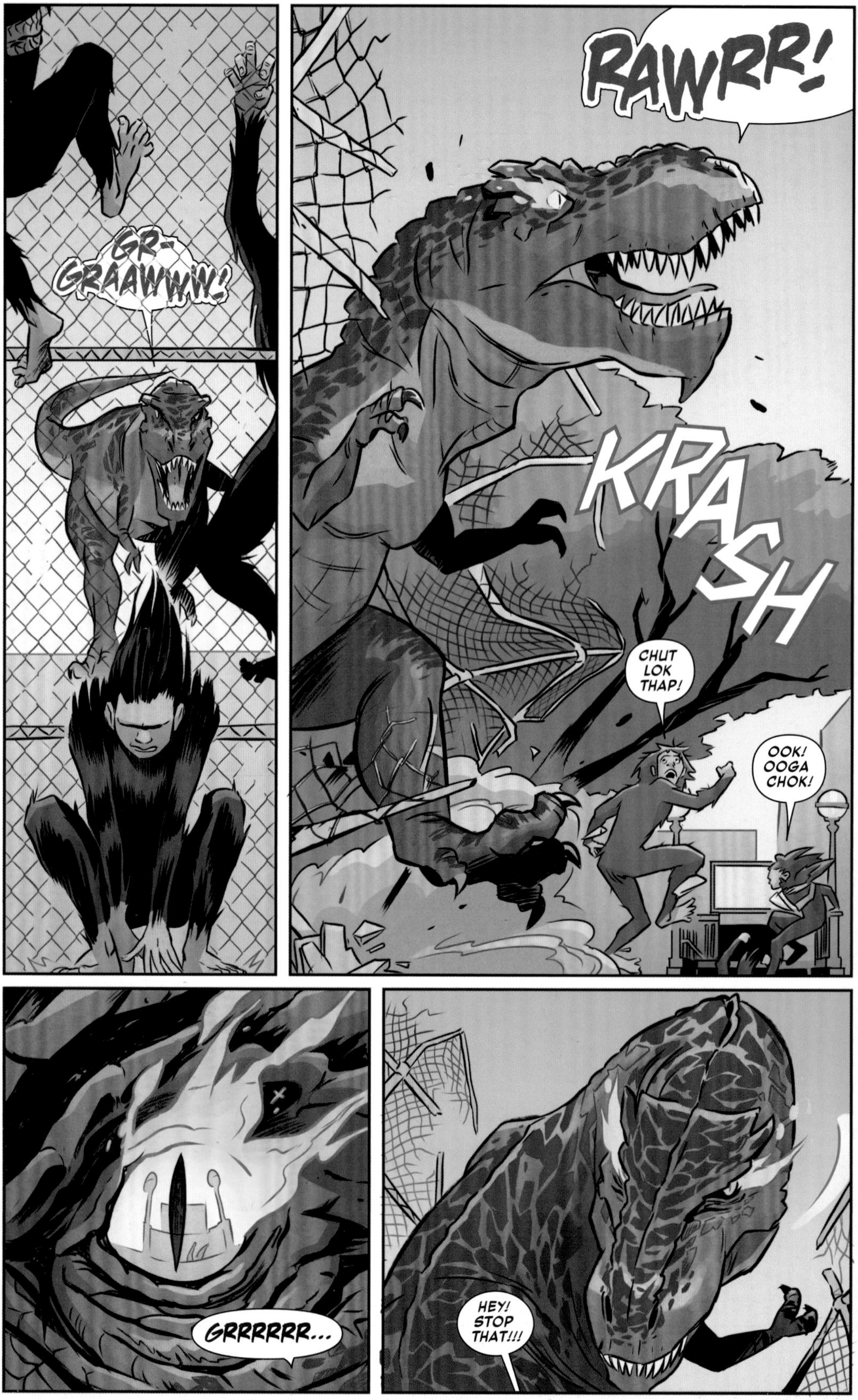
GR-
GRAAWWW!
RAWRR!
KRASH
CHUT LOK THAP!
OOK! OOGA CHOK!
GRRRRRR...
HEY! STOP THAT!!!

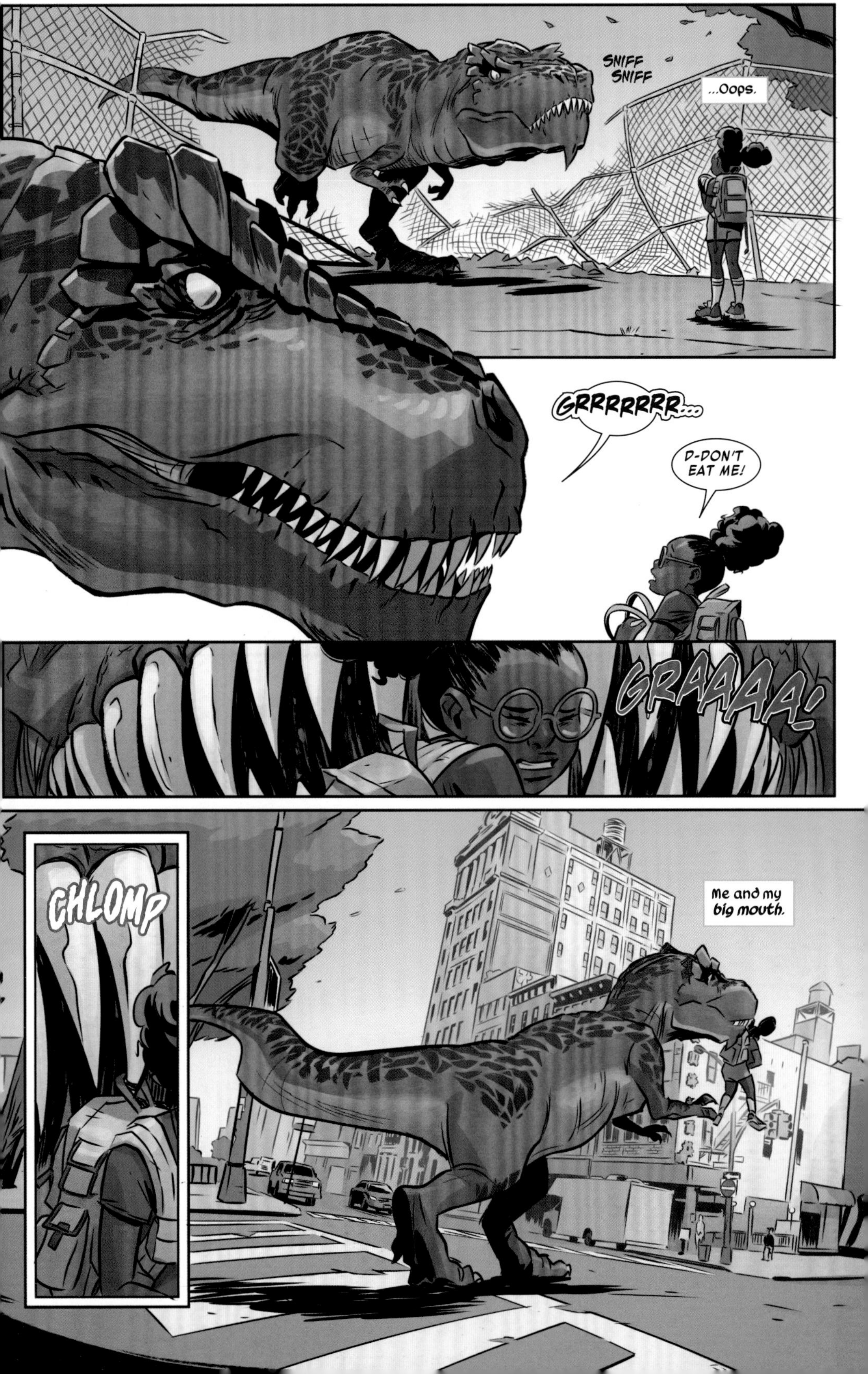
SNIFF
SNIFF
...Oops.
GRRRRRRR...
D-DON'T EAT ME!
GRAAAAA!
CHLOMP
Me and my big mouth.

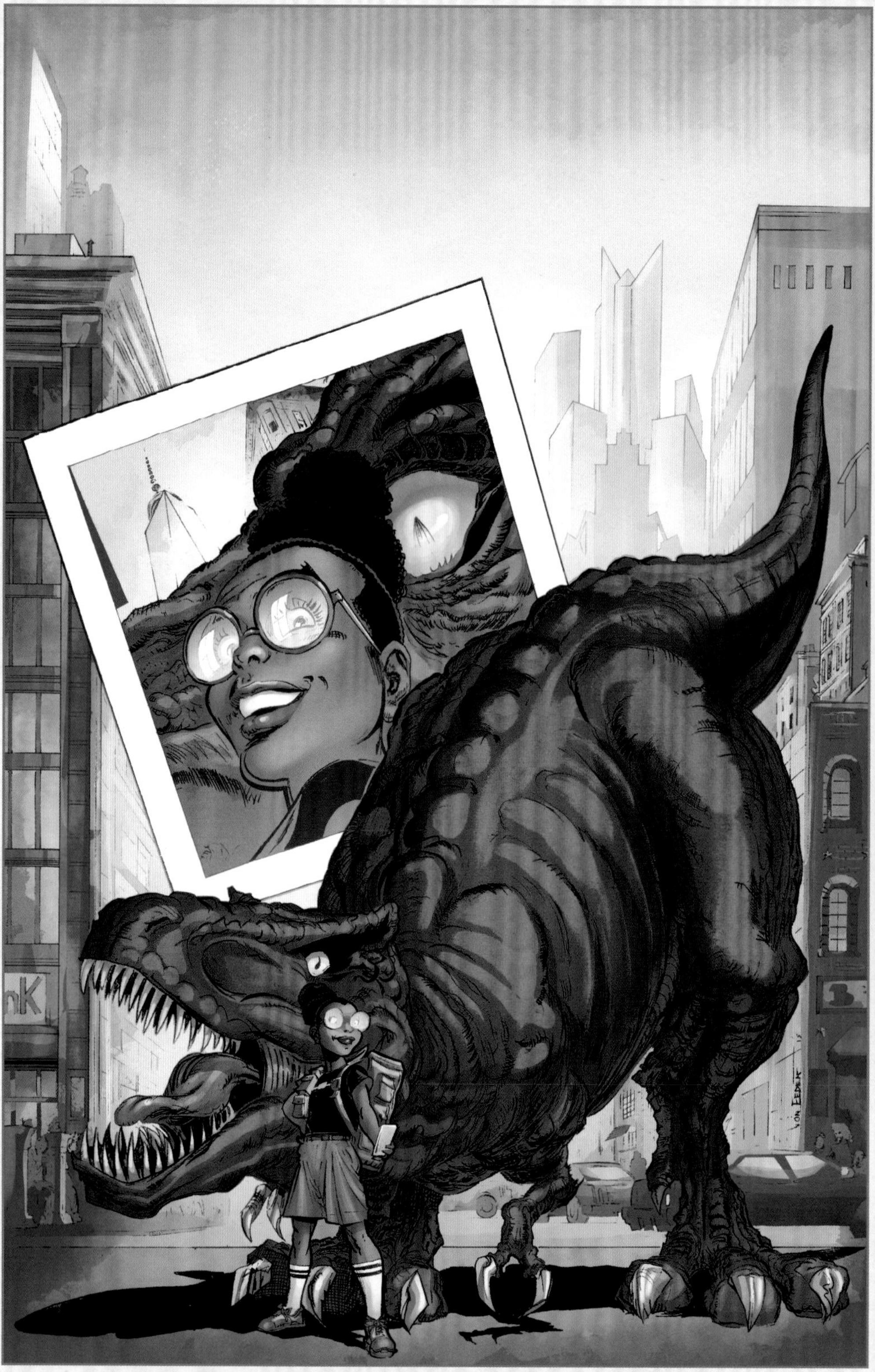

MOON GIRL AND DEVIL DINOSAUR #1 VARIANT
BY TREVOR VON EEDEN

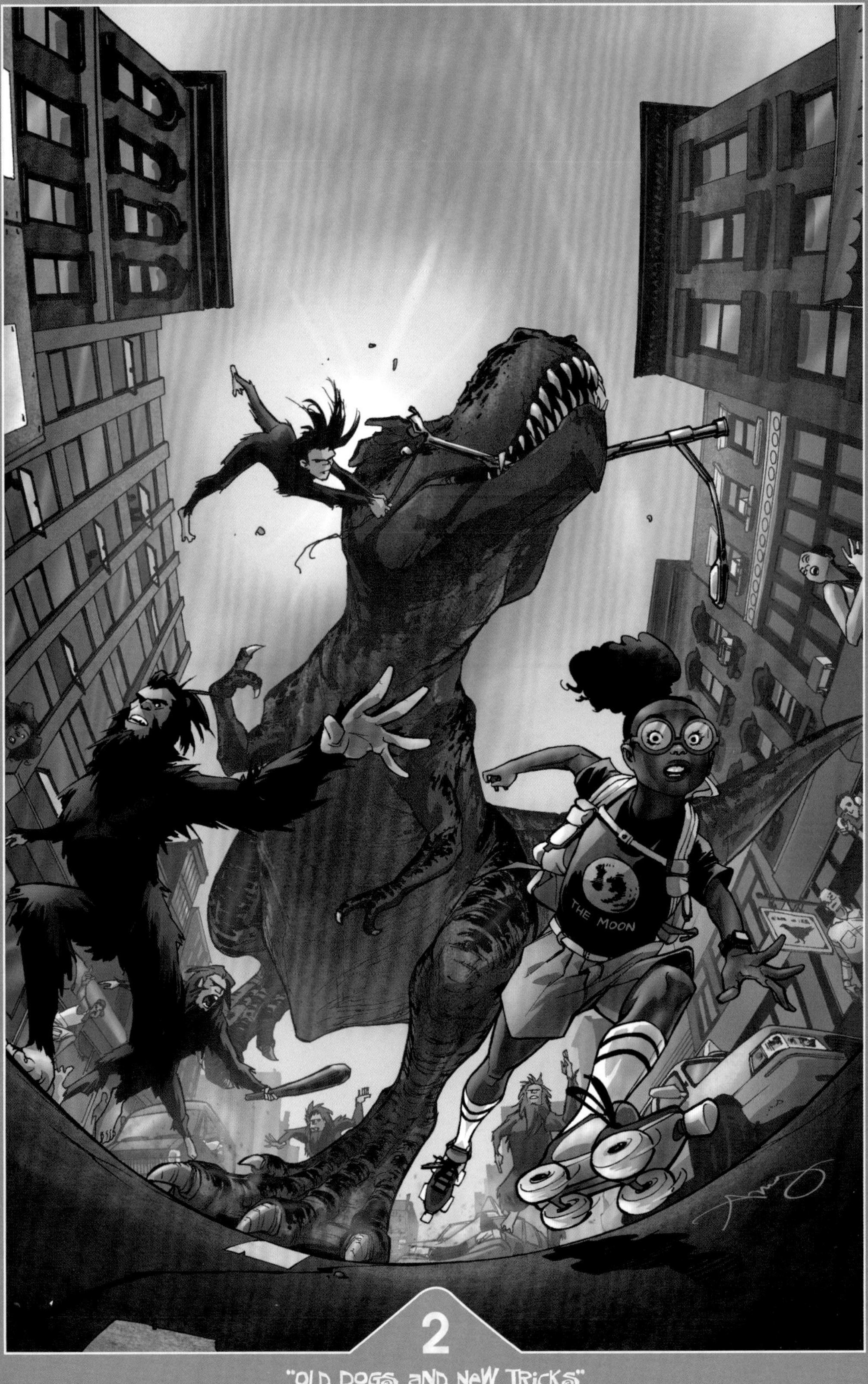
THE MOON

2

"OLD DOGS AND NEW TRICKS"

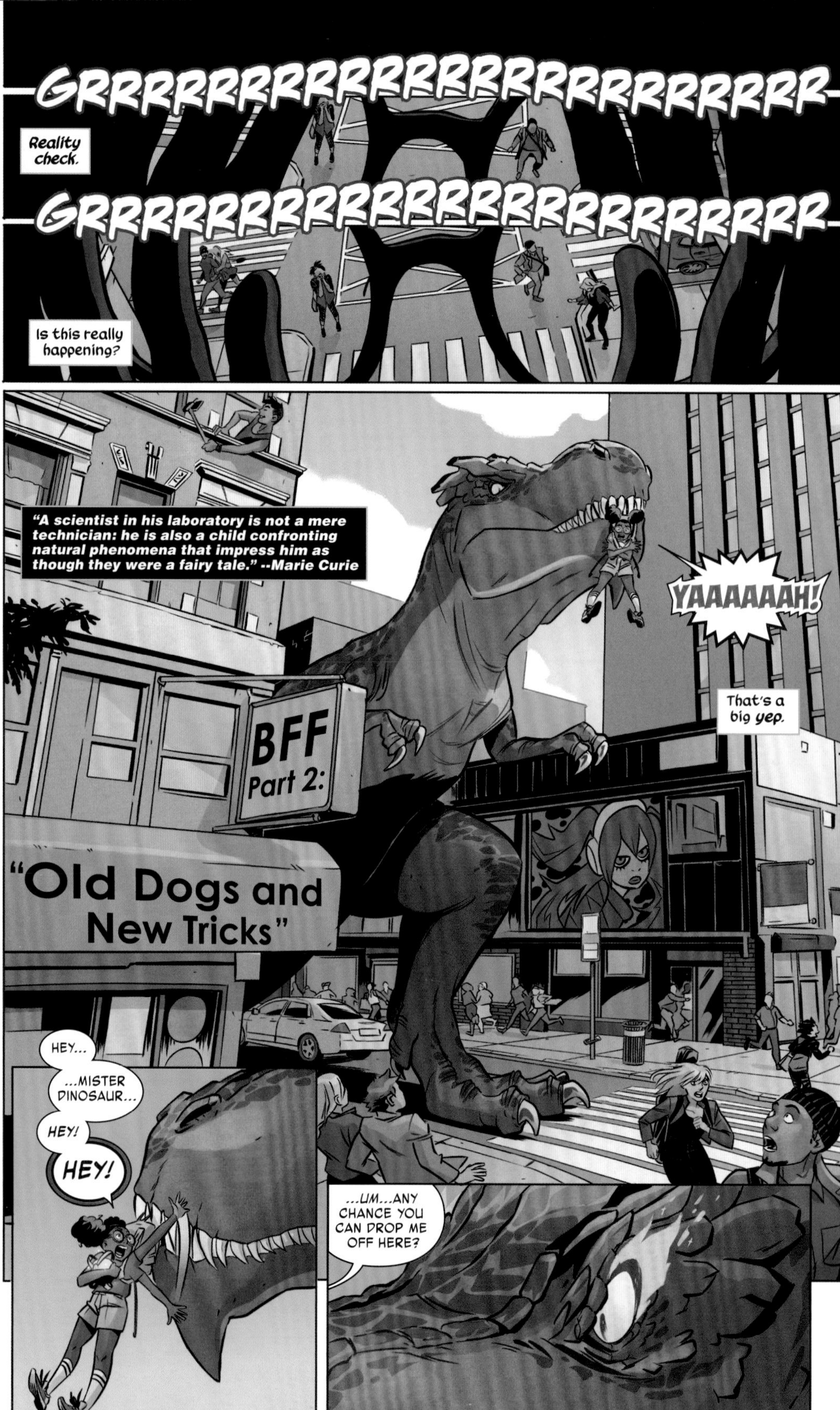
GRRRRRRRRRRRRRRRRRRRRRRRRR
Reality check.
GRRRRRRRRRRRRRRRRRRRRRRRRR
Is this really happening?
"A scientist in his laboratory is not a mere technician: he is also a child confronting natural phenomena that impress him as though they were a fairy tale." --Marie Curie
YAAAAAAH!
That's a big yep.
BFF Part 2:
"Old Dogs and New Tricks"
HEY...
...MISTER DINOSAUR...
HEY!
HEY!
...UM...ANY CHANCE YOU CAN DROP ME OFF HERE?

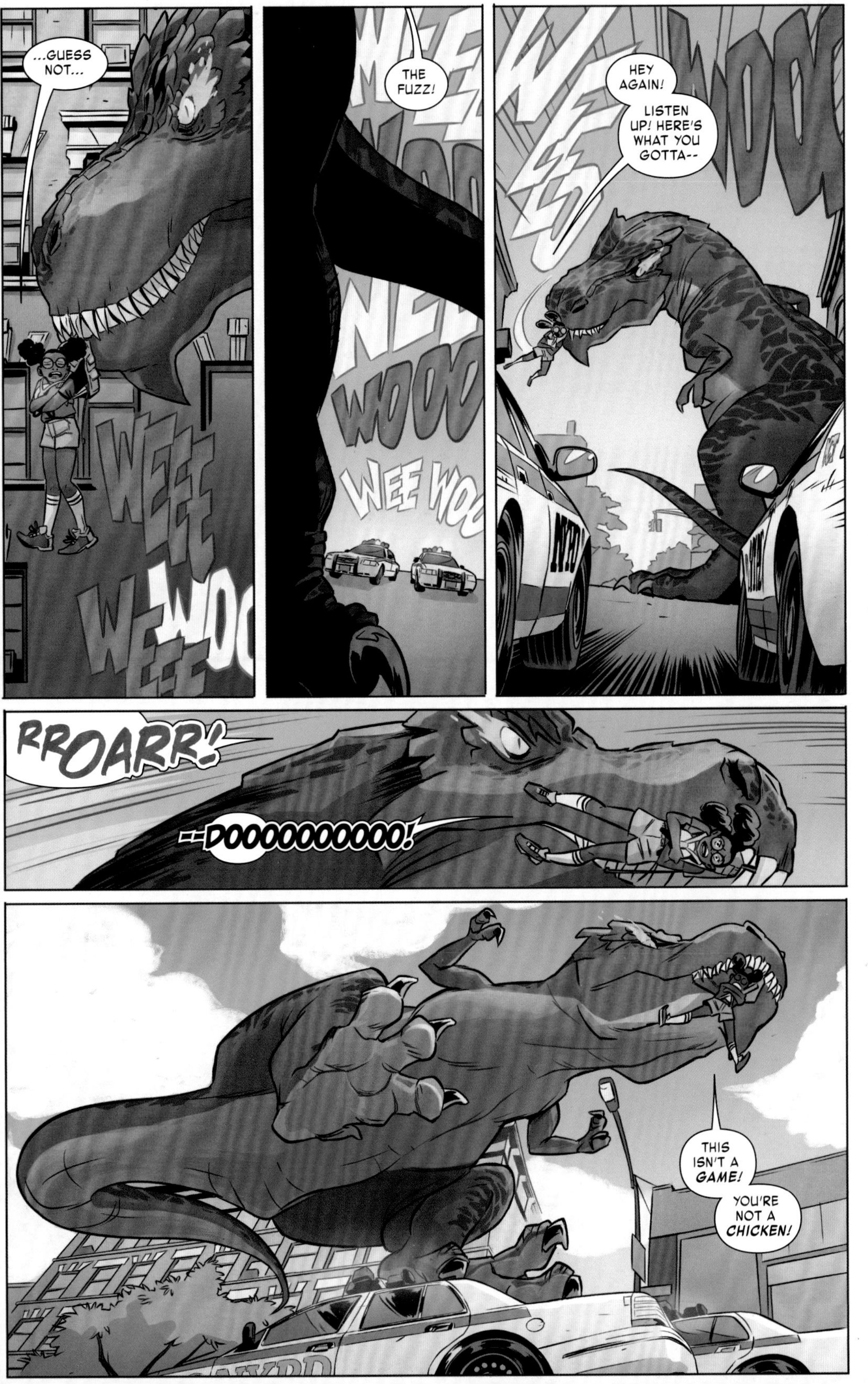
...GUESS NOT...
WEEE WEEE WOO
THE FUZZ!
WEE WOO WEE WOO
HEY AGAIN!
LISTEN UP! HERE'S WHAT YOU GOTTA--
RROARR!
--DOOOOOOOOOO!
THIS ISN'T A *GAME!*
YOU'RE NOT A *CHICKEN!*

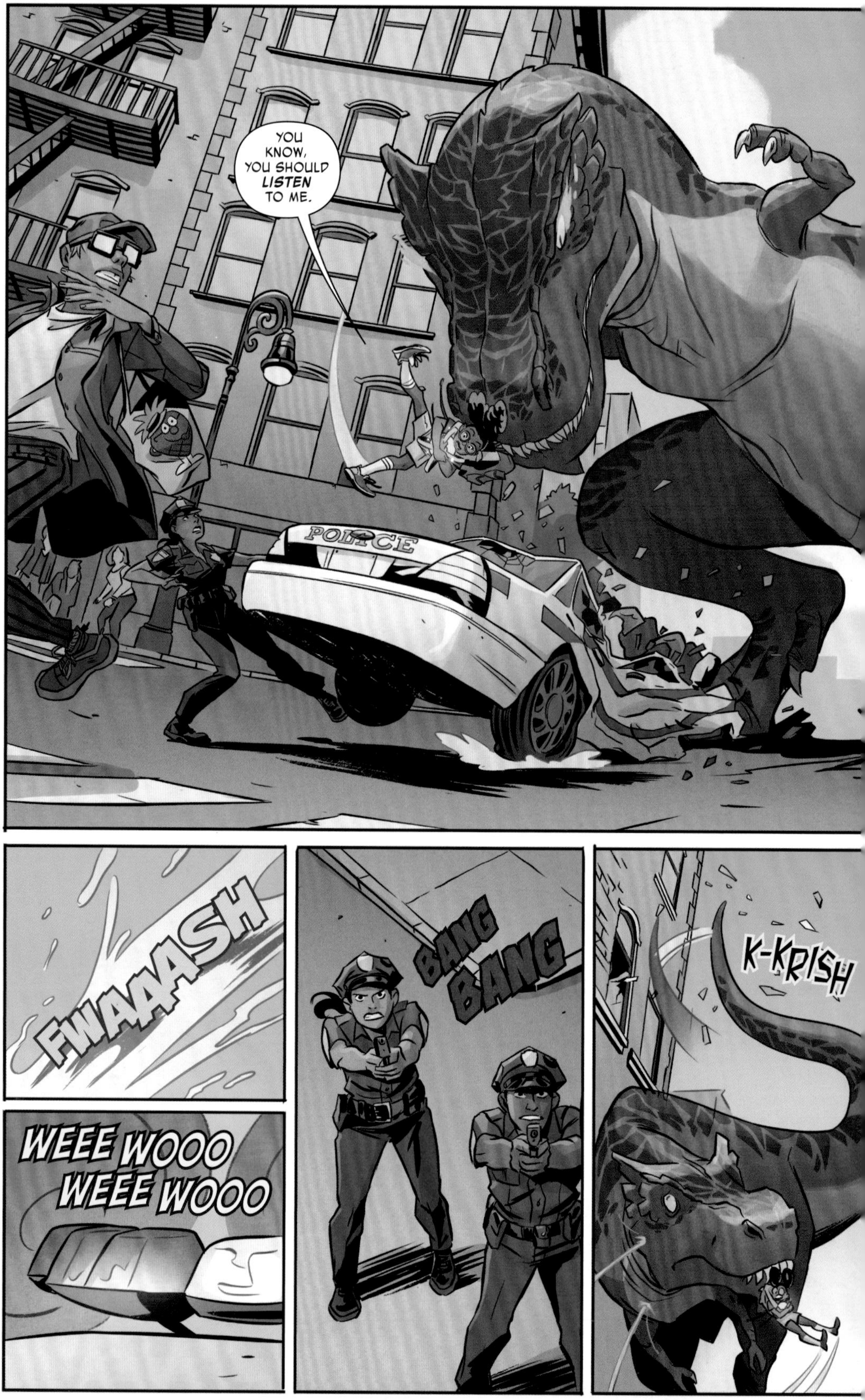
YOU KNOW, YOU SHOULD *LISTEN* TO ME.
POLICE
FWAAASH
BANG BANG
K-KRISH
WEEE WOOO WEEE WOOO

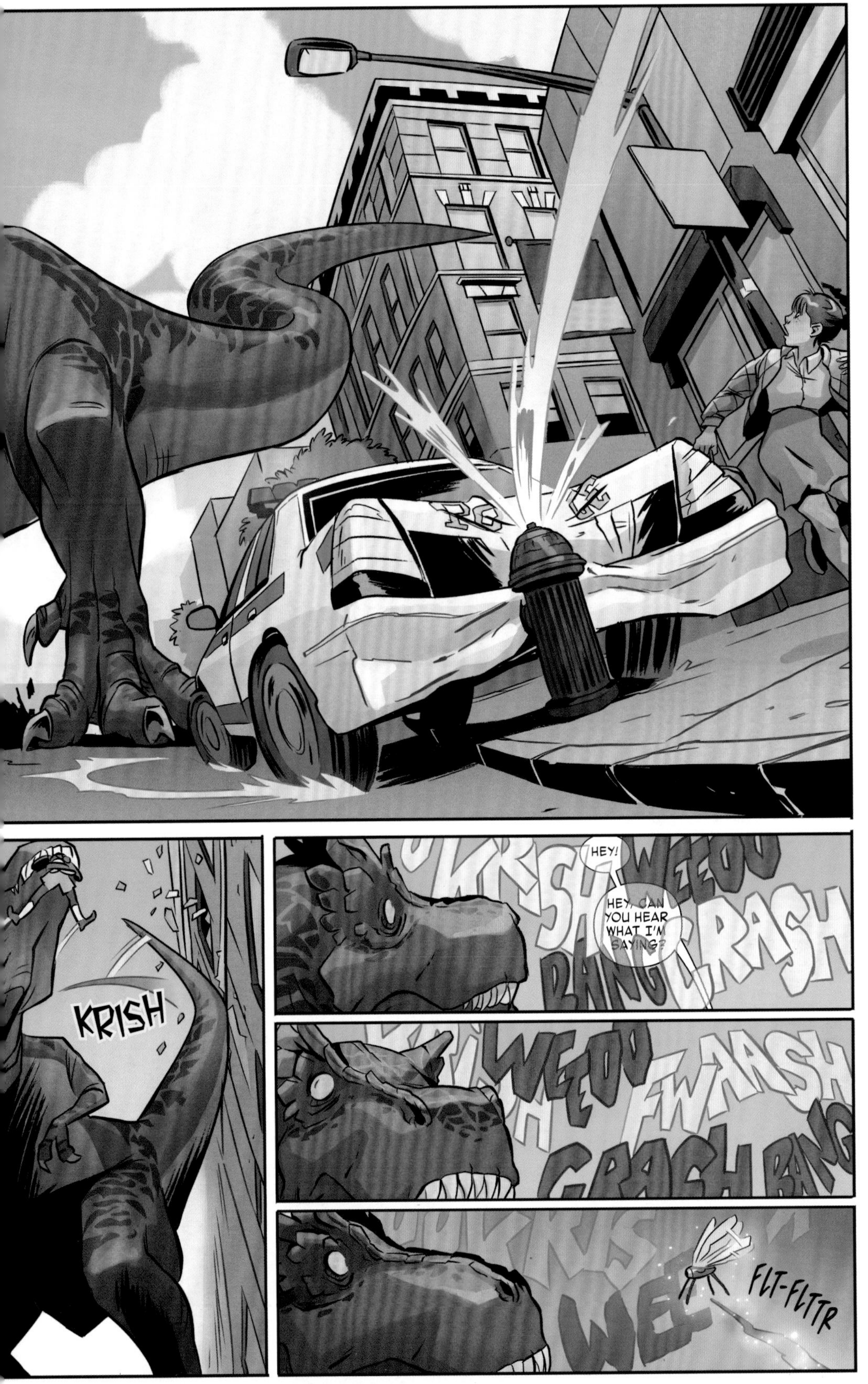
KRISH
HEY!
HEY, CAN YOU HEAR WHAT I'M SAYING?
WEEOO
CRASH
BANG
WEEOO
FWAASH
CRASH
BANG
FLT-FLTTR

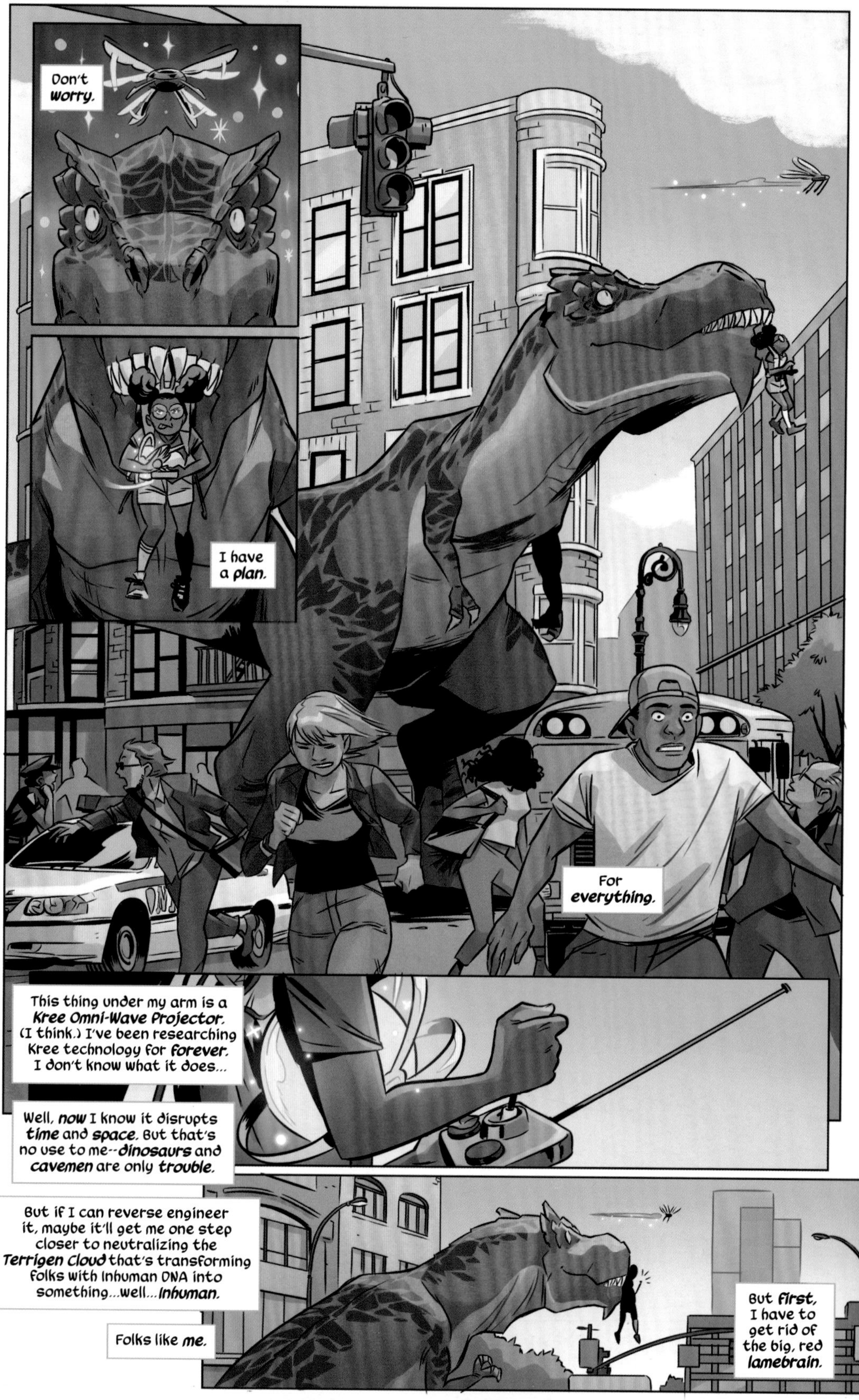
Don't worry.
I have a plan.
For everything.
This thing under my arm is a Kree Omni-Wave Projector. (I think.) I've been researching Kree technology for forever. I don't know what it does...
Well, now I know it disrupts time and space. But that's no use to me--dinosaurs and cavemen are only trouble.
But if I can reverse engineer it, maybe it'll get me one step closer to neutralizing the Terrigen Cloud that's transforming folks with Inhuman DNA into something...well...Inhuman.
Folks like me.
But first, I have to get rid of the big, red lamebrain.

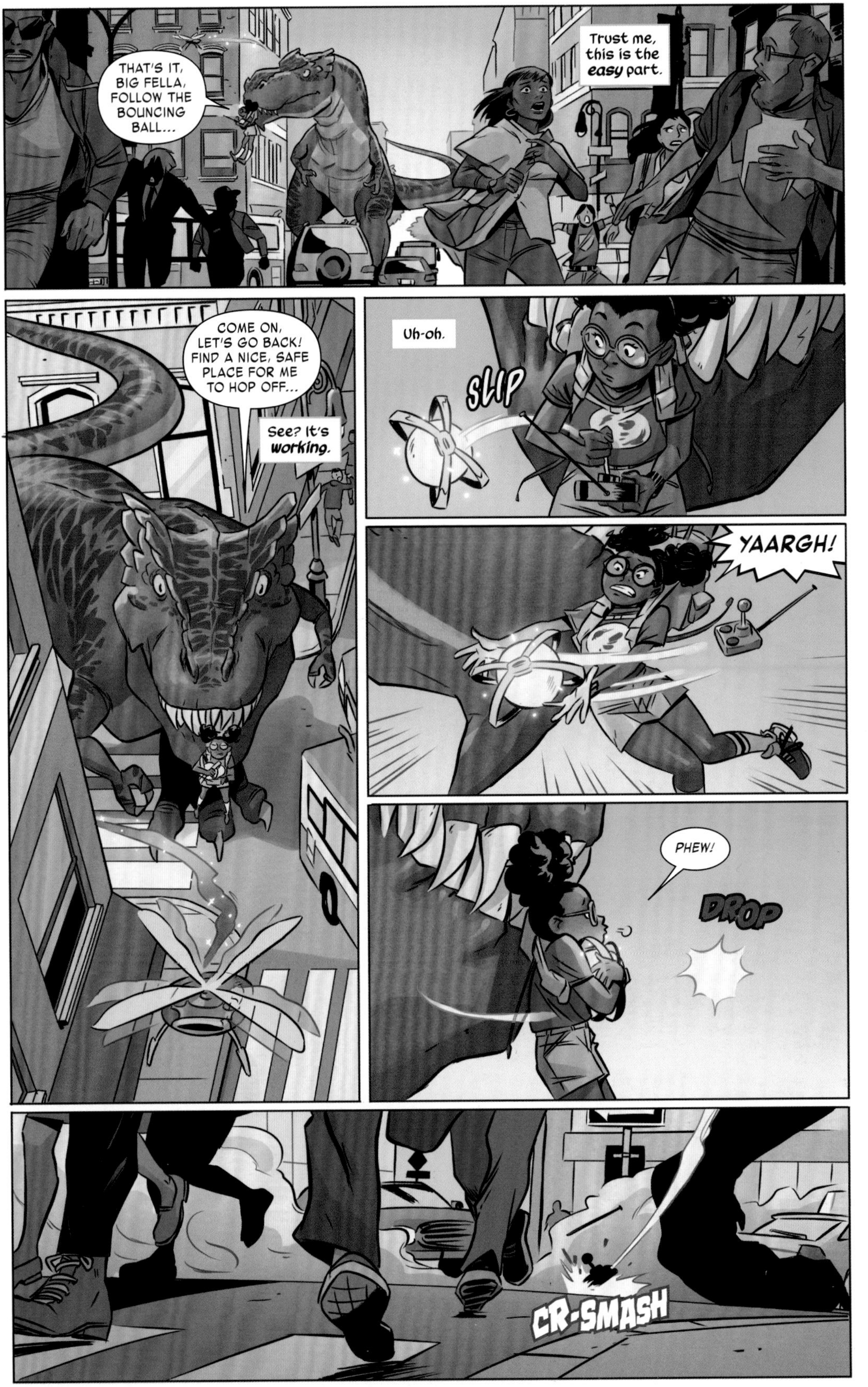
THAT'S IT, BIG FELLA, FOLLOW THE BOUNCING BALL...
Trust me, this is the *easy* part.
COME ON, LET'S GO BACK! FIND A NICE, SAFE PLACE FOR ME TO HOP OFF...
See? It's **working.**
Uh-oh.
SLIP
YAARGH!
PHEW!
DROP
CR-SMASH

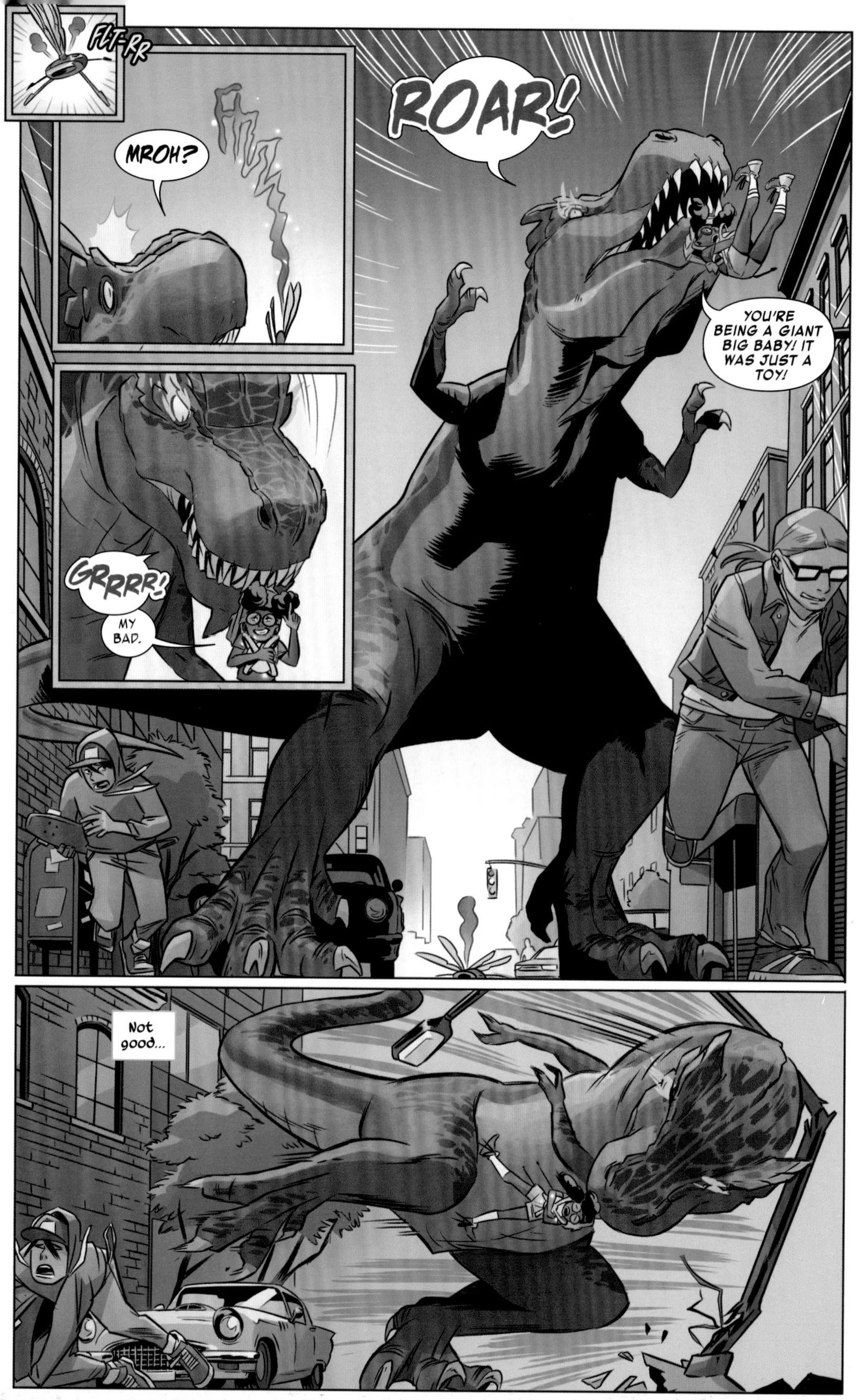
FLT-RR
MROH?
ROAR!
YOU'RE BEING A GIANT BIG BABY! IT WAS JUST A TOY!
GRRRR!
MY BAD.
Not good...

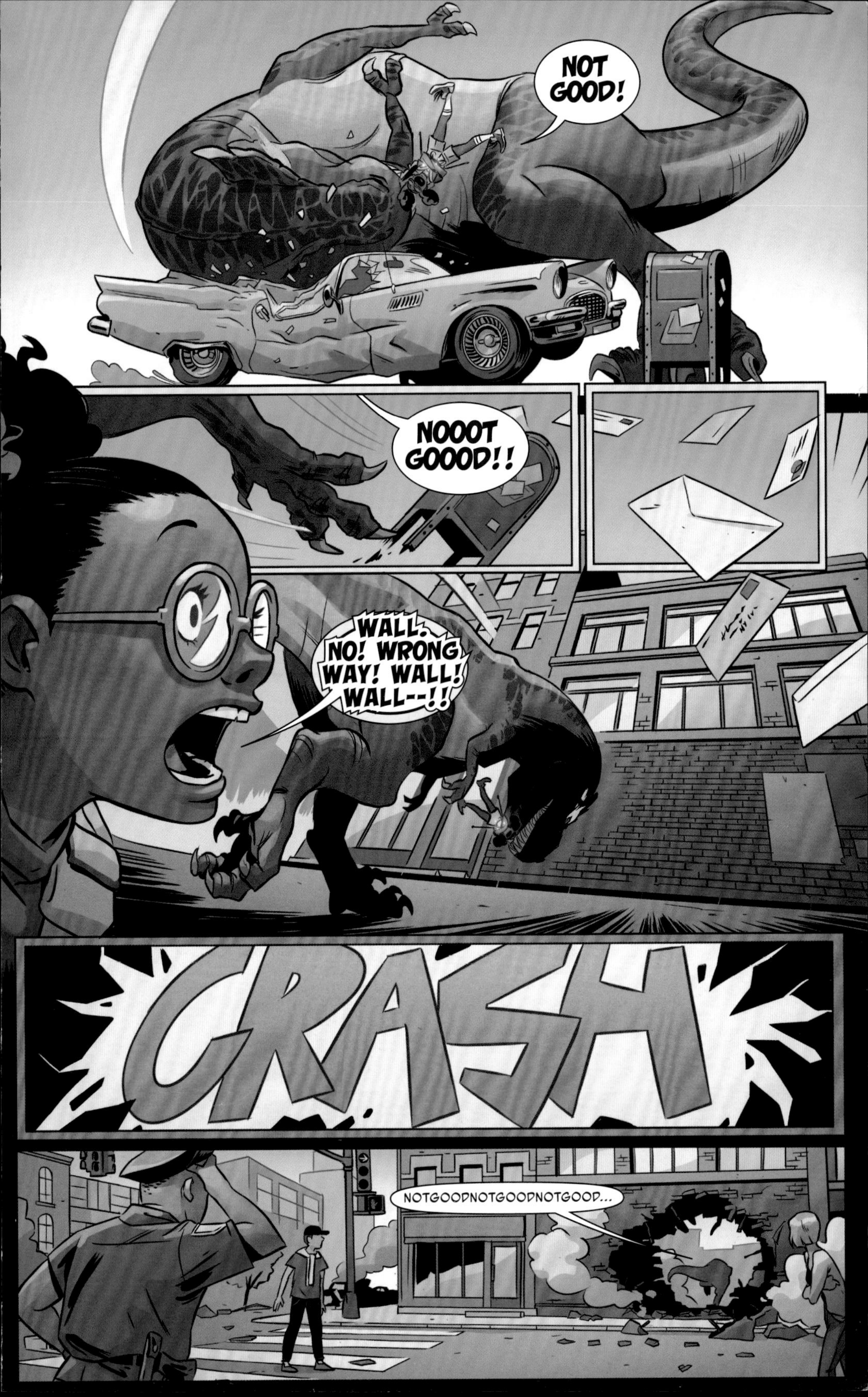
NOT GOOD!
NOOOT GOOOD!!
WALL. NO! WRONG WAY! WALL! WALL--!!
CRASH
NOTGOODNOTGOODNOTGOOD...

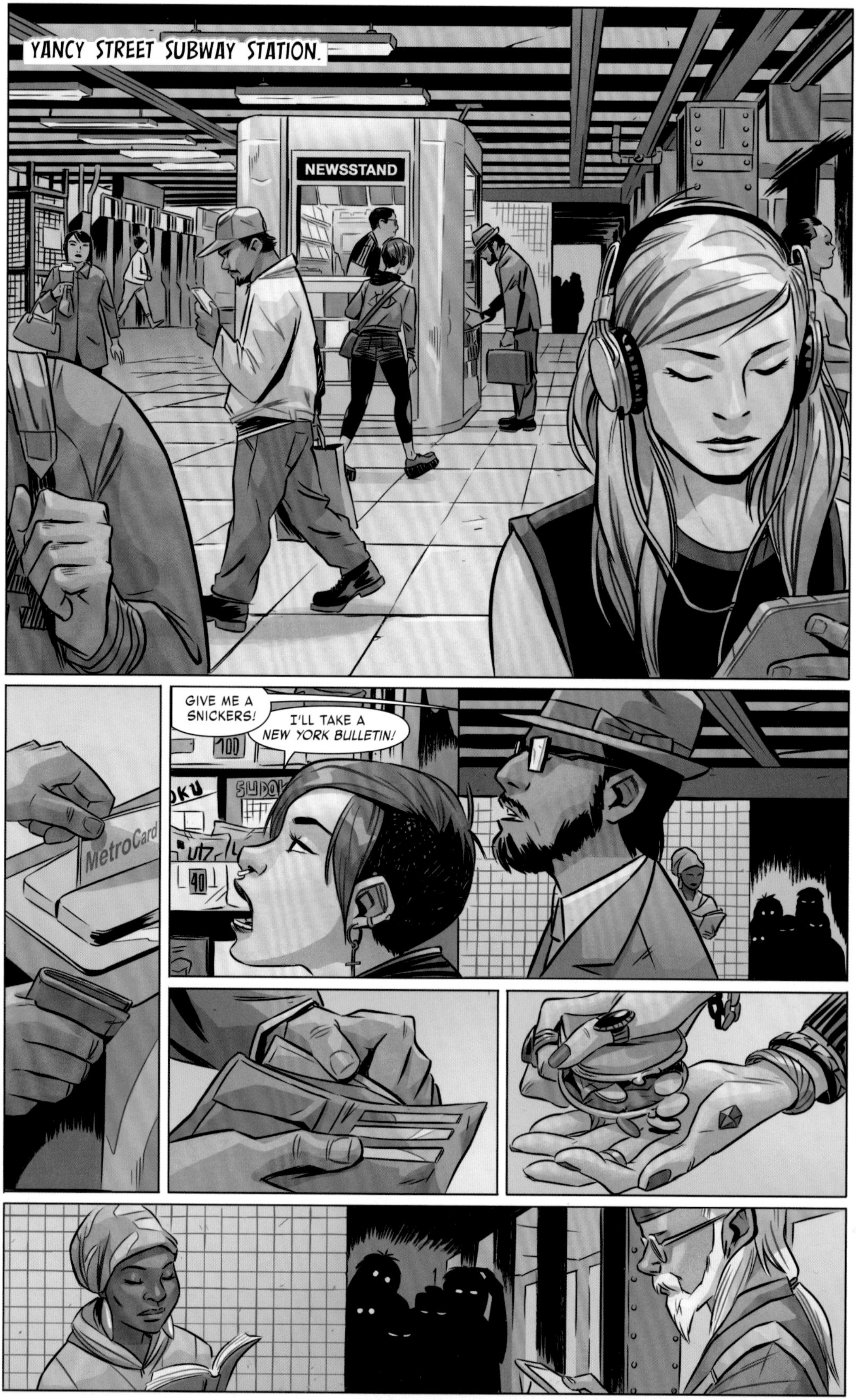
YANCY STREET SUBWAY STATION.
NEWSSTAND
GIVE ME A SNICKERS!
I'LL TAKE A NEW YORK BULLETIN!
MetroCard
SUDOKU

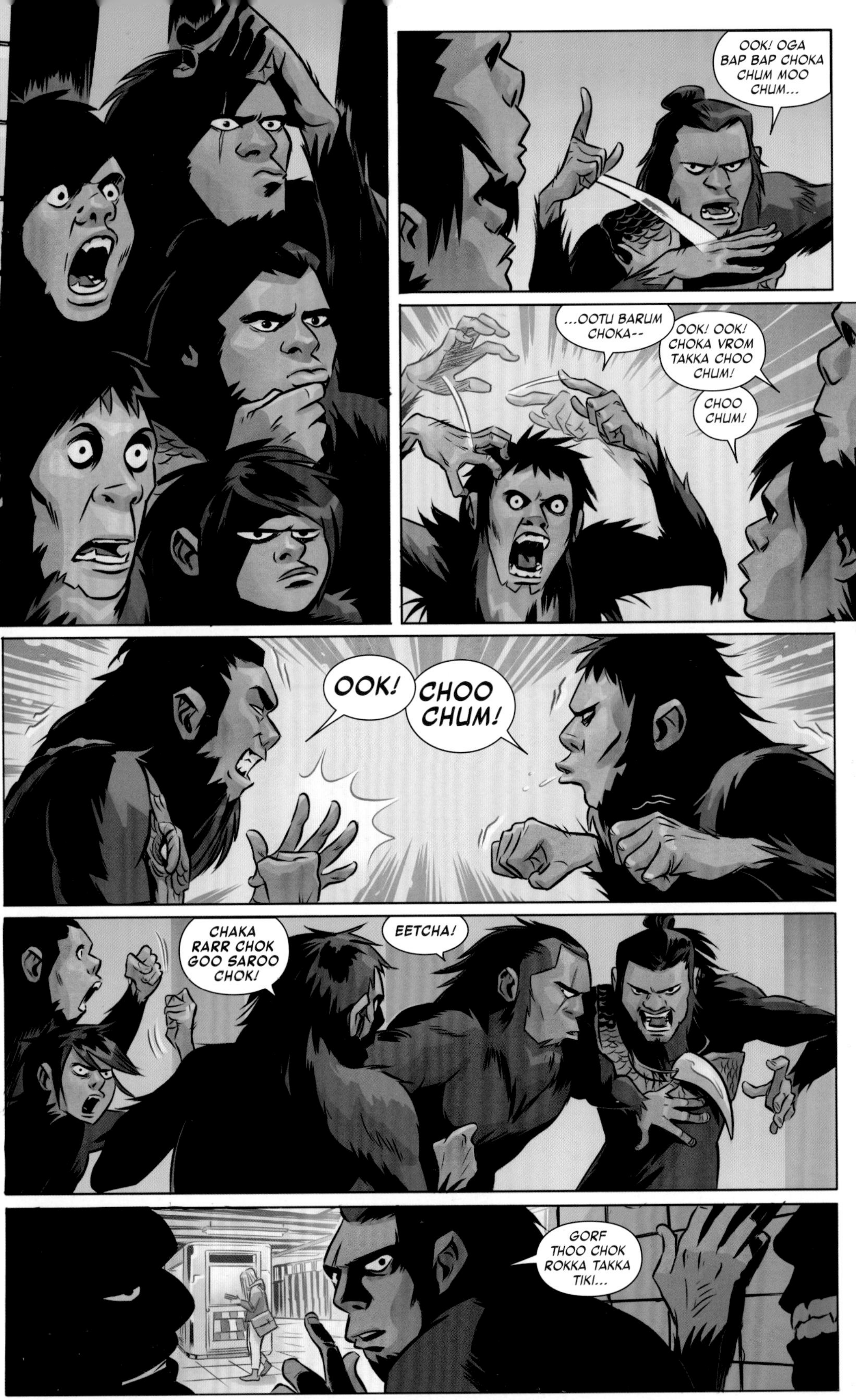
OOK! OGA BAP BAP CHOKA CHUM MOO CHUM...
...OOTU BARUM CHOKA--
OOK! OOK! CHOKA VROM TAKKA CHOO CHUM!
CHOO CHUM!
OOK!
CHOO CHUM!
CHAKA RARR CHOK GOO SAROO CHOK!
EETCHA!
GORF THOO CHOK ROKKA TAKKA TIKI...

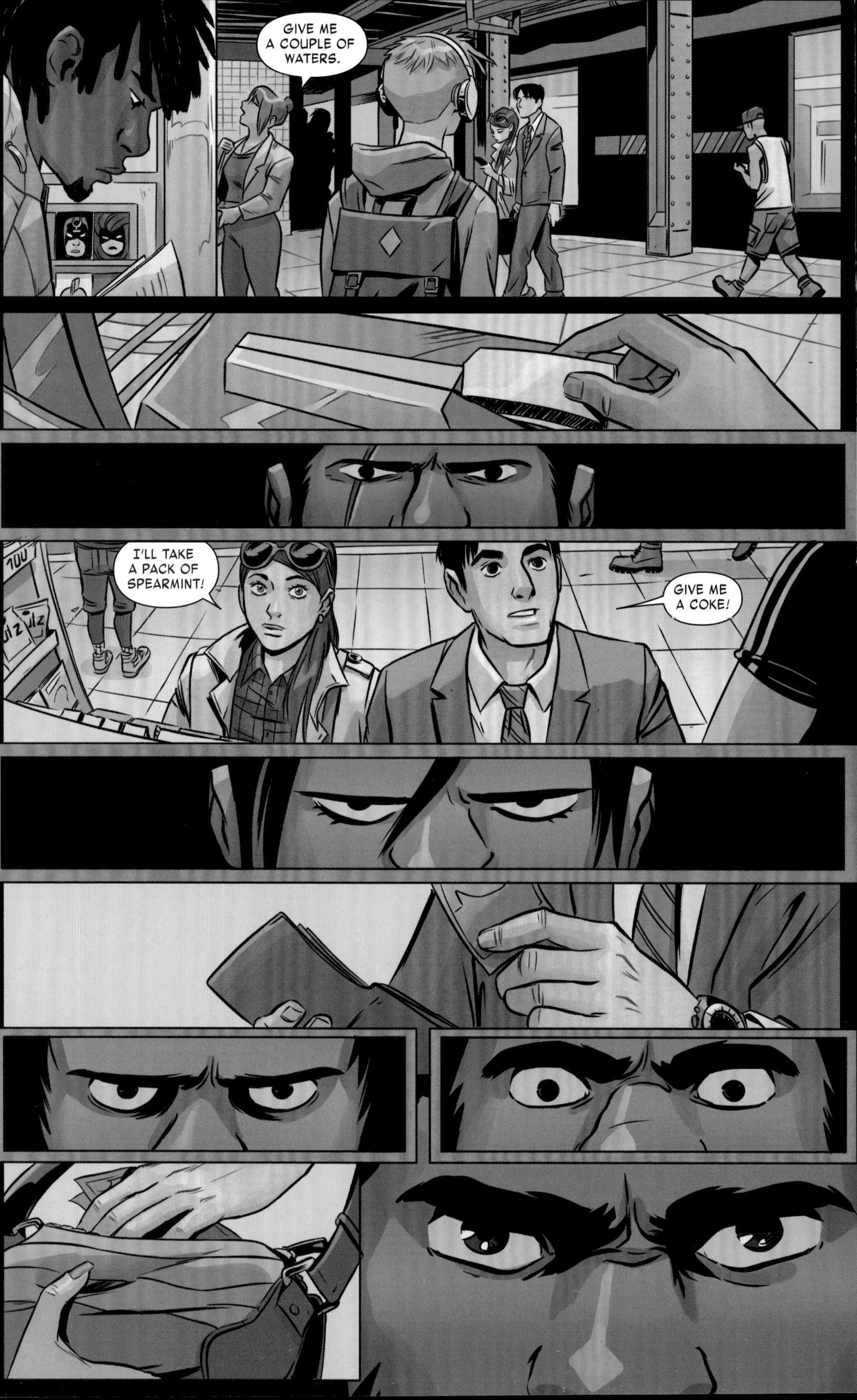
GIVE ME A COUPLE OF WATERS.
I'LL TAKE A PACK OF SPEARMINT!
GIVE ME A COKE!

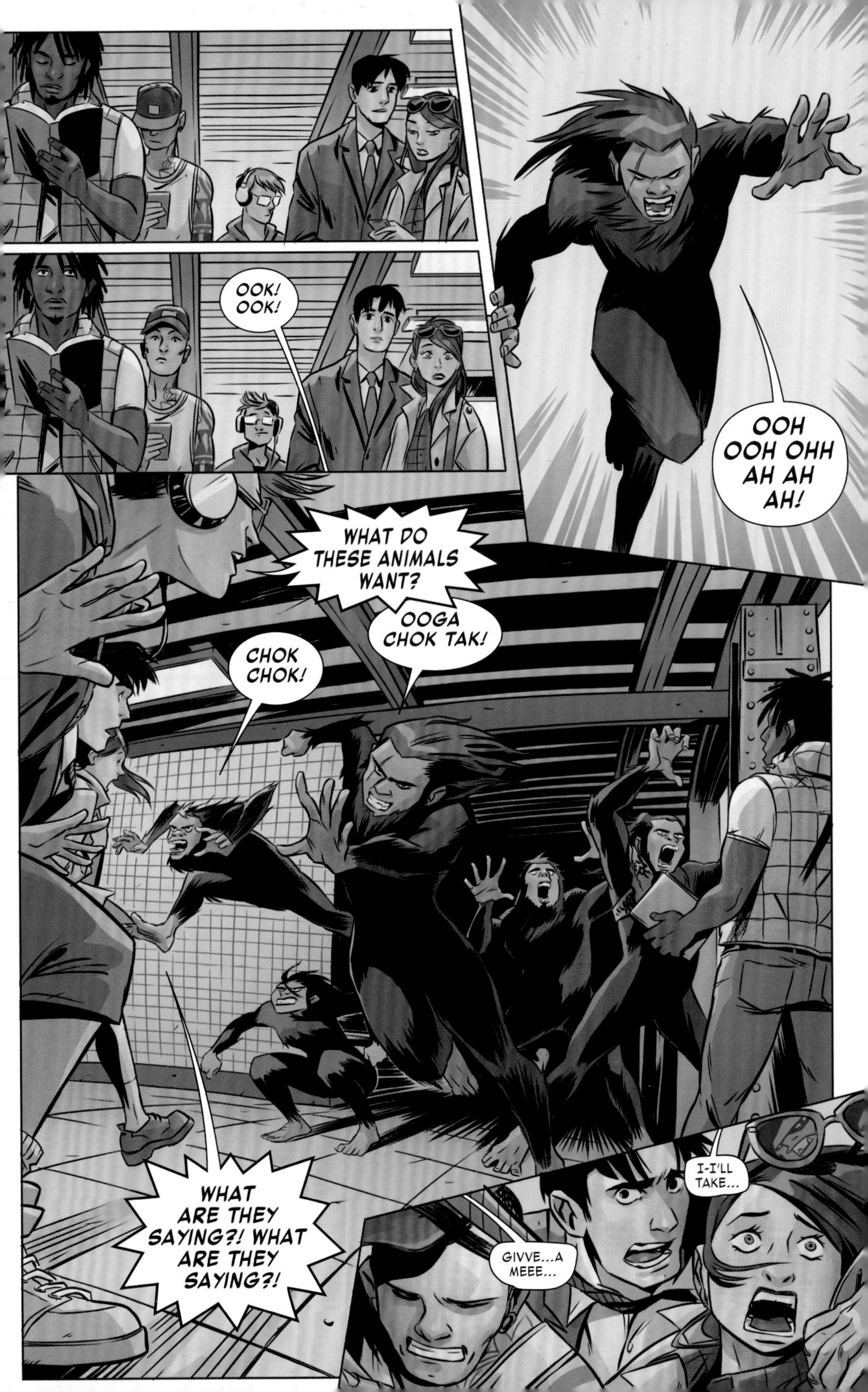
OOK! OOK!
OOH OOH OHH AH AH AH!
WHAT DO THESE ANIMALS WANT?
OOGA CHOK TAK!
CHOK CHOK!
WHAT ARE THEY SAYING?! WHAT ARE THEY SAYING?!
I-I'LL TAKE...
GIVVE...A MEEE...

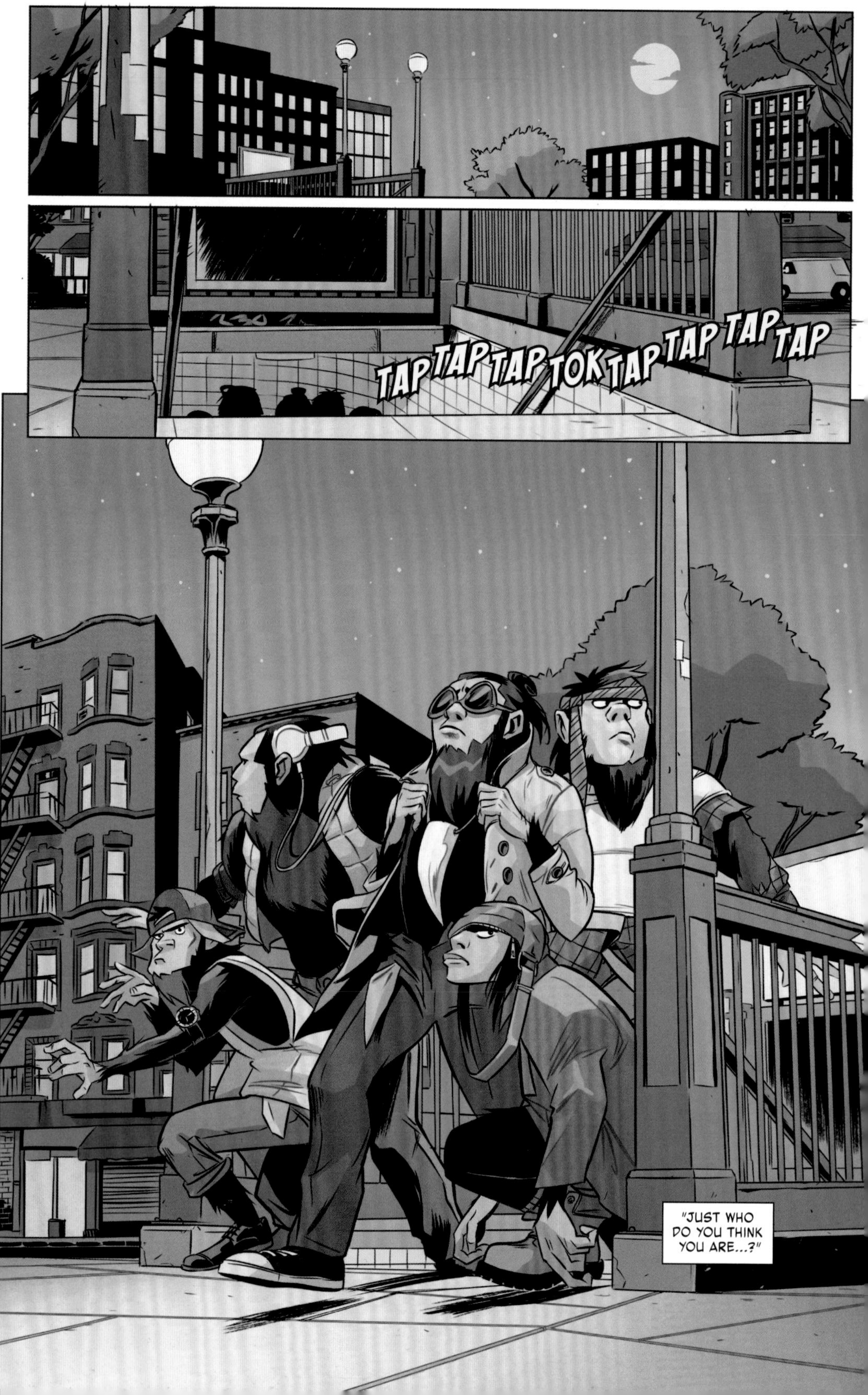
TAP TAP TAP TOK TAP TAP TAP TAP
"JUST WHO DO YOU THINK YOU ARE...?"

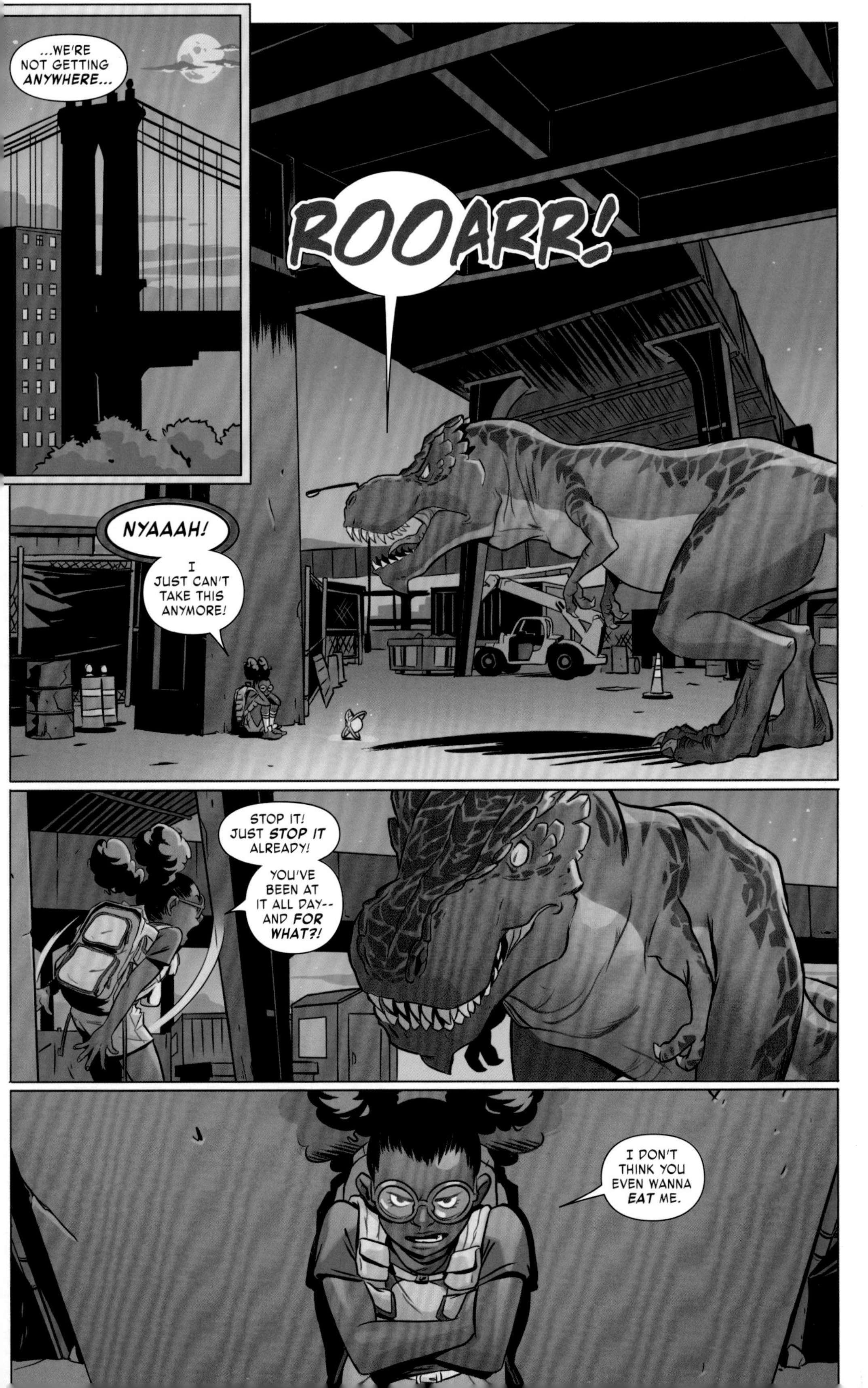
...WE'RE NOT GETTING ANYWHERE...
ROOARR!
NYAAAH!
I JUST CAN'T TAKE THIS ANYMORE!
STOP IT! JUST STOP IT ALREADY!
YOU'VE BEEN AT IT ALL DAY-- AND FOR WHAT?!
I DON'T THINK YOU EVEN WANNA EAT ME.

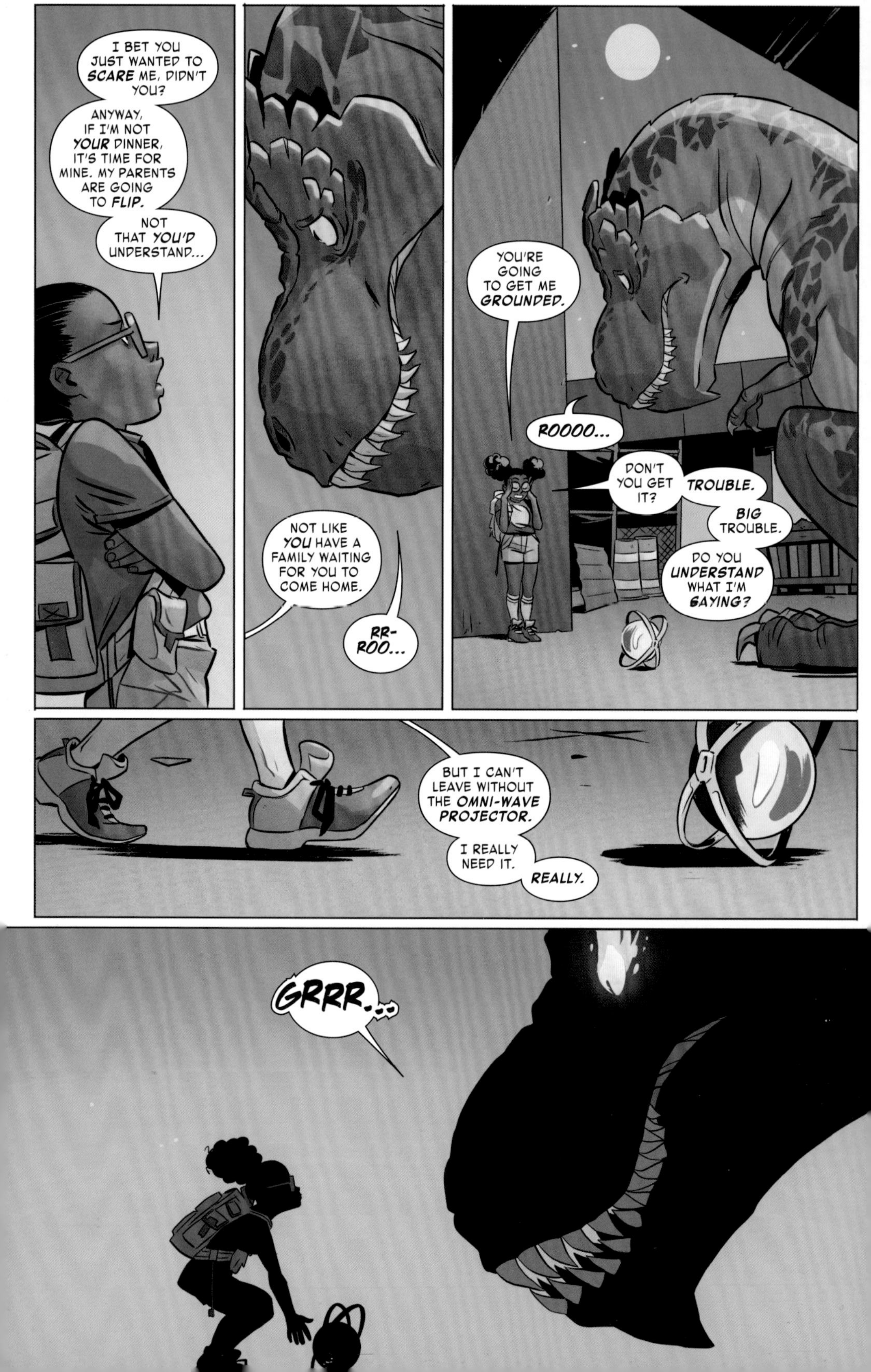
I BET YOU JUST WANTED TO SCARE ME, DIDN'T YOU?
ANYWAY, IF I'M NOT YOUR DINNER, IT'S TIME FOR MINE. MY PARENTS ARE GOING TO FLIP.
NOT THAT YOU'D UNDERSTAND...
NOT LIKE YOU HAVE A FAMILY WAITING FOR YOU TO COME HOME.
RR-ROO...
YOU'RE GOING TO GET ME GROUNDED.
ROOOO...
DON'T YOU GET IT?
TROUBLE.
BIG TROUBLE.
DO YOU UNDERSTAND WHAT I'M SAYING?
BUT I CAN'T LEAVE WITHOUT THE OMNI-WAVE PROJECTOR.
I REALLY NEED IT.
REALLY.
GRRR...

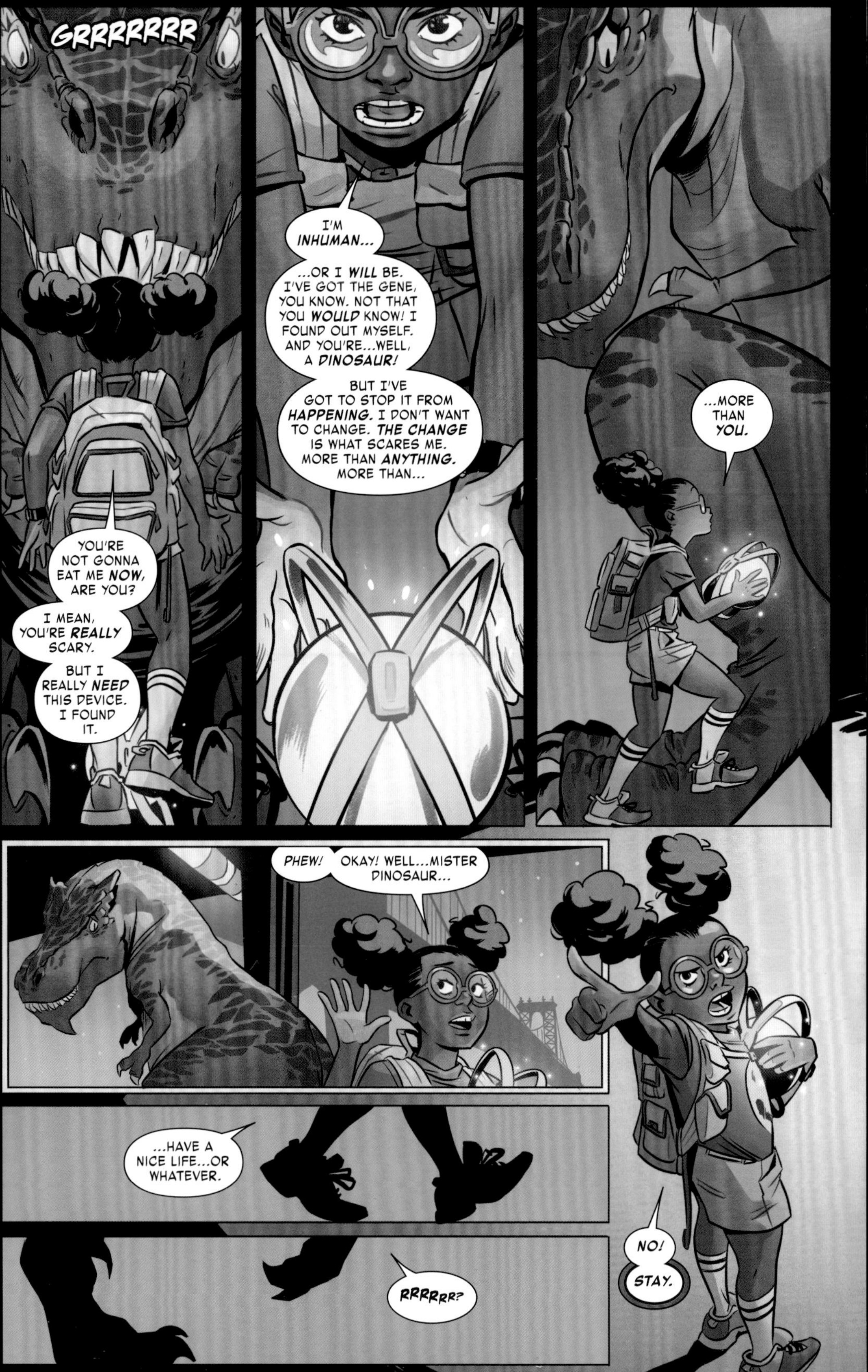

GRRRRRRR
YOU'RE NOT GONNA EAT ME NOW, ARE YOU?
I MEAN, YOU'RE REALLY SCARY.
BUT I REALLY NEED THIS DEVICE. I FOUND IT.
I'M INHUMAN...
...OR I WILL BE. I'VE GOT THE GENE, YOU KNOW. NOT THAT YOU WOULD KNOW! I FOUND OUT MYSELF. AND YOU'RE...WELL, A DINOSAUR!
BUT I'VE GOT TO STOP IT FROM HAPPENING. I DON'T WANT TO CHANGE. THE CHANGE IS WHAT SCARES ME. MORE THAN ANYTHING. MORE THAN...
...MORE THAN YOU.
PHEW!
OKAY! WELL...MISTER DINOSAUR...
...HAVE A NICE LIFE...OR WHATEVER.
RRRRRR?
NO!
STAY.

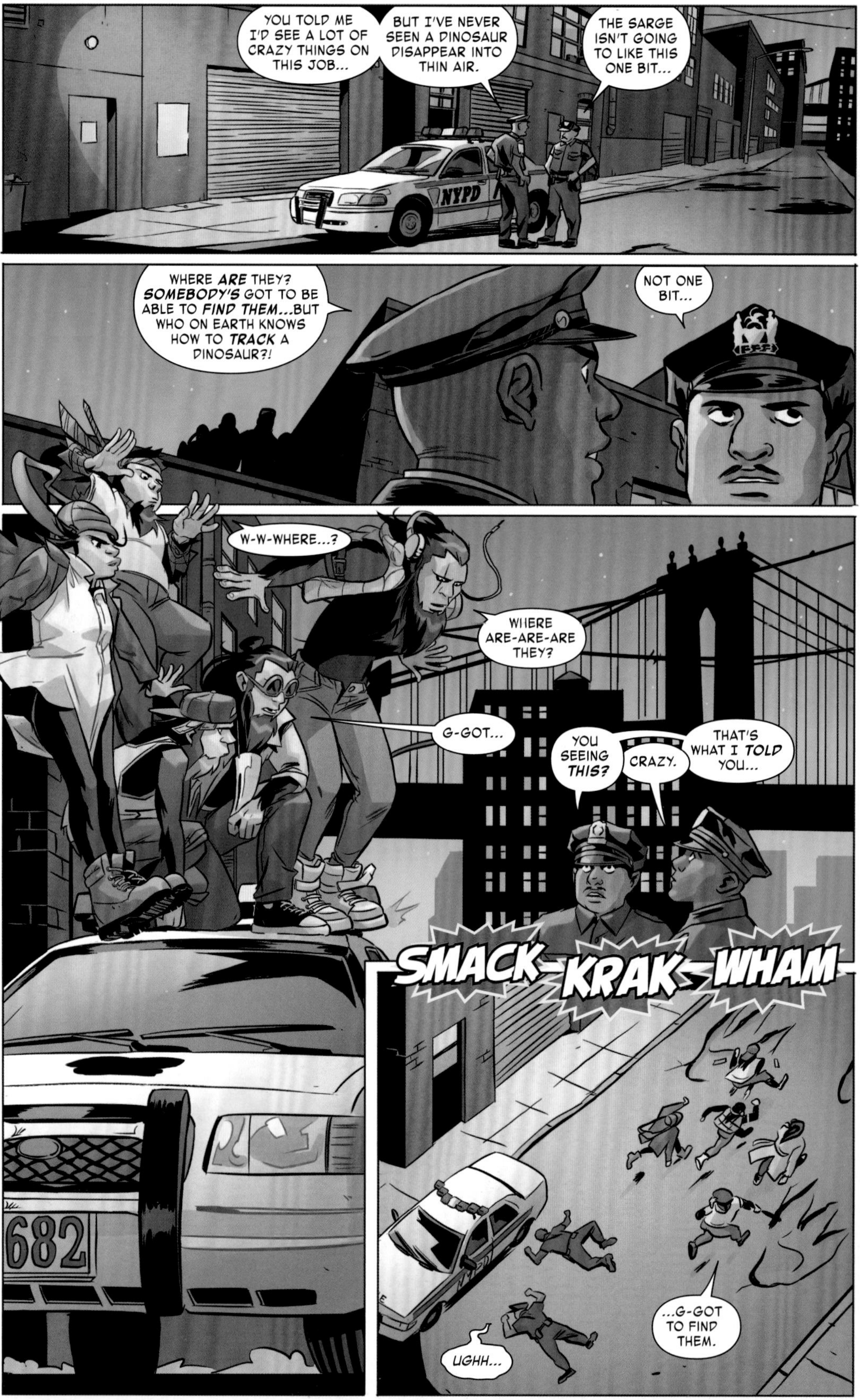
YOU TOLD ME I'D SEE A LOT OF CRAZY THINGS ON THIS JOB...
BUT I'VE NEVER SEEN A DINOSAUR DISAPPEAR INTO THIN AIR.
THE SARGE ISN'T GOING TO LIKE THIS ONE BIT...
NYPD
WHERE ARE THEY? SOMEBODY'S GOT TO BE ABLE TO FIND THEM...BUT WHO ON EARTH KNOWS HOW TO TRACK A DINOSAUR?!
NOT ONE BIT...
W-W-WHERE...?
WHERE ARE-ARE-ARE THEY?
G-GOT...
YOU SEEING THIS?
CRAZY.
THAT'S WHAT I TOLD YOU...
682
SMACK
KRAK
WHAM
...G-GOT TO FIND THEM.
UGHH...

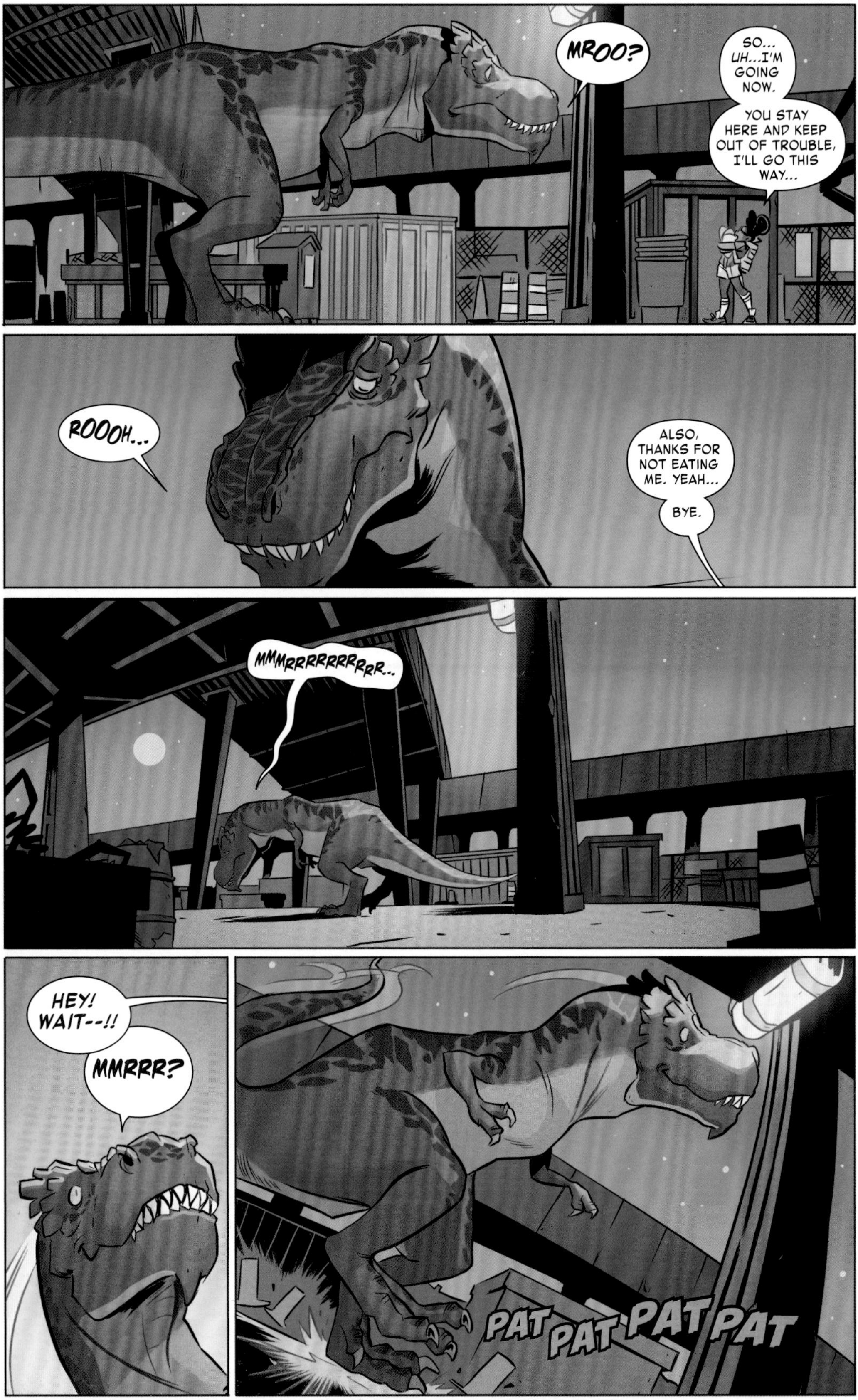
MROO?
SO... UH...I'M GOING NOW.
YOU STAY HERE AND KEEP OUT OF TROUBLE, I'LL GO THIS WAY...
ROOOH...
ALSO, THANKS FOR NOT EATING ME. YEAH...
BYE.
MMMRRRRRRRRRR...
HEY! WAIT--!!
MMRRR?
PAT PAT PAT PAT

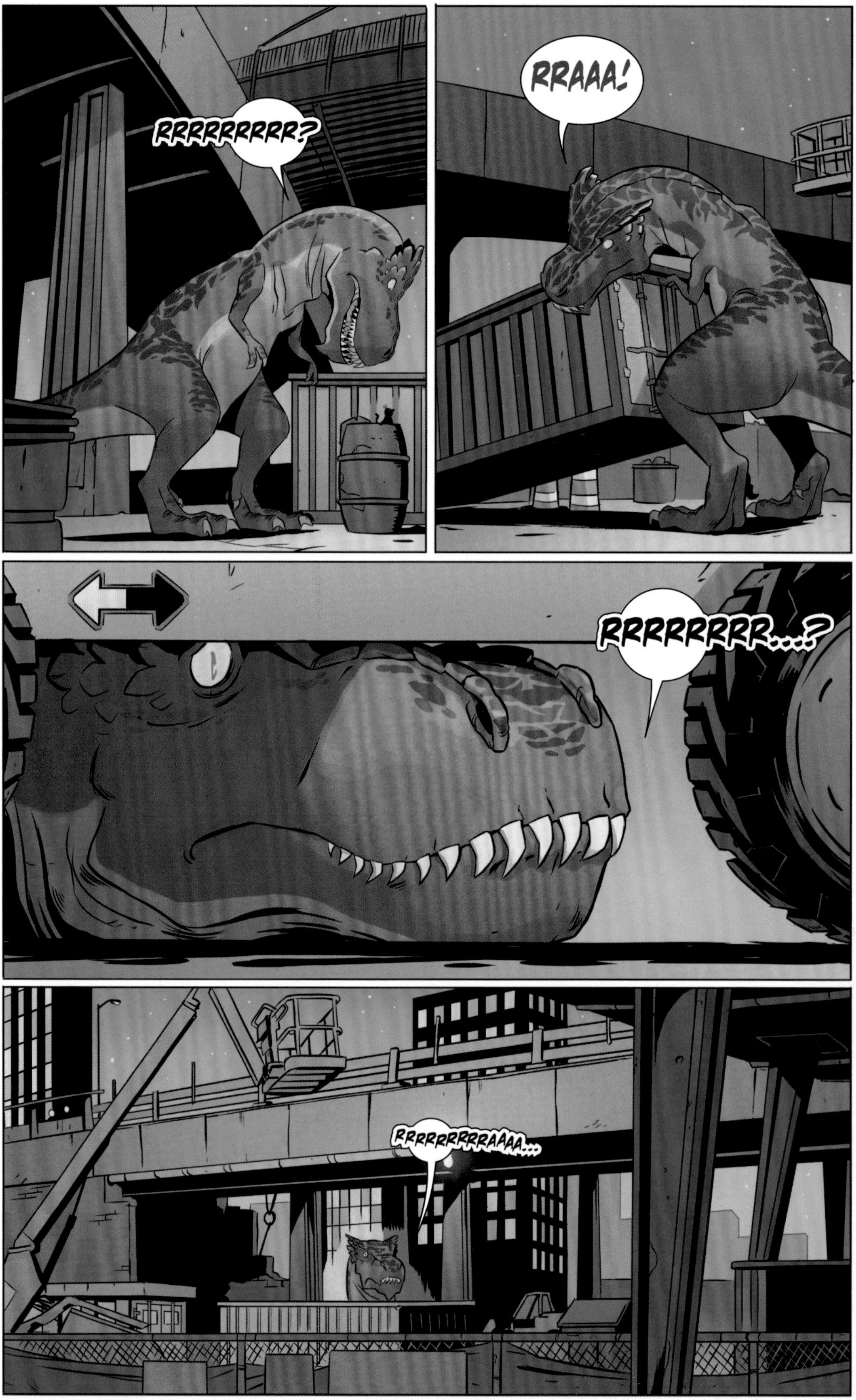
RRRRRRRRR?
RRAAA!
RRRRRRRR...?
RRRRRRRRRAAAA...

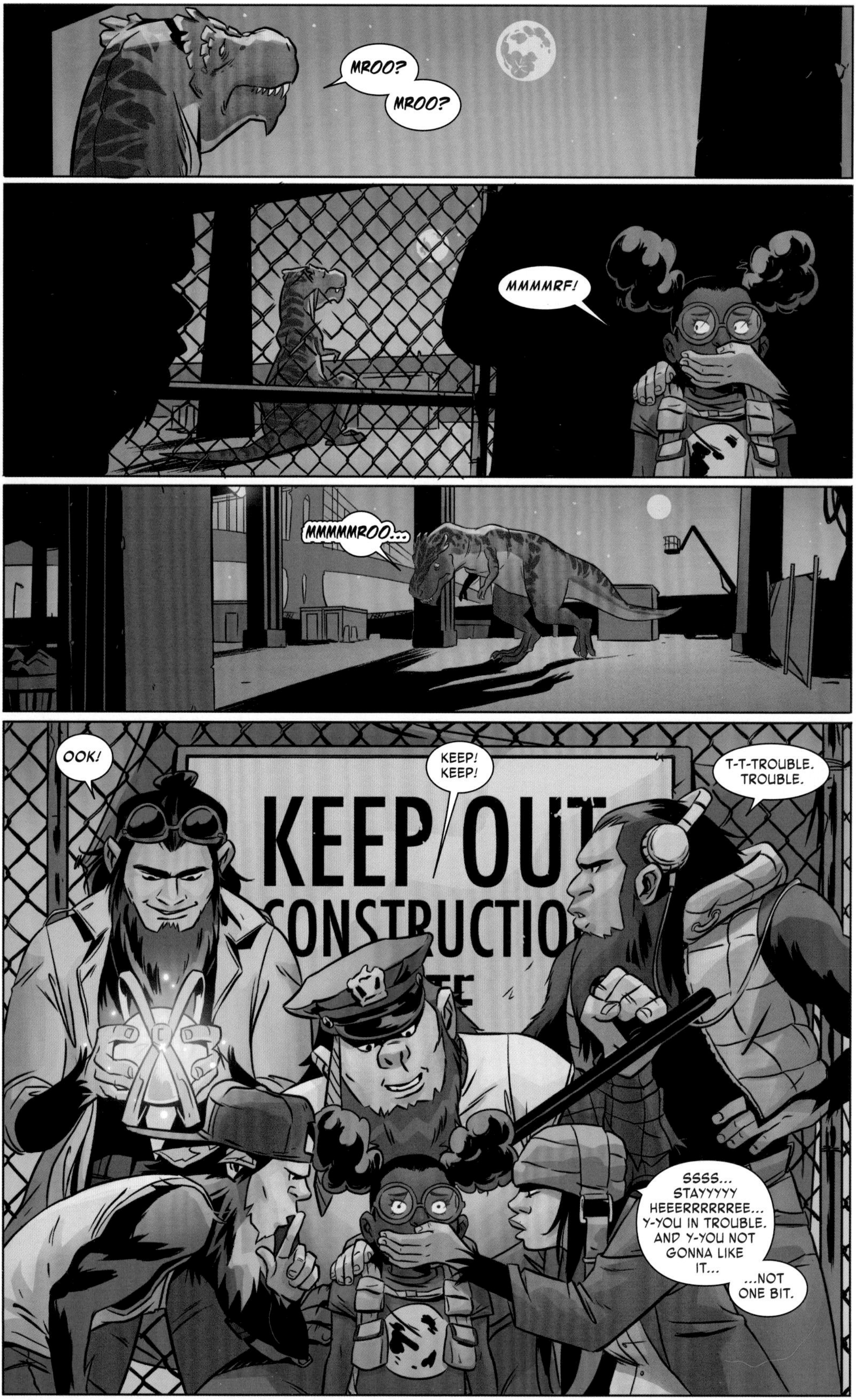
MROO?
MROO?
MMMMRF!
MMMMMROO...
OOK!
KEEP! KEEP!
T-T-TROUBLE. TROUBLE.
KEEP OUT
CONSTRUCTIO
SSSS... STAYYYYY HEEERRRRRREE... Y-YOU IN TROUBLE. AND Y-YOU NOT GONNA LIKE IT...
...NOT ONE BIT.

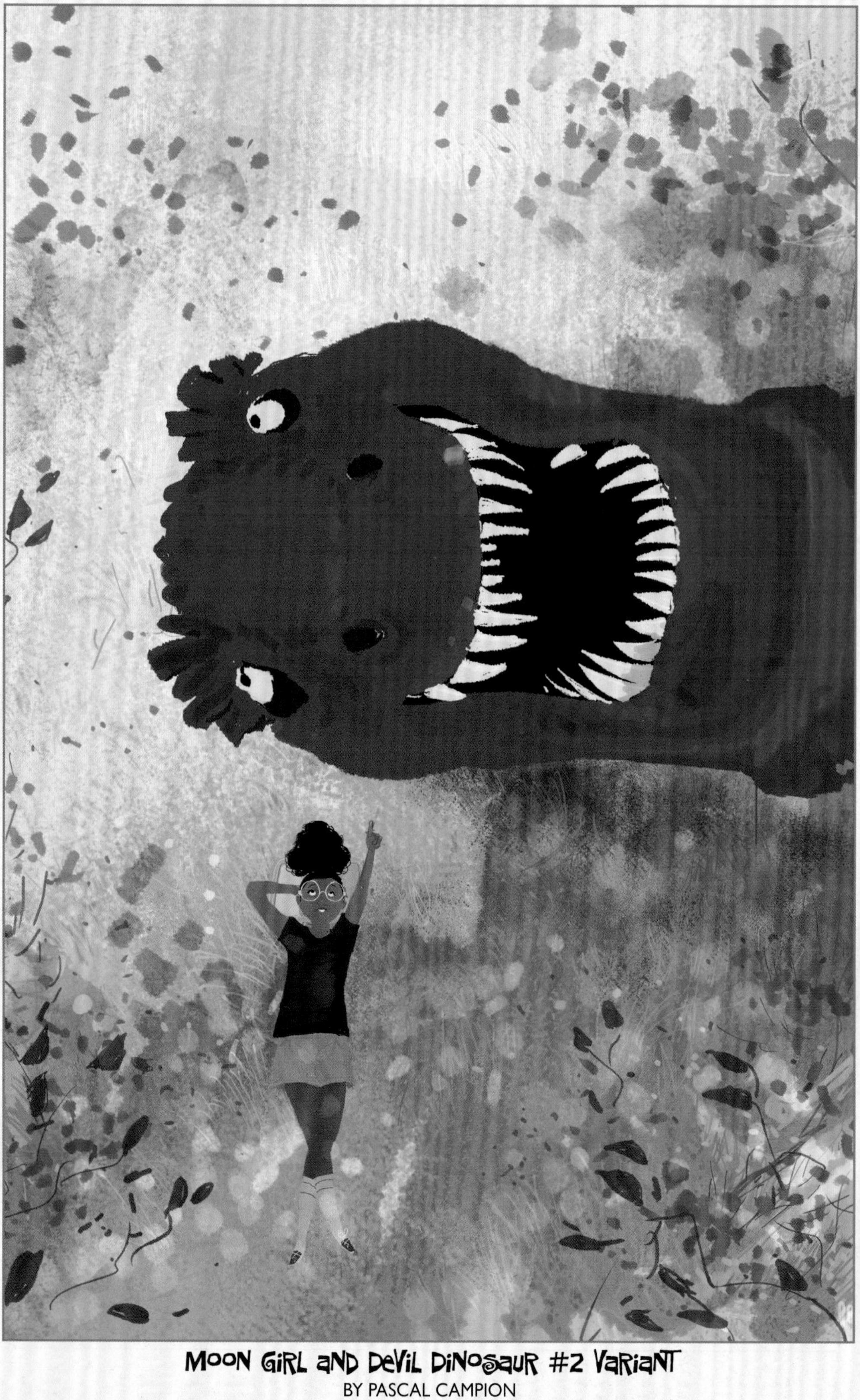

MOON GIRL AND DEVIL DINOSAUR #2 VARIANT
BY PASCAL CAMPION

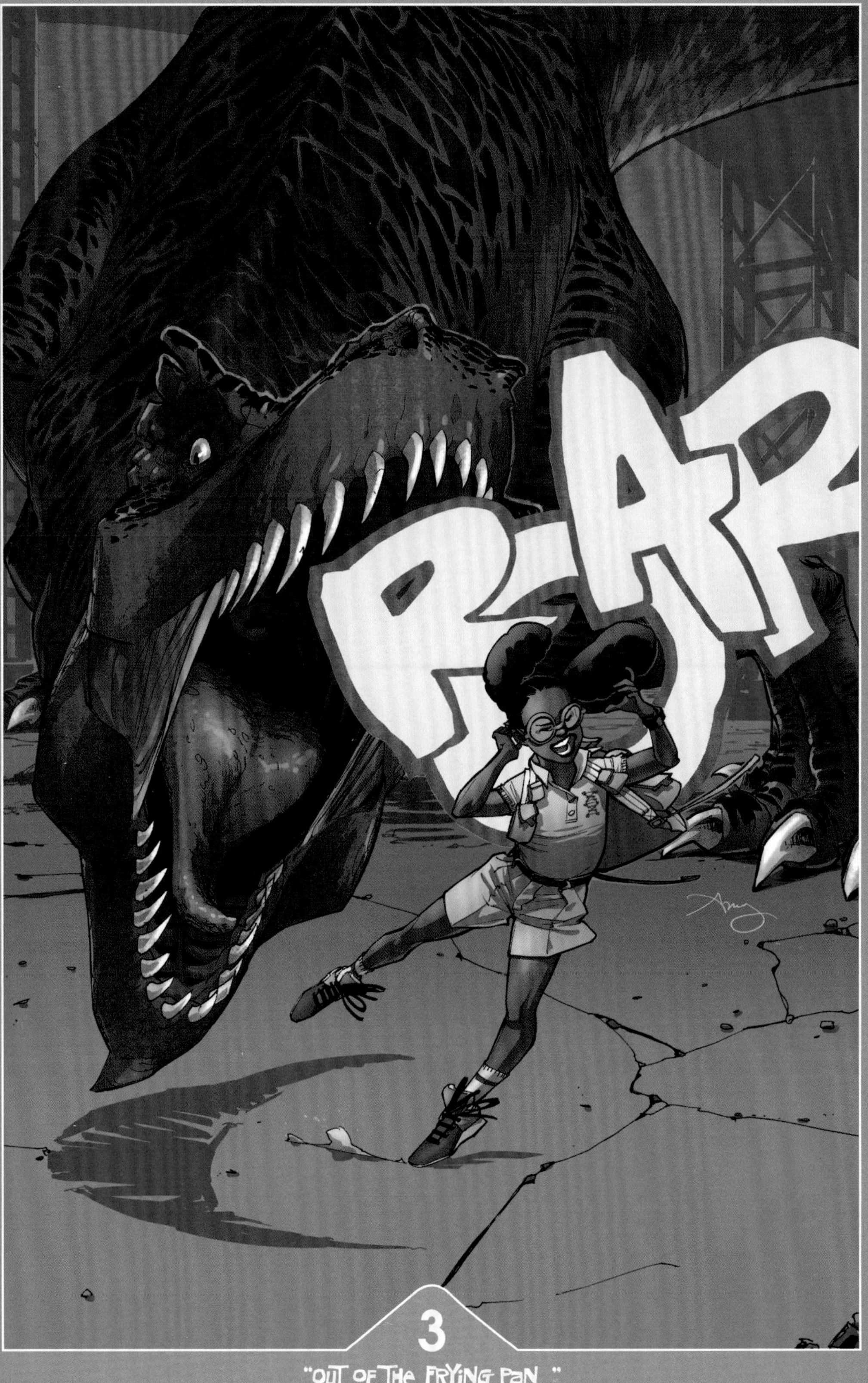
RAR

3

"OUT OF THE FRYING PAN..."

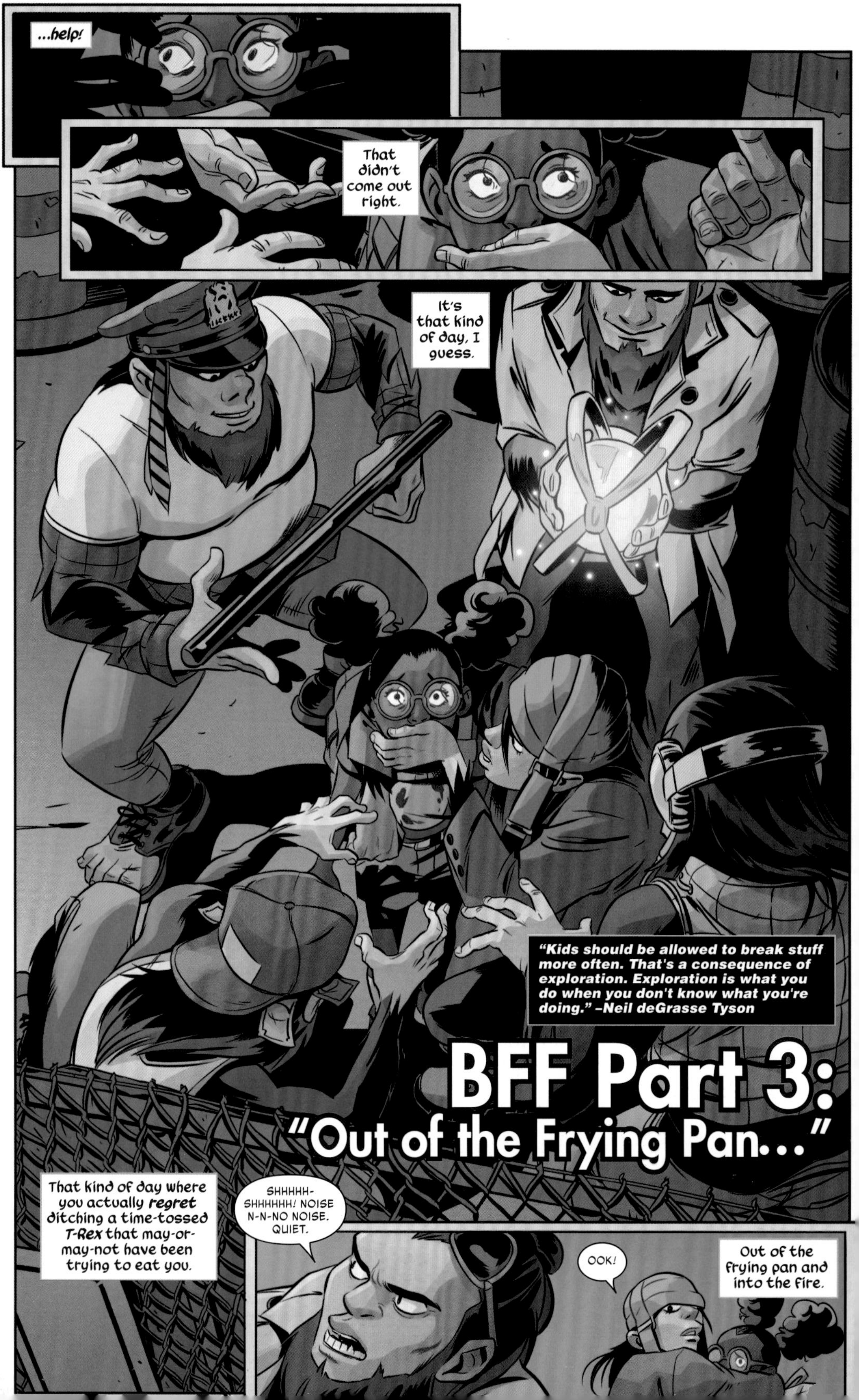
...help!
That didn't come out right.
It's that kind of day, I guess.
"Kids should be allowed to break stuff more often. That's a consequence of exploration. Exploration is what you do when you don't know what you're doing." –Neil deGrasse Tyson
BFF Part 3: "Out of the Frying Pan..."
That kind of day where you actually regret ditching a time-tossed T-Rex that may-or-may-not have been trying to eat you.
SHHHHH-SHHHHHH! NOISE N-N-NO NOISE. QUIET.
OOK!
Out of the frying pan and into the fire.

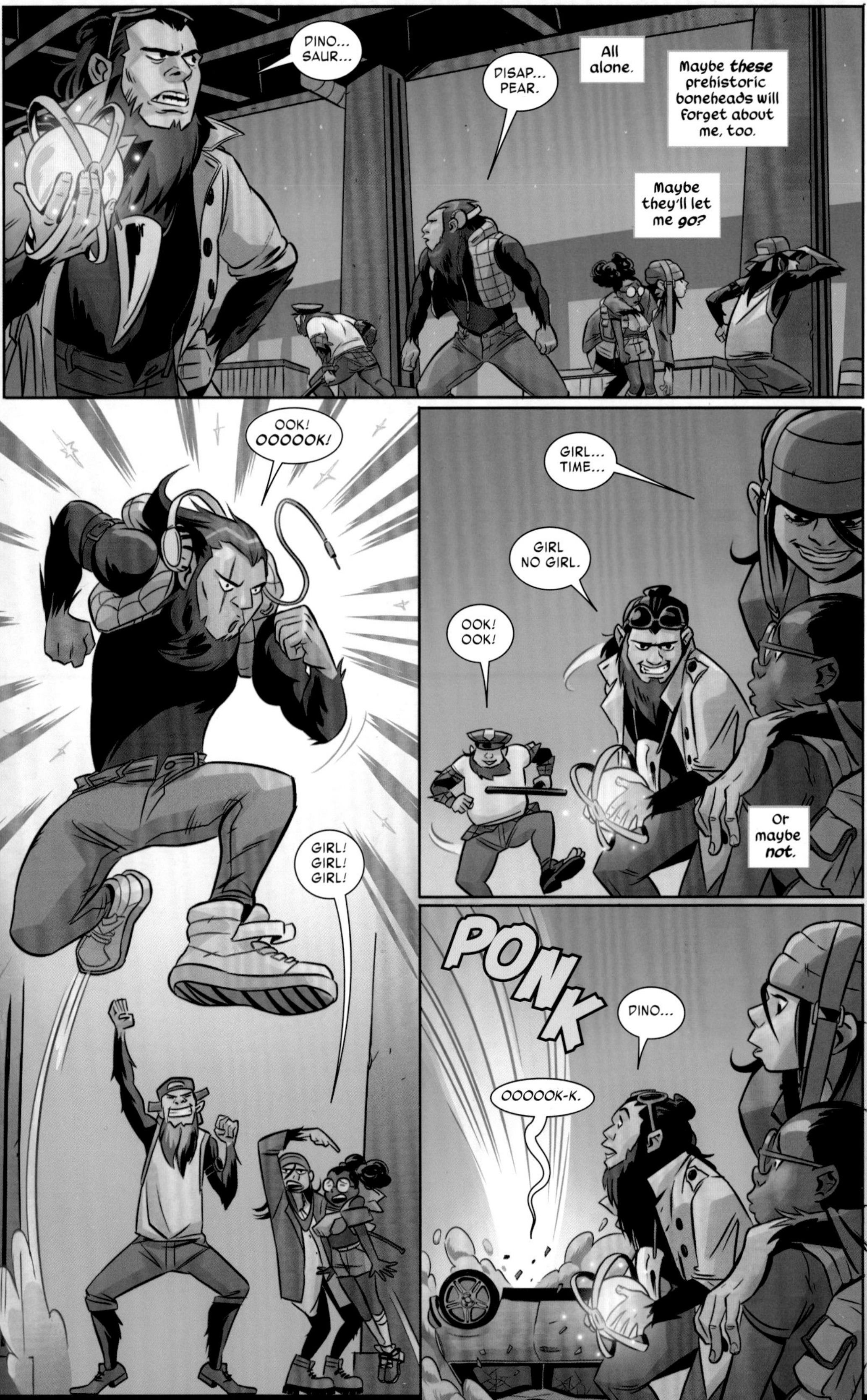
DINO... SAUR...
DISAP... PEAR.
All alone.
Maybe *these* prehistoric boneheads will forget about me, too.
Maybe they'll let me *go?*
OOK! OOOOOK!
GIRL! GIRL! GIRL!
GIRL... TIME...
GIRL NO GIRL.
OOK! OOK!
Or maybe *not.*
PONK
DINO...
OOOOOK-K.

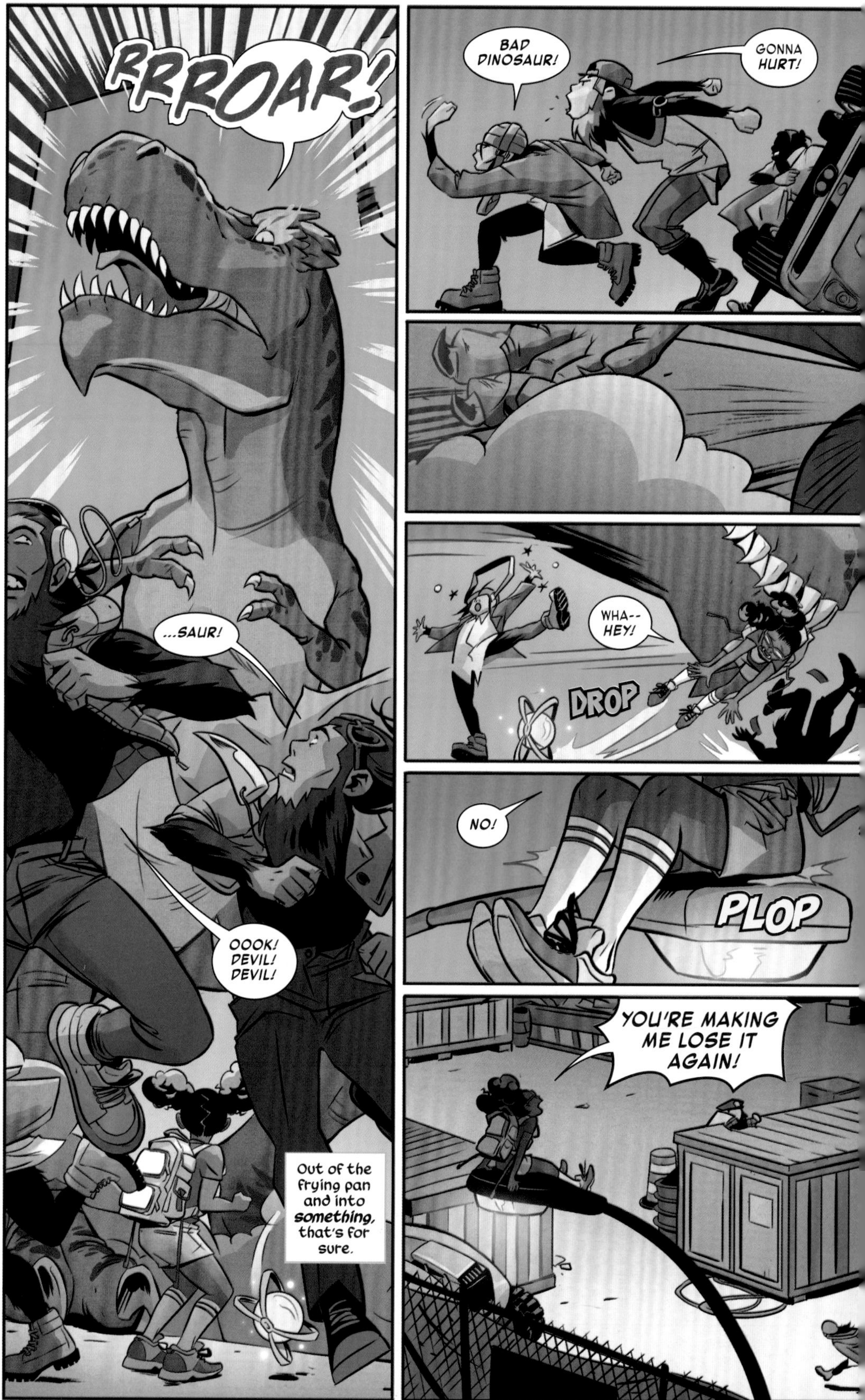
RRROAR!
...SAUR!
OOOK! DEVIL! DEVIL!
Out of the frying pan and into *something,* that's for sure.
BAD DINOSAUR!
GONNA HURT!
WHA-- HEY!
DROP
NO!
PLOP
YOU'RE MAKING ME LOSE IT AGAIN!

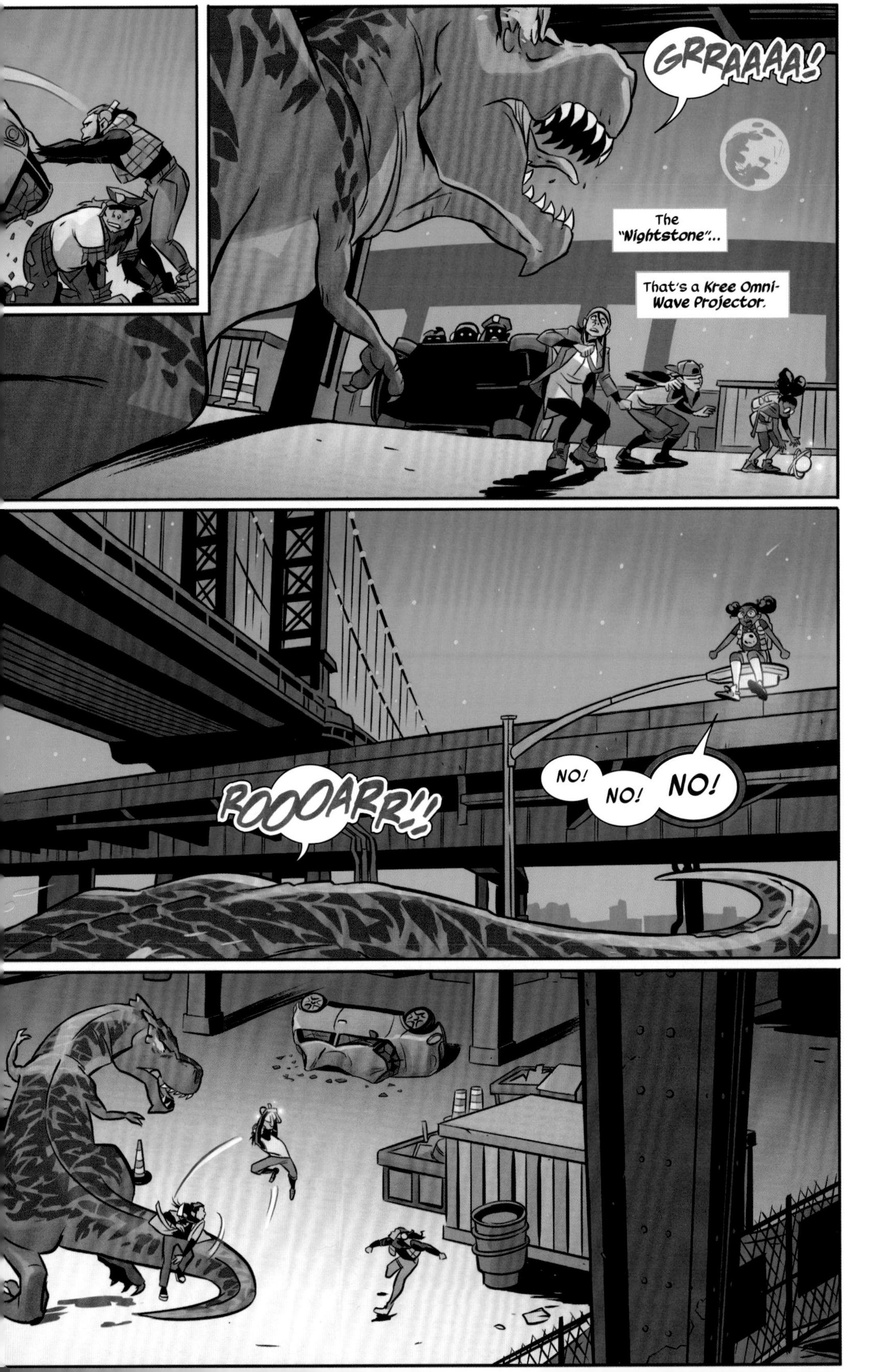
GRRAAAA!
The "Nightstone"...
That's a Kree Omni-Wave Projector.
ROOOARR!!
NO!
NO!
NO!

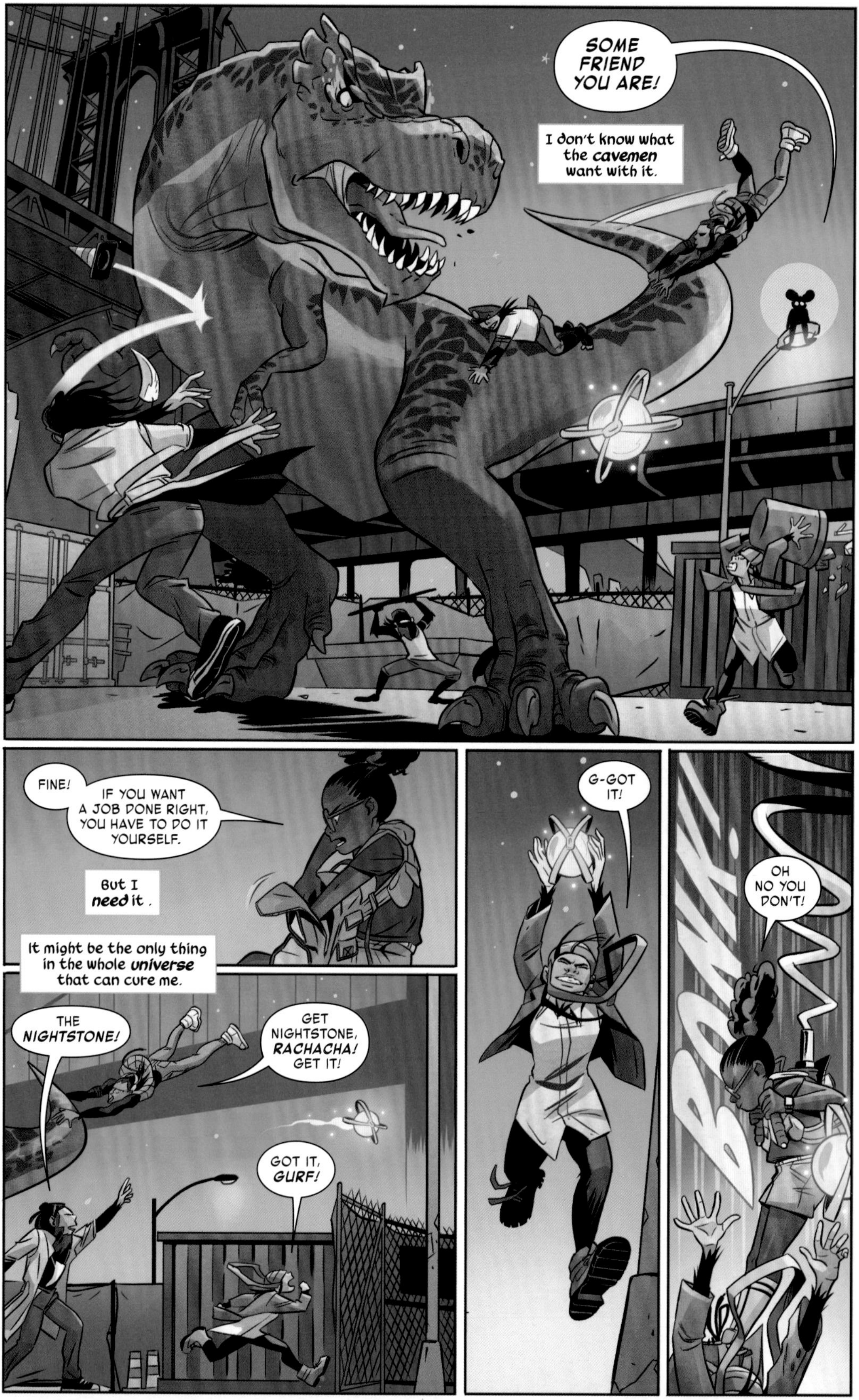

SOME FRIEND YOU ARE!
I don't know what the *cavemen* want with it.
FINE!
IF YOU WANT A JOB DONE RIGHT, YOU HAVE TO DO IT YOURSELF.
But I *need* it.
It might be the only thing in the whole *universe* that can cure me.
THE *NIGHTSTONE!*
GET NIGHTSTONE, *RACHACHA!* GET IT!
GOT IT, *GURF!*
G-GOT IT!
OH NO YOU DON'T!

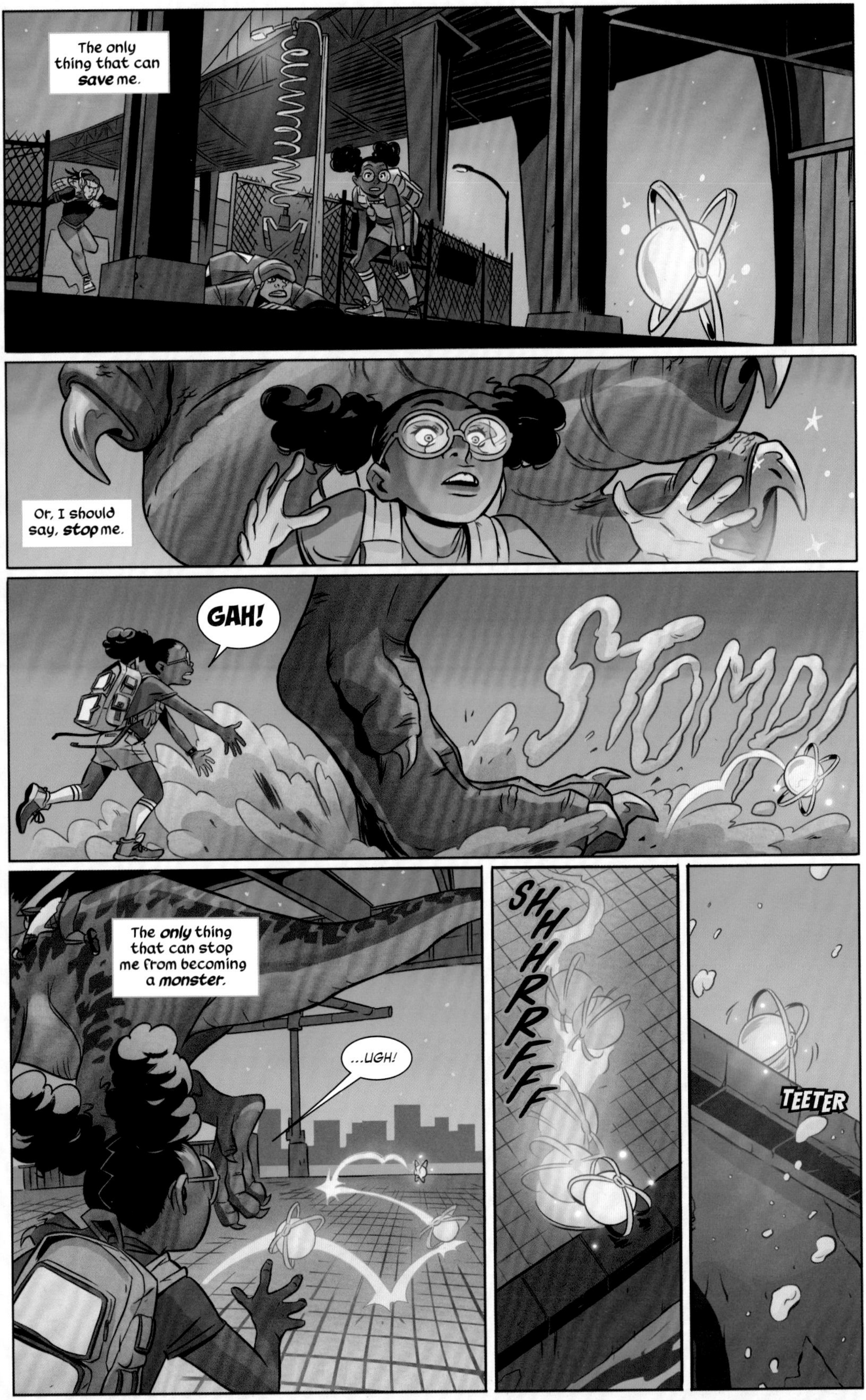
The only thing that can *save* me.
Or, I should say, *stop* me.
GAH!
STOMP!
The *only* thing that can stop me from becoming a *monster*.
...UGH!
SHHHRRFFF
TEETER

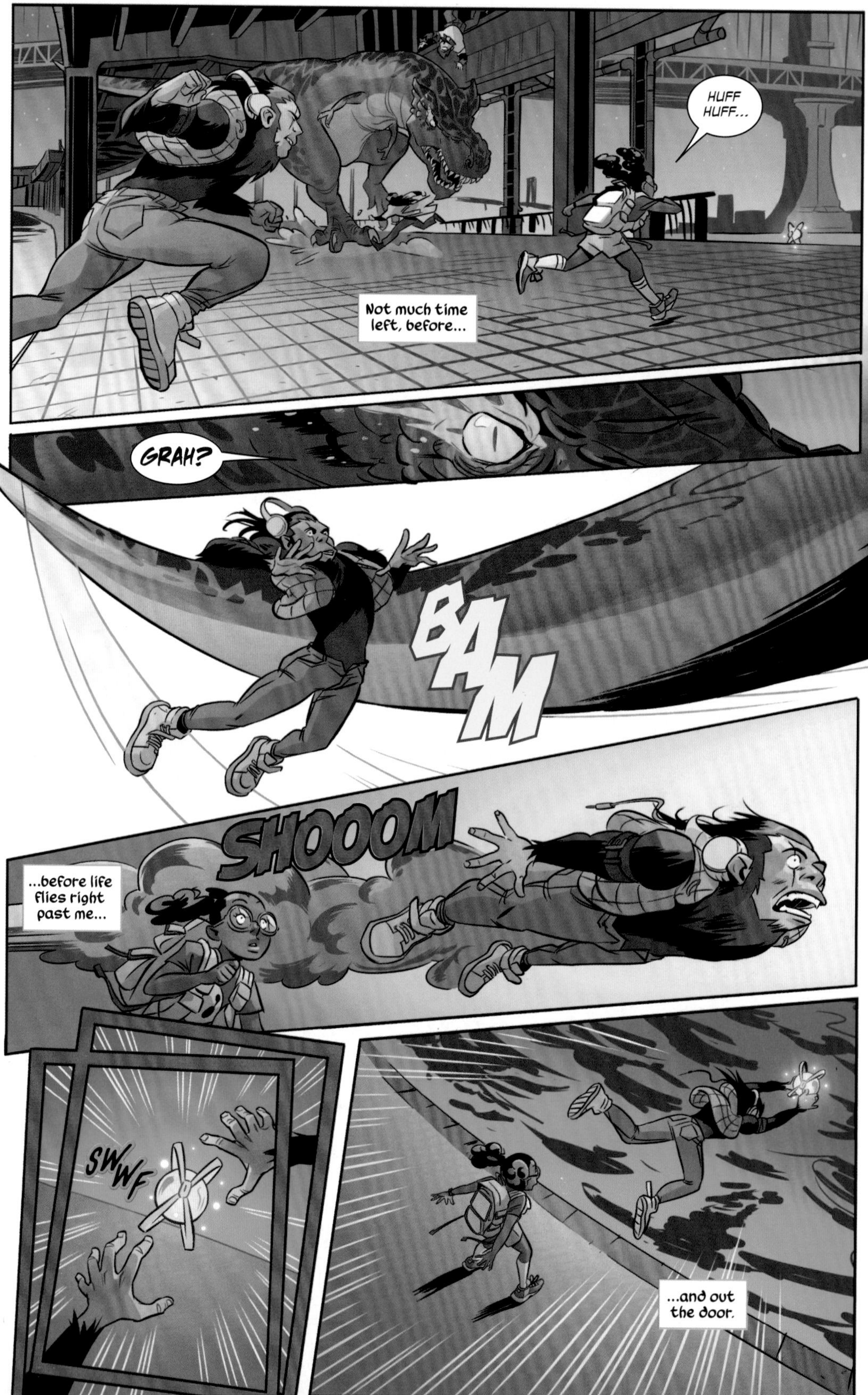
HUFF HUFF...
Not much time left, before...
GRAH?
BAM
SHOOOM
...before life flies right past me...
SWWF
...and out the door.

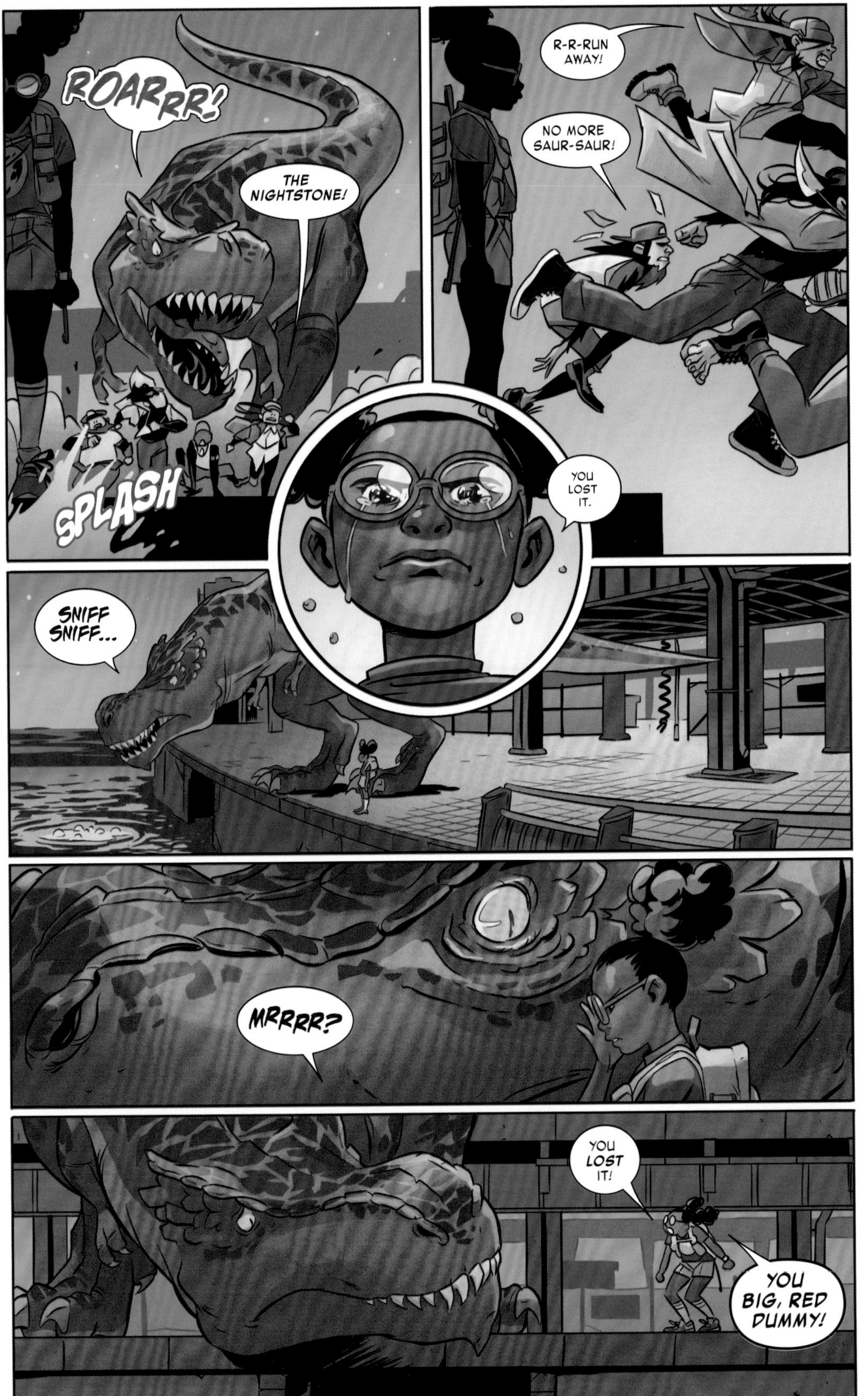
ROARRR!
THE NIGHTSTONE!
SPLASH
R-R-RUN AWAY!
NO MORE SAUR-SAUR!
YOU LOST IT.
SNIFF SNIFF...
MRRRR?
YOU LOST IT!
YOU BIG, RED DUMMY!

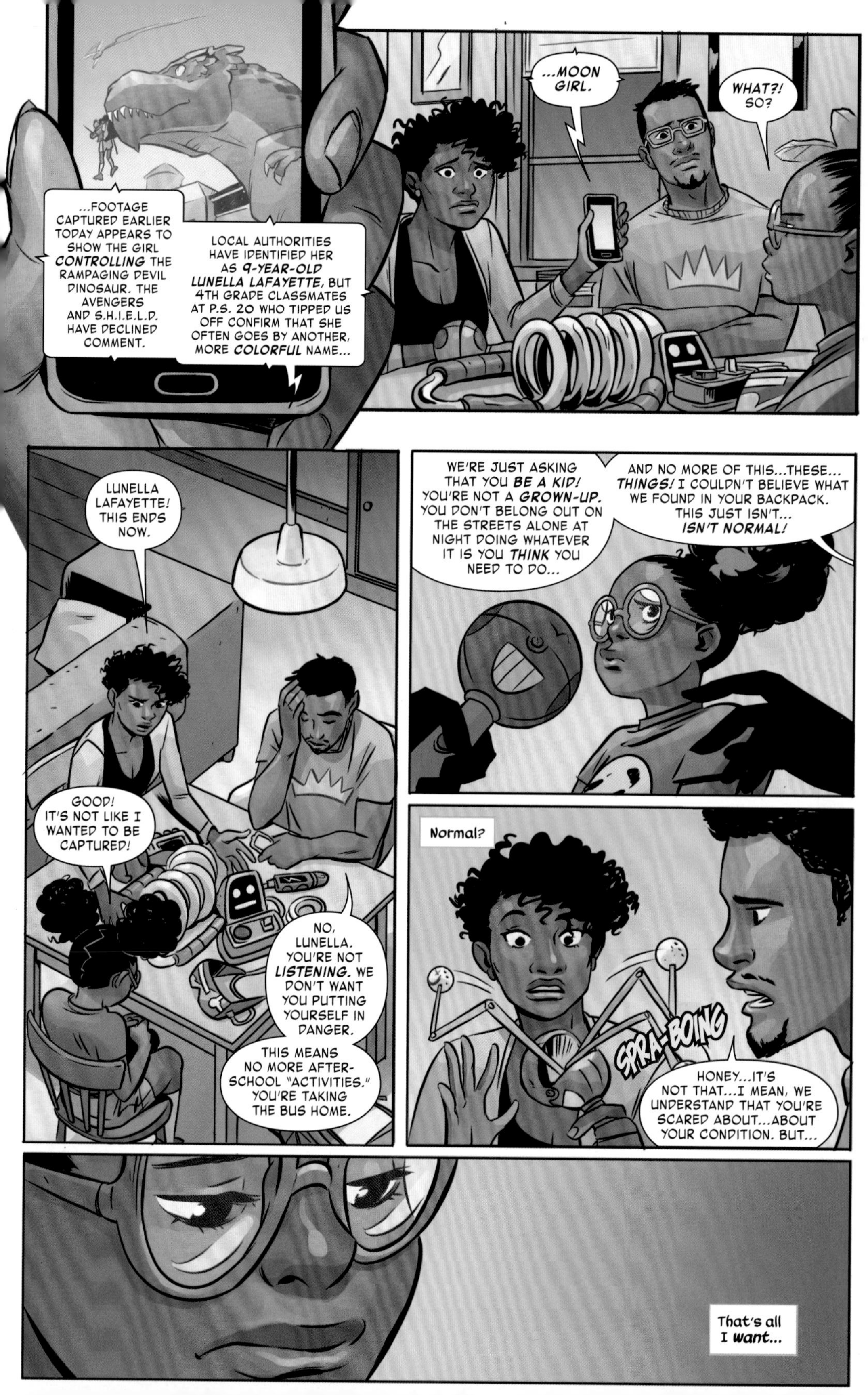
...FOOTAGE CAPTURED EARLIER TODAY APPEARS TO SHOW THE GIRL CONTROLLING THE RAMPAGING DEVIL DINOSAUR. THE AVENGERS AND S.H.I.E.L.D. HAVE DECLINED COMMENT.
LOCAL AUTHORITIES HAVE IDENTIFIED HER AS 9-YEAR-OLD LUNELLA LAFAYETTE, BUT 4TH GRADE CLASSMATES AT P.S. 20 WHO TIPPED US OFF CONFIRM THAT SHE OFTEN GOES BY ANOTHER, MORE COLORFUL NAME...
...MOON GIRL.
WHAT?! SO?
LUNELLA LAFAYETTE! THIS ENDS NOW.
GOOD! IT'S NOT LIKE I WANTED TO BE CAPTURED!
NO, LUNELLA. YOU'RE NOT LISTENING. WE DON'T WANT YOU PUTTING YOURSELF IN DANGER.
THIS MEANS NO MORE AFTER-SCHOOL "ACTIVITIES." YOU'RE TAKING THE BUS HOME.
WE'RE JUST ASKING THAT YOU BE A KID! YOU'RE NOT A GROWN-UP. YOU DON'T BELONG OUT ON THE STREETS ALONE AT NIGHT DOING WHATEVER IT IS YOU THINK YOU NEED TO DO...
AND NO MORE OF THIS...THESE... THINGS! I COULDN'T BELIEVE WHAT WE FOUND IN YOUR BACKPACK. THIS JUST ISN'T... ISN'T NORMAL!
Normal?
SPRA-BOING
HONEY...IT'S NOT THAT...I MEAN, WE UNDERSTAND THAT YOU'RE SCARED ABOUT...ABOUT YOUR CONDITION. BUT...
That's all I want...

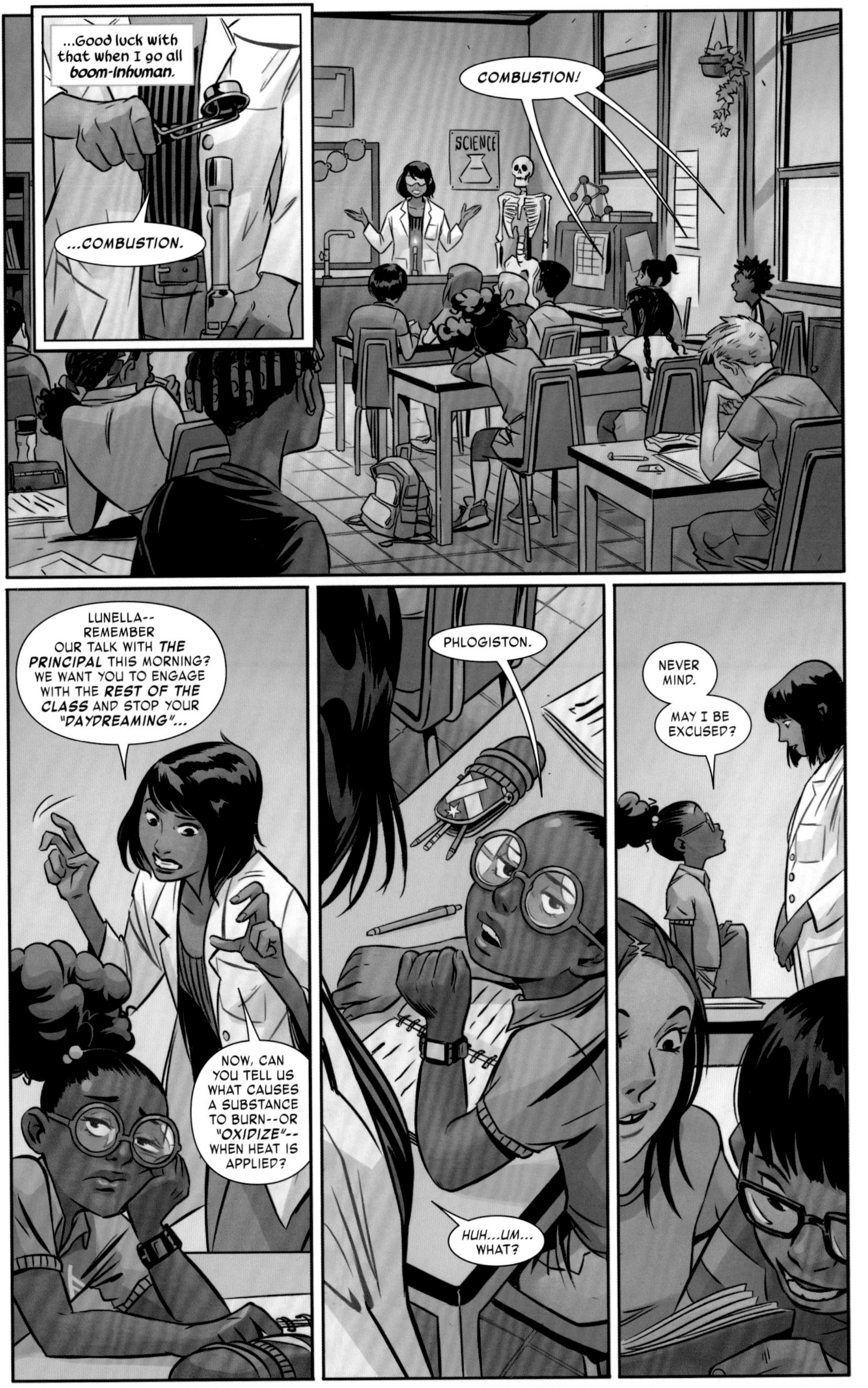
...Good luck with that when I go all *boom-Inhuman*.
...COMBUSTION.
COMBUSTION!
SCIENCE
LUNELLA-- REMEMBER OUR TALK WITH *THE PRINCIPAL* THIS MORNING? WE WANT YOU TO ENGAGE WITH THE *REST OF THE CLASS* AND STOP YOUR *"DAYDREAMING"*...
NOW, CAN YOU TELL US WHAT CAUSES A SUBSTANCE TO BURN--OR *"OXIDIZE"*-- WHEN HEAT IS APPLIED?
HUH...UM... WHAT?
PHLOGISTON.
NEVER MIND.
MAY I BE EXCUSED?

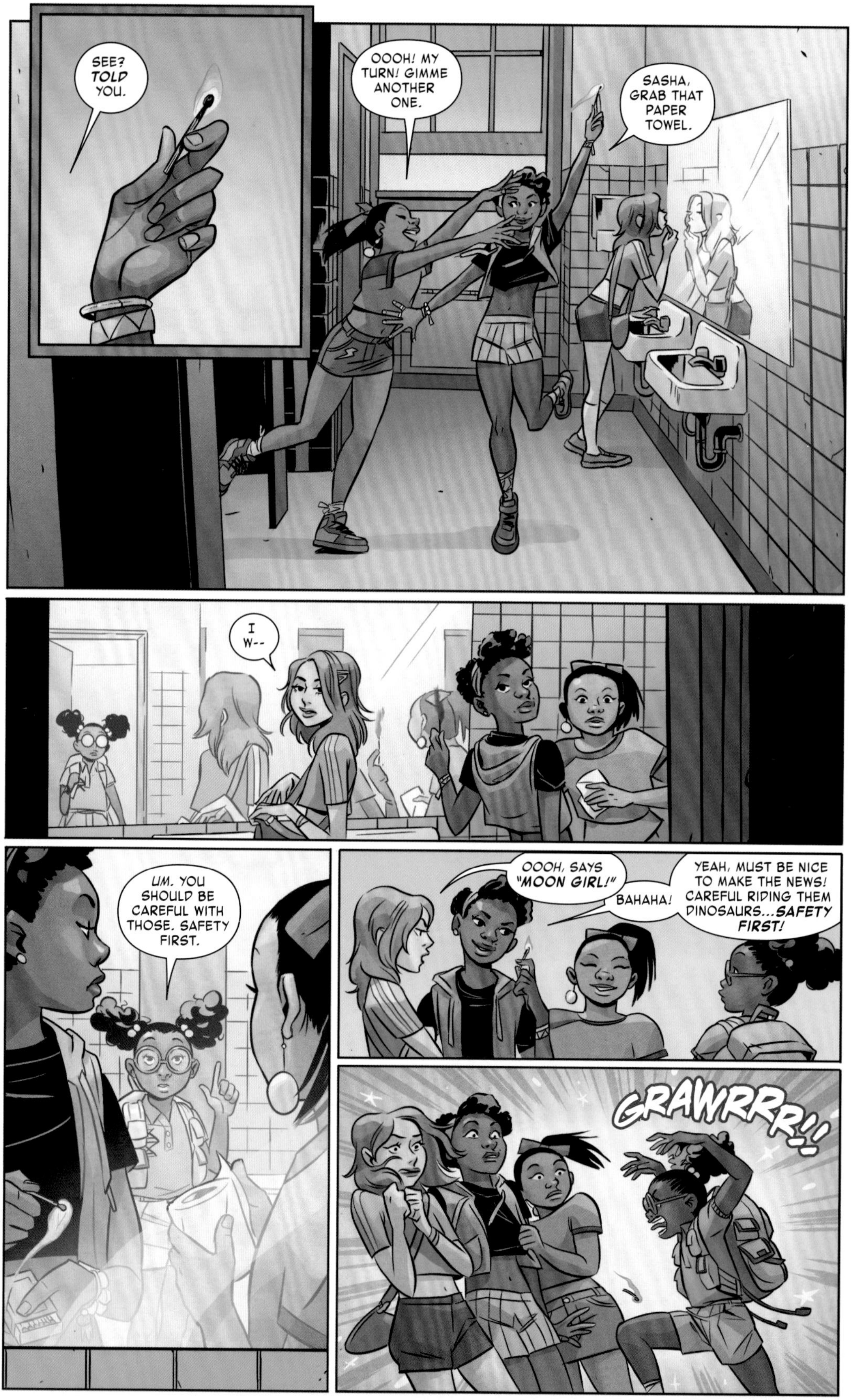
SEE? TOLD YOU.
OOOH! MY TURN! GIMME ANOTHER ONE.
SASHA, GRAB THAT PAPER TOWEL.
I W--
UM. YOU SHOULD BE CAREFUL WITH THOSE. SAFETY FIRST.
OOOH, SAYS "MOON GIRL!"
BAHAHA!
YEAH, MUST BE NICE TO MAKE THE NEWS! CAREFUL RIDING THEM DINOSAURS...SAFETY FIRST!
GRAWRRR!!

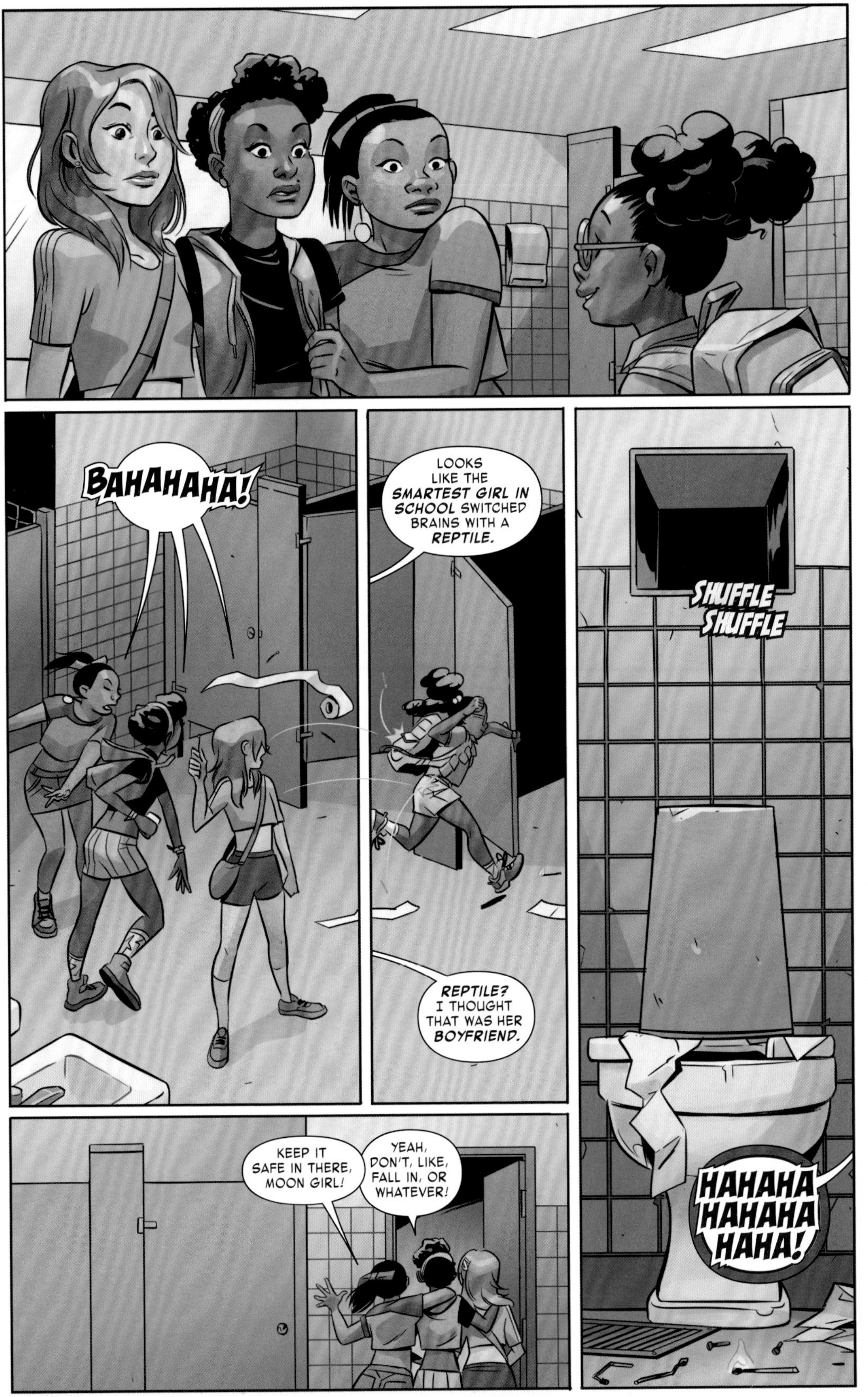
BAHAHAHA!
LOOKS LIKE THE SMARTEST GIRL IN SCHOOL SWITCHED BRAINS WITH A REPTILE.
REPTILE? I THOUGHT THAT WAS HER BOYFRIEND.
SHUFFLE SHUFFLE
KEEP IT SAFE IN THERE, MOON GIRL!
YEAH, DON'T, LIKE, FALL IN, OR WHATEVER!
HAHAHA HAHAHA HAHA!

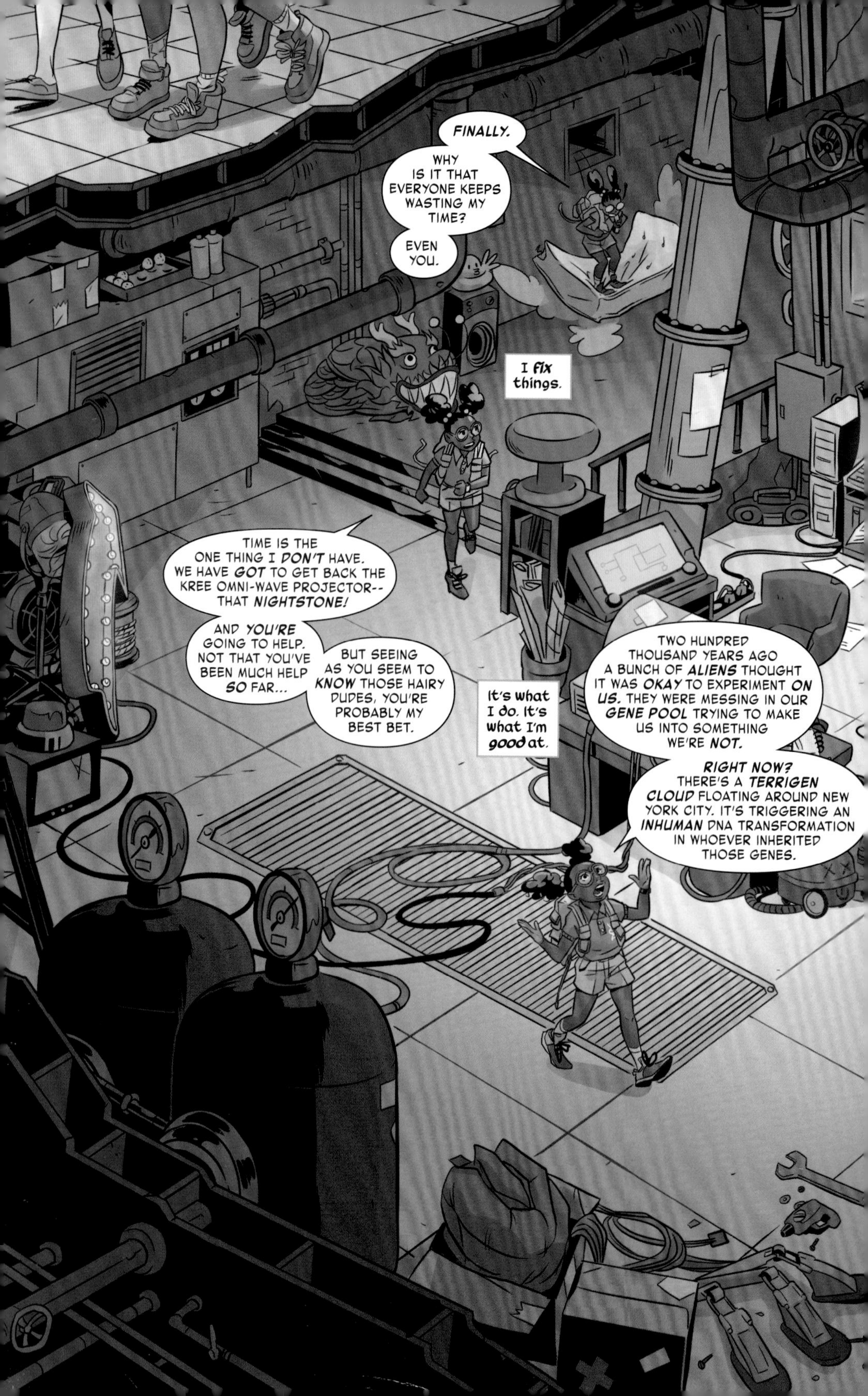
FINALLY.
WHY IS IT THAT EVERYONE KEEPS WASTING MY TIME?
EVEN YOU.
I fix things.
TIME IS THE ONE THING I DON'T HAVE. WE HAVE GOT TO GET BACK THE KREE OMNI-WAVE PROJECTOR-- THAT NIGHTSTONE!
AND YOU'RE GOING TO HELP. NOT THAT YOU'VE BEEN MUCH HELP SO FAR...
BUT SEEING AS YOU SEEM TO KNOW THOSE HAIRY DUDES, YOU'RE PROBABLY MY BEST BET.
It's what I do. It's what I'm good at.
TWO HUNDRED THOUSAND YEARS AGO A BUNCH OF ALIENS THOUGHT IT WAS OKAY TO EXPERIMENT ON US. THEY WERE MESSING IN OUR GENE POOL TRYING TO MAKE US INTO SOMETHING WE'RE NOT.
RIGHT NOW? THERE'S A TERRIGEN CLOUD FLOATING AROUND NEW YORK CITY. IT'S TRIGGERING AN INHUMAN DNA TRANSFORMATION IN WHOEVER INHERITED THOSE GENES.

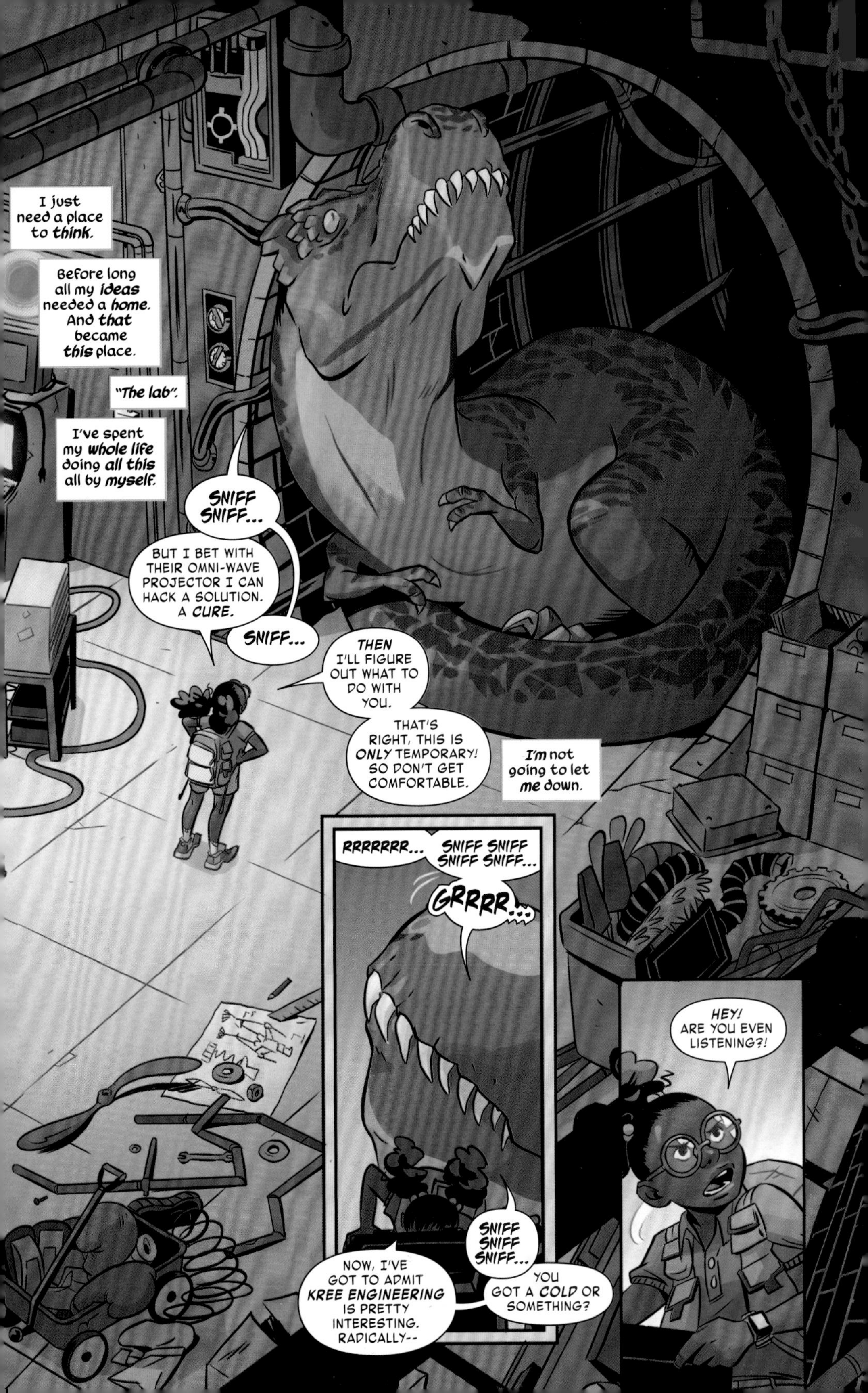
I just need a place to think.
Before long all my ideas needed a home. And that became this place.
"The lab".
I've spent my whole life doing all this all by myself.
SNIFF SNIFF...
BUT I BET WITH THEIR OMNI-WAVE PROJECTOR I CAN HACK A SOLUTION. A CURE.
SNIFF...
THEN I'LL FIGURE OUT WHAT TO DO WITH YOU.
THAT'S RIGHT, THIS IS ONLY TEMPORARY! SO DON'T GET COMFORTABLE.
I'm not going to let me down.
RRRRRRR...
SNIFF SNIFF SNIFF SNIFF...
GRRRR...
SNIFF SNIFF SNIFF...
NOW, I'VE GOT TO ADMIT KREE ENGINEERING IS PRETTY INTERESTING. RADICALLY--
YOU GOT A COLD OR SOMETHING?
HEY! ARE YOU EVEN LISTENING?!

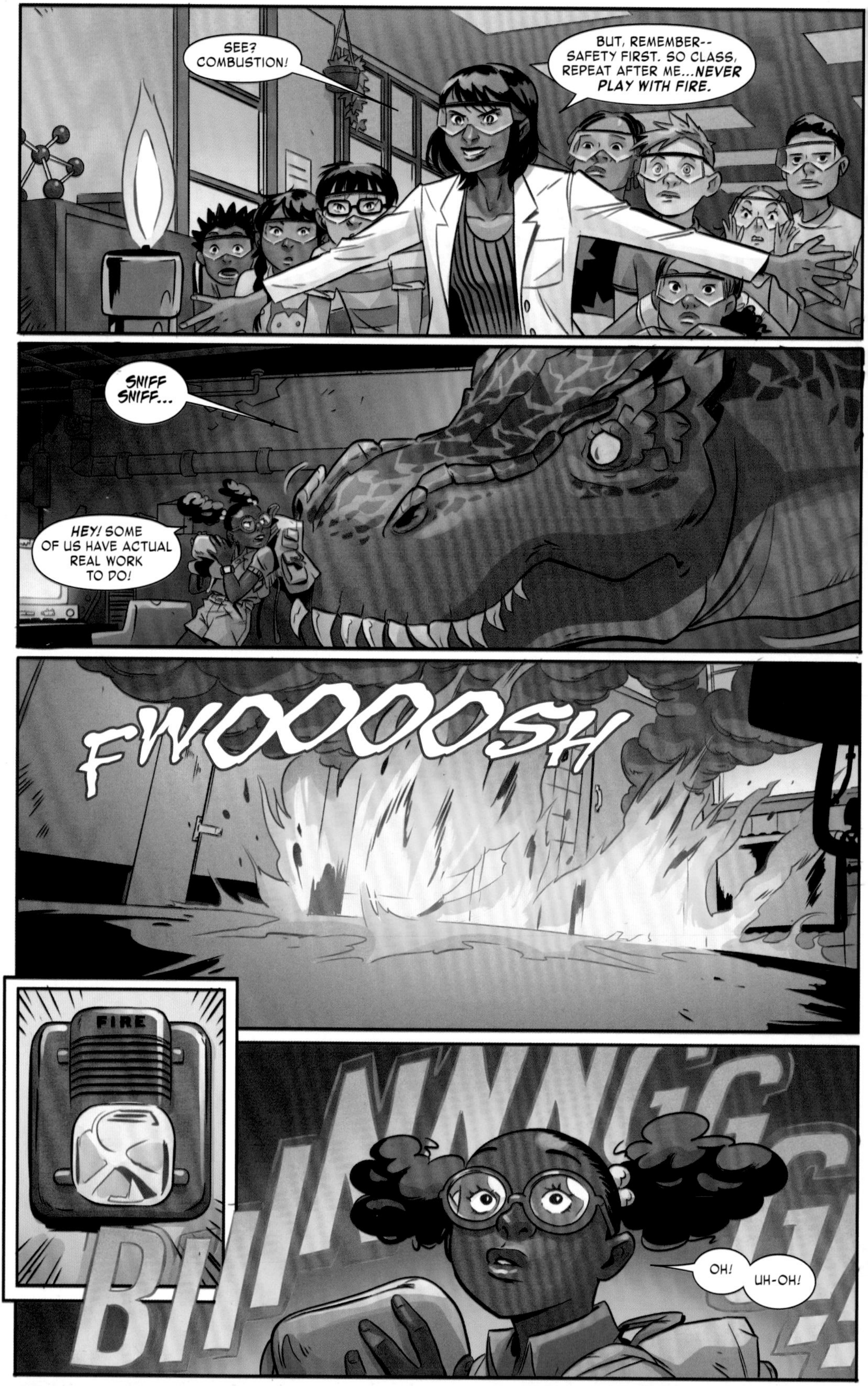
SEE? COMBUSTION!
BUT, REMEMBER-- SAFETY FIRST. SO CLASS, REPEAT AFTER ME...**NEVER PLAY WITH FIRE.**
SNIFF SNIFF...
HEY! SOME OF US HAVE ACTUAL REAL WORK TO DO!
FWOOOOSH
FIRE
OH!
UH-OH!

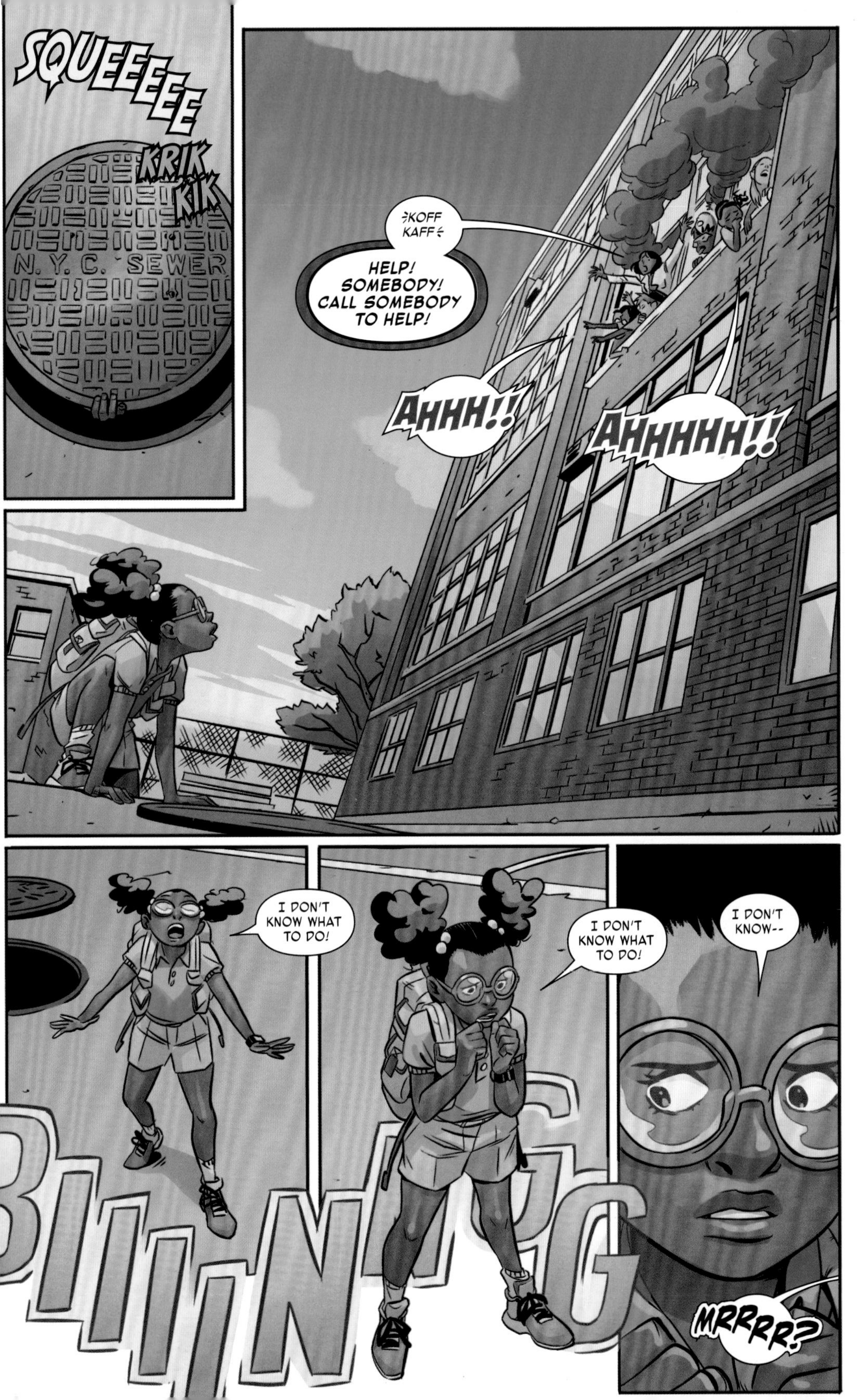
SQUEEEEEE
KRIK KIK
N. Y. C. SEWER
KOFF KAFF
HELP! SOMEBODY! CALL SOMEBODY TO HELP!
AHHH!!
AHHHHH!!
I DON'T KNOW WHAT TO DO!
I DON'T KNOW WHAT TO DO!
I DON'T KNOW--
MRRRR?

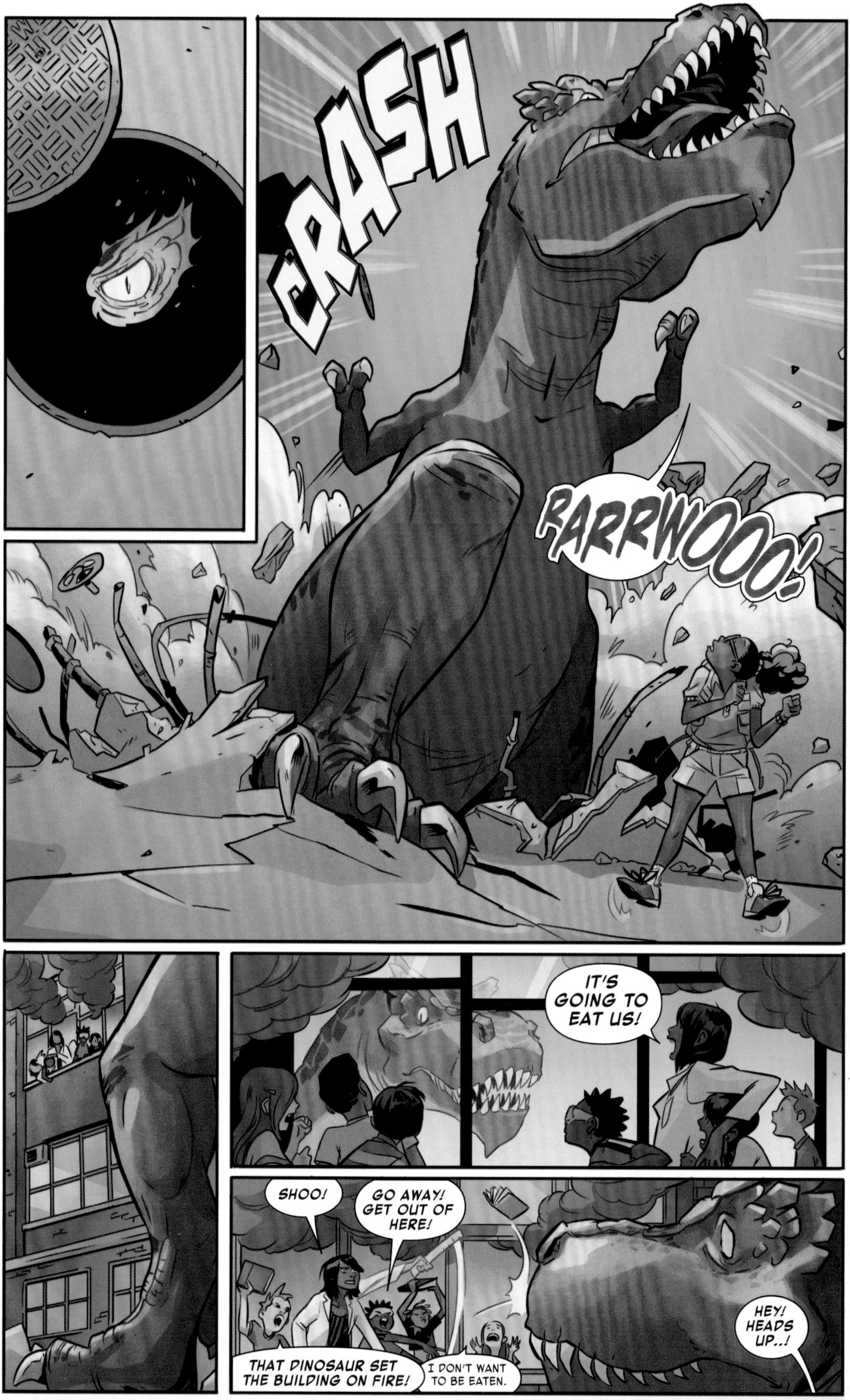
CRASH
RARRWOOO!
IT'S GOING TO EAT US!
SHOO!
GO AWAY! GET OUT OF HERE!
THAT DINOSAUR SET THE BUILDING ON FIRE!
I DON'T WANT TO BE EATEN.
HEY! HEADS UP..!

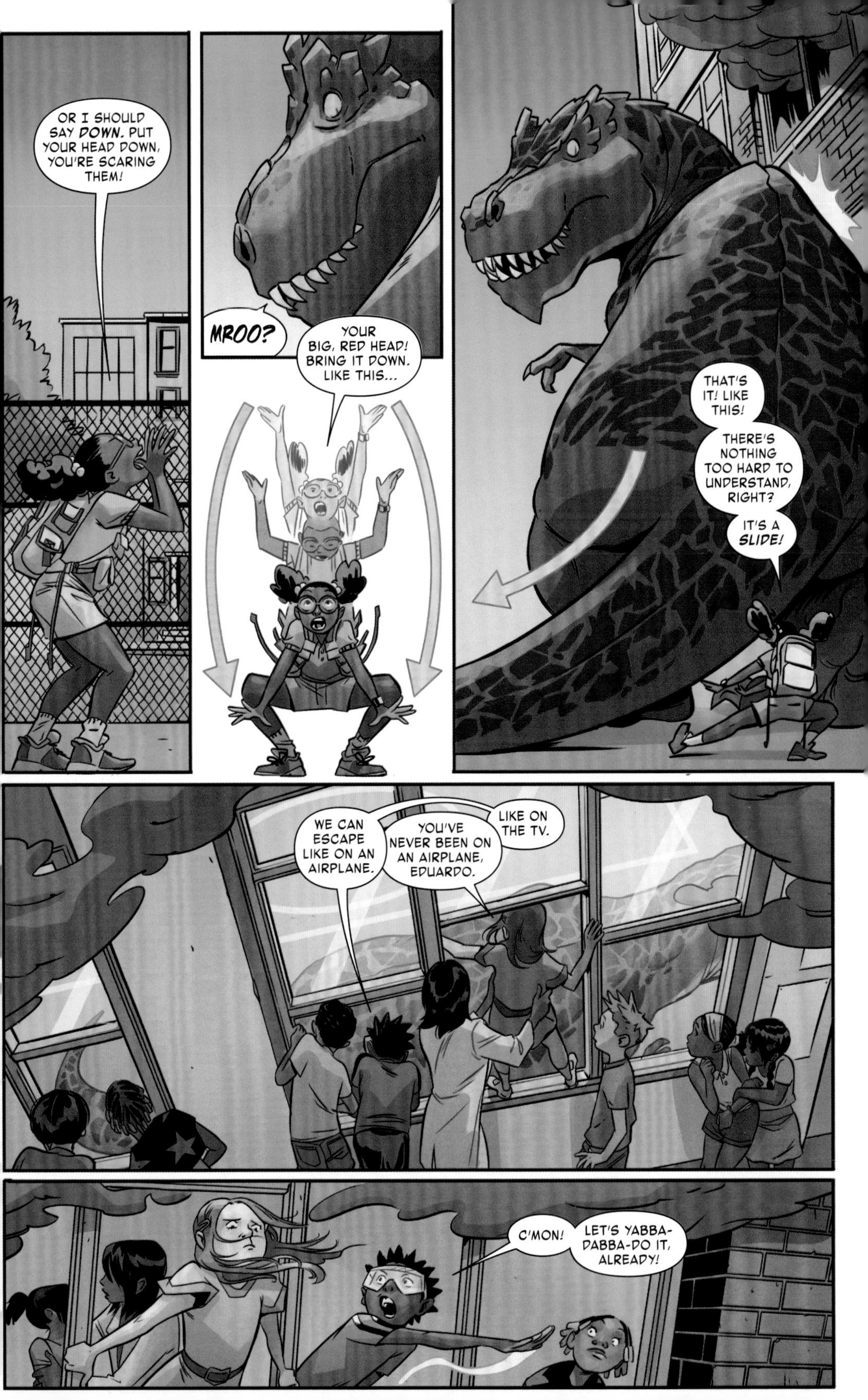
OR I SHOULD SAY DOWN. PUT YOUR HEAD DOWN, YOU'RE SCARING THEM!
MROO?
YOUR BIG, RED HEAD! BRING IT DOWN. LIKE THIS...
THAT'S IT! LIKE THIS!
THERE'S NOTHING TOO HARD TO UNDERSTAND, RIGHT?
IT'S A SLIDE!
WE CAN ESCAPE LIKE ON AN AIRPLANE.
YOU'VE NEVER BEEN ON AN AIRPLANE, EDUARDO.
LIKE ON THE TV.
C'MON!
LET'S YABBA-DABBA-DO IT, ALREADY!

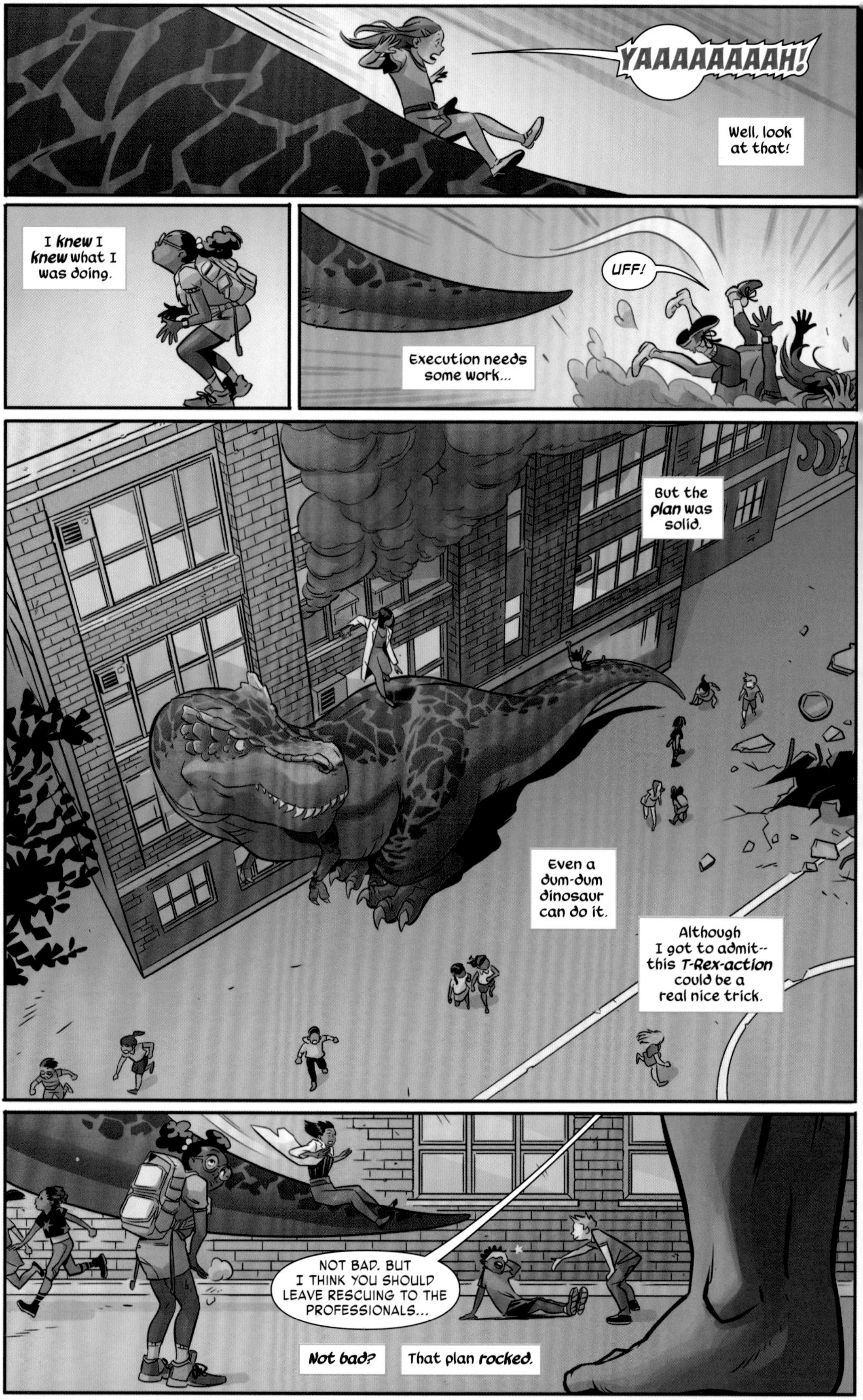

YAAAAAAAAH!
Well, look at that!
I *knew* I *knew* what I was doing.
UFF!
Execution needs some work...
But the *plan* was solid.
Even a dum-dum dinosaur can do it.
Although I got to admit-- this *T-Rex-action* could be a real nice trick.
NOT BAD. BUT I THINK YOU SHOULD LEAVE RESCUING TO THE PROFESSIONALS...
Not bad?
That plan *rocked.*

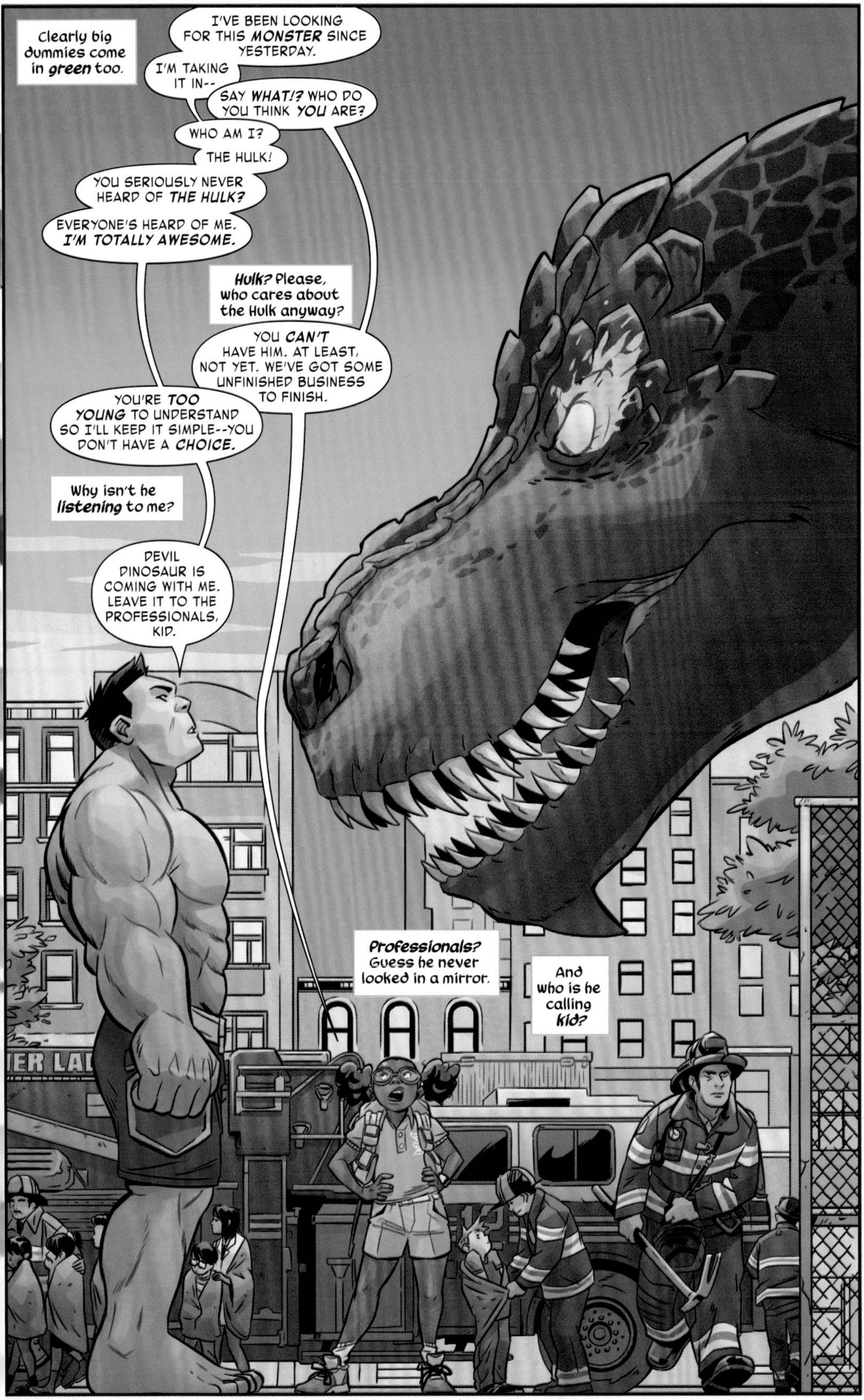
Clearly big dummies come in green too.
I'VE BEEN LOOKING FOR THIS MONSTER SINCE YESTERDAY.
I'M TAKING IT IN--
SAY WHAT!? WHO DO YOU THINK YOU ARE?
WHO AM I?
THE HULK!
YOU SERIOUSLY NEVER HEARD OF THE HULK?
EVERYONE'S HEARD OF ME. I'M TOTALLY AWESOME.
Hulk? Please, who cares about the Hulk anyway?
YOU CAN'T HAVE HIM. AT LEAST, NOT YET. WE'VE GOT SOME UNFINISHED BUSINESS TO FINISH.
YOU'RE TOO YOUNG TO UNDERSTAND SO I'LL KEEP IT SIMPLE--YOU DON'T HAVE A CHOICE.
Why isn't he listening to me?
DEVIL DINOSAUR IS COMING WITH ME. LEAVE IT TO THE PROFESSIONALS, KID.
Professionals? Guess he never looked in a mirror.
And who is he calling kid?

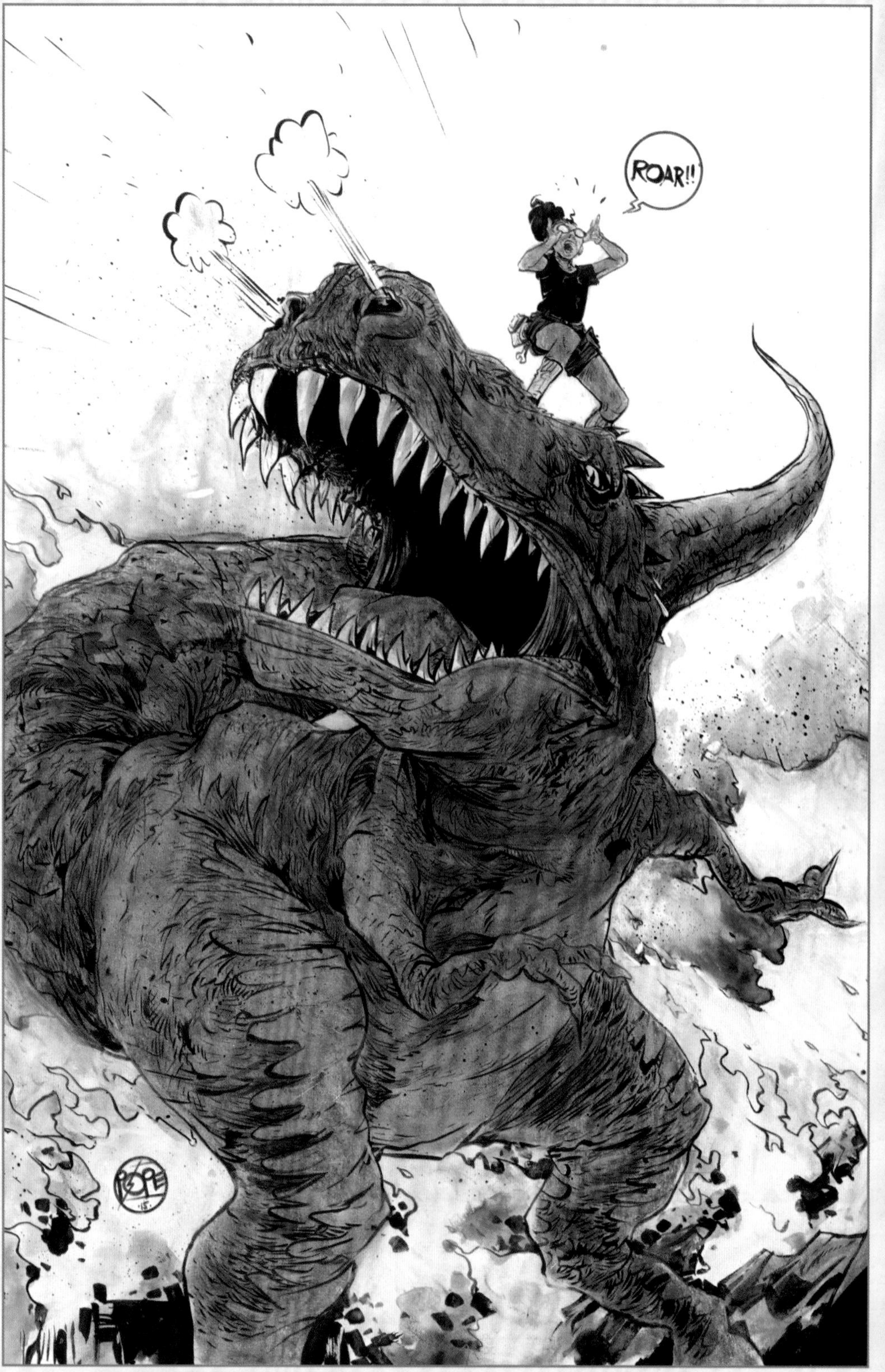
ROAR!!

MOON GIRL AND DEVIL DINOSAUR #3 VARIANT
BY PAUL POPE

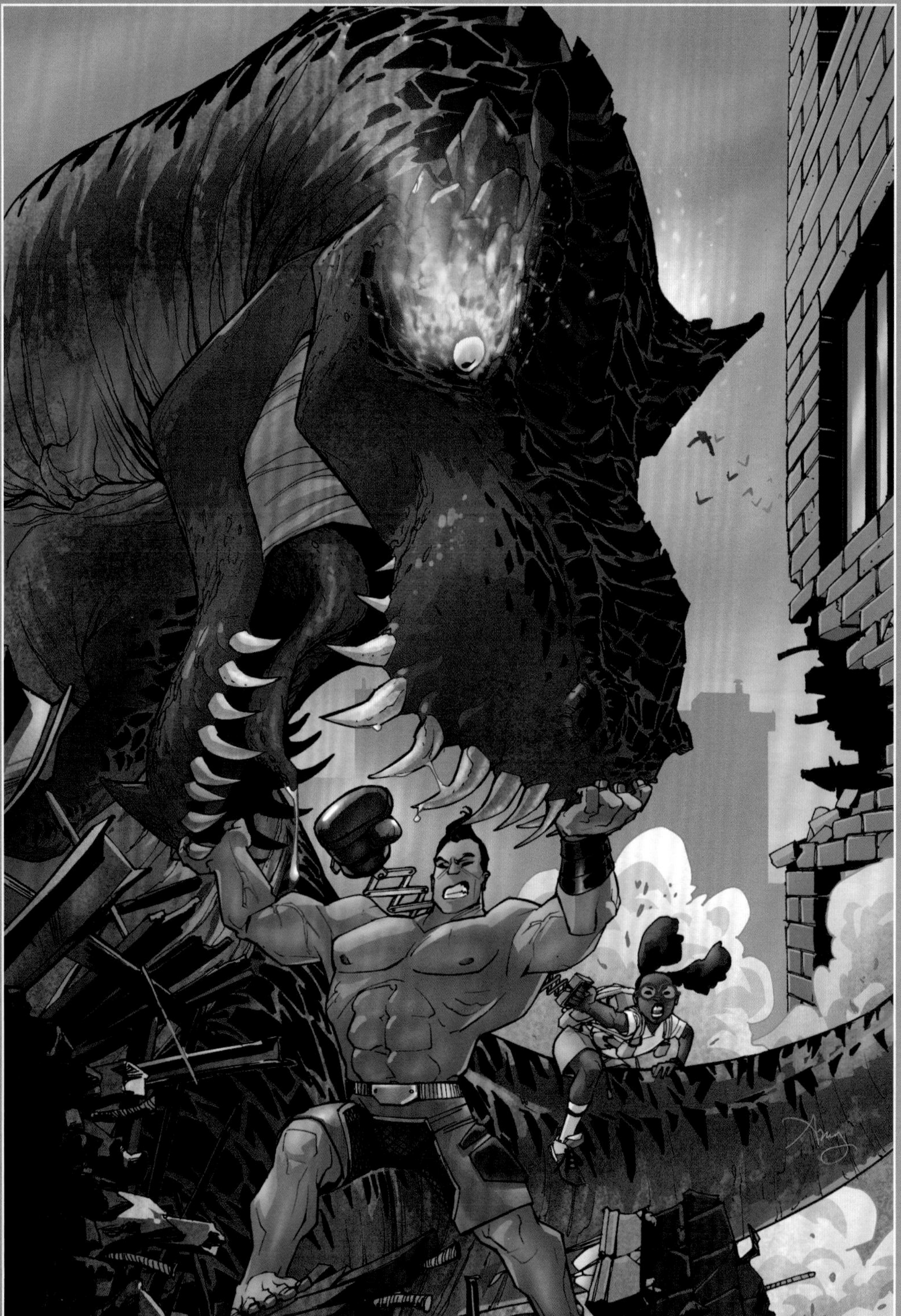

4

"HULK + DEVIL DINOSAUR = 'NUFF SAID"

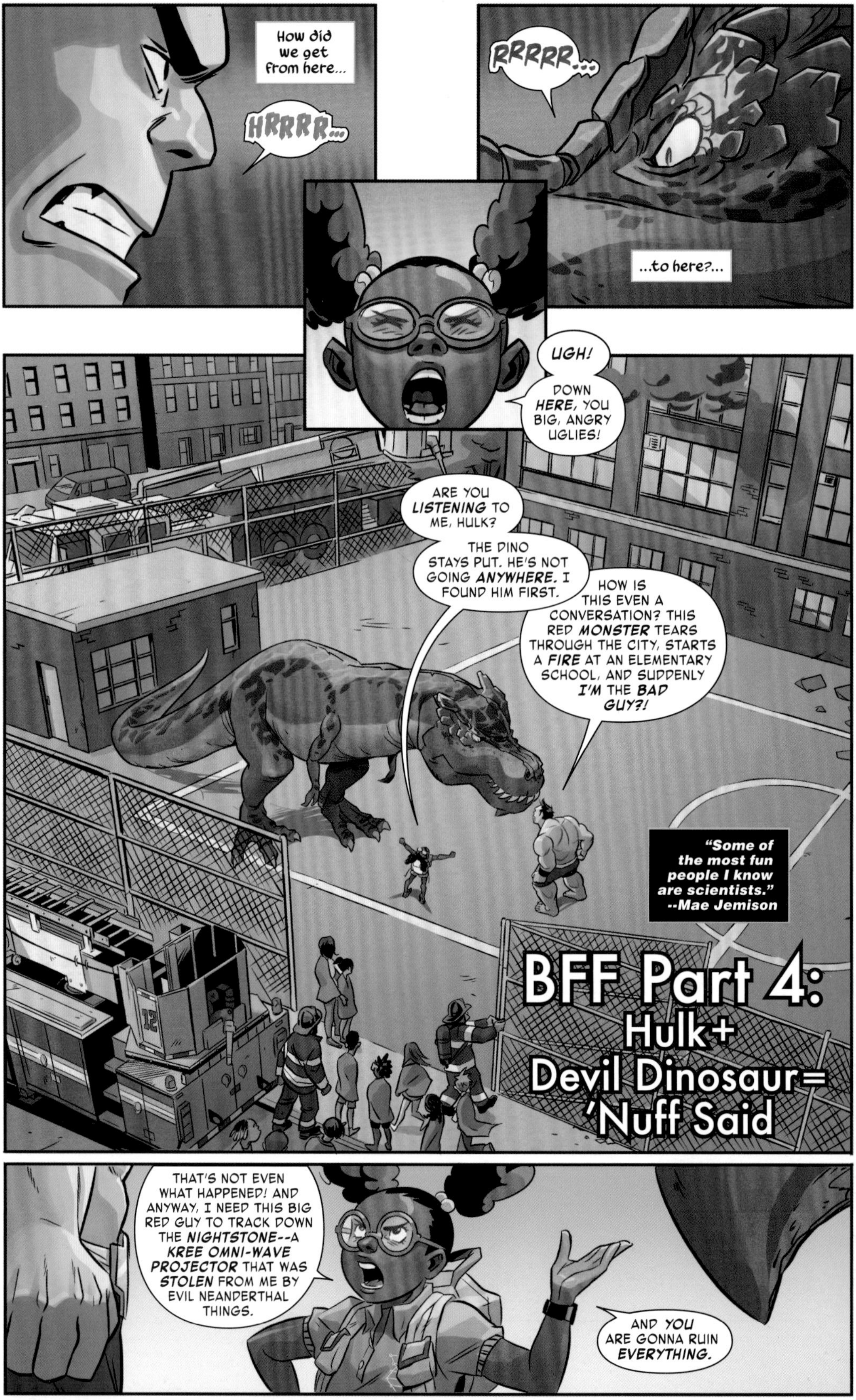

How did we get from here...
HRRRR...
RRRRR...
...to here?...
UGH!
DOWN HERE, YOU BIG, ANGRY UGLIES!
ARE YOU LISTENING TO ME, HULK?
THE DINO STAYS PUT. HE'S NOT GOING ANYWHERE. I FOUND HIM FIRST.
HOW IS THIS EVEN A CONVERSATION? THIS RED MONSTER TEARS THROUGH THE CITY, STARTS A FIRE AT AN ELEMENTARY SCHOOL, AND SUDDENLY I'M THE BAD GUY?!
"Some of the most fun people I know are scientists." --Mae Jemison
BFF Part 4:
Hulk+ Devil Dinosaur= 'Nuff Said
12
THAT'S NOT EVEN WHAT HAPPENED! AND ANYWAY, I NEED THIS BIG RED GUY TO TRACK DOWN THE NIGHTSTONE--A KREE OMNI-WAVE PROJECTOR THAT WAS STOLEN FROM ME BY EVIL NEANDERTHAL THINGS.
AND YOU ARE GONNA RUIN EVERYTHING.

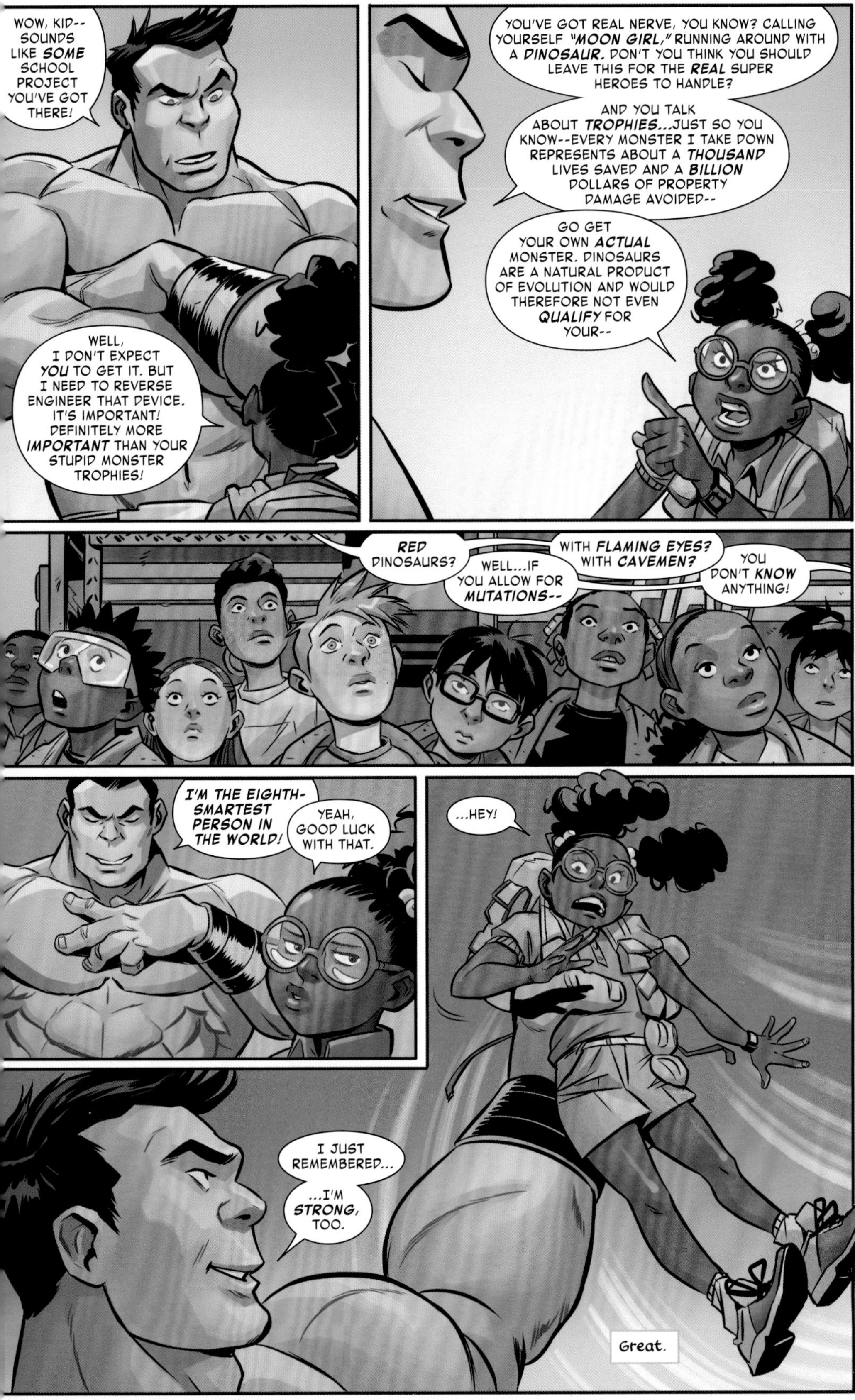
WOW, KID--SOUNDS LIKE SOME SCHOOL PROJECT YOU'VE GOT THERE!
WELL, I DON'T EXPECT YOU TO GET IT. BUT I NEED TO REVERSE ENGINEER THAT DEVICE. IT'S IMPORTANT! DEFINITELY MORE IMPORTANT THAN YOUR STUPID MONSTER TROPHIES!
YOU'VE GOT REAL NERVE, YOU KNOW? CALLING YOURSELF "MOON GIRL," RUNNING AROUND WITH A DINOSAUR. DON'T YOU THINK YOU SHOULD LEAVE THIS FOR THE REAL SUPER HEROES TO HANDLE?
AND YOU TALK ABOUT TROPHIES...JUST SO YOU KNOW--EVERY MONSTER I TAKE DOWN REPRESENTS ABOUT A THOUSAND LIVES SAVED AND A BILLION DOLLARS OF PROPERTY DAMAGE AVOIDED--
GO GET YOUR OWN ACTUAL MONSTER. DINOSAURS ARE A NATURAL PRODUCT OF EVOLUTION AND WOULD THEREFORE NOT EVEN QUALIFY FOR YOUR--
RED DINOSAURS?
WITH FLAMING EYES? WITH CAVEMEN?
WELL...IF YOU ALLOW FOR MUTATIONS--
YOU DON'T KNOW ANYTHING!
I'M THE EIGHTH-SMARTEST PERSON IN THE WORLD!
YEAH, GOOD LUCK WITH THAT.
...HEY!
I JUST REMEMBERED...
...I'M STRONG, TOO.
Great.

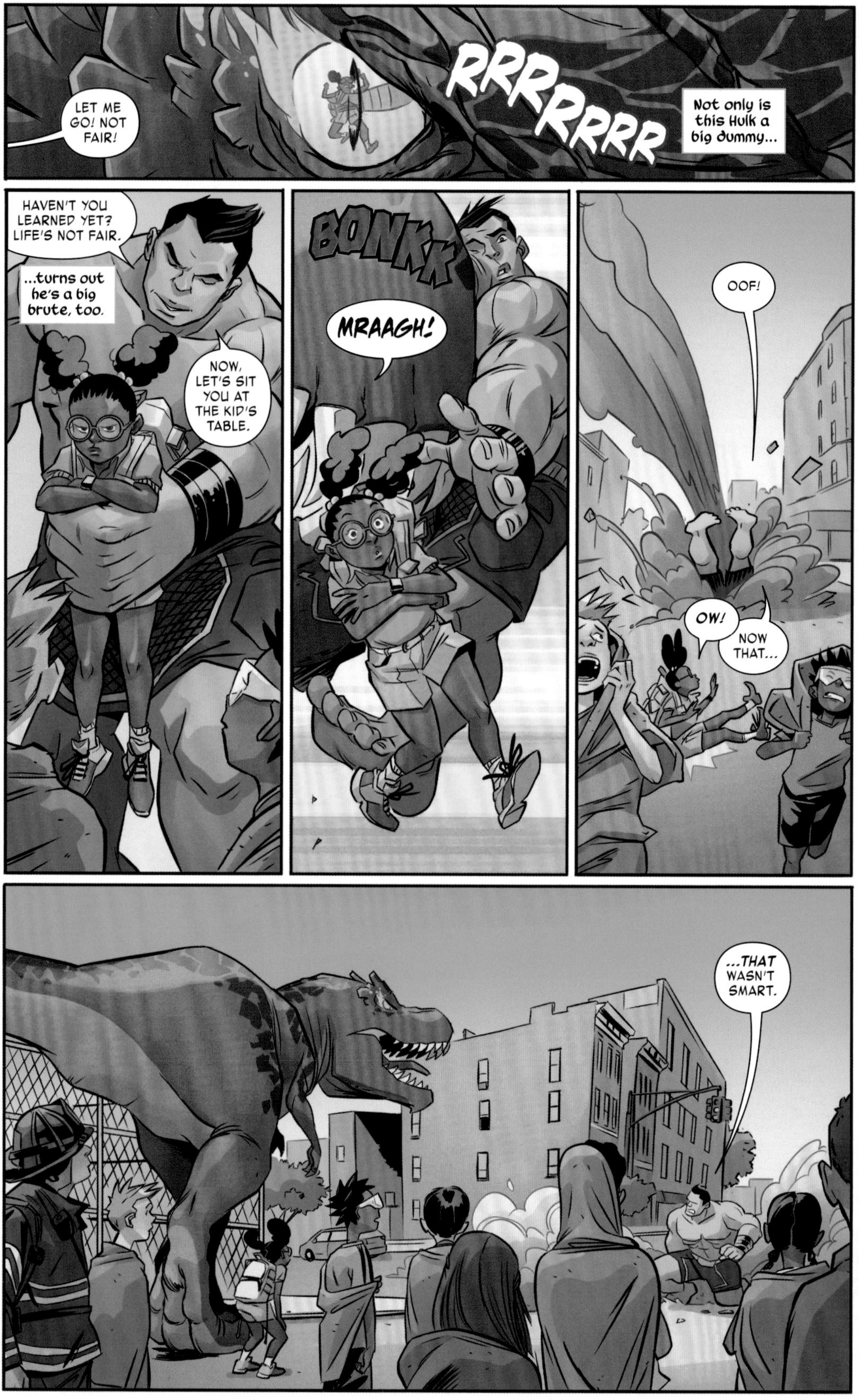
LET ME GO! NOT FAIR!
RRRRRRR
Not only is this Hulk a big dummy...
HAVEN'T YOU LEARNED YET? LIFE'S NOT FAIR.
...turns out he's a big brute, too.
NOW, LET'S SIT YOU AT THE KID'S TABLE.
BONKK
MRAAGH!
OOF!
OW!
NOW THAT...
...THAT WASN'T SMART.

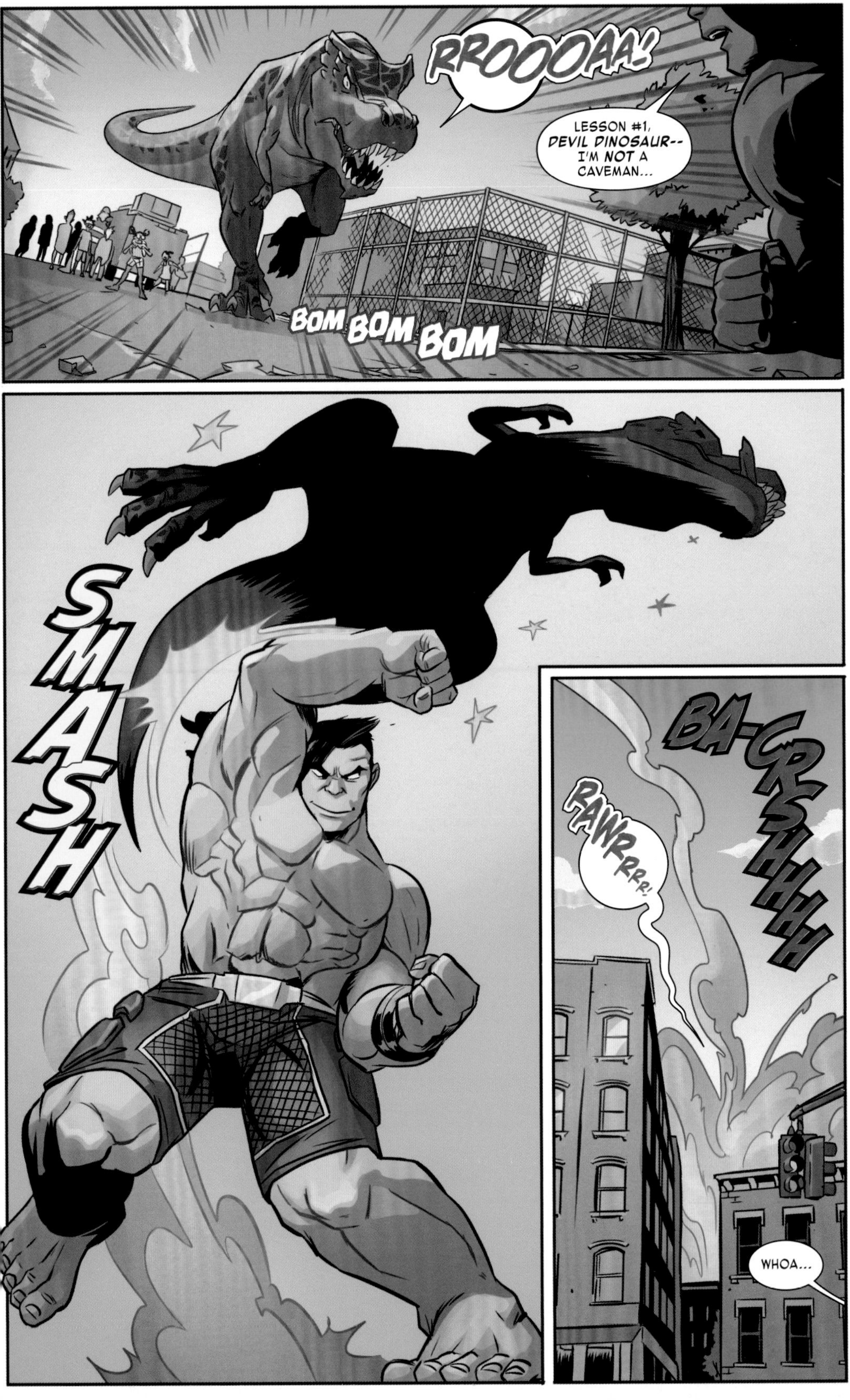
RRROOOAA!
LESSON #1, DEVIL DINOSAUR-- I'M NOT A CAVEMAN...
BOM BOM BOM
SMASH
BA-CRSHHHHH
RAWRrrr!
WHOA...

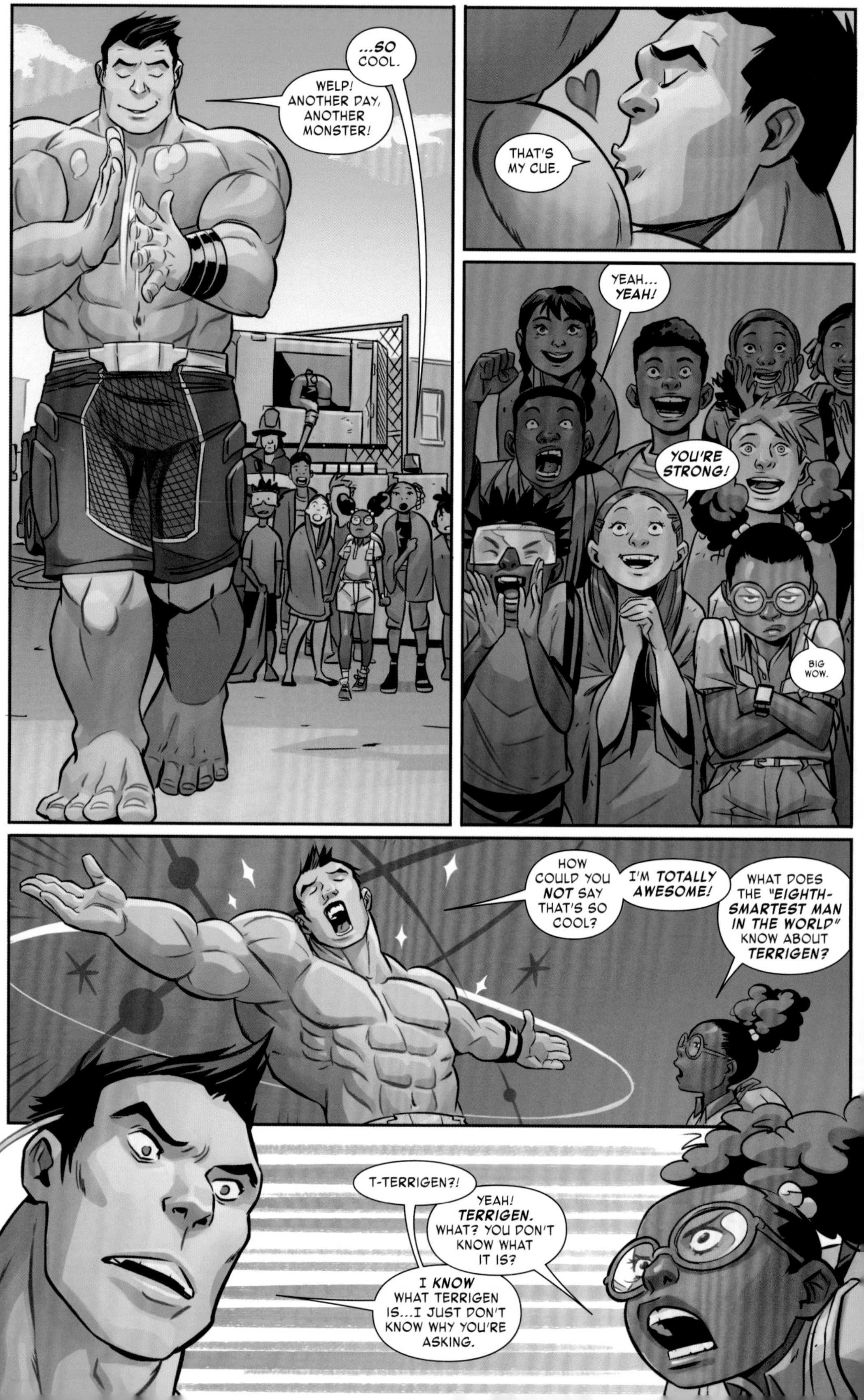
WELP! ANOTHER DAY, ANOTHER MONSTER!
...SO COOL.
THAT'S MY CUE.
YEAH... YEAH!
YOU'RE STRONG!
BIG WOW.
HOW COULD YOU NOT SAY THAT'S SO COOL?
I'M TOTALLY AWESOME!
WHAT DOES THE "EIGHTH-SMARTEST MAN IN THE WORLD" KNOW ABOUT TERRIGEN?
T-TERRIGEN?!
YEAH! TERRIGEN. WHAT? YOU DON'T KNOW WHAT IT IS?
I KNOW WHAT TERRIGEN IS...I JUST DON'T KNOW WHY YOU'RE ASKING.

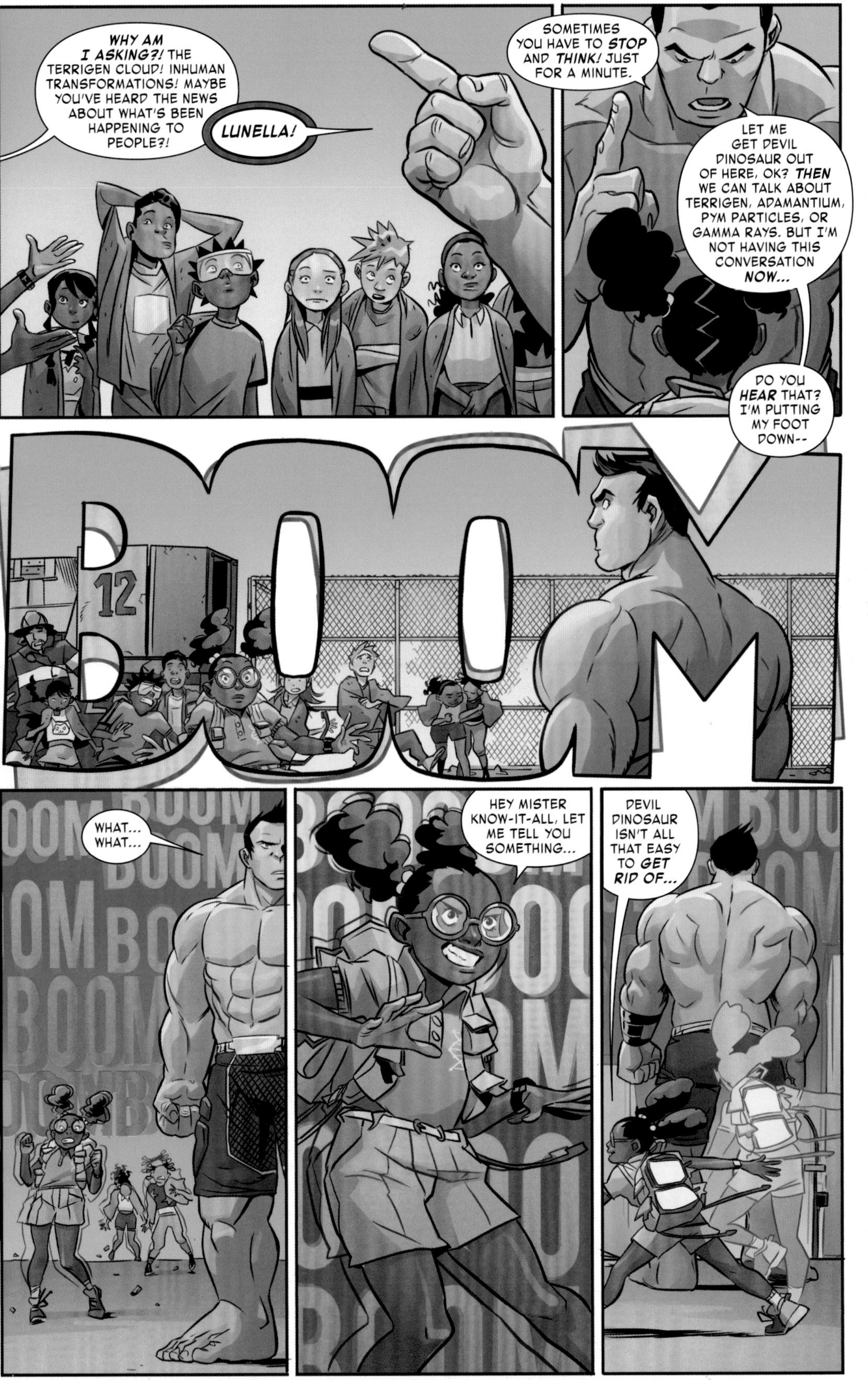
WHY AM I ASKING?! THE TERRIGEN CLOUD! INHUMAN TRANSFORMATIONS! MAYBE YOU'VE HEARD THE NEWS ABOUT WHAT'S BEEN HAPPENING TO PEOPLE?!
LUNELLA!
SOMETIMES YOU HAVE TO STOP AND THINK! JUST FOR A MINUTE.
LET ME GET DEVIL DINOSAUR OUT OF HERE, OK? THEN WE CAN TALK ABOUT TERRIGEN, ADAMANTIUM, PYM PARTICLES, OR GAMMA RAYS. BUT I'M NOT HAVING THIS CONVERSATION NOW...
DO YOU HEAR THAT? I'M PUTTING MY FOOT DOWN--
BOOM
12
WHAT... WHAT...
HEY MISTER KNOW-IT-ALL, LET ME TELL YOU SOMETHING...
DEVIL DINOSAUR ISN'T ALL THAT EASY TO GET RID OF...

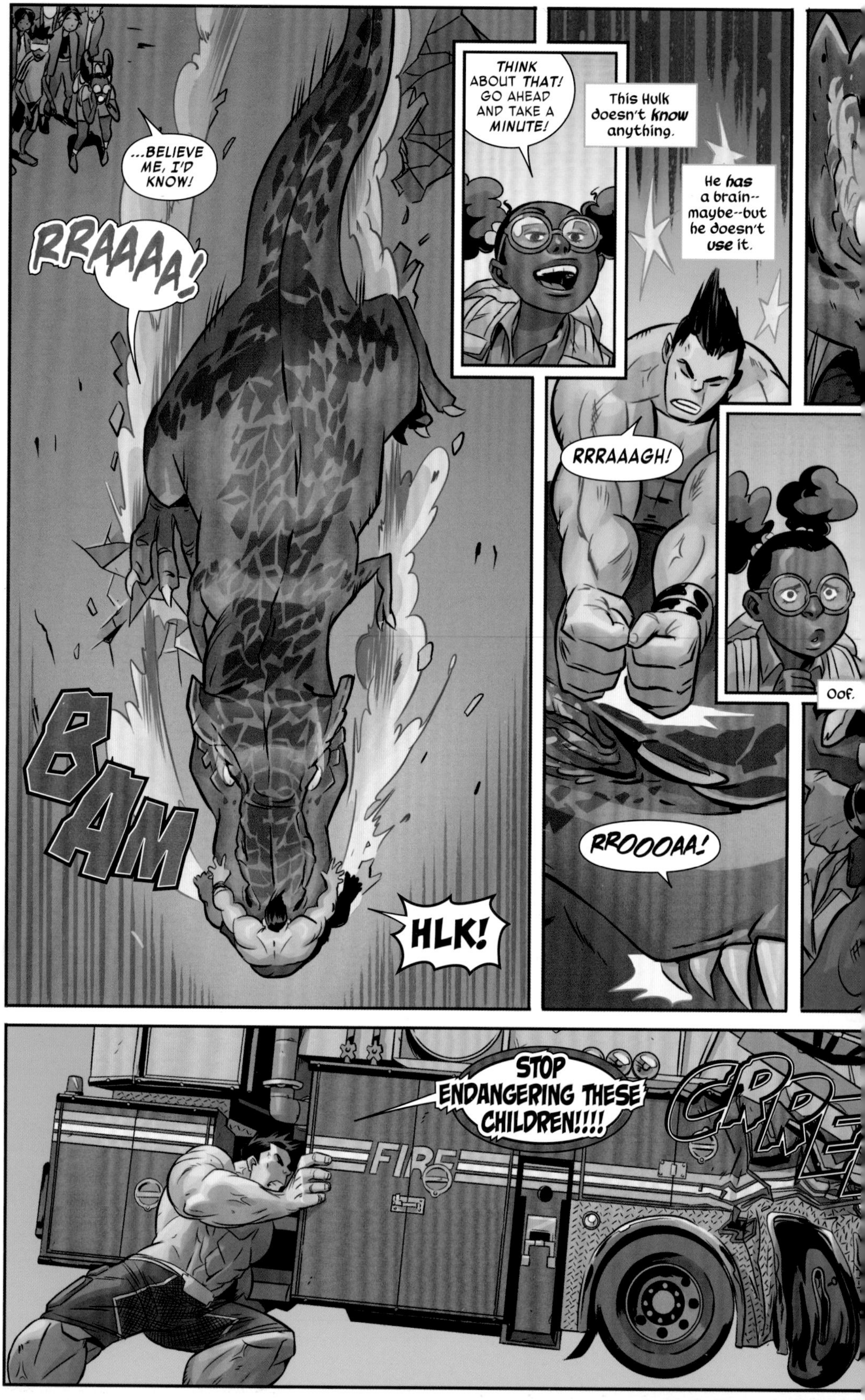
...BELIEVE ME, I'D KNOW!
RRAAAAA!
BAM
HLK!
THINK ABOUT THAT! GO AHEAD AND TAKE A MINUTE!
This Hulk doesn't know anything.
He has a brain-- maybe--but he doesn't use it.
RRRAAAGH!
RROOOAA!
Oof.
STOP ENDANGERING THESE CHILDREN!!!!
FIRE

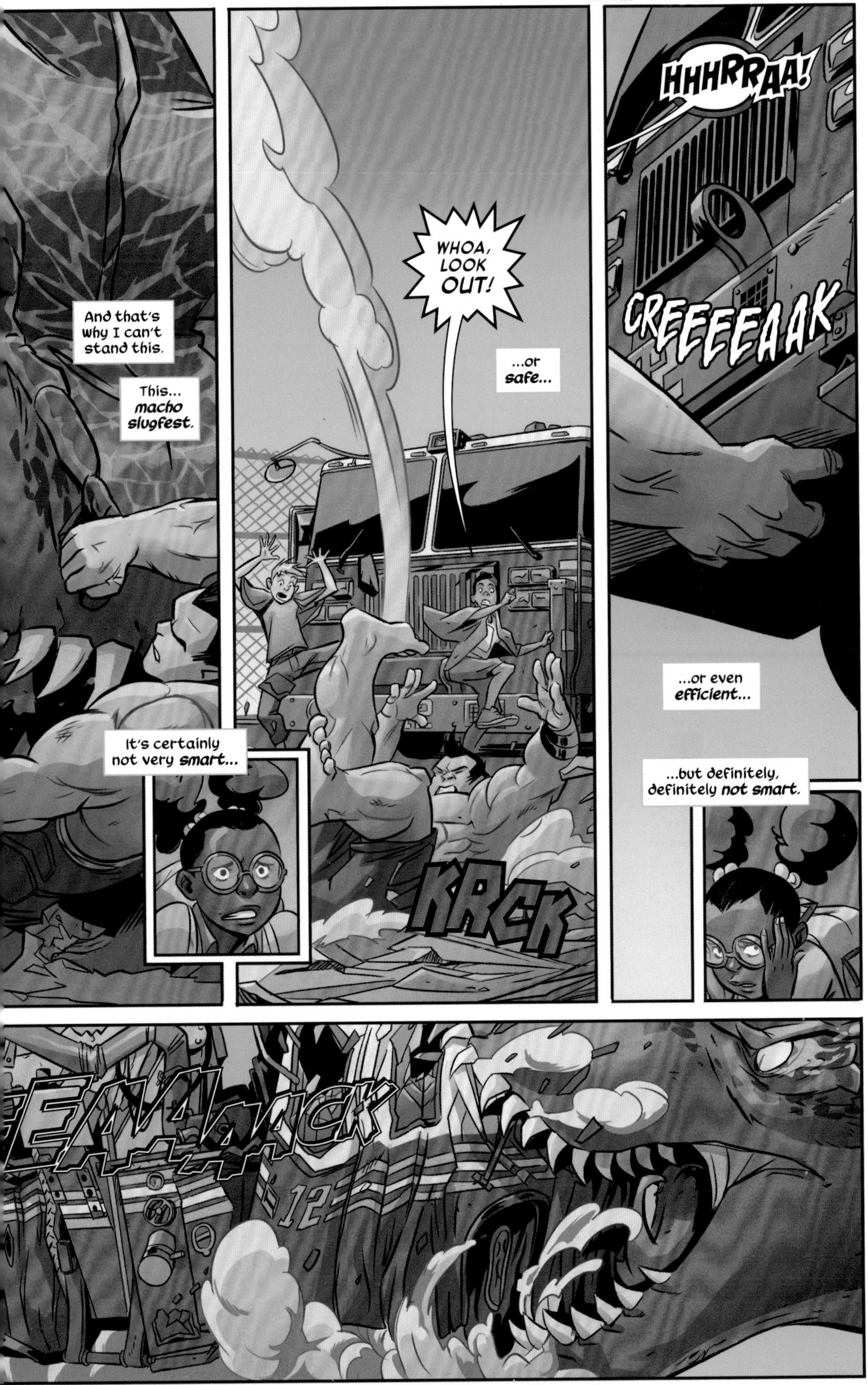

And that's why I can't stand this.
This... macho slugfest.
It's certainly not very smart...
WHOA, LOOK OUT!
...or safe...
KRCK
HHHRRAA!
CREEEEAAK
...or even efficient...
...but definitely, definitely not smart.

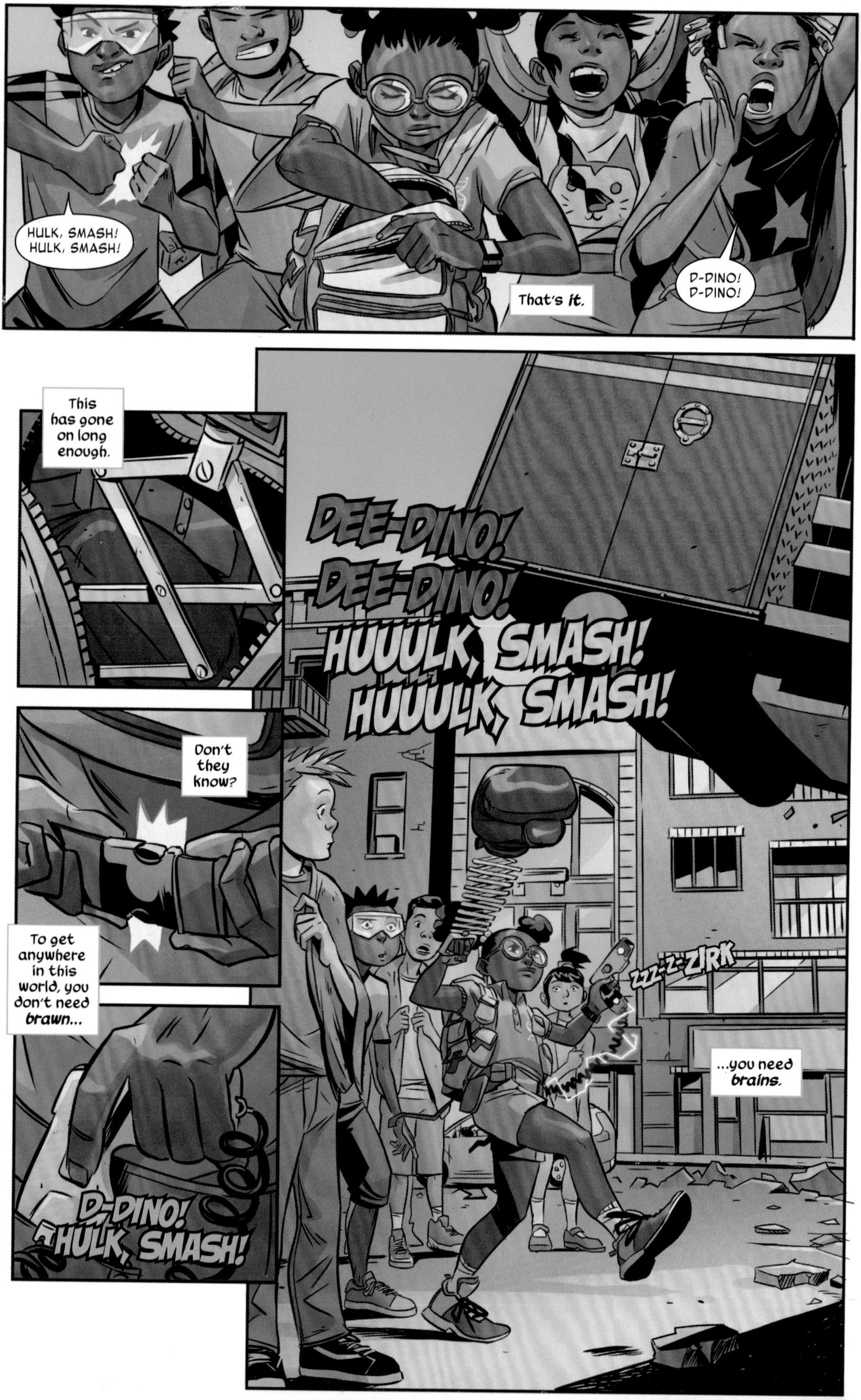
HULK, SMASH! HULK, SMASH!
That's *it.*
D-DINO! D-DINO!
This has gone on long enough.
Don't they know?
To get anywhere in this world, you don't need *brawn...*
D-DINO! HULK, SMASH!
DEE-DINO! DEE-DINO!
HUUULK, SMASH! HUUULK, SMASH!
ZZZ-Z-ZIRK
...you need *brains.*

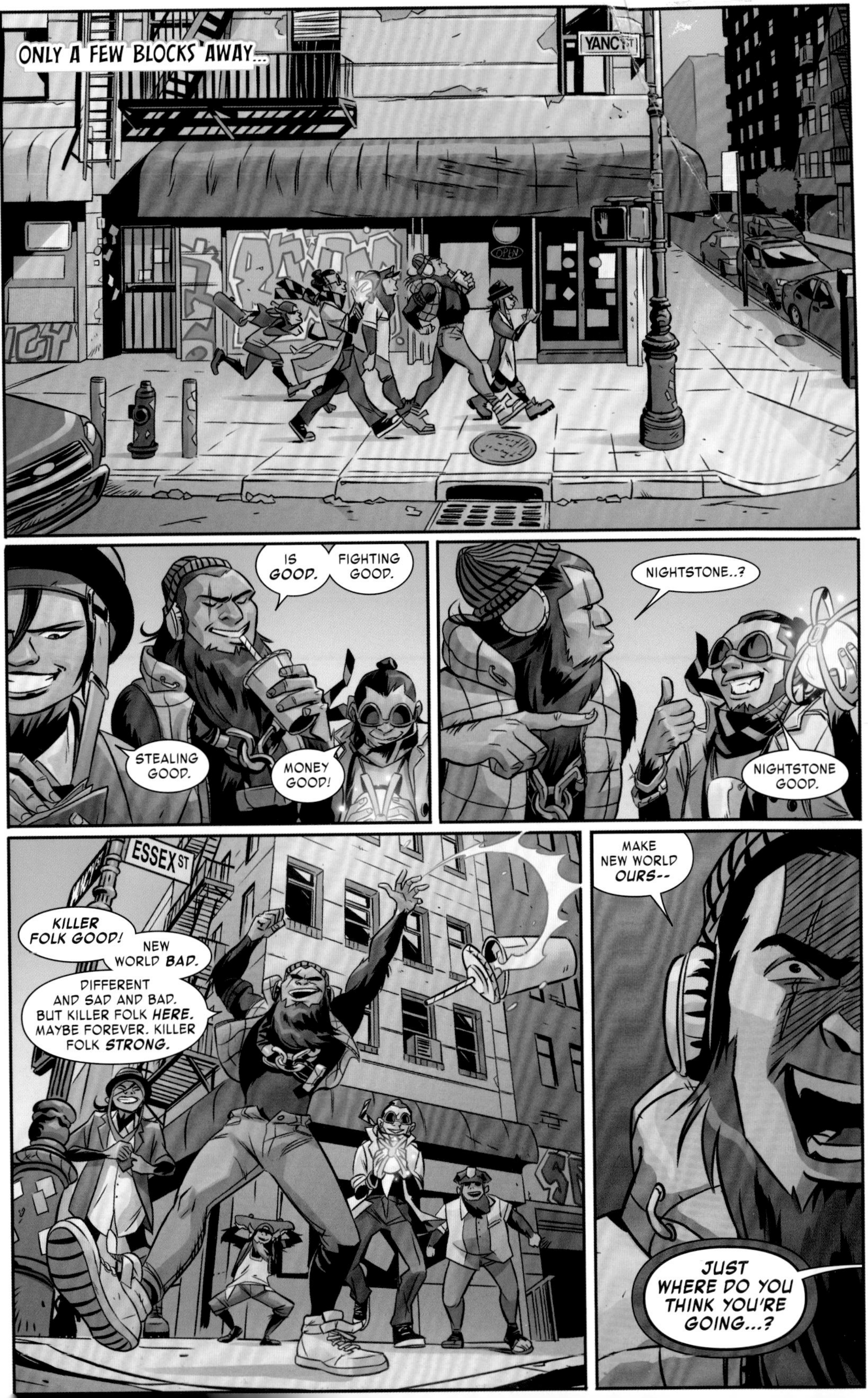
ONLY A FEW BLOCKS AWAY...
YANCY ST
IS GOOD.
FIGHTING GOOD.
STEALING GOOD.
MONEY GOOD!
NIGHTSTONE..?
NIGHTSTONE GOOD.
ESSEX ST
KILLER FOLK GOOD!
NEW WORLD BAD.
DIFFERENT AND SAD AND BAD. BUT KILLER FOLK HERE. MAYBE FOREVER. KILLER FOLK STRONG.
MAKE NEW WORLD OURS--
JUST WHERE DO YOU THINK YOU'RE GOING...?

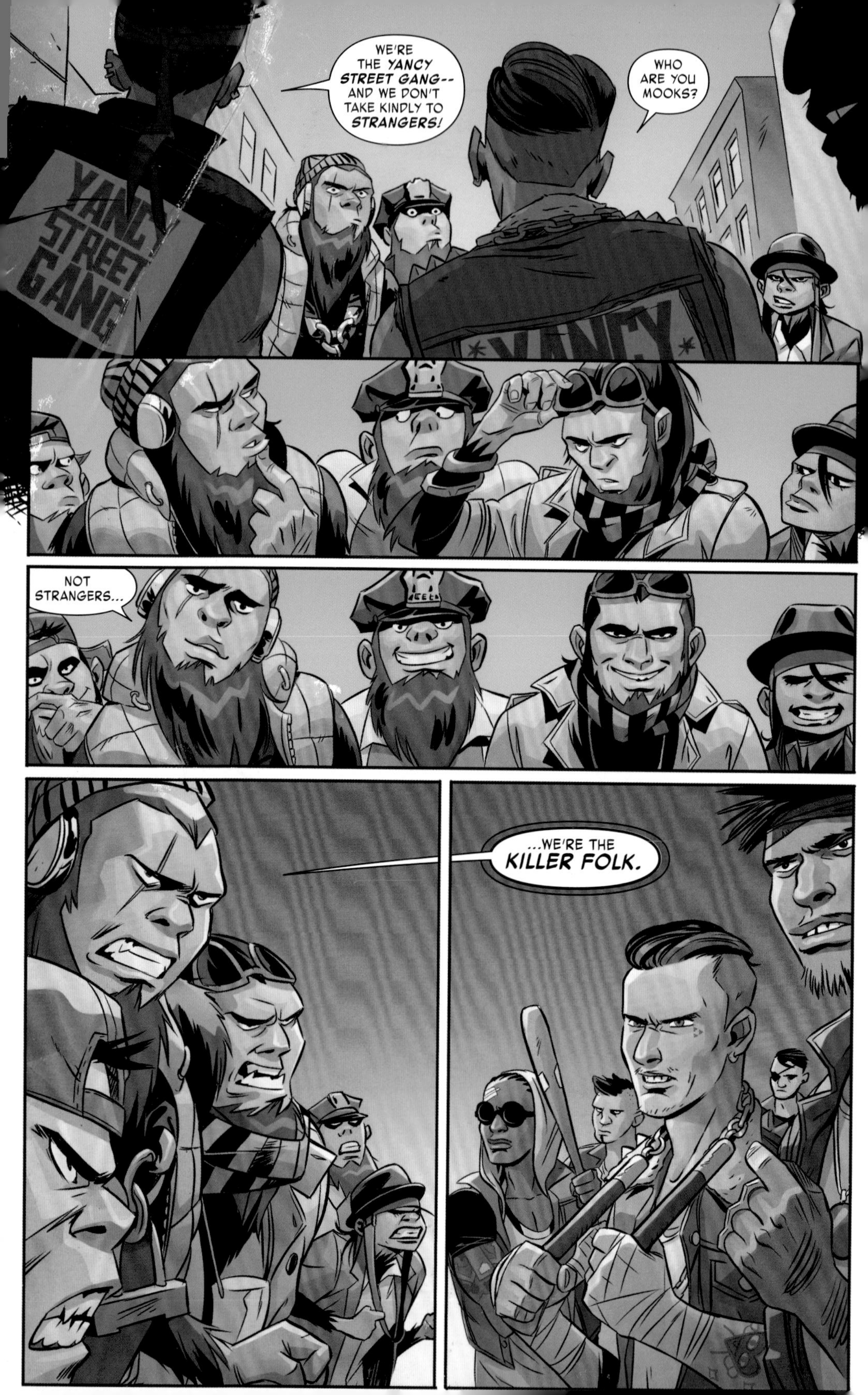
WE'RE THE YANCY STREET GANG-- AND WE DON'T TAKE KINDLY TO STRANGERS!
WHO ARE YOU MOOKS?
YANCY STREET GANG
YANCY
NOT STRANGERS...
...WE'RE THE KILLER FOLK.

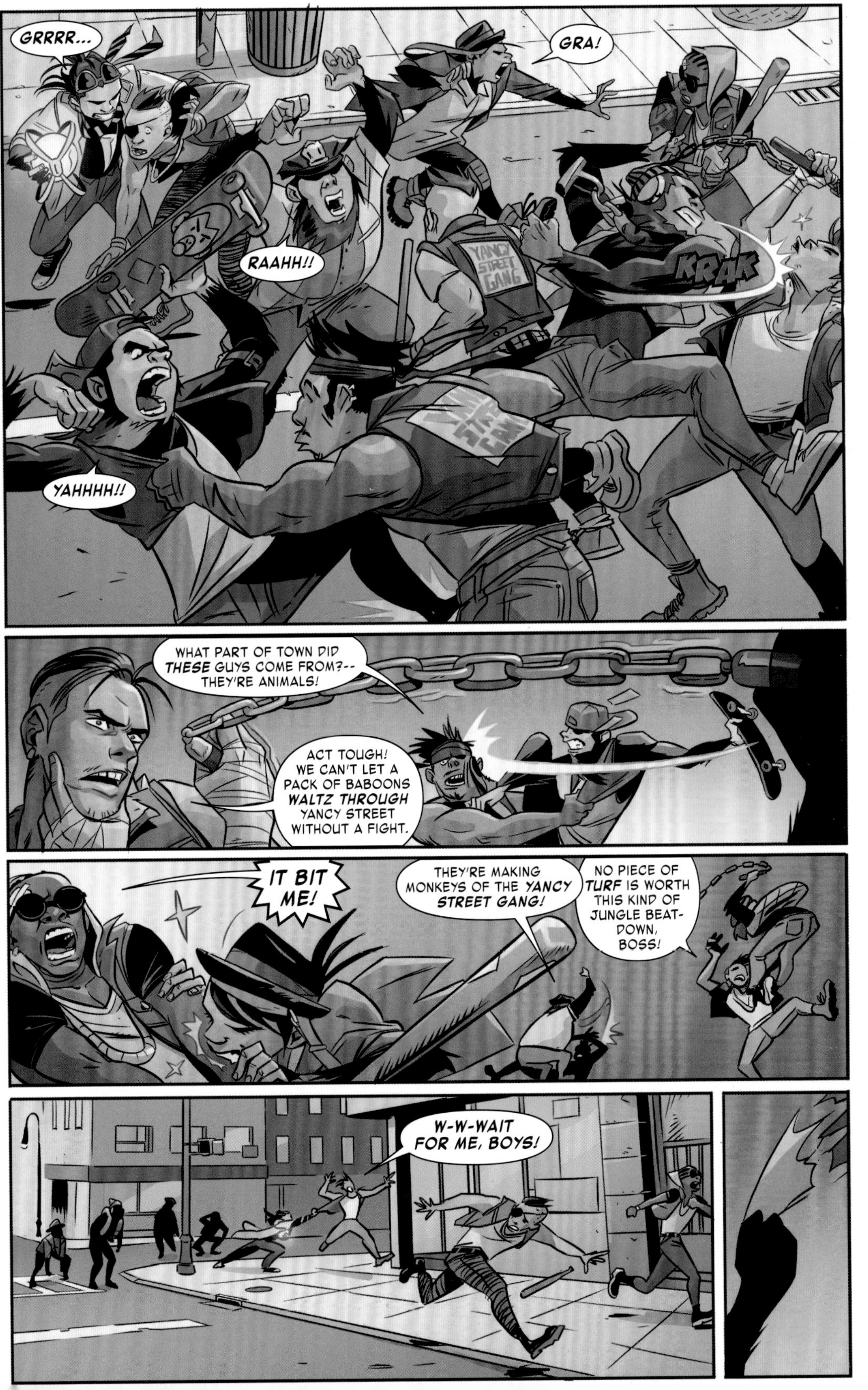
GRRRR...
GRA!
RAAHH!!
KRAK
YAHHHH!!
WHAT PART OF TOWN DID THESE GUYS COME FROM?-- THEY'RE ANIMALS!
ACT TOUGH! WE CAN'T LET A PACK OF BABOONS WALTZ THROUGH YANCY STREET WITHOUT A FIGHT.
IT BIT ME!
THEY'RE MAKING MONKEYS OF THE YANCY STREET GANG!
NO PIECE OF TURF IS WORTH THIS KIND OF JUNGLE BEAT-DOWN, BOSS!
W-W-WAIT FOR ME, BOYS!

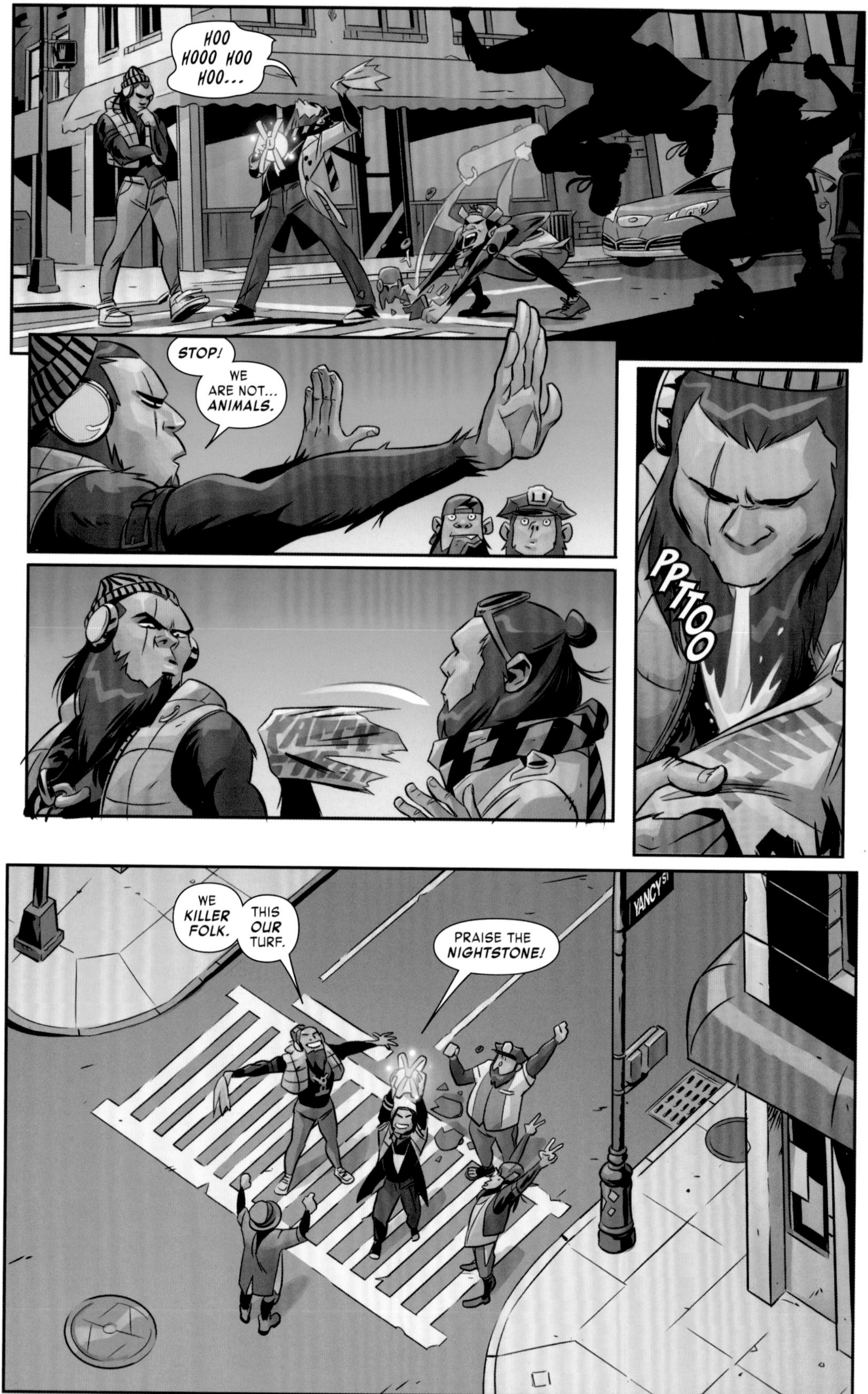
HOO HOOO HOO HOO...
STOP!
WE ARE NOT... ANIMALS.
PPTTOO
WE KILLER FOLK.
THIS OUR TURF.
PRAISE THE NIGHTSTONE!
YANCY ST

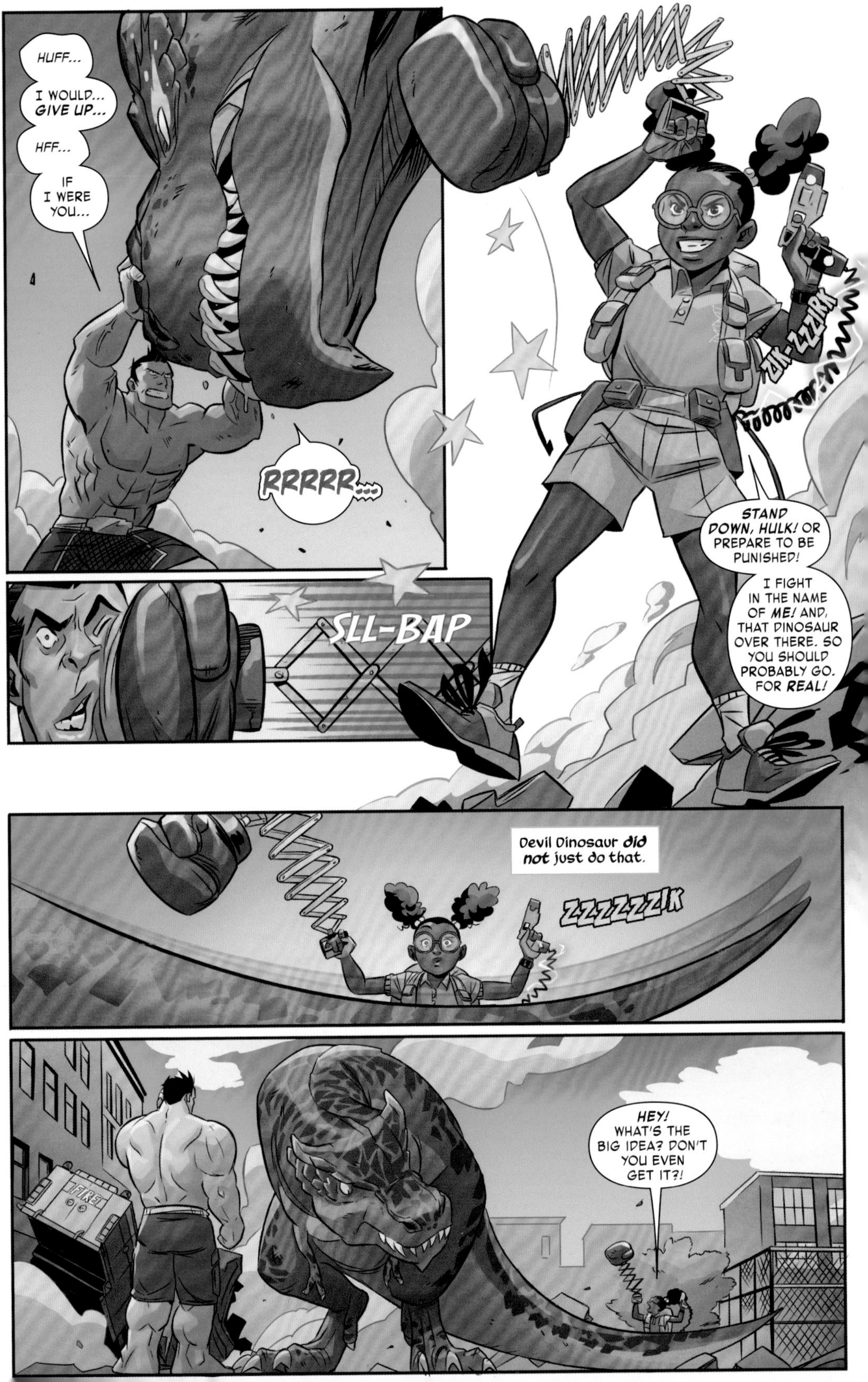
HUFF...
I WOULD... GIVE UP...
HFF...
IF I WERE YOU...
RRRRR...
ZIK-ZZZIRK
STAND DOWN, HULK! OR PREPARE TO BE PUNISHED!
I FIGHT IN THE NAME OF ME! AND, THAT DINOSAUR OVER THERE. SO YOU SHOULD PROBABLY GO. FOR REAL!
SLL-BAP
Devil Dinosaur did not just do that.
ZZZZZZIK
HEY! WHAT'S THE BIG IDEA? DON'T YOU EVEN GET IT?!
FIRE

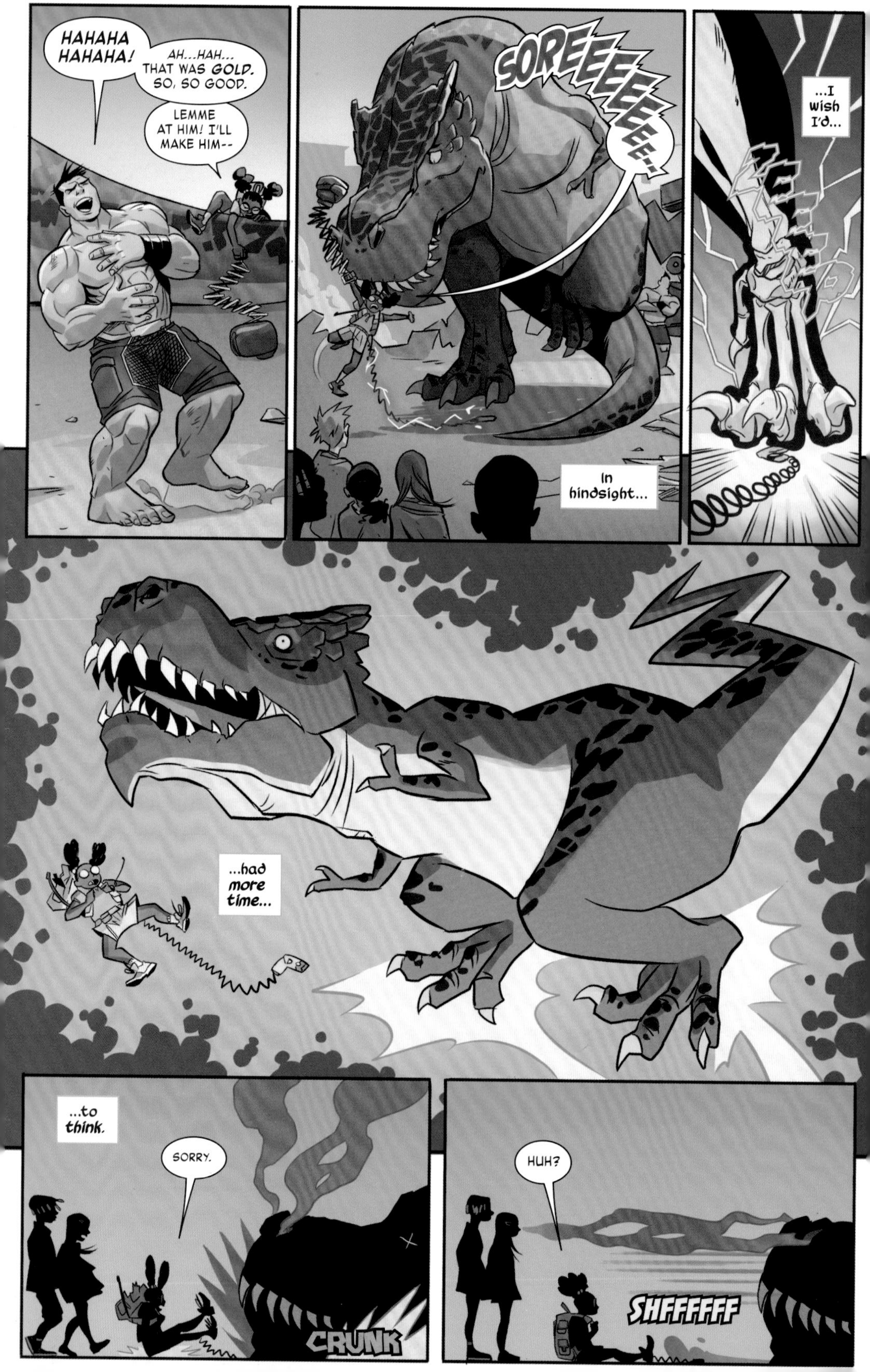

HAHAHA HAHAHA!
AH...HAH... THAT WAS GOLD. SO, SO GOOD.
LEMME AT HIM! I'LL MAKE HIM--
SOREEEEEEEEE..
In hindsight...
...I wish I'd...
...had more time...
...to think.
SORRY.
CRUNK
HUH?
SHFFFFFF

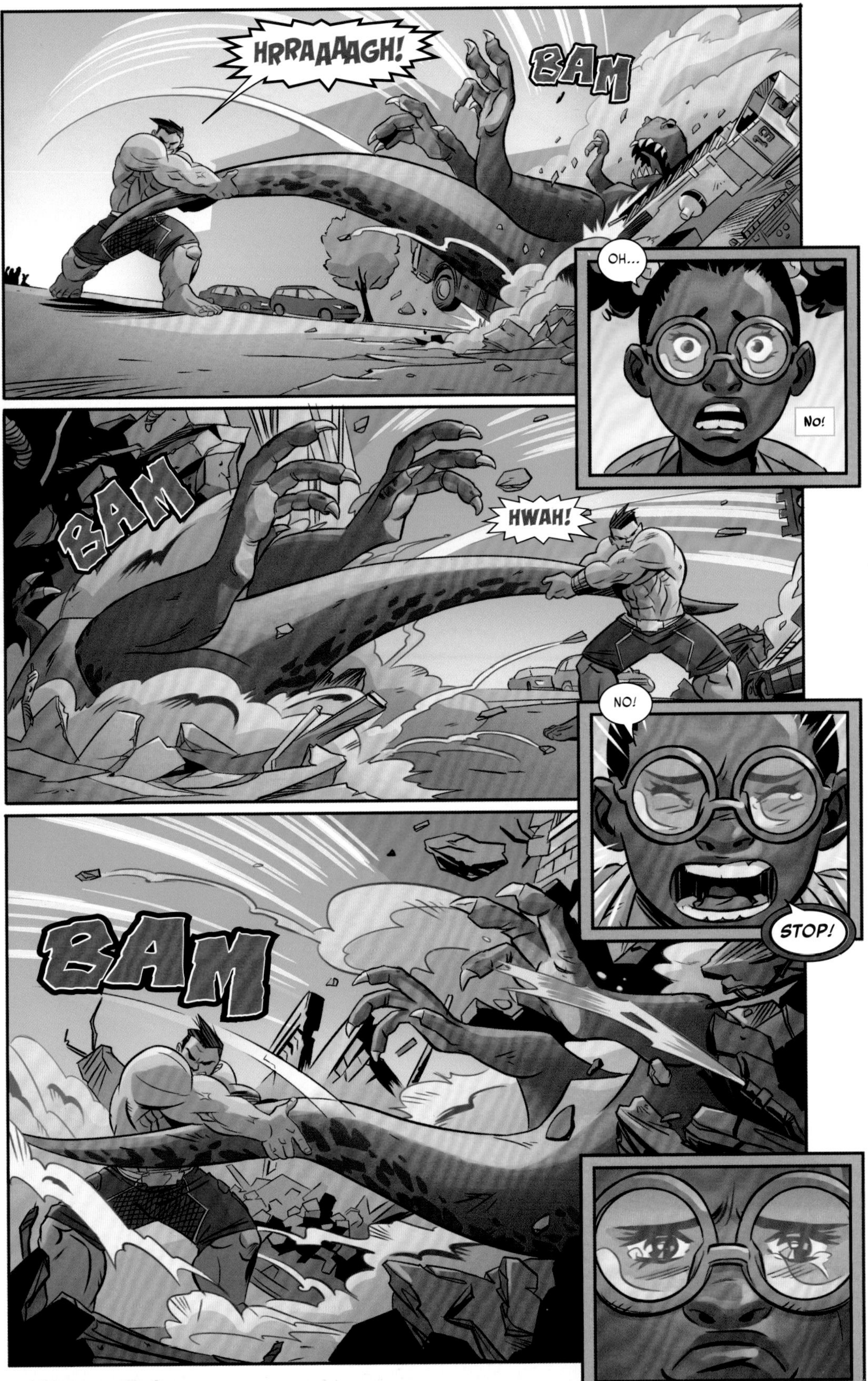
HRRAAAAGH!
BAM
OH...
NO!
BAM
HWAH!
NO!
STOP!
BAM

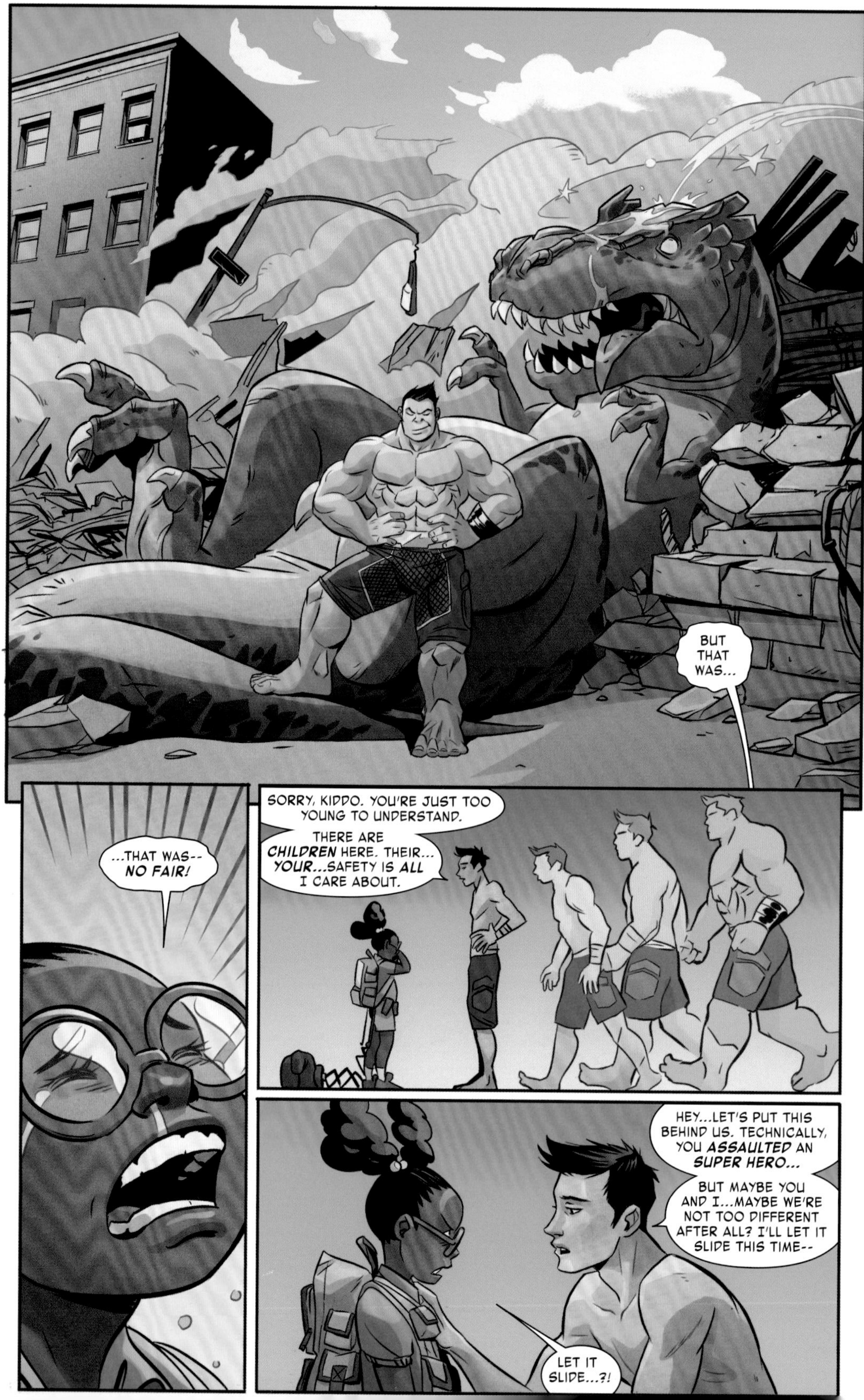
BUT THAT WAS...
...THAT WAS-- NO FAIR!
SORRY, KIDDO. YOU'RE JUST TOO YOUNG TO UNDERSTAND.
THERE ARE CHILDREN HERE. THEIR... YOUR...SAFETY IS ALL I CARE ABOUT.
HEY...LET'S PUT THIS BEHIND US. TECHNICALLY, YOU ASSAULTED AN SUPER HERO...
BUT MAYBE YOU AND I...MAYBE WE'RE NOT TOO DIFFERENT AFTER ALL? I'LL LET IT SLIDE THIS TIME--
LET IT SLIDE...?!

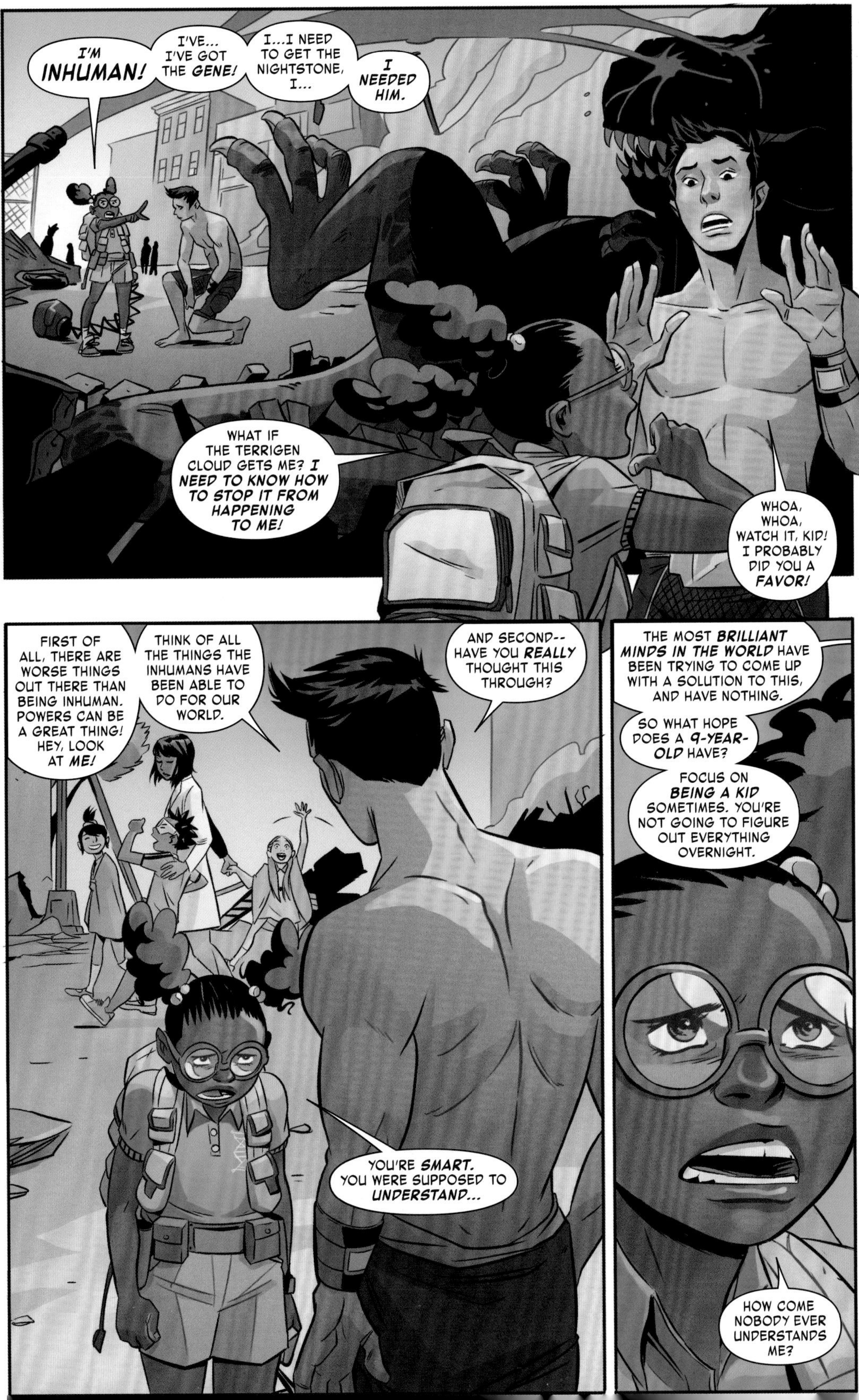
I'M INHUMAN!
I'VE... I'VE GOT THE GENE!
I...I NEED TO GET THE NIGHTSTONE, I...
I NEEDED HIM.
WHAT IF THE TERRIGEN CLOUD GETS ME? I NEED TO KNOW HOW TO STOP IT FROM HAPPENING TO ME!
WHOA, WHOA, WATCH IT, KID! I PROBABLY DID YOU A FAVOR!
FIRST OF ALL, THERE ARE WORSE THINGS OUT THERE THAN BEING INHUMAN. POWERS CAN BE A GREAT THING! HEY, LOOK AT ME!
THINK OF ALL THE THINGS THE INHUMANS HAVE BEEN ABLE TO DO FOR OUR WORLD.
AND SECOND-- HAVE YOU REALLY THOUGHT THIS THROUGH?
YOU'RE SMART. YOU WERE SUPPOSED TO UNDERSTAND...
THE MOST BRILLIANT MINDS IN THE WORLD HAVE BEEN TRYING TO COME UP WITH A SOLUTION TO THIS, AND HAVE NOTHING.
SO WHAT HOPE DOES A 9-YEAR-OLD HAVE?
FOCUS ON BEING A KID SOMETIMES. YOU'RE NOT GOING TO FIGURE OUT EVERYTHING OVERNIGHT.
HOW COME NOBODY EVER UNDERSTANDS ME?

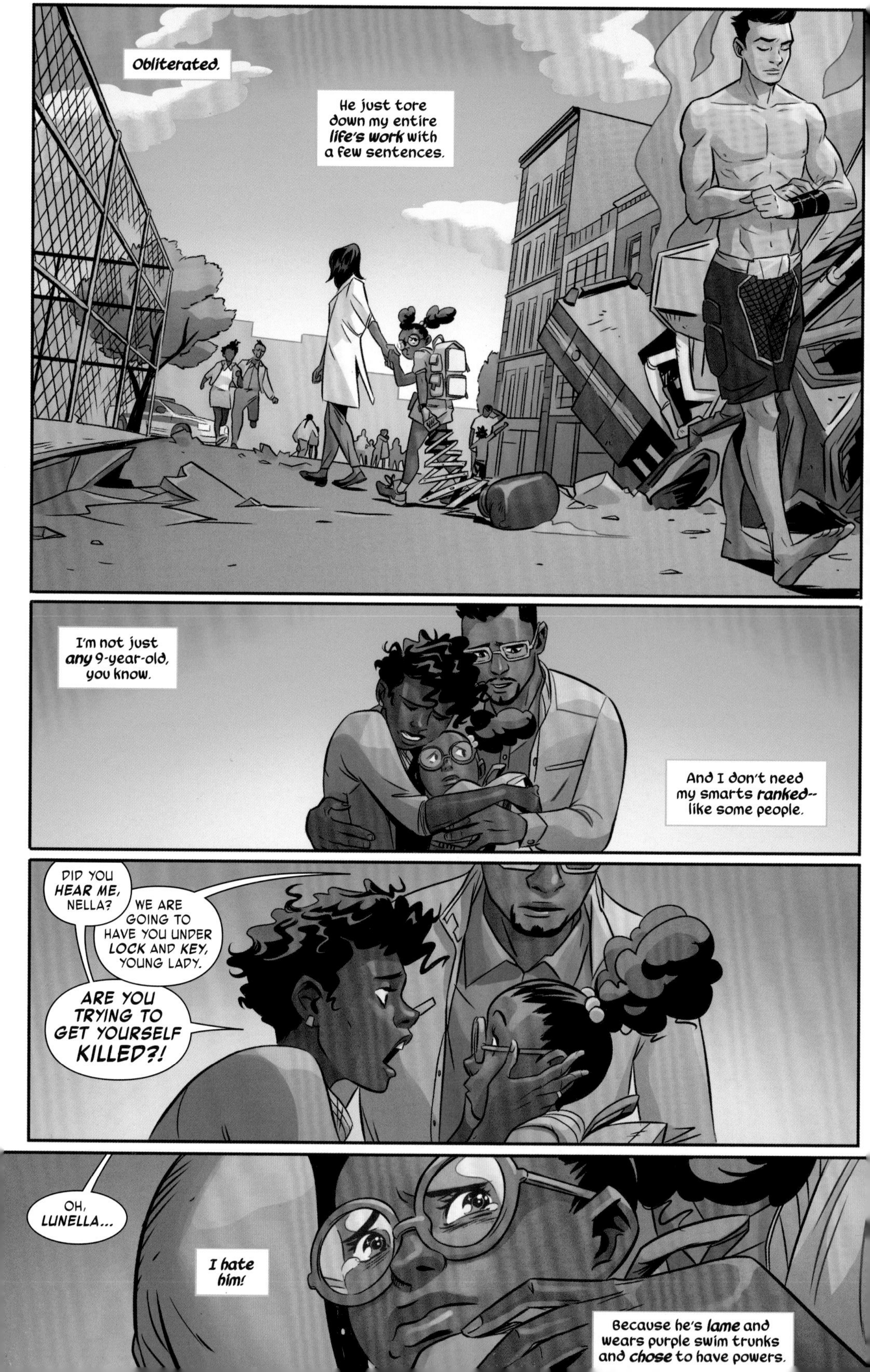
Obliterated.
He just tore down my entire life's work with a few sentences.
I'm not just any 9-year-old, you know.
And I don't need my smarts ranked-- like some people.
DID YOU HEAR ME, NELLA?
WE ARE GOING TO HAVE YOU UNDER LOCK AND KEY, YOUNG LADY.
ARE YOU TRYING TO GET YOURSELF KILLED?!
OH, LUNELLA...
I hate him!
Because he's lame and wears purple swim trunks and chose to have powers.

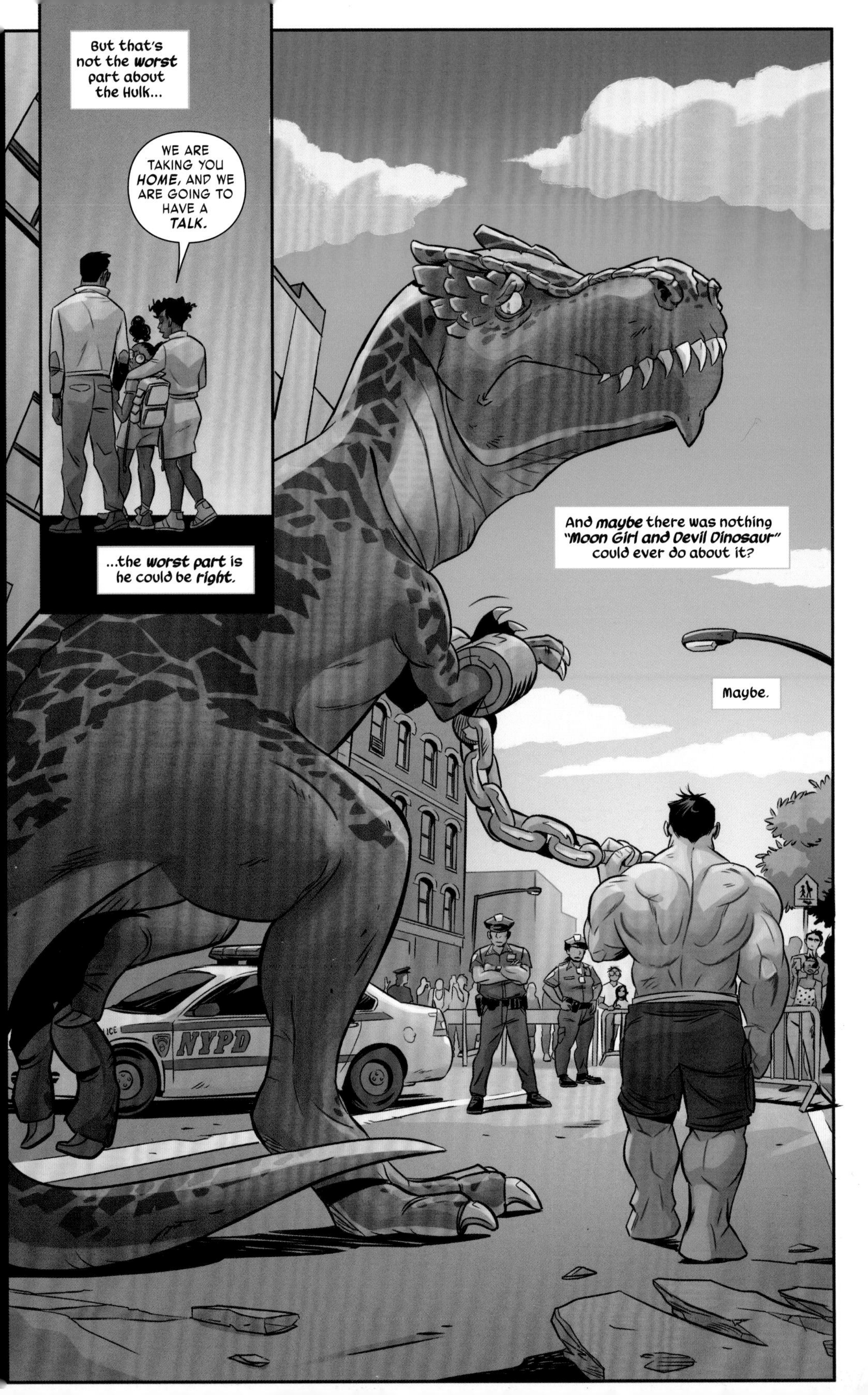
But that's not the *worst* part about the Hulk...
WE ARE TAKING YOU *HOME*, AND WE ARE GOING TO HAVE A *TALK*.
...the *worst part* is he could be *right*.
And *maybe* there was nothing *"Moon Girl and Devil Dinosaur"* could ever do about it?
Maybe.
NYPD

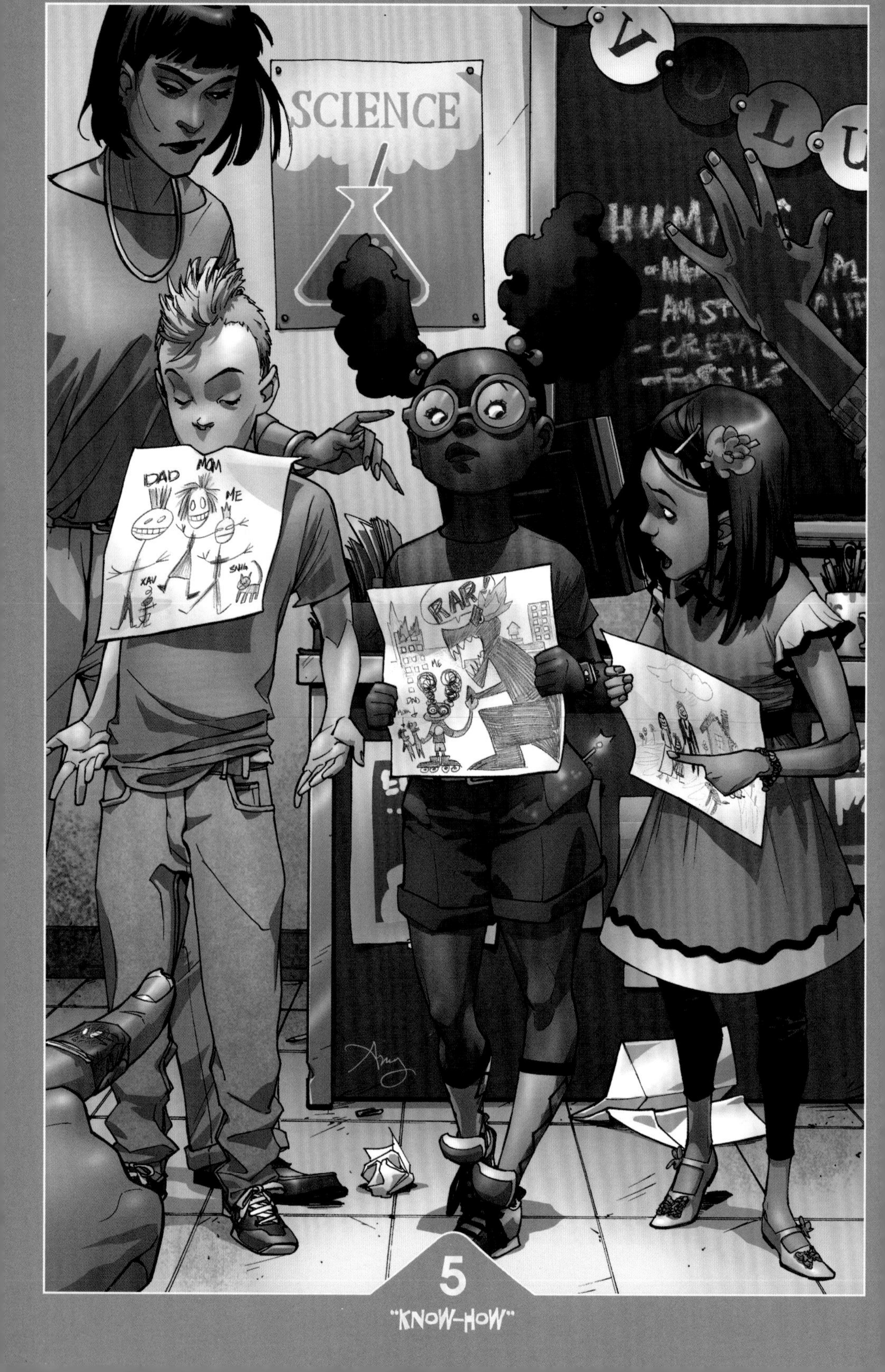
SCIENCE
DAD
MOM
ME
RAR!

5
"KNOW-HOW"

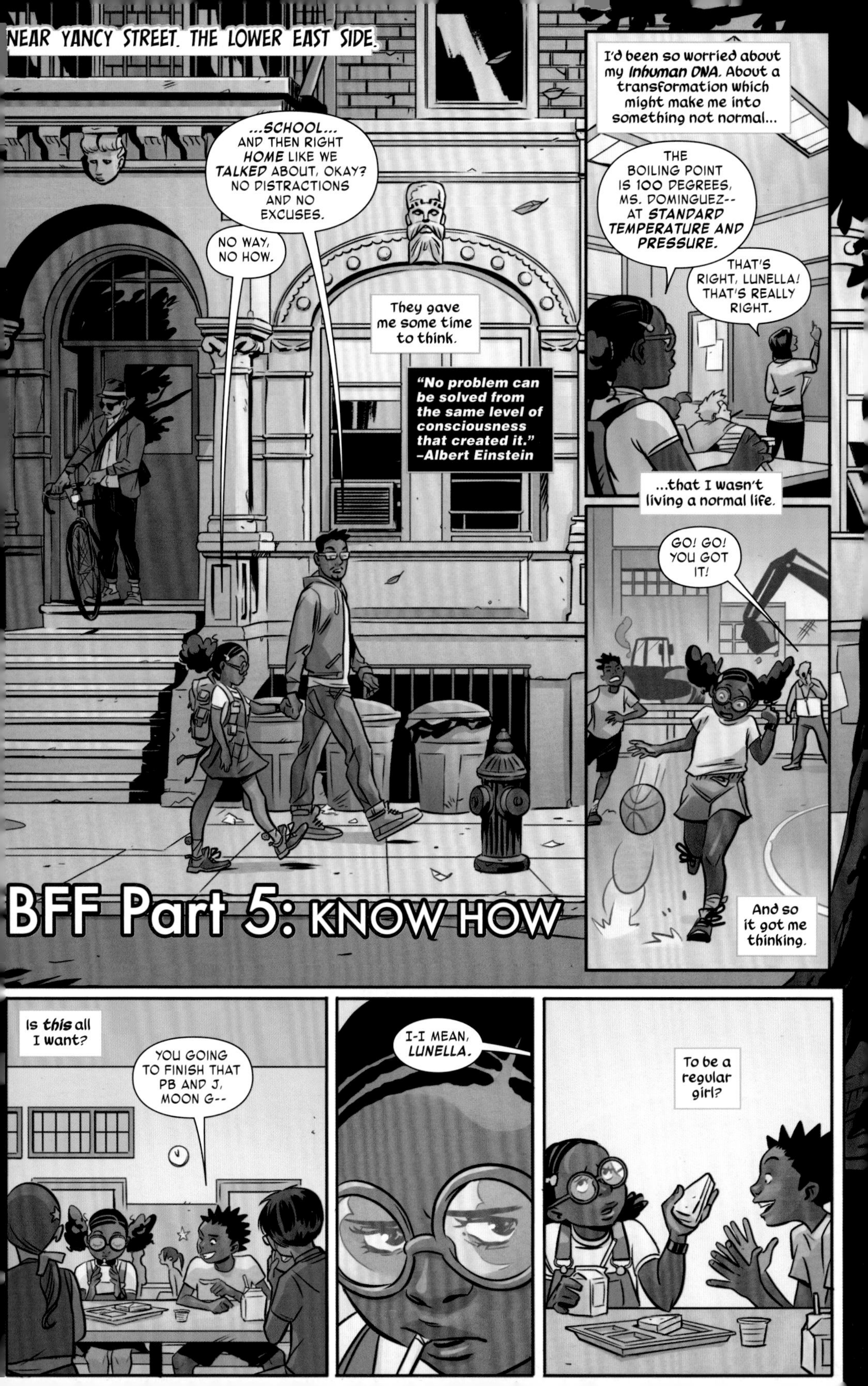
NEAR YANCY STREET. THE LOWER EAST SIDE.
...SCHOOL... AND THEN RIGHT HOME LIKE WE TALKED ABOUT, OKAY? NO DISTRACTIONS AND NO EXCUSES.
NO WAY, NO HOW.
They gave me some time to think.
"No problem can be solved from the same level of consciousness that created it." –Albert Einstein
I'd been so worried about my Inhuman DNA. About a transformation which might make me into something not normal...
THE BOILING POINT IS 100 DEGREES, MS. DOMINGUEZ-- AT STANDARD TEMPERATURE AND PRESSURE.
THAT'S RIGHT, LUNELLA! THAT'S REALLY RIGHT.
...that I wasn't living a normal life.
GO! GO! YOU GOT IT!
And so it got me thinking.
BFF Part 5: KNOW HOW
Is this all I want?
YOU GOING TO FINISH THAT PB AND J, MOON G--
I-I MEAN, LUNELLA.
To be a regular girl?

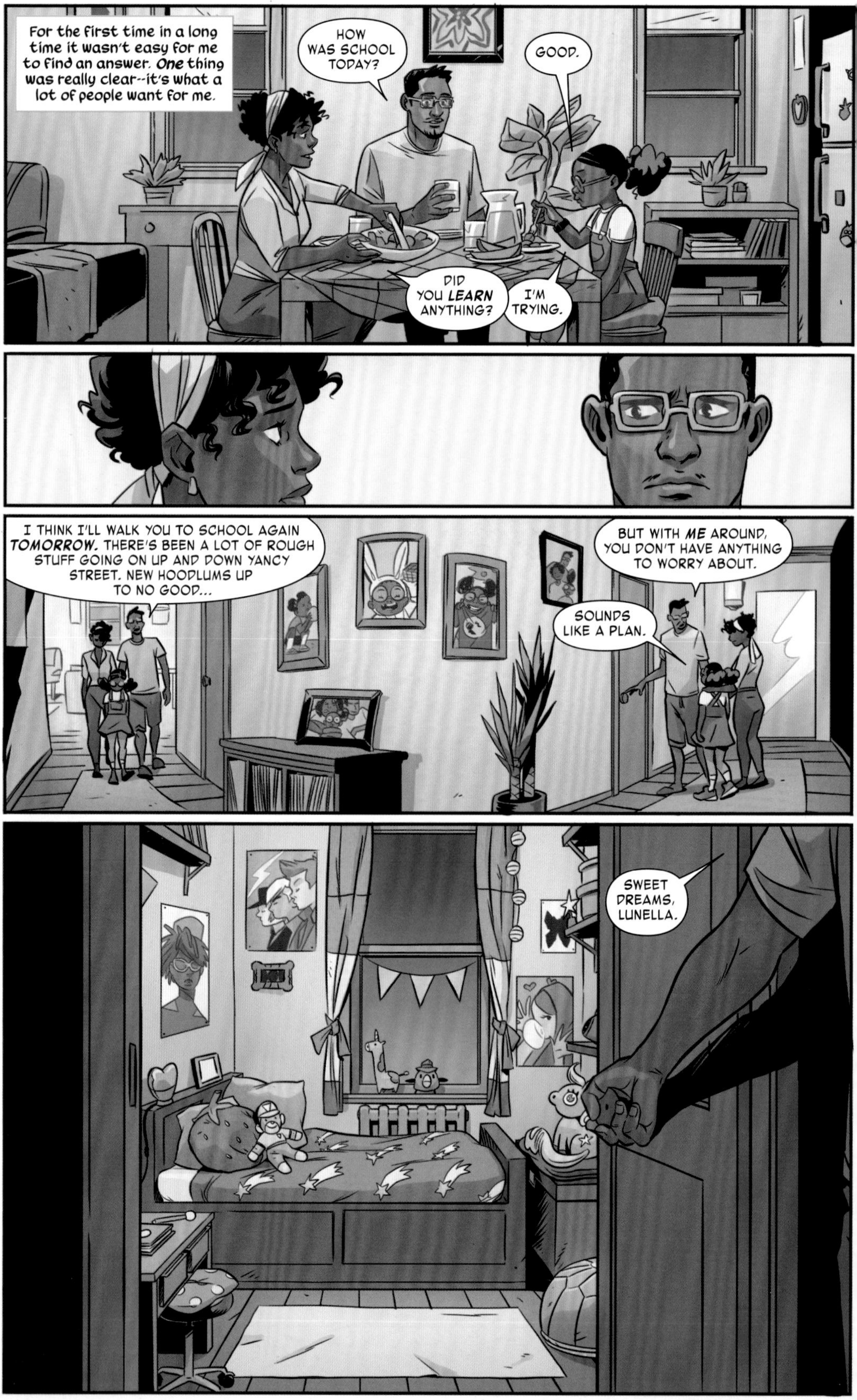
For the first time in a long time it wasn't easy for me to find an answer. *One* thing was really clear--it's what a lot of people want for me.
HOW WAS SCHOOL TODAY?
GOOD.
DID YOU **LEARN** ANYTHING?
I'M TRYING.
I THINK I'LL WALK YOU TO SCHOOL AGAIN **TOMORROW.** THERE'S BEEN A LOT OF ROUGH STUFF GOING ON UP AND DOWN YANCY STREET. NEW HOODLUMS UP TO NO GOOD...
BUT WITH **ME** AROUND, YOU DON'T HAVE ANYTHING TO WORRY ABOUT.
SOUNDS LIKE A PLAN.
SWEET DREAMS, LUNELLA.

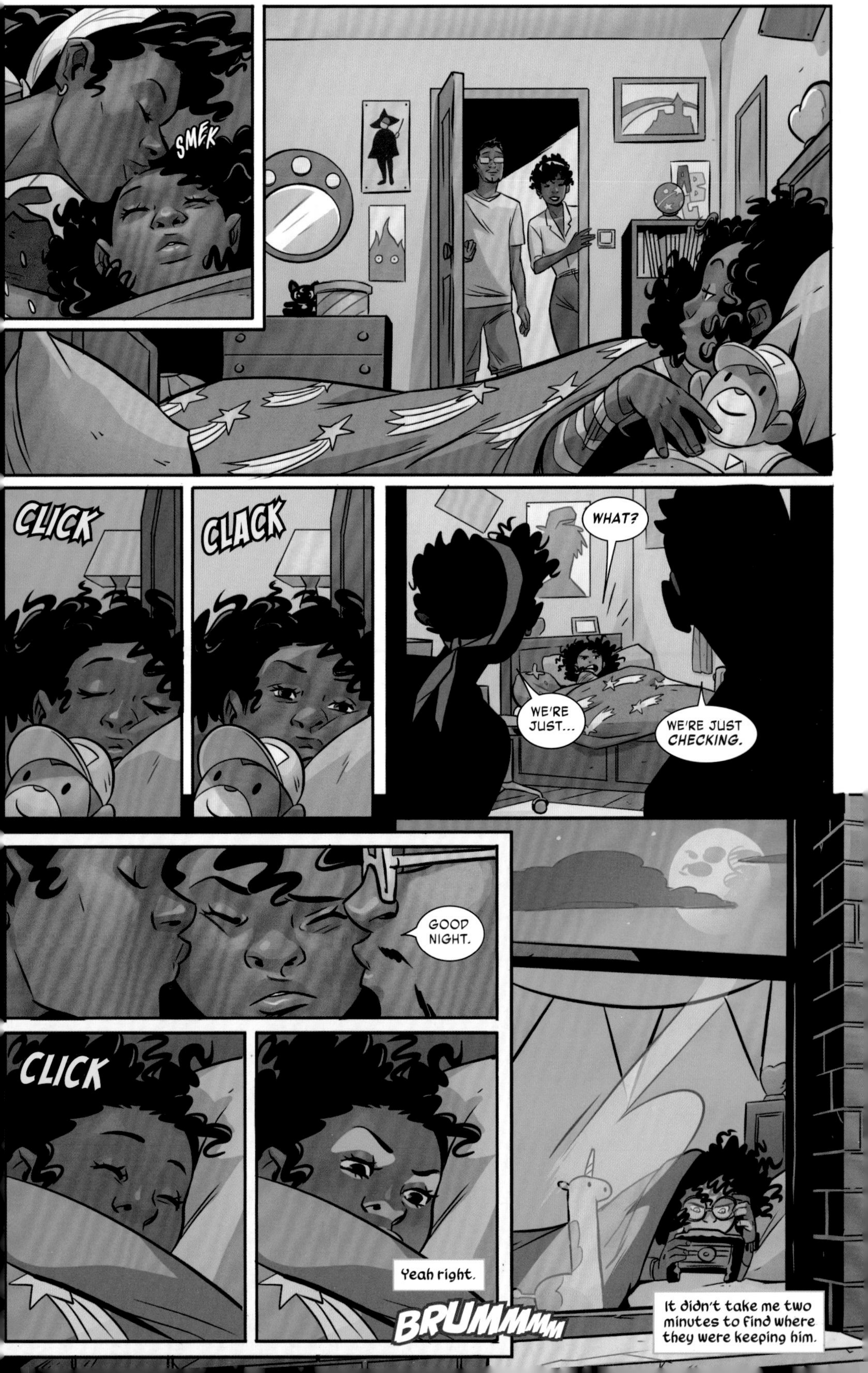
SMEK
CLICK
CLACK
WHAT?
WE'RE JUST...
WE'RE JUST CHECKING.
GOOD NIGHT.
CLICK
Yeah right.
BRUMMMM
It didn't take me two minutes to find where they were keeping him.

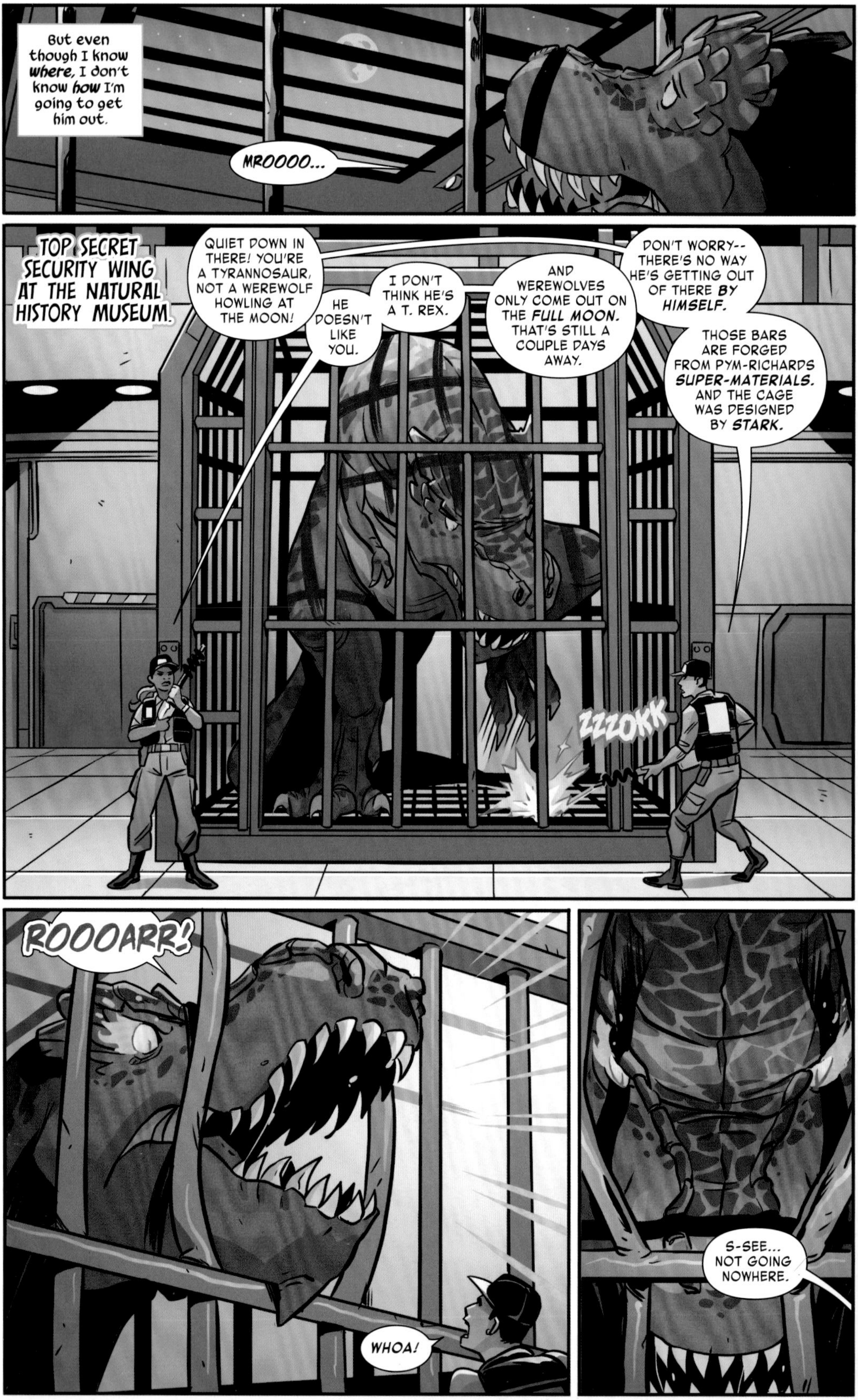
But even though I know *where*, I don't know *how* I'm going to get him out.
MROOOO...
TOP SECRET SECURITY WING AT THE NATURAL HISTORY MUSEUM.
QUIET DOWN IN THERE! YOU'RE A TYRANNOSAUR, NOT A WEREWOLF HOWLING AT THE MOON!
HE DOESN'T LIKE YOU.
I DON'T THINK HE'S A T. REX.
AND WEREWOLVES ONLY COME OUT ON THE *FULL MOON.* THAT'S STILL A COUPLE DAYS AWAY.
DON'T WORRY-- THERE'S NO WAY HE'S GETTING OUT OF THERE *BY HIMSELF.*
THOSE BARS ARE FORGED FROM PYM-RICHARDS *SUPER-MATERIALS.* AND THE CAGE WAS DESIGNED BY *STARK.*
ZZZOKK
ROOOARR!
WHOA!
S-SEE... NOT GOING NOWHERE.

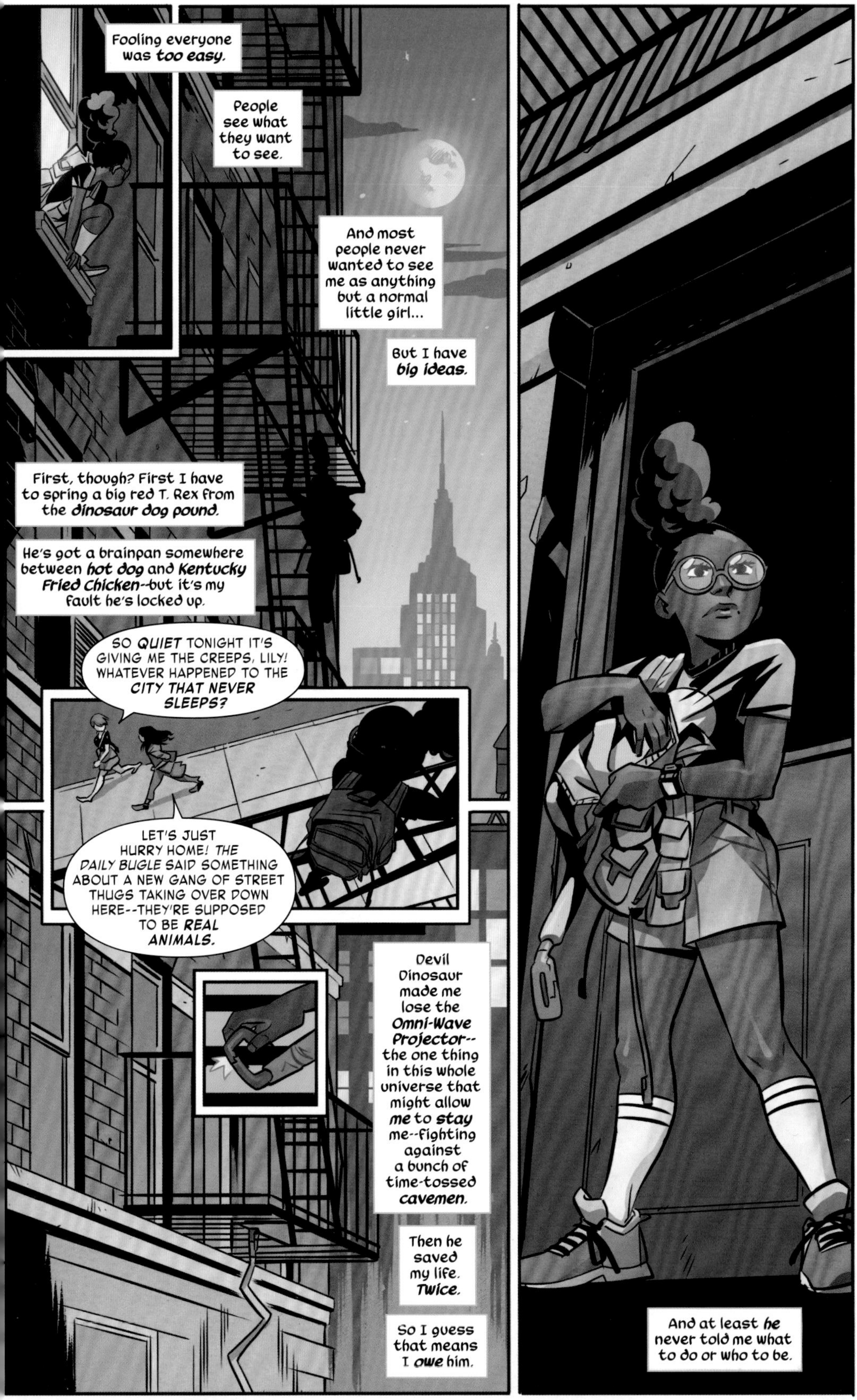
Fooling everyone was too easy.
People see what they want to see.
And most people never wanted to see me as anything but a normal little girl...
But I have big ideas.
First, though? First I have to spring a big red T. Rex from the dinosaur dog pound.
He's got a brainpan somewhere between hot dog and Kentucky Fried Chicken--but it's my fault he's locked up.
SO QUIET TONIGHT IT'S GIVING ME THE CREEPS, LILY! WHATEVER HAPPENED TO THE CITY THAT NEVER SLEEPS?
LET'S JUST HURRY HOME! THE DAILY BUGLE SAID SOMETHING ABOUT A NEW GANG OF STREET THUGS TAKING OVER DOWN HERE--THEY'RE SUPPOSED TO BE REAL ANIMALS.
Devil Dinosaur made me lose the Omni-Wave Projector--the one thing in this whole universe that might allow me to stay me--fighting against a bunch of time-tossed cavemen.
Then he saved my life. Twice.
So I guess that means I owe him.
And at least he never told me what to do or who to be.

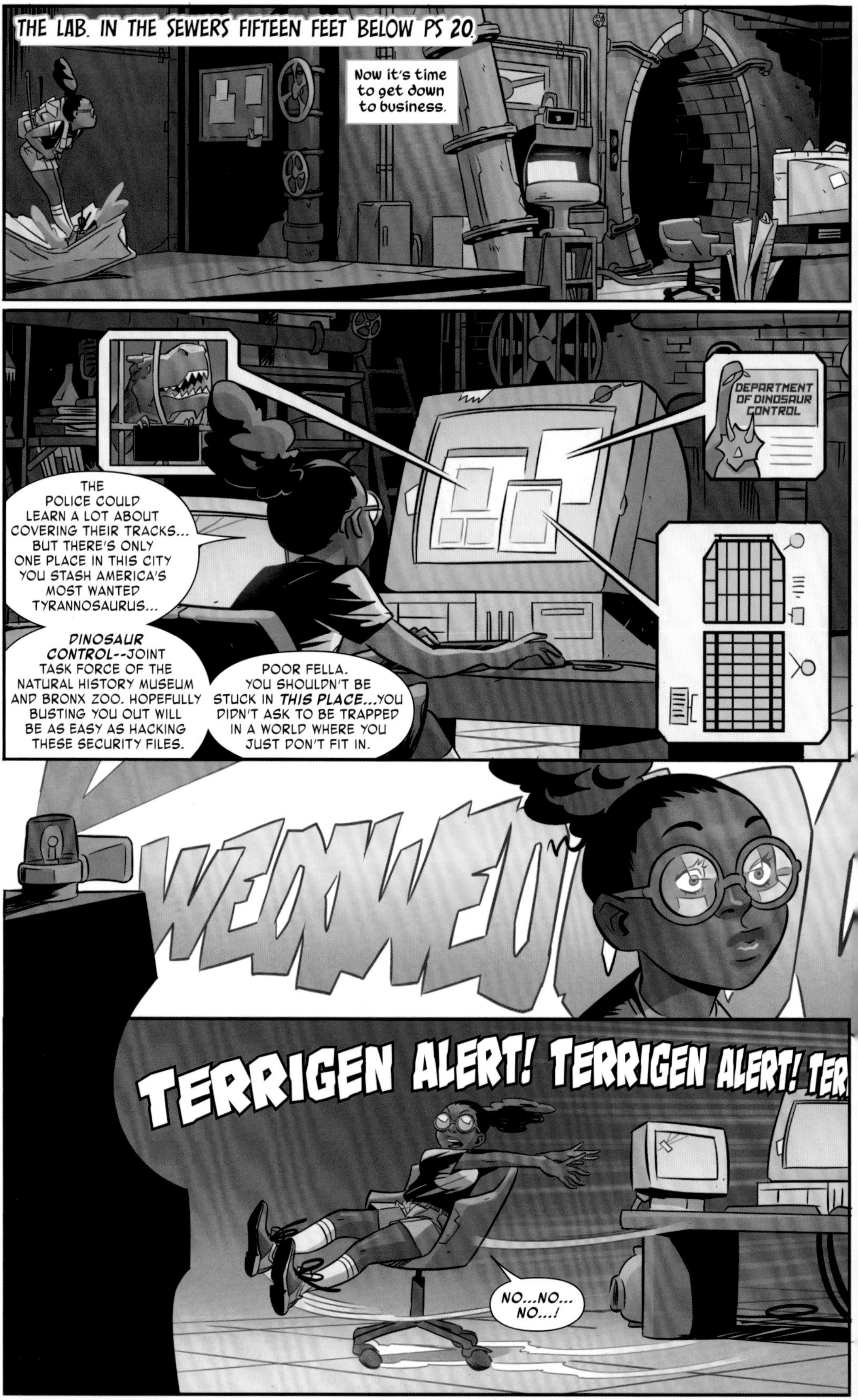
THE LAB. IN THE SEWERS FIFTEEN FEET BELOW PS 20.
Now it's time to get down to business.
DEPARTMENT OF DINOSAUR CONTROL
THE POLICE COULD LEARN A LOT ABOUT COVERING THEIR TRACKS... BUT THERE'S ONLY ONE PLACE IN THIS CITY YOU STASH AMERICA'S MOST WANTED TYRANNOSAURUS...
DINOSAUR CONTROL--JOINT TASK FORCE OF THE NATURAL HISTORY MUSEUM AND BRONX ZOO. HOPEFULLY BUSTING YOU OUT WILL BE AS EASY AS HACKING THESE SECURITY FILES.
POOR FELLA. YOU SHOULDN'T BE STUCK IN THIS PLACE...YOU DIDN'T ASK TO BE TRAPPED IN A WORLD WHERE YOU JUST DON'T FIT IN.
TERRIGEN ALERT! TERRIGEN ALERT! TER
NO...NO... NO...!

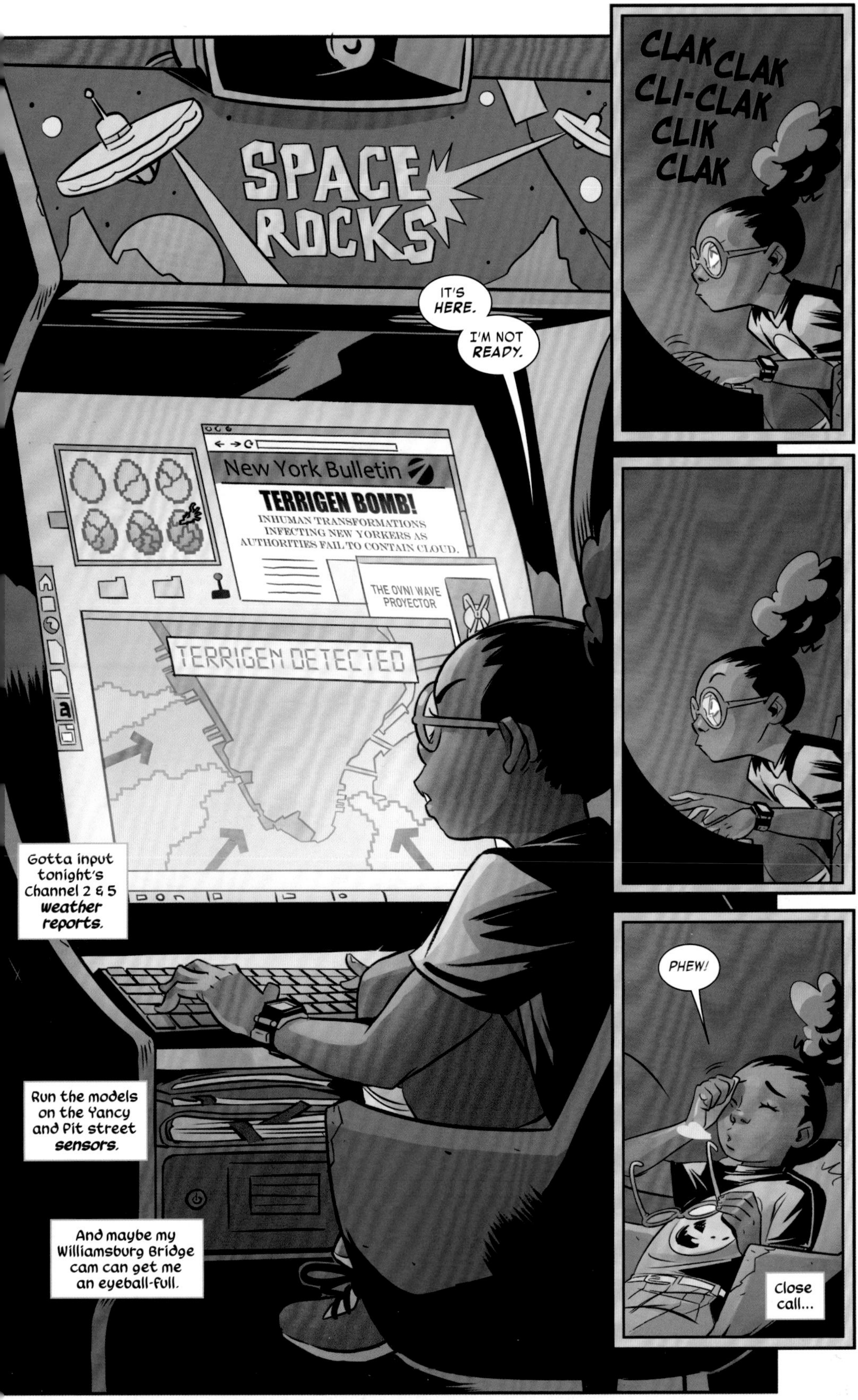
SPACE ROCKS
IT'S HERE.
I'M NOT READY.
New York Bulletin
TERRIGEN BOMB!
INHUMAN TRANSFORMATIONS INFECTING NEW YORKERS AS AUTHORITIES FAIL TO CONTAIN CLOUD.
THE OVNI WAVE PROYECTOR
TERRIGEN DETECTED
Gotta input tonight's Channel 2 & 5 weather reports.
Run the models on the Yancy and Pit street sensors.
And maybe my Williamsburg Bridge cam can get me an eyeball-full.
CLAK CLAK CLI-CLAK CLIK CLAK
PHEW!
Close call...

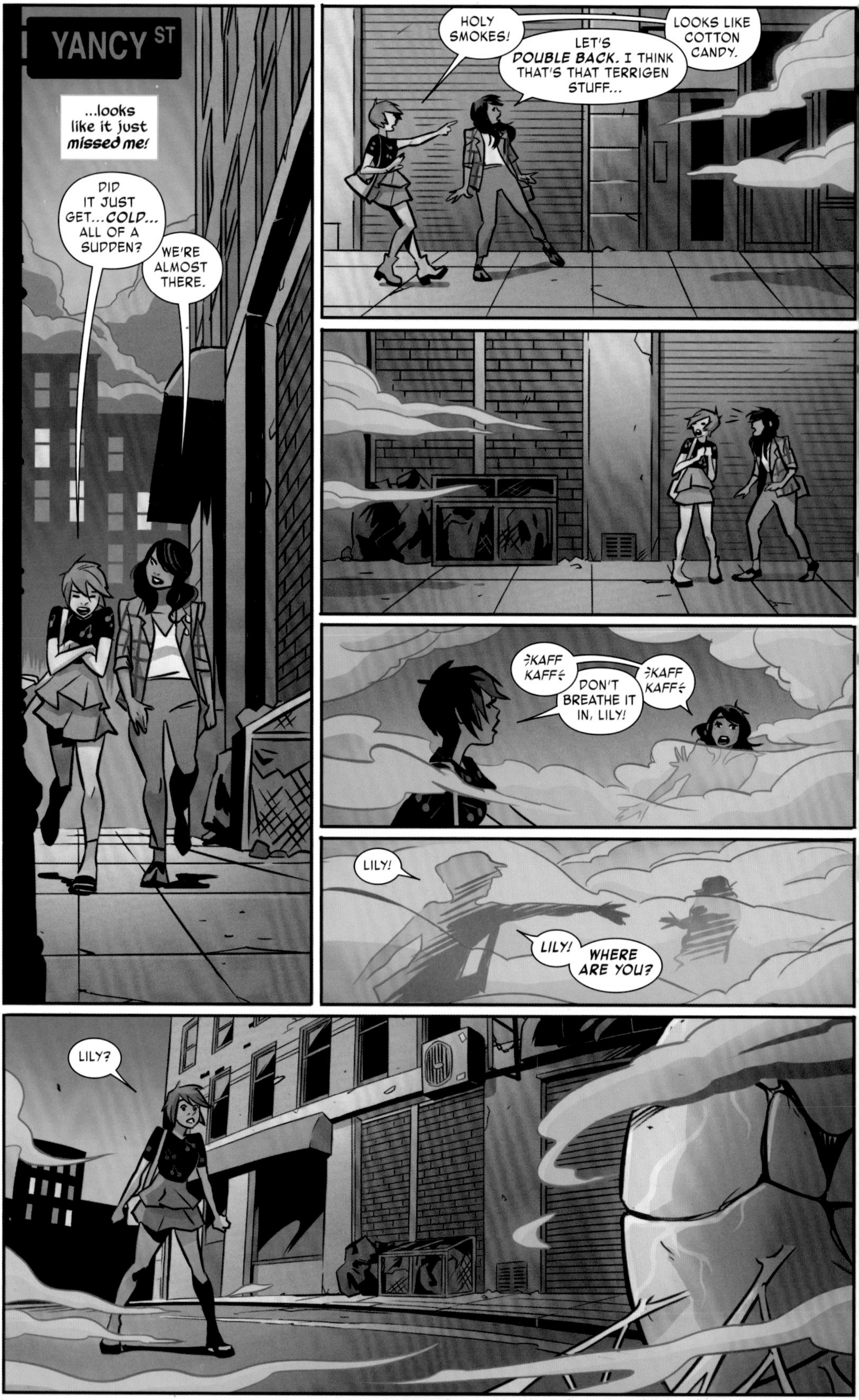

YANCY ST
...looks like it just missed me!
DID IT JUST GET...COLD... ALL OF A SUDDEN?
WE'RE ALMOST THERE.
HOLY SMOKES!
LOOKS LIKE COTTON CANDY.
LET'S DOUBLE BACK. I THINK THAT'S THAT TERRIGEN STUFF...
KAFF KAFF
KAFF KAFF
DON'T BREATHE IT IN, LILY!
LILY!
LILY!
WHERE ARE YOU?
LILY?

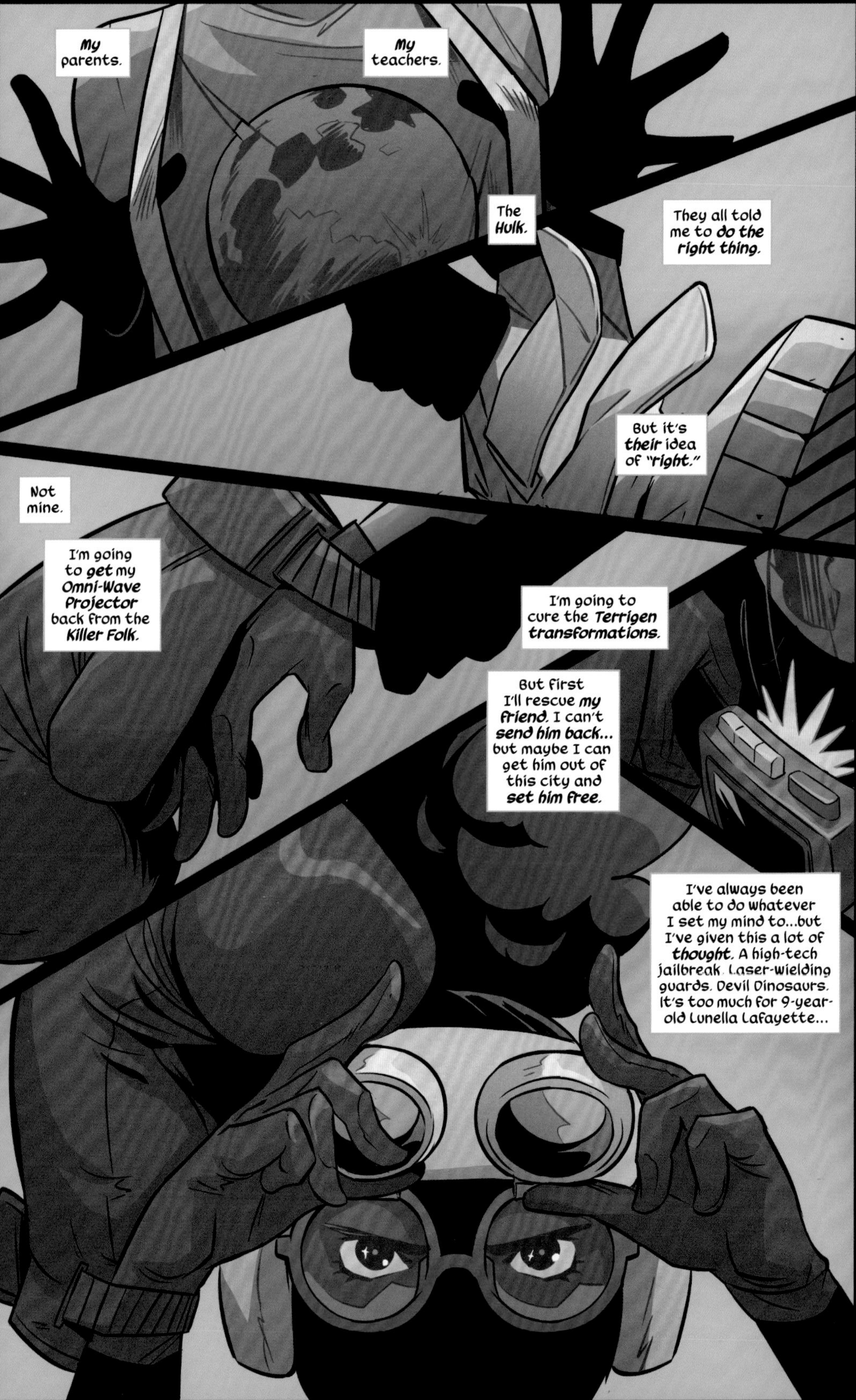
My parents.
My teachers.
The Hulk.
They all told me to do the right thing.
But it's their idea of "right."
Not mine.
I'm going to get my Omni-Wave Projector back from the Killer Folk.
I'm going to cure the Terrigen transformations.
But first I'll rescue my friend. I can't send him back... but maybe I can get him out of this city and set him free.
I've always been able to do whatever I set my mind to...but I've given this a lot of thought. A high-tech jailbreak. Laser-wielding guards. Devil Dinosaurs. It's too much for 9-year-old Lunella Lafayette...

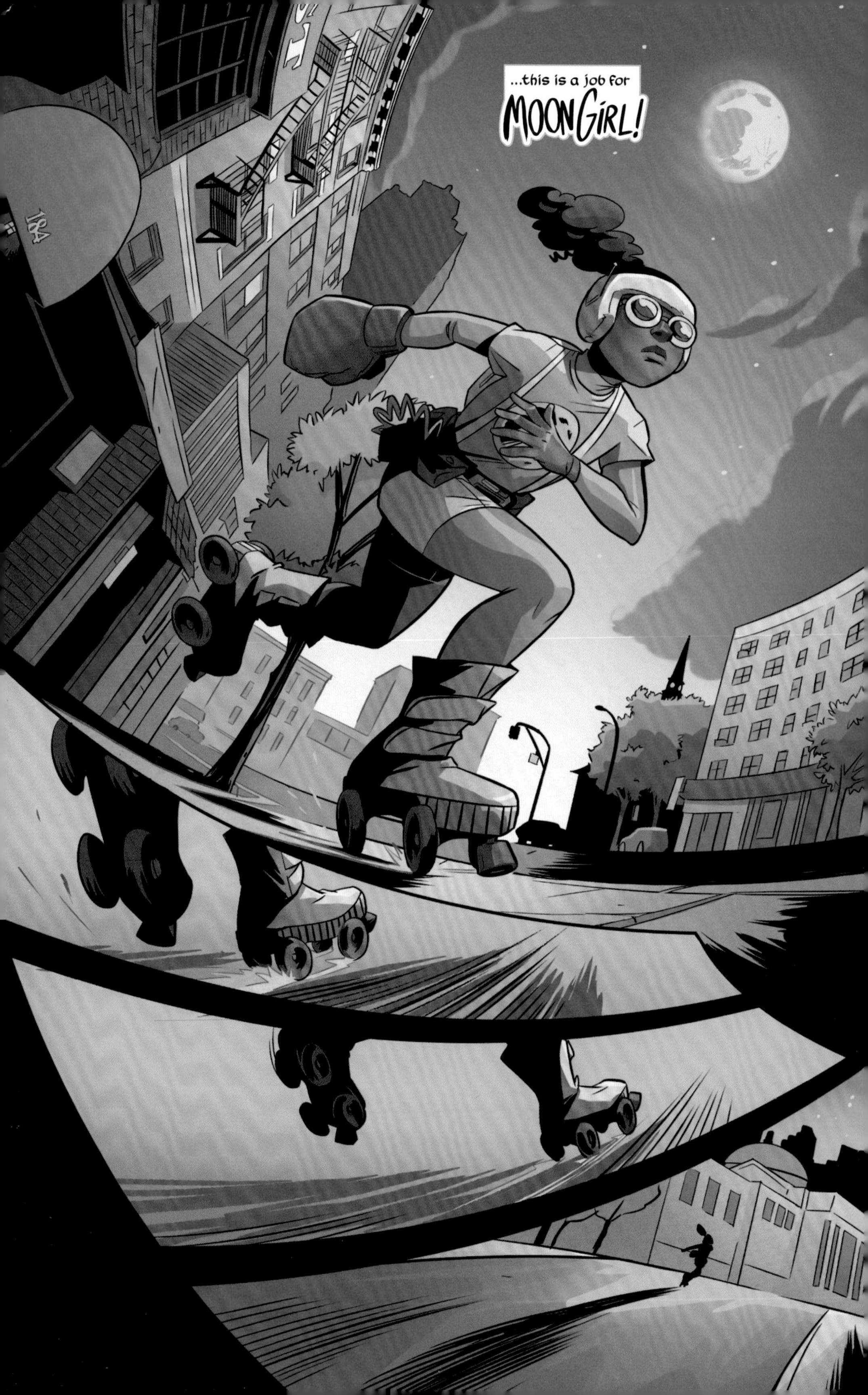
...this is a job for
MOON GIRL!

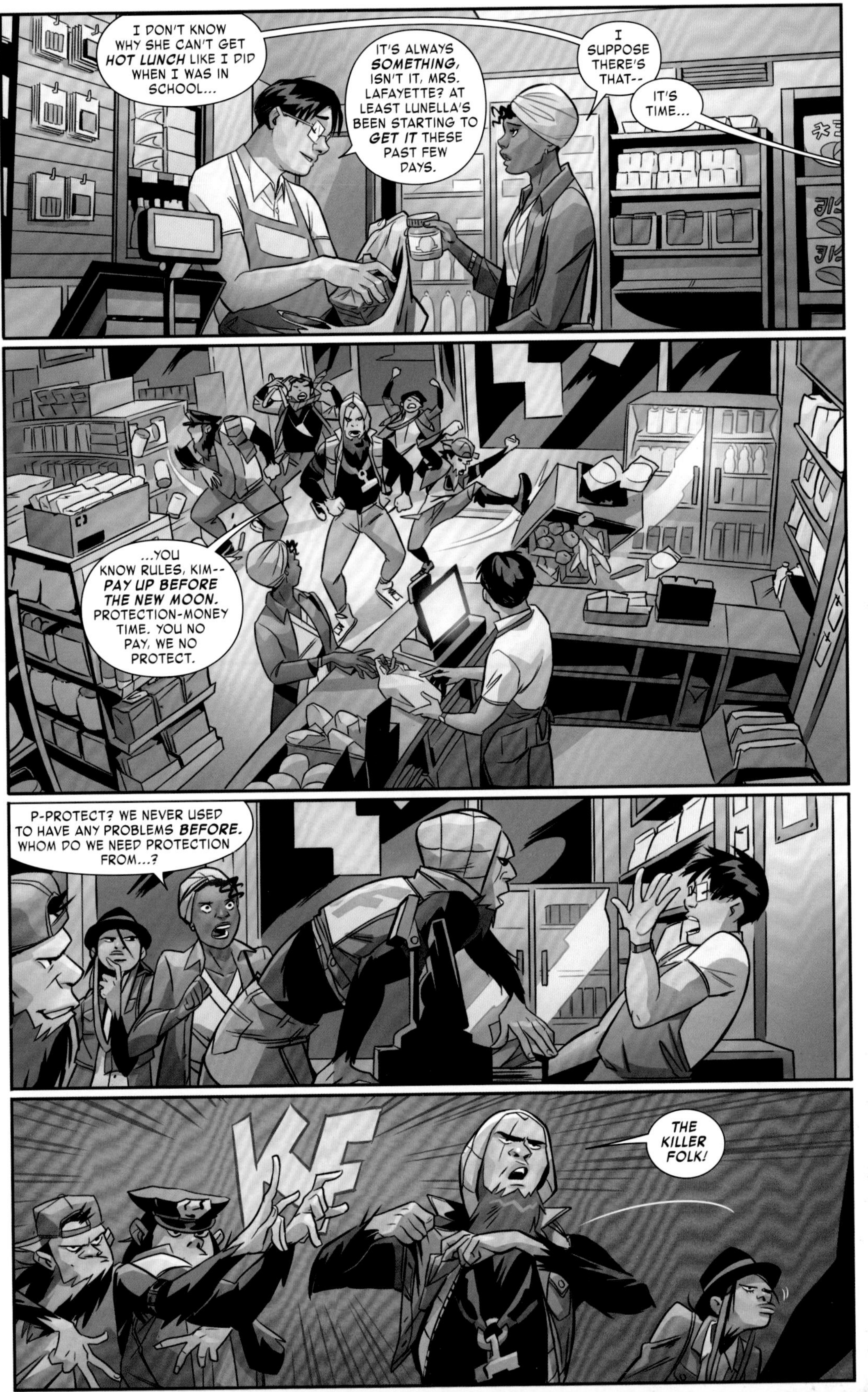
I DON'T KNOW WHY SHE CAN'T GET HOT LUNCH LIKE I DID WHEN I WAS IN SCHOOL...
IT'S ALWAYS SOMETHING, ISN'T IT, MRS. LAFAYETTE? AT LEAST LUNELLA'S BEEN STARTING TO GET IT THESE PAST FEW DAYS.
I SUPPOSE THERE'S THAT--
IT'S TIME...
...YOU KNOW RULES, KIM-- PAY UP BEFORE THE NEW MOON. PROTECTION-MONEY TIME. YOU NO PAY, WE NO PROTECT.
P-PROTECT? WE NEVER USED TO HAVE ANY PROBLEMS BEFORE. WHOM DO WE NEED PROTECTION FROM...?
THE KILLER FOLK!

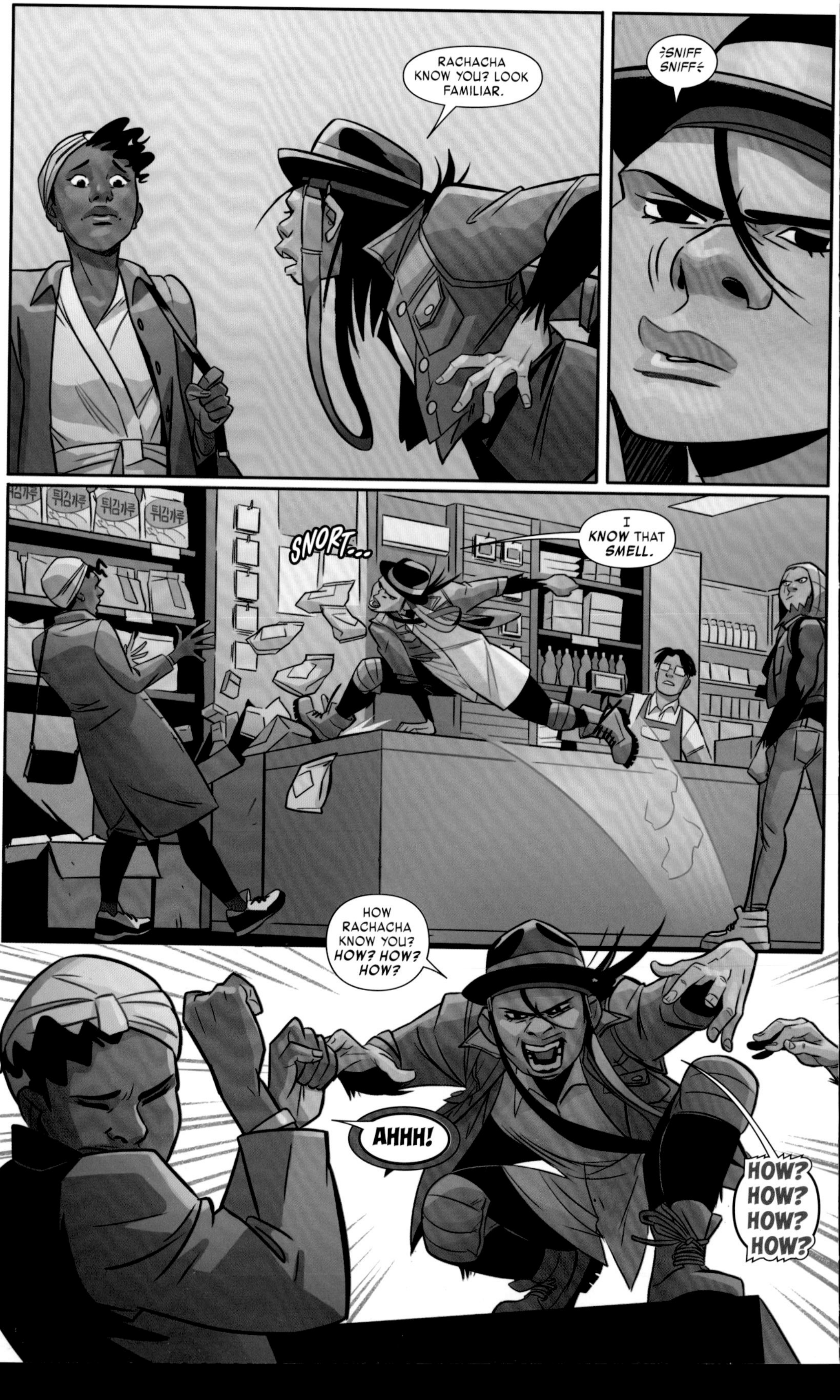

RACHACHA KNOW YOU? LOOK FAMILIAR.
SNIFF SNIFF
튀김가루
SNORT...
I KNOW THAT SMELL.
HOW RACHACHA KNOW YOU? HOW? HOW? HOW?
AHHH!
HOW? HOW? HOW? HOW?

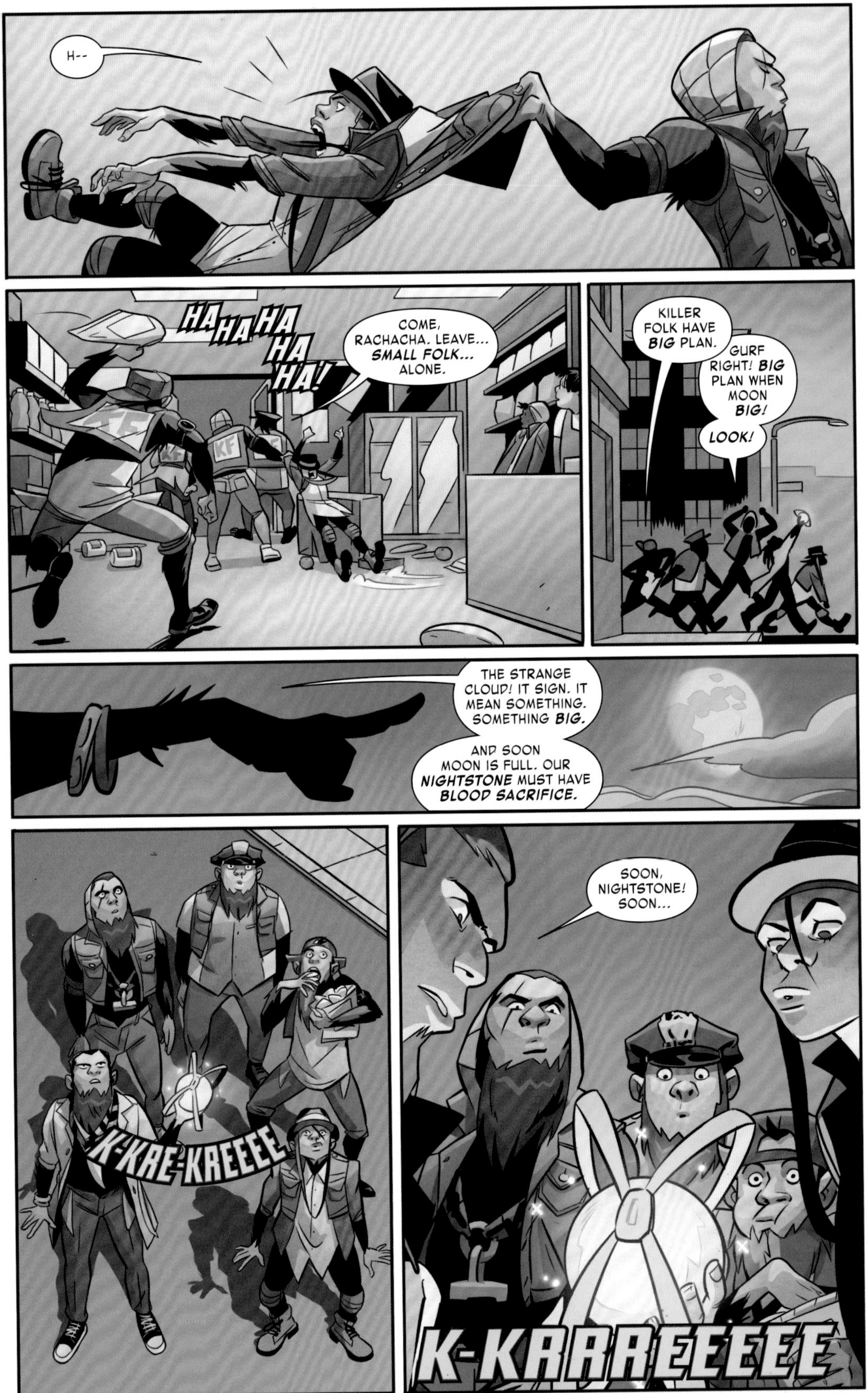

H--
HA HA HA HA HA HA!
COME, RACHACHA. LEAVE... SMALL FOLK... ALONE.
KILLER FOLK HAVE BIG PLAN.
GURF RIGHT! BIG PLAN WHEN MOON BIG!
LOOK!
THE STRANGE CLOUD! IT SIGN. IT MEAN SOMETHING. SOMETHING BIG.
AND SOON MOON IS FULL. OUR NIGHTSTONE MUST HAVE BLOOD SACRIFICE.
K-KRE-KREEEE
SOON, NIGHTSTONE! SOON...
K-KRRREEEEE

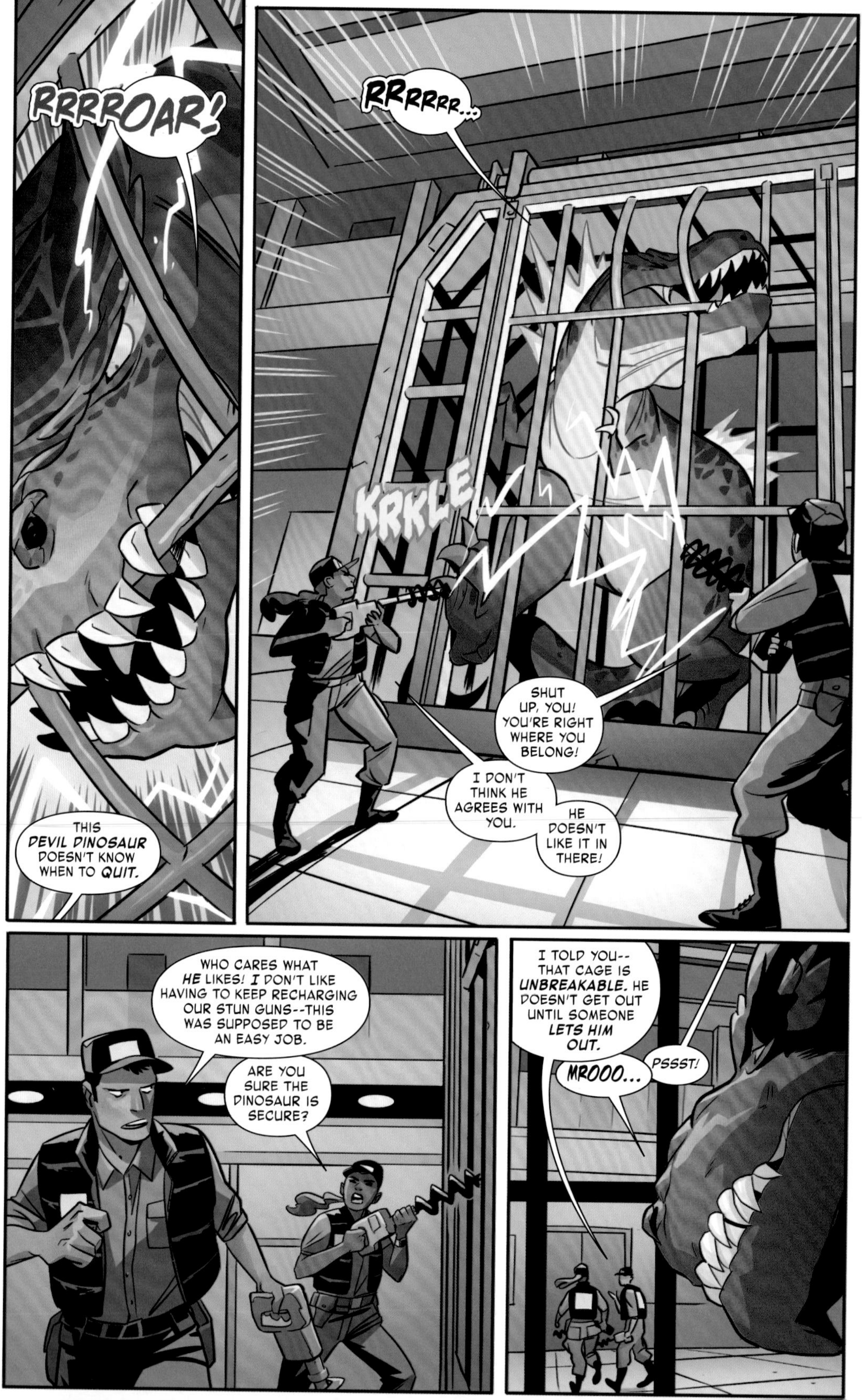
RRRROAR!
THIS DEVIL DINOSAUR DOESN'T KNOW WHEN TO QUIT.
RRRRRR...
KRKLE
SHUT UP, YOU! YOU'RE RIGHT WHERE YOU BELONG!
I DON'T THINK HE AGREES WITH YOU.
HE DOESN'T LIKE IT IN THERE!
WHO CARES WHAT HE LIKES! I DON'T LIKE HAVING TO KEEP RECHARGING OUR STUN GUNS--THIS WAS SUPPOSED TO BE AN EASY JOB.
ARE YOU SURE THE DINOSAUR IS SECURE?
I TOLD YOU--THAT CAGE IS UNBREAKABLE. HE DOESN'T GET OUT UNTIL SOMEONE LETS HIM OUT.
MROOO...
PSSST!

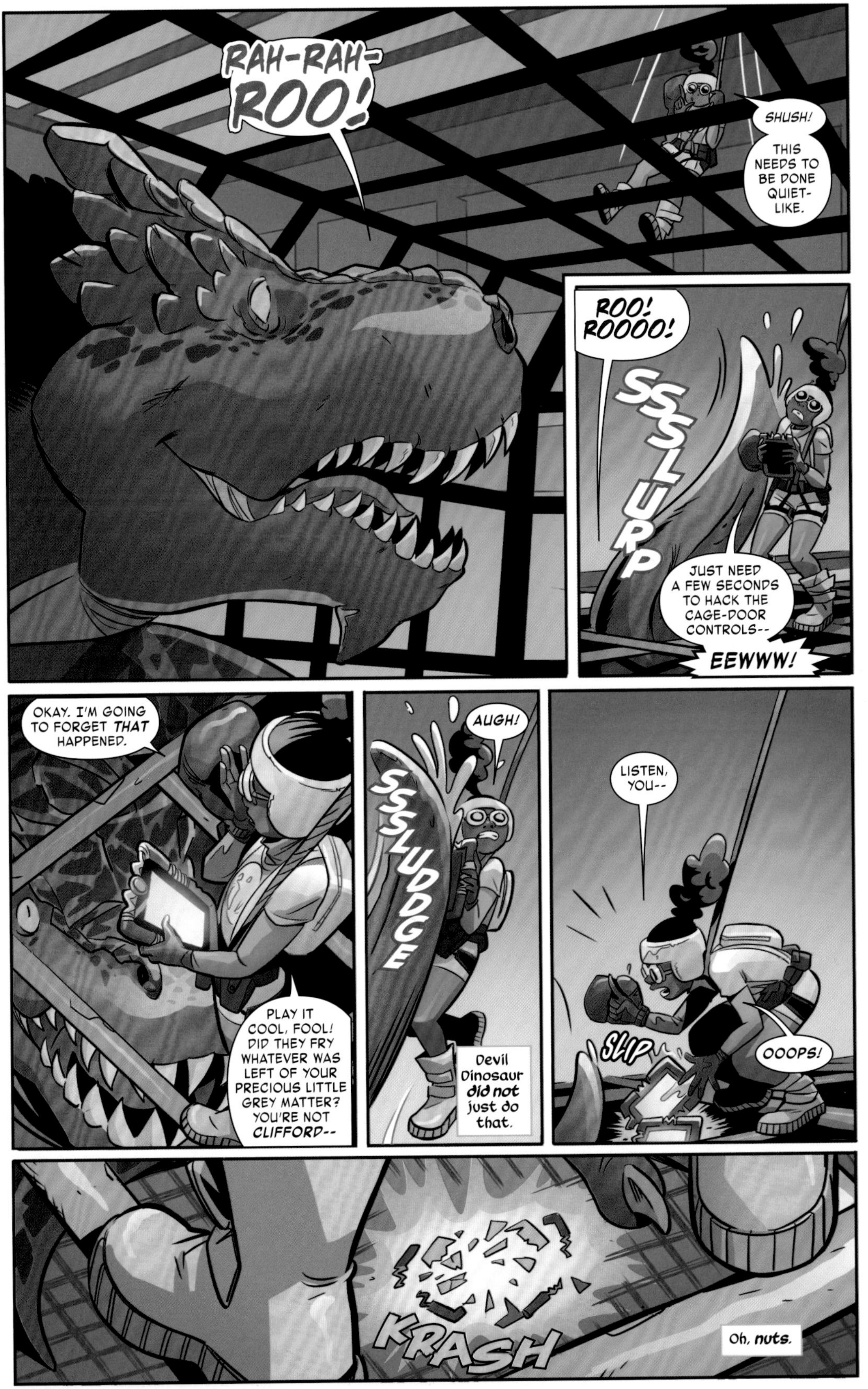
RAH-RAH-ROO!
SHUSH!
THIS NEEDS TO BE DONE QUIET-LIKE.
ROO! ROOOO!
SSSLURP
JUST NEED A FEW SECONDS TO HACK THE CAGE-DOOR CONTROLS--
EEWWW!
OKAY. I'M GOING TO FORGET THAT HAPPENED.
PLAY IT COOL, FOOL! DID THEY FRY WHATEVER WAS LEFT OF YOUR PRECIOUS LITTLE GREY MATTER? YOU'RE NOT CLIFFORD--
AUGH!
SSSLUDDGE
Devil Dinosaur did not just do that.
LISTEN, YOU--
SLIP
OOOPS!
KRASH
Oh, nuts.

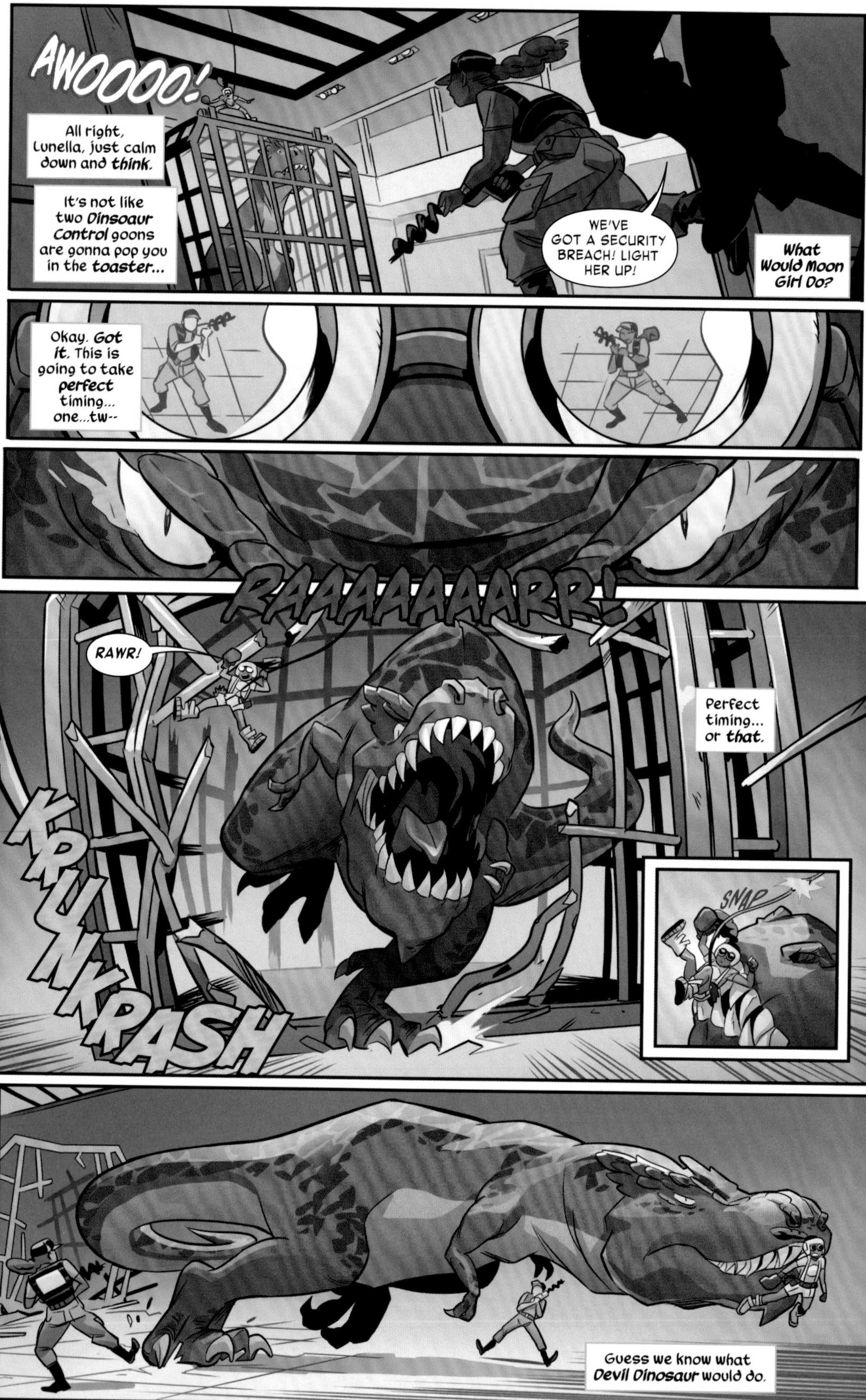
AWOOOO!
All right, Lunella, just calm down and think.
It's not like two Dinosaur Control goons are gonna pop you in the toaster...
WE'VE GOT A SECURITY BREACH! LIGHT HER UP!
What Would Moon Girl Do?
Okay. Got it. This is going to take perfect timing... one...tw--
RAAAAAAAARR!
RAWR!
Perfect timing... or that.
KRUNKRASH
SNAP
Guess we know what Devil Dinosaur would do.

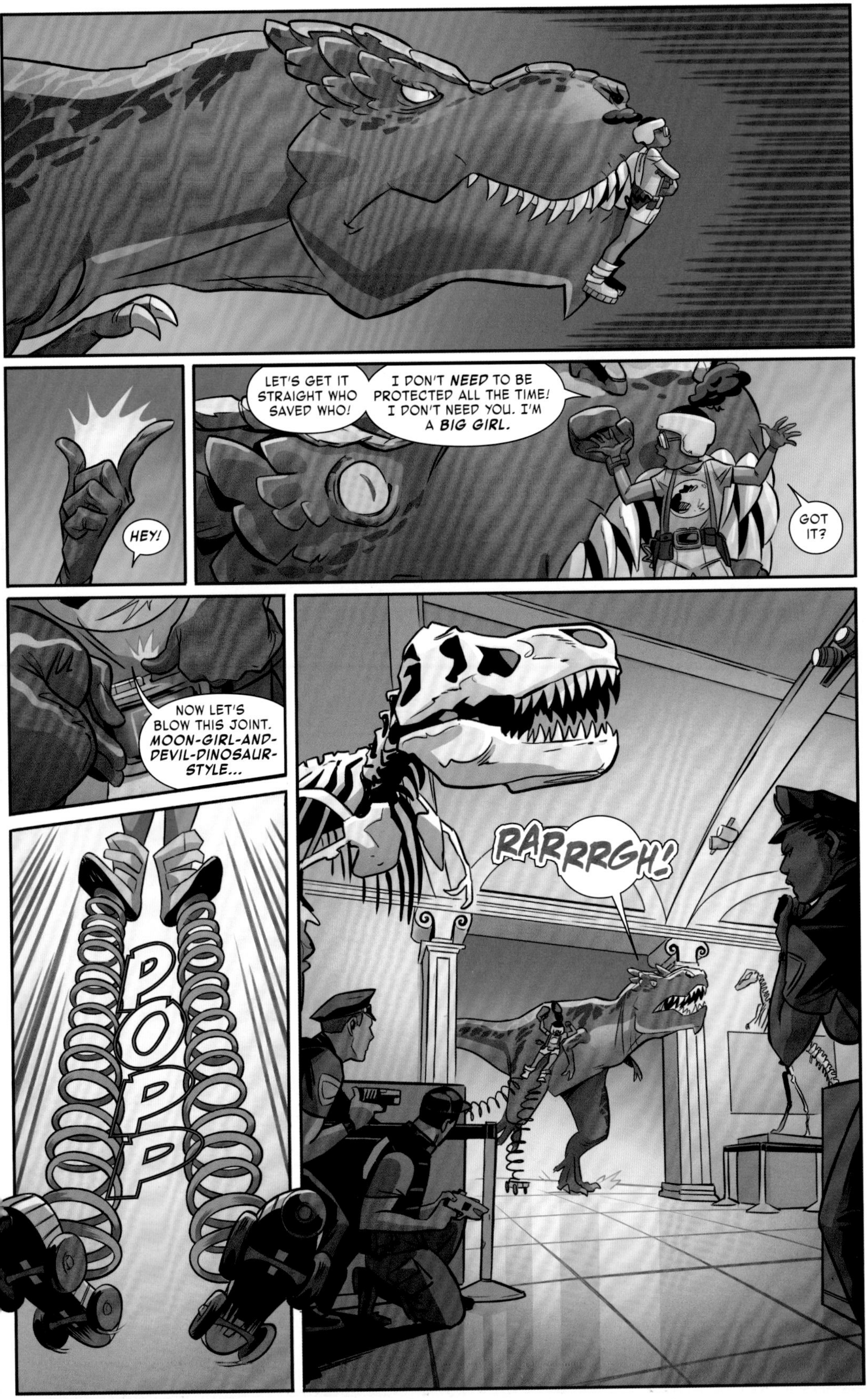
HEY!
LET'S GET IT STRAIGHT WHO SAVED WHO!
I DON'T NEED TO BE PROTECTED ALL THE TIME! I DON'T NEED YOU. I'M A BIG GIRL.
GOT IT?
NOW LET'S BLOW THIS JOINT. MOON-GIRL-AND-DEVIL-DINOSAUR-STYLE...
POPP
RARRRGH!

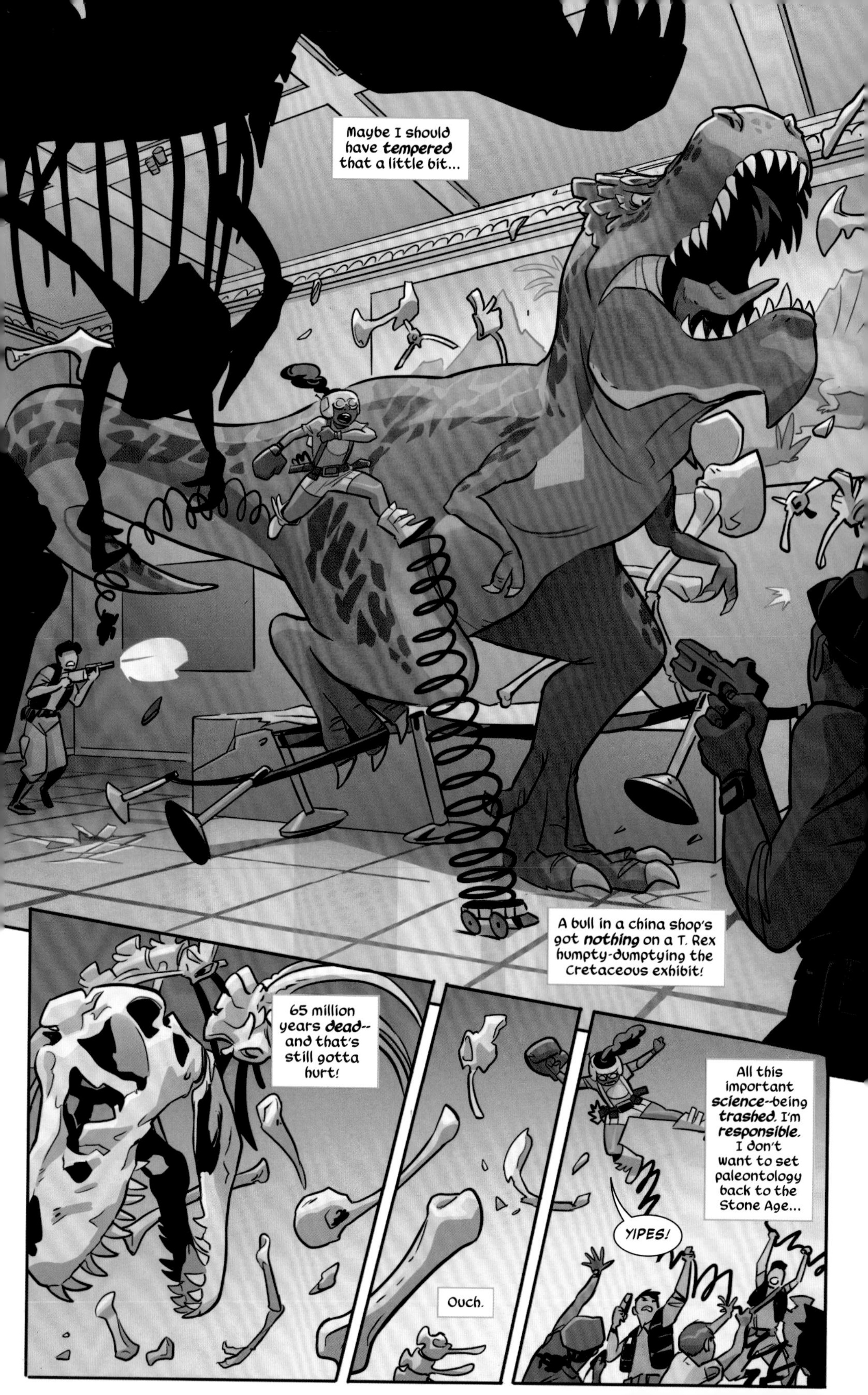
Maybe I should have tempered that a little bit...
A bull in a china shop's got nothing on a T. Rex humpty-dumptying the Cretaceous exhibit!
65 million years dead--and that's still gotta hurt!
Ouch.
All this important science--being trashed. I'm responsible. I don't want to set paleontology back to the Stone Age...
YIPES!

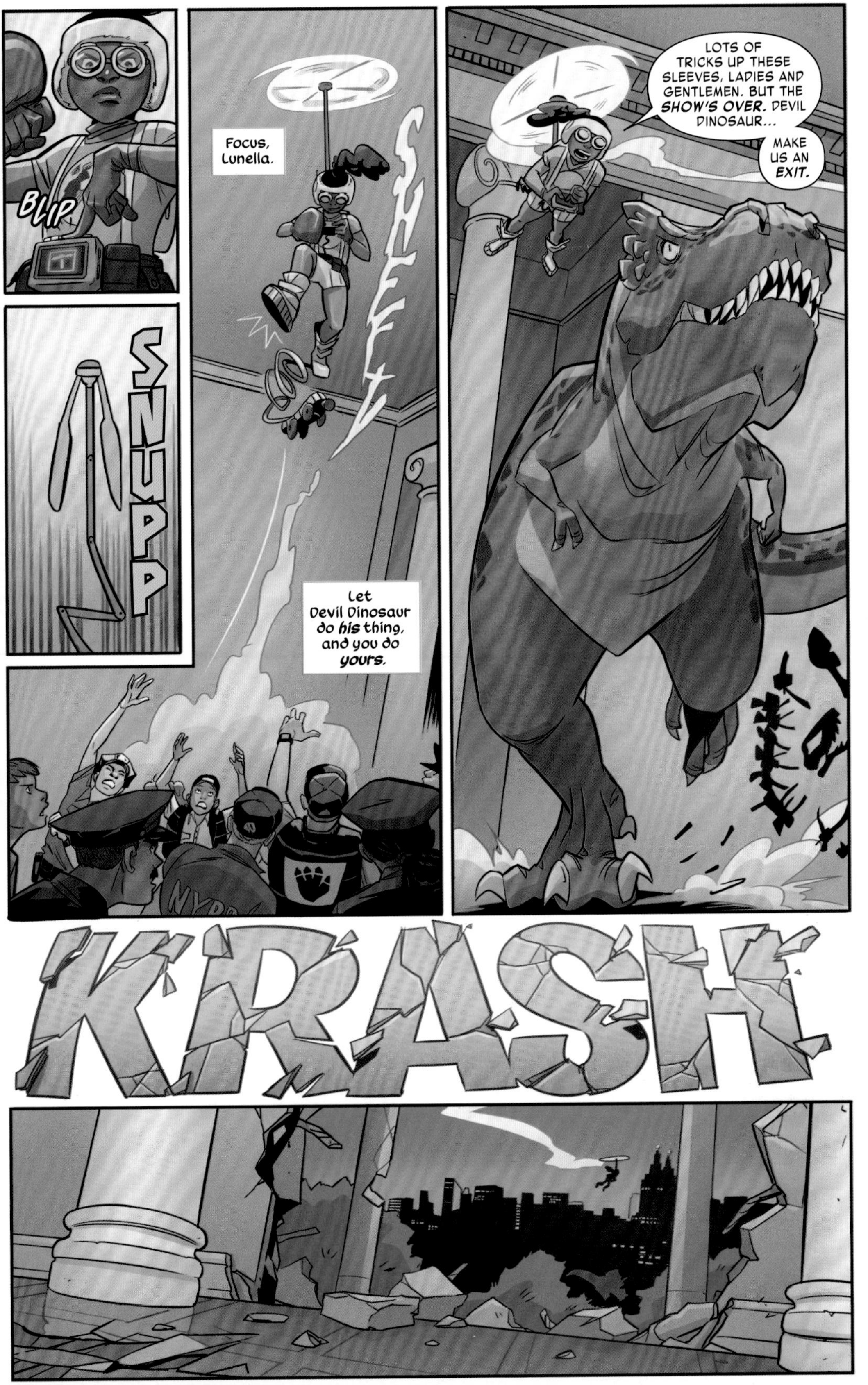
BLIP
SNUPP
Focus, Lunella.
SHEEEW
Let Devil Dinosaur do his thing, and you do yours.
NYPD
LOTS OF TRICKS UP THESE SLEEVES, LADIES AND GENTLEMEN. BUT THE SHOW'S OVER. DEVIL DINOSAUR...
MAKE US AN EXIT.
KRASH

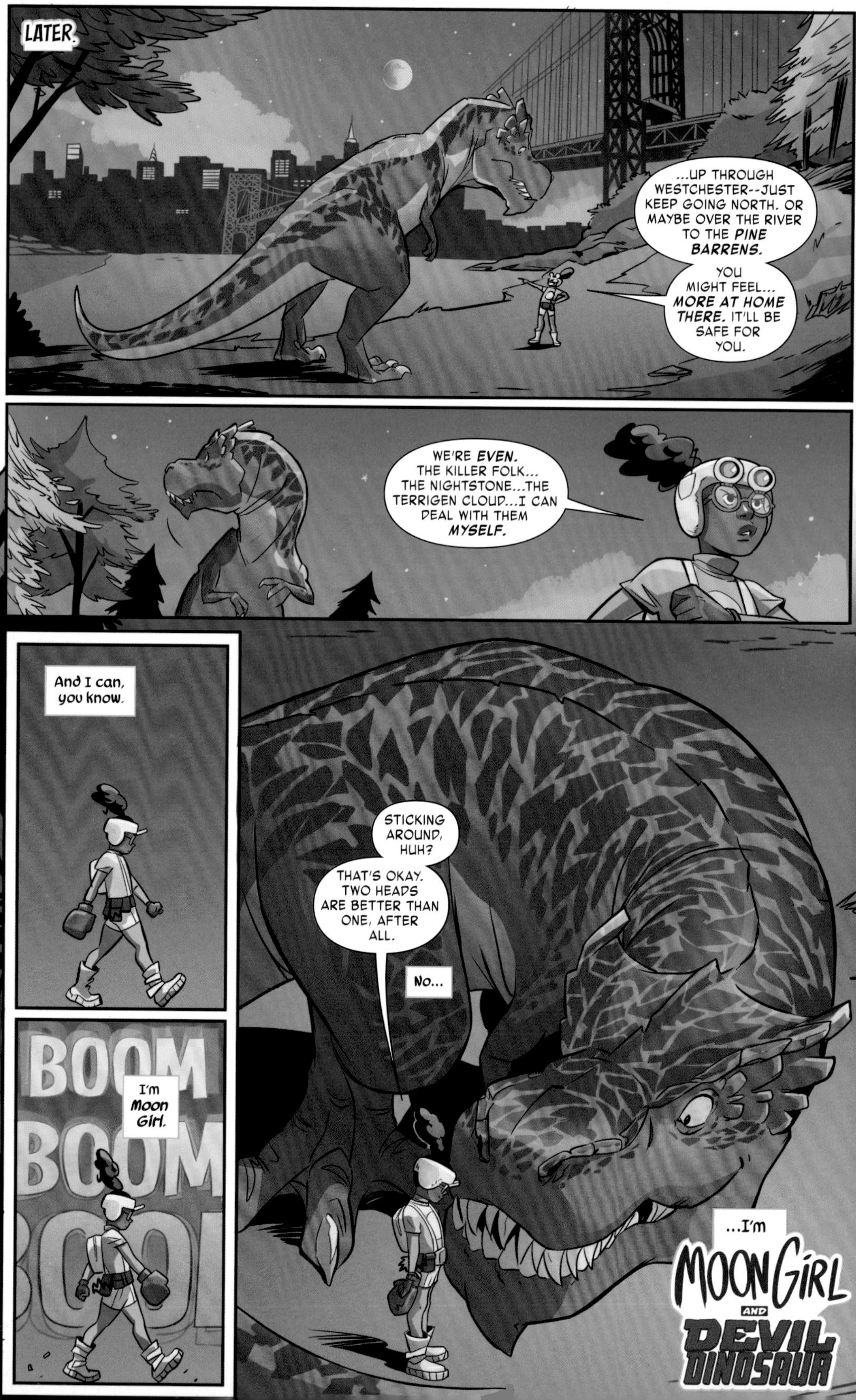
LATER.
...UP THROUGH WESTCHESTER--JUST KEEP GOING NORTH. OR MAYBE OVER THE RIVER TO THE PINE BARRENS.
YOU MIGHT FEEL... MORE AT HOME THERE. IT'LL BE SAFE FOR YOU.
WE'RE EVEN. THE KILLER FOLK... THE NIGHTSTONE...THE TERRIGEN CLOUD...I CAN DEAL WITH THEM MYSELF.
And I can, you know.
I'm Moon Girl.
BOOM
BOOM
STICKING AROUND, HUH?
THAT'S OKAY. TWO HEADS ARE BETTER THAN ONE, AFTER ALL.
No...
...I'm
MOON GIRL
AND
DEVIL DINOSAUR

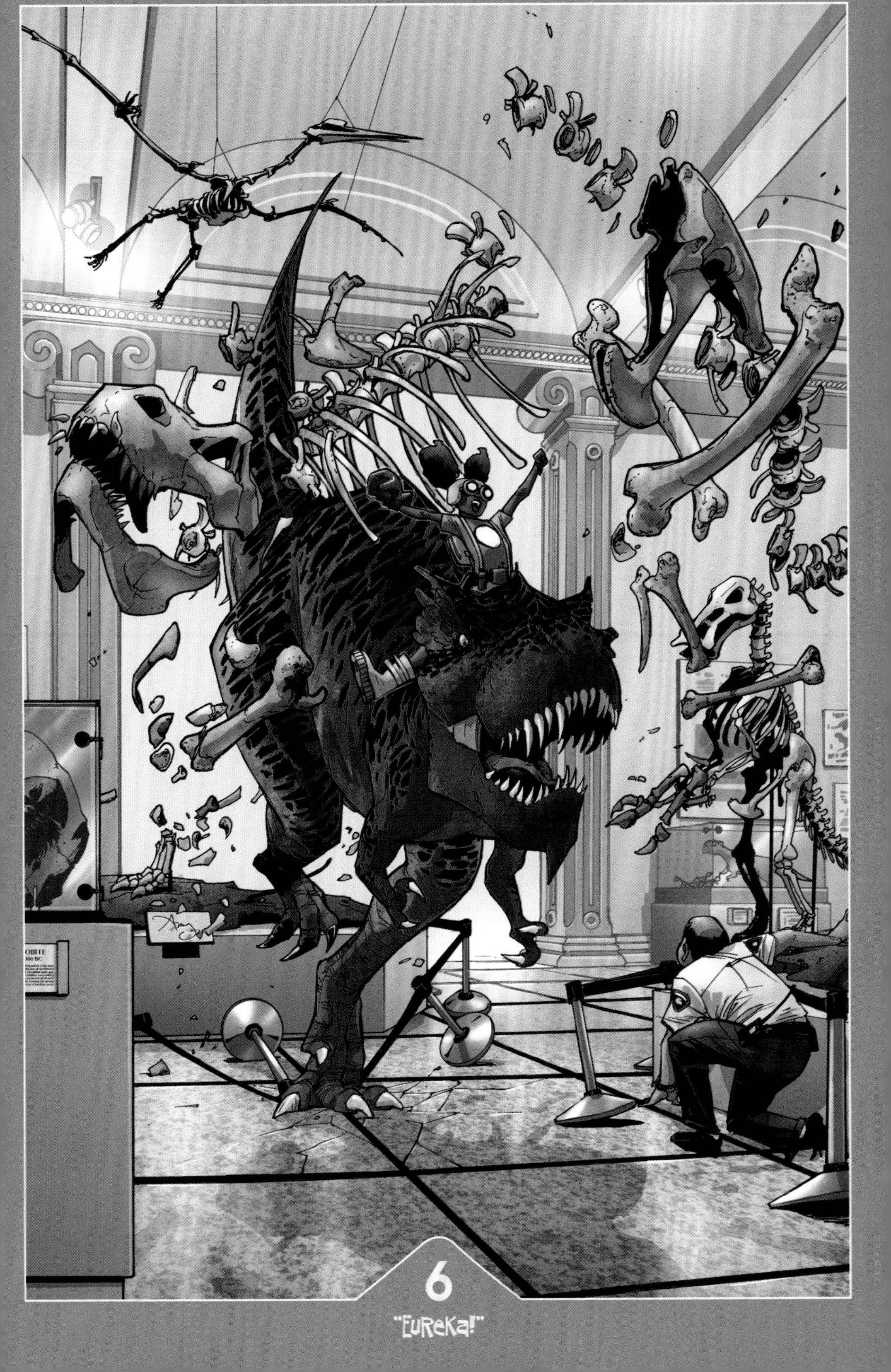

6

"EUREKA!"

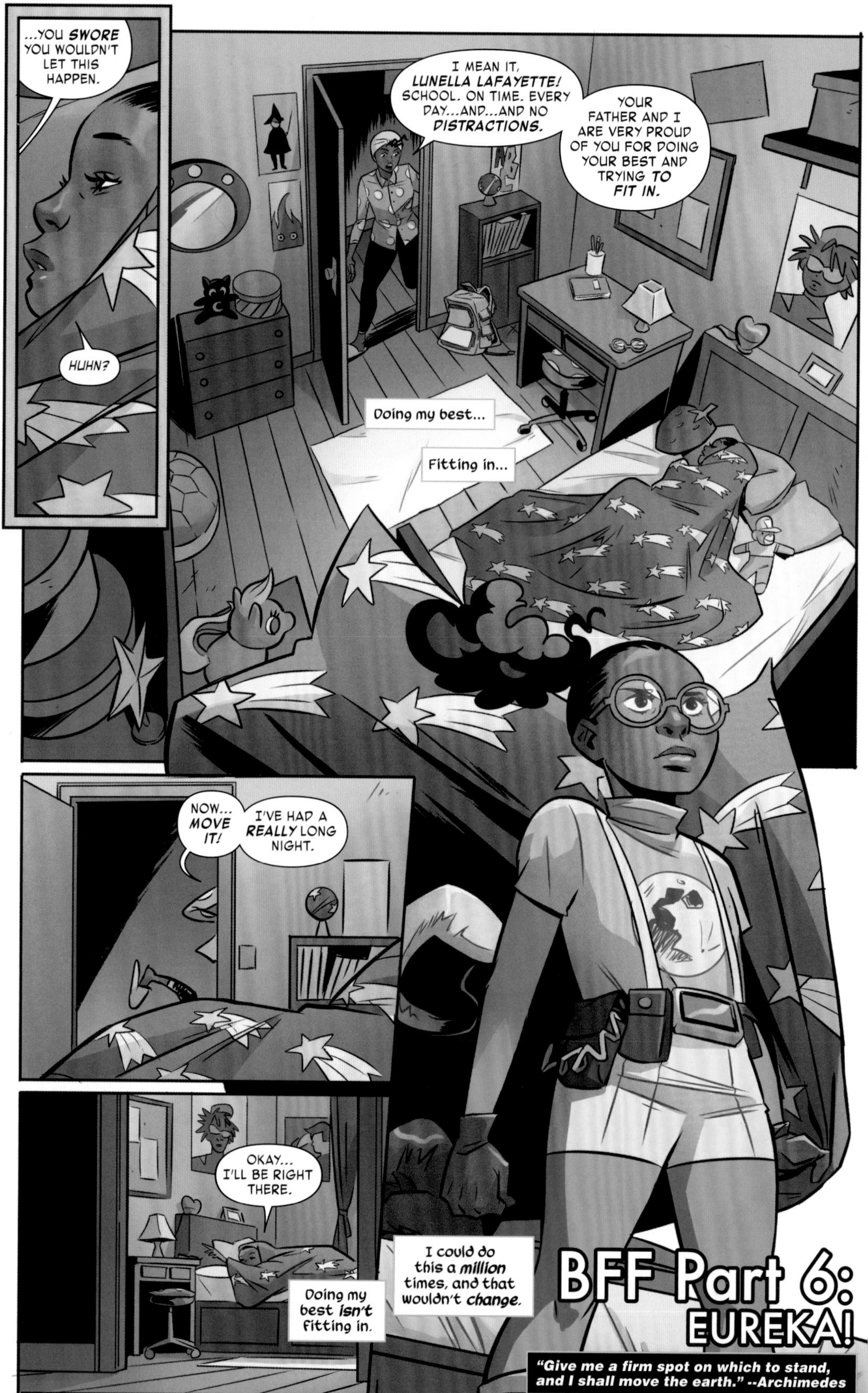

...YOU SWORE YOU WOULDN'T LET THIS HAPPEN.
HUHN?
I MEAN IT, LUNELLA LAFAYETTE! SCHOOL. ON TIME. EVERY DAY...AND...AND NO DISTRACTIONS.
YOUR FATHER AND I ARE VERY PROUD OF YOU FOR DOING YOUR BEST AND TRYING TO FIT IN.
Doing my best...
Fitting in...
NOW... MOVE IT!
I'VE HAD A REALLY LONG NIGHT.
OKAY... I'LL BE RIGHT THERE.
Doing my best isn't fitting in.
I could do this a million times, and that wouldn't change.
BFF Part 6:
EUREKA!
"Give me a firm spot on which to stand, and I shall move the earth." --Archimedes

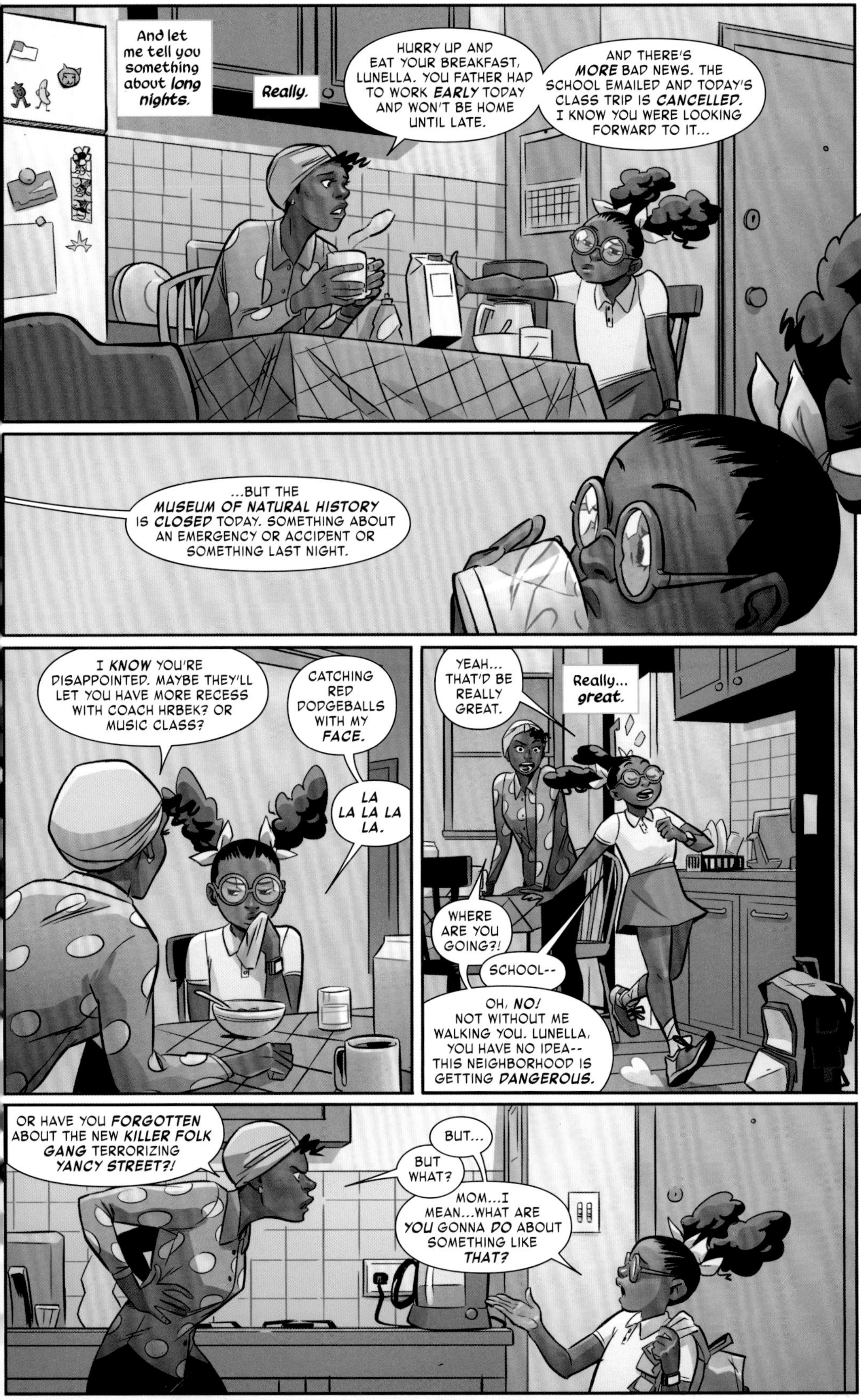
And let me tell you something about long nights.
Really.
HURRY UP AND EAT YOUR BREAKFAST, LUNELLA. YOU FATHER HAD TO WORK EARLY TODAY AND WON'T BE HOME UNTIL LATE.
AND THERE'S MORE BAD NEWS. THE SCHOOL EMAILED AND TODAY'S CLASS TRIP IS CANCELLED. I KNOW YOU WERE LOOKING FORWARD TO IT...
...BUT THE MUSEUM OF NATURAL HISTORY IS CLOSED TODAY. SOMETHING ABOUT AN EMERGENCY OR ACCIDENT OR SOMETHING LAST NIGHT.
I KNOW YOU'RE DISAPPOINTED. MAYBE THEY'LL LET YOU HAVE MORE RECESS WITH COACH HRBEK? OR MUSIC CLASS?
CATCHING RED DODGEBALLS WITH MY FACE.
LA LA LA LA LA.
YEAH... THAT'D BE REALLY GREAT.
Really... great.
WHERE ARE YOU GOING?!
SCHOOL--
OH, NO! NOT WITHOUT ME WALKING YOU. LUNELLA, YOU HAVE NO IDEA-- THIS NEIGHBORHOOD IS GETTING DANGEROUS.
OR HAVE YOU FORGOTTEN ABOUT THE NEW KILLER FOLK GANG TERRORIZING YANCY STREET?!
BUT...
BUT WHAT?
MOM...I MEAN...WHAT ARE YOU GONNA DO ABOUT SOMETHING LIKE THAT?

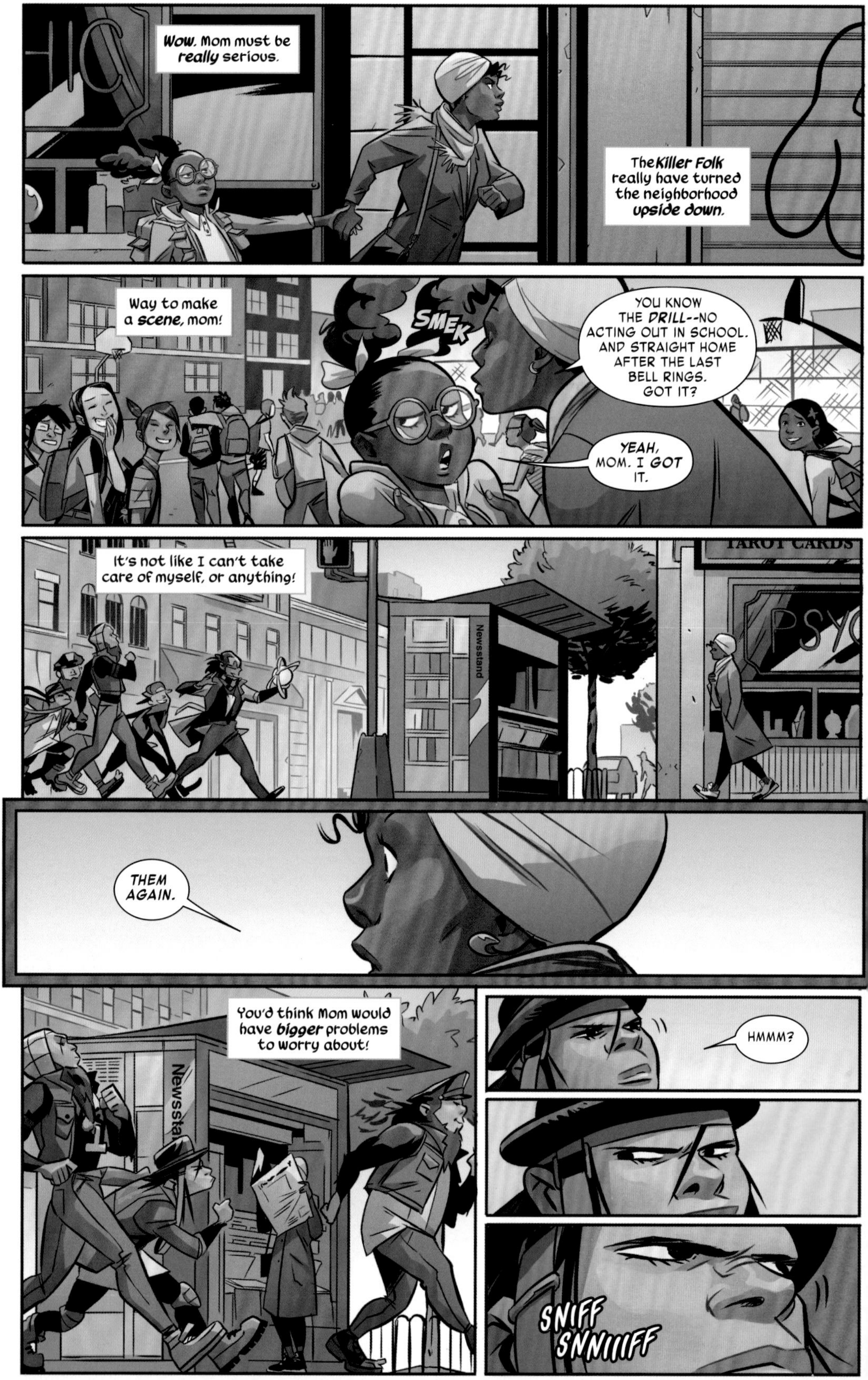

Wow. Mom must be really serious.
The Killer Folk really have turned the neighborhood upside down.
Way to make a scene, mom!
SMEK
YOU KNOW THE DRILL--NO ACTING OUT IN SCHOOL. AND STRAIGHT HOME AFTER THE LAST BELL RINGS. GOT IT?
YEAH, MOM. I GOT IT.
It's not like I can't take care of myself, or anything!
TAROT CARDS
Newsstand
PSYC
THEM AGAIN.
You'd think Mom would have bigger problems to worry about!
Newssta
HMMM?
SNIFF
SNNIIIFF

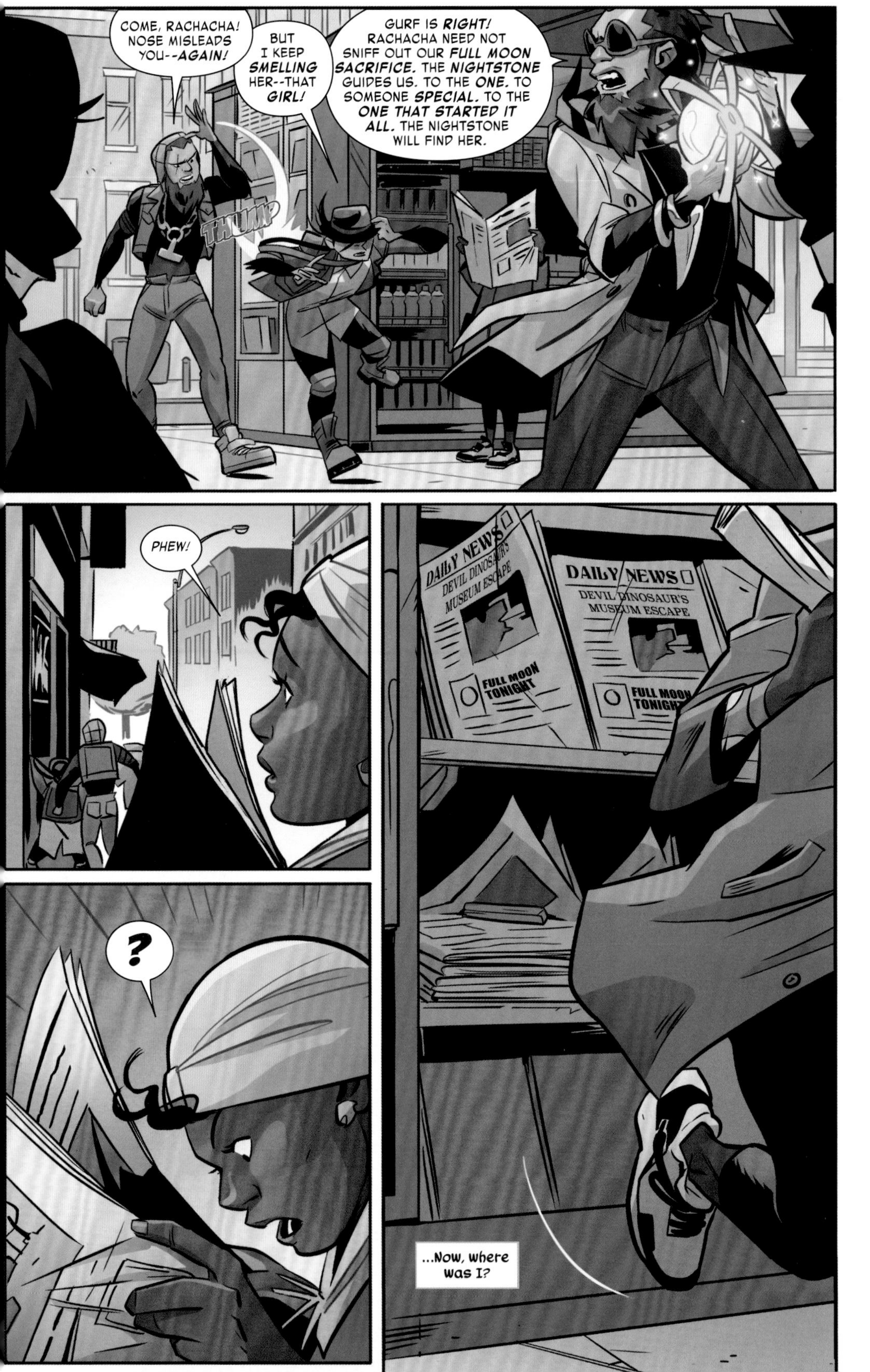
COME, RACHACHA! NOSE MISLEADS YOU--AGAIN!
BUT I KEEP SMELLING HER--THAT GIRL!
GURF IS RIGHT! RACHACHA NEED NOT SNIFF OUT OUR FULL MOON SACRIFICE. THE NIGHTSTONE GUIDES US. TO THE ONE. TO SOMEONE SPECIAL. TO THE ONE THAT STARTED IT ALL. THE NIGHTSTONE WILL FIND HER.
THUMP
PHEW!
?
DAILY NEWS
DEVIL DINOSAUR'S MUSEUM ESCAPE
FULL MOON TONIGHT
...Now, where was I?

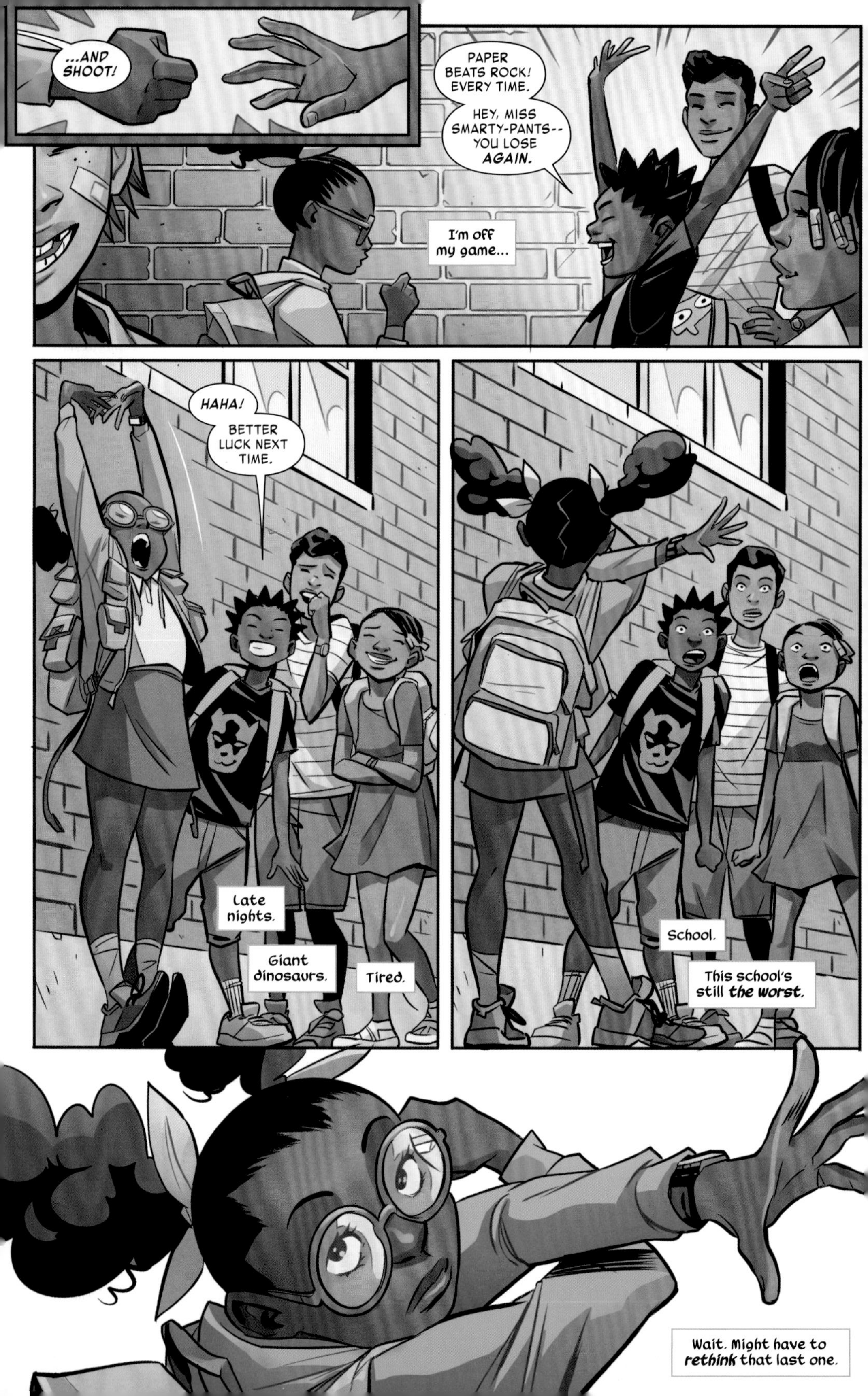
...AND SHOOT!
PAPER BEATS ROCK! EVERY TIME.
HEY, MISS SMARTY-PANTS-- YOU LOSE AGAIN.
I'm off my game...
HAHA!
BETTER LUCK NEXT TIME.
Late nights.
Giant dinosaurs.
Tired.
School.
This school's still the worst.
Wait. Might have to rethink that last one.

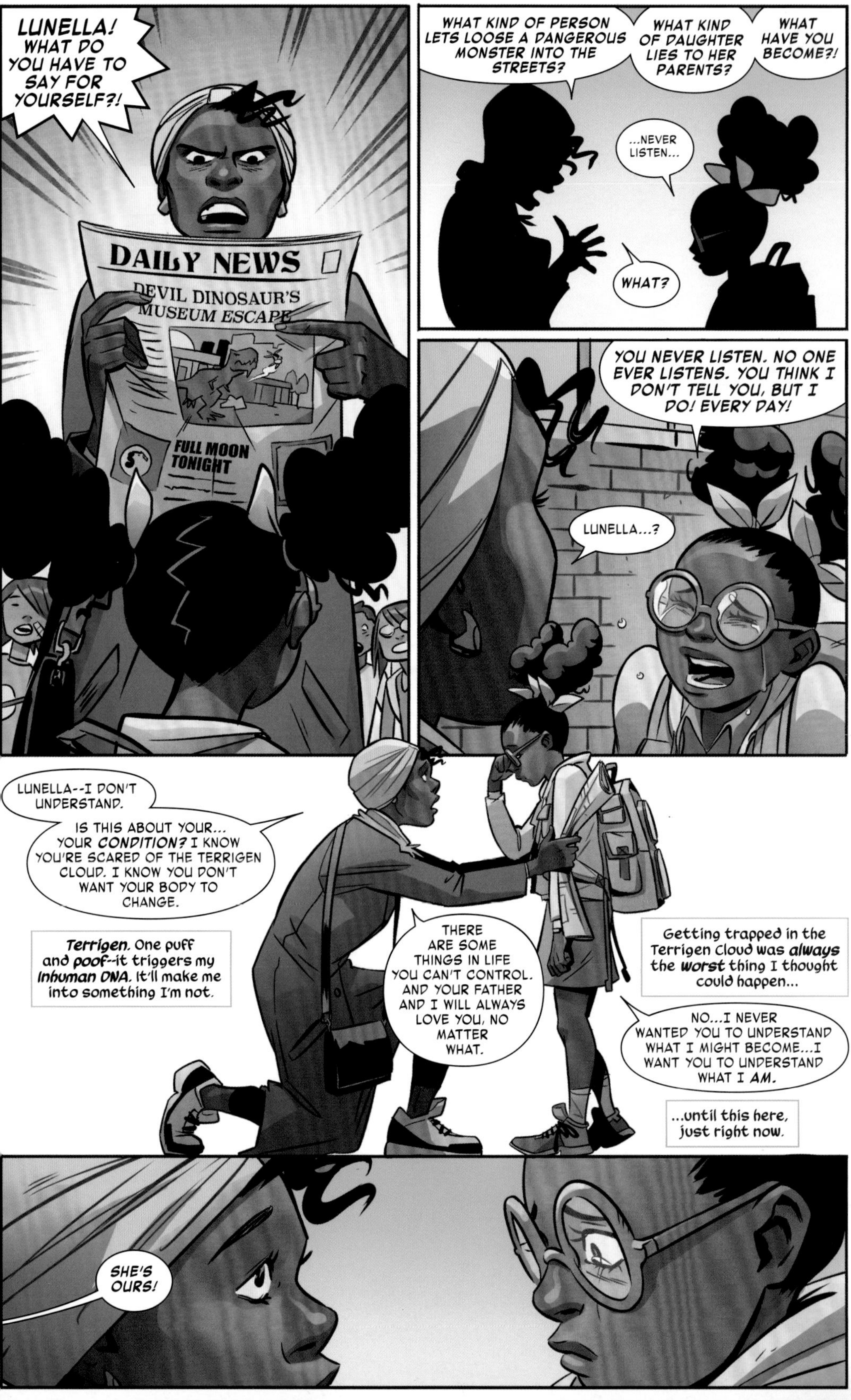
LUNELLA! WHAT DO YOU HAVE TO SAY FOR YOURSELF?!
DAILY NEWS
DEVIL DINOSAUR'S MUSEUM ESCAPE
FULL MOON TONIGHT
WHAT KIND OF PERSON LETS LOOSE A DANGEROUS MONSTER INTO THE STREETS?
WHAT KIND OF DAUGHTER LIES TO HER PARENTS?
WHAT HAVE YOU BECOME?!
...NEVER LISTEN...
WHAT?
YOU NEVER LISTEN. NO ONE EVER LISTENS. YOU THINK I DON'T TELL YOU, BUT I DO! EVERY DAY!
LUNELLA...?
LUNELLA--I DON'T UNDERSTAND.
IS THIS ABOUT YOUR... YOUR CONDITION? I KNOW YOU'RE SCARED OF THE TERRIGEN CLOUD. I KNOW YOU DON'T WANT YOUR BODY TO CHANGE.
Terrigen. One puff and poof--it triggers my Inhuman DNA. It'll make me into something I'm not.
THERE ARE SOME THINGS IN LIFE YOU CAN'T CONTROL. AND YOUR FATHER AND I WILL ALWAYS LOVE YOU, NO MATTER WHAT.
Getting trapped in the Terrigen Cloud was always the worst thing I thought could happen...
NO...I NEVER WANTED YOU TO UNDERSTAND WHAT I MIGHT BECOME...I WANT YOU TO UNDERSTAND WHAT I AM.
...until this here, just right now.
SHE'S OURS!

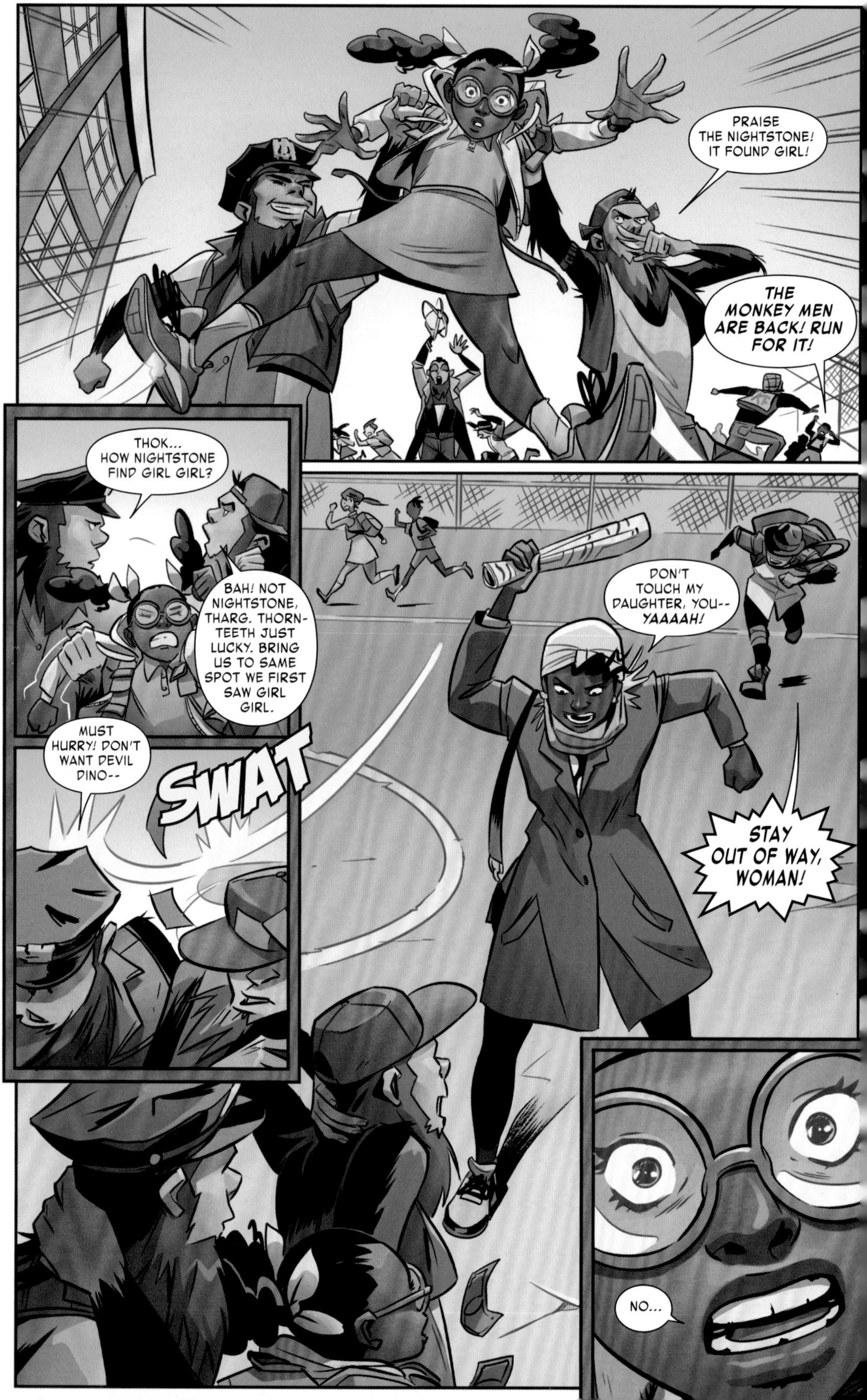
PRAISE THE NIGHTSTONE! IT FOUND GIRL!
THE MONKEY MEN ARE BACK! RUN FOR IT!
THOK... HOW NIGHTSTONE FIND GIRL GIRL?
BAH! NOT NIGHTSTONE, THARG. THORN-TEETH JUST LUCKY. BRING US TO SAME SPOT WE FIRST SAW GIRL GIRL.
MUST HURRY! DON'T WANT DEVIL DINO--
SWAT
DON'T TOUCH MY DAUGHTER, YOU-- YAAAAH!
STAY OUT OF WAY, WOMAN!
NO...

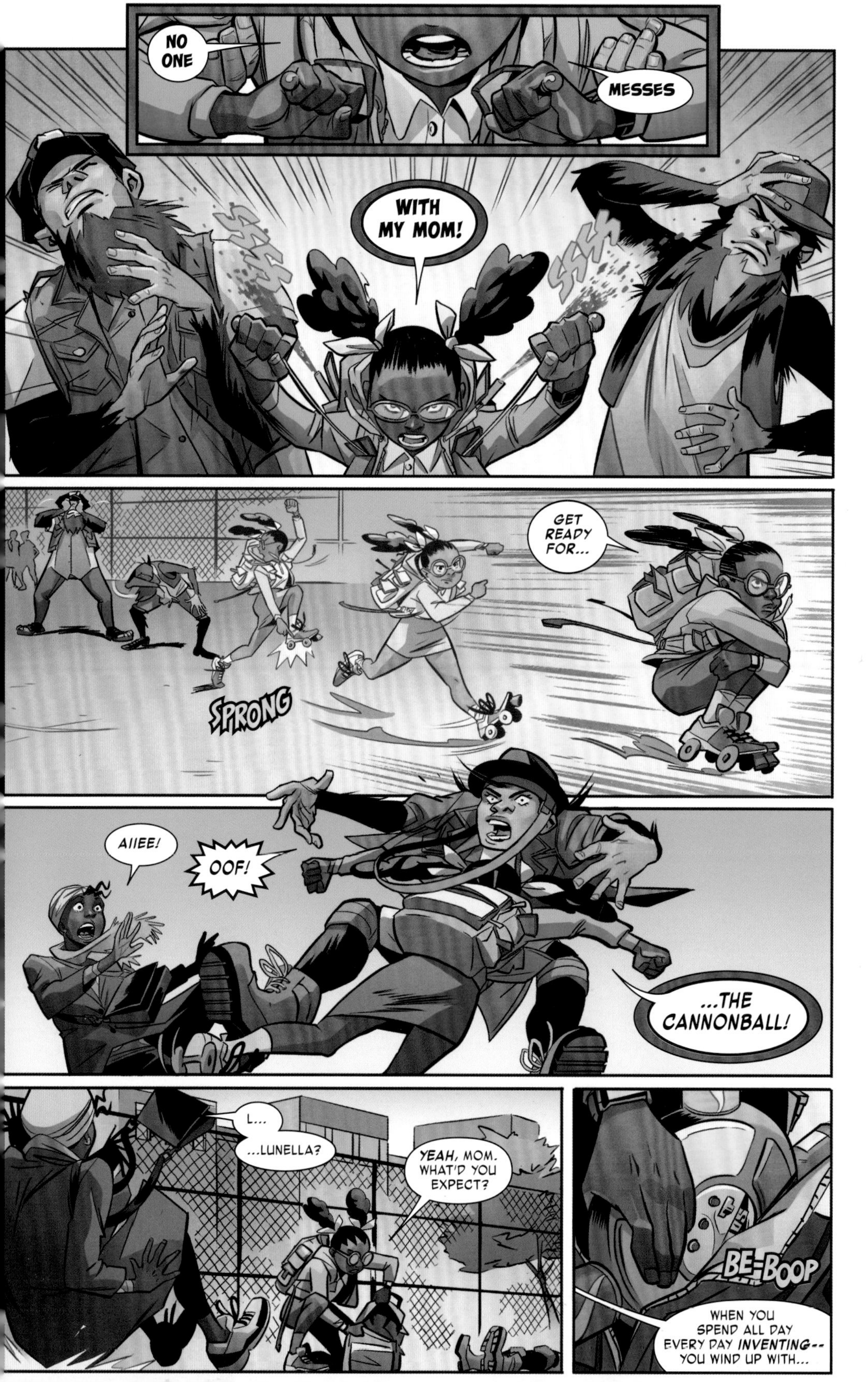

NO ONE
MESSES
WITH MY MOM!
SSSH
SSSH
GET READY FOR...
SPRONG
AIIEE!
OOF!
...THE CANNONBALL!
L...
...LUNELLA?
YEAH, MOM. WHAT'D YOU EXPECT?
BE-BOOP
WHEN YOU SPEND ALL DAY EVERY DAY INVENTING--
YOU WIND UP WITH...

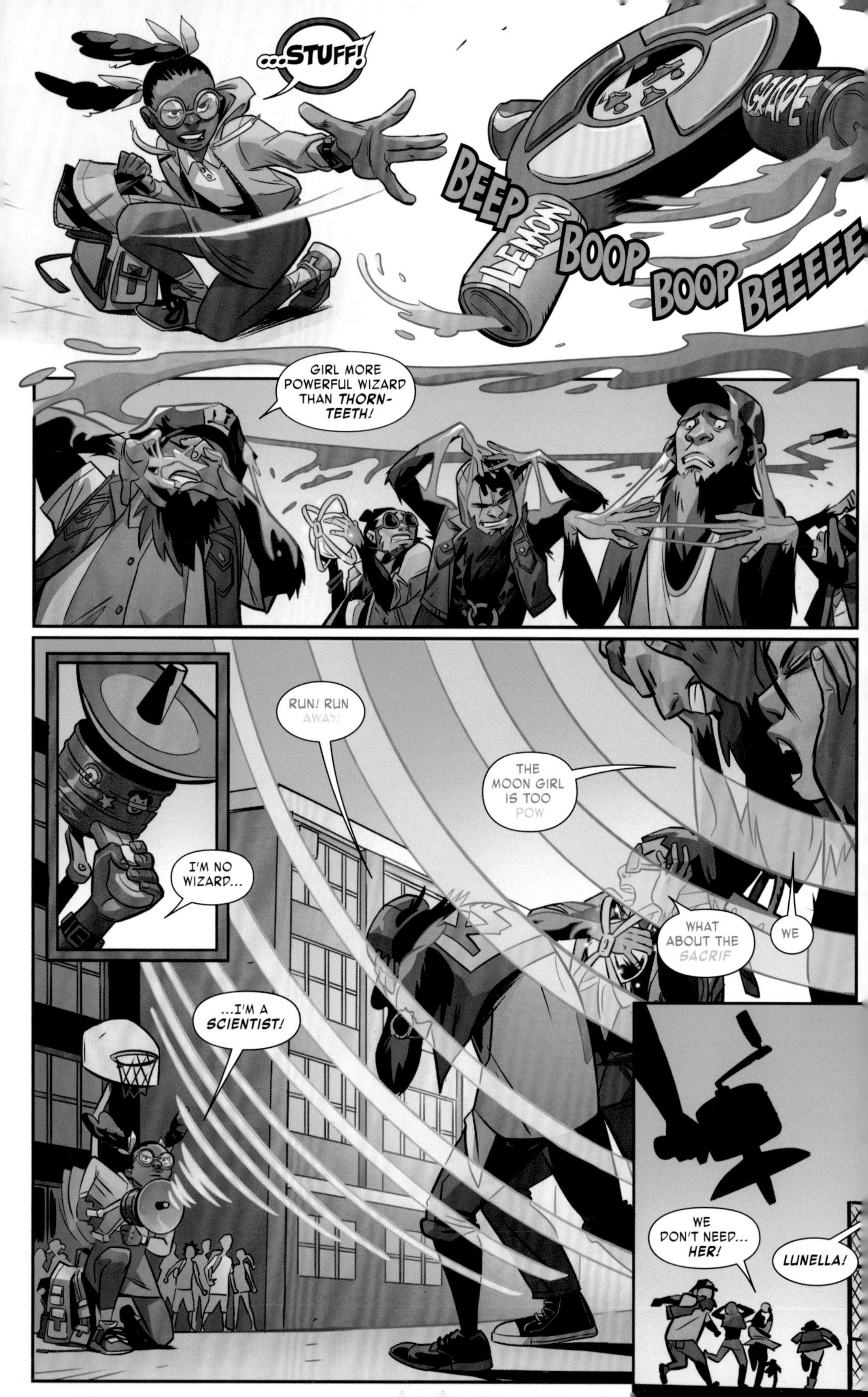
...STUFF!
GRAPE
LEMON
BEEP
BOOP
BOOP
BEEEEE
GIRL MORE POWERFUL WIZARD THAN THORN-TEETH!
I'M NO WIZARD...
RUN! RUN AWAY!
THE MOON GIRL IS TOO POW
...I'M A SCIENTIST!
WHAT ABOUT THE SACRIF
WE
WE DON'T NEED... HER!
LUNELLA!

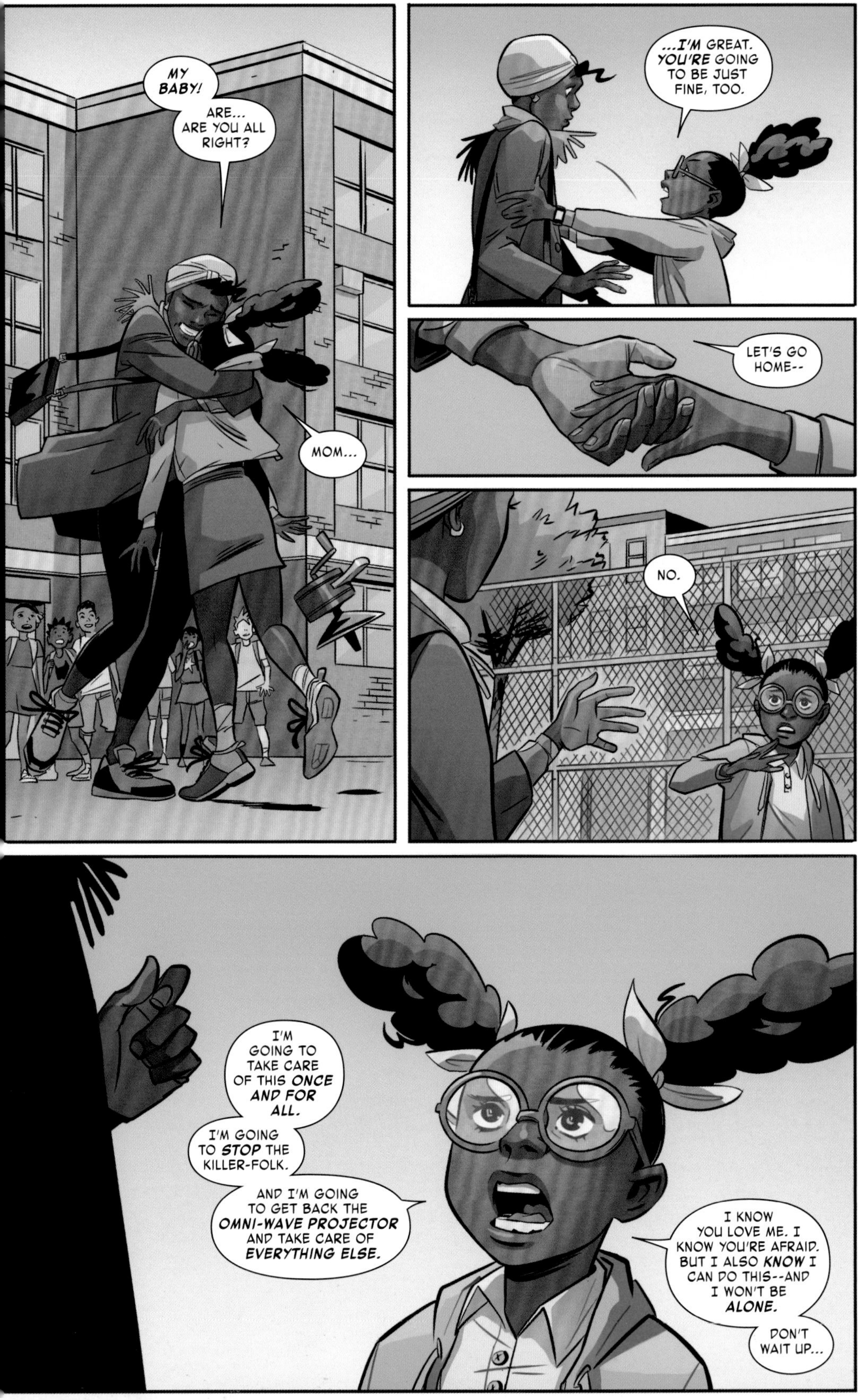
MY BABY!
ARE... ARE YOU ALL RIGHT?
MOM...
...I'M GREAT. YOU'RE GOING TO BE JUST FINE, TOO.
LET'S GO HOME--
NO.
I'M GOING TO TAKE CARE OF THIS ONCE AND FOR ALL.
I'M GOING TO STOP THE KILLER-FOLK.
AND I'M GOING TO GET BACK THE OMNI-WAVE PROJECTOR AND TAKE CARE OF EVERYTHING ELSE.
I KNOW YOU LOVE ME. I KNOW YOU'RE AFRAID. BUT I ALSO KNOW I CAN DO THIS--AND I WON'T BE ALONE.
DON'T WAIT UP...

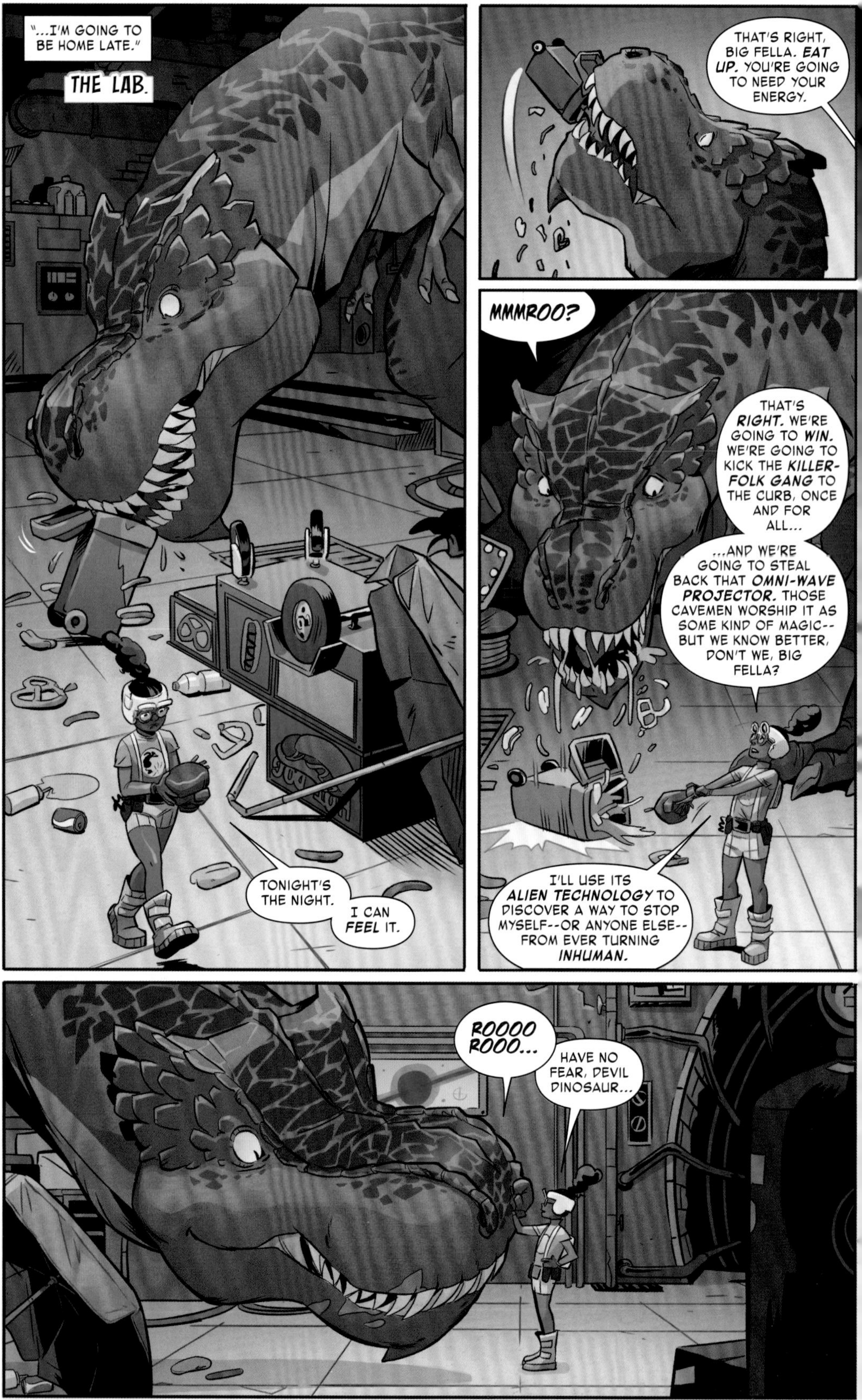
"...I'M GOING TO BE HOME LATE."
THE LAB.
TONIGHT'S THE NIGHT.
I CAN FEEL IT.
THAT'S RIGHT, BIG FELLA. EAT UP. YOU'RE GOING TO NEED YOUR ENERGY.
MMMROO?
THAT'S RIGHT. WE'RE GOING TO WIN. WE'RE GOING TO KICK THE KILLER-FOLK GANG TO THE CURB, ONCE AND FOR ALL...
...AND WE'RE GOING TO STEAL BACK THAT OMNI-WAVE PROJECTOR. THOSE CAVEMEN WORSHIP IT AS SOME KIND OF MAGIC--BUT WE KNOW BETTER, DON'T WE, BIG FELLA?
I'LL USE ITS ALIEN TECHNOLOGY TO DISCOVER A WAY TO STOP MYSELF--OR ANYONE ELSE--FROM EVER TURNING INHUMAN.
ROOOO ROOO...
HAVE NO FEAR, DEVIL DINOSAUR...

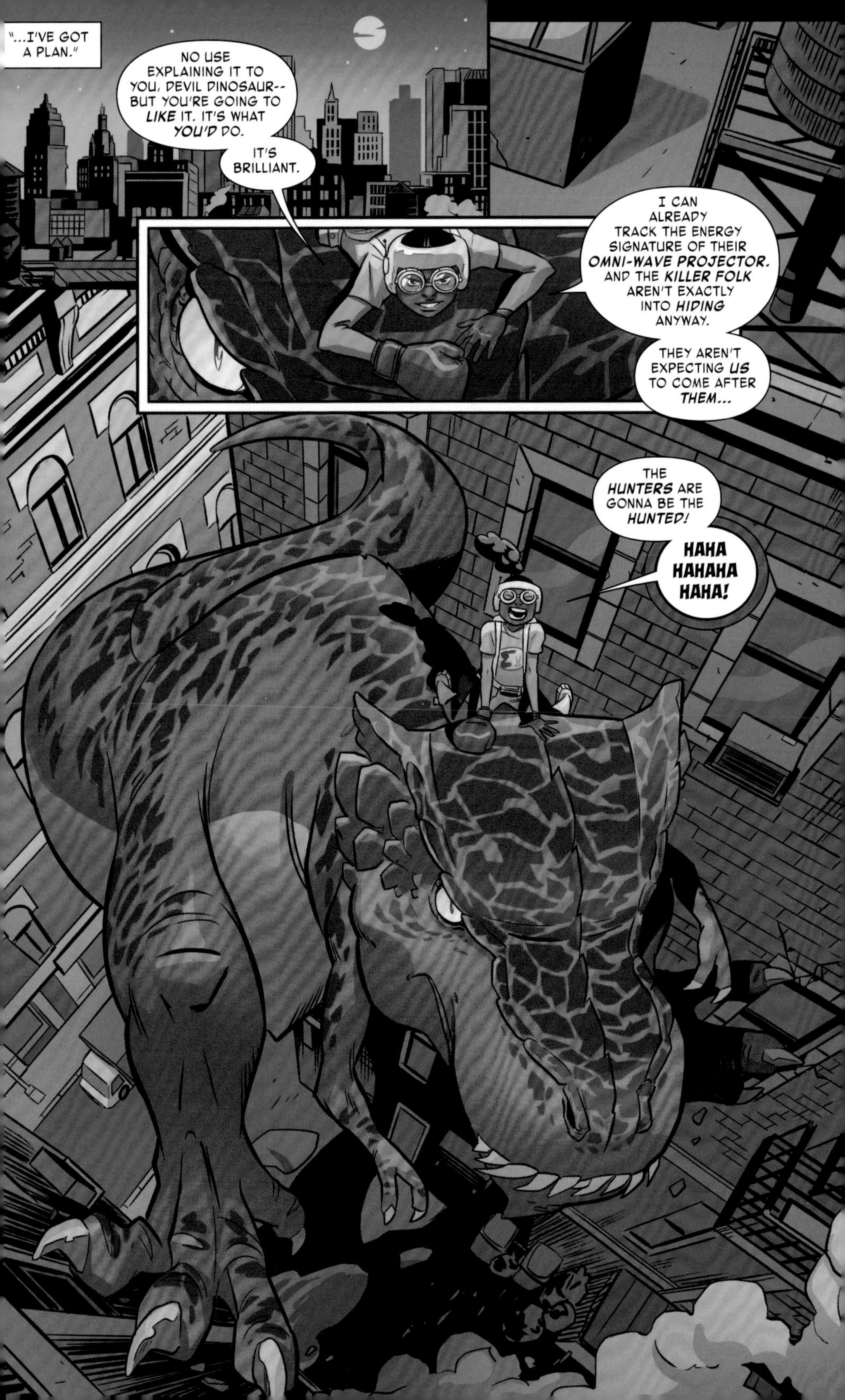
"...I'VE GOT A PLAN."
NO USE EXPLAINING IT TO YOU, DEVIL DINOSAUR-- BUT YOU'RE GOING TO *LIKE* IT. IT'S WHAT *YOU'D* DO.
IT'S BRILLIANT.
I CAN ALREADY TRACK THE ENERGY SIGNATURE OF THEIR *OMNI-WAVE PROJECTOR.* AND THE *KILLER FOLK* AREN'T EXACTLY INTO *HIDING* ANYWAY.
THEY AREN'T EXPECTING *US* TO COME AFTER *THEM...*
THE *HUNTERS* ARE GONNA BE THE *HUNTED!*
HAHA HAHAHA HAHA!

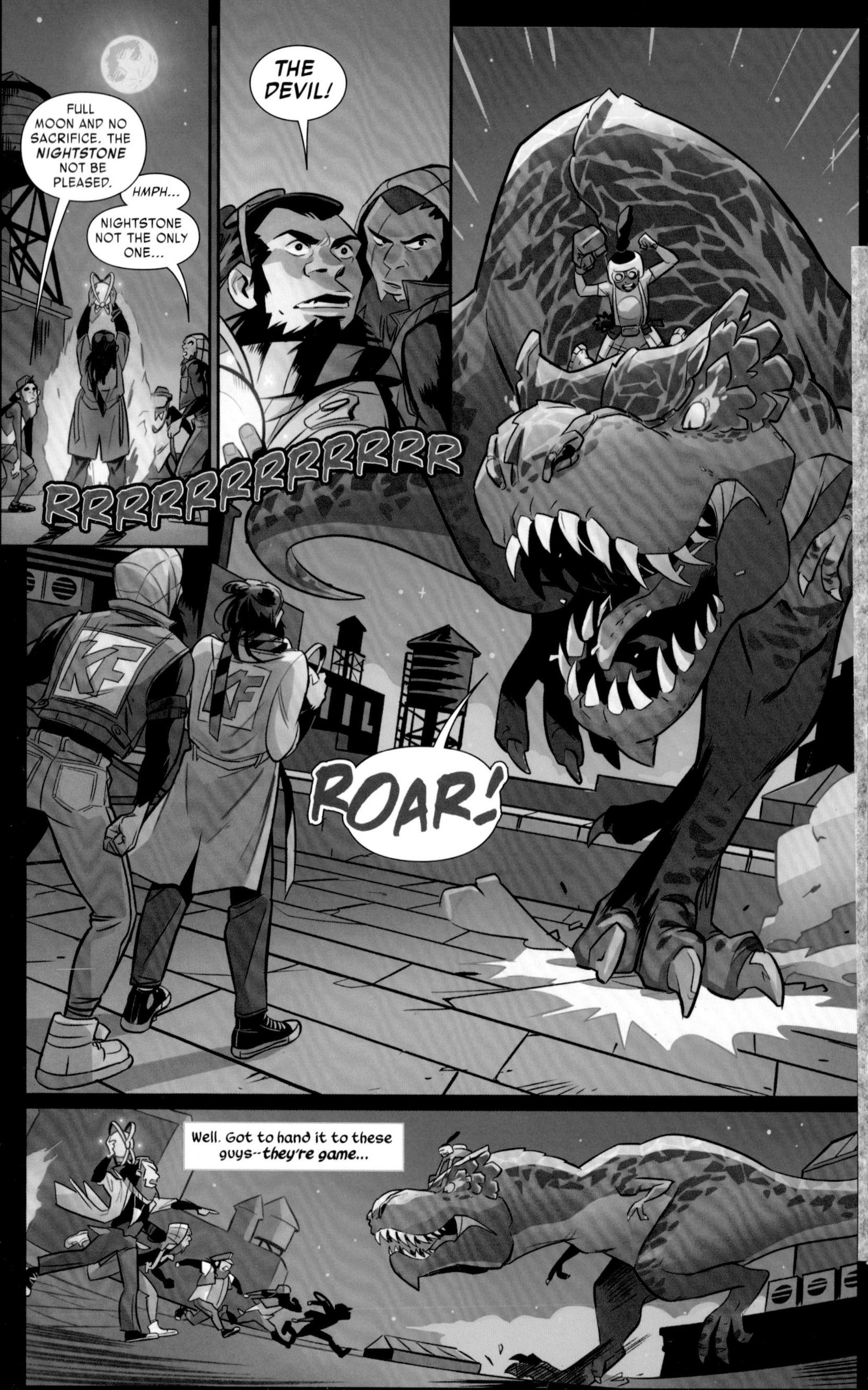
FULL MOON AND NO SACRIFICE. THE *NIGHTSTONE* NOT BE PLEASED.
HMPH...
NIGHTSTONE NOT THE ONLY ONE...
THE DEVIL!
RRRRRRRRRRRRRRR
ROAR!
Well. Got to hand it to these guys--*they're game...*

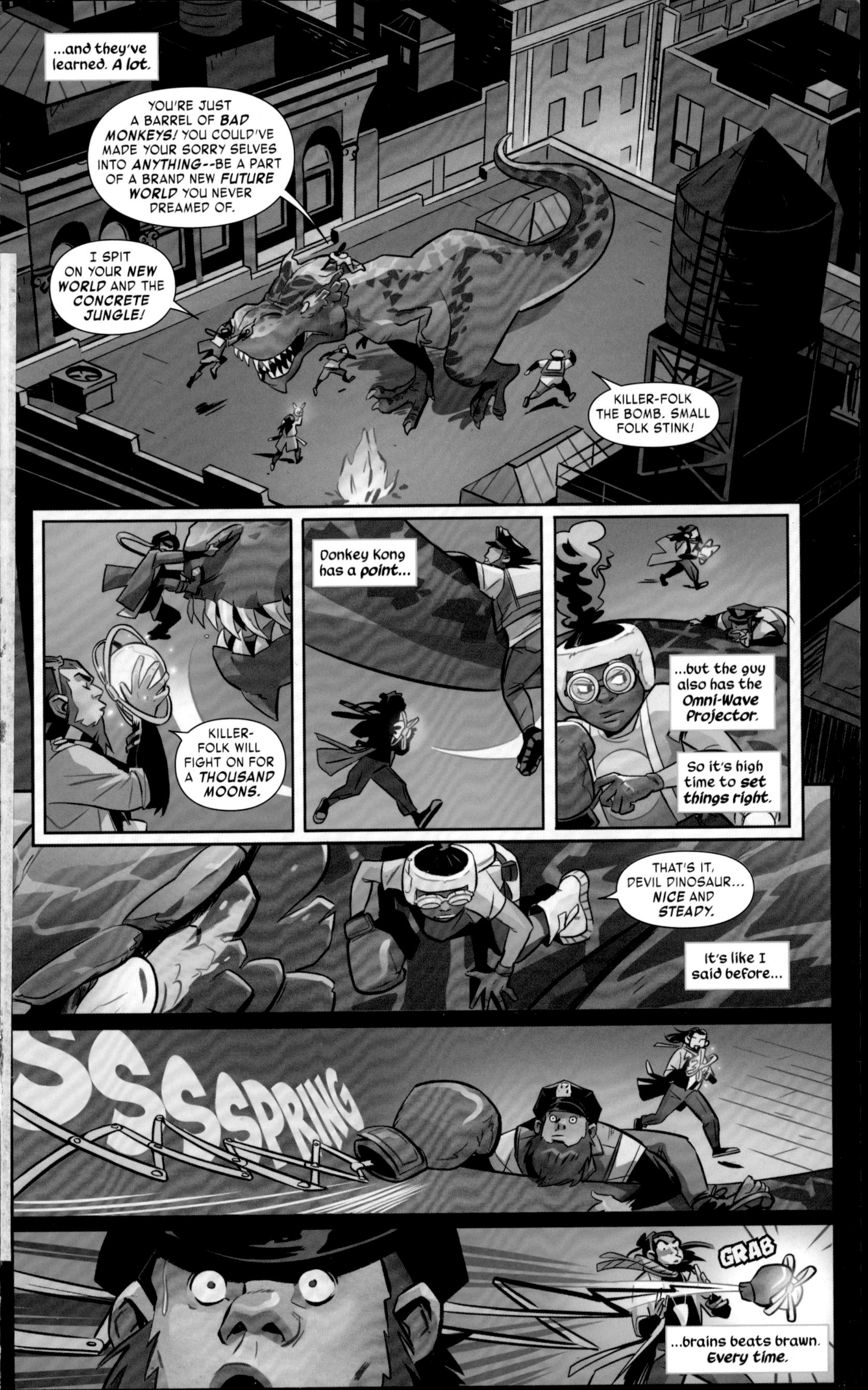
...and they've learned. A lot.
YOU'RE JUST A BARREL OF BAD MONKEYS! YOU COULD'VE MADE YOUR SORRY SELVES INTO ANYTHING--BE A PART OF A BRAND NEW FUTURE WORLD YOU NEVER DREAMED OF.
I SPIT ON YOUR NEW WORLD AND THE CONCRETE JUNGLE!
KILLER-FOLK THE BOMB. SMALL FOLK STINK!
KILLER-FOLK WILL FIGHT ON FOR A THOUSAND MOONS.
Donkey Kong has a point...
...but the guy also has the Omni-Wave Projector.
So it's high time to set things right.
THAT'S IT, DEVIL DINOSAUR... NICE AND STEADY.
It's like I said before...
SSSSPRING
GRAB
...brains beats brawn. Every time.

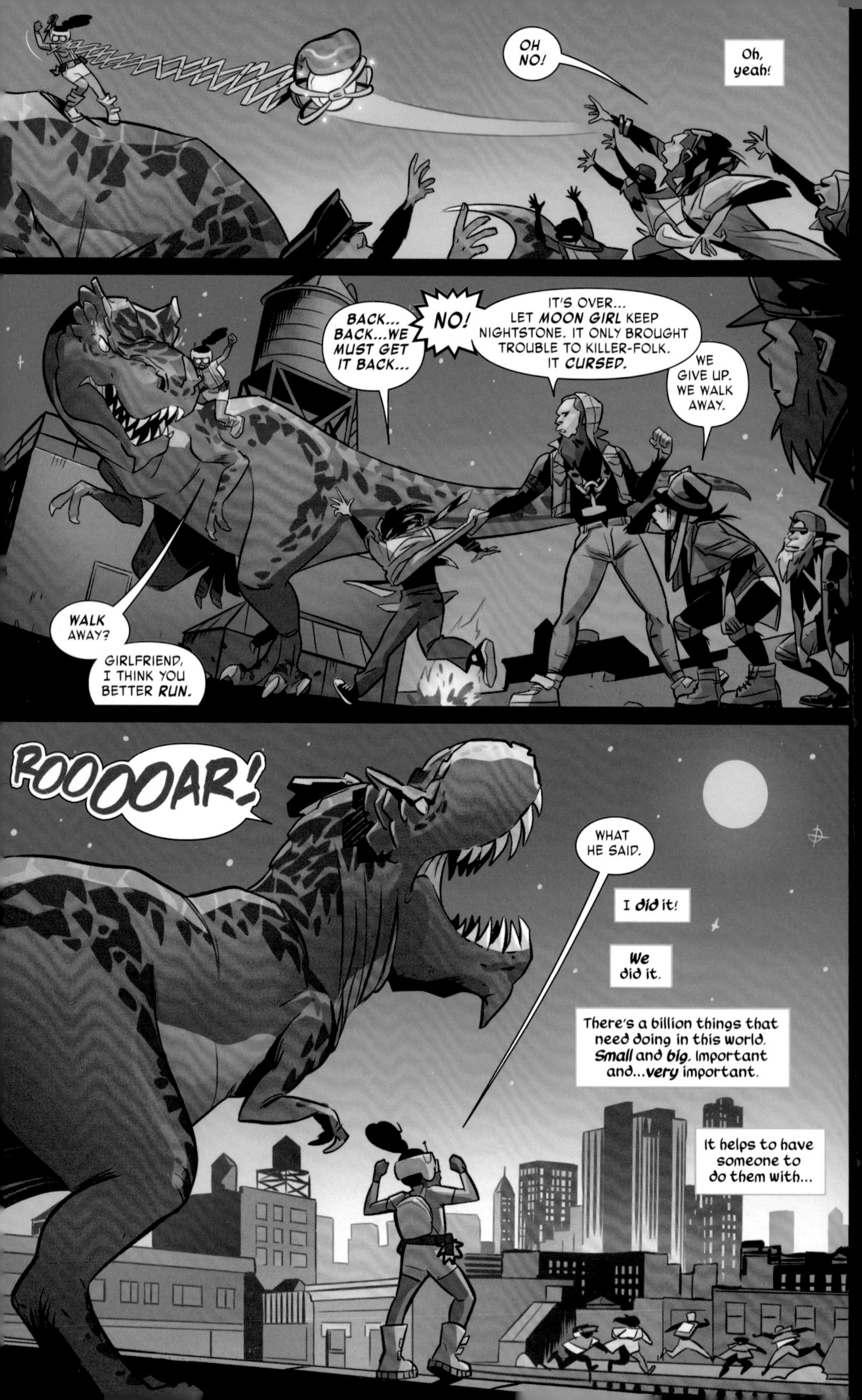
OH NO!
Oh, yeah!
BACK... BACK...WE MUST GET IT BACK...
NO!
IT'S OVER... LET MOON GIRL KEEP NIGHTSTONE. IT ONLY BROUGHT TROUBLE TO KILLER-FOLK. IT CURSED.
WE GIVE UP. WE WALK AWAY.
WALK AWAY?
GIRLFRIEND, I THINK YOU BETTER RUN.
ROOOOAR!
WHAT HE SAID.
I did it!
We did it.
There's a billion things that need doing in this world. Small and big. Important and...very important.
It helps to have someone to do them with...

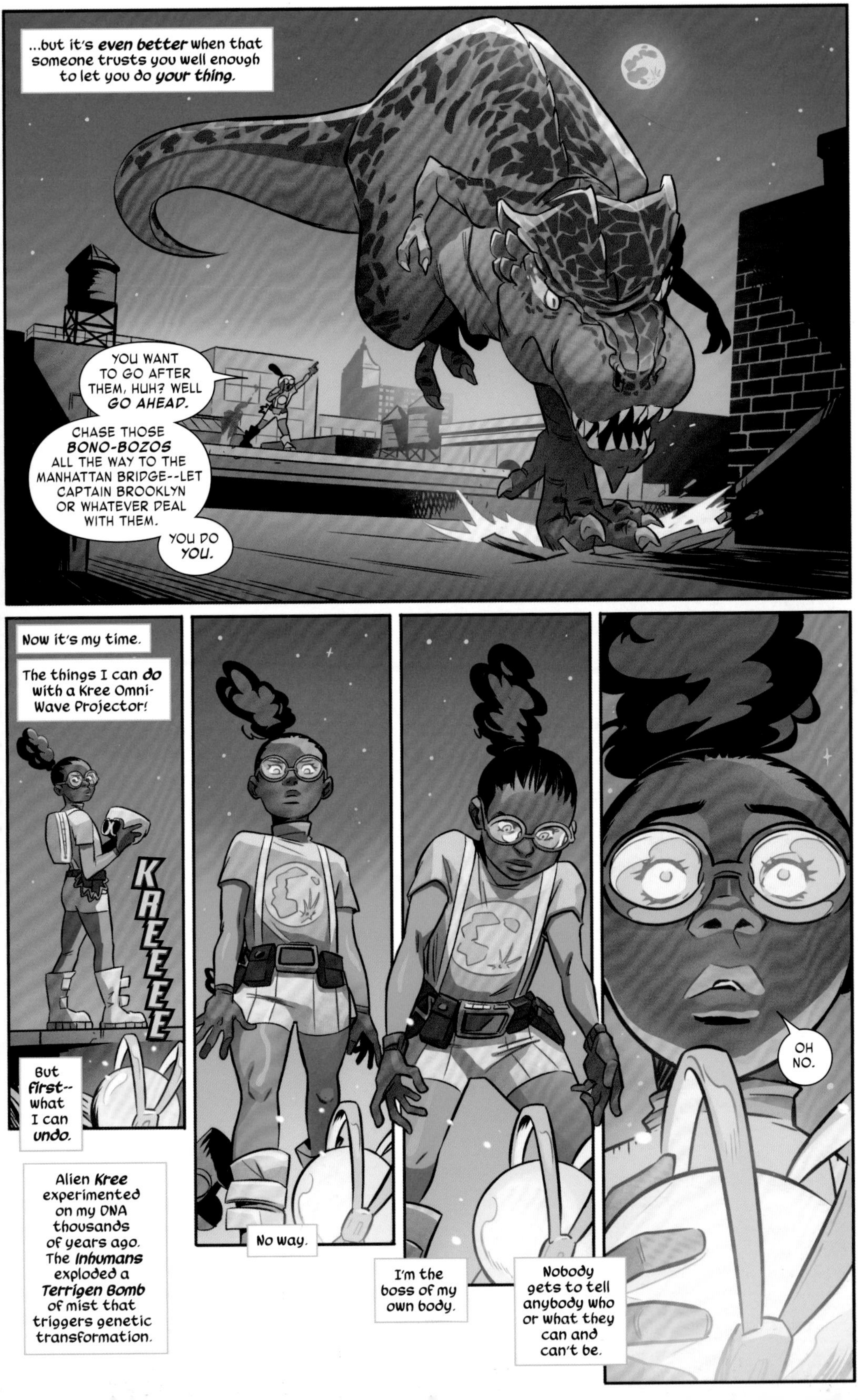
...but it's even better when that someone trusts you well enough to let you do your thing.
YOU WANT TO GO AFTER THEM, HUH? WELL GO AHEAD.
CHASE THOSE BONO-BOZOS ALL THE WAY TO THE MANHATTAN BRIDGE--LET CAPTAIN BROOKLYN OR WHATEVER DEAL WITH THEM.
YOU DO YOU.
Now it's my time.
The things I can do with a Kree Omni-Wave Projector!
KREEEEE
But first--what I can undo.
Alien Kree experimented on my DNA thousands of years ago. The Inhumans exploded a Terrigen Bomb of mist that triggers genetic transformation.
No way.
I'm the boss of my own body.
Nobody gets to tell anybody who or what they can and can't be.
OH NO.

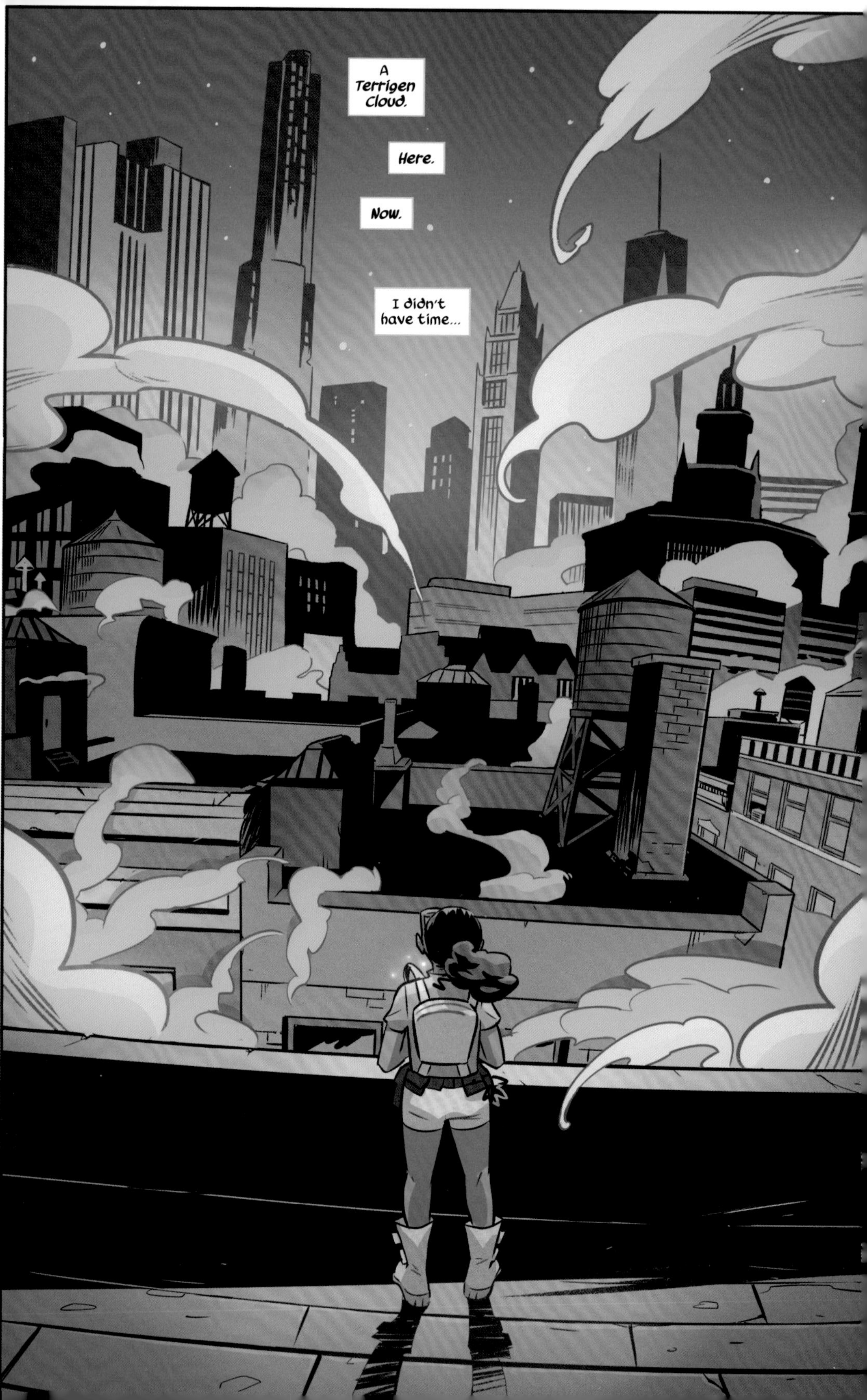
A Terrigen Cloud.
Here.
Now.
I didn't have time...

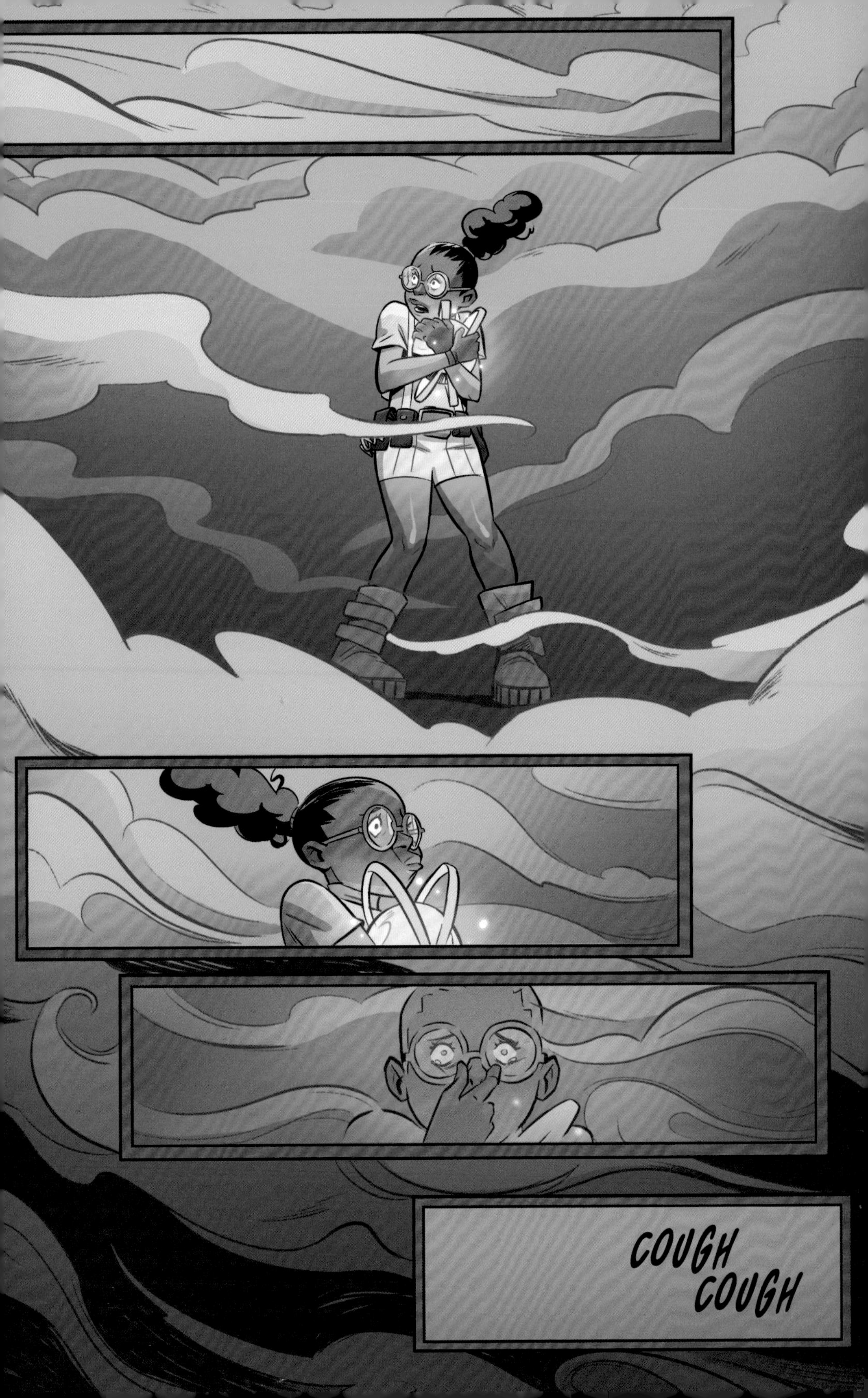
COUGH COUGH

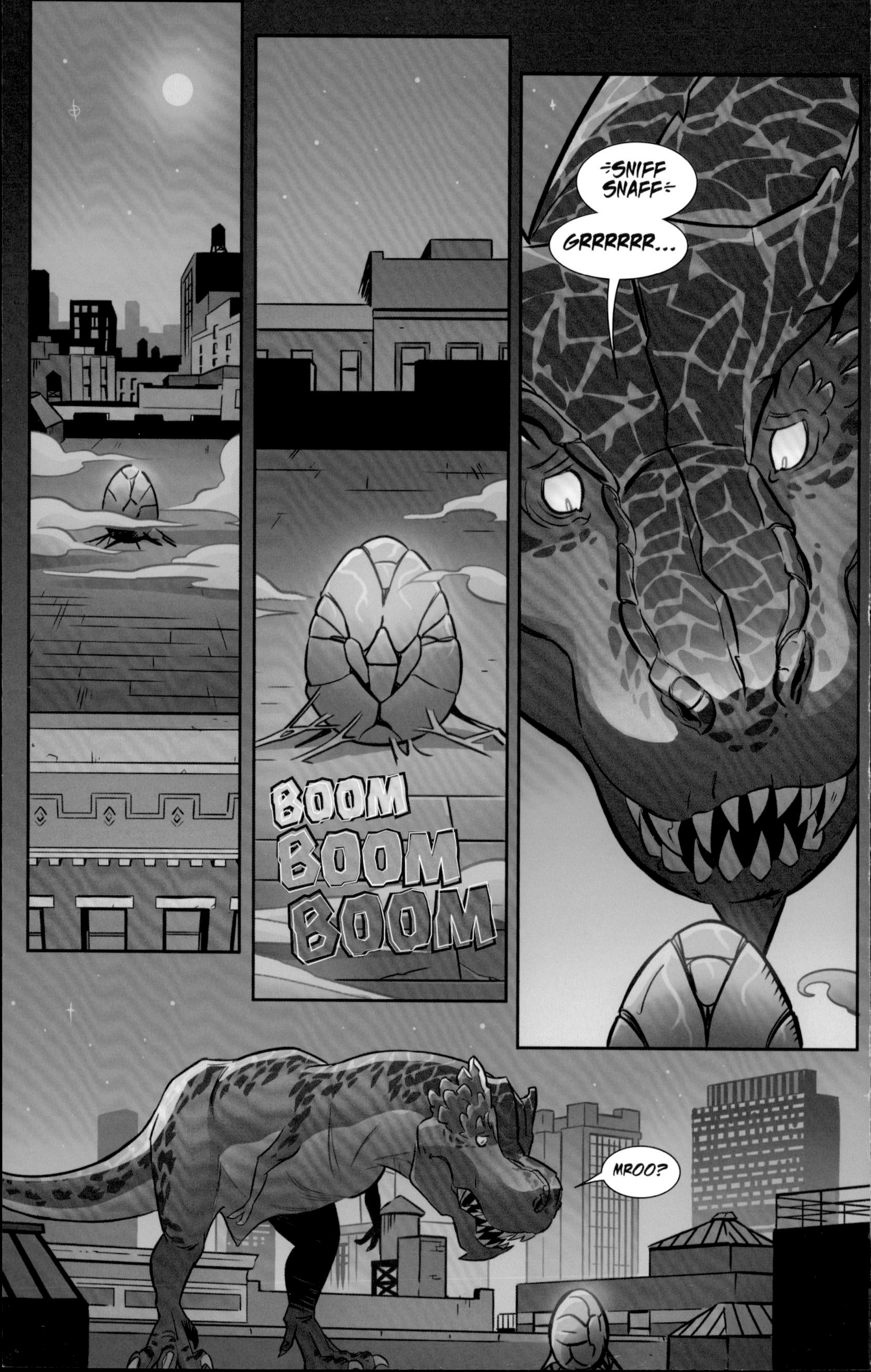
BOOM
BOOM
BOOM
SNIFF SNAFF
GRRRRRR...
MROO?

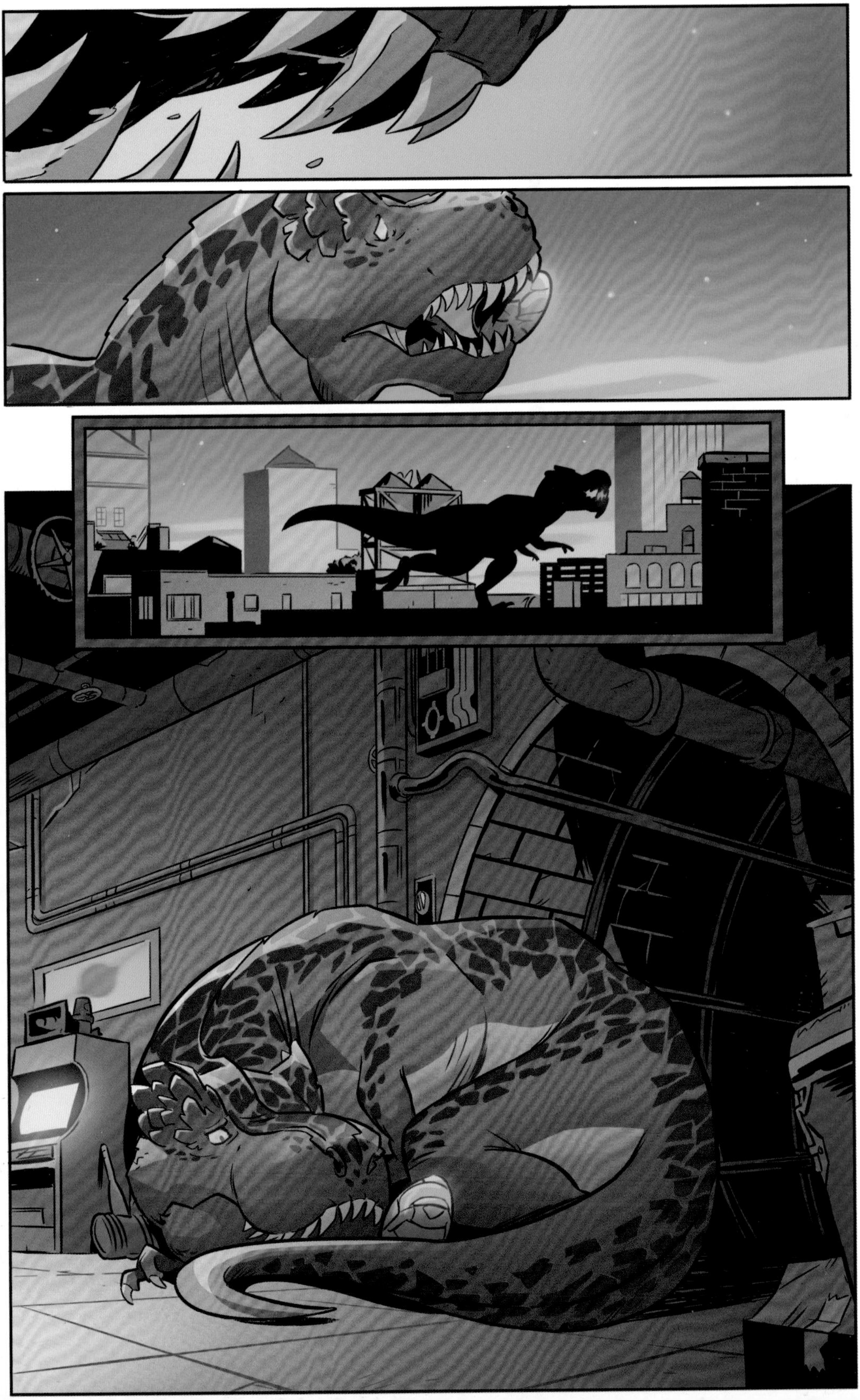

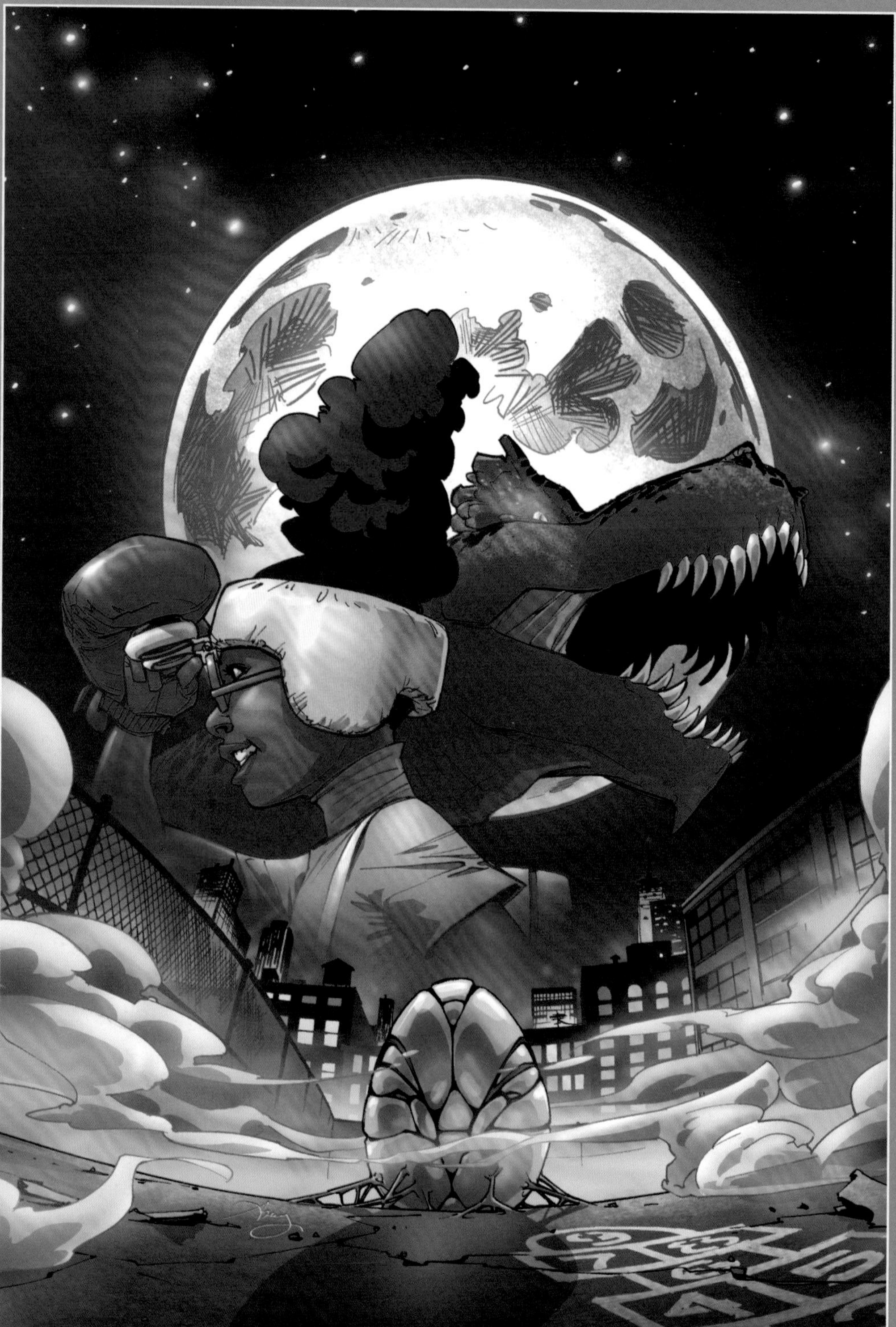

7

"GROWING UP IS HARD"

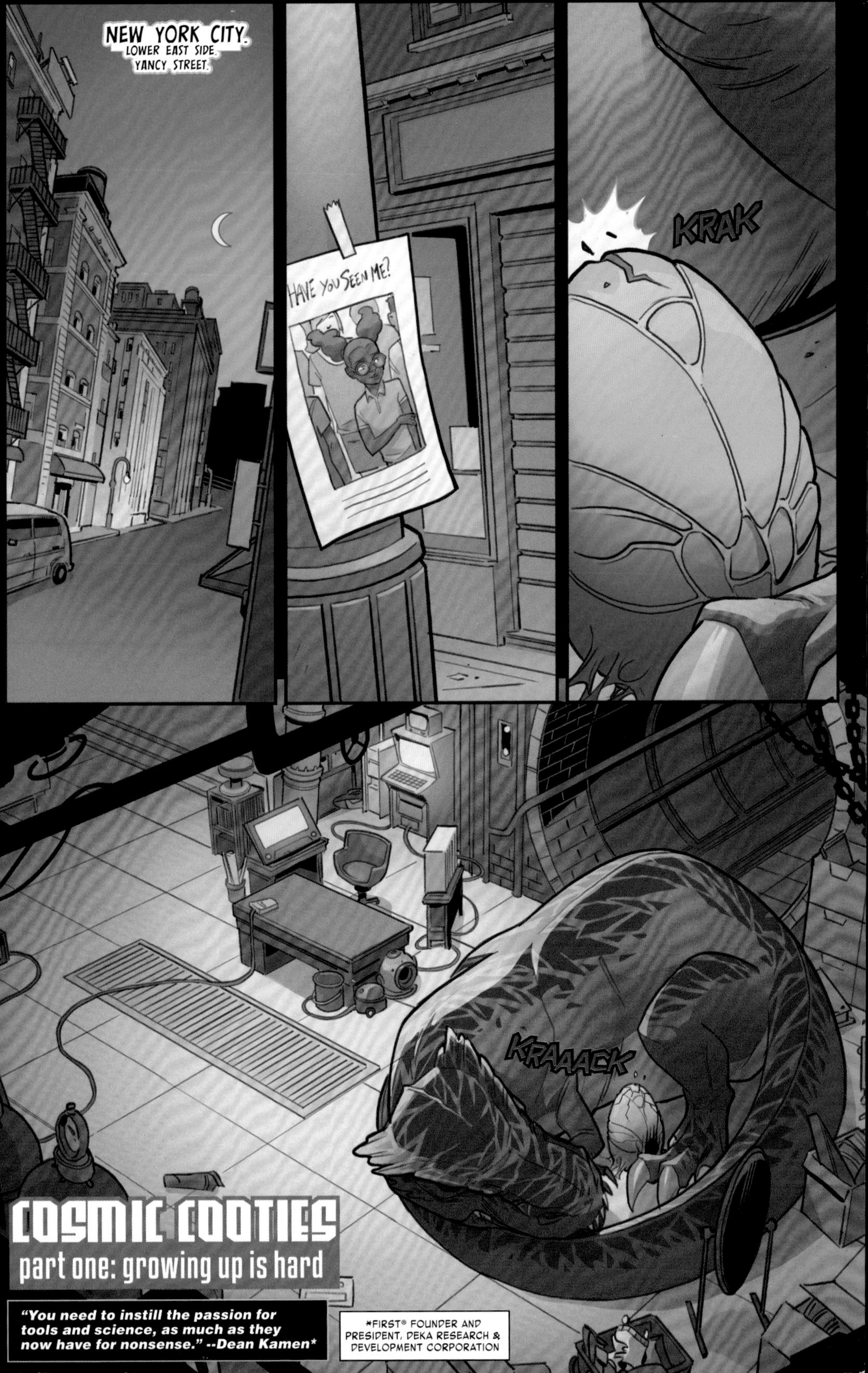
NEW YORK CITY.
LOWER EAST SIDE.
YANCY STREET.
HAVE YOU SEEN ME?
KRAK
KRAAACK
COSMIC COOTIES
part one: growing up is hard
"You need to instill the passion for tools and science, as much as they now have for nonsense." --Dean Kamen*
*FIRST® FOUNDER AND PRESIDENT, DEKA RESEARCH & DEVELOPMENT CORPORATION

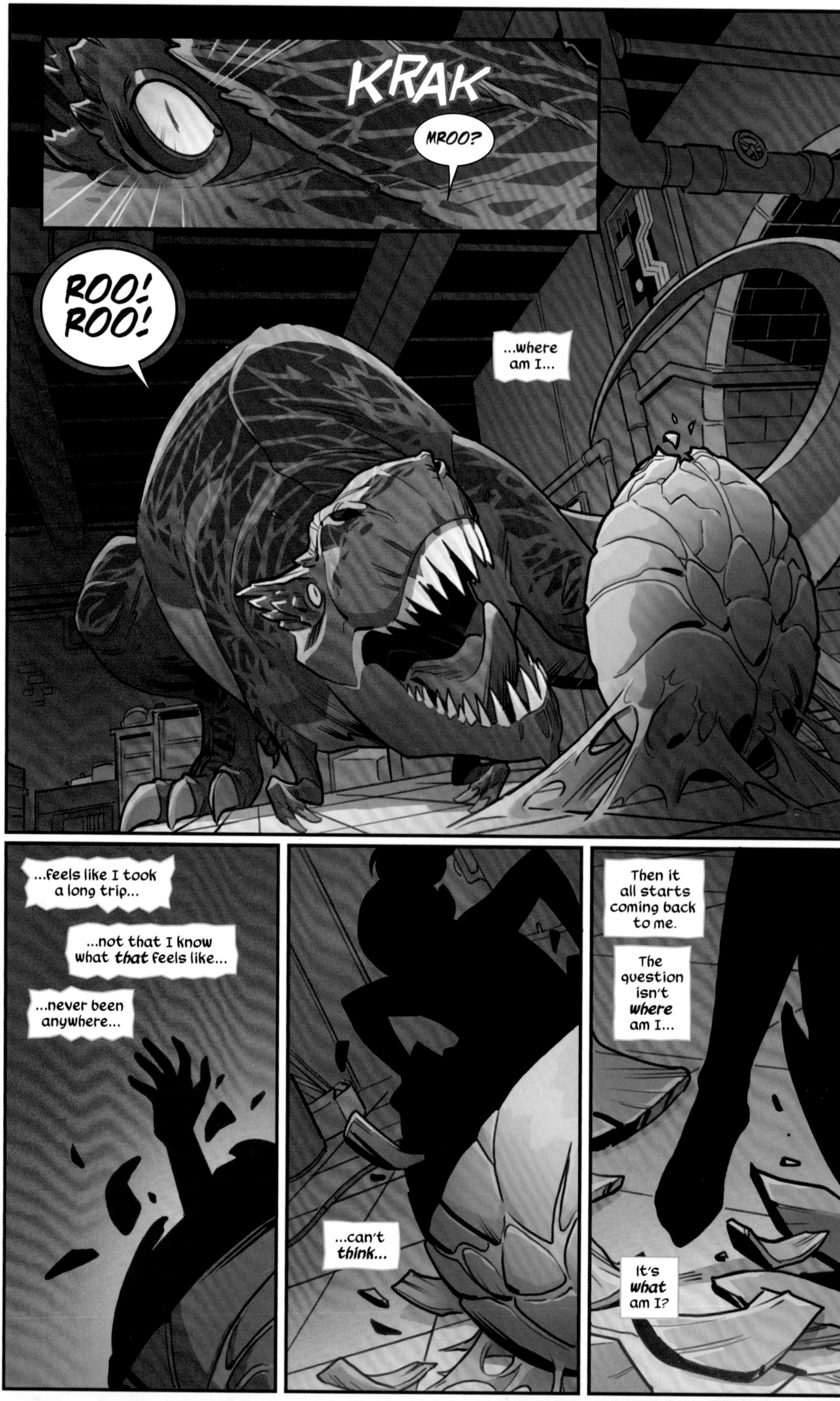
KRAK
MROO?
ROO! ROO!
...where am I...
...feels like I took a long trip...
...not that I know what *that* feels like...
...never been anywhere...
...can't *think*...
Then it all starts coming back to me.
The question isn't *where* am I...
It's *what* am I?

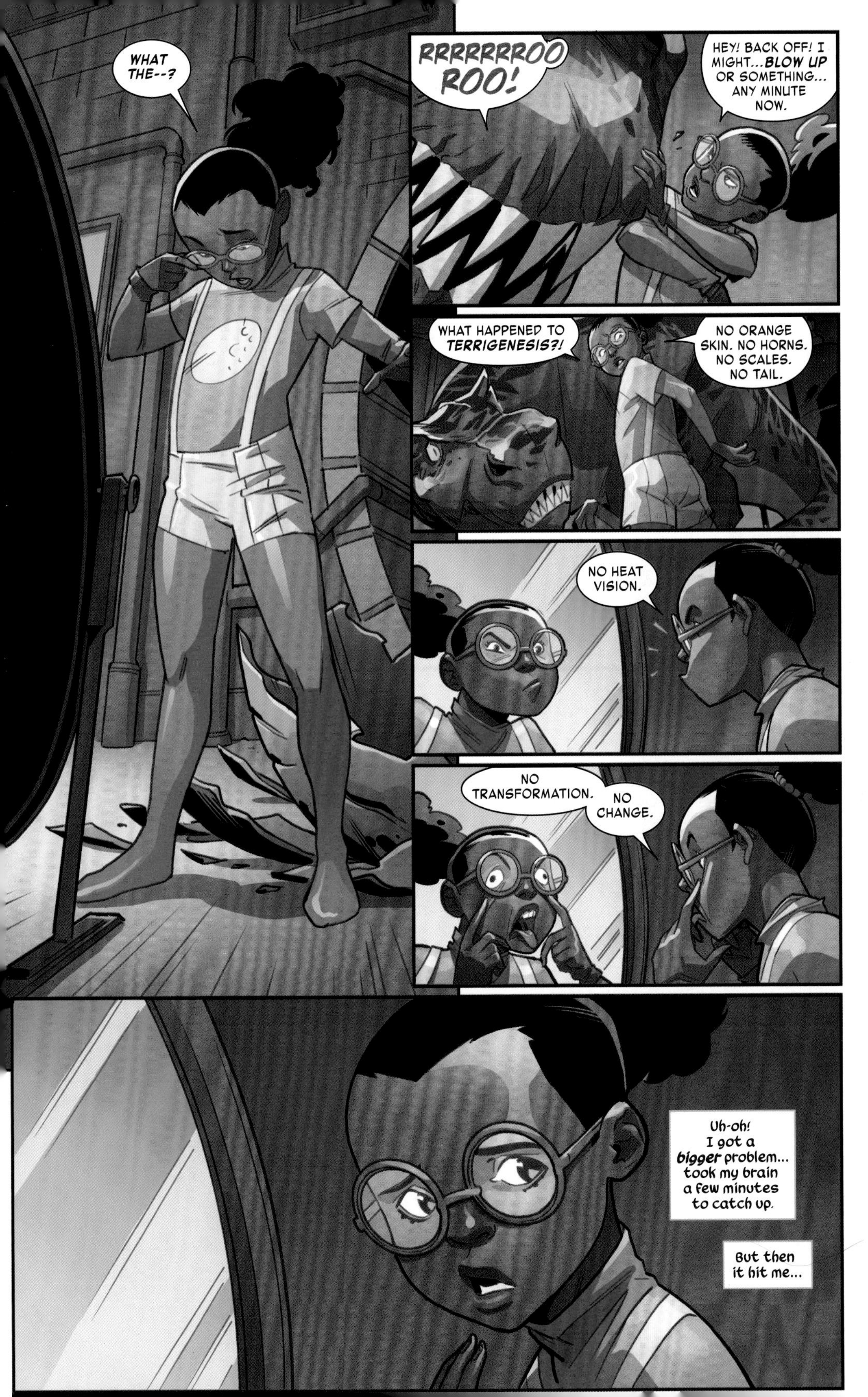
WHAT THE--?
RRRRRRROO ROO!
HEY! BACK OFF! I MIGHT...BLOW UP OR SOMETHING... ANY MINUTE NOW.
WHAT HAPPENED TO TERRIGENESIS?!
NO ORANGE SKIN. NO HORNS. NO SCALES. NO TAIL.
NO HEAT VISION.
NO TRANSFORMATION.
NO CHANGE.
Uh-oh! I got a bigger problem... took my brain a few minutes to catch up.
But then it hit me...

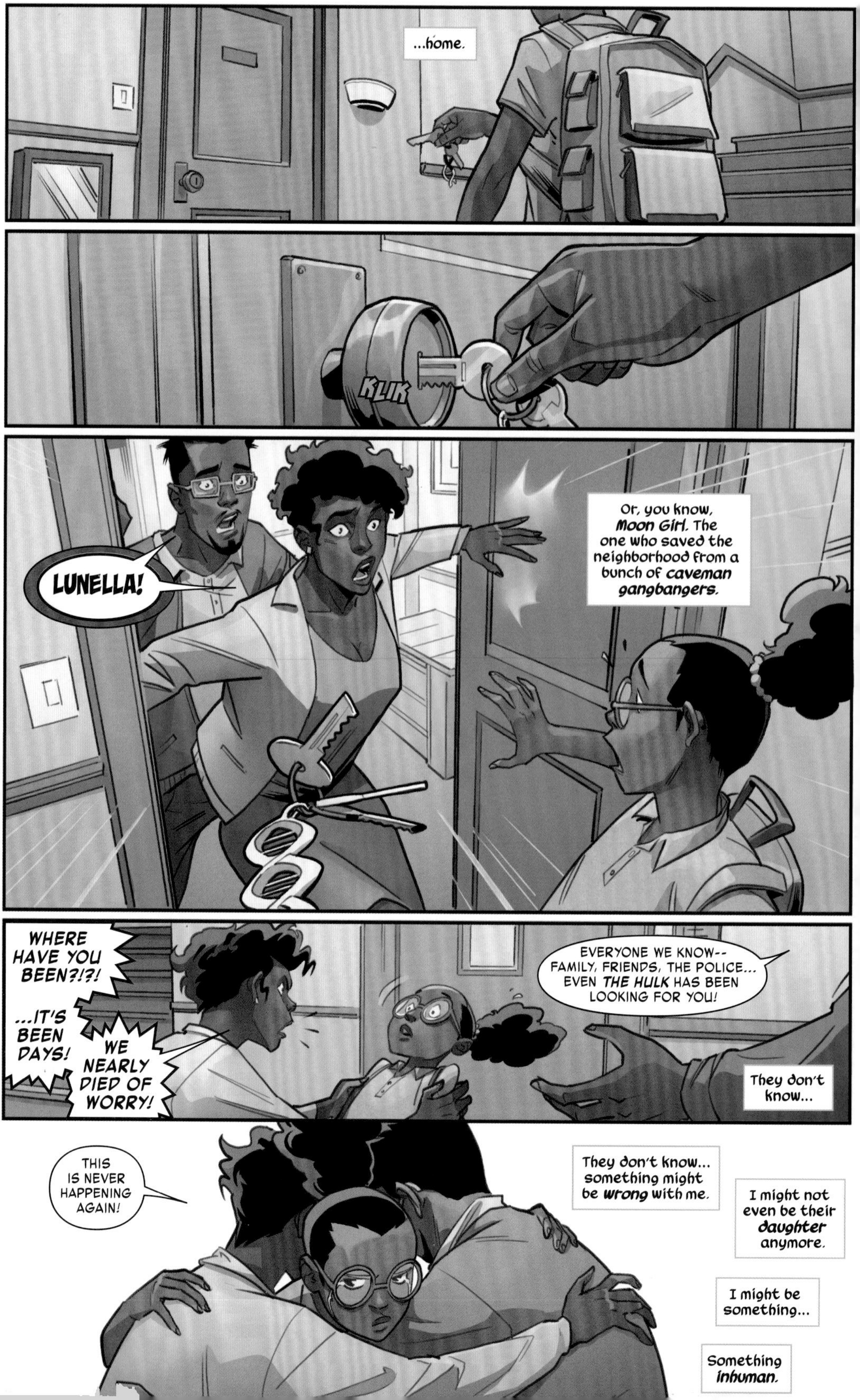
...home.
KLIK
LUNELLA!
Or, you know, Moon Girl. The one who saved the neighborhood from a bunch of caveman gangbangers.
WHERE HAVE YOU BEEN?!?!
...IT'S BEEN DAYS!
WE NEARLY DIED OF WORRY!
EVERYONE WE KNOW-- FAMILY, FRIENDS, THE POLICE... EVEN THE HULK HAS BEEN LOOKING FOR YOU!
They don't know...
THIS IS NEVER HAPPENING AGAIN!
They don't know... something might be wrong with me.
I might not even be their daughter anymore.
I might be something...
Something inhuman.

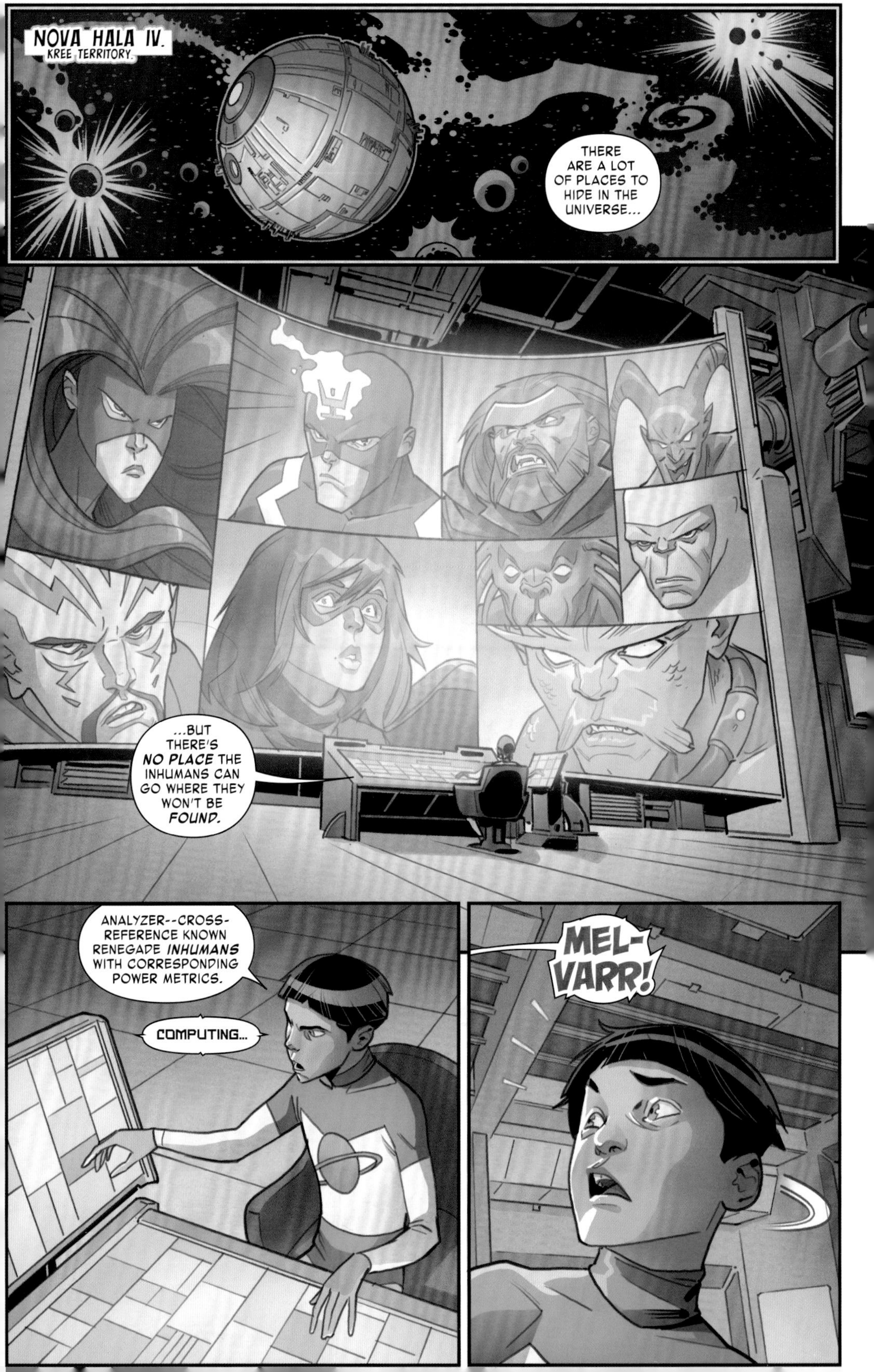
NOVA HALA IV.
KREE TERRITORY.
THERE ARE A LOT OF PLACES TO HIDE IN THE UNIVERSE...
...BUT THERE'S NO PLACE THE INHUMANS CAN GO WHERE THEY WON'T BE FOUND.
ANALYZER--CROSS-REFERENCE KNOWN RENEGADE INHUMANS WITH CORRESPONDING POWER METRICS.
COMPUTING...
MEL-VARR!

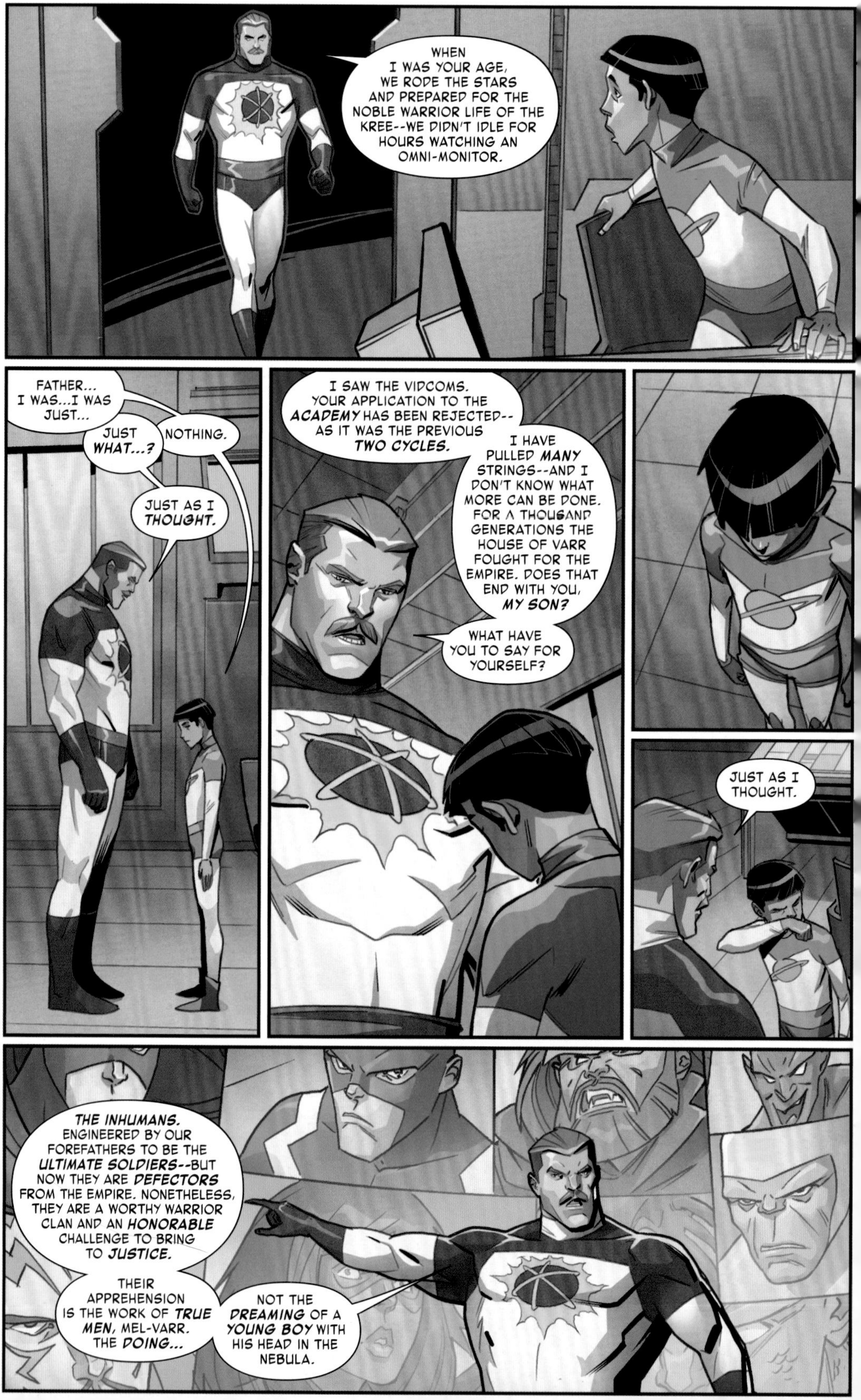
WHEN I WAS YOUR AGE, WE RODE THE STARS AND PREPARED FOR THE NOBLE WARRIOR LIFE OF THE KREE--WE DIDN'T IDLE FOR HOURS WATCHING AN OMNI-MONITOR.
FATHER... I WAS...I WAS JUST...
JUST WHAT...?
NOTHING.
JUST AS I THOUGHT.
I SAW THE VIDCOMS. YOUR APPLICATION TO THE ACADEMY HAS BEEN REJECTED-- AS IT WAS THE PREVIOUS TWO CYCLES.
I HAVE PULLED MANY STRINGS--AND I DON'T KNOW WHAT MORE CAN BE DONE. FOR A THOUSAND GENERATIONS THE HOUSE OF VARR FOUGHT FOR THE EMPIRE. DOES THAT END WITH YOU, MY SON?
WHAT HAVE YOU TO SAY FOR YOURSELF?
JUST AS I THOUGHT.
THE INHUMANS. ENGINEERED BY OUR FOREFATHERS TO BE THE ULTIMATE SOLDIERS--BUT NOW THEY ARE DEFECTORS FROM THE EMPIRE. NONETHELESS, THEY ARE A WORTHY WARRIOR CLAN AND AN HONORABLE CHALLENGE TO BRING TO JUSTICE.
THEIR APPREHENSION IS THE WORK OF TRUE MEN, MEL-VARR. THE DOING...
NOT THE DREAMING OF A YOUNG BOY WITH HIS HEAD IN THE NEBULA.

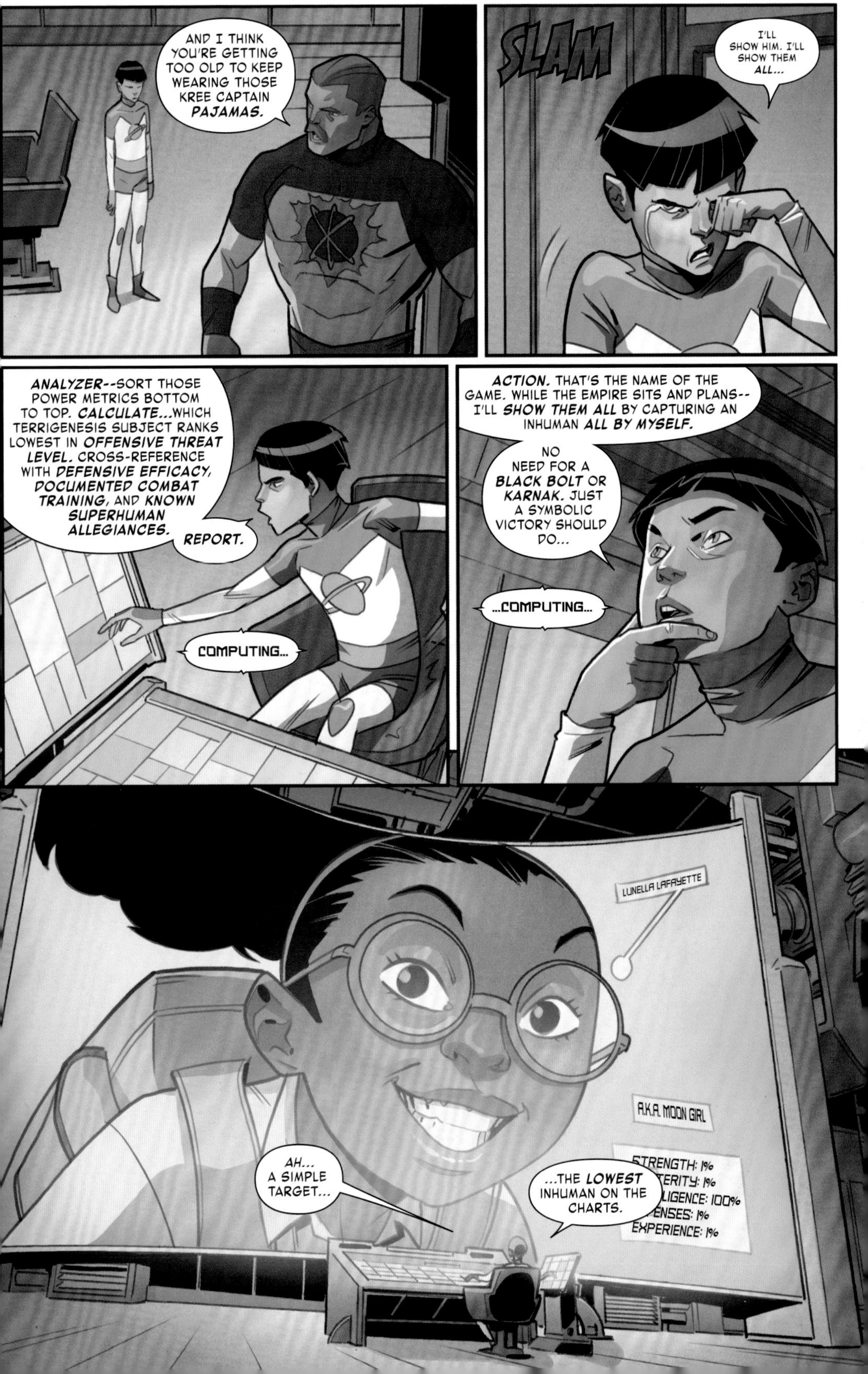
AND I THINK YOU'RE GETTING TOO OLD TO KEEP WEARING THOSE KREE CAPTAIN PAJAMAS.
SLAM
I'LL SHOW HIM. I'LL SHOW THEM ALL...
ANALYZER--SORT THOSE POWER METRICS BOTTOM TO TOP. CALCULATE...WHICH TERRIGENESIS SUBJECT RANKS LOWEST IN OFFENSIVE THREAT LEVEL. CROSS-REFERENCE WITH DEFENSIVE EFFICACY, DOCUMENTED COMBAT TRAINING, AND KNOWN SUPERHUMAN ALLEGIANCES.
REPORT.
COMPUTING...
ACTION. THAT'S THE NAME OF THE GAME. WHILE THE EMPIRE SITS AND PLANS--I'LL SHOW THEM ALL BY CAPTURING AN INHUMAN ALL BY MYSELF.
NO NEED FOR A BLACK BOLT OR KARNAK. JUST A SYMBOLIC VICTORY SHOULD DO...
...COMPUTING...
LUNELLA LAFAYETTE
A.K.A. MOON GIRL
STRENGTH: 1%
TERITY: 1%
LIGENCE: 100%
ENSES: 1%
EXPERIENCE: 1%
AH... A SIMPLE TARGET...
...THE LOWEST INHUMAN ON THE CHARTS.

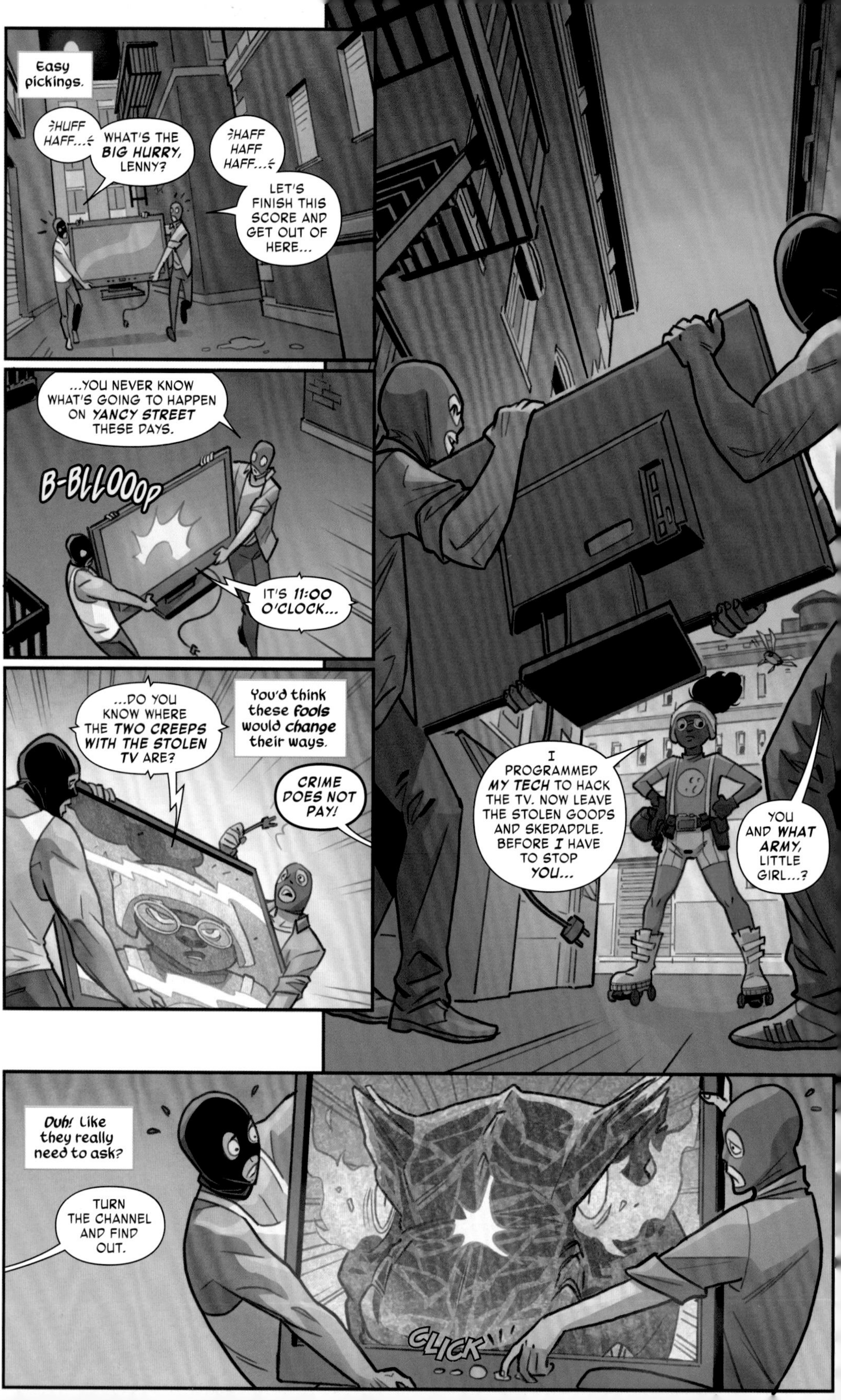
Easy pickings.
HUFF HAFF...
WHAT'S THE BIG HURRY, LENNY?
HAFF HAFF HAFF...
LET'S FINISH THIS SCORE AND GET OUT OF HERE...
...YOU NEVER KNOW WHAT'S GOING TO HAPPEN ON YANCY STREET THESE DAYS.
B-BLLOOOP
IT'S 11:00 O'CLOCK...
...DO YOU KNOW WHERE THE TWO CREEPS WITH THE STOLEN TV ARE?
You'd think these fools would change their ways.
CRIME DOES NOT PAY!
I PROGRAMMED MY TECH TO HACK THE TV. NOW LEAVE THE STOLEN GOODS AND SKEDADDLE. BEFORE I HAVE TO STOP YOU...
YOU AND WHAT ARMY, LITTLE GIRL...?
Duh! Like they really need to ask?
TURN THE CHANNEL AND FIND OUT.
CLICK

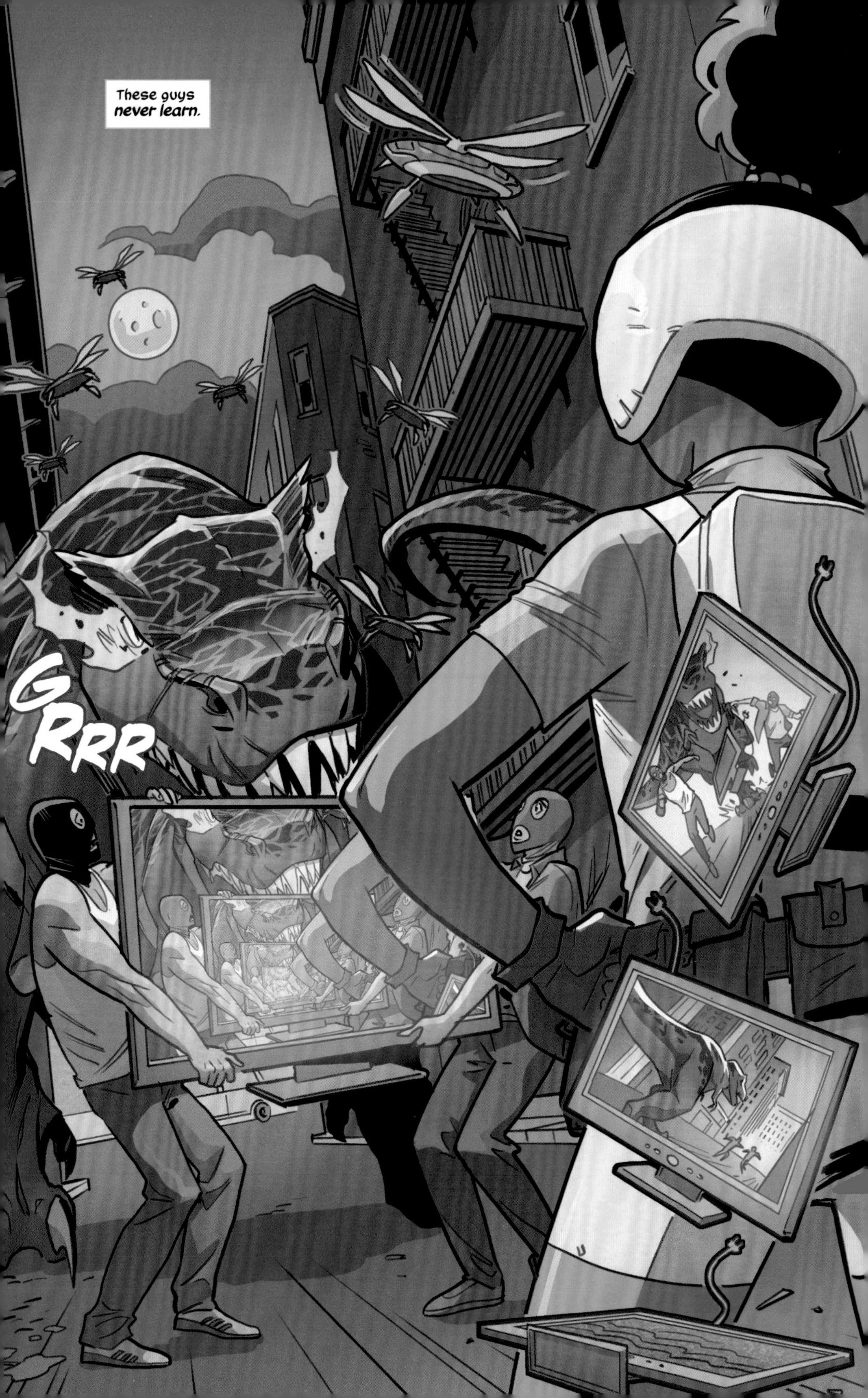
These guys never learn.
GRRR

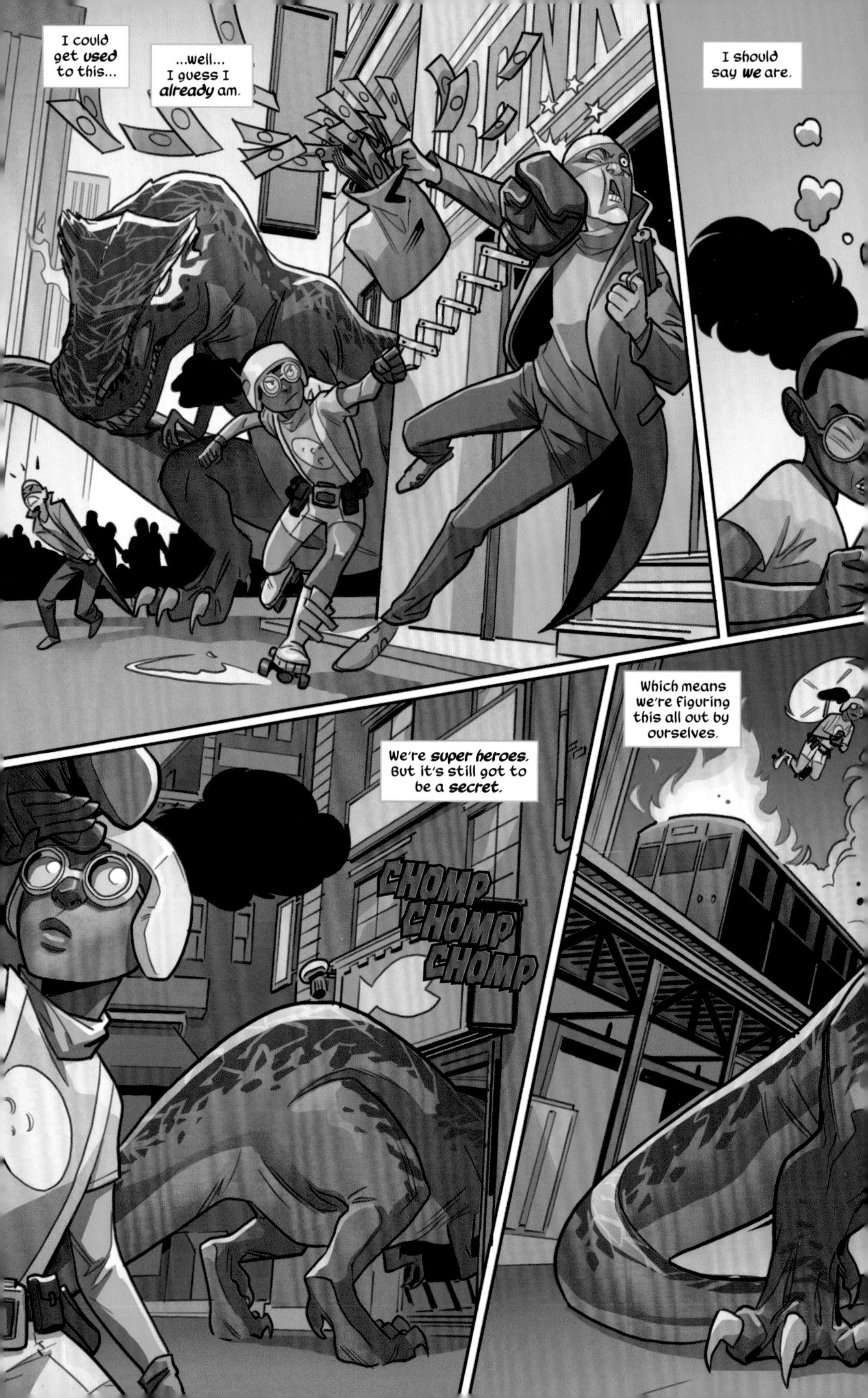
I could get used to this...
...well... I guess I already am.
I should say we are.
We're super heroes. But it's still got to be a secret.
CHOMP CHOMP CHOMP
Which means we're figuring this all out by ourselves.

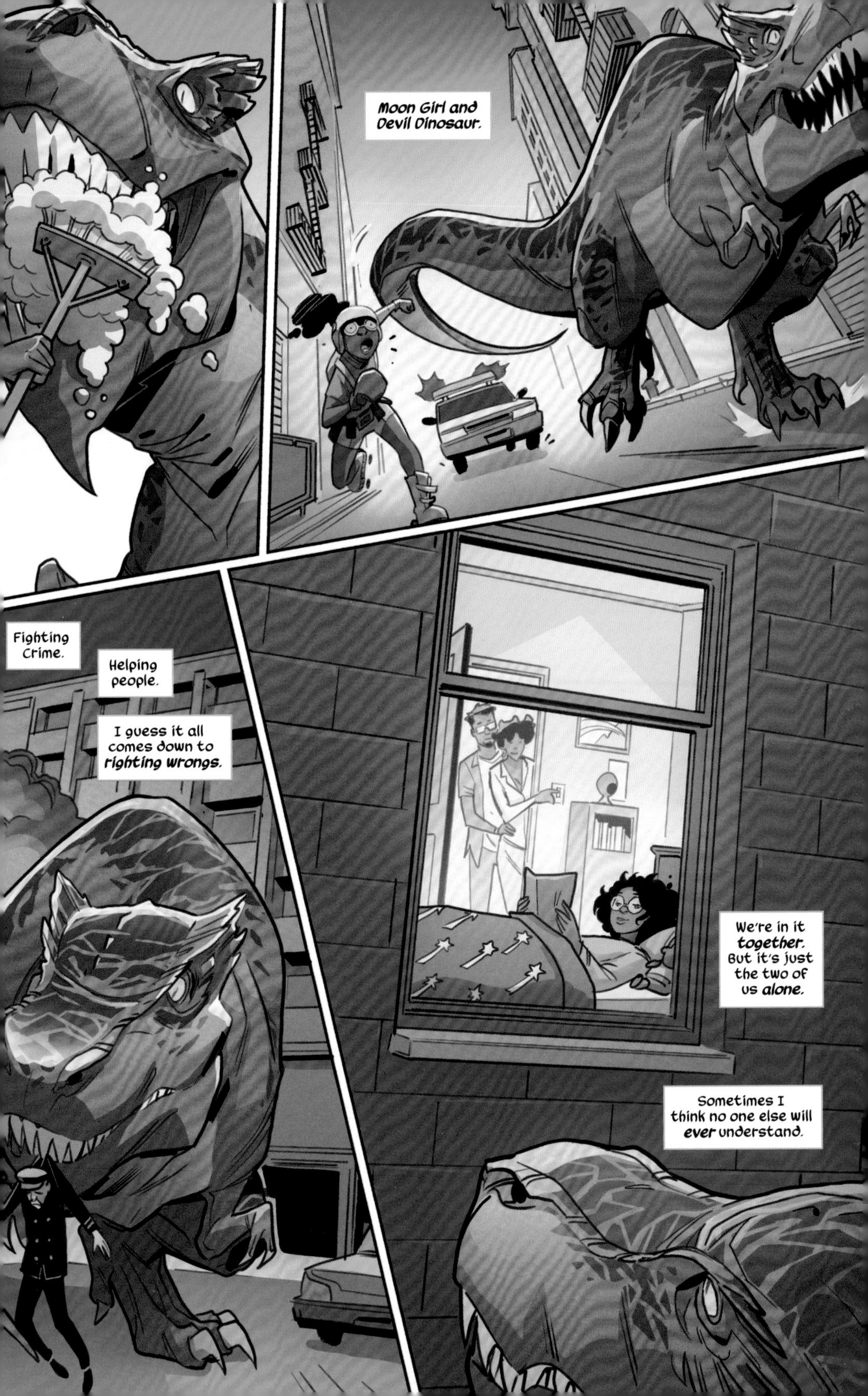
Moon Girl and Devil Dinosaur.
Fighting Crime.
Helping people.
I guess it all comes down to righting wrongs.
We're in it together. But it's just the two of us alone.
Sometimes I think no one else will ever understand.

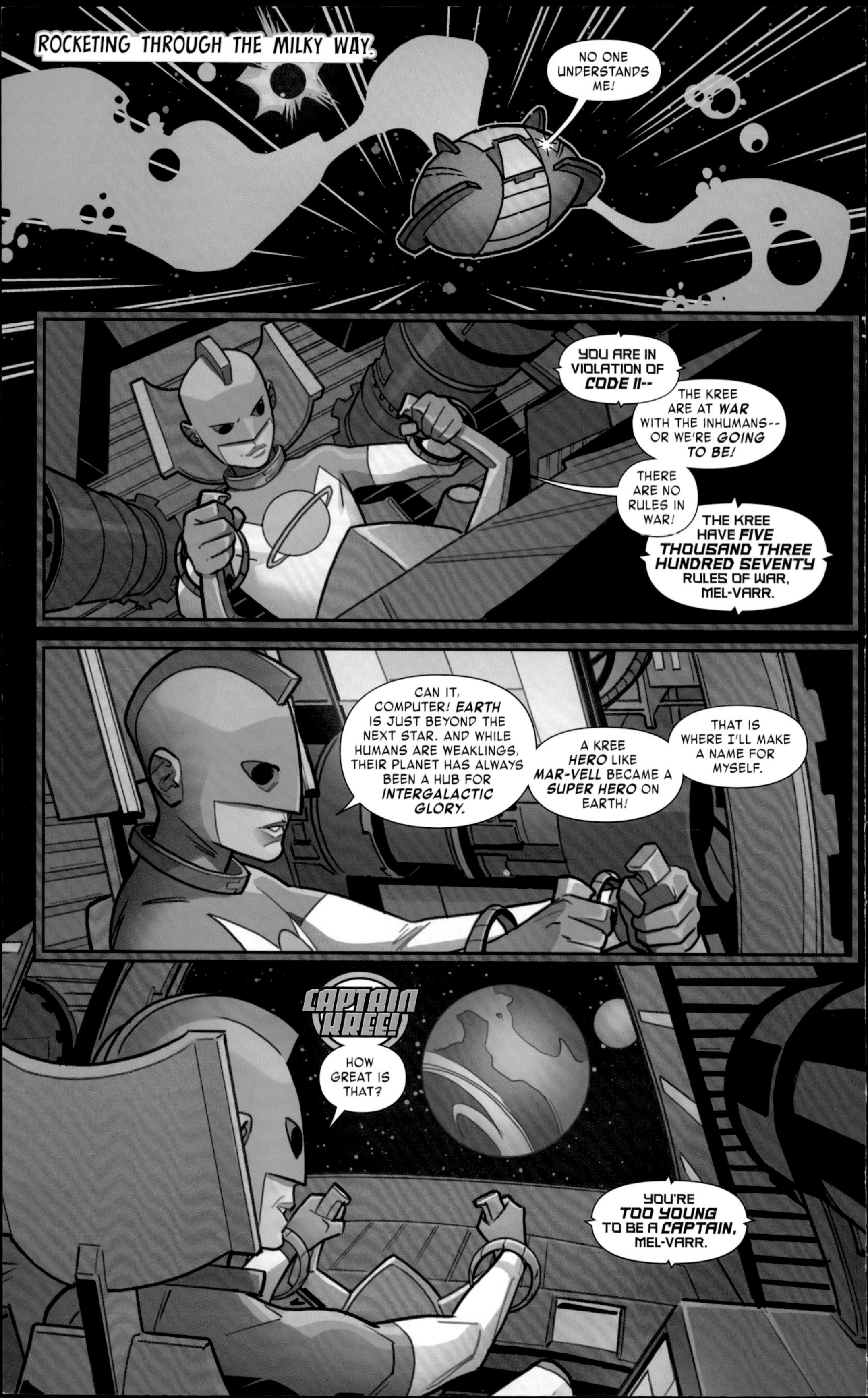
ROCKETING THROUGH THE MILKY WAY.
NO ONE UNDERSTANDS ME!
YOU ARE IN VIOLATION OF CODE 11--
THE KREE ARE AT WAR WITH THE INHUMANS-- OR WE'RE GOING TO BE!
THERE ARE NO RULES IN WAR!
THE KREE HAVE FIVE THOUSAND THREE HUNDRED SEVENTY RULES OF WAR, MEL-VARR.
CAN IT, COMPUTER! EARTH IS JUST BEYOND THE NEXT STAR. AND WHILE HUMANS ARE WEAKLINGS, THEIR PLANET HAS ALWAYS BEEN A HUB FOR INTERGALACTIC GLORY.
A KREE HERO LIKE MAR-VELL BECAME A SUPER HERO ON EARTH!
THAT IS WHERE I'LL MAKE A NAME FOR MYSELF.
CAPTAIN KREE!
HOW GREAT IS THAT?
YOU'RE TOO YOUNG TO BE A CAPTAIN, MEL-VARR.

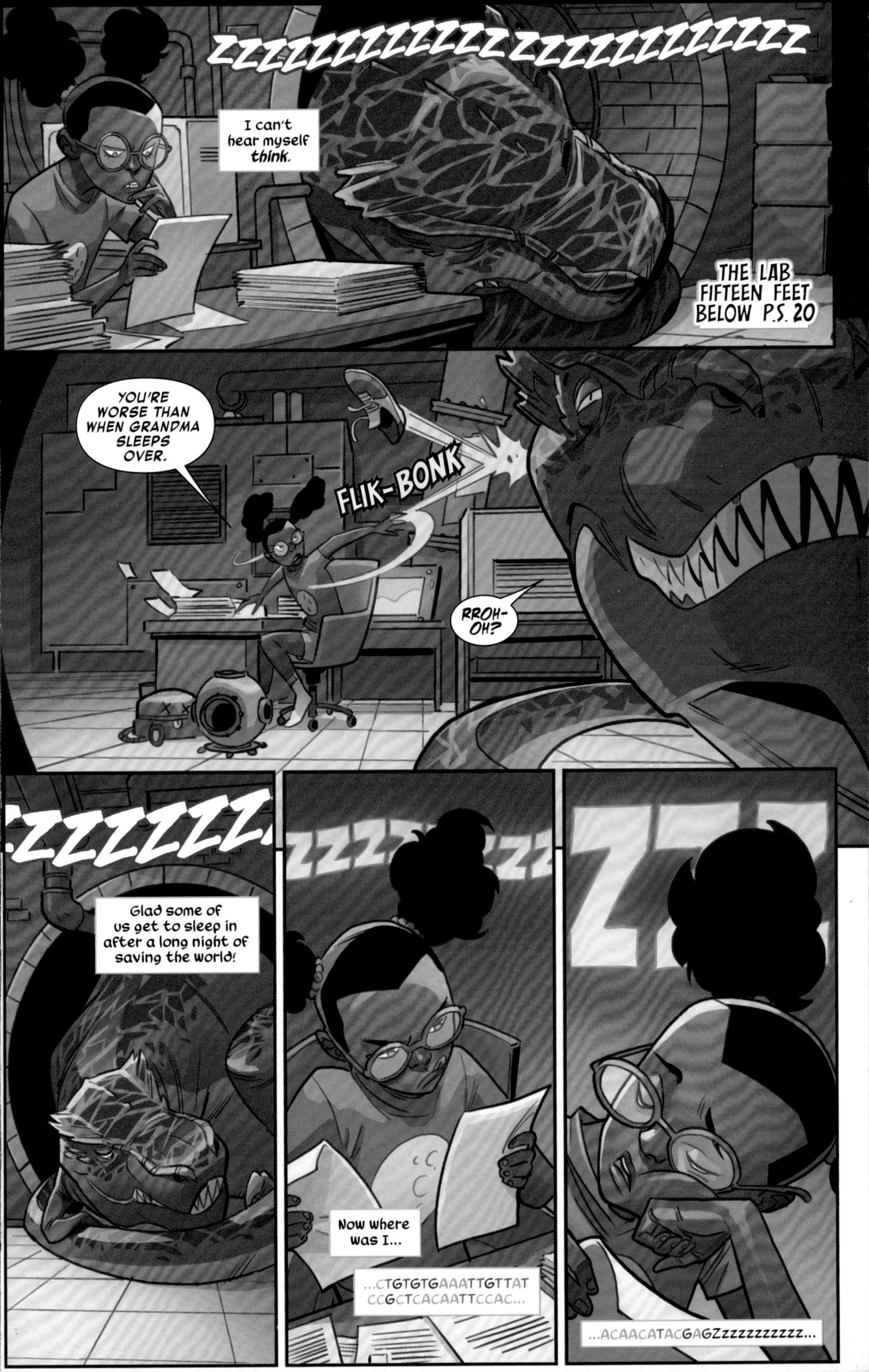
ZZZZZZZZZZZZZZZZZZZZZZZZZZZZZ
I can't hear myself think.
THE LAB FIFTEEN FEET BELOW P.S. 20
YOU'RE WORSE THAN WHEN GRANDMA SLEEPS OVER.
FLIK-BONK
RROH-OH?
ZZZZZZZ
Glad some of us get to sleep in after a long night of saving the world!
ZZZZZZZZZZZ
Now where was I...
...CTGTGTGAAATTGTTAT CCGCTCACAATTCCAC...
ZZ
...ACAACATACGAGZzzzzzzzzz...

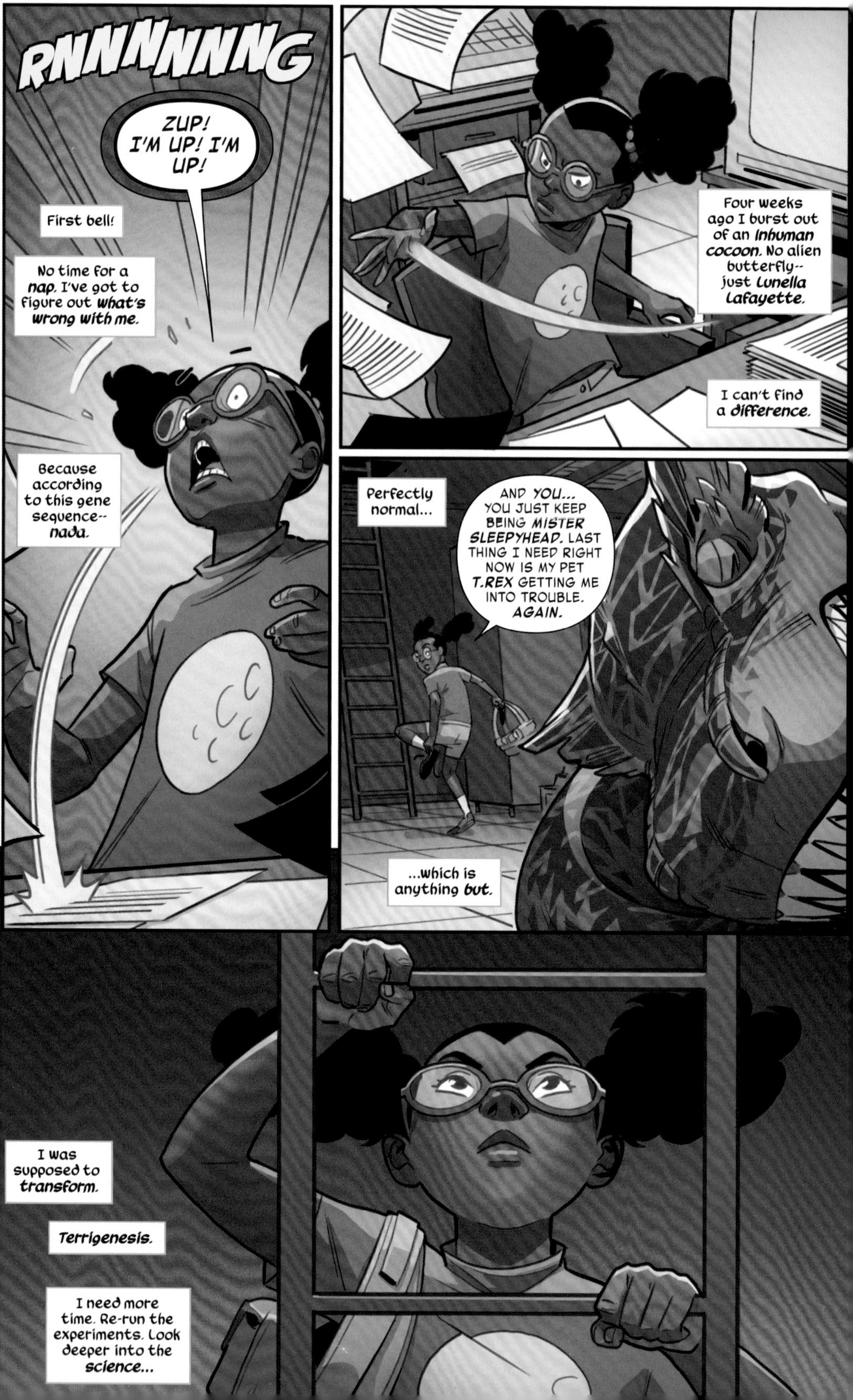

RNNNNNNG
ZUP! I'M UP! I'M UP!
First bell!
No time for a nap. I've got to figure out what's wrong with me.
Because according to this gene sequence-- nada.
Four weeks ago I burst out of an Inhuman cocoon. No alien butterfly-- just Lunella Lafayette.
I can't find a difference.
Perfectly normal...
AND YOU... YOU JUST KEEP BEING MISTER SLEEPYHEAD. LAST THING I NEED RIGHT NOW IS MY PET T.REX GETTING ME INTO TROUBLE. AGAIN.
...which is anything but.
I was supposed to transform.
Terrigenesis.
I need more time. Re-run the experiments. Look deeper into the science...

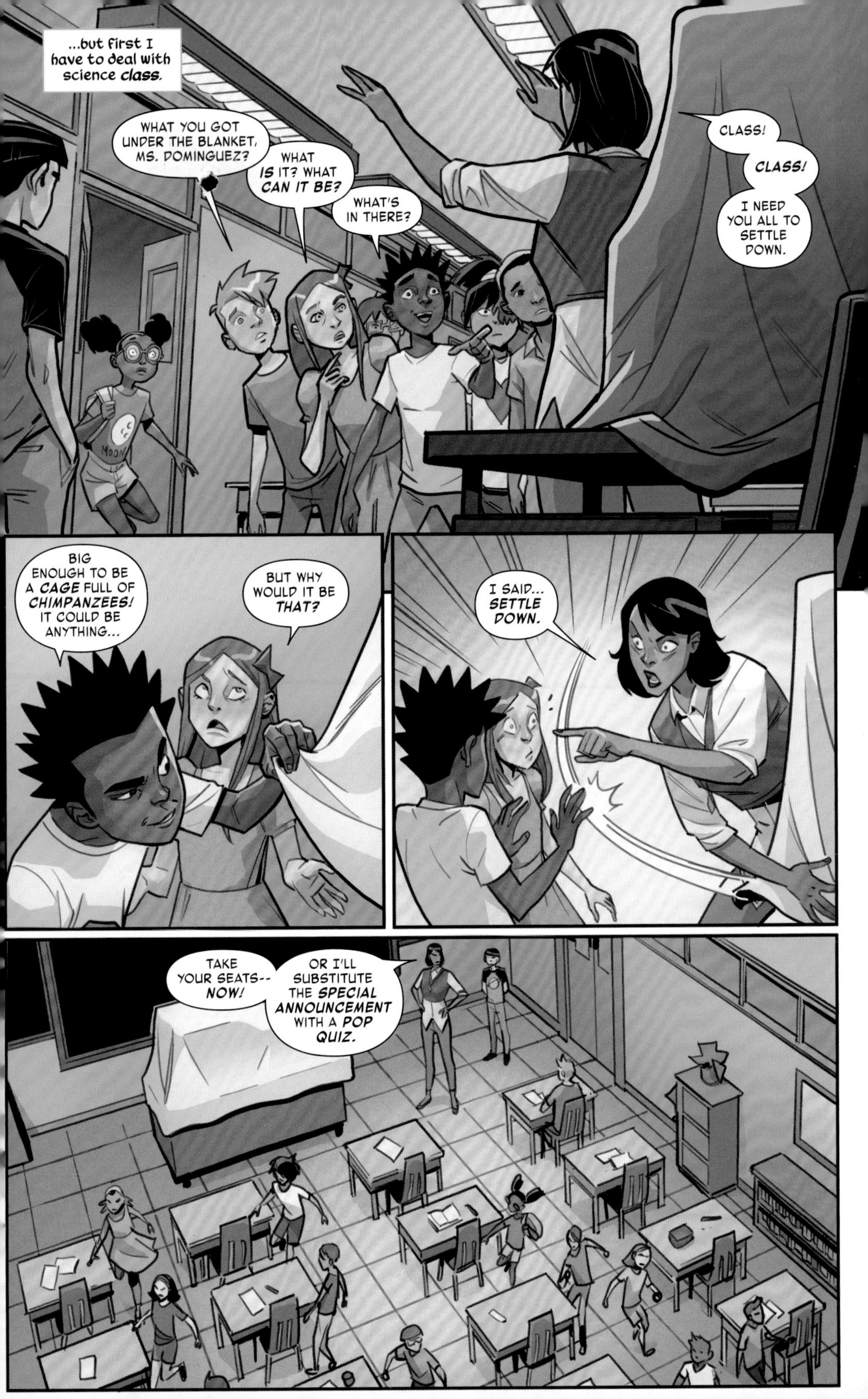
...but first I have to deal with science class.
WHAT YOU GOT UNDER THE BLANKET, MS. DOMINGUEZ?
WHAT IS IT? WHAT CAN IT BE?
WHAT'S IN THERE?
CLASS!
CLASS!
I NEED YOU ALL TO SETTLE DOWN.
MOON
BIG ENOUGH TO BE A CAGE FULL OF CHIMPANZEES! IT COULD BE ANYTHING...
BUT WHY WOULD IT BE THAT?
I SAID... SETTLE DOWN.
TAKE YOUR SEATS-- NOW!
OR I'LL SUBSTITUTE THE SPECIAL ANNOUNCEMENT WITH A POP QUIZ.

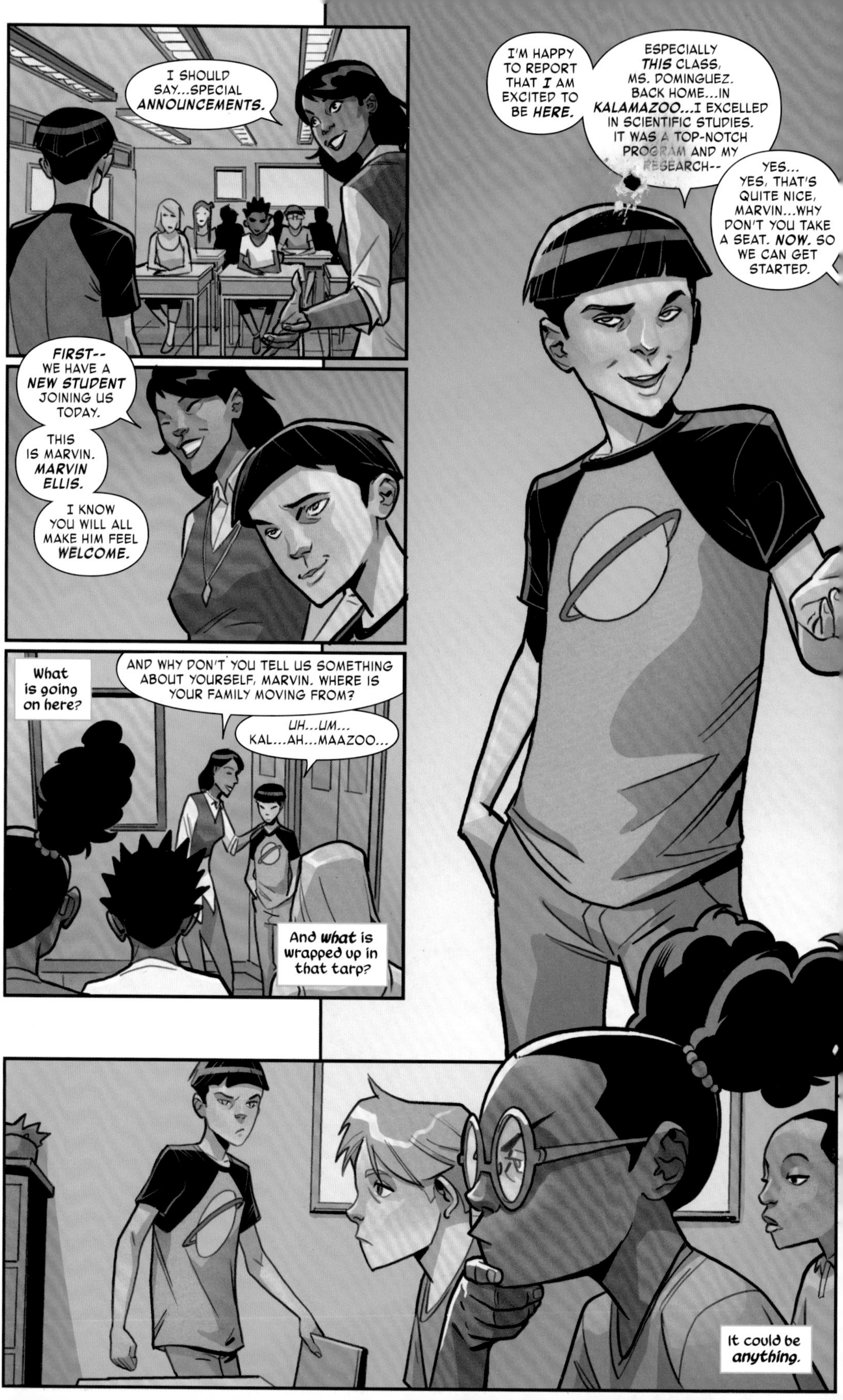
I SHOULD SAY...SPECIAL ANNOUNCEMENTS.
FIRST-- WE HAVE A NEW STUDENT JOINING US TODAY.
THIS IS MARVIN. MARVIN ELLIS.
I KNOW YOU WILL ALL MAKE HIM FEEL WELCOME.
What is going on here?
AND WHY DON'T YOU TELL US SOMETHING ABOUT YOURSELF, MARVIN. WHERE IS YOUR FAMILY MOVING FROM?
UH...UM... KAL...AH...MAAZOO...
And what is wrapped up in that tarp?
I'M HAPPY TO REPORT THAT I AM EXCITED TO BE HERE.
ESPECIALLY THIS CLASS, MS. DOMINGUEZ. BACK HOME...IN KALAMAZOO...I EXCELLED IN SCIENTIFIC STUDIES. IT WAS A TOP-NOTCH PROGRAM AND MY RESEARCH--
YES... YES, THAT'S QUITE NICE, MARVIN...WHY DON'T YOU TAKE A SEAT. NOW. SO WE CAN GET STARTED.
It could be anything.

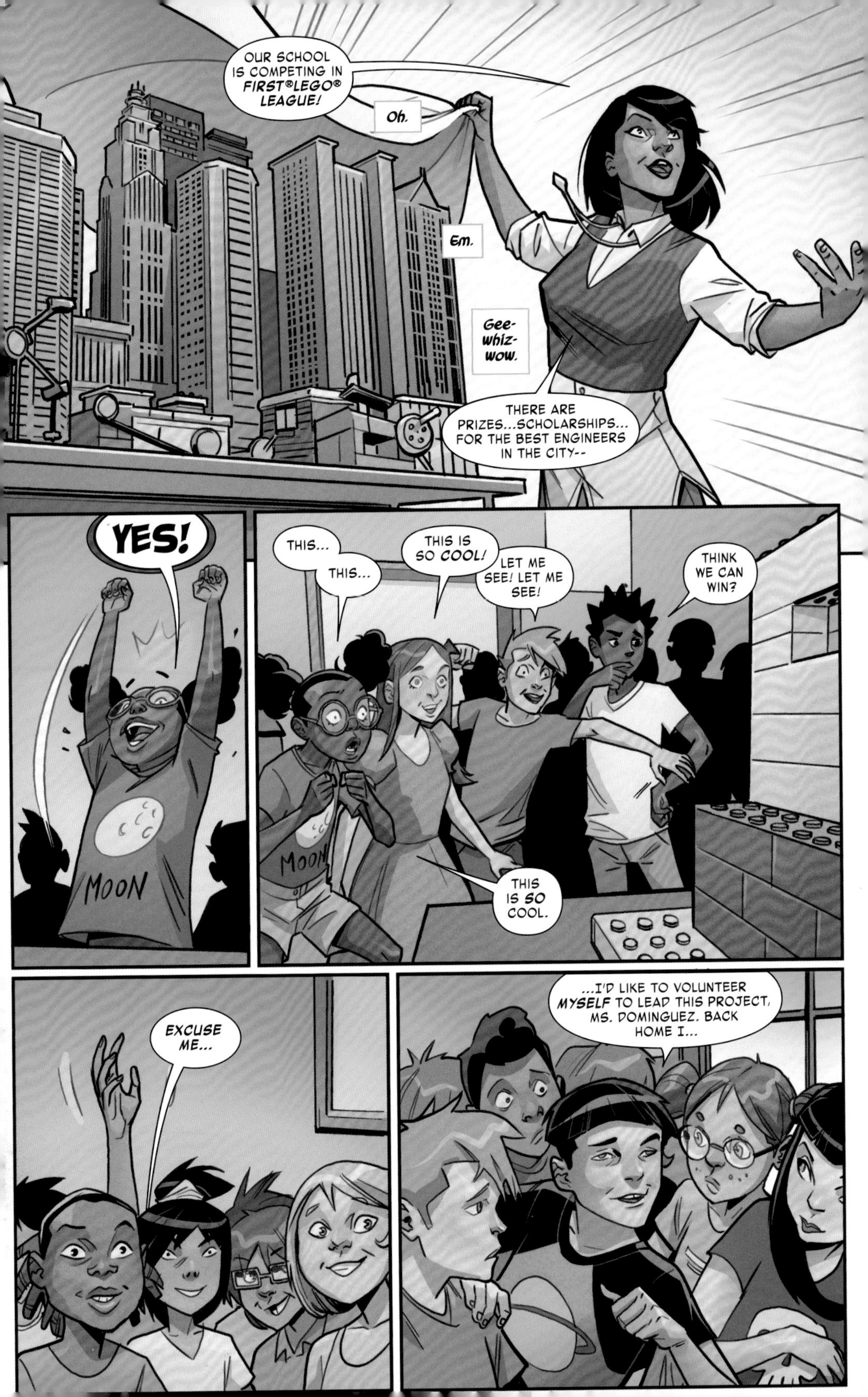
OUR SCHOOL IS COMPETING IN FIRST®LEGO® LEAGUE!
Oh.
Em.
Gee-whiz-wow.
THERE ARE PRIZES...SCHOLARSHIPS... FOR THE BEST ENGINEERS IN THE CITY--
YES!
THIS...
THIS...
THIS IS SO COOL!
LET ME SEE! LET ME SEE!
THINK WE CAN WIN?
MOON
THIS IS SO COOL.
EXCUSE ME...
...I'D LIKE TO VOLUNTEER MYSELF TO LEAD THIS PROJECT, MS. DOMINGUEZ. BACK HOME I...

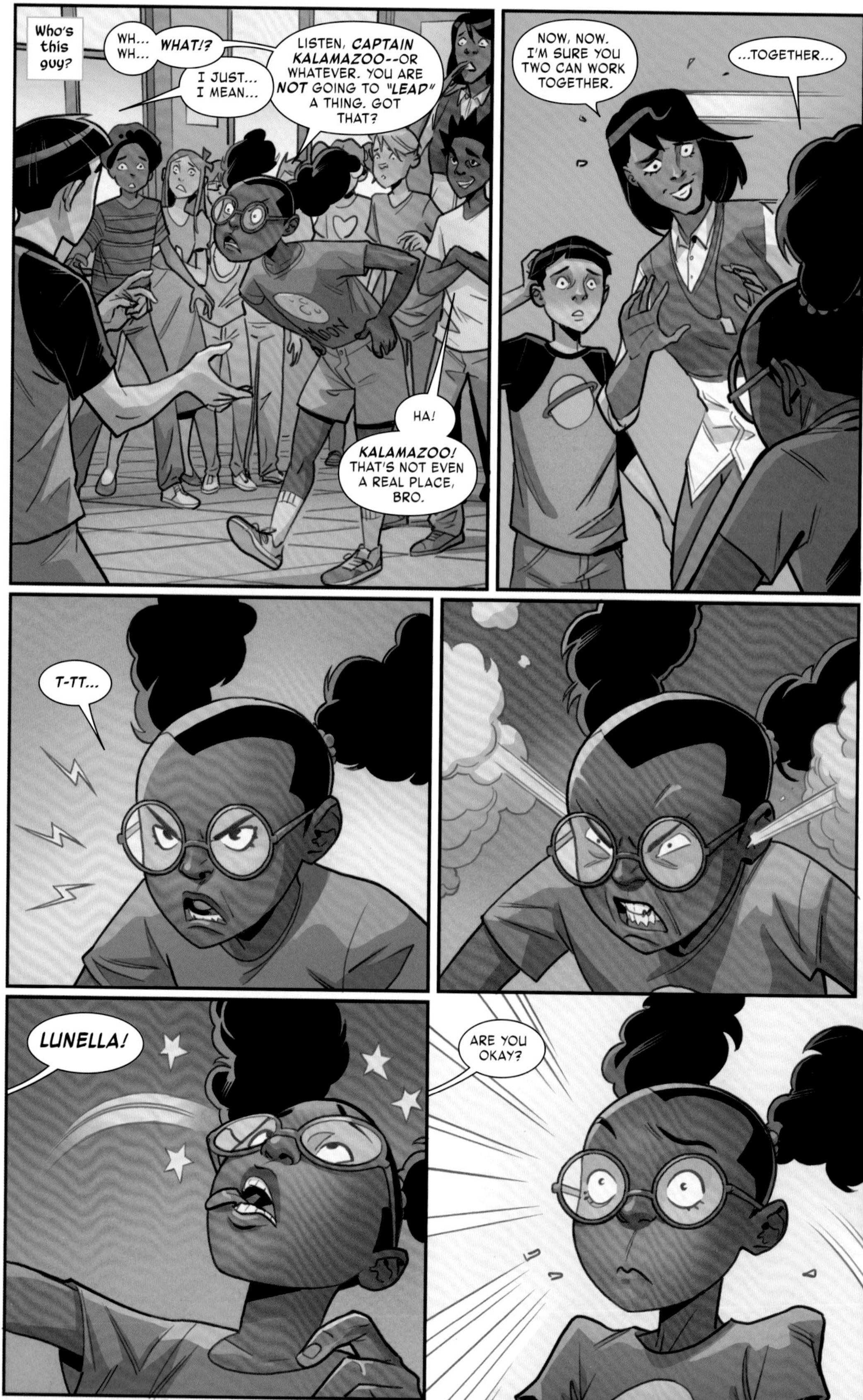
Who's this guy?
WH... WH... WHAT!?
I JUST... I MEAN...
LISTEN, CAPTAIN KALAMAZOO--OR WHATEVER. YOU ARE NOT GOING TO "LEAD" A THING. GOT THAT?
HA!
KALAMAZOO! THAT'S NOT EVEN A REAL PLACE, BRO.
NOW, NOW. I'M SURE YOU TWO CAN WORK TOGETHER.
...TOGETHER...
T-TT...
LUNELLA!
ARE YOU OKAY?

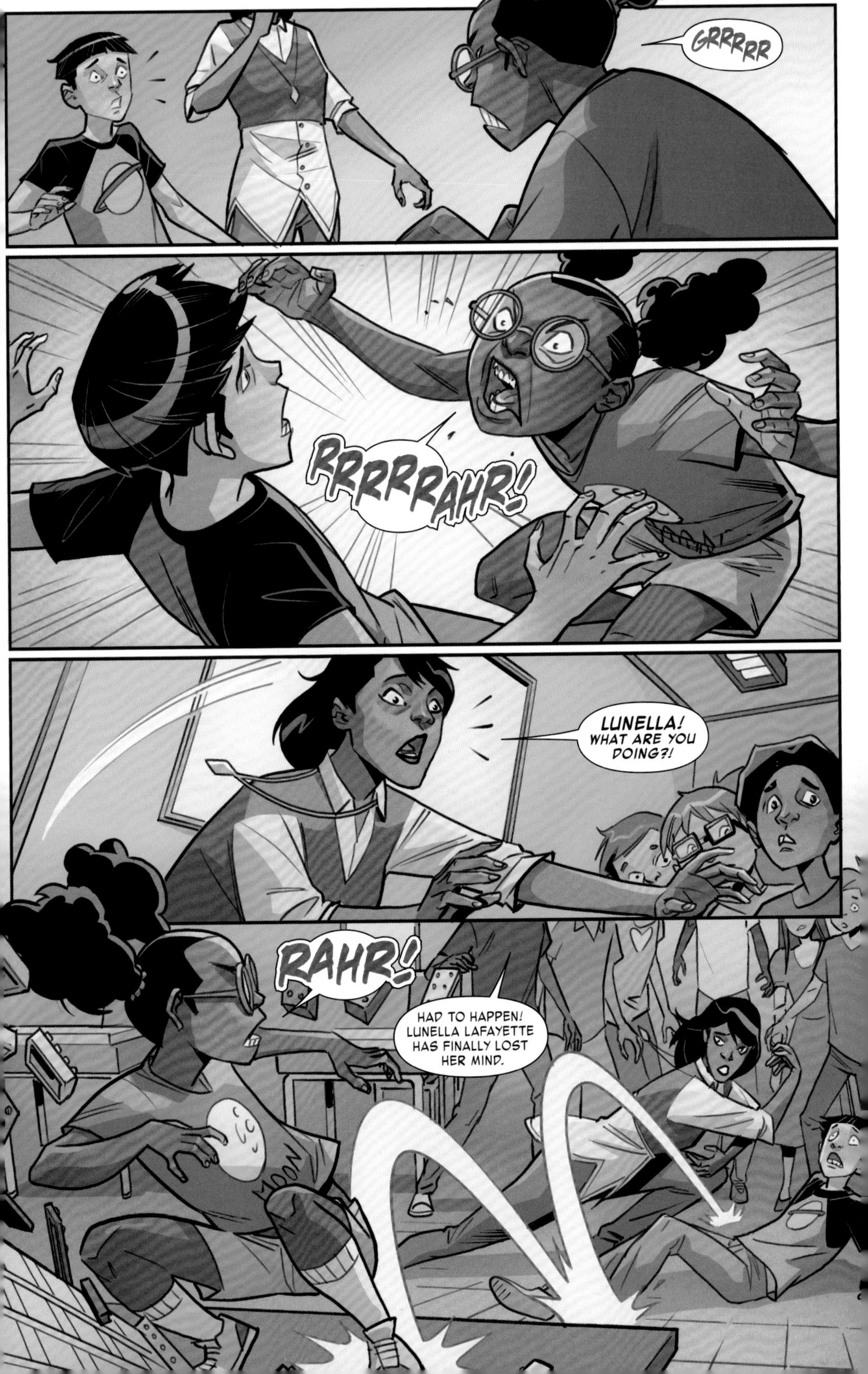
GRRRRR
RRRRRAHR!
LUNELLA! WHAT ARE YOU DOING?!
RAHR!
HAD TO HAPPEN! LUNELLA LAFAYETTE HAS FINALLY LOST HER MIND.

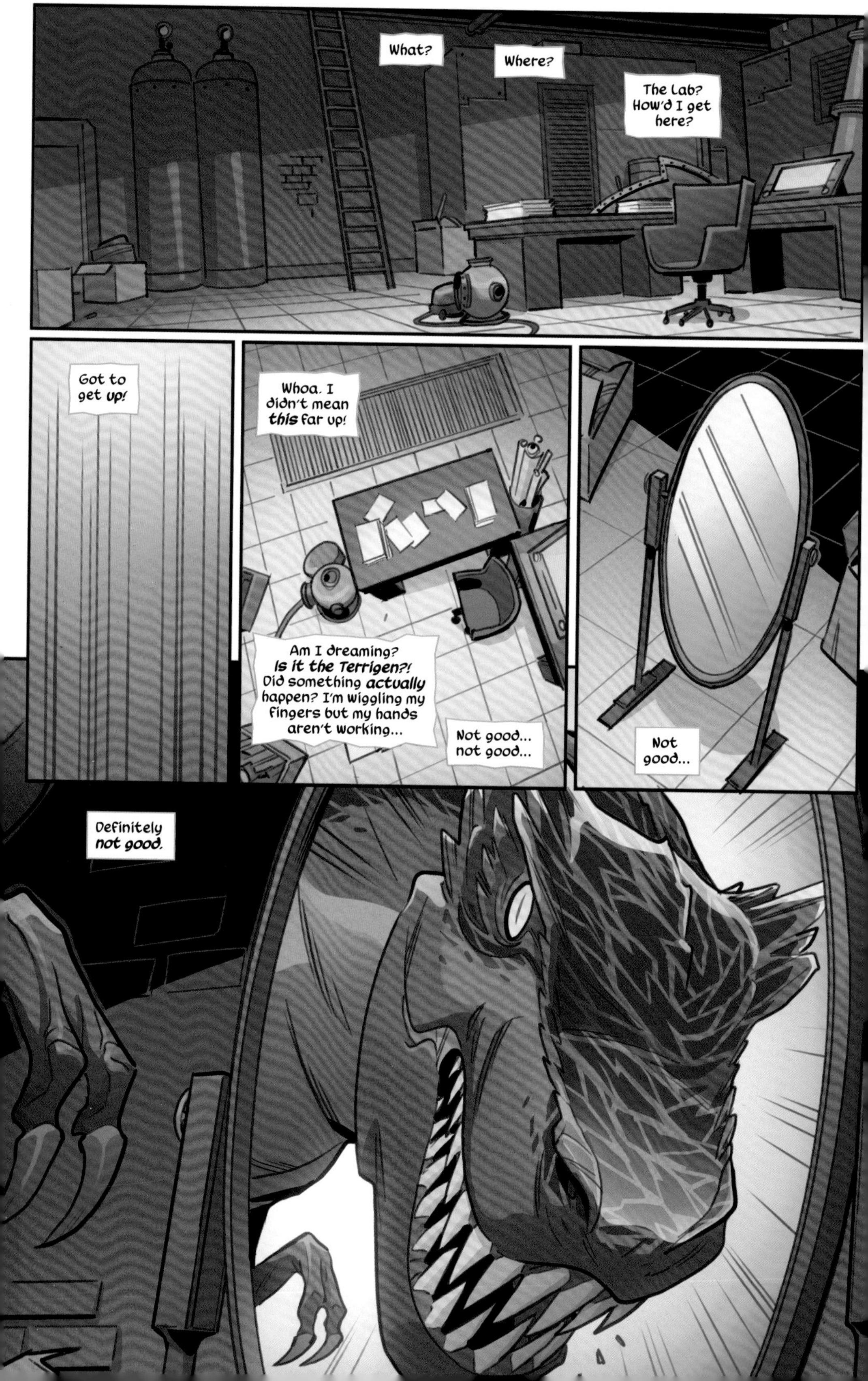
What?
Where?
The Lab? How'd I get here?
Got to get *up!*
Whoa. I didn't mean **this** far up!
Am I dreaming? ***Is it the Terrigen?!*** Did something ***actually*** happen? I'm wiggling my fingers but my hands aren't working...
Not good... not good...
Not good...
Definitely ***not good.***

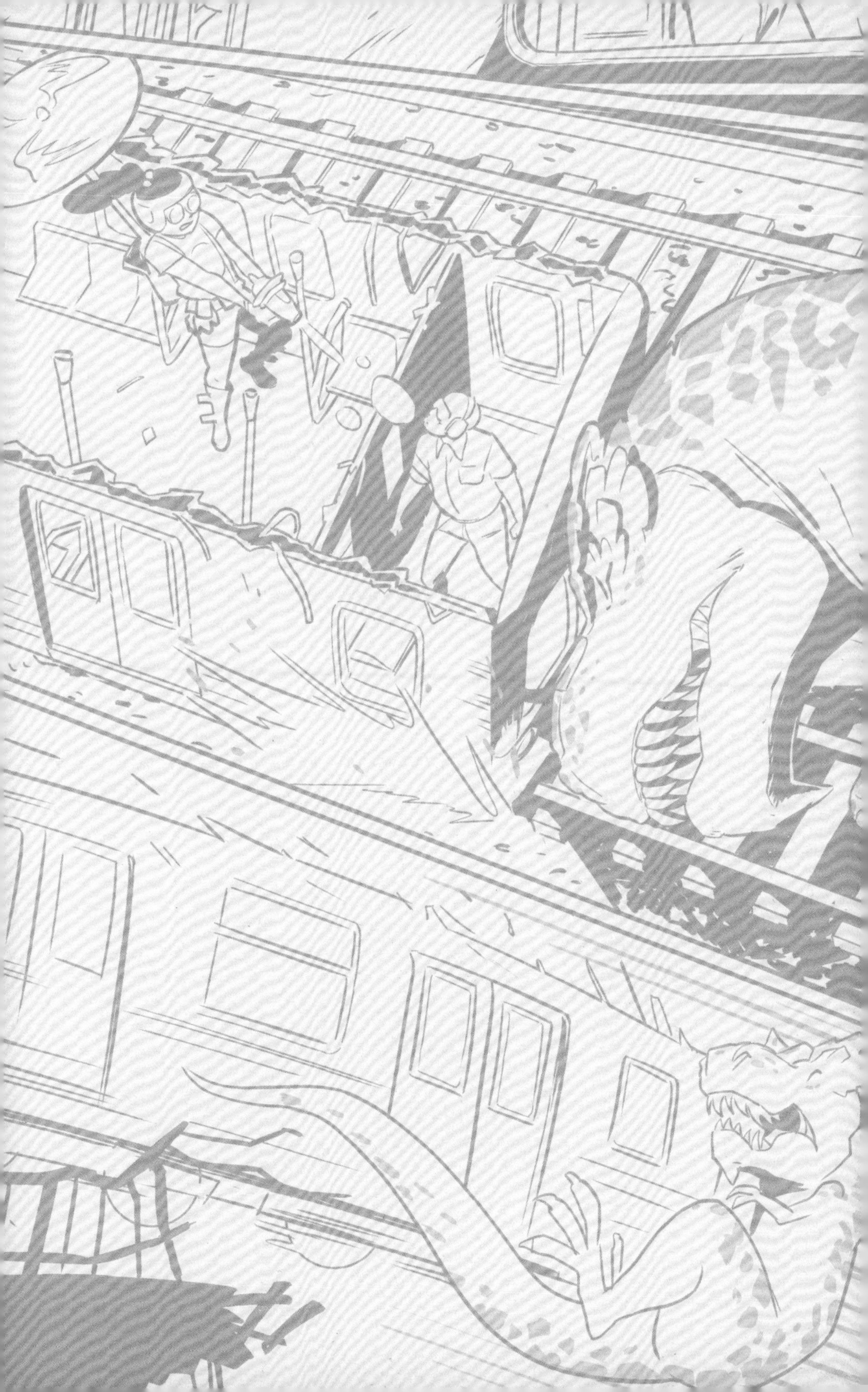

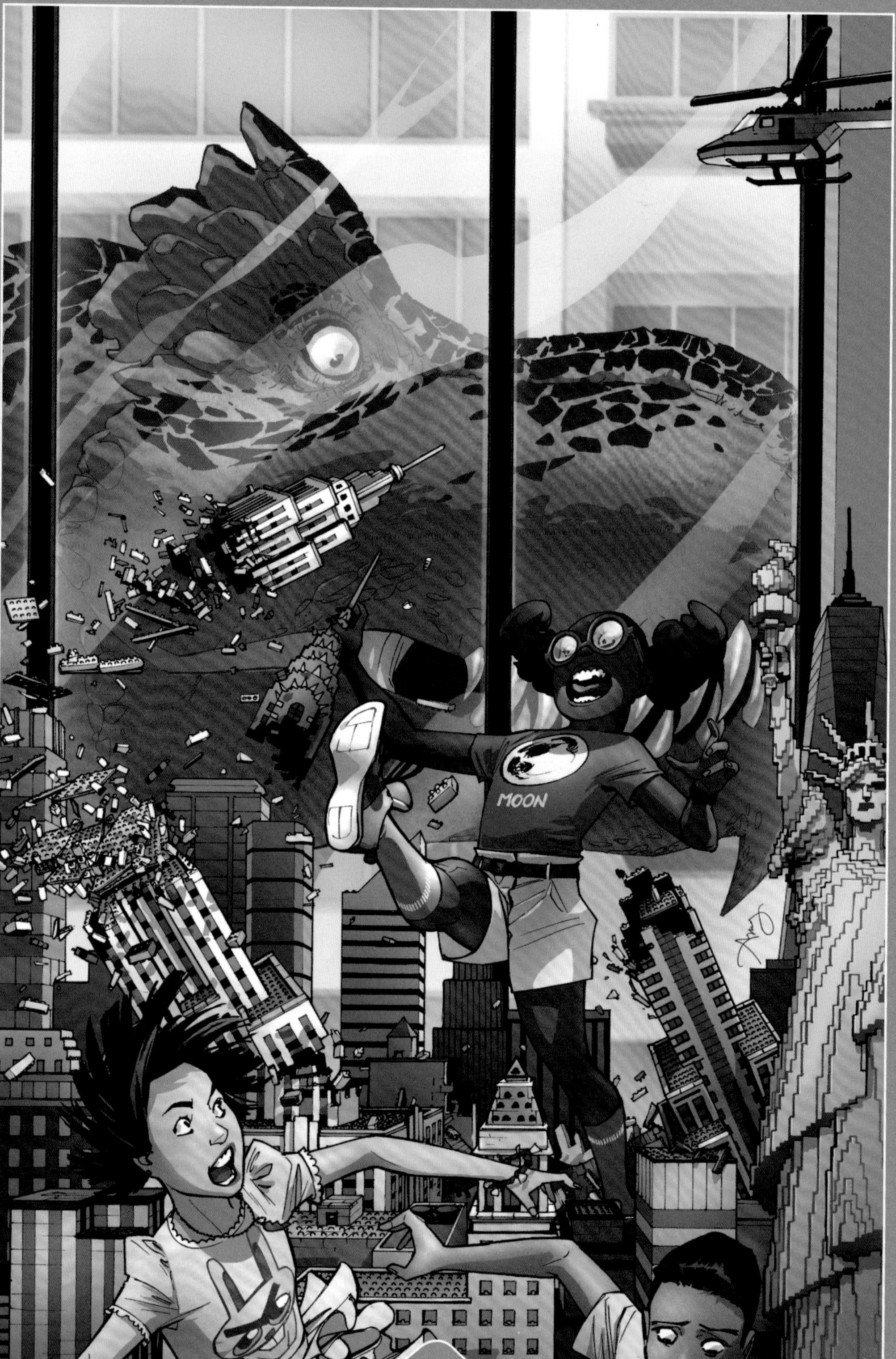
MOON

8

"SWITCHEROO"

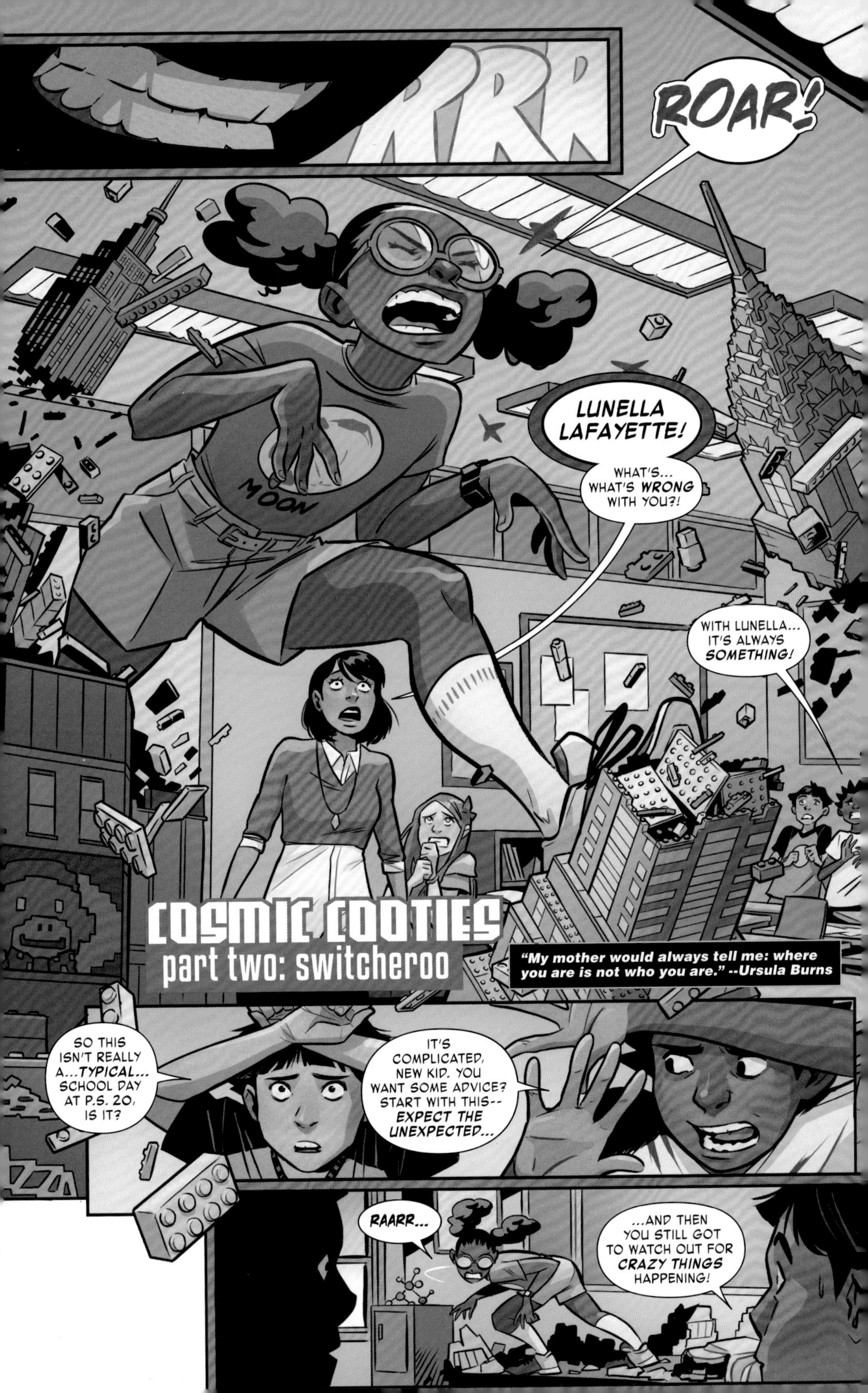
RRR
ROAR!
LUNELLA LAFAYETTE!
WHAT'S... WHAT'S WRONG WITH YOU?!
WITH LUNELLA... IT'S ALWAYS SOMETHING!
MOON
COSMIC COOTIES
part two: switcheroo
"My mother would always tell me: where you are is not who you are." --Ursula Burns
SO THIS ISN'T REALLY A...TYPICAL... SCHOOL DAY AT P.S. 20, IS IT?
IT'S COMPLICATED, NEW KID. YOU WANT SOME ADVICE? START WITH THIS-- EXPECT THE UNEXPECTED...
RAARR...
...AND THEN YOU STILL GOT TO WATCH OUT FOR CRAZY THINGS HAPPENING!

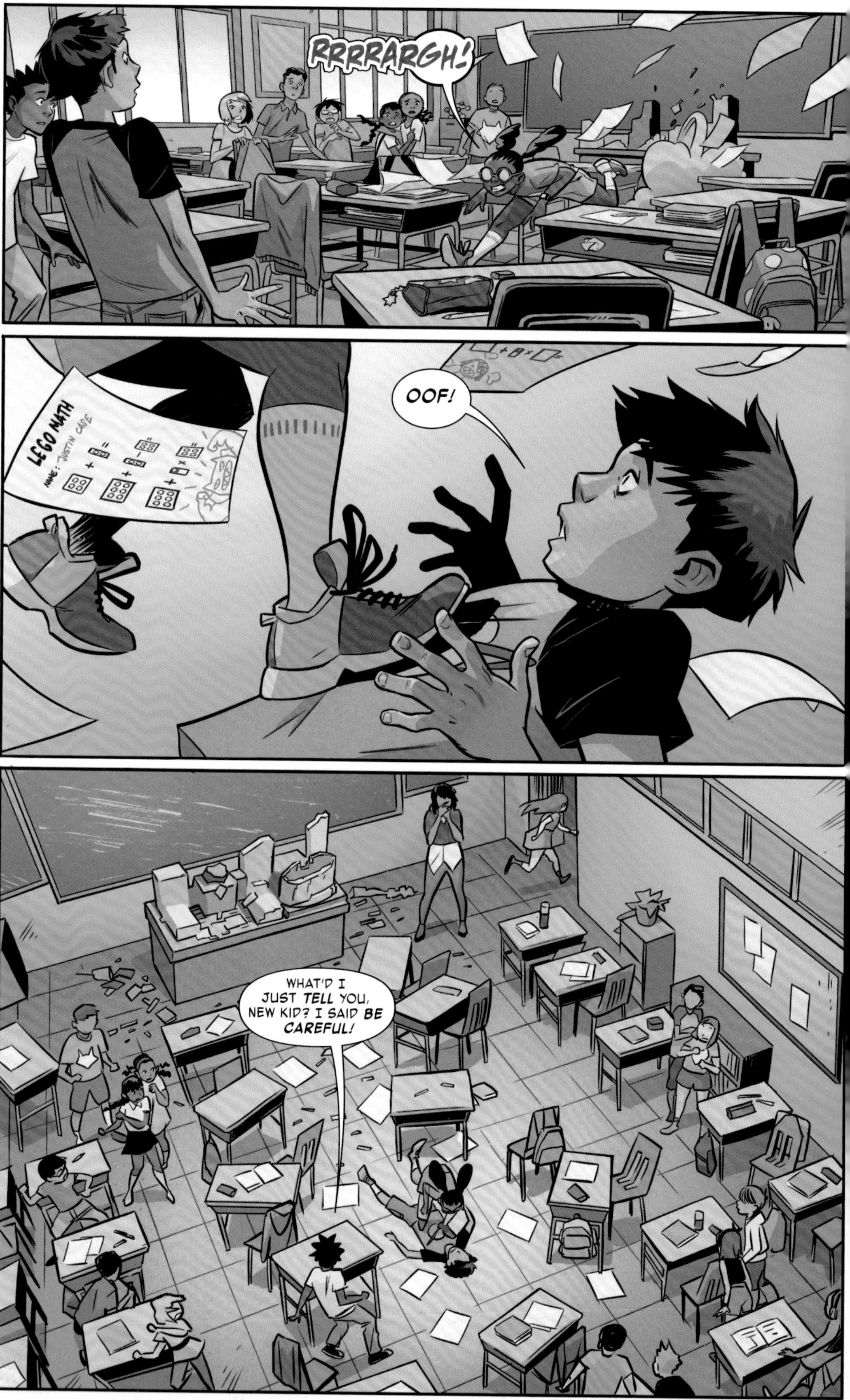
RRRRARGH!
OOF!
LEGO MATH
NAME: JUSTIN CASE
WHAT'D I JUST TELL YOU, NEW KID? I SAID BE CAREFUL!

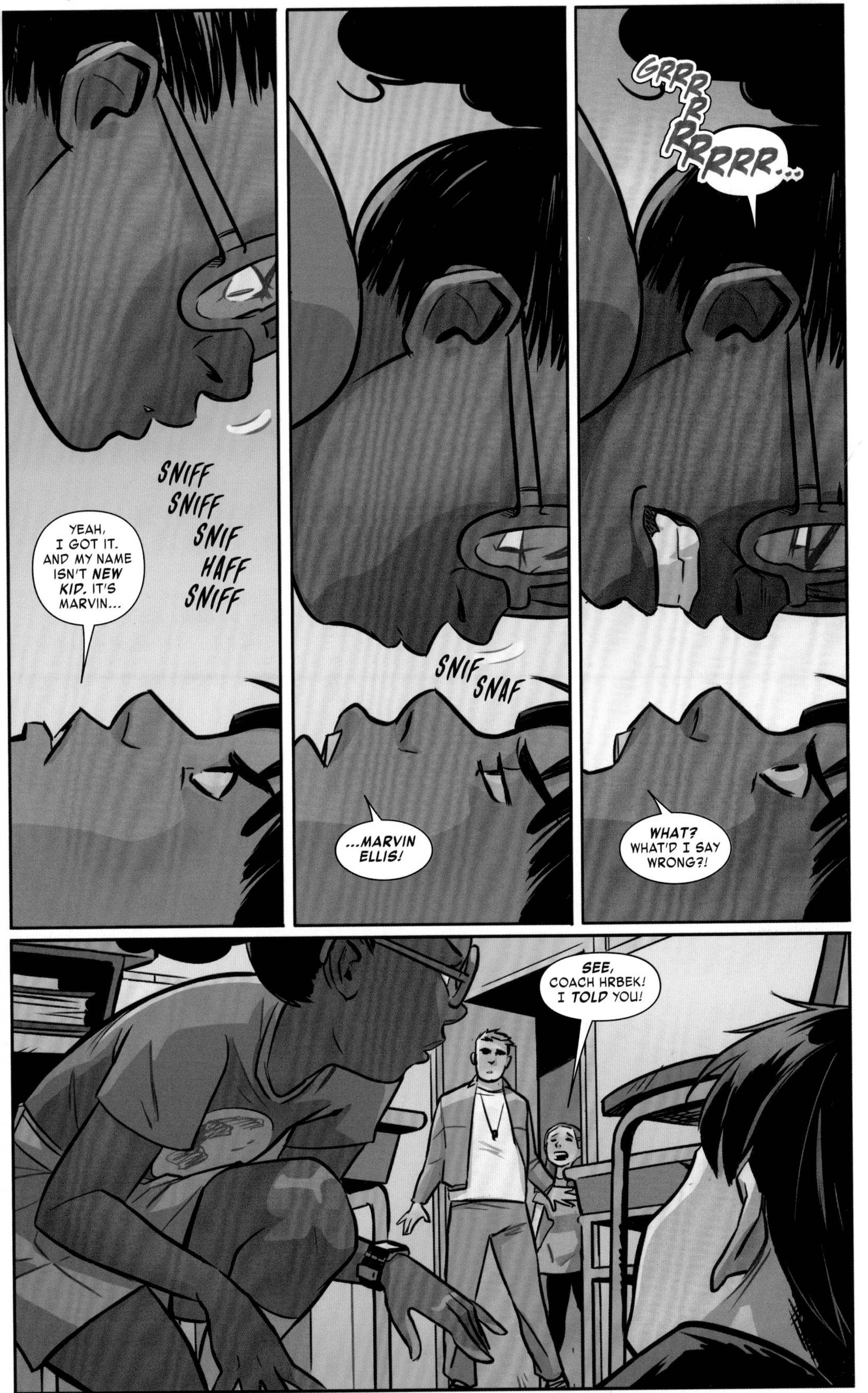
SNIFF SNIFF SNIF HAFF SNIFF
YEAH, I GOT IT. AND MY NAME ISN'T NEW KID. IT'S MARVIN...
SNIF SNAF
...MARVIN ELLIS!
GRRRRRRRRR...
WHAT? WHAT'D I SAY WRONG?!
SEE, COACH HRBEK! I TOLD YOU!

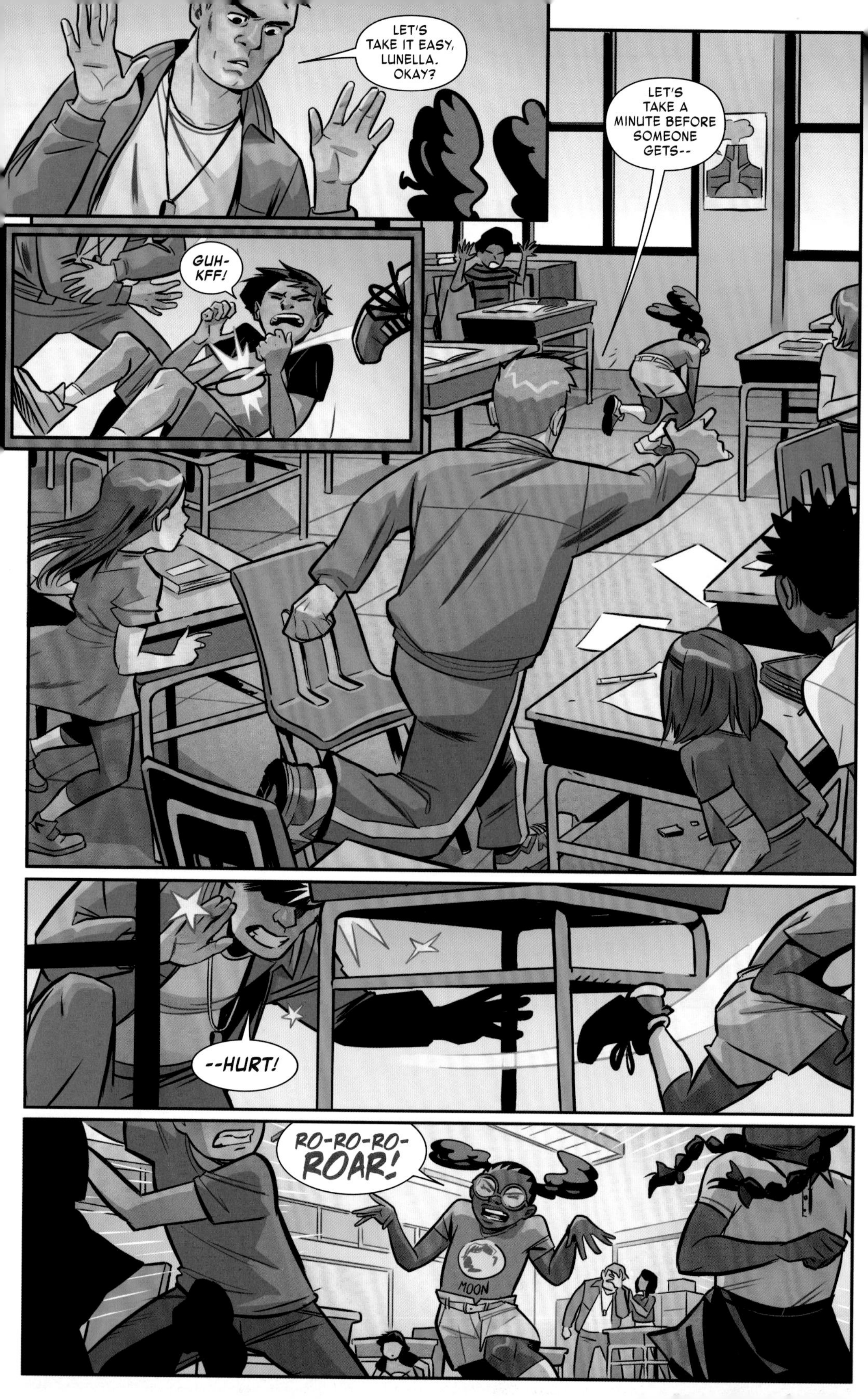

LET'S TAKE IT EASY, LUNELLA. OKAY?
LET'S TAKE A MINUTE BEFORE SOMEONE GETS--
GUH-KFF!
--HURT!
RO-RO-RO-ROAR!
MOON

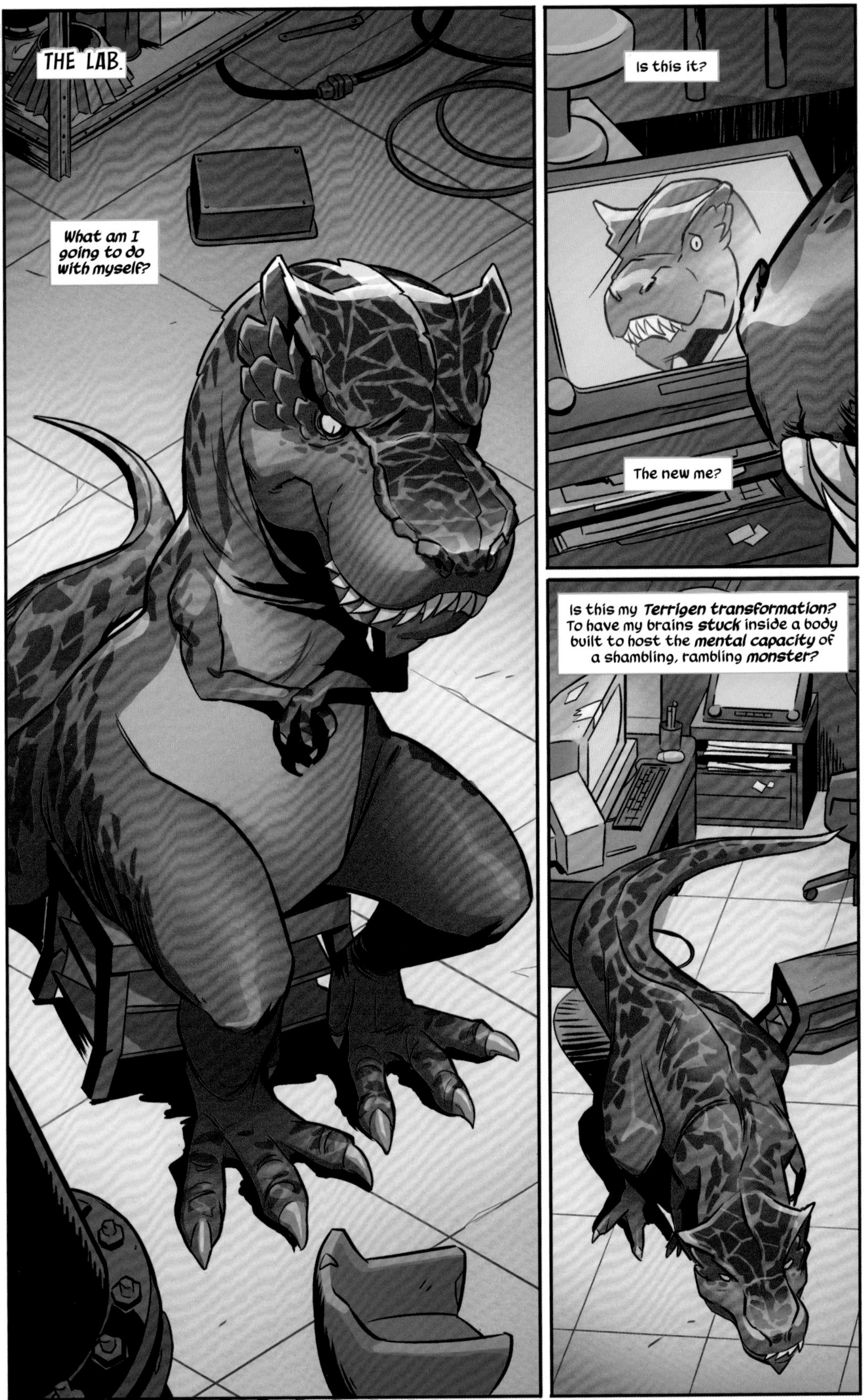
THE LAB.
What am I going to do with myself?
Is this it?
The new me?
Is this my *Terrigen transformation?* To have my brains **stuck** inside a body built to host the *mental capacity* of a shambling, rambling *monster?*

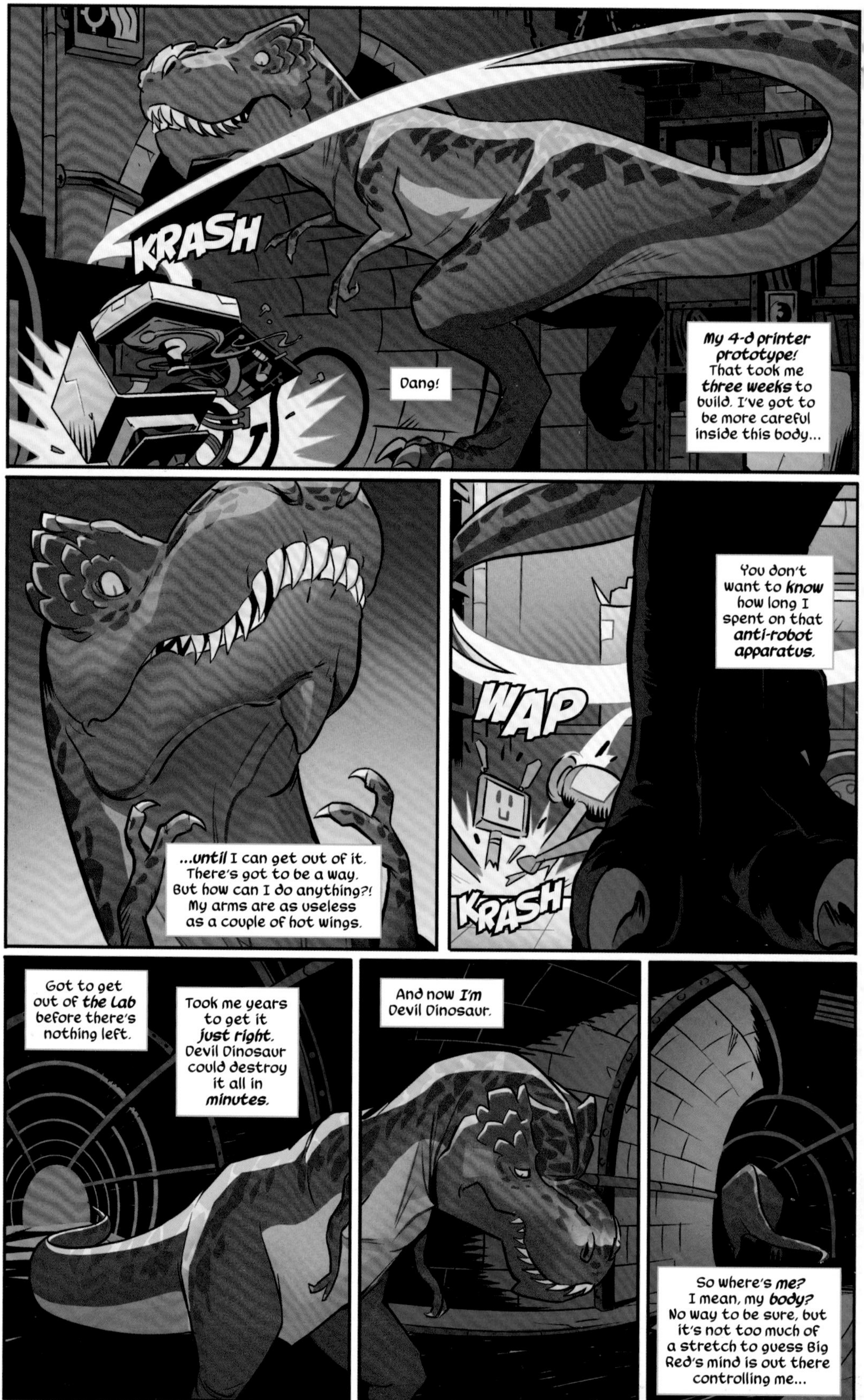
KRASH
Dang!
My 4-d printer prototype! That took me three weeks to build. I've got to be more careful inside this body...
...until I can get out of it. There's got to be a way. But how can I do anything?! My arms are as useless as a couple of hot wings.
You don't want to know how long I spent on that anti-robot apparatus.
WAP
KRASH
Got to get out of the Lab before there's nothing left.
Took me years to get it just right. Devil Dinosaur could destroy it all in minutes.
And now I'm Devil Dinosaur.
So where's me? I mean, my body? No way to be sure, but it's not too much of a stretch to guess Big Red's mind is out there controlling me...

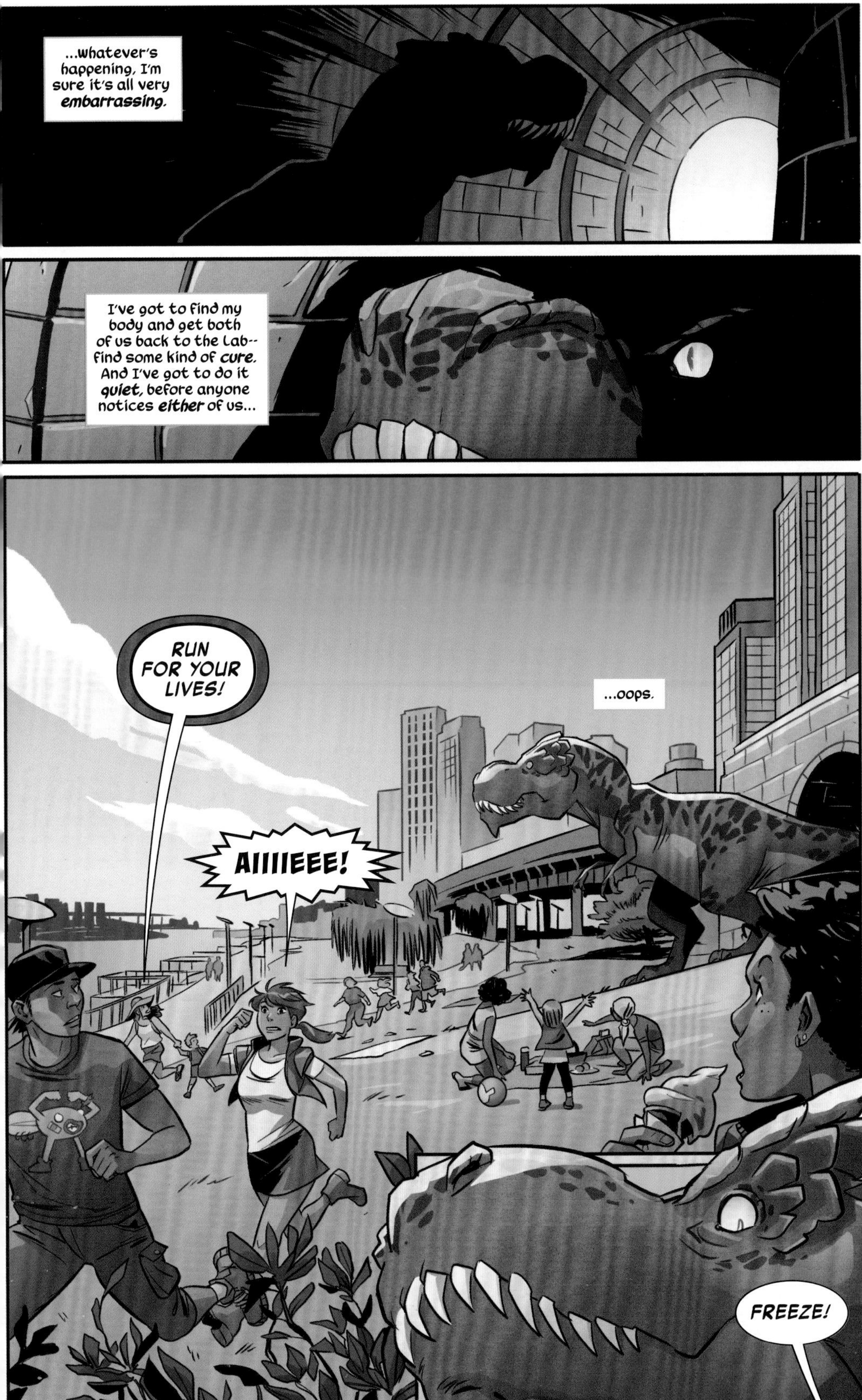
...whatever's happening, I'm sure it's all very *embarrassing.*
I've got to find my body and get both of us back to the Lab-- find some kind of *cure.* And I've got to do it *quiet,* before anyone notices *either* of us...
RUN FOR YOUR LIVES!
...oops.
AIIIIEEE!
FREEZE!

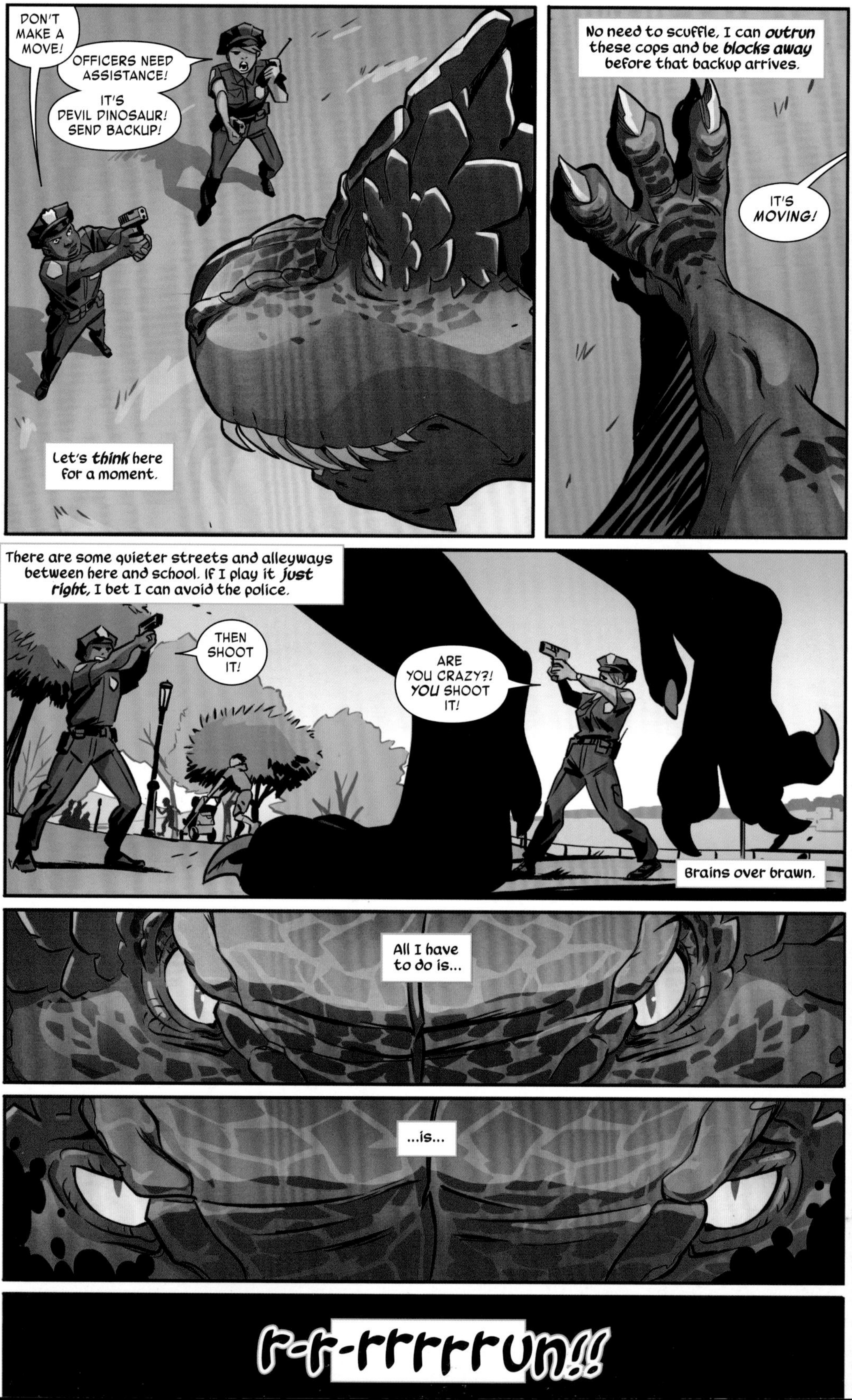
DON'T MAKE A MOVE!
OFFICERS NEED ASSISTANCE!
IT'S DEVIL DINOSAUR! SEND BACKUP!
Let's *think* here for a moment.
No need to scuffle, I can *outrun* these cops and be *blocks away* before that backup arrives.
IT'S *MOVING!*
There are some quieter streets and alleyways between here and school. If I play it *just right*, I bet I can avoid the police.
THEN SHOOT IT!
ARE YOU CRAZY?! *YOU* SHOOT IT!
Brains over brawn.
All I have to do is...
...is...
R-R-RRRRRUN!!

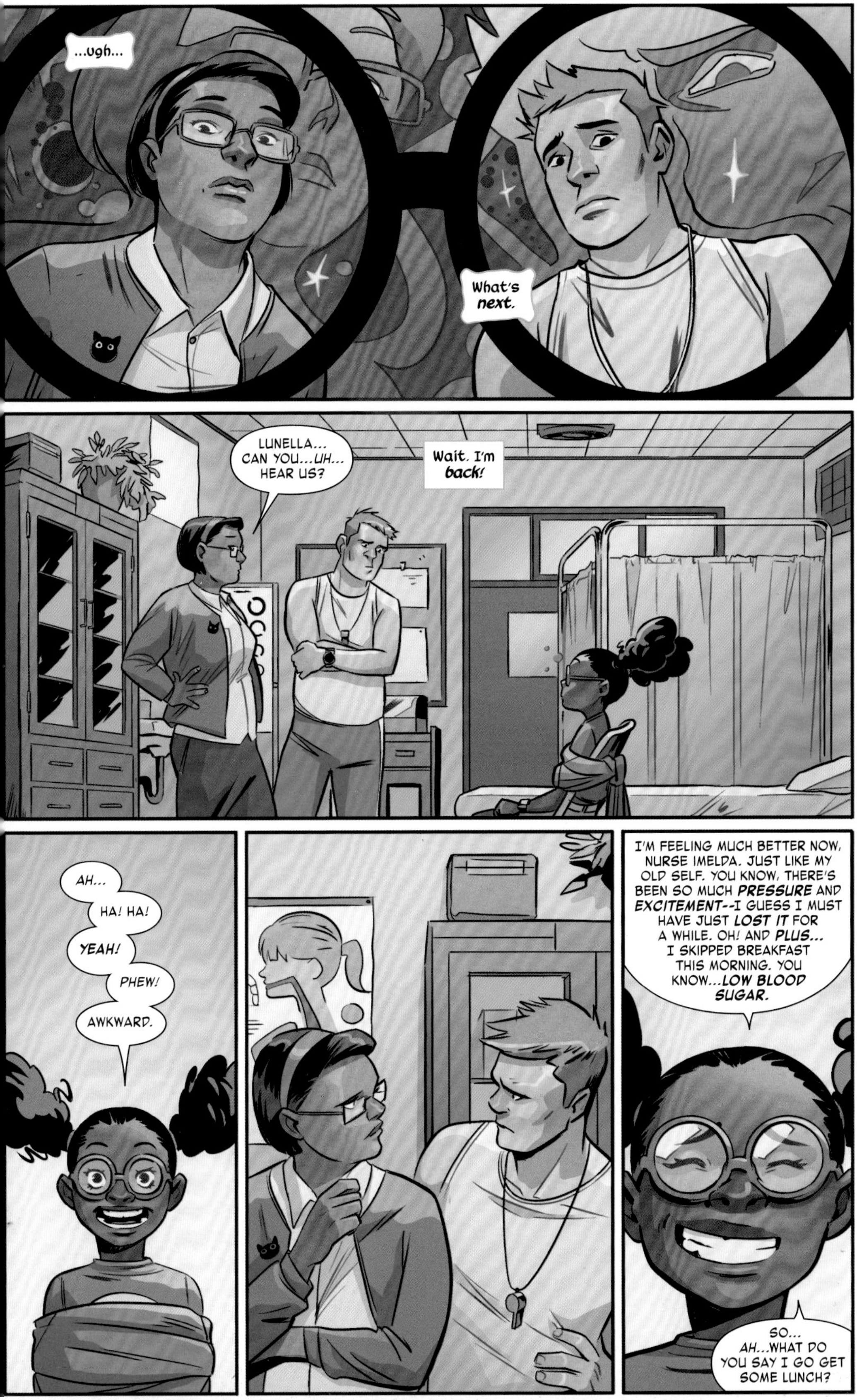
...ugh...
What's next.
LUNELLA... CAN YOU...UH... HEAR US?
Wait. I'm back!
AH...
HA! HA!
YEAH!
PHEW!
AWKWARD.
I'M FEELING MUCH BETTER NOW, NURSE IMELDA. JUST LIKE MY OLD SELF. YOU KNOW, THERE'S BEEN SO MUCH PRESSURE AND EXCITEMENT--I GUESS I MUST HAVE JUST LOST IT FOR A WHILE. OH! AND PLUS... I SKIPPED BREAKFAST THIS MORNING. YOU KNOW...LOW BLOOD SUGAR.
SO... AH...WHAT DO YOU SAY I GO GET SOME LUNCH?

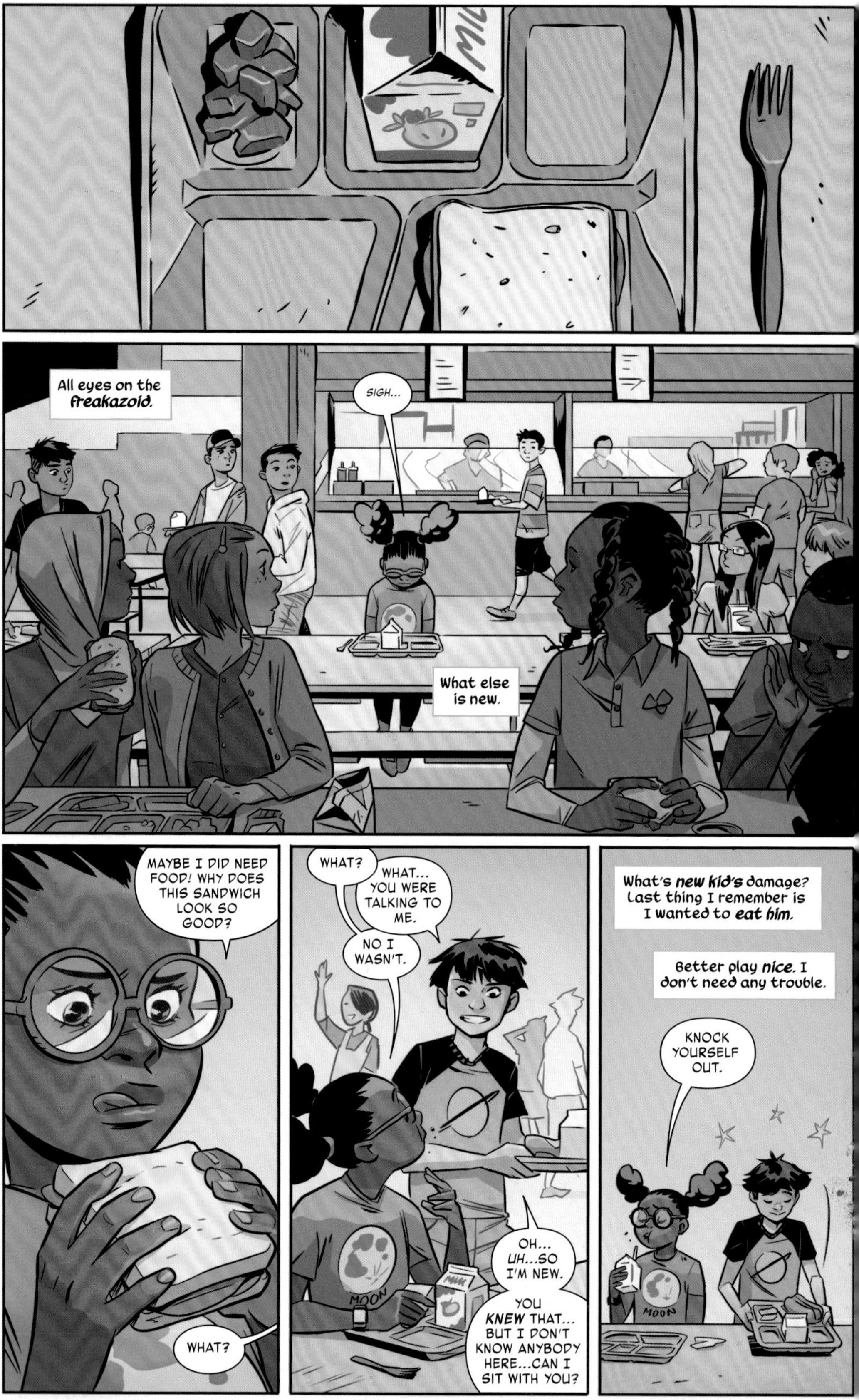
MILK
All eyes on the *freakazoid.*
SIGH...
What else is new.
MAYBE I DID NEED FOOD! WHY DOES THIS SANDWICH LOOK SO GOOD?
WHAT?
WHAT?
WHAT... YOU WERE TALKING TO ME.
NO I WASN'T.
OH... UH...SO I'M NEW.
YOU *KNEW* THAT... BUT I DON'T KNOW ANYBODY HERE...CAN I SIT WITH YOU?
MOON
What's *new kid's* damage? Last thing I remember is I wanted to *eat him.*
Better play *nice.* I don't need any trouble.
KNOCK YOURSELF OUT.
MOON

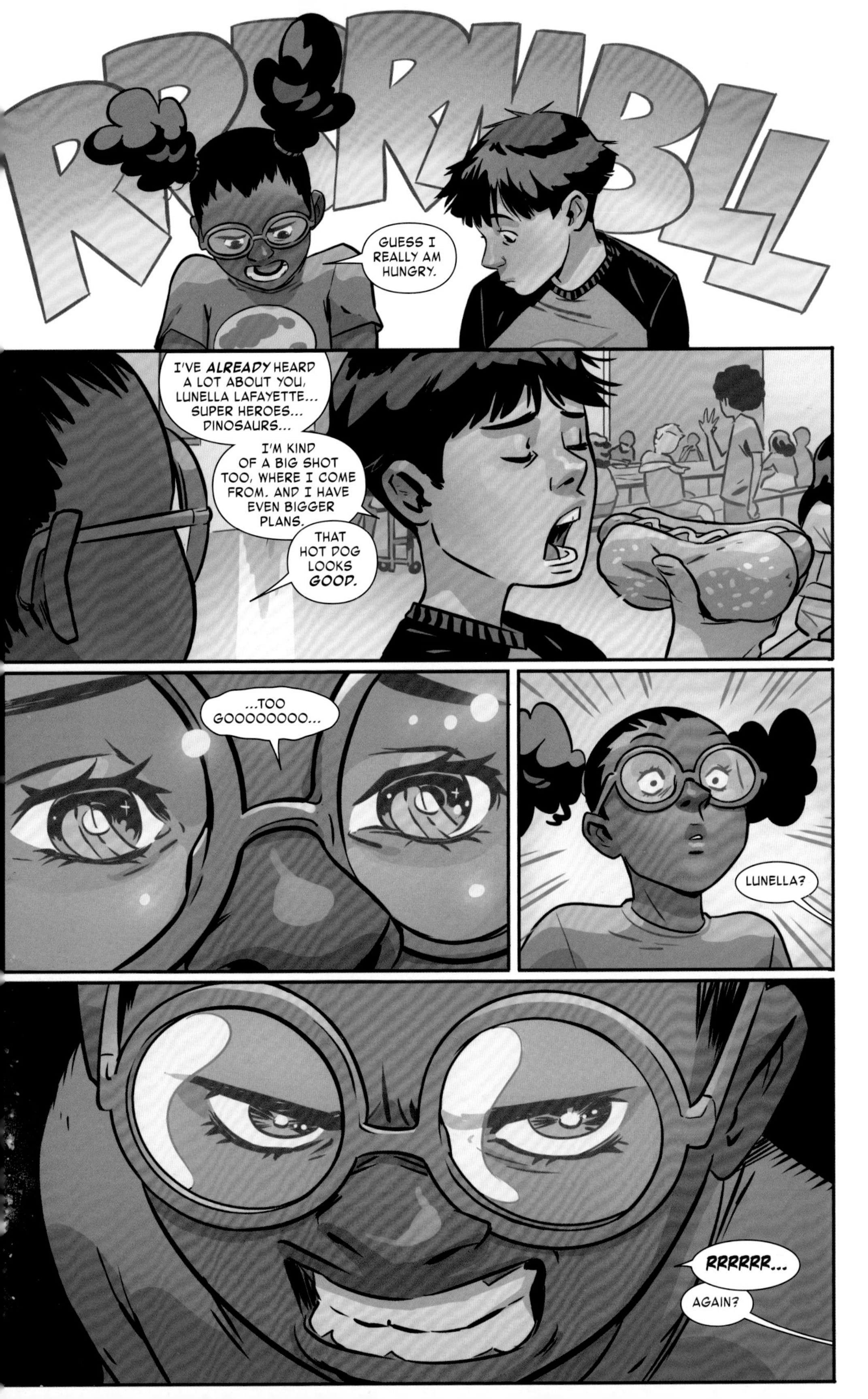
RRRUMBLLL
GUESS I REALLY AM HUNGRY.
I'VE ALREADY HEARD A LOT ABOUT YOU, LUNELLA LAFAYETTE... SUPER HEROES... DINOSAURS...
I'M KIND OF A BIG SHOT TOO, WHERE I COME FROM. AND I HAVE EVEN BIGGER PLANS.
THAT HOT DOG LOOKS GOOD.
...TOO GOOOOOOOO...
LUNELLA?
RRRRRR...
AGAIN?

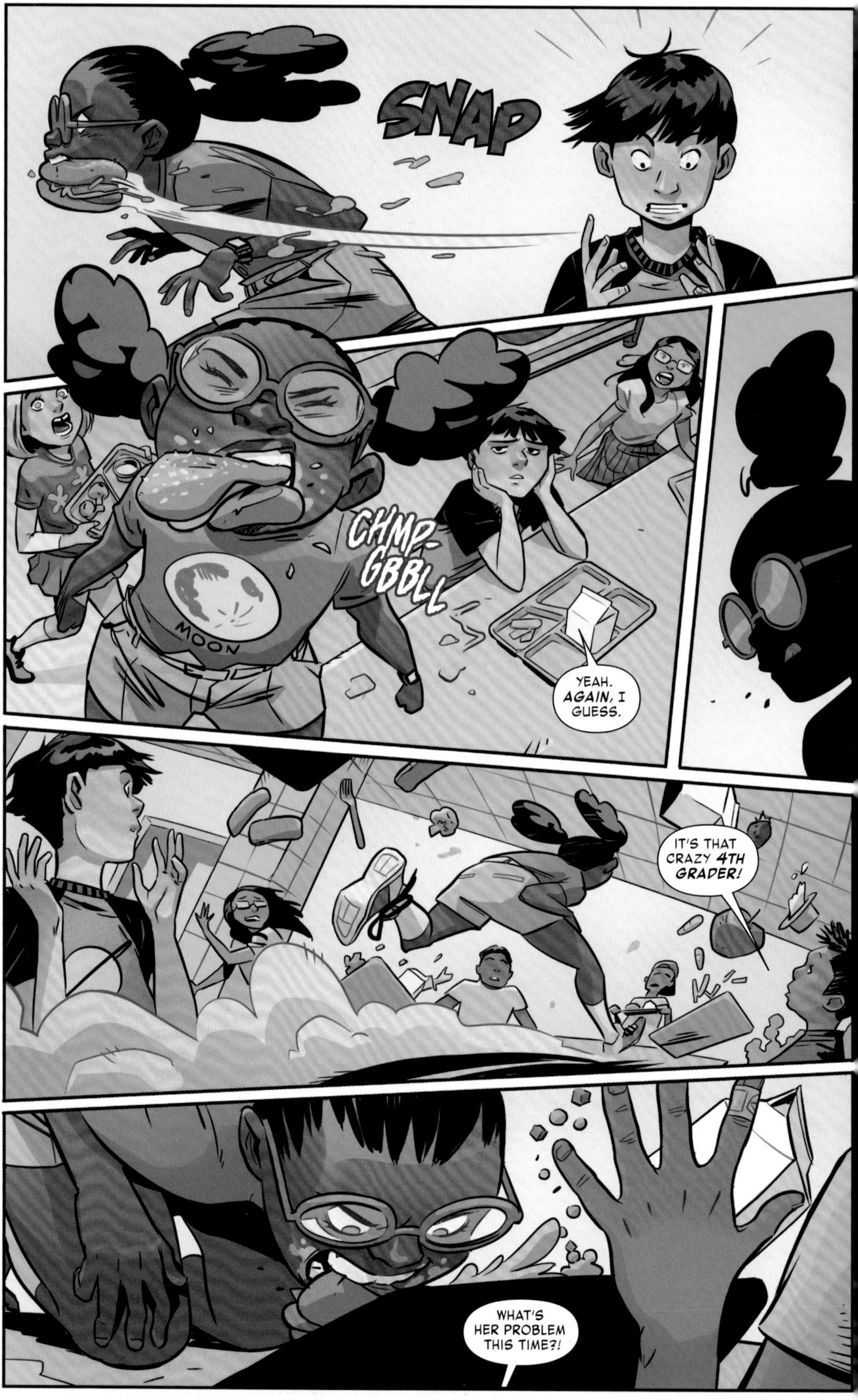
SNAP
CHMP-GBBLL
YEAH. AGAIN, I GUESS.
IT'S THAT CRAZY 4TH GRADER!
WHAT'S HER PROBLEM THIS TIME?!

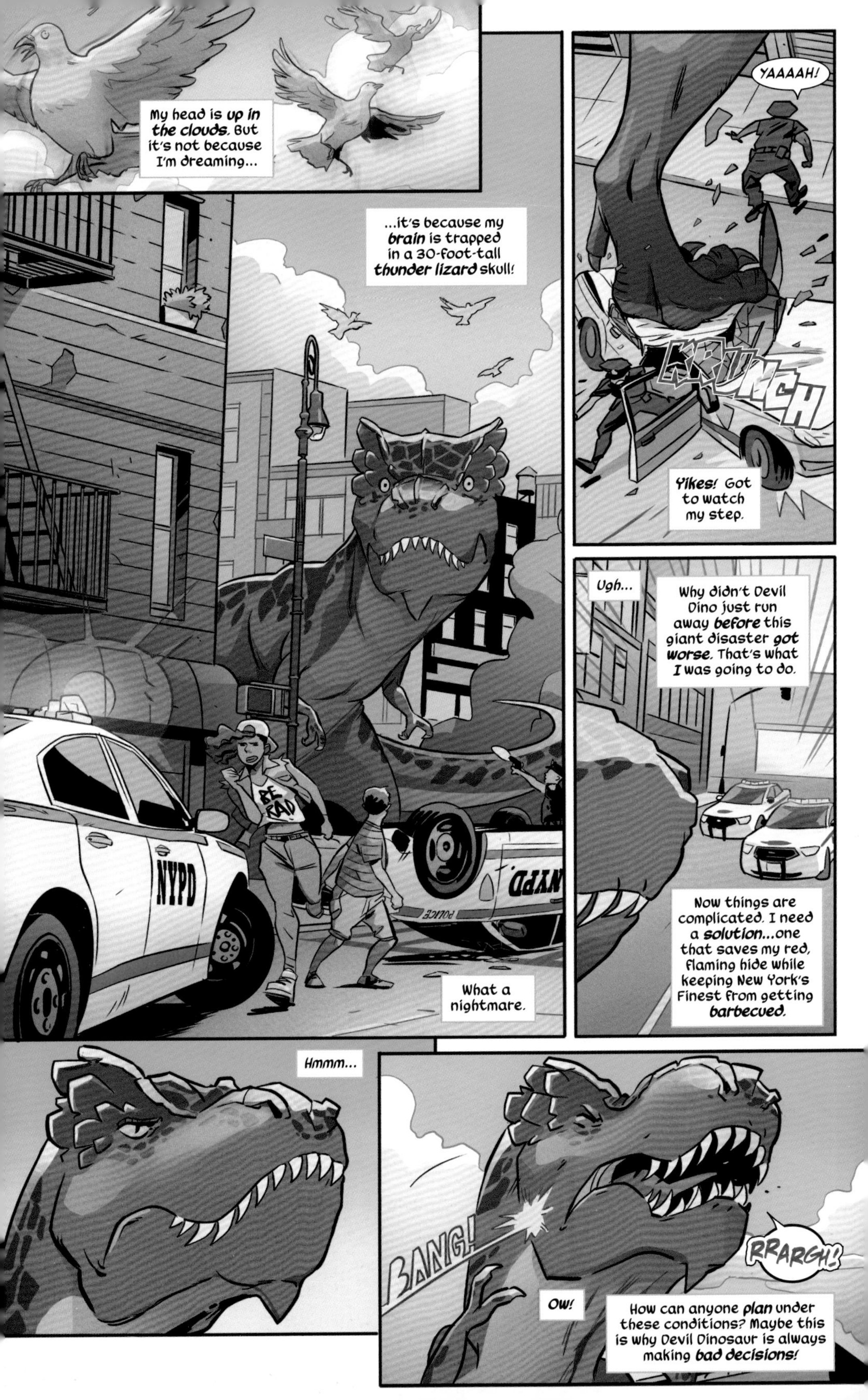
My head is up in the clouds. But it's not because I'm dreaming...
...it's because my brain is trapped in a 30-foot-tall thunder lizard skull!
BE RAD
NYPD
POLICE
NYPD
What a nightmare.
YAAAAH!
KRUNCH
Yikes! Got to watch my step.
Ugh...
Why didn't Devil Dino just run away before this giant disaster got worse. That's what I was going to do.
Now things are complicated. I need a solution...one that saves my red, flaming hide while keeping New York's Finest from getting barbecued.
Hmmm...
BANG!
RRARGH!
OW!
How can anyone plan under these conditions? Maybe this is why Devil Dinosaur is always making bad decisions!

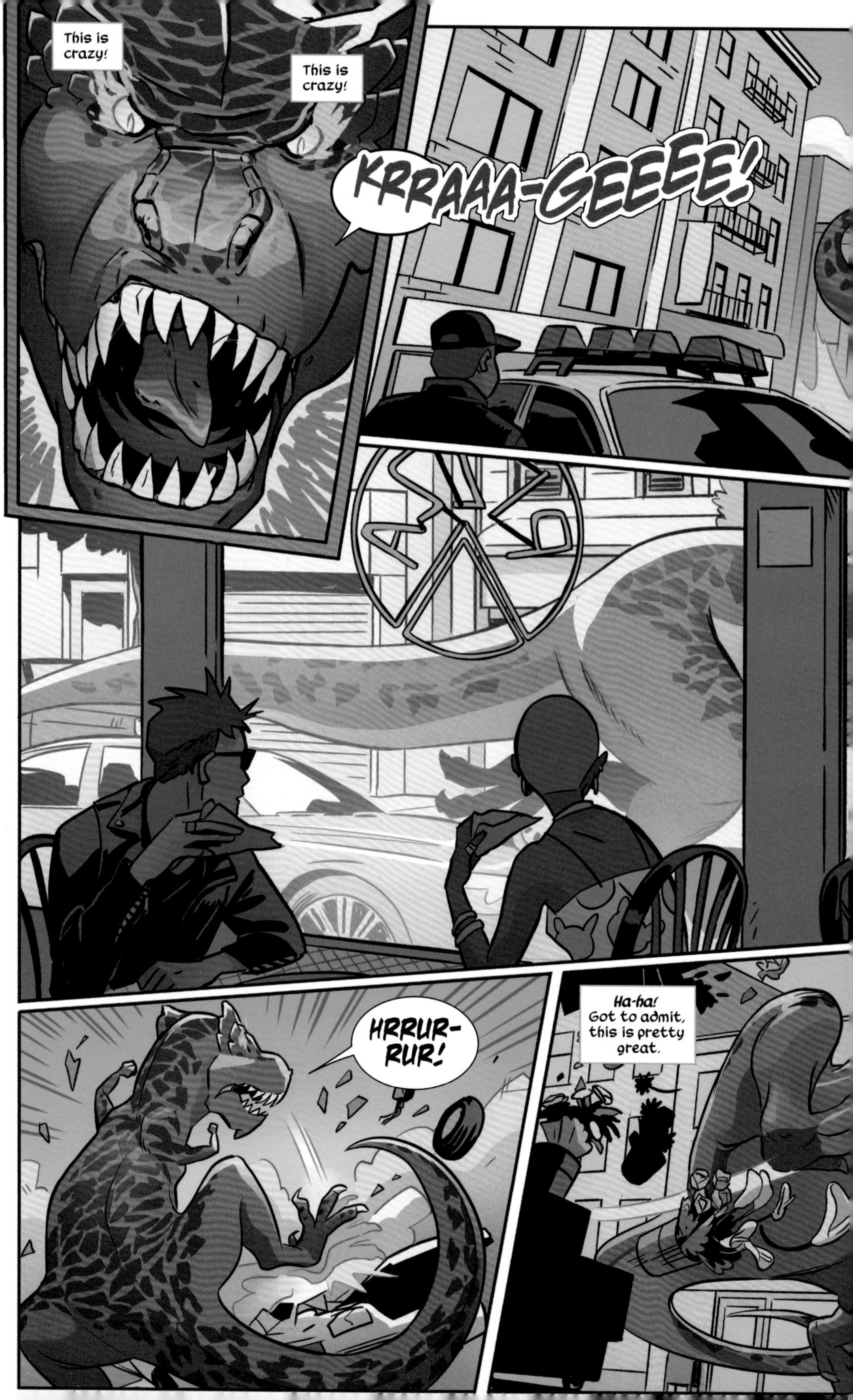
This is crazy!
This is crazy!
KRRAAA-GEEEEE!
HRRUR-RUR!
Ha-ha! Got to admit, this is pretty great.

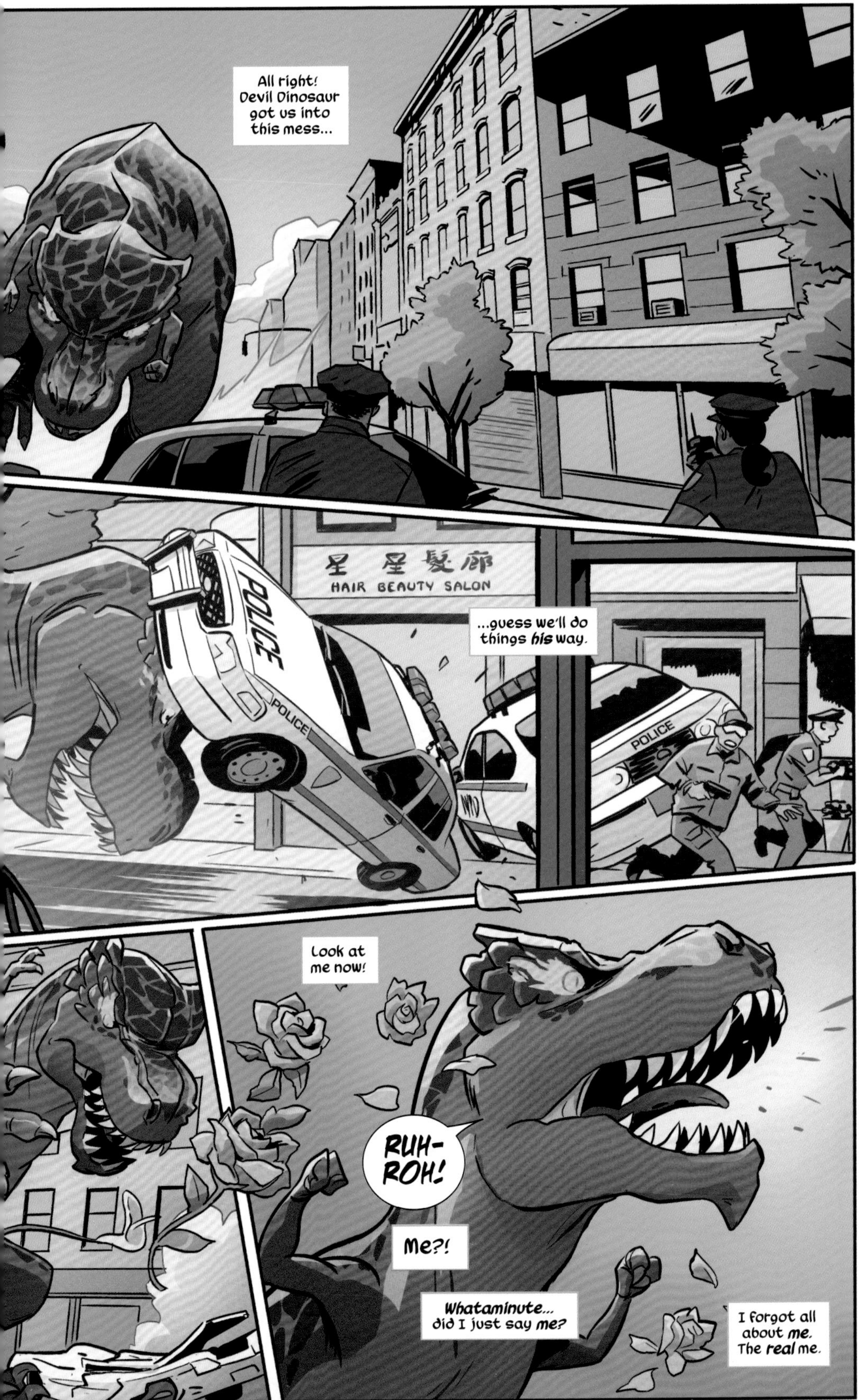
All right! Devil Dinosaur got us into this mess...
星 星 髮 廊
HAIR BEAUTY SALON
POLICE
...guess we'll do things *his* way.
POLICE
POLICE
Look at me now!
RUH-ROH!
Me?!
Whataminute... did I just say *me?*
I forgot all about *me.* The *real* me.

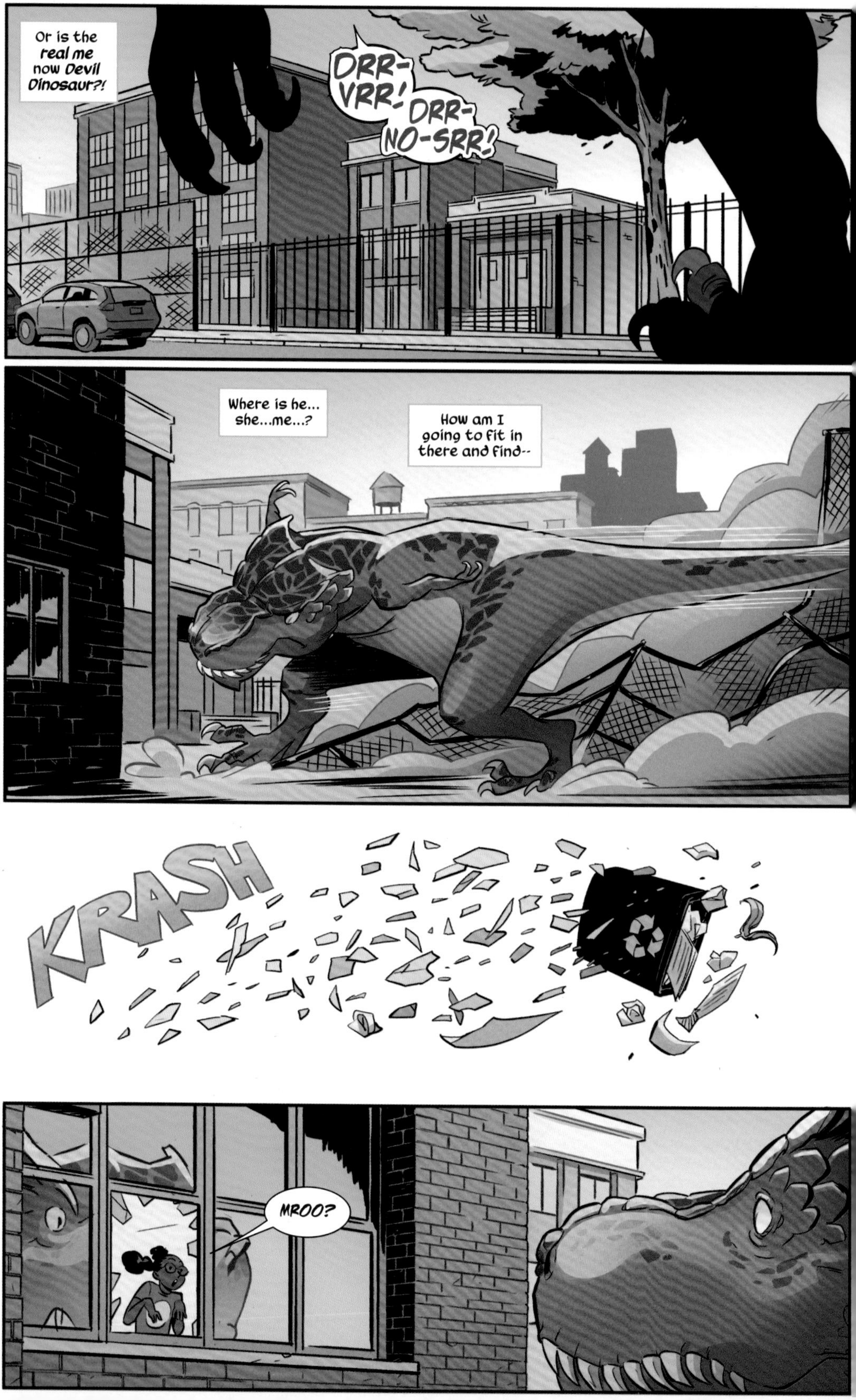
Or is the real me now Devil Dinosaur?!
DRR-VRR!
DRR-NO-SRR!
Where is he... she...me...?
How am I going to fit in there and find--
KRASH
MROO?

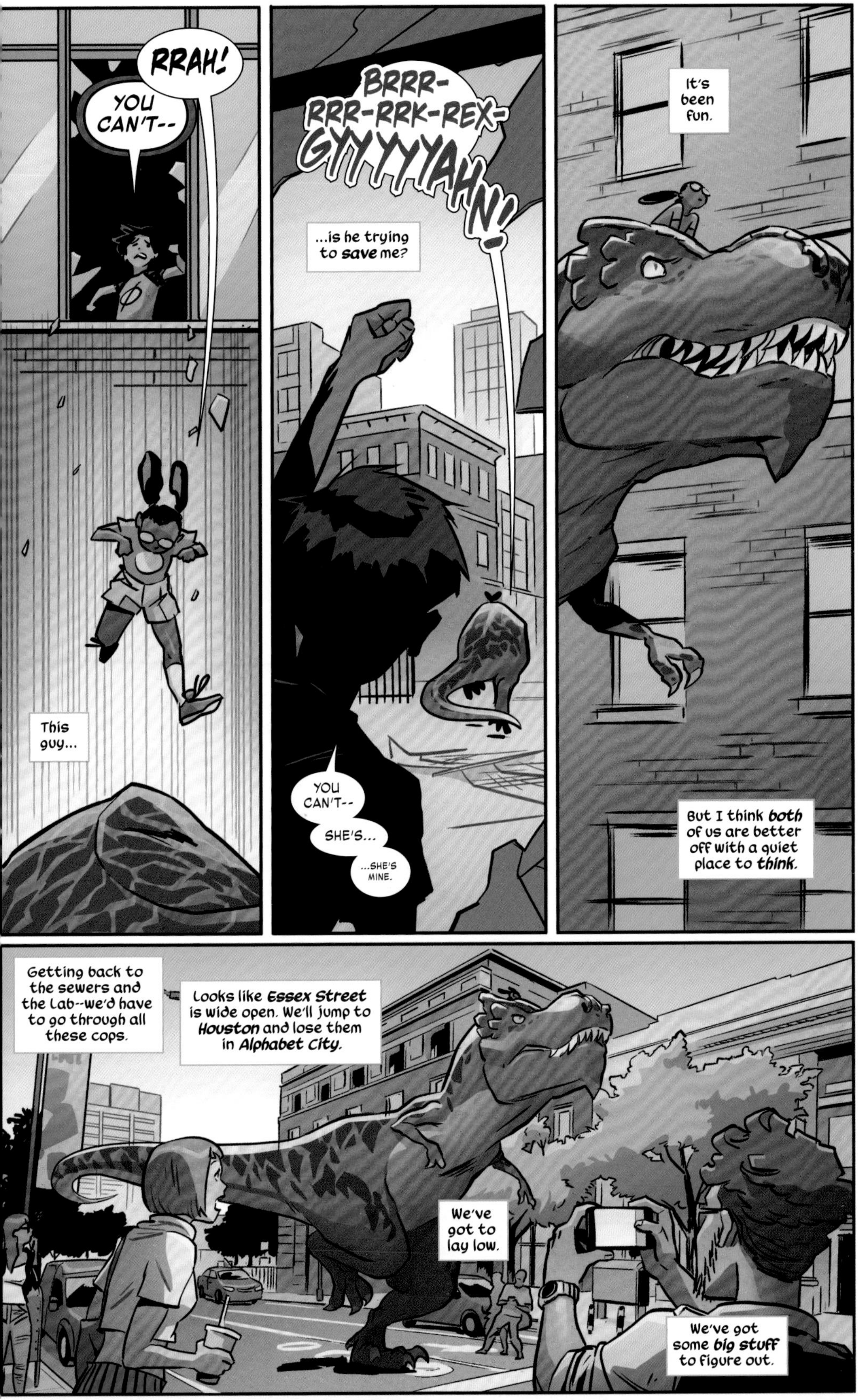
RRAH!
YOU CAN'T--
This guy...
BRRRR-RRR-RRK-REX-GYYYYYAHN!
...is he trying to **save** me?
YOU CAN'T--
SHE'S...
...SHE'S MINE.
It's been fun.
But I think **both** of us are better off with a quiet place to **think**.
Getting back to the sewers and the Lab--we'd have to go through all these cops.
Looks like **Essex Street** is wide open. We'll jump to **Houston** and lose them in **Alphabet City**.
We've got to lay low.
We've got some **big stuff** to figure out.

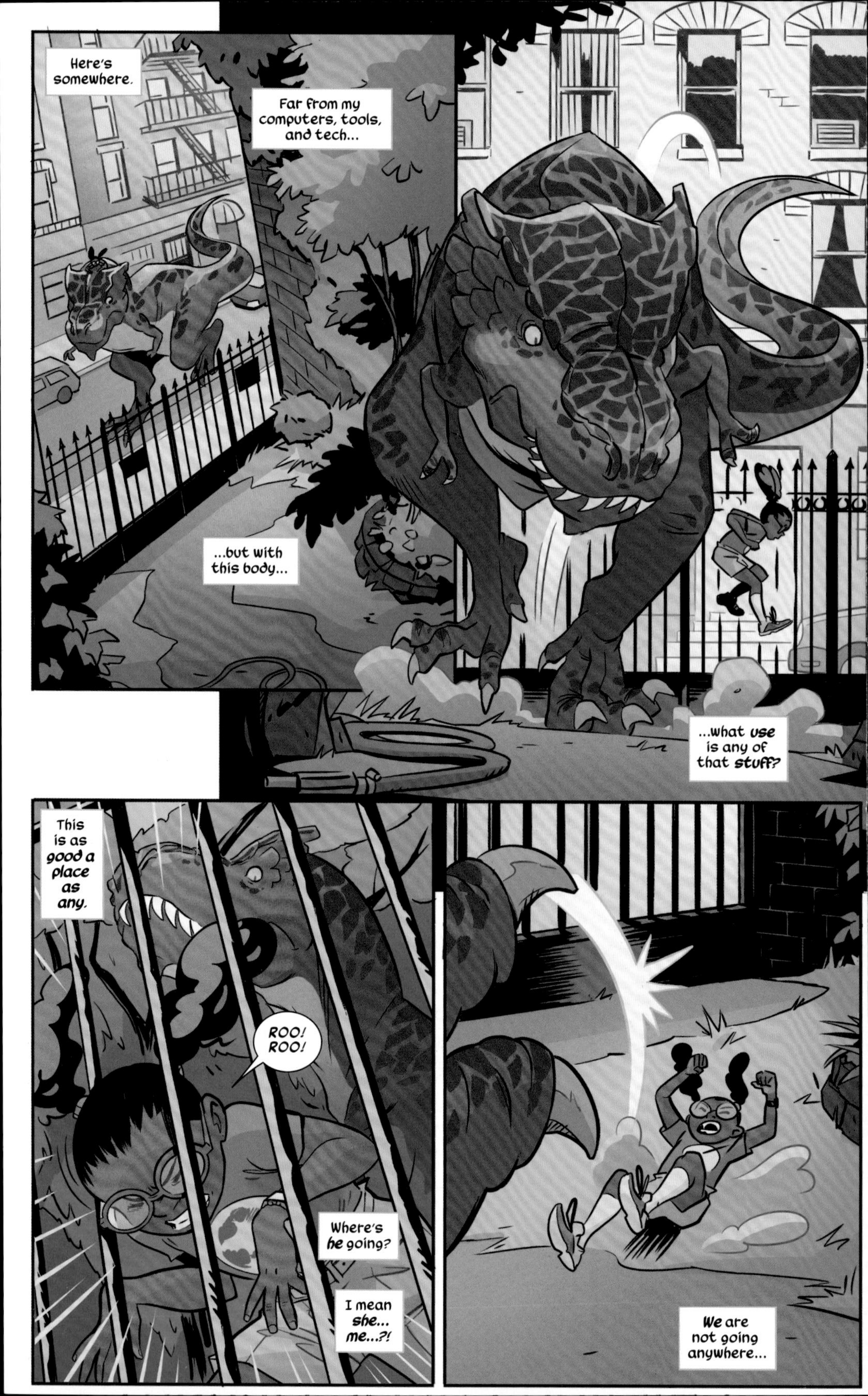
Here's somewhere.
Far from my computers, tools, and tech...
...but with this body...
...what use is any of that stuff?
This is as good a place as any.
ROO! ROO!
Where's he going?
I mean she... me...?!
We are not going anywhere...

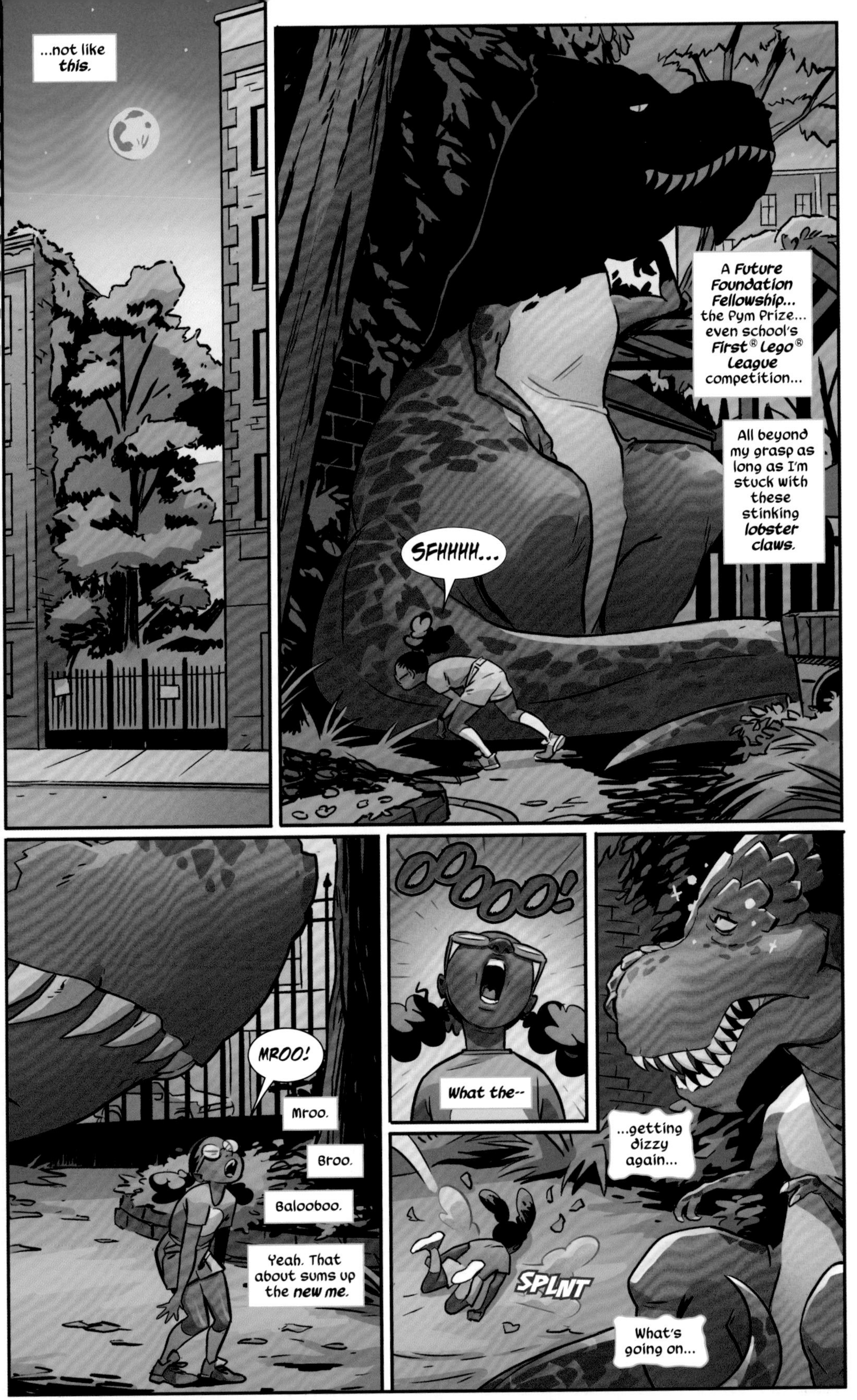
...not like this.
A Future Foundation Fellowship... the Pym Prize... even school's First® Lego® League competition...
All beyond my grasp as long as I'm stuck with these stinking lobster claws.
SFHHHH...
MROO!
Mroo.
Broo.
Balooboo.
Yeah. That about sums up the new me.
OOOOOO!
What the--
...getting dizzy again...
SPLNT
What's going on...

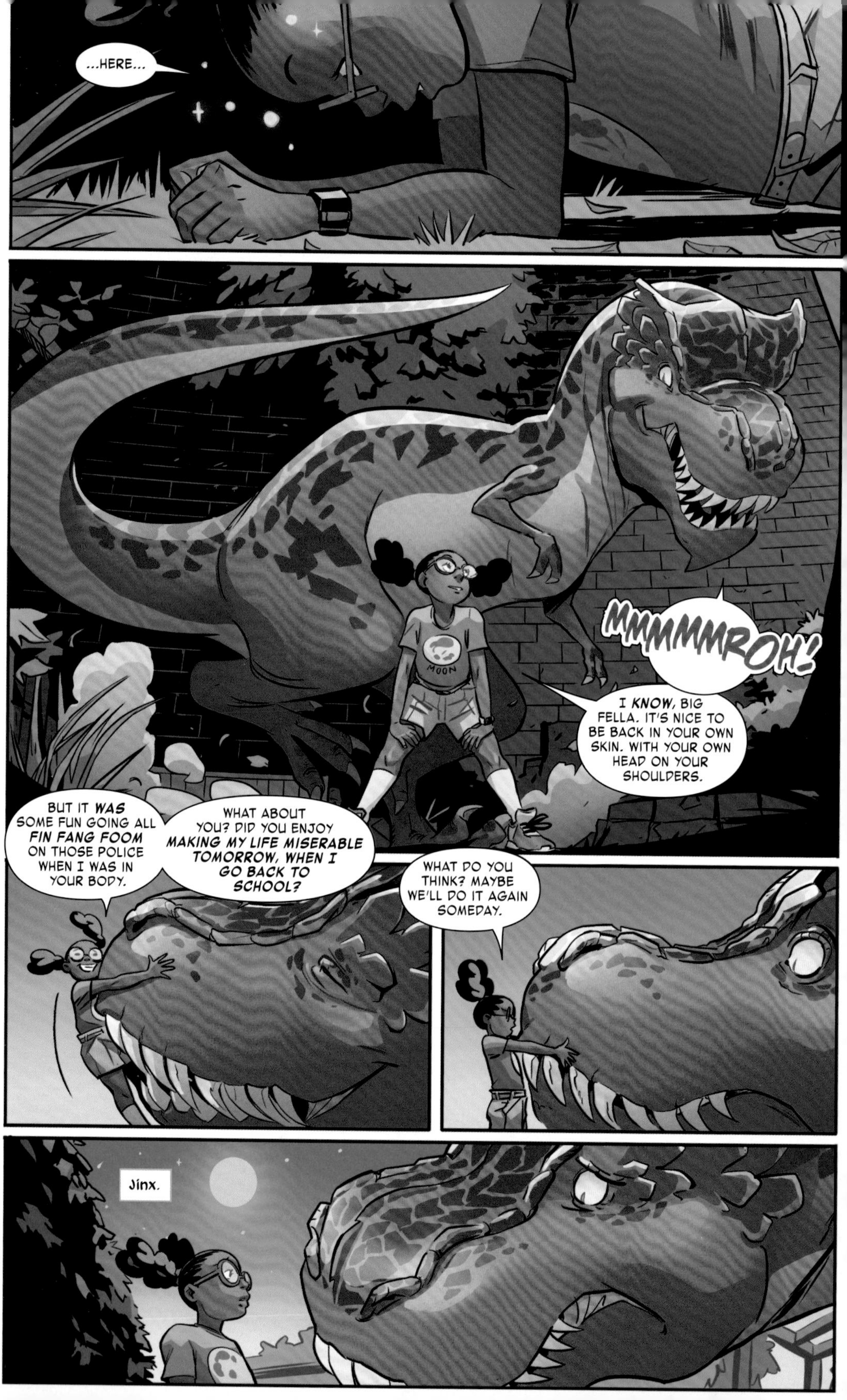
...HERE...
MMMMMROH!
I *KNOW*, BIG FELLA. IT'S NICE TO BE BACK IN YOUR OWN SKIN. WITH YOUR OWN HEAD ON YOUR SHOULDERS.
BUT IT *WAS* SOME FUN GOING ALL *FIN FANG FOOM* ON THOSE POLICE WHEN I WAS IN YOUR BODY.
WHAT ABOUT YOU? DID YOU ENJOY *MAKING MY LIFE MISERABLE TOMORROW, WHEN I GO BACK TO SCHOOL?*
WHAT DO YOU THINK? MAYBE WE'LL DO IT AGAIN SOMEDAY.
Jinx.

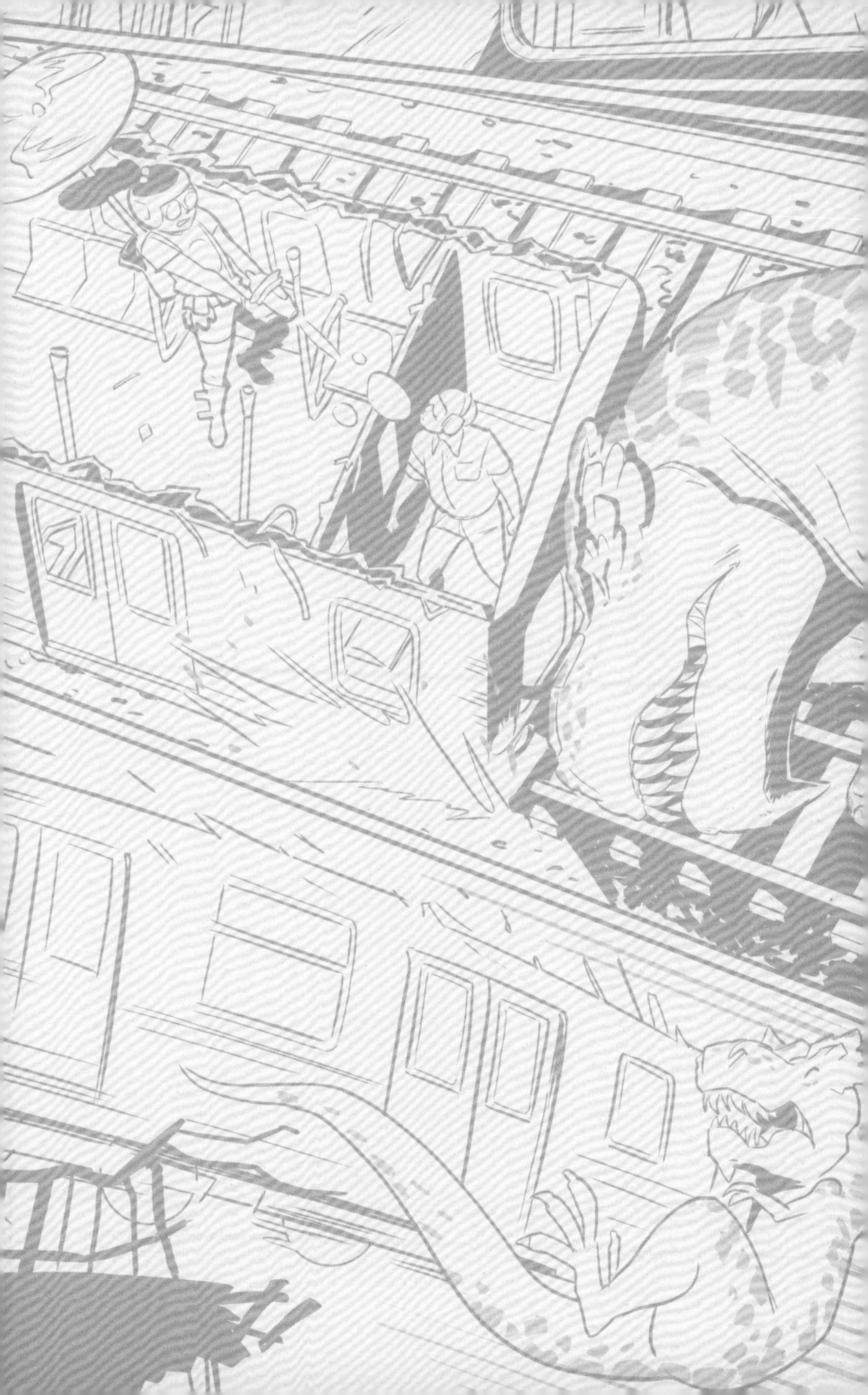

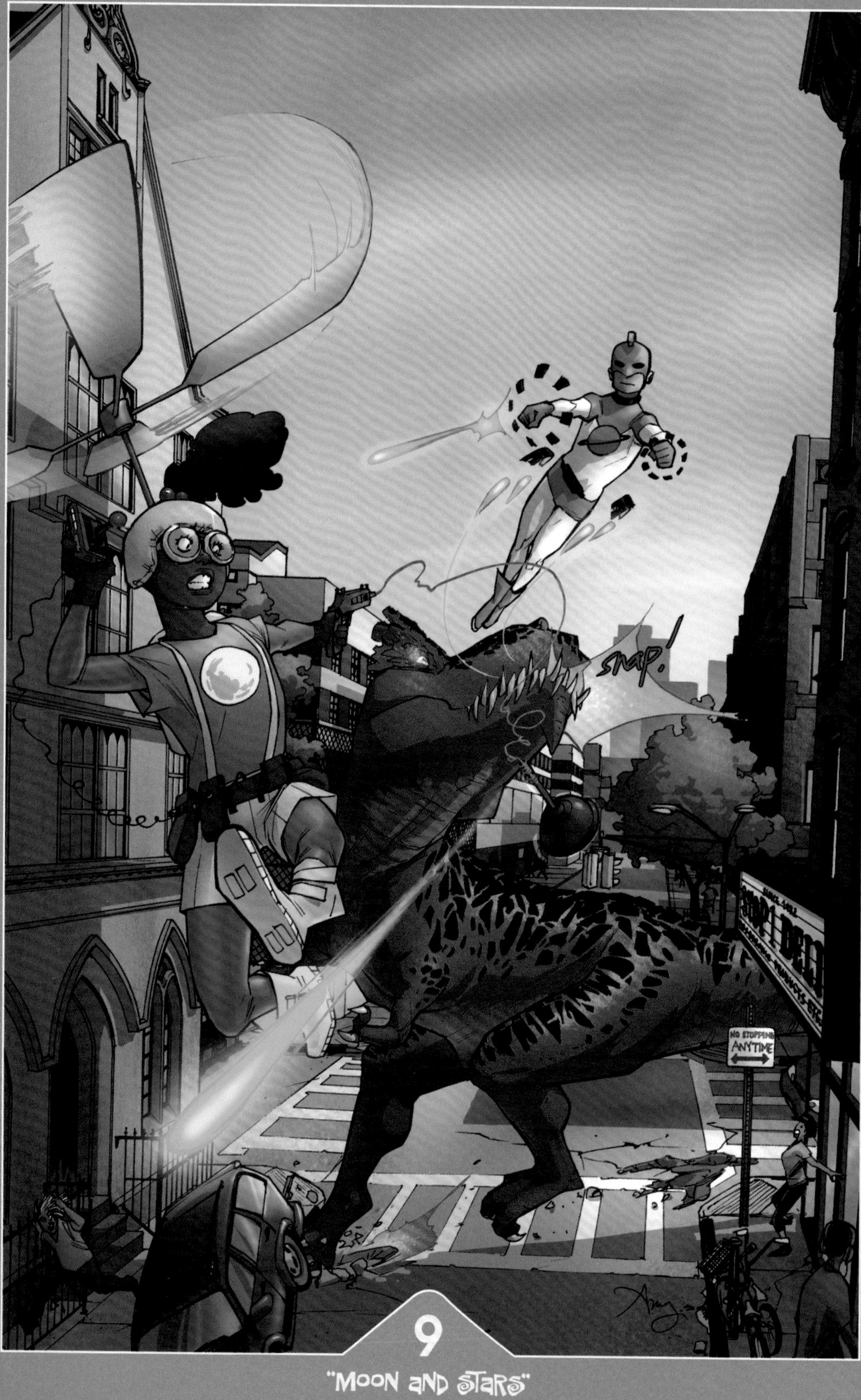
snap!
NO STOPPING
ANYTIME

9

"MOON AND STARS"

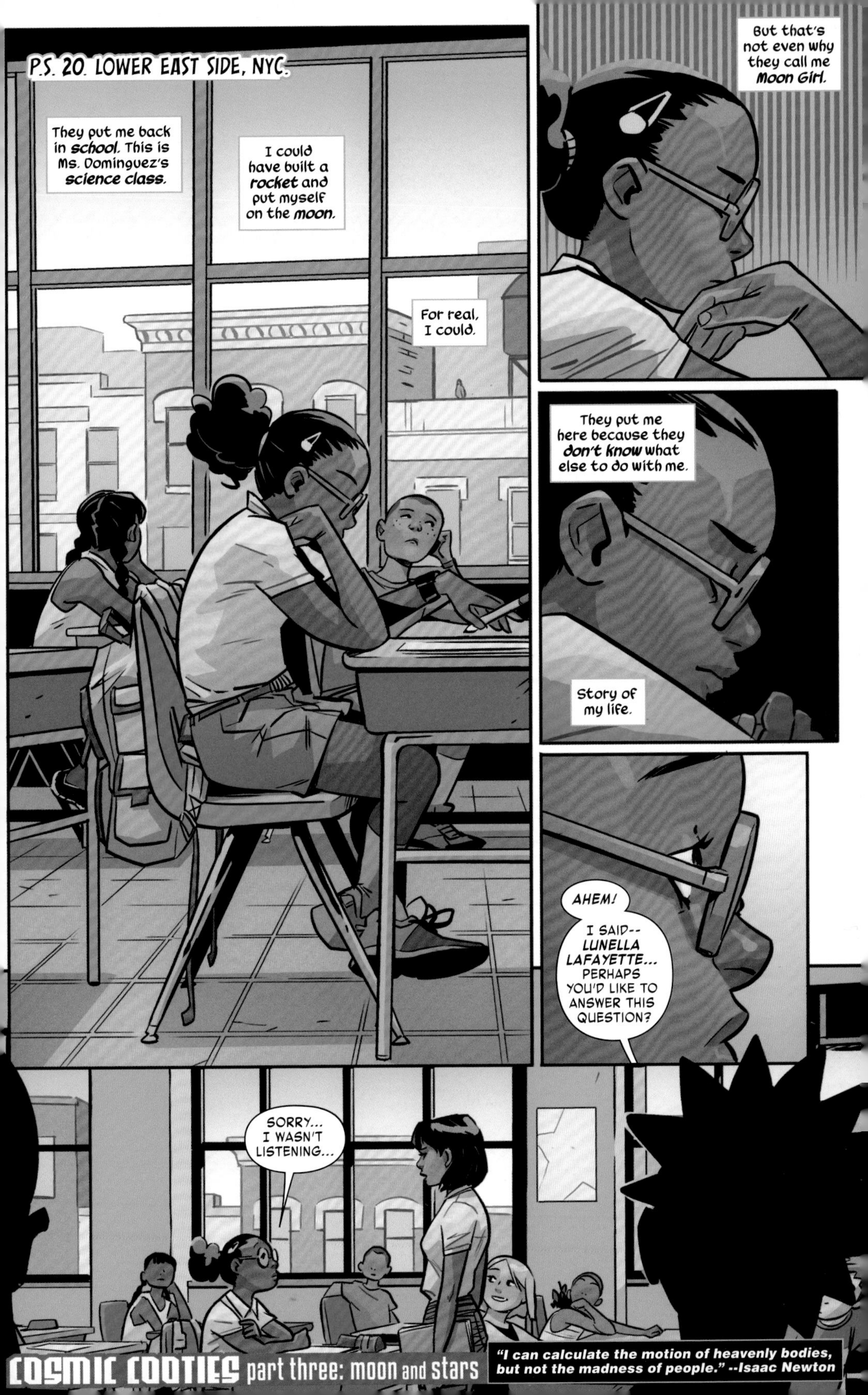
P.S. 20. LOWER EAST SIDE, NYC.
They put me back in school. This is Ms. Dominguez's science class.
I could have built a rocket and put myself on the moon.
For real, I could.
But that's not even why they call me Moon Girl.
They put me here because they don't know what else to do with me.
Story of my life.
AHEM!
I SAID-- LUNELLA LAFAYETTE... PERHAPS YOU'D LIKE TO ANSWER THIS QUESTION?
SORRY... I WASN'T LISTENING...
COSMIC COOTIES part three: moon and stars
"I can calculate the motion of heavenly bodies, but not the madness of people." --Isaac Newton

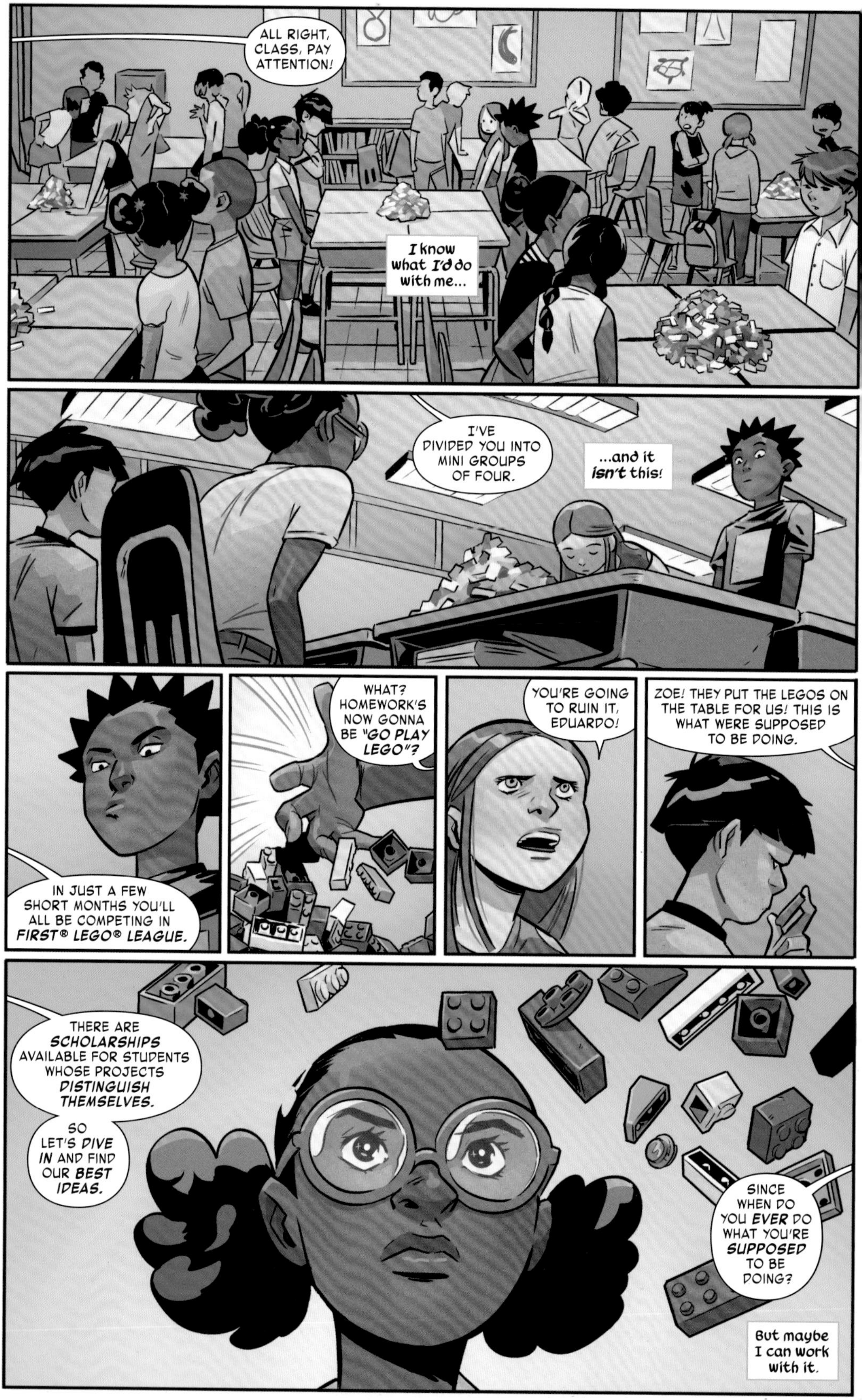
ALL RIGHT, CLASS, PAY ATTENTION!
I know what I'd do with me...
I'VE DIVIDED YOU INTO MINI GROUPS OF FOUR.
...and it isn't this!
IN JUST A FEW SHORT MONTHS YOU'LL ALL BE COMPETING IN FIRST® LEGO® LEAGUE.
WHAT? HOMEWORK'S NOW GONNA BE "GO PLAY LEGO"?
YOU'RE GOING TO RUIN IT, EDUARDO!
ZOE! THEY PUT THE LEGOS ON THE TABLE FOR US! THIS IS WHAT WERE SUPPOSED TO BE DOING.
THERE ARE SCHOLARSHIPS AVAILABLE FOR STUDENTS WHOSE PROJECTS DISTINGUISH THEMSELVES.
SO LET'S DIVE IN AND FIND OUR BEST IDEAS.
SINCE WHEN DO YOU EVER DO WHAT YOU'RE SUPPOSED TO BE DOING?
But maybe I can work with it.

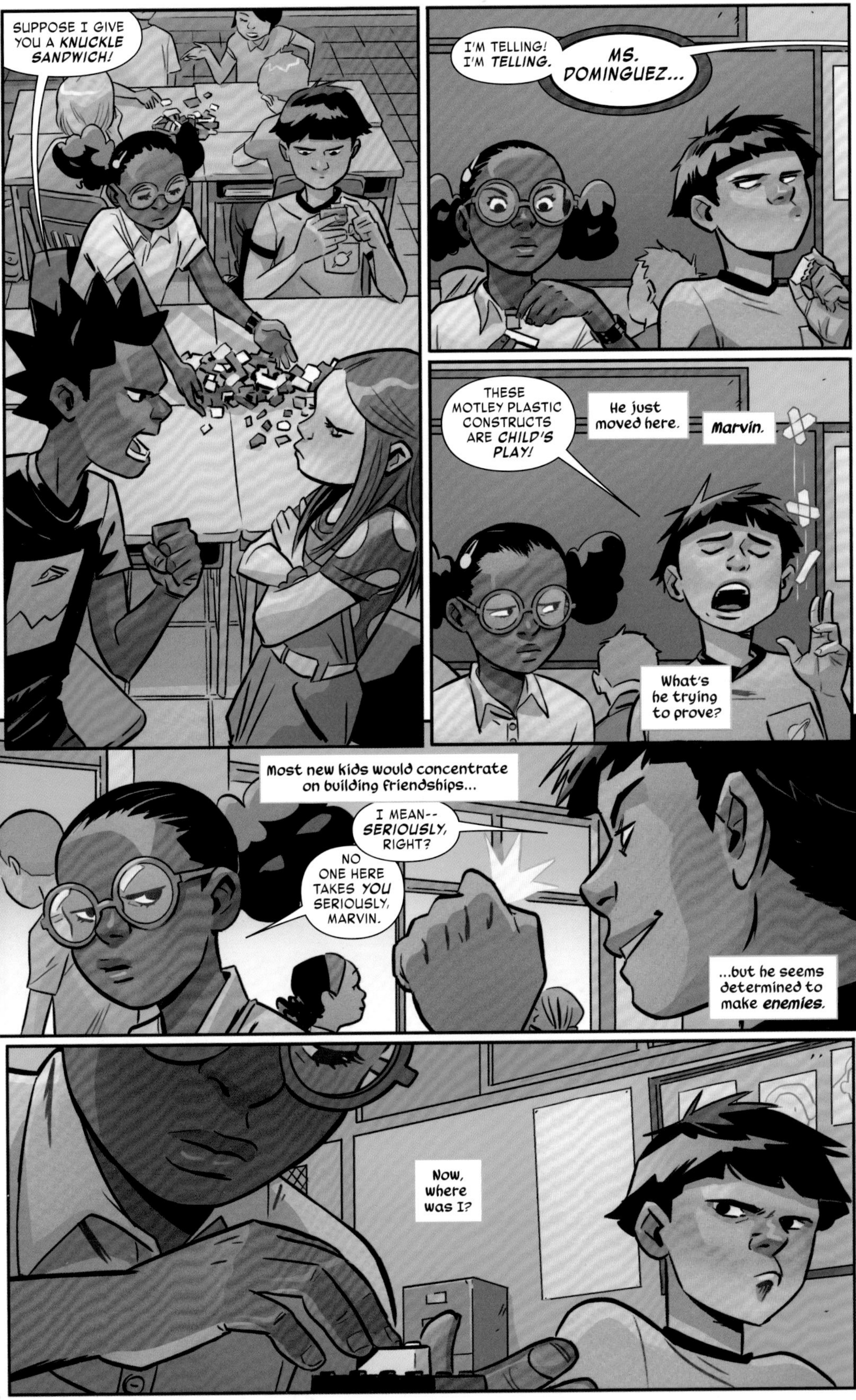
SUPPOSE I GIVE YOU A KNUCKLE SANDWICH!
I'M TELLING! I'M TELLING.
MS. DOMINGUEZ...
THESE MOTLEY PLASTIC CONSTRUCTS ARE CHILD'S PLAY!
He just moved here.
Marvin.
What's he trying to prove?
Most new kids would concentrate on building friendships...
I MEAN-- SERIOUSLY, RIGHT?
NO ONE HERE TAKES YOU SERIOUSLY, MARVIN.
...but he seems determined to make enemies.
Now, where was I?

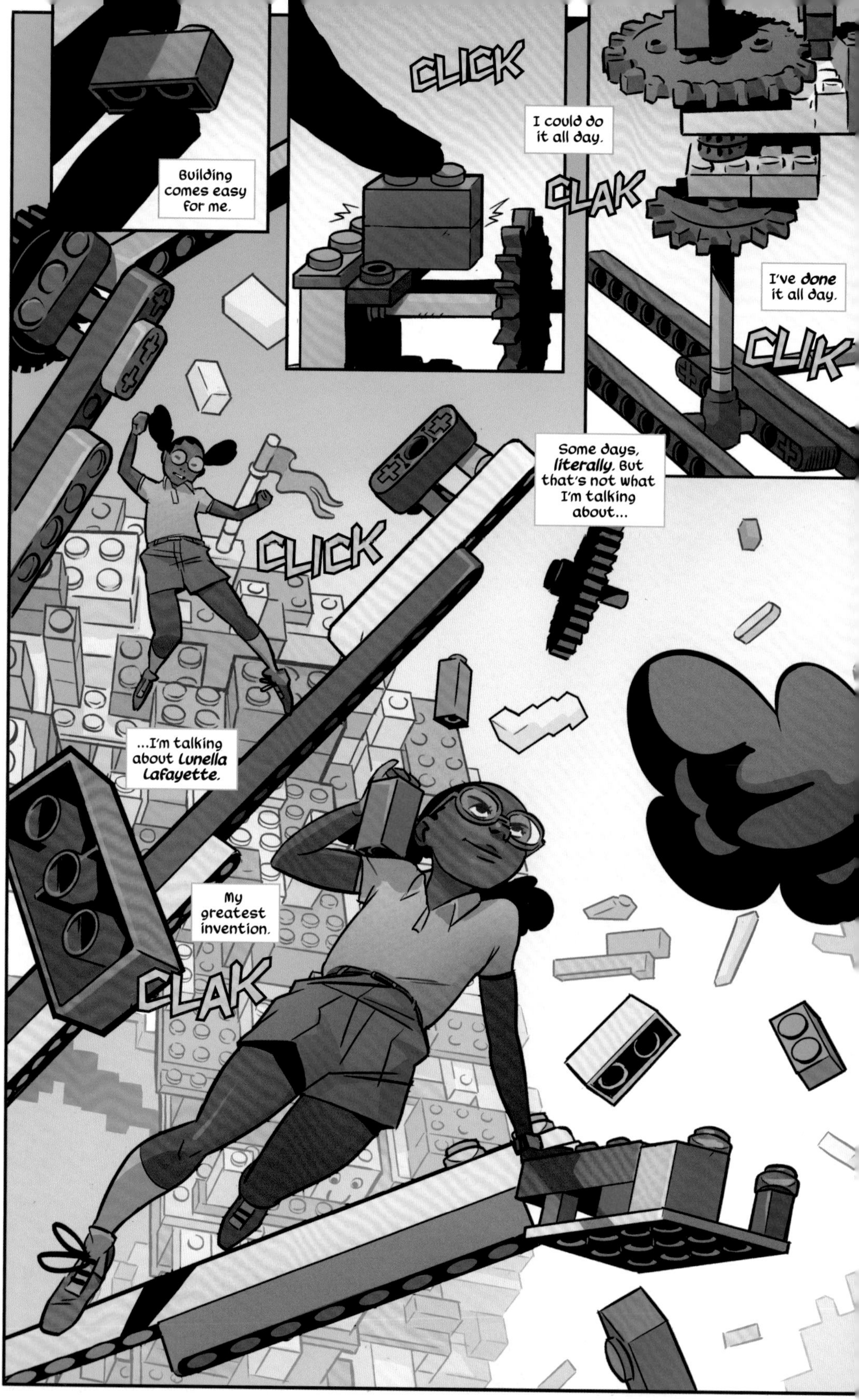
Building comes easy for me.
CLICK
I could do it all day.
CLAK
I've *done* it all day.
CLIK
Some days, *literally.* But that's not what I'm talking about...
CLICK
...I'm talking about *Lunella Lafayette.*
My greatest invention.
CLAK

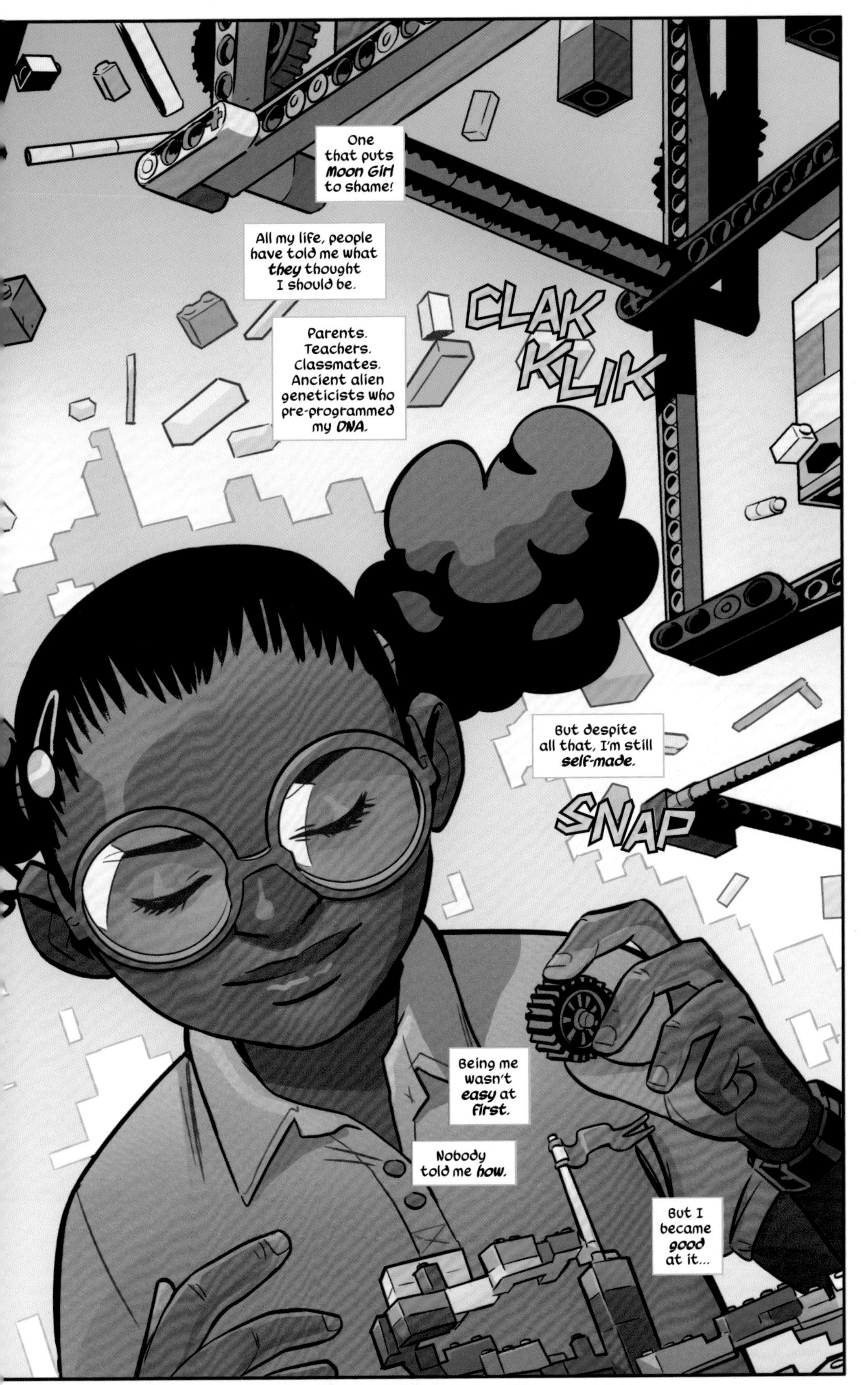

One that puts Moon Girl to shame!
All my life, people have told me what they thought I should be.
Parents. Teachers. Classmates. Ancient alien geneticists who pre-programmed my DNA.
CLAK
KLIK
But despite all that, I'm still self-made.
SNAP
Being me wasn't easy at first.
Nobody told me how.
But I became good at it...

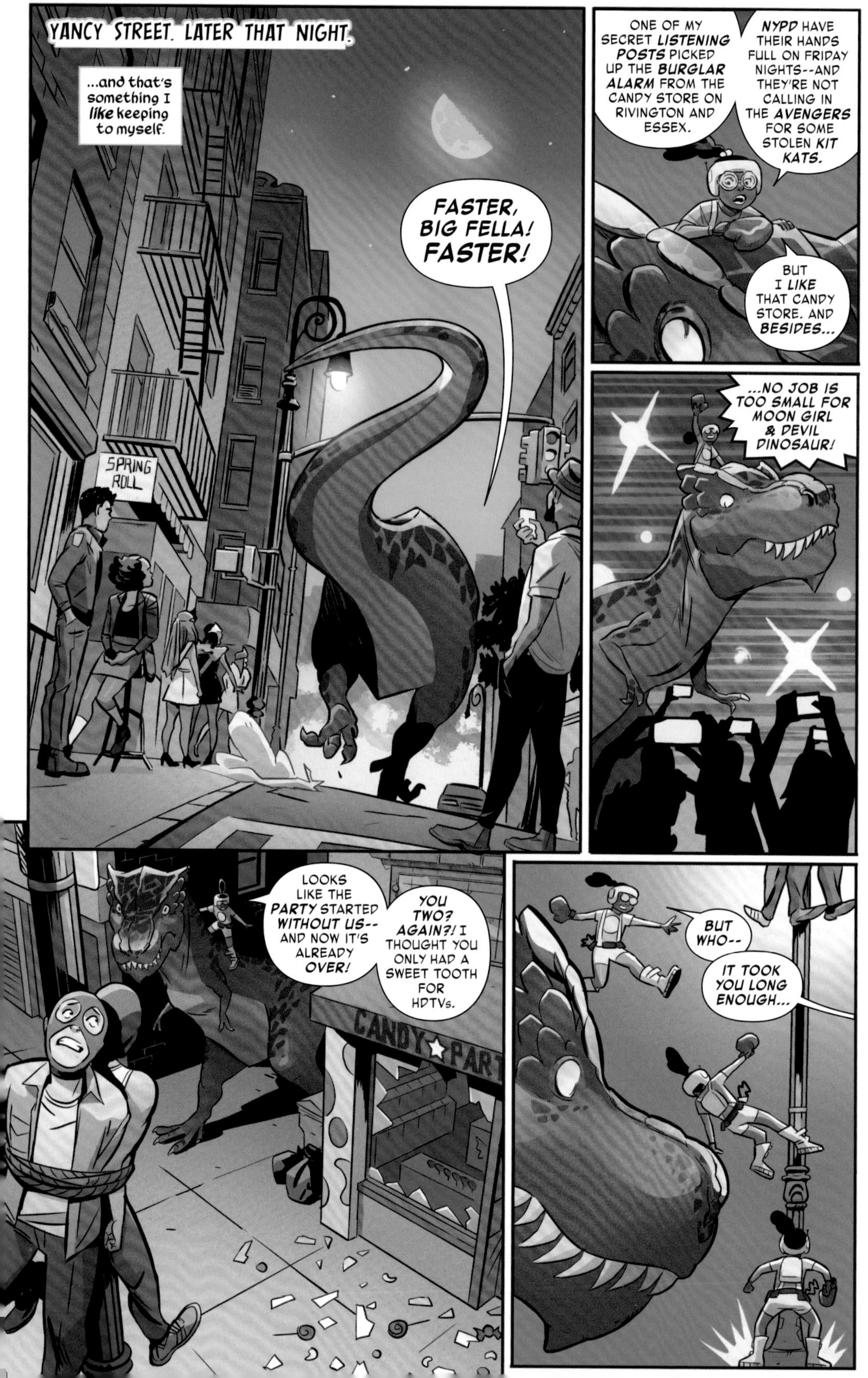
YANCY STREET. LATER THAT NIGHT.
...and that's something I like keeping to myself.
FASTER, BIG FELLA! FASTER!
SPRING ROLL
ONE OF MY SECRET LISTENING POSTS PICKED UP THE BURGLAR ALARM FROM THE CANDY STORE ON RIVINGTON AND ESSEX.
NYPD HAVE THEIR HANDS FULL ON FRIDAY NIGHTS--AND THEY'RE NOT CALLING IN THE AVENGERS FOR SOME STOLEN KIT KATS.
BUT I LIKE THAT CANDY STORE. AND BESIDES...
...NO JOB IS TOO SMALL FOR MOON GIRL & DEVIL DINOSAUR!
LOOKS LIKE THE PARTY STARTED WITHOUT US--AND NOW IT'S ALREADY OVER!
YOU TWO? AGAIN?! I THOUGHT YOU ONLY HAD A SWEET TOOTH FOR HDTVs.
CANDY PART
BUT WHO--
IT TOOK YOU LONG ENOUGH...

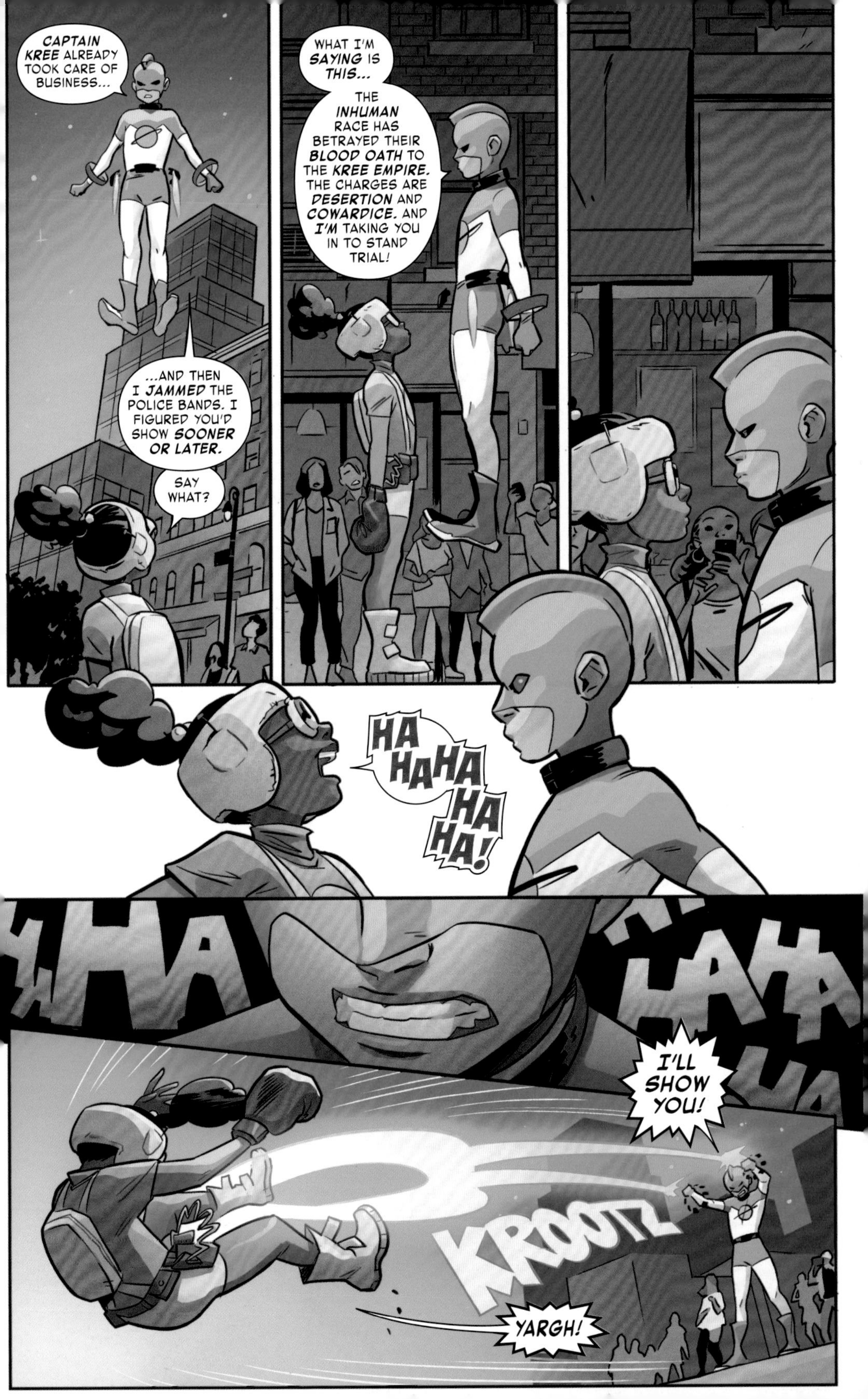
CAPTAIN KREE ALREADY TOOK CARE OF BUSINESS...
...AND THEN I JAMMED THE POLICE BANDS. I FIGURED YOU'D SHOW SOONER OR LATER.
SAY WHAT?
WHAT I'M SAYING IS THIS...
THE INHUMAN RACE HAS BETRAYED THEIR BLOOD OATH TO THE KREE EMPIRE. THE CHARGES ARE DESERTION AND COWARDICE. AND I'M TAKING YOU IN TO STAND TRIAL!
HA HAHA HA HA!
HA
I'LL SHOW YOU!
KROOTZ
YARGH!

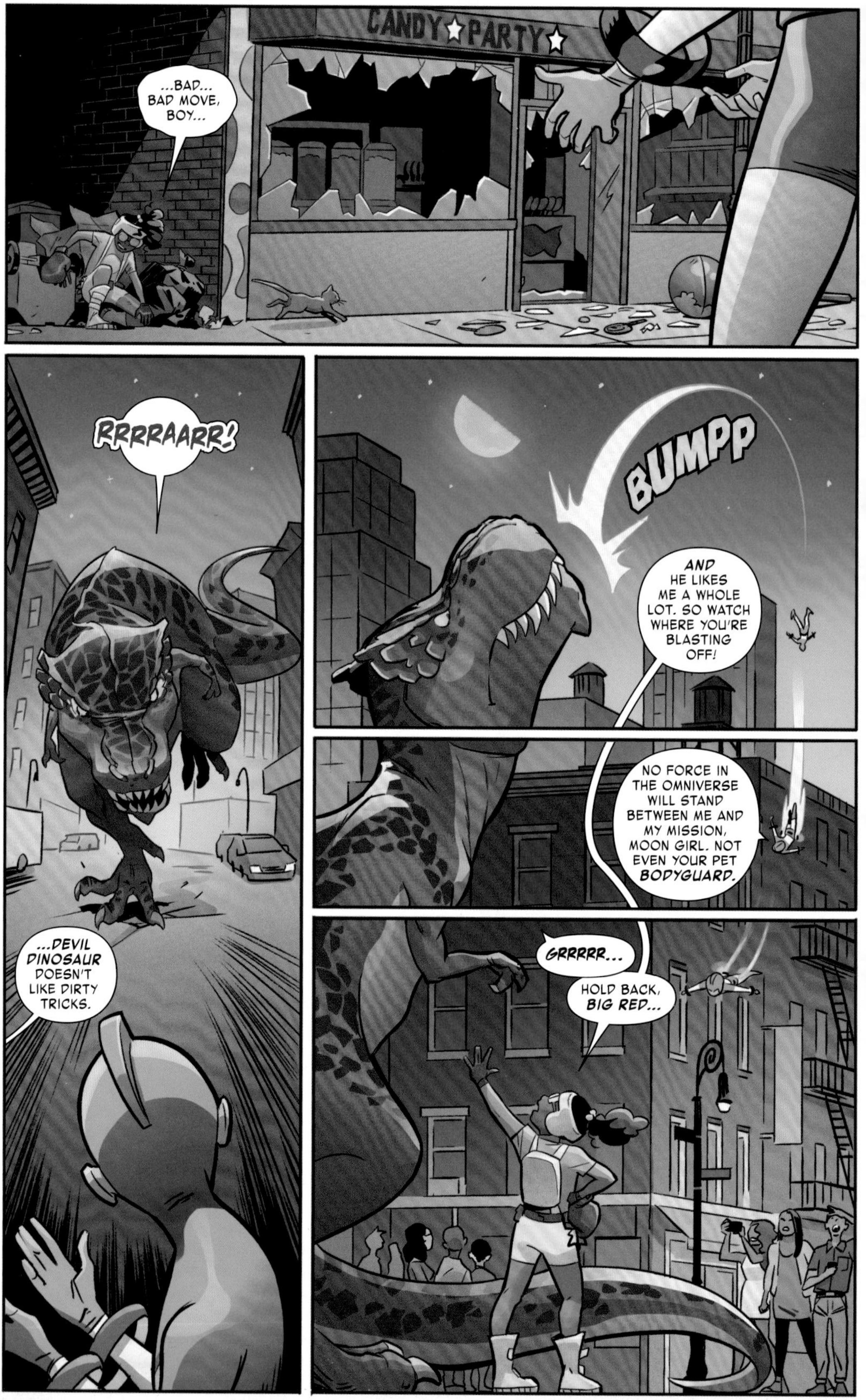
CANDY PARTY
...BAD... BAD MOVE, BOY...
RRRRAARR!
...DEVIL DINOSAUR DOESN'T LIKE DIRTY TRICKS.
BUMPP
AND HE LIKES ME A WHOLE LOT. SO WATCH WHERE YOU'RE BLASTING OFF!
NO FORCE IN THE OMNIVERSE WILL STAND BETWEEN ME AND MY MISSION, MOON GIRL. NOT EVEN YOUR PET BODYGUARD.
GRRRRR...
HOLD BACK, BIG RED...

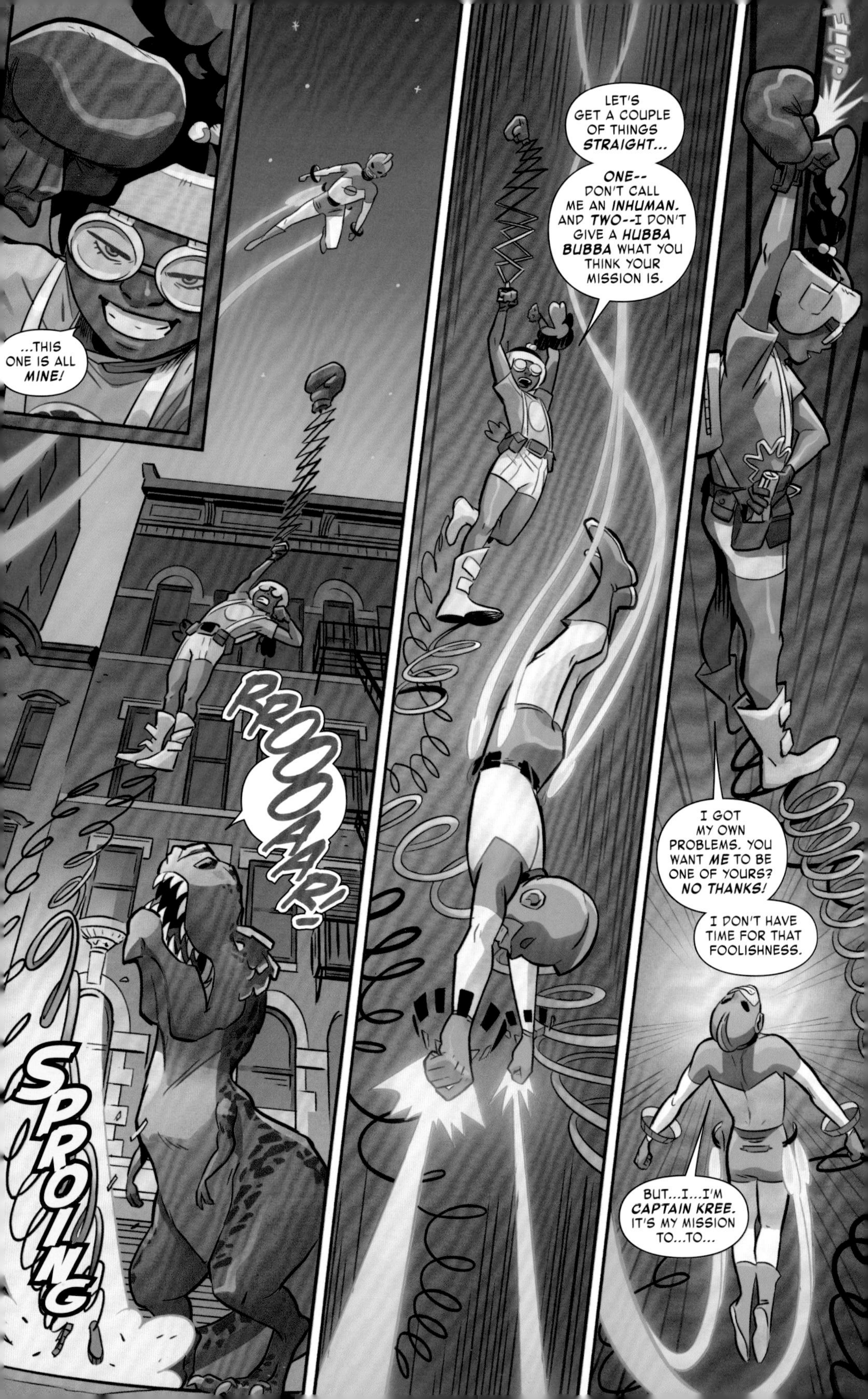

...THIS ONE IS ALL MINE!
RROOOAAAR!
SPROING
LET'S GET A COUPLE OF THINGS STRAIGHT...
ONE-- DON'T CALL ME AN INHUMAN. AND TWO--I DON'T GIVE A HUBBA BUBBA WHAT YOU THINK YOUR MISSION IS.
FLOP
I GOT MY OWN PROBLEMS. YOU WANT ME TO BE ONE OF YOURS? NO THANKS!
I DON'T HAVE TIME FOR THAT FOOLISHNESS.
BUT...I...I'M CAPTAIN KREE. IT'S MY MISSION TO...TO...

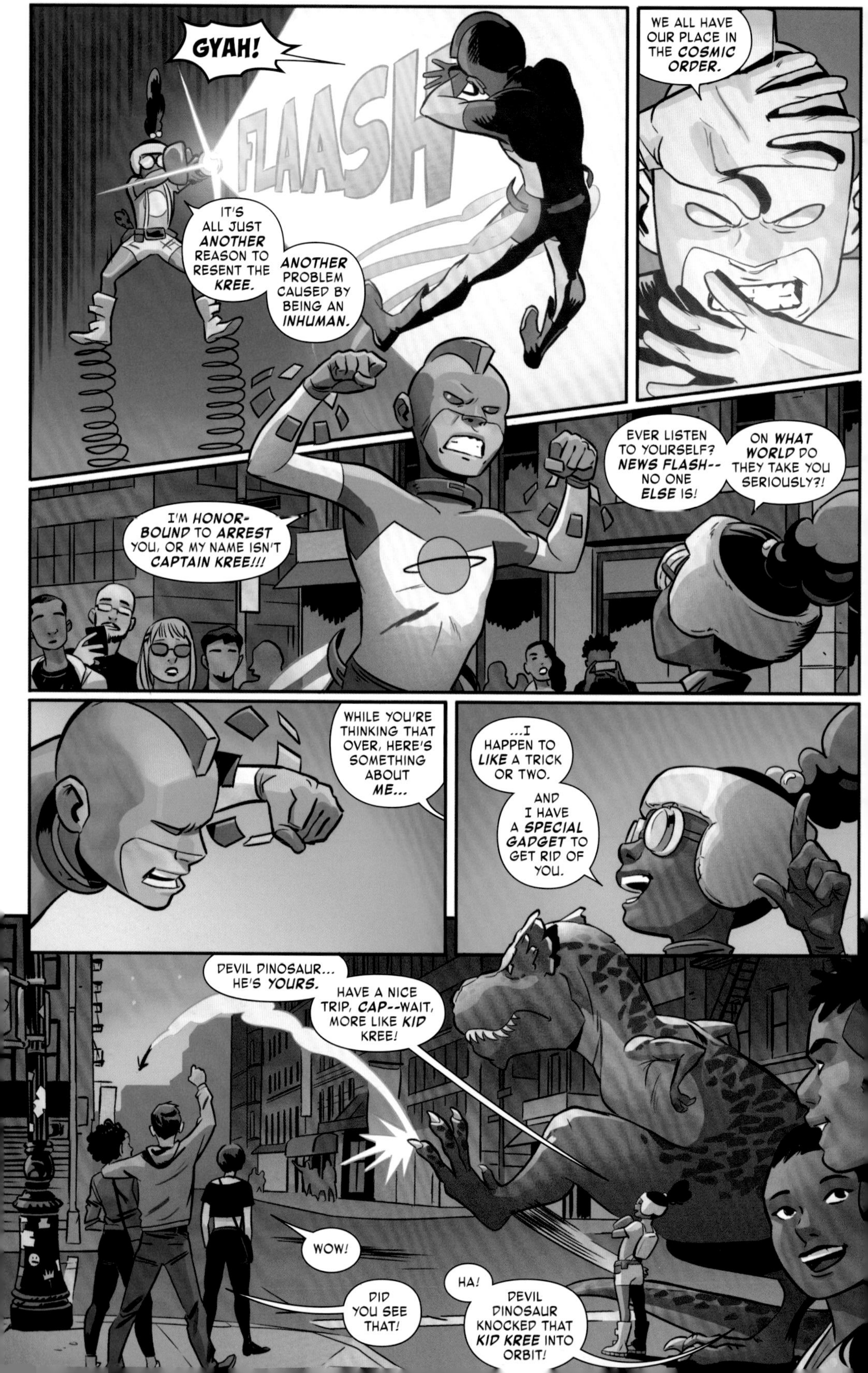
GYAH!
FLAASH
IT'S ALL JUST ANOTHER REASON TO RESENT THE KREE.
ANOTHER PROBLEM CAUSED BY BEING AN INHUMAN.
WE ALL HAVE OUR PLACE IN THE COSMIC ORDER.
I'M HONOR-BOUND TO ARREST YOU, OR MY NAME ISN'T CAPTAIN KREE!!!
EVER LISTEN TO YOURSELF? NEWS FLASH-- NO ONE ELSE IS!
ON WHAT WORLD DO THEY TAKE YOU SERIOUSLY?!
WHILE YOU'RE THINKING THAT OVER, HERE'S SOMETHING ABOUT ME...
...I HAPPEN TO LIKE A TRICK OR TWO.
AND I HAVE A SPECIAL GADGET TO GET RID OF YOU.
DEVIL DINOSAUR... HE'S YOURS.
HAVE A NICE TRIP, CAP--WAIT, MORE LIKE KID KREE!
WOW!
DID YOU SEE THAT!
HA!
DEVIL DINOSAUR KNOCKED THAT KID KREE INTO ORBIT!

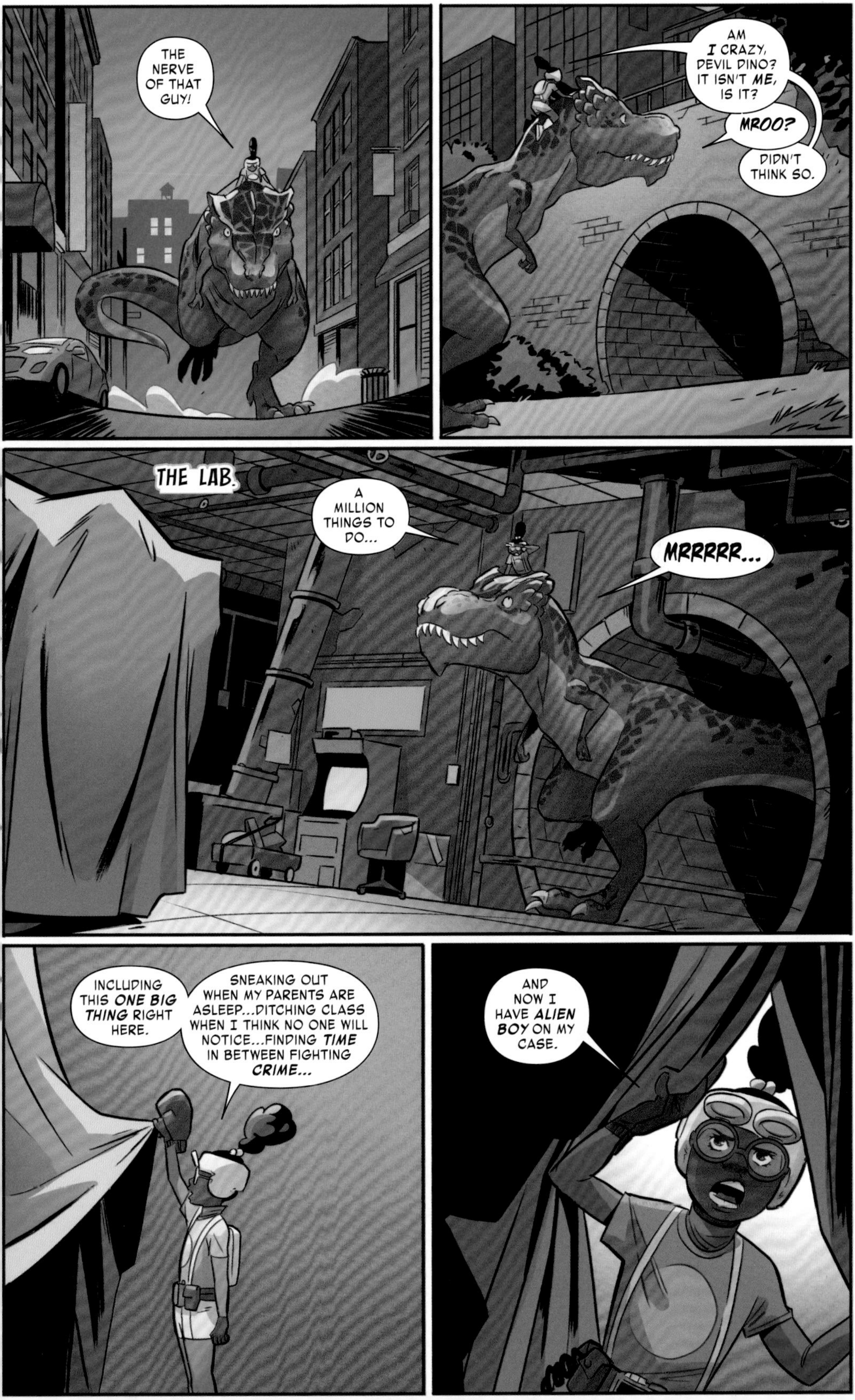
THE NERVE OF THAT GUY!
AM I CRAZY, DEVIL DINO? IT ISN'T ME, IS IT?
MROO?
DIDN'T THINK SO.
THE LAB.
A MILLION THINGS TO DO...
MRRRRR...
INCLUDING THIS ONE BIG THING RIGHT HERE.
SNEAKING OUT WHEN MY PARENTS ARE ASLEEP...DITCHING CLASS WHEN I THINK NO ONE WILL NOTICE...FINDING TIME IN BETWEEN FIGHTING CRIME...
AND NOW I HAVE ALIEN BOY ON MY CASE.

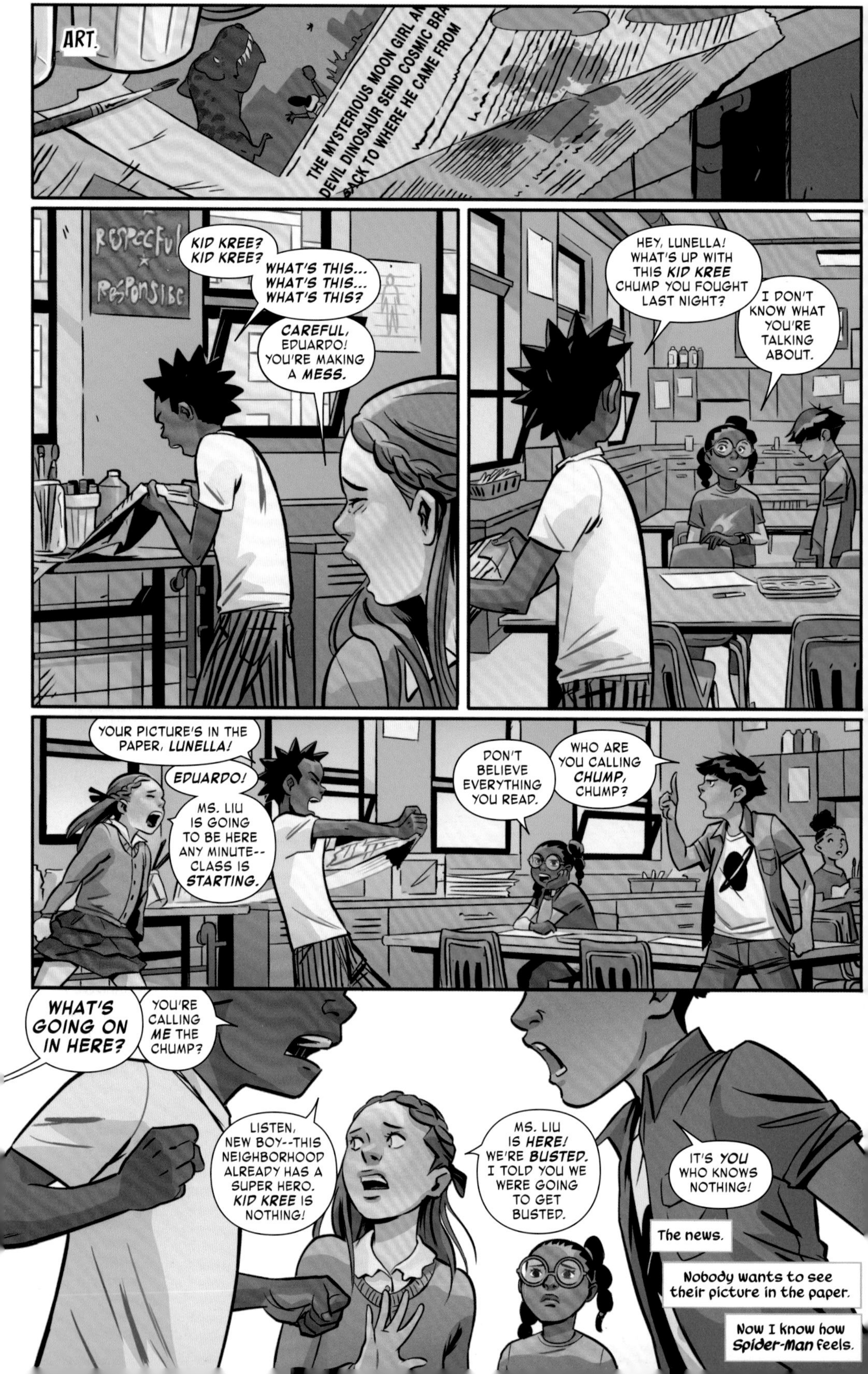
ART.
THE MYSTERIOUS MOON GIRL AN
DEVIL DINOSAUR SEND COSMIC BRA
BACK TO WHERE HE CAME FROM
KID KREE? KID KREE?
WHAT'S THIS... WHAT'S THIS... WHAT'S THIS?
CAREFUL, EDUARDO! YOU'RE MAKING A MESS.
HEY, LUNELLA! WHAT'S UP WITH THIS KID KREE CHUMP YOU FOUGHT LAST NIGHT?
I DON'T KNOW WHAT YOU'RE TALKING ABOUT.
YOUR PICTURE'S IN THE PAPER, LUNELLA!
EDUARDO!
MS. LIU IS GOING TO BE HERE ANY MINUTE-- CLASS IS STARTING.
DON'T BELIEVE EVERYTHING YOU READ.
WHO ARE YOU CALLING CHUMP, CHUMP?
WHAT'S GOING ON IN HERE?
YOU'RE CALLING ME THE CHUMP?
LISTEN, NEW BOY--THIS NEIGHBORHOOD ALREADY HAS A SUPER HERO. KID KREE IS NOTHING!
MS. LIU IS HERE! WE'RE BUSTED. I TOLD YOU WE WERE GOING TO GET BUSTED.
IT'S YOU WHO KNOWS NOTHING!
The news.
Nobody wants to see their picture in the paper.
Now I know how Spider-Man feels.

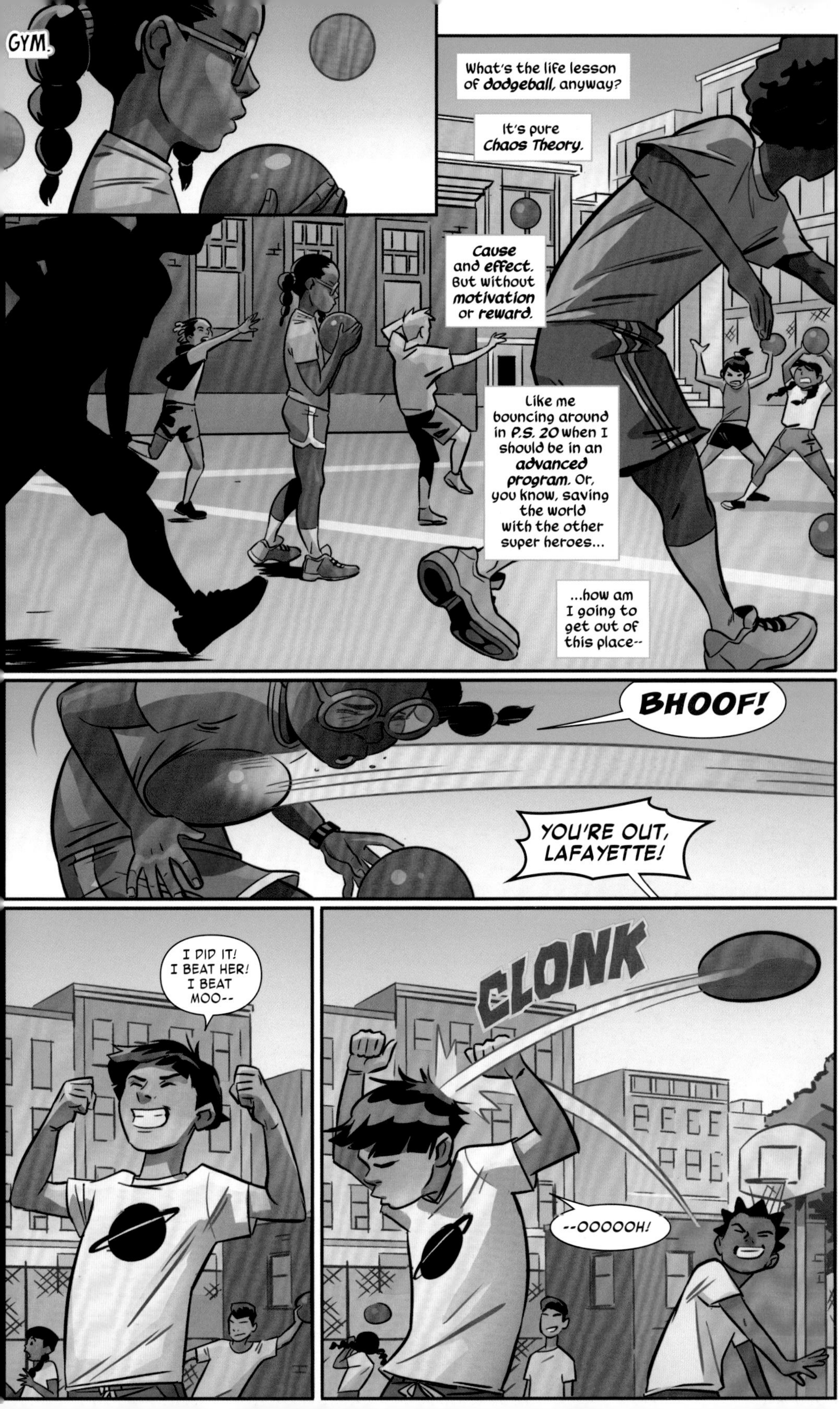
GYM.
What's the life lesson of dodgeball, anyway?
It's pure Chaos Theory.
Cause and effect. But without motivation or reward.
Like me bouncing around in P.S. 20 when I should be in an advanced program. Or, you know, saving the world with the other super heroes...
...how am I going to get out of this place--
BHOOF!
YOU'RE OUT, LAFAYETTE!
I DID IT! I BEAT HER! I BEAT MOO--
CLONK
--OOOOOH!

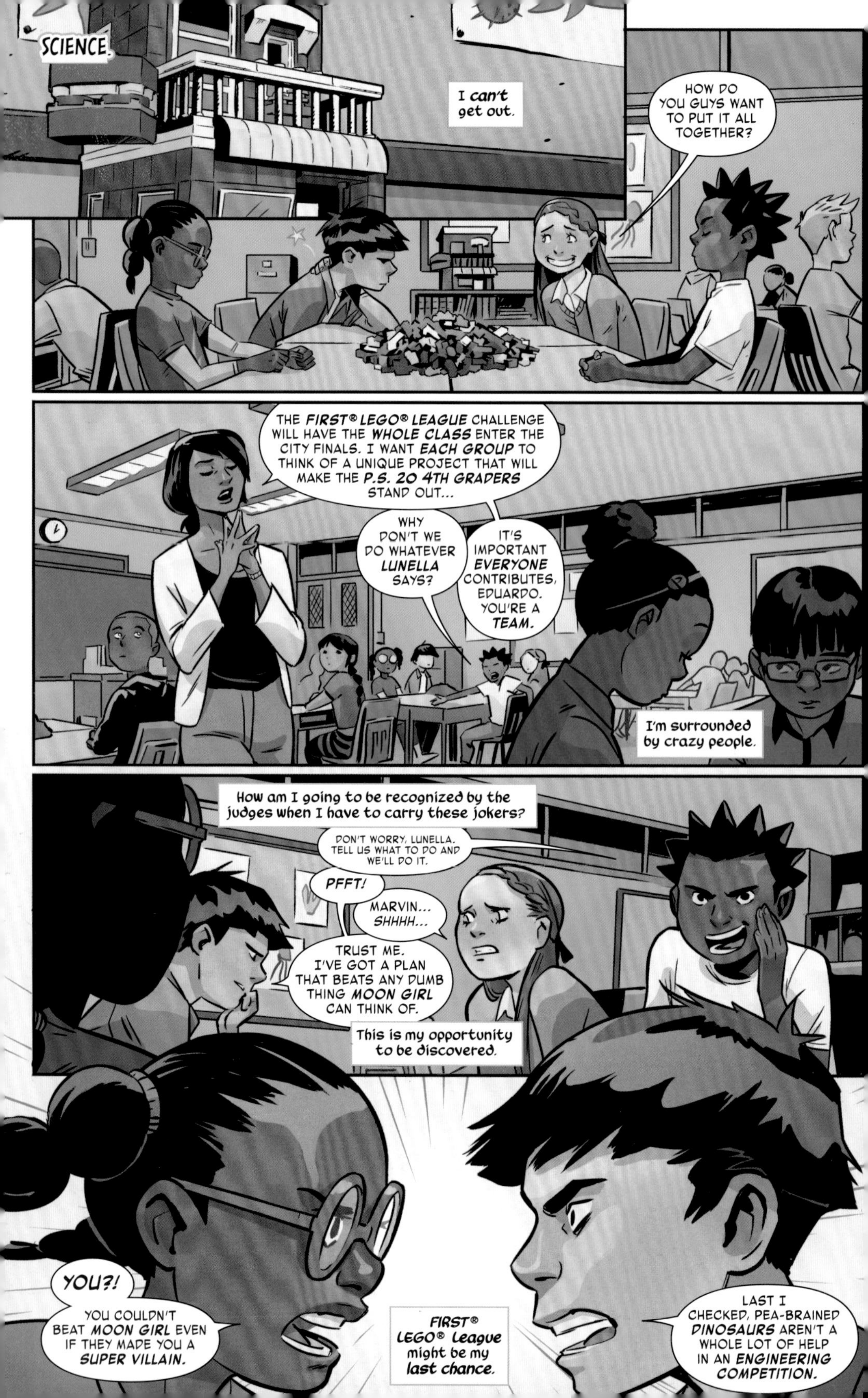
SCIENCE.
I can't get out.
HOW DO YOU GUYS WANT TO PUT IT ALL TOGETHER?
THE FIRST® LEGO® LEAGUE CHALLENGE WILL HAVE THE WHOLE CLASS ENTER THE CITY FINALS. I WANT EACH GROUP TO THINK OF A UNIQUE PROJECT THAT WILL MAKE THE P.S. 20 4TH GRADERS STAND OUT...
WHY DON'T WE DO WHATEVER LUNELLA SAYS?
IT'S IMPORTANT EVERYONE CONTRIBUTES, EDUARDO. YOU'RE A TEAM.
I'm surrounded by crazy people.
How am I going to be recognized by the judges when I have to carry these jokers?
DON'T WORRY, LUNELLA. TELL US WHAT TO DO AND WE'LL DO IT.
PFFT!
MARVIN... SHHHH...
TRUST ME. I'VE GOT A PLAN THAT BEATS ANY DUMB THING MOON GIRL CAN THINK OF.
This is my opportunity to be discovered.
YOU?!
YOU COULDN'T BEAT MOON GIRL EVEN IF THEY MADE YOU A SUPER VILLAIN.
FIRST® LEGO® League might be my last chance.
LAST I CHECKED, PEA-BRAINED DINOSAURS AREN'T A WHOLE LOT OF HELP IN AN ENGINEERING COMPETITION.

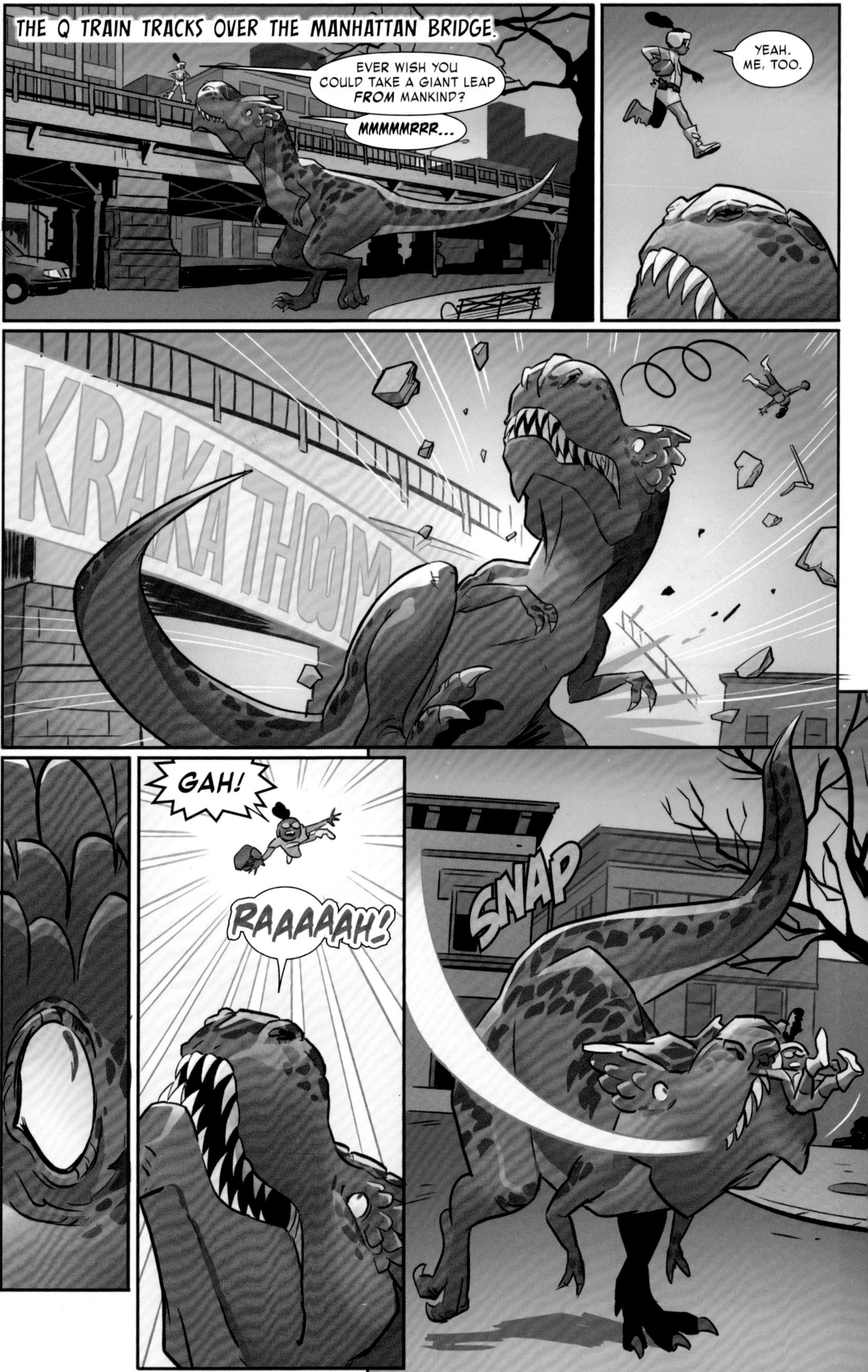
THE Q TRAIN TRACKS OVER THE MANHATTAN BRIDGE.
EVER WISH YOU COULD TAKE A GIANT LEAP FROM MANKIND?
MMMMMRRR...
YEAH. ME, TOO.
KRAKATHOOM
GAH!
RAAAAAH!
SNAP

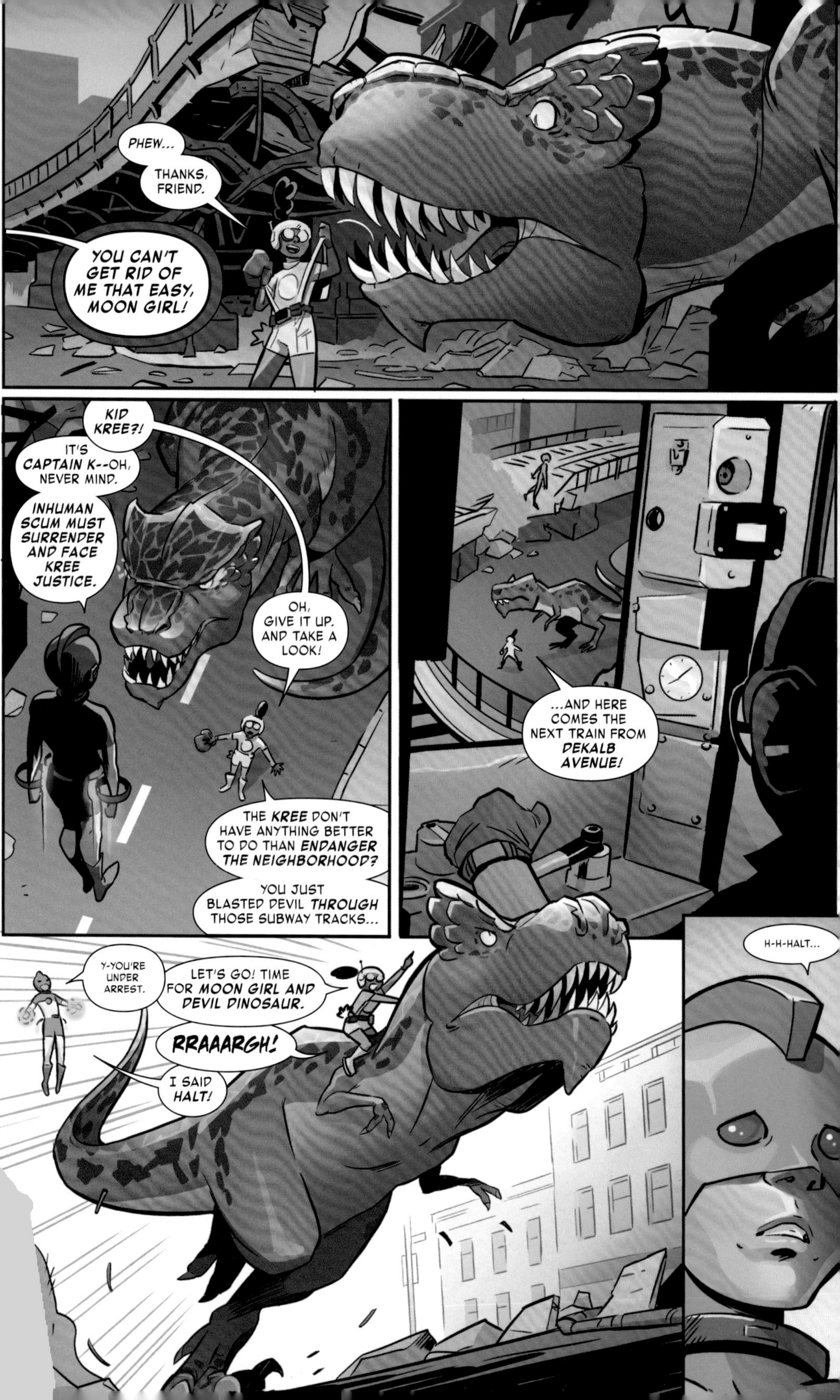
PHEW...
THANKS, FRIEND.
YOU CAN'T GET RID OF ME THAT EASY, MOON GIRL!
KID KREE?!
IT'S CAPTAIN K--OH, NEVER MIND.
INHUMAN SCUM MUST SURRENDER AND FACE KREE JUSTICE.
OH, GIVE IT UP. AND TAKE A LOOK!
THE KREE DON'T HAVE ANYTHING BETTER TO DO THAN ENDANGER THE NEIGHBORHOOD?
YOU JUST BLASTED DEVIL THROUGH THOSE SUBWAY TRACKS...
...AND HERE COMES THE NEXT TRAIN FROM DEKALB AVENUE!
Y-YOU'RE UNDER ARREST.
LET'S GO! TIME FOR MOON GIRL AND DEVIL DINOSAUR.
RRAAARGH!
I SAID HALT!
H-H-HALT...

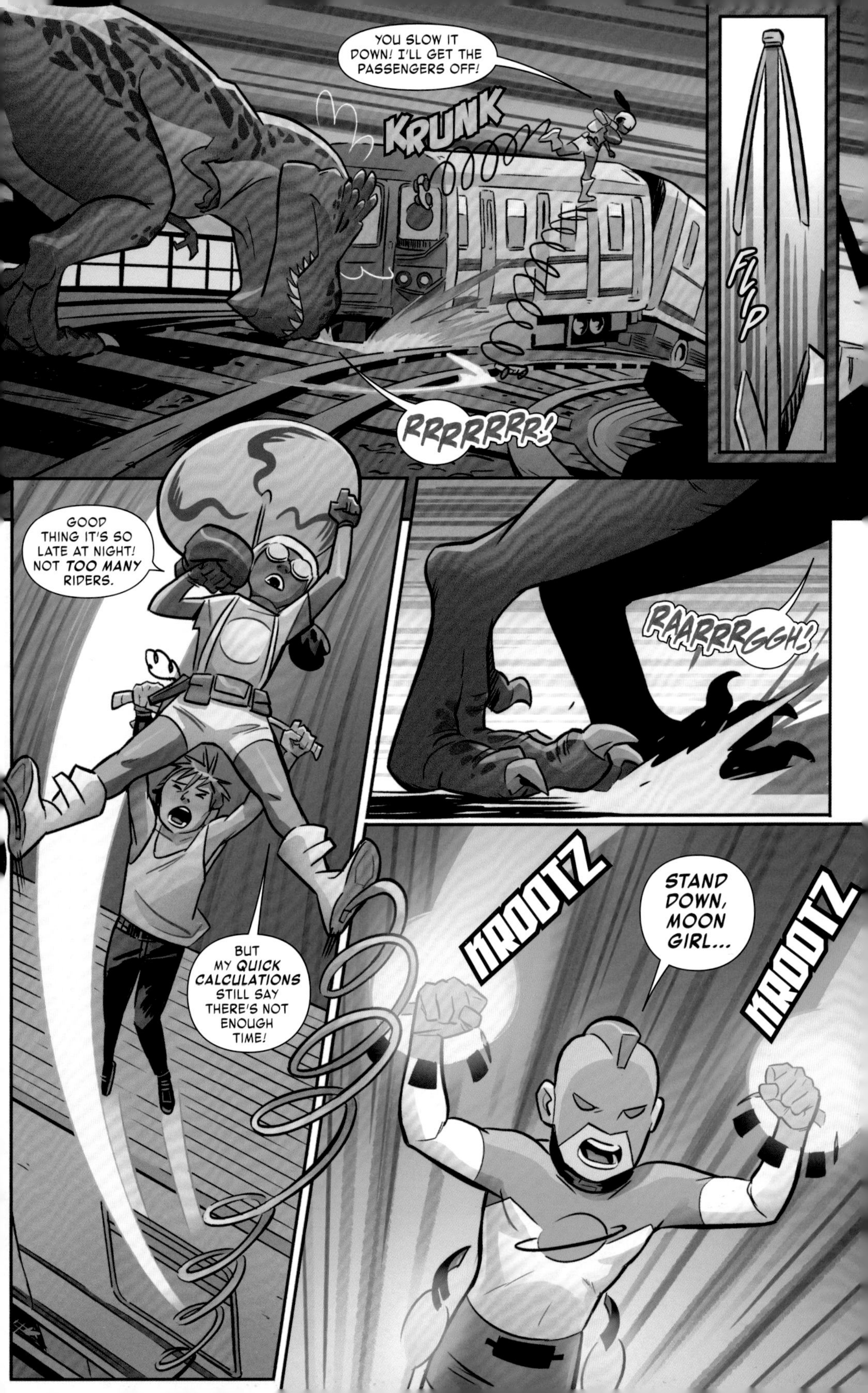
YOU SLOW IT DOWN! I'LL GET THE PASSENGERS OFF!
KRUNK
FLIP
RRRRRRR!
GOOD THING IT'S SO LATE AT NIGHT! NOT *TOO MANY* RIDERS.
RAARRRGGH!
BUT MY *QUICK CALCULATIONS* STILL SAY THERE'S NOT ENOUGH TIME!
KROOTZ
STAND DOWN, MOON GIRL...
KROOTZ

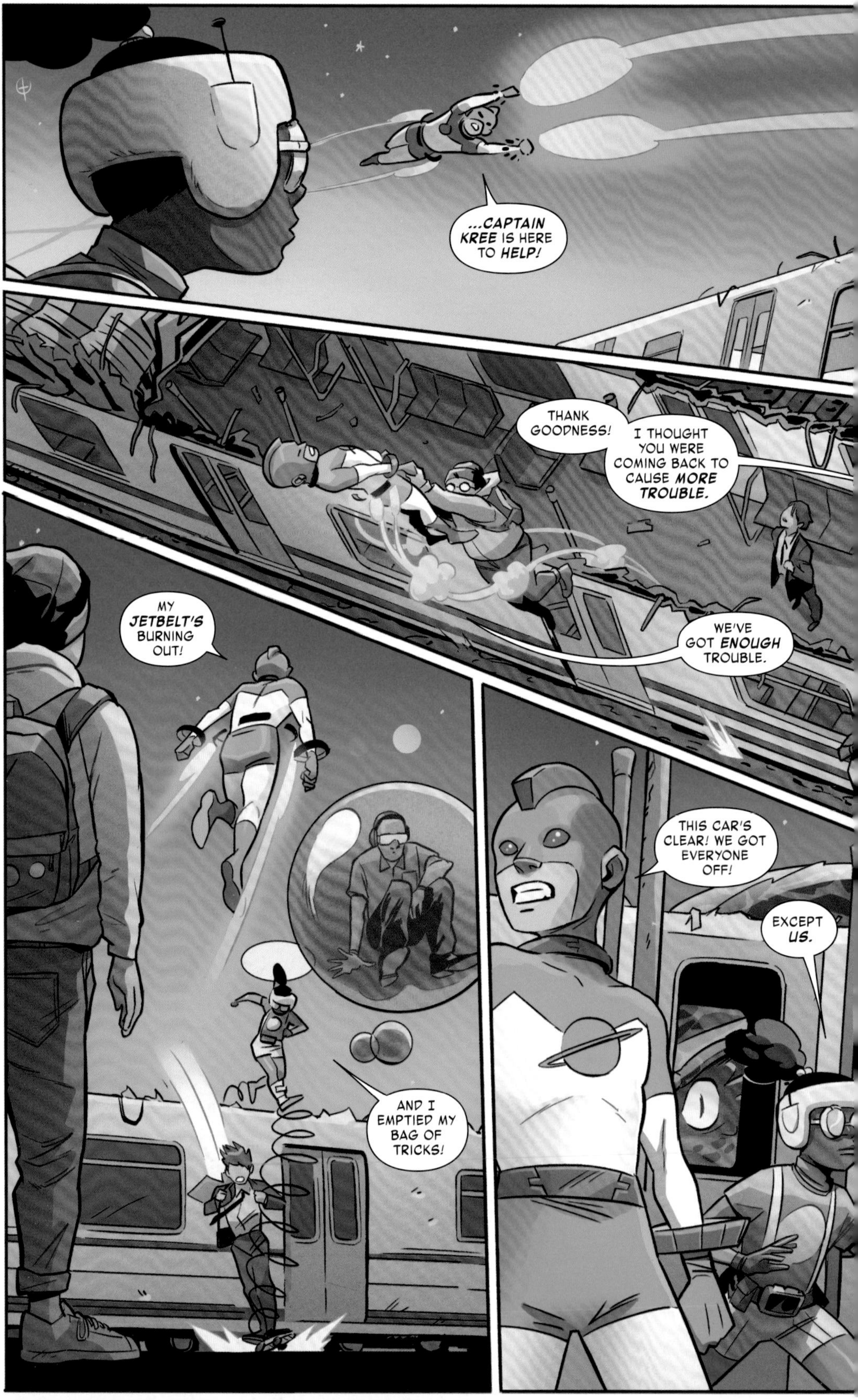
...CAPTAIN KREE IS HERE TO HELP!
THANK GOODNESS!
I THOUGHT YOU WERE COMING BACK TO CAUSE MORE TROUBLE.
WE'VE GOT ENOUGH TROUBLE.
MY JETBELT'S BURNING OUT!
AND I EMPTIED MY BAG OF TRICKS!
THIS CAR'S CLEAR! WE GOT EVERYONE OFF!
EXCEPT US.

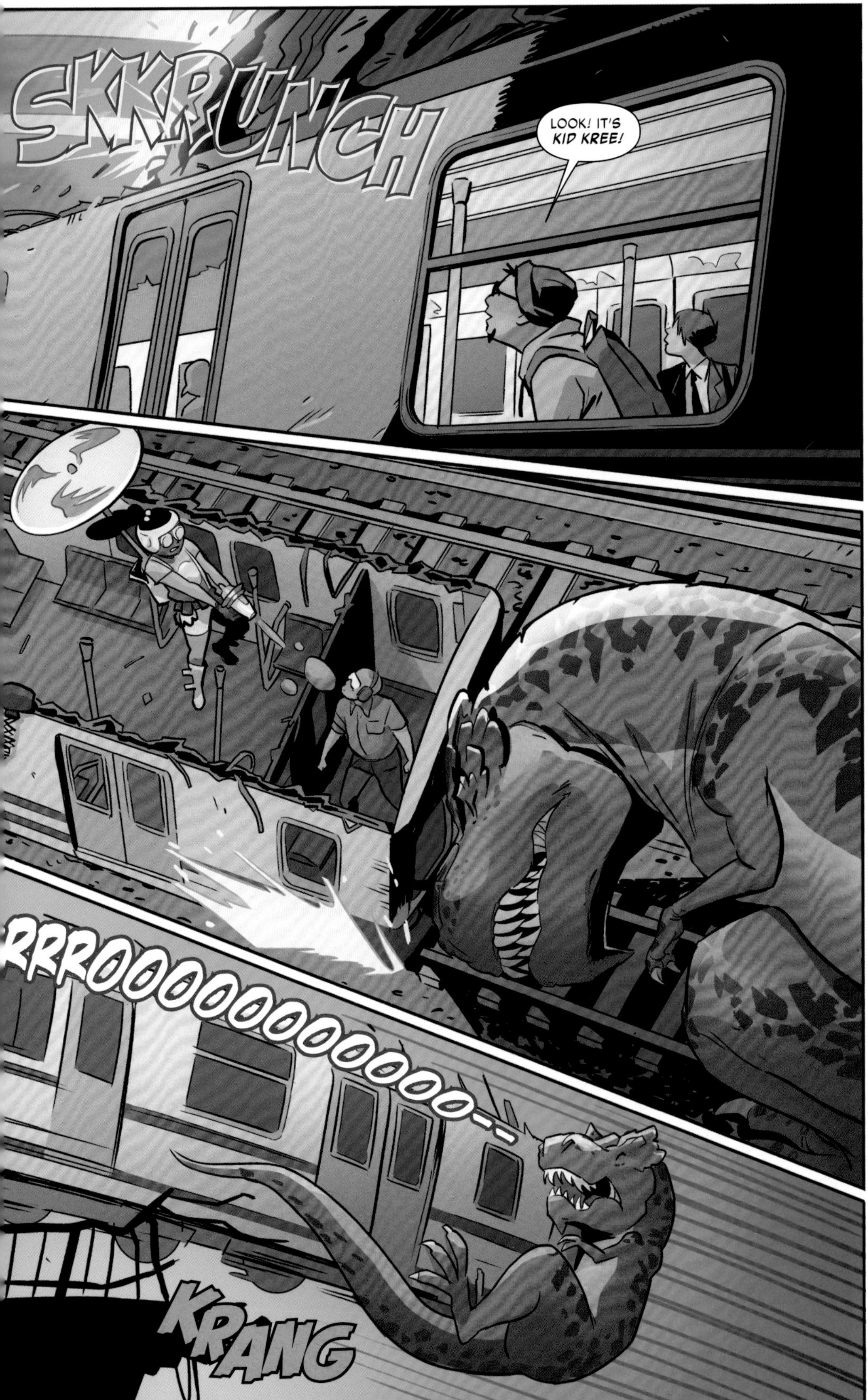
SKKRUNCH
LOOK! IT'S KID KREE!
RRROOOOOOOOOOOOOO--
KRANG

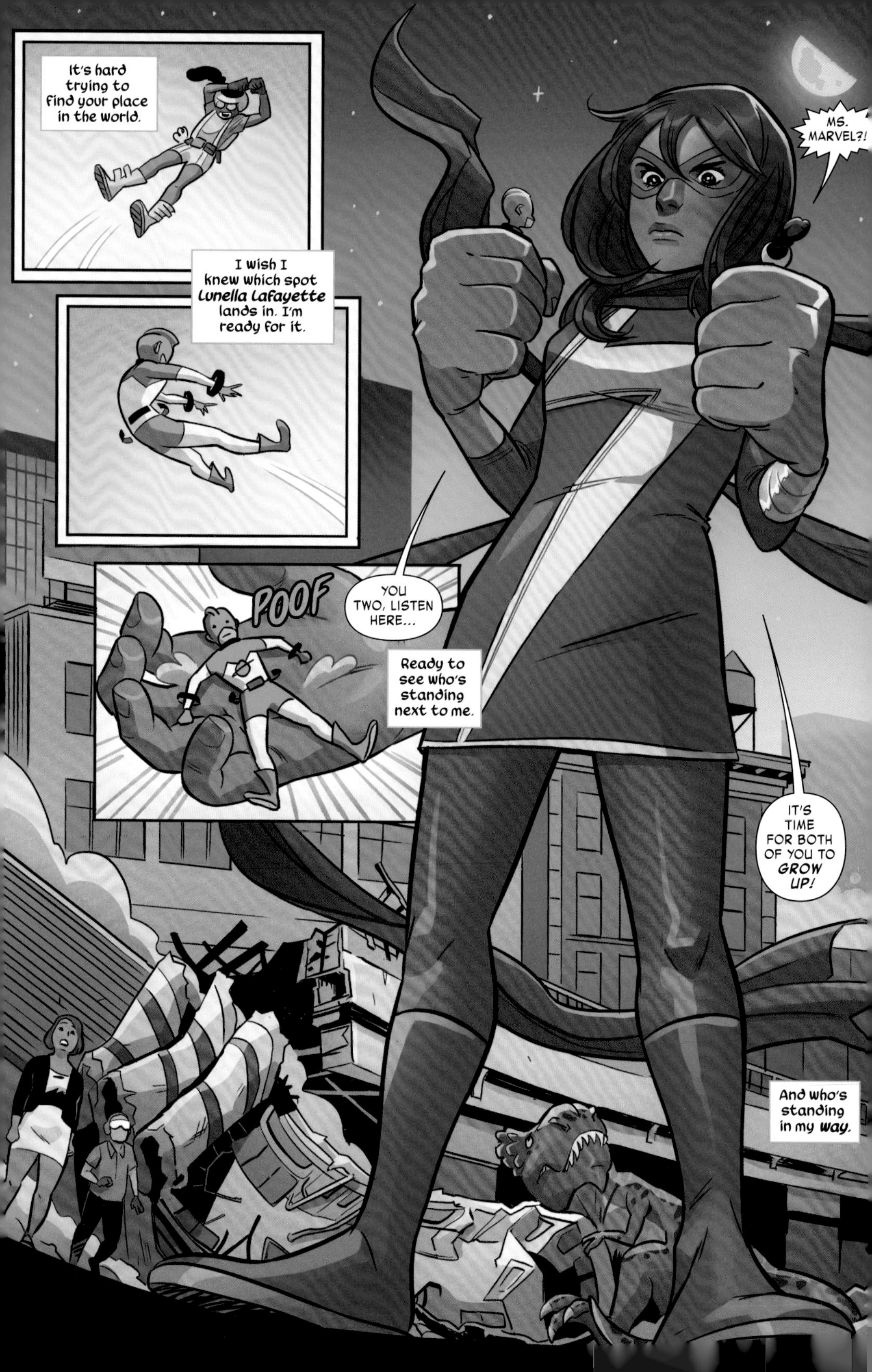
It's hard trying to find your place in the world.
I wish I knew which spot Lunella Lafayette lands in. I'm ready for it.
POOF
YOU TWO, LISTEN HERE...
Ready to see who's standing next to me.
MS. MARVEL?!
IT'S TIME FOR BOTH OF YOU TO GROW UP!
And who's standing in my way.

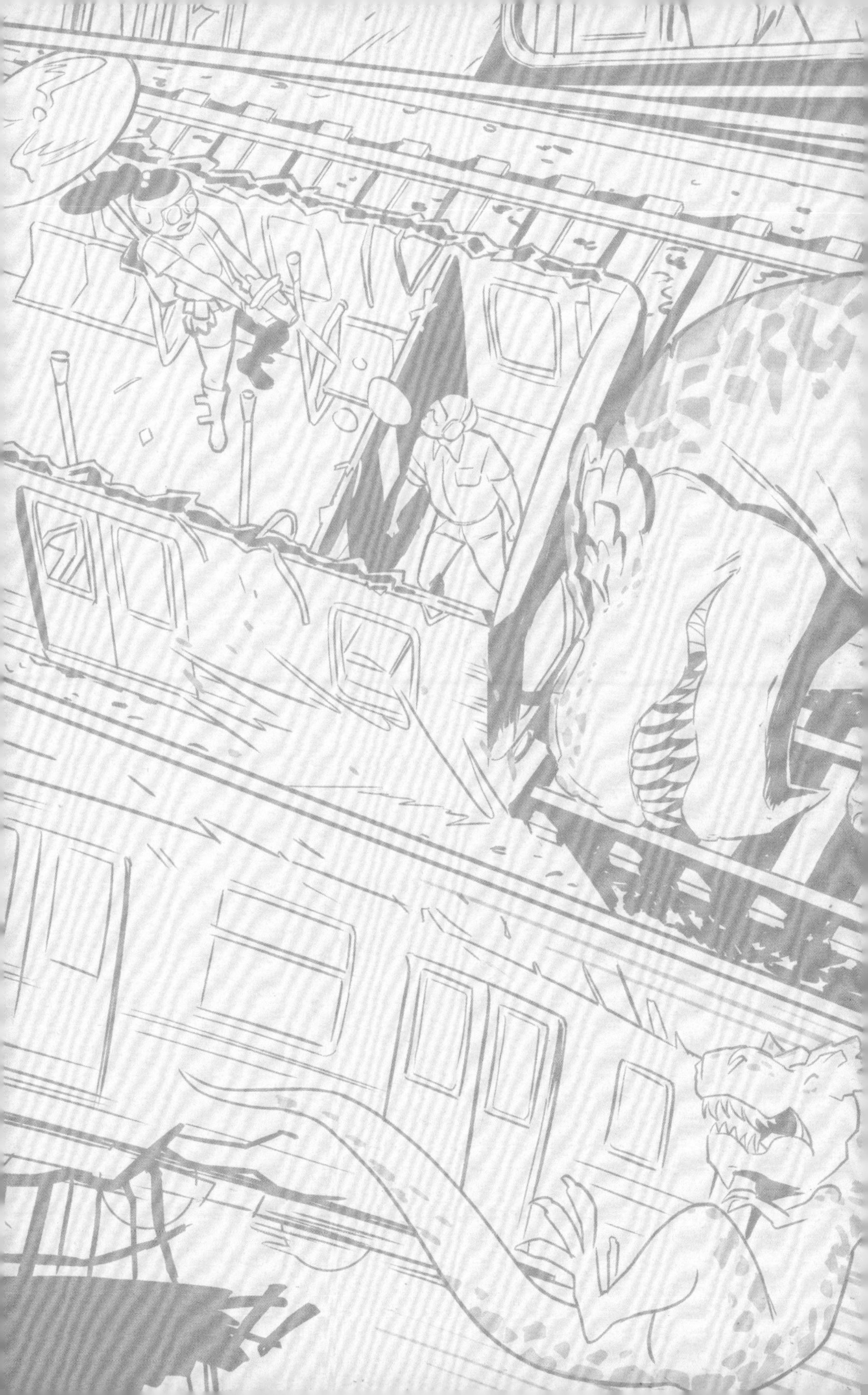

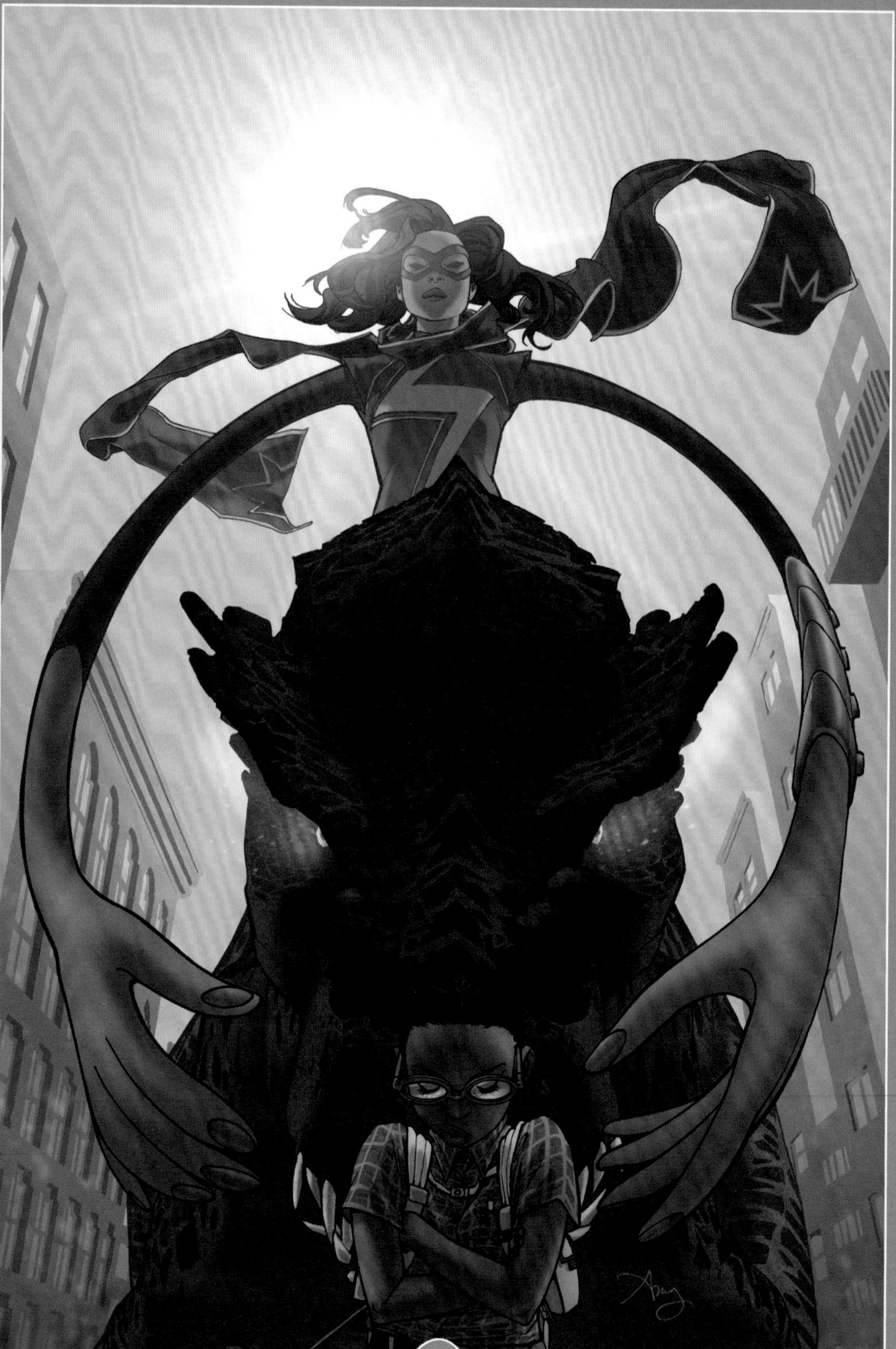

10

"THE IN-CROWD"

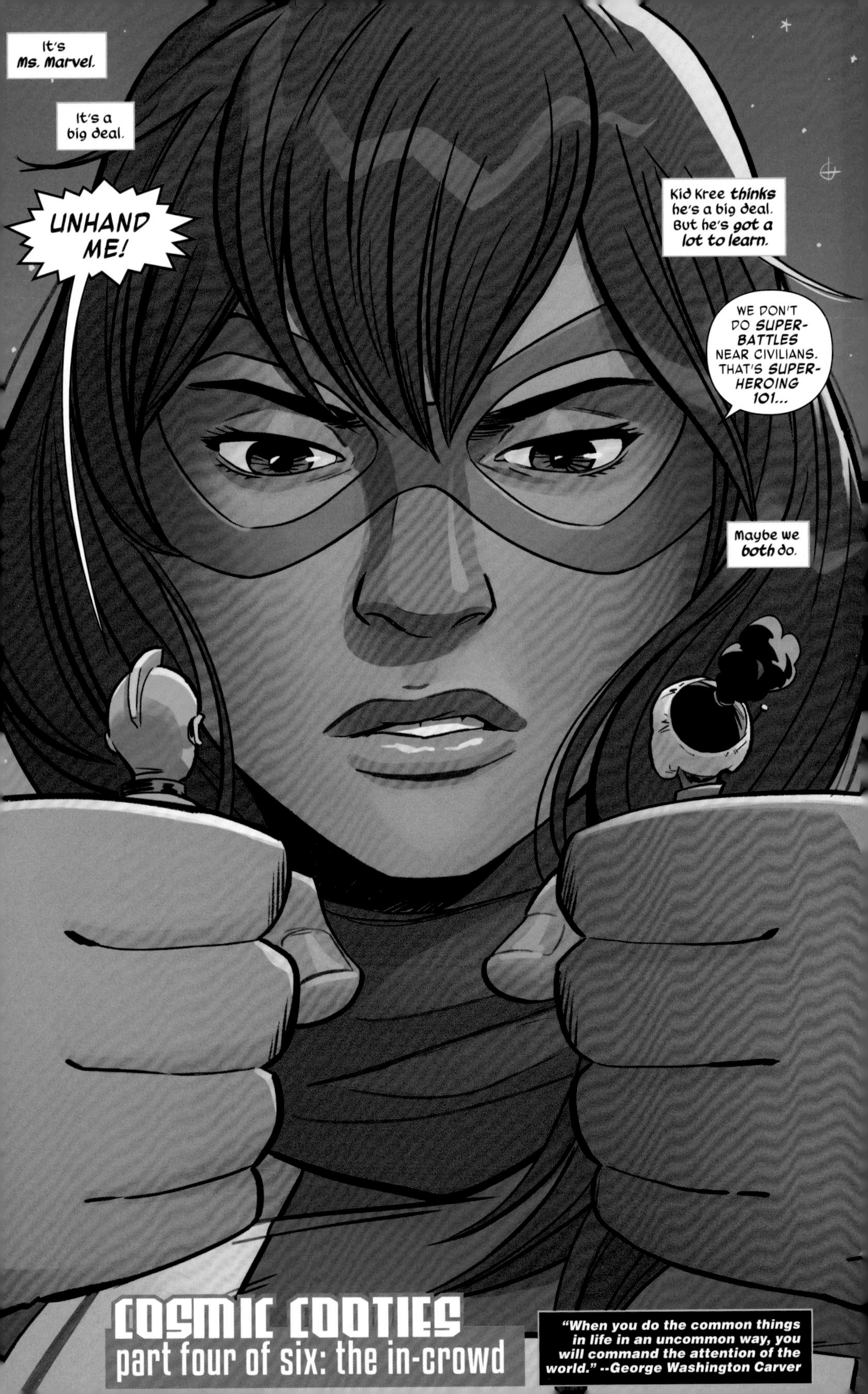

It's Ms. Marvel.
It's a big deal.
UNHAND ME!
Kid Kree thinks he's a big deal. But he's got a lot to learn.
WE DON'T DO SUPER-BATTLES NEAR CIVILIANS. THAT'S SUPER-HEROING 101...
Maybe we both do.
COSMIC COOTIES
part four of six: the in-crowd
"When you do the common things in life in an uncommon way, you will command the attention of the world." --George Washington Carver

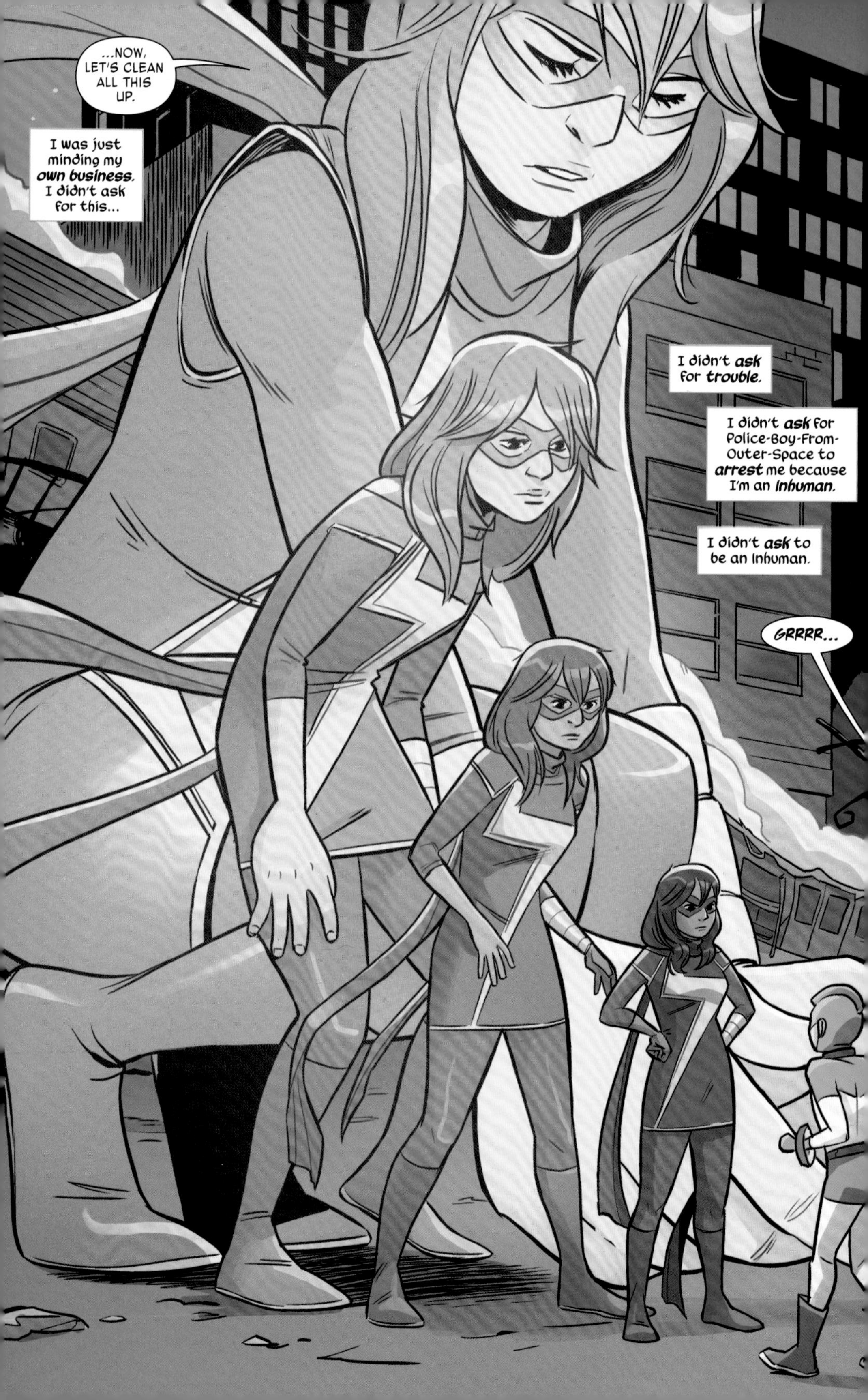
...NOW, LET'S CLEAN ALL THIS UP.
I was just minding my ***own business.*** I didn't ask for this...
I didn't ***ask*** for ***trouble.***
I didn't ***ask*** for Police-Boy-From-Outer-Space to ***arrest*** me because I'm an ***Inhuman.***
I didn't ***ask*** to be an Inhuman.
GRRRR...

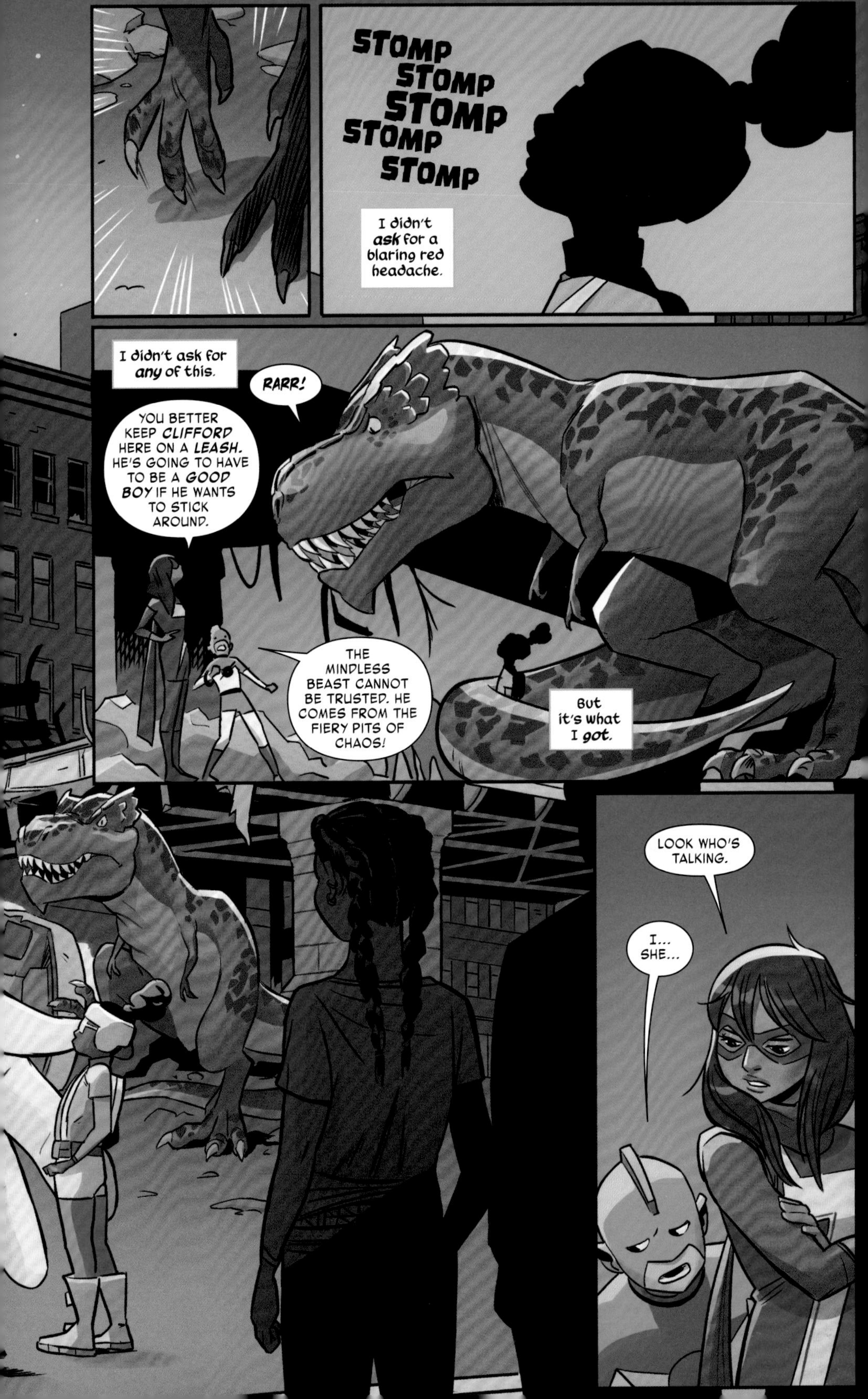
STOMP
STOMP
STOMP
STOMP
STOMP
I didn't ask for a blaring red headache.
I didn't ask for any of this.
RARR!
YOU BETTER KEEP CLIFFORD HERE ON A LEASH. HE'S GOING TO HAVE TO BE A GOOD BOY IF HE WANTS TO STICK AROUND.
THE MINDLESS BEAST CANNOT BE TRUSTED. HE COMES FROM THE FIERY PITS OF CHAOS!
But it's what I got.
LOOK WHO'S TALKING.
I... SHE...

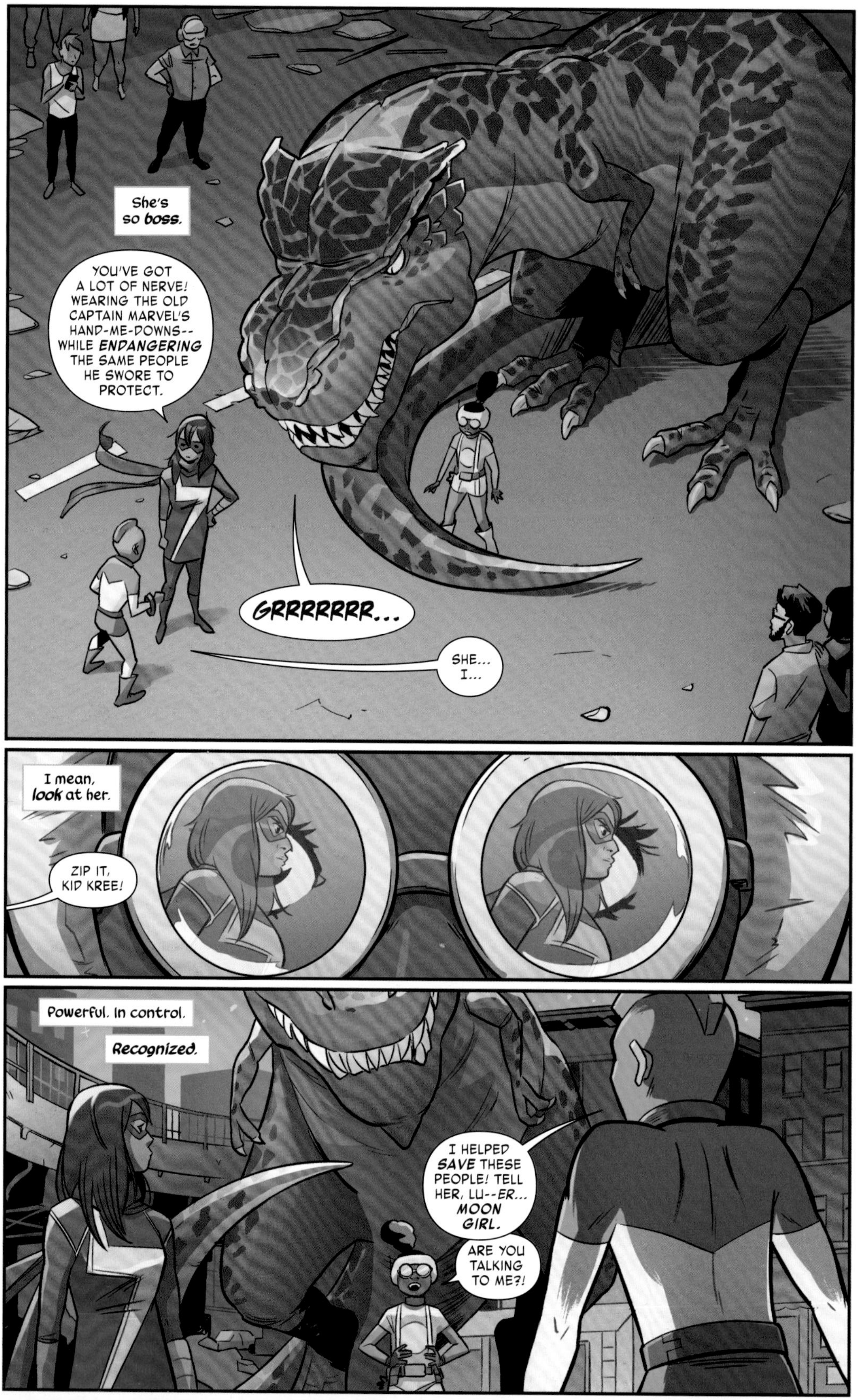
She's so boss.
YOU'VE GOT A LOT OF NERVE! WEARING THE OLD CAPTAIN MARVEL'S HAND-ME-DOWNS--WHILE ENDANGERING THE SAME PEOPLE HE SWORE TO PROTECT.
GRRRRRRR...
SHE... I...
I mean, look at her.
ZIP IT, KID KREE!
Powerful. In control.
Recognized.
I HELPED SAVE THESE PEOPLE! TELL HER, LU--ER... MOON GIRL.
ARE YOU TALKING TO ME?!

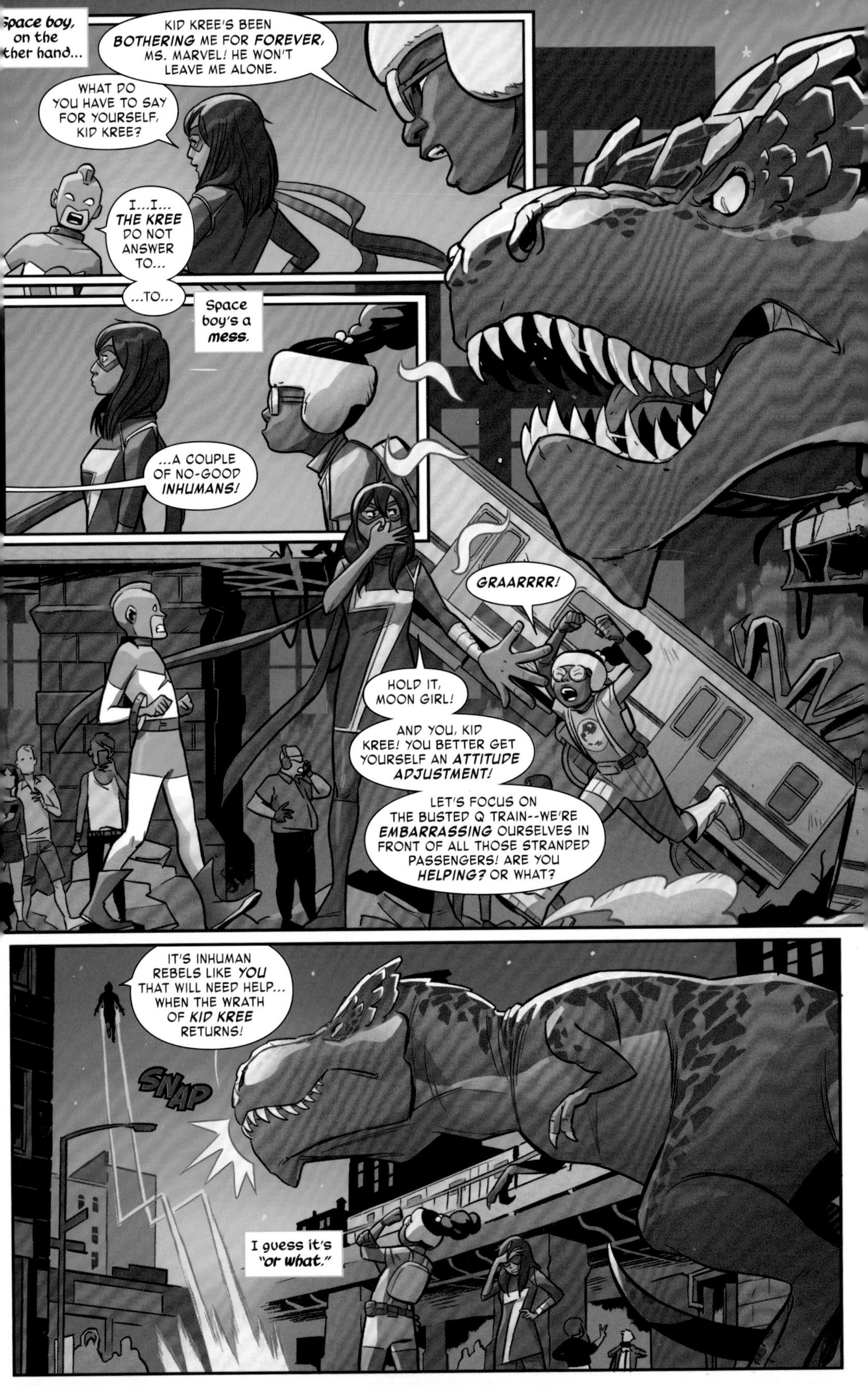

Space boy, on the other hand...
KID KREE'S BEEN BOTHERING ME FOR FOREVER, MS. MARVEL! HE WON'T LEAVE ME ALONE.
WHAT DO YOU HAVE TO SAY FOR YOURSELF, KID KREE?
I...I... THE KREE DO NOT ANSWER TO...
...TO...
Space boy's a mess.
...A COUPLE OF NO-GOOD INHUMANS!
GRAARRRR!
HOLD IT, MOON GIRL!
AND YOU, KID KREE! YOU BETTER GET YOURSELF AN ATTITUDE ADJUSTMENT!
LET'S FOCUS ON THE BUSTED Q TRAIN--WE'RE EMBARRASSING OURSELVES IN FRONT OF ALL THOSE STRANDED PASSENGERS! ARE YOU HELPING? OR WHAT?
IT'S INHUMAN REBELS LIKE YOU THAT WILL NEED HELP... WHEN THE WRATH OF KID KREE RETURNS!
SNAP
I guess it's "or what."

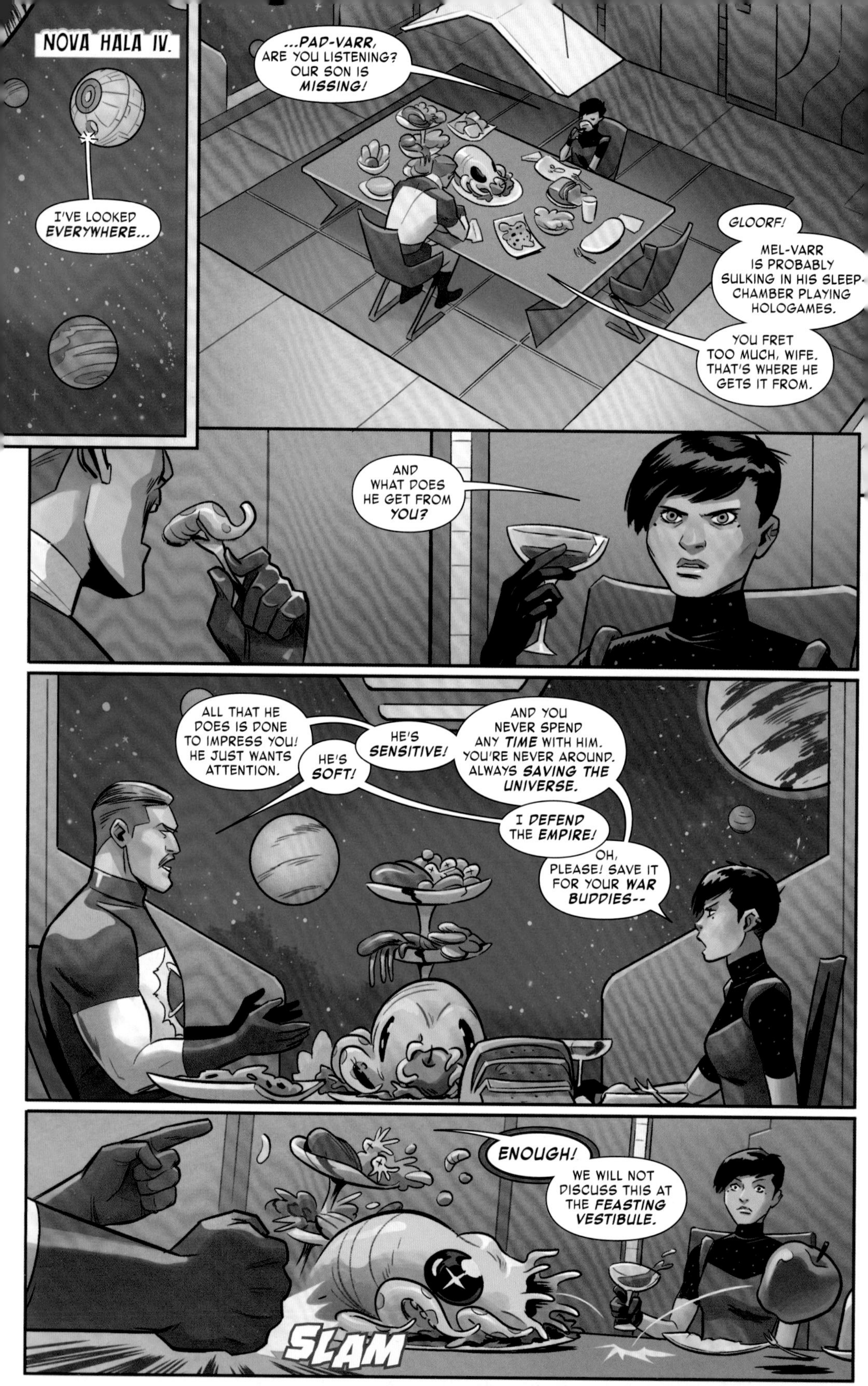
NOVA HALA IV.
I'VE LOOKED EVERYWHERE...
...PAD-VARR, ARE YOU LISTENING? OUR SON IS MISSING!
GLOORF!
MEL-VARR IS PROBABLY SULKING IN HIS SLEEP-CHAMBER PLAYING HOLOGAMES.
YOU FRET TOO MUCH, WIFE. THAT'S WHERE HE GETS IT FROM.
AND WHAT DOES HE GET FROM YOU?
ALL THAT HE DOES IS DONE TO IMPRESS YOU! HE JUST WANTS ATTENTION.
HE'S SOFT!
HE'S SENSITIVE!
AND YOU NEVER SPEND ANY TIME WITH HIM. YOU'RE NEVER AROUND. ALWAYS SAVING THE UNIVERSE.
I DEFEND THE EMPIRE!
OH, PLEASE! SAVE IT FOR YOUR WAR BUDDIES--
ENOUGH!
WE WILL NOT DISCUSS THIS AT THE FEASTING VESTIBULE.
SLAM

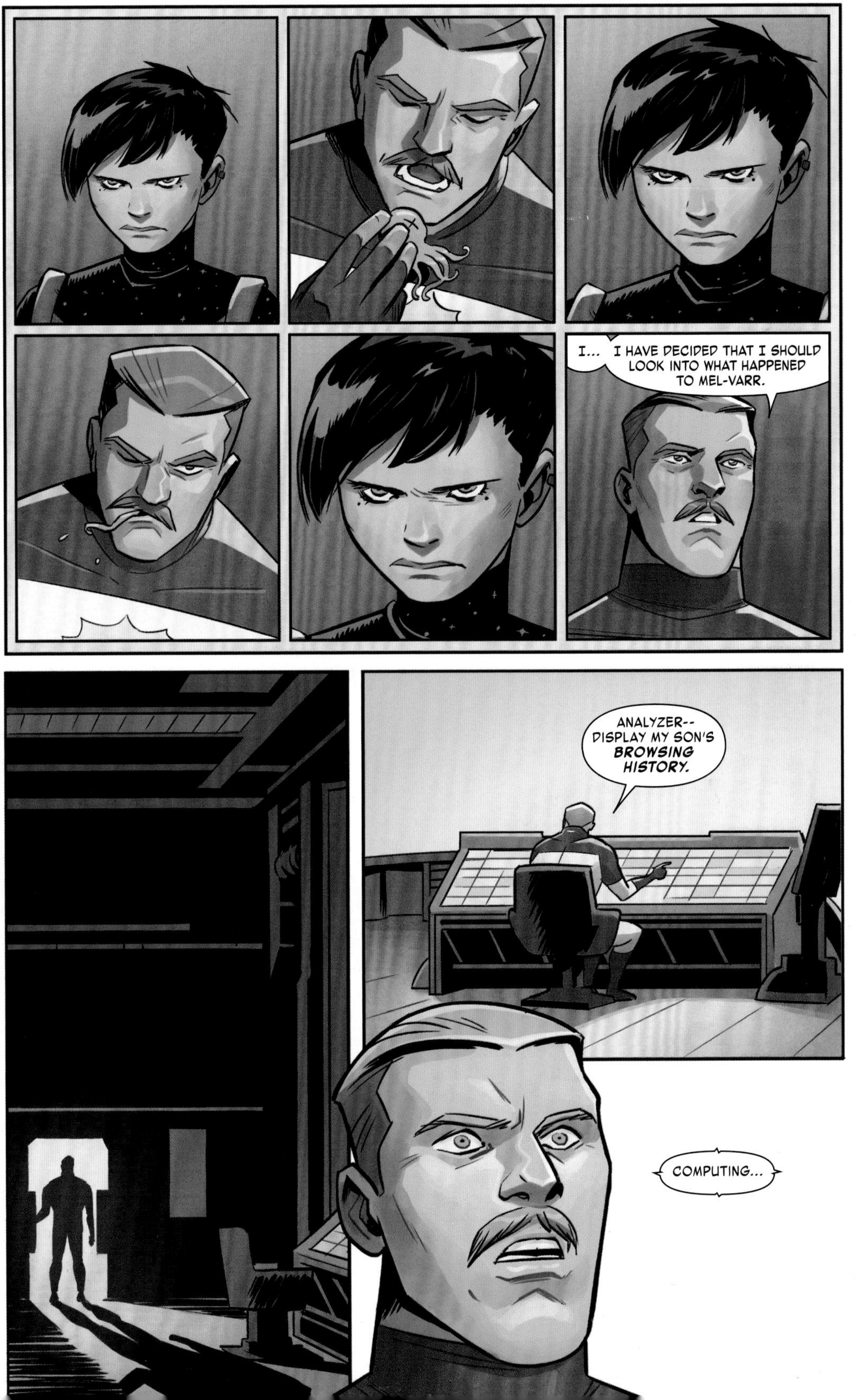
I... I HAVE DECIDED THAT I SHOULD LOOK INTO WHAT HAPPENED TO MEL-VARR.
ANALYZER-- DISPLAY MY SON'S **BROWSING HISTORY.**
COMPUTING...

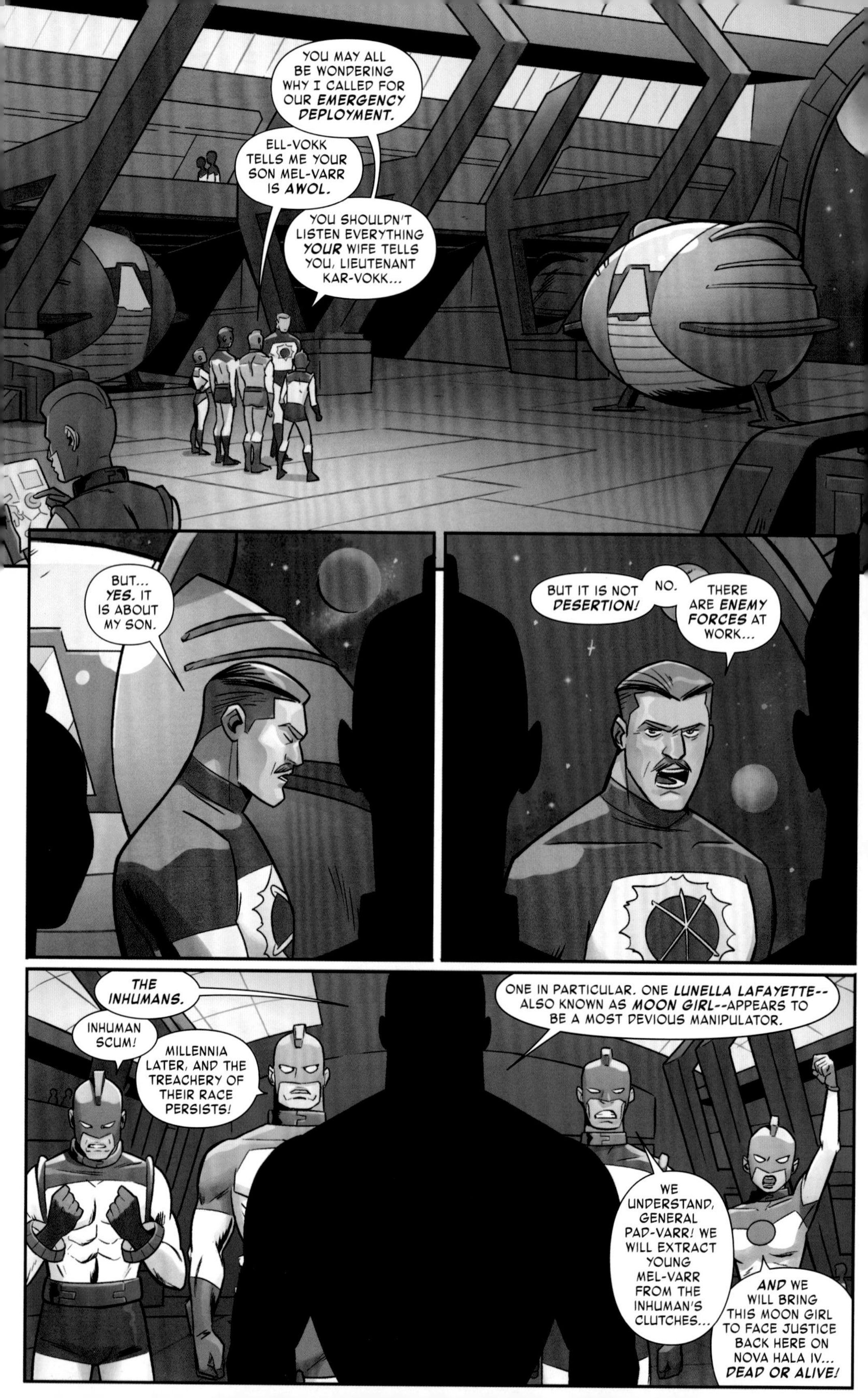
YOU MAY ALL BE WONDERING WHY I CALLED FOR OUR EMERGENCY DEPLOYMENT.
ELL-VOKK TELLS ME YOUR SON MEL-VARR IS AWOL.
YOU SHOULDN'T LISTEN EVERYTHING YOUR WIFE TELLS YOU, LIEUTENANT KAR-VOKK...
BUT... YES. IT IS ABOUT MY SON.
BUT IT IS NOT DESERTION!
NO.
THERE ARE ENEMY FORCES AT WORK...
THE INHUMANS.
INHUMAN SCUM!
MILLENNIA LATER, AND THE TREACHERY OF THEIR RACE PERSISTS!
ONE IN PARTICULAR. ONE LUNELLA LAFAYETTE--ALSO KNOWN AS MOON GIRL--APPEARS TO BE A MOST DEVIOUS MANIPULATOR.
WE UNDERSTAND, GENERAL PAD-VARR! WE WILL EXTRACT YOUNG MEL-VARR FROM THE INHUMAN'S CLUTCHES...
AND WE WILL BRING THIS MOON GIRL TO FACE JUSTICE BACK HERE ON NOVA HALA IV... DEAD OR ALIVE!

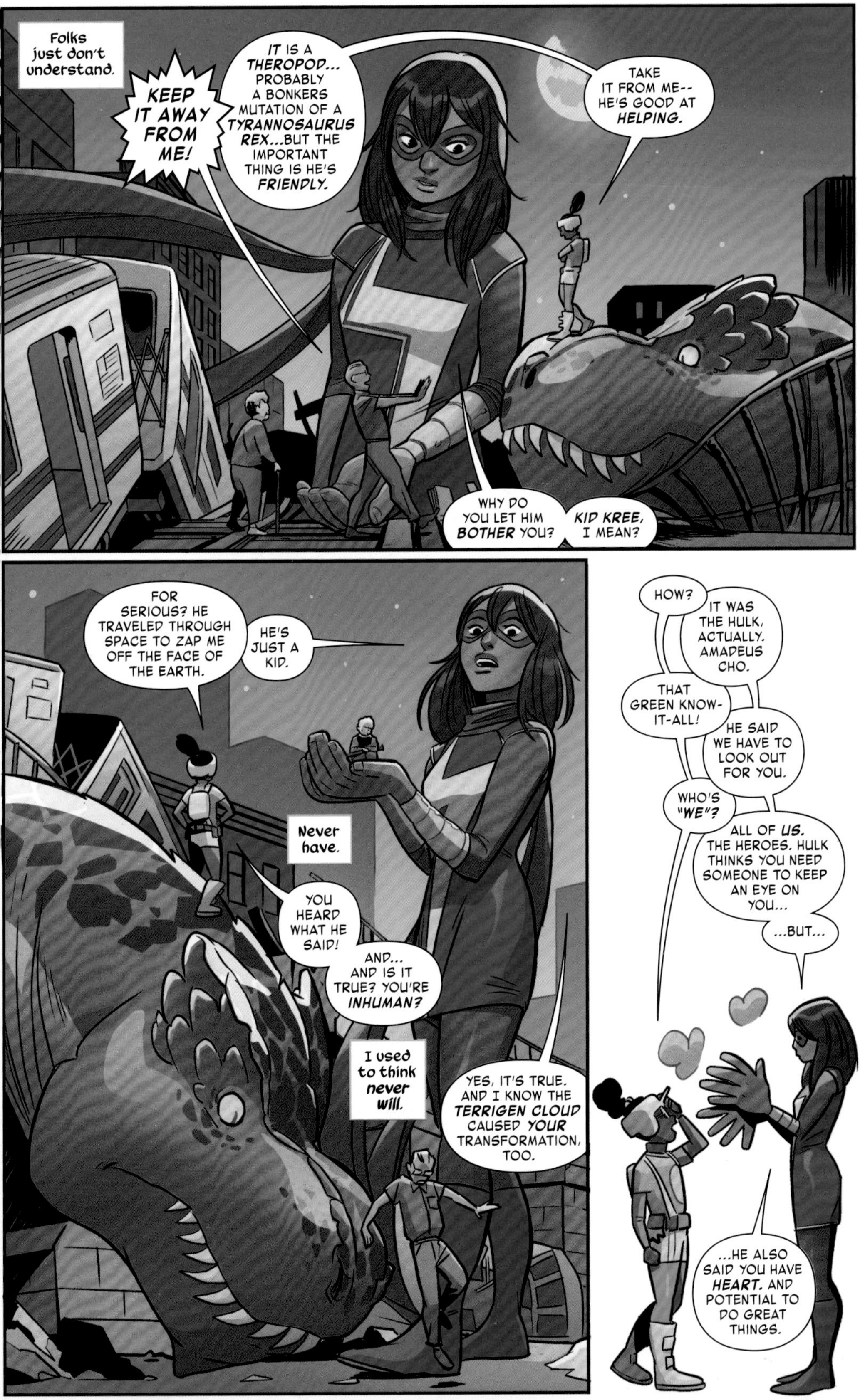
Folks just don't understand.
KEEP IT AWAY FROM ME!
IT IS A THEROPOD... PROBABLY A BONKERS MUTATION OF A TYRANNOSAURUS REX...BUT THE IMPORTANT THING IS HE'S FRIENDLY.
TAKE IT FROM ME-- HE'S GOOD AT HELPING.
WHY DO YOU LET HIM BOTHER YOU?
KID KREE, I MEAN?
FOR SERIOUS? HE TRAVELED THROUGH SPACE TO ZAP ME OFF THE FACE OF THE EARTH.
HE'S JUST A KID.
Never have.
YOU HEARD WHAT HE SAID!
AND... AND IS IT TRUE? YOU'RE INHUMAN?
I used to think never will.
YES, IT'S TRUE. AND I KNOW THE TERRIGEN CLOUD CAUSED YOUR TRANSFORMATION, TOO.
HOW?
IT WAS THE HULK, ACTUALLY. AMADEUS CHO.
THAT GREEN KNOW-IT-ALL!
HE SAID WE HAVE TO LOOK OUT FOR YOU.
WHO'S "WE"?
ALL OF US. THE HEROES. HULK THINKS YOU NEED SOMEONE TO KEEP AN EYE ON YOU...
...BUT...
...HE ALSO SAID YOU HAVE HEART. AND POTENTIAL TO DO GREAT THINGS.

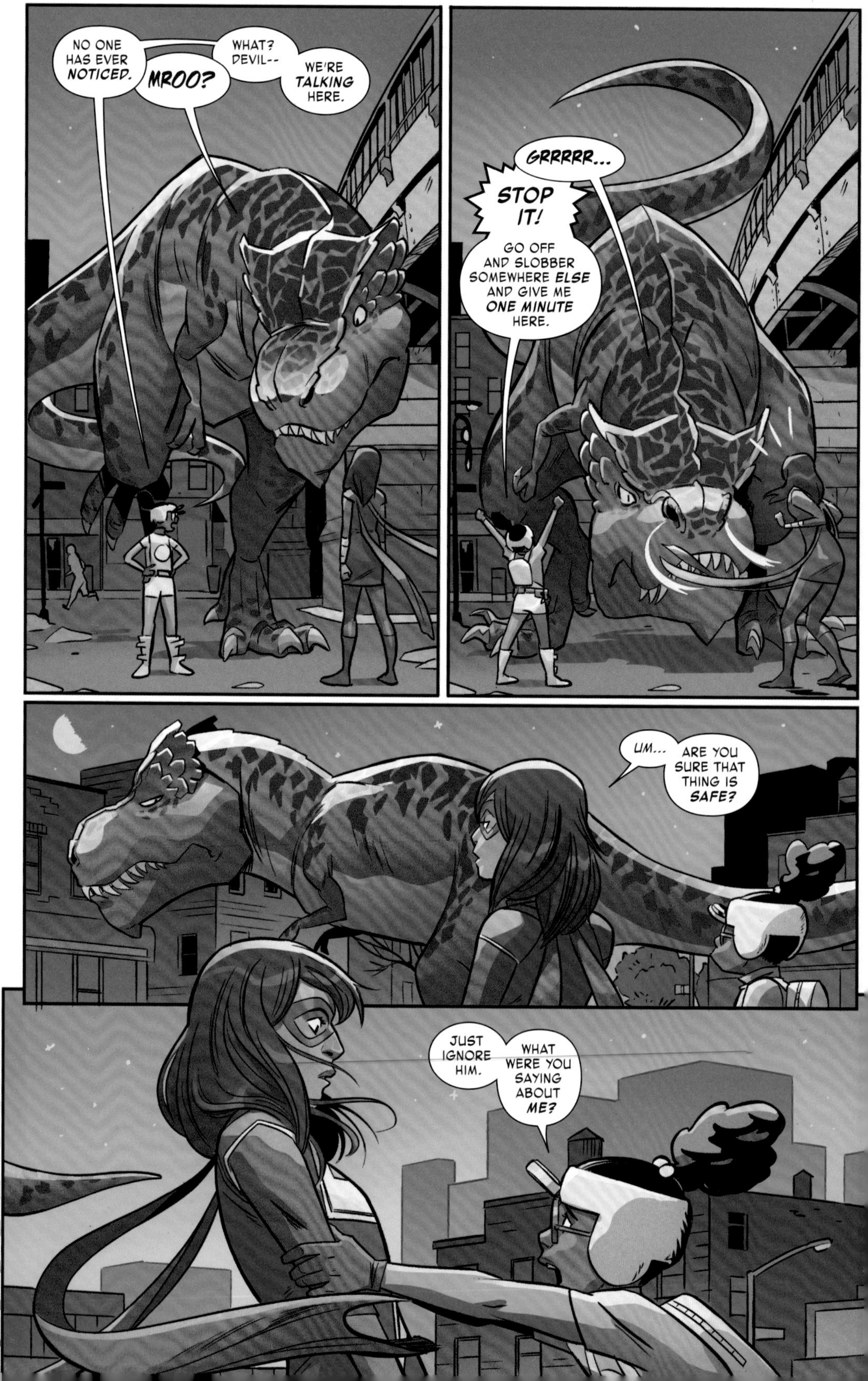
NO ONE HAS EVER NOTICED.
MROO?
WHAT? DEVIL--
WE'RE TALKING HERE.
GRRRRR...
STOP IT!
GO OFF AND SLOBBER SOMEWHERE ELSE AND GIVE ME ONE MINUTE HERE.
UM...
ARE YOU SURE THAT THING IS SAFE?
JUST IGNORE HIM.
WHAT WERE YOU SAYING ABOUT ME?

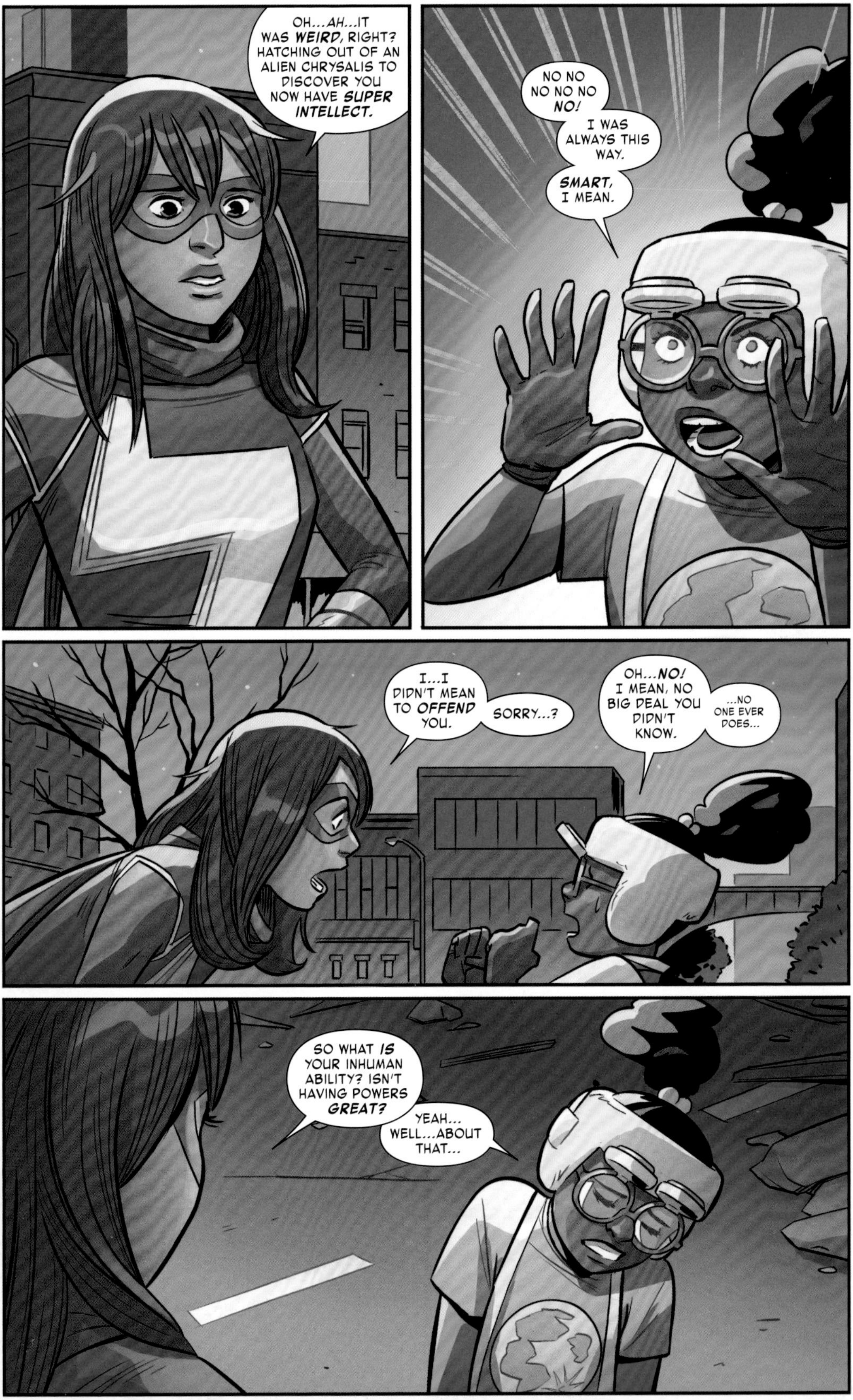
OH...AH...IT WAS WEIRD, RIGHT? HATCHING OUT OF AN ALIEN CHRYSALIS TO DISCOVER YOU NOW HAVE SUPER INTELLECT.
NO NO NO NO NO NO NO!
I WAS ALWAYS THIS WAY.
SMART, I MEAN.
I...I DIDN'T MEAN TO OFFEND YOU.
SORRY...?
OH...NO! I MEAN, NO BIG DEAL YOU DIDN'T KNOW.
...NO ONE EVER DOES...
SO WHAT IS YOUR INHUMAN ABILITY? ISN'T HAVING POWERS GREAT?
YEAH... WELL...ABOUT THAT...

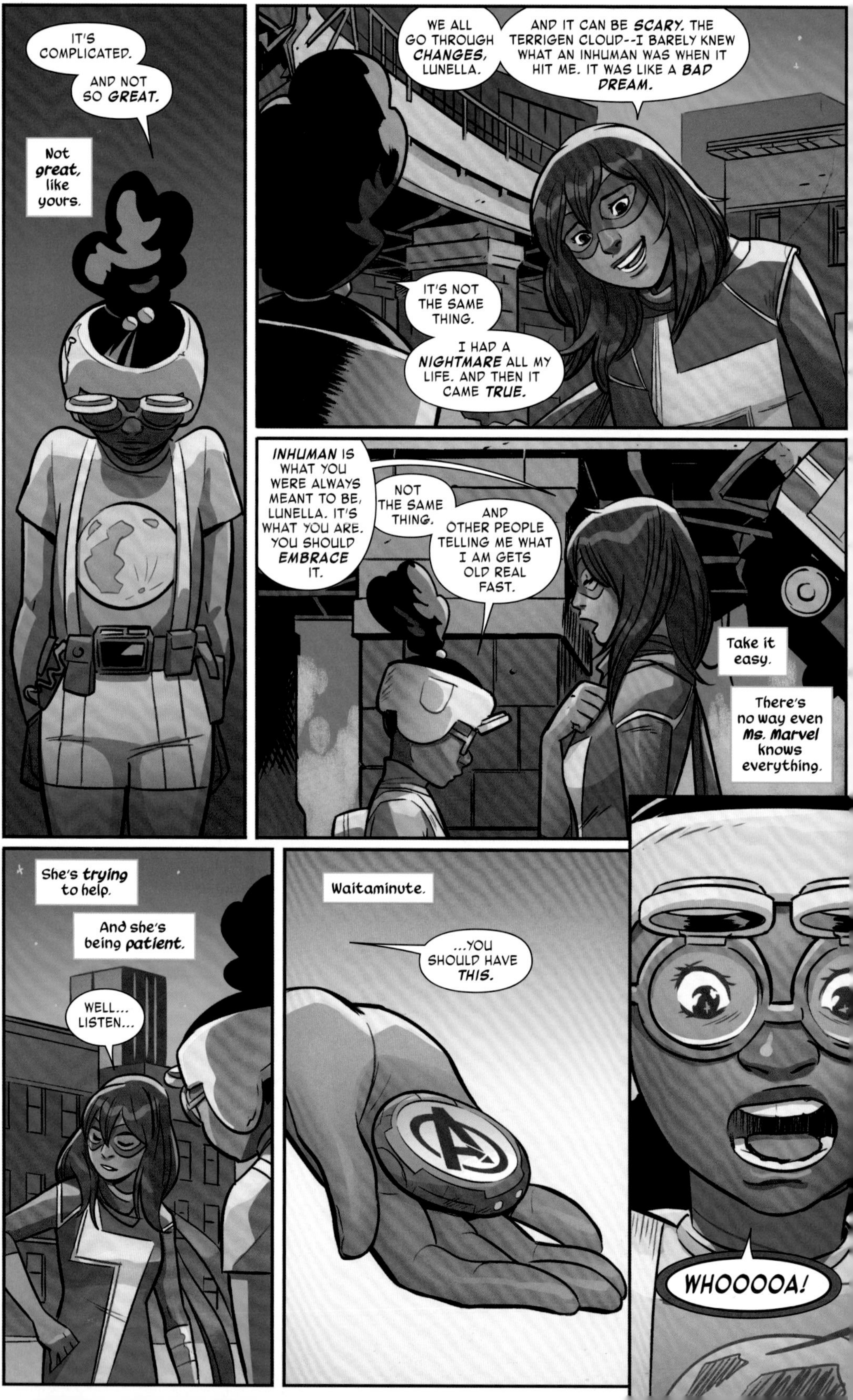

IT'S COMPLICATED.
AND NOT SO GREAT.
Not great, like yours.
WE ALL GO THROUGH CHANGES, LUNELLA.
AND IT CAN BE SCARY. THE TERRIGEN CLOUD--I BARELY KNEW WHAT AN INHUMAN WAS WHEN IT HIT ME. IT WAS LIKE A BAD DREAM.
IT'S NOT THE SAME THING.
I HAD A NIGHTMARE ALL MY LIFE. AND THEN IT CAME TRUE.
INHUMAN IS WHAT YOU WERE ALWAYS MEANT TO BE, LUNELLA. IT'S WHAT YOU ARE. YOU SHOULD EMBRACE IT.
NOT THE SAME THING.
AND OTHER PEOPLE TELLING ME WHAT I AM GETS OLD REAL FAST.
Take it easy.
There's no way even Ms. Marvel knows everything.
She's trying to help.
And she's being patient.
WELL... LISTEN...
Waitaminute.
...YOU SHOULD HAVE THIS.
WHOOOOA!

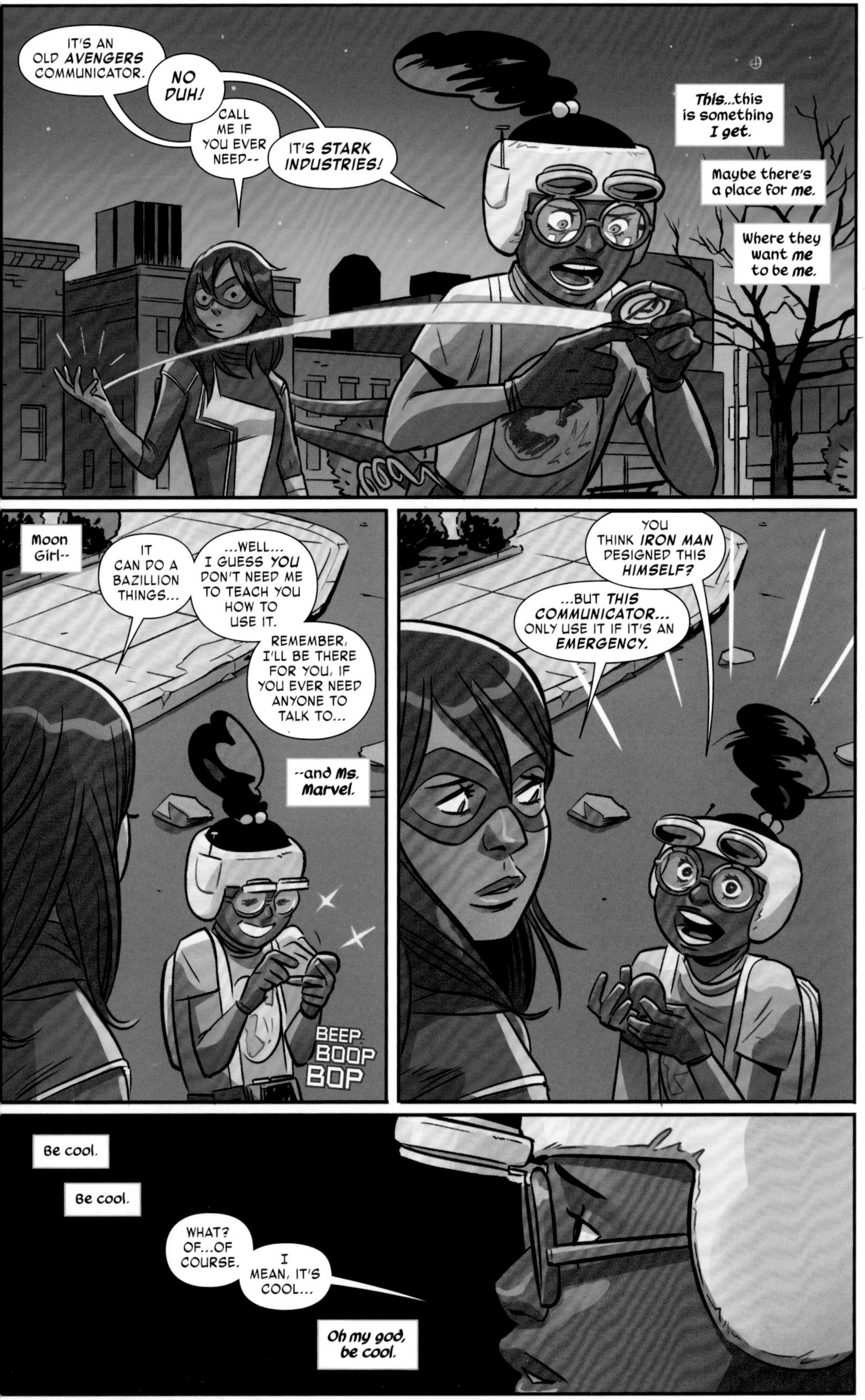

IT'S AN OLD AVENGERS COMMUNICATOR.
NO DUH!
CALL ME IF YOU EVER NEED--
IT'S STARK INDUSTRIES!
This...this is something I get.
Maybe there's a place for me.
Where they want me to be me.
Moon Girl--
IT CAN DO A BAZILLION THINGS...
...WELL... I GUESS YOU DON'T NEED ME TO TEACH YOU HOW TO USE IT.
REMEMBER, I'LL BE THERE FOR YOU, IF YOU EVER NEED ANYONE TO TALK TO...
--and Ms. Marvel.
BEEP BOOP BOP
YOU THINK IRON MAN DESIGNED THIS HIMSELF?
...BUT THIS COMMUNICATOR... ONLY USE IT IF IT'S AN EMERGENCY.
Be cool.
Be cool.
WHAT? OF...OF COURSE.
I MEAN, IT'S COOL...
Oh my god, be cool.

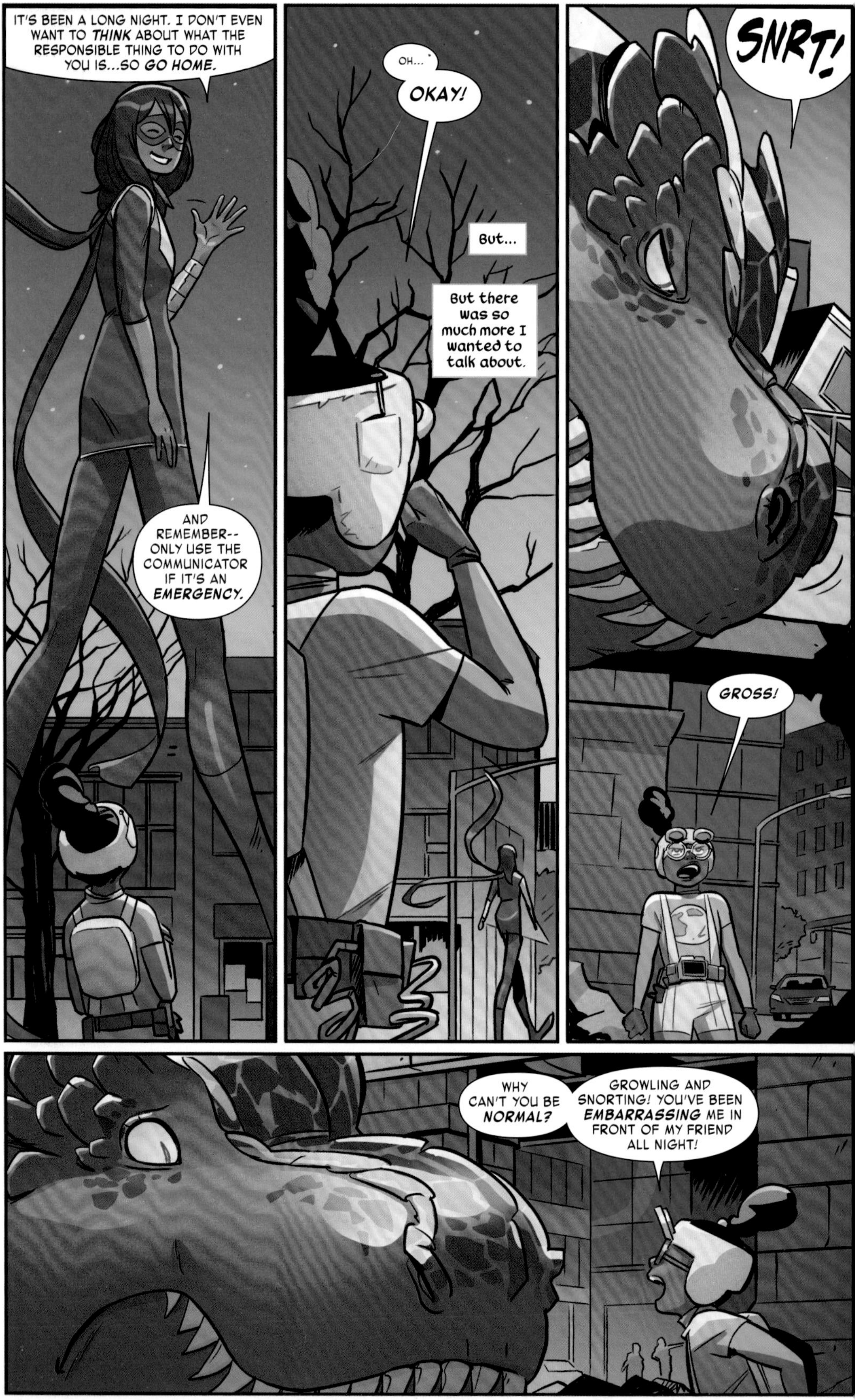
IT'S BEEN A LONG NIGHT. I DON'T EVEN WANT TO *THINK* ABOUT WHAT THE RESPONSIBLE THING TO DO WITH YOU IS...SO *GO HOME.*
AND REMEMBER-- ONLY USE THE COMMUNICATOR IF IT'S AN *EMERGENCY.*
OH...
OKAY!
But...
But there was so much more I wanted to talk about.
SNRT!
GROSS!
WHY CAN'T YOU BE *NORMAL?*
GROWLING AND SNORTING! YOU'VE BEEN *EMBARRASSING* ME IN FRONT OF MY FRIEND ALL NIGHT!

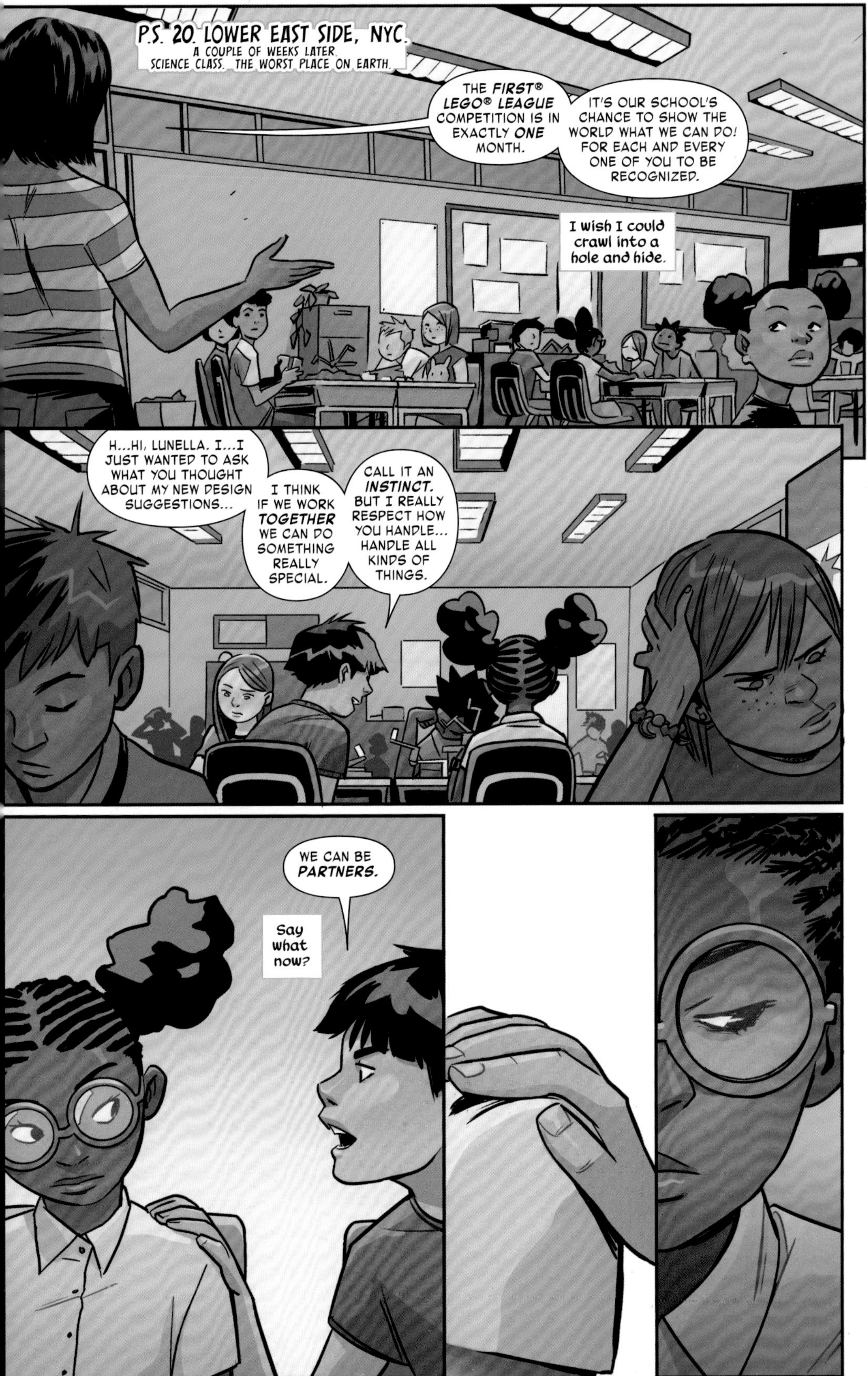
P.S. 20. LOWER EAST SIDE, NYC.
A COUPLE OF WEEKS LATER.
SCIENCE CLASS. THE WORST PLACE ON EARTH.
THE FIRST® LEGO® LEAGUE COMPETITION IS IN EXACTLY ONE MONTH.
IT'S OUR SCHOOL'S CHANCE TO SHOW THE WORLD WHAT WE CAN DO! FOR EACH AND EVERY ONE OF YOU TO BE RECOGNIZED.
I wish I could crawl into a hole and hide.
H...HI, LUNELLA. I...I JUST WANTED TO ASK WHAT YOU THOUGHT ABOUT MY NEW DESIGN SUGGESTIONS...
I THINK IF WE WORK TOGETHER WE CAN DO SOMETHING REALLY SPECIAL.
CALL IT AN INSTINCT. BUT I REALLY RESPECT HOW YOU HANDLE... HANDLE ALL KINDS OF THINGS.
WE CAN BE PARTNERS.
Say what now?

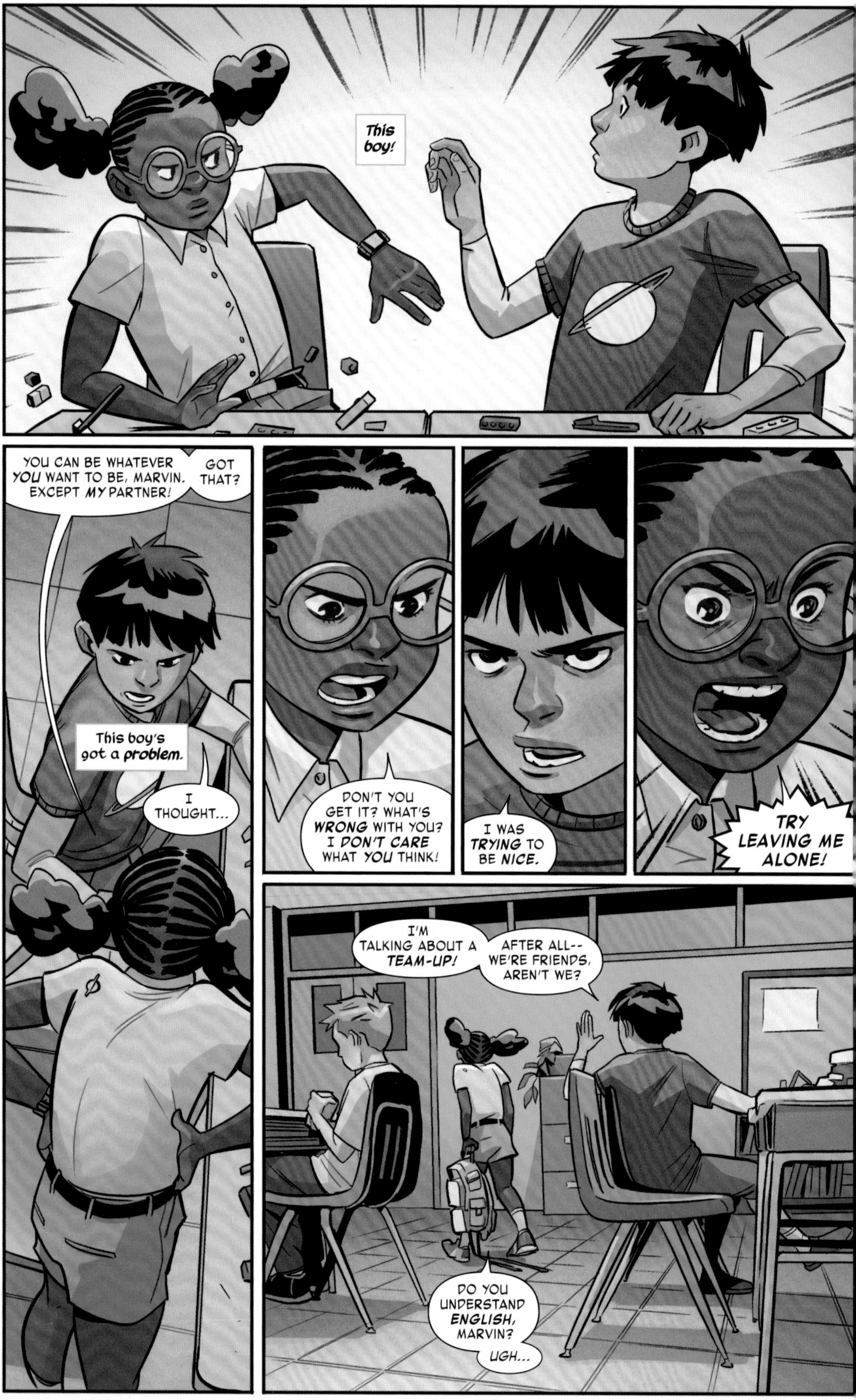

This boy!
YOU CAN BE WHATEVER YOU WANT TO BE, MARVIN. EXCEPT MY PARTNER!
GOT THAT?
This boy's got a problem.
I THOUGHT...
DON'T YOU GET IT? WHAT'S WRONG WITH YOU? I DON'T CARE WHAT YOU THINK!
I WAS TRYING TO BE NICE.
TRY LEAVING ME ALONE!
I'M TALKING ABOUT A TEAM-UP!
AFTER ALL-- WE'RE FRIENDS, AREN'T WE?
DO YOU UNDERSTAND ENGLISH, MARVIN?
UGH...

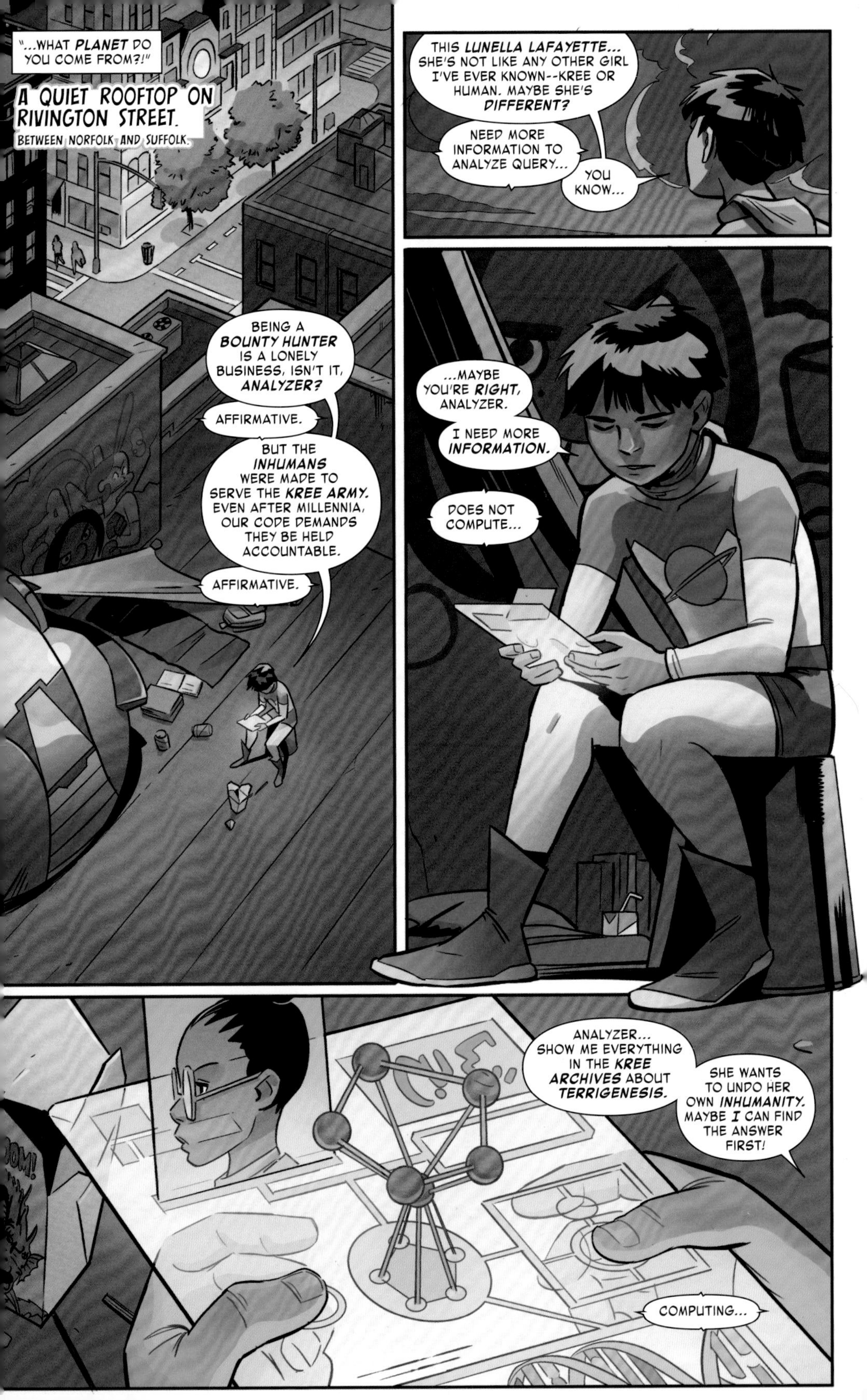
"...WHAT PLANET DO YOU COME FROM?!"
A QUIET ROOFTOP ON RIVINGTON STREET.
BETWEEN NORFOLK AND SUFFOLK.
BEING A BOUNTY HUNTER IS A LONELY BUSINESS, ISN'T IT, ANALYZER?
AFFIRMATIVE.
BUT THE INHUMANS WERE MADE TO SERVE THE KREE ARMY. EVEN AFTER MILLENNIA, OUR CODE DEMANDS THEY BE HELD ACCOUNTABLE.
AFFIRMATIVE.
THIS LUNELLA LAFAYETTE... SHE'S NOT LIKE ANY OTHER GIRL I'VE EVER KNOWN--KREE OR HUMAN. MAYBE SHE'S DIFFERENT?
NEED MORE INFORMATION TO ANALYZE QUERY...
YOU KNOW...
...MAYBE YOU'RE RIGHT, ANALYZER.
I NEED MORE INFORMATION.
DOES NOT COMPUTE...
ANALYZER... SHOW ME EVERYTHING IN THE KREE ARCHIVES ABOUT TERRIGENESIS.
SHE WANTS TO UNDO HER OWN INHUMANITY. MAYBE I CAN FIND THE ANSWER FIRST!
COMPUTING...

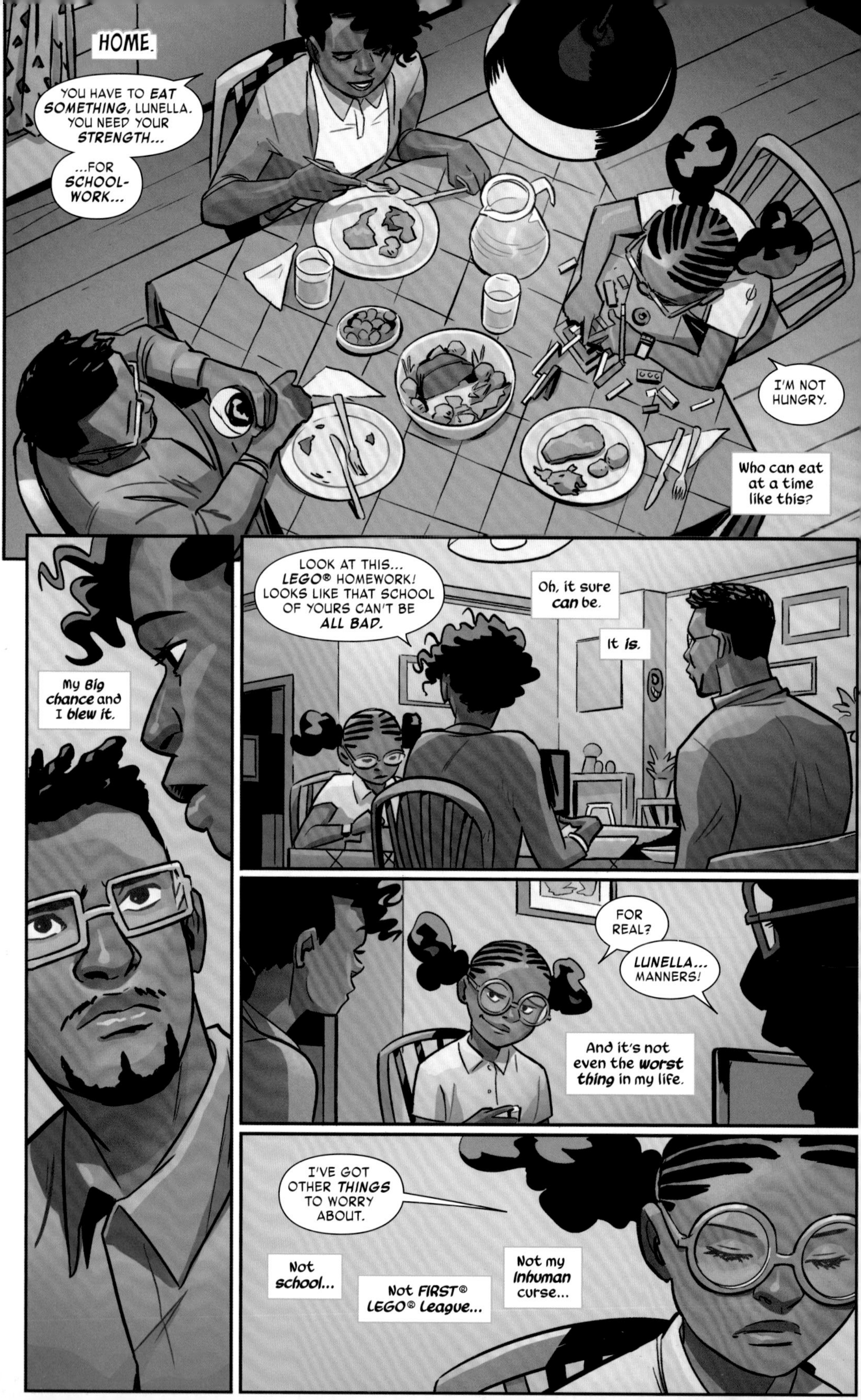
HOME.
YOU HAVE TO EAT SOMETHING, LUNELLA. YOU NEED YOUR STRENGTH...
...FOR SCHOOL-WORK...
I'M NOT HUNGRY.
Who can eat at a time like this?
My Big chance and I blew it.
LOOK AT THIS... LEGO® HOMEWORK! LOOKS LIKE THAT SCHOOL OF YOURS CAN'T BE ALL BAD.
Oh, it sure can be.
It is.
FOR REAL?
LUNELLA... MANNERS!
And it's not even the worst thing in my life.
I'VE GOT OTHER THINGS TO WORRY ABOUT.
Not school...
Not FIRST® LEGO® League...
Not my Inhuman curse...

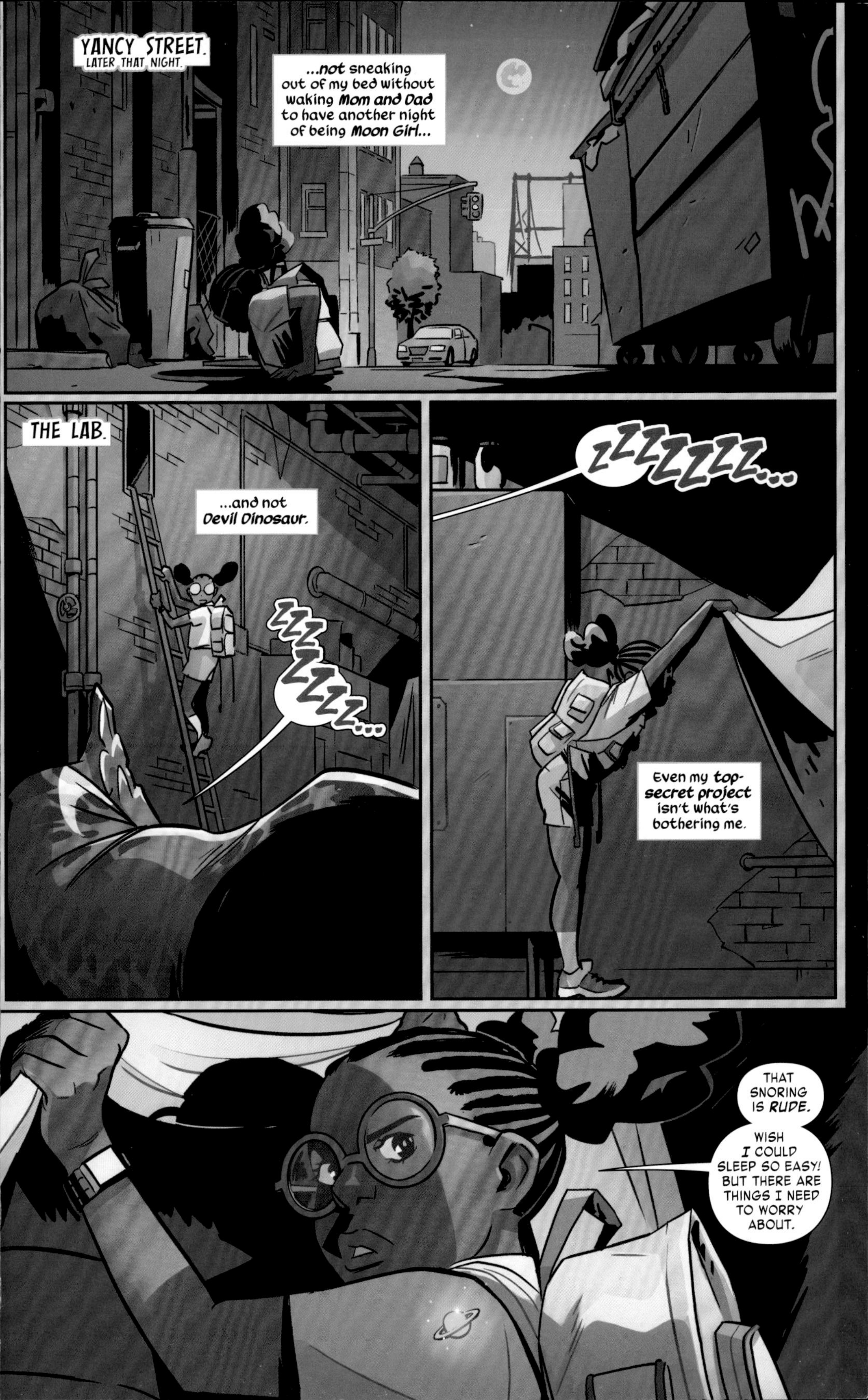
YANCY STREET. LATER THAT NIGHT.
...not sneaking out of my bed without waking Mom and Dad to have another night of being Moon Girl...
THE LAB.
...and not Devil Dinosaur.
ZZZZZZZ...
ZZZZZZZZZ...
Even my top-secret project isn't what's bothering me.
THAT SNORING IS RUDE.
WISH I COULD SLEEP SO EASY! BUT THERE ARE THINGS I NEED TO WORRY ABOUT.

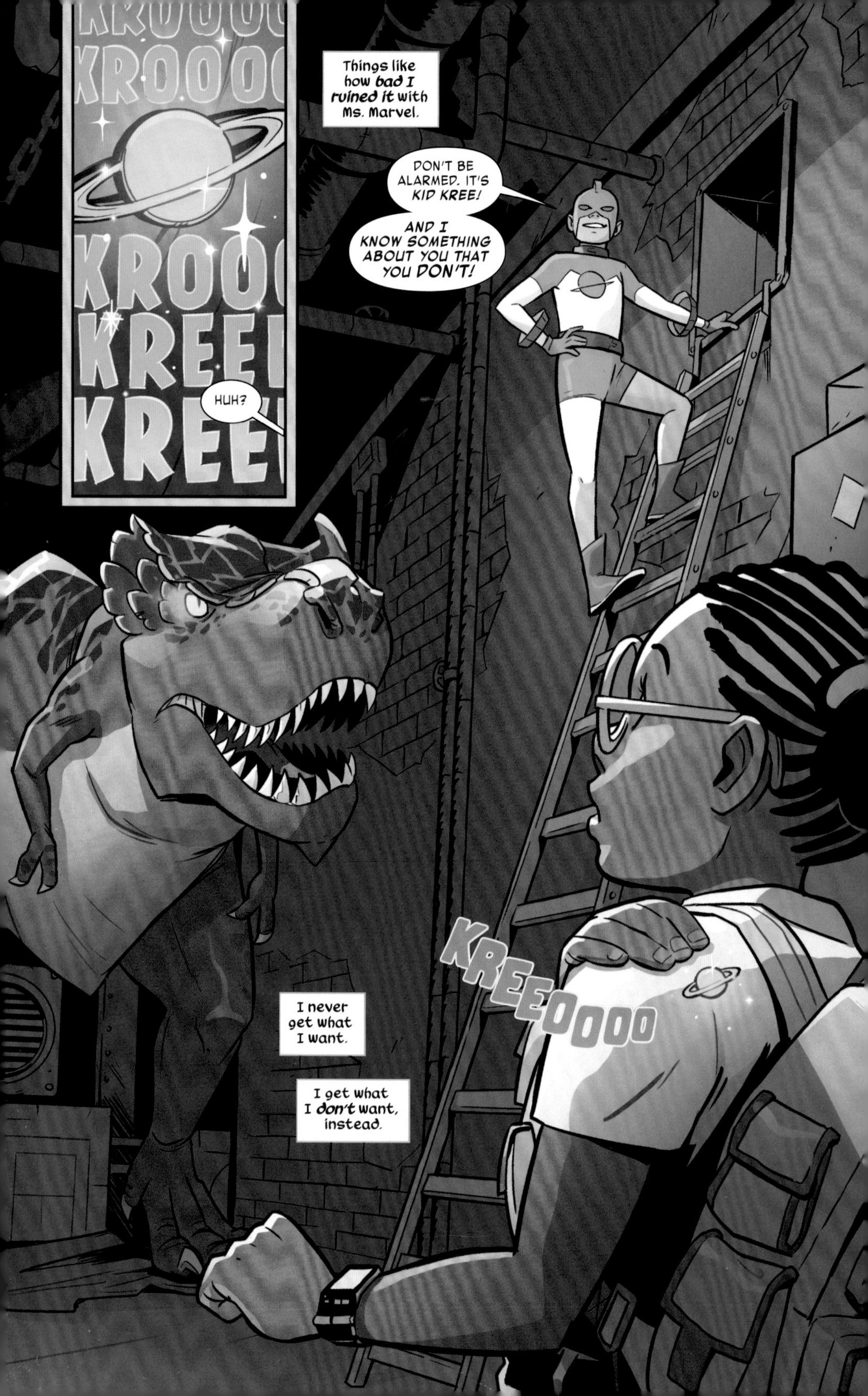
KROOOO
KROOOO
KROOOO
KREEE
KREEE
Things like how bad I ruined it with Ms. Marvel.
DON'T BE ALARMED. IT'S KID KREE!
AND I KNOW SOMETHING ABOUT YOU THAT YOU DON'T!
HUH?
KREEOOOO
I never get what I want.
I get what I don't want, instead.

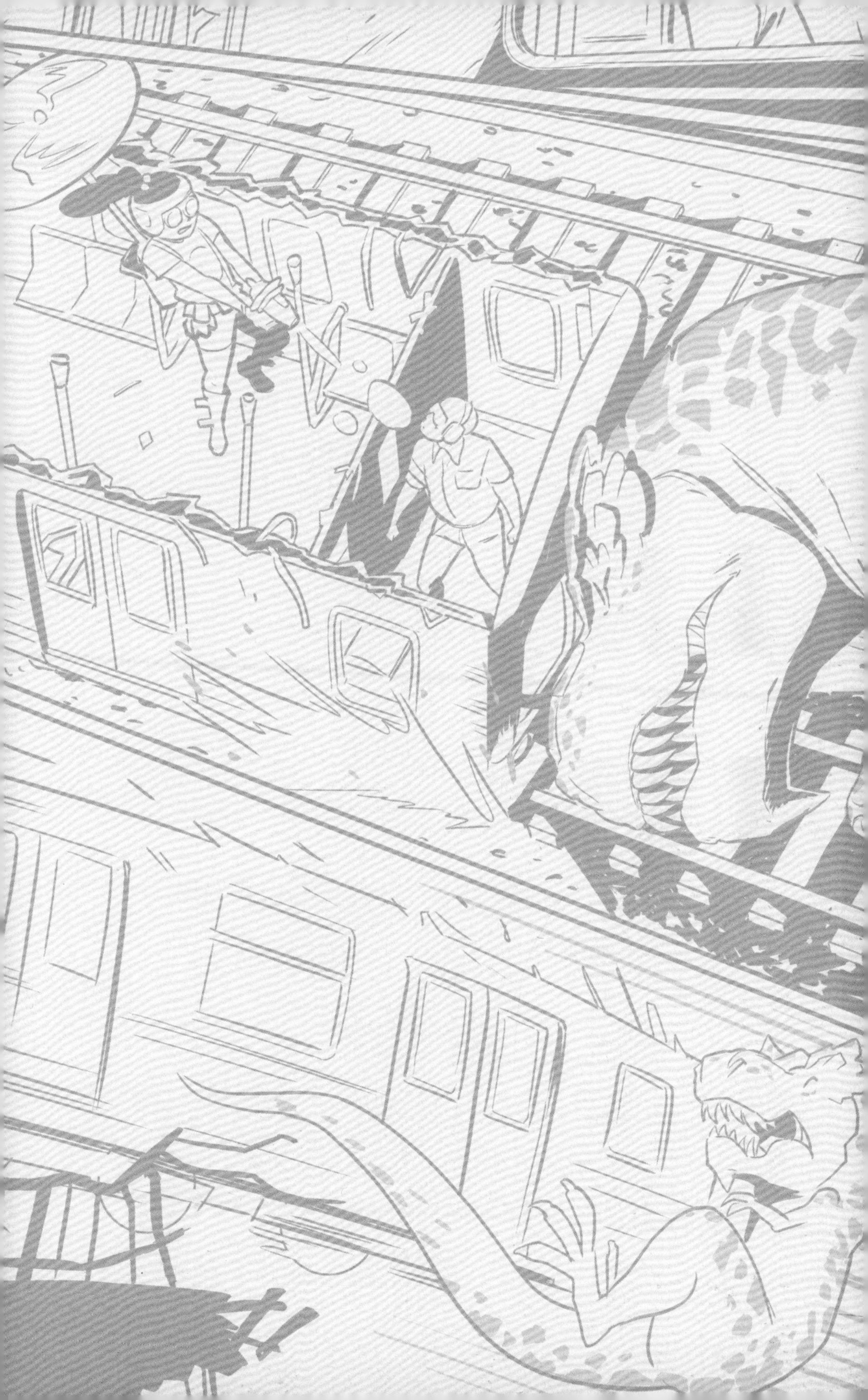

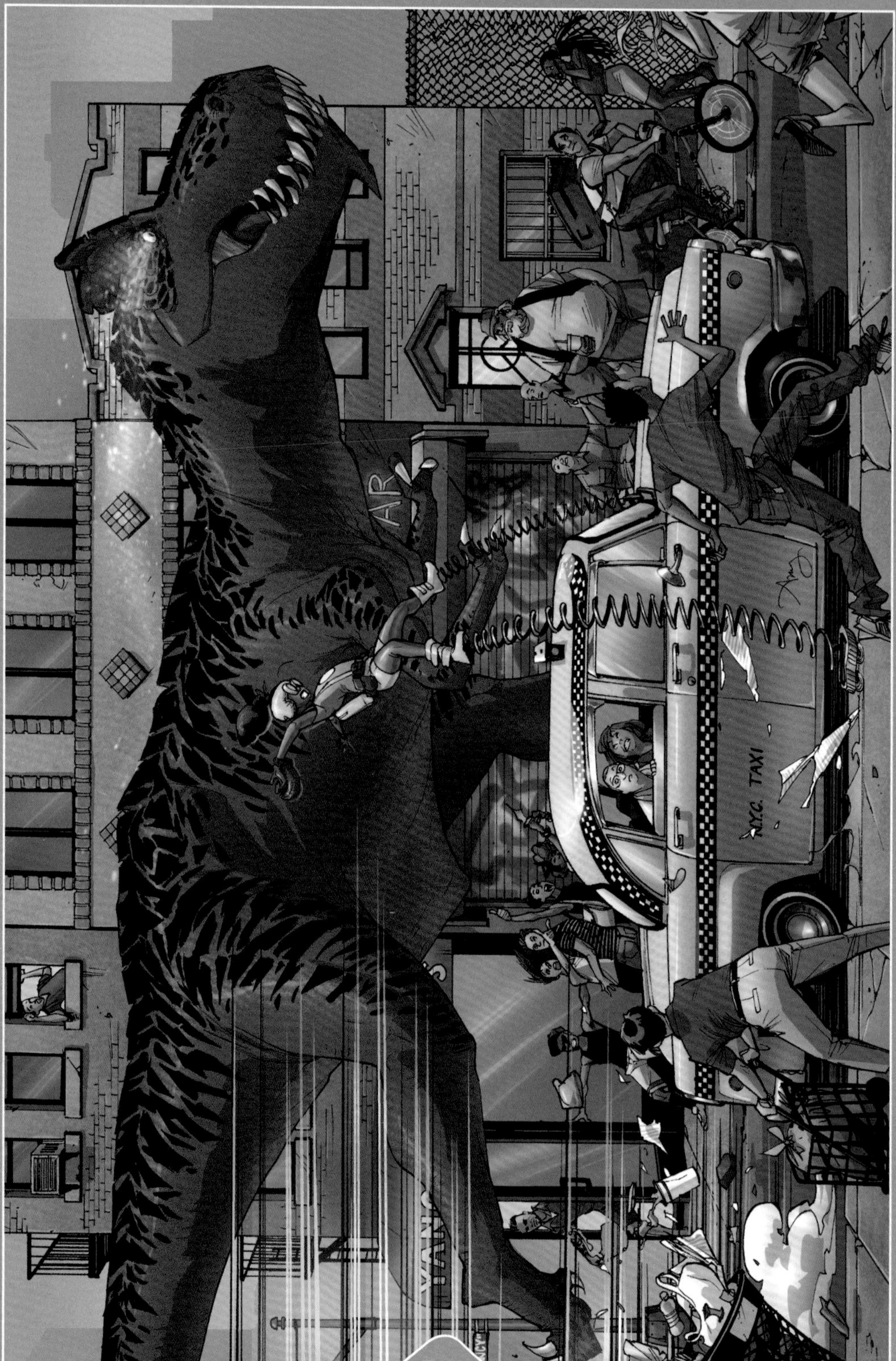
N.Y.C. TAXI

11

"The Inhuman Thing To Do"

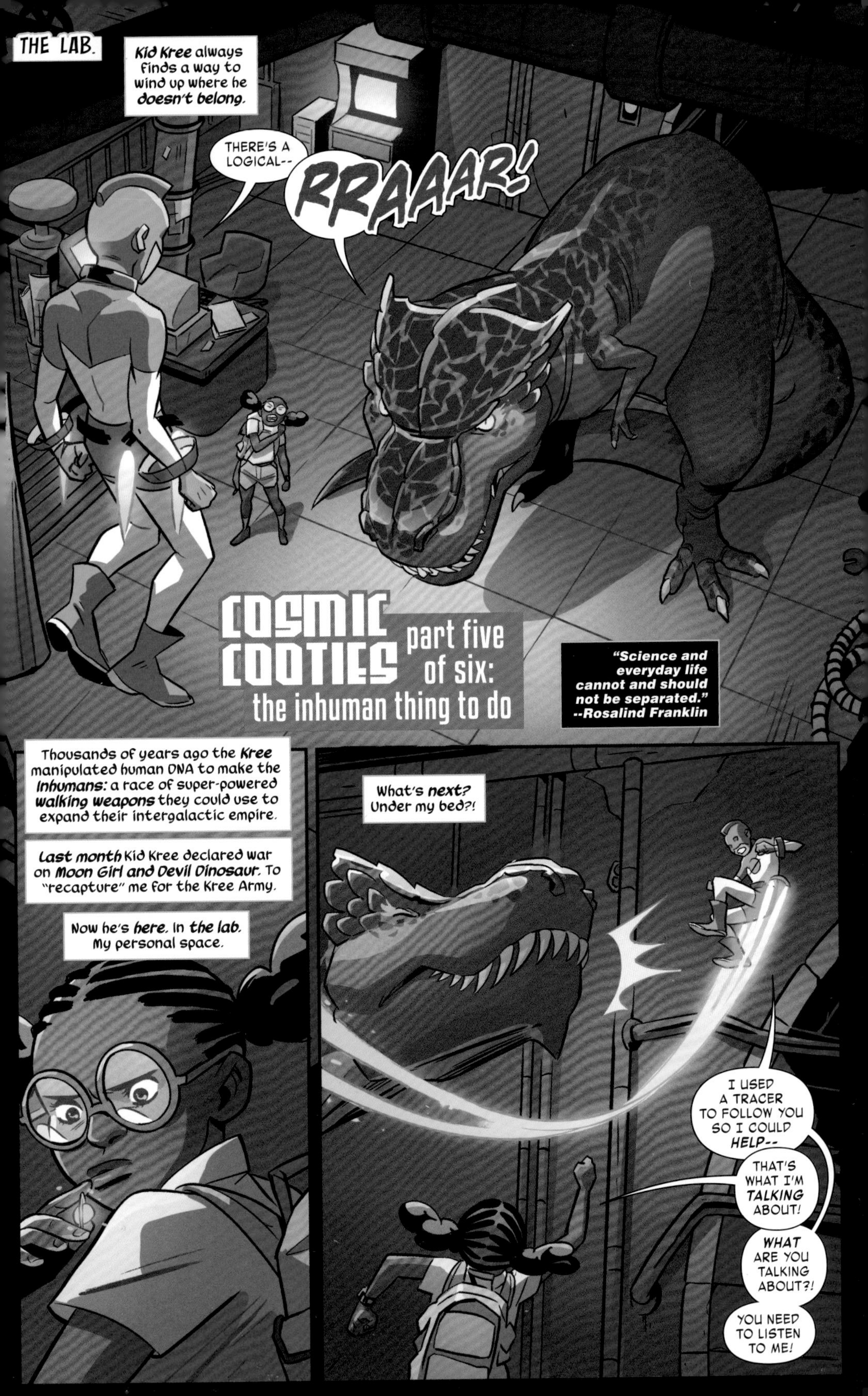
THE LAB.
Kid Kree always finds a way to wind up where he doesn't belong.
THERE'S A LOGICAL--
RRAAAR!
COSMIC COOTIES part five of six: the inhuman thing to do
"Science and everyday life cannot and should not be separated." --Rosalind Franklin
Thousands of years ago the Kree manipulated human DNA to make the Inhumans: a race of super-powered walking weapons they could use to expand their intergalactic empire.
Last month Kid Kree declared war on Moon Girl and Devil Dinosaur. To "recapture" me for the Kree Army.
Now he's here. In the lab. My personal space.
What's next? Under my bed?!
I USED A TRACER TO FOLLOW YOU SO I COULD HELP--
THAT'S WHAT I'M TALKING ABOUT!
WHAT ARE YOU TALKING ABOUT?!
YOU NEED TO LISTEN TO ME!

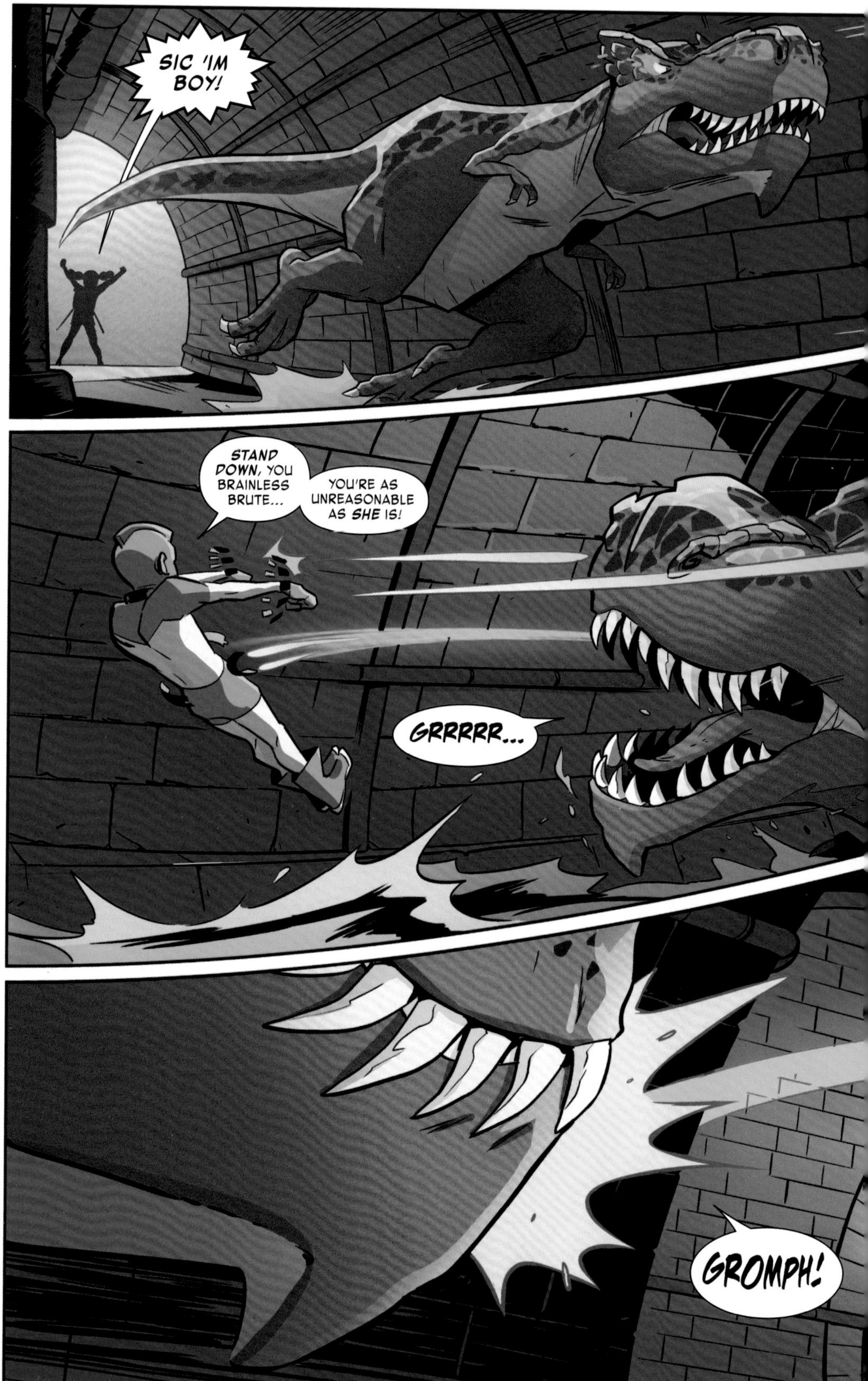
SIC 'IM BOY!
STAND DOWN, YOU BRAINLESS BRUTE...
YOU'RE AS UNREASONABLE AS SHE IS!
GRRRRR...
GROMPH!

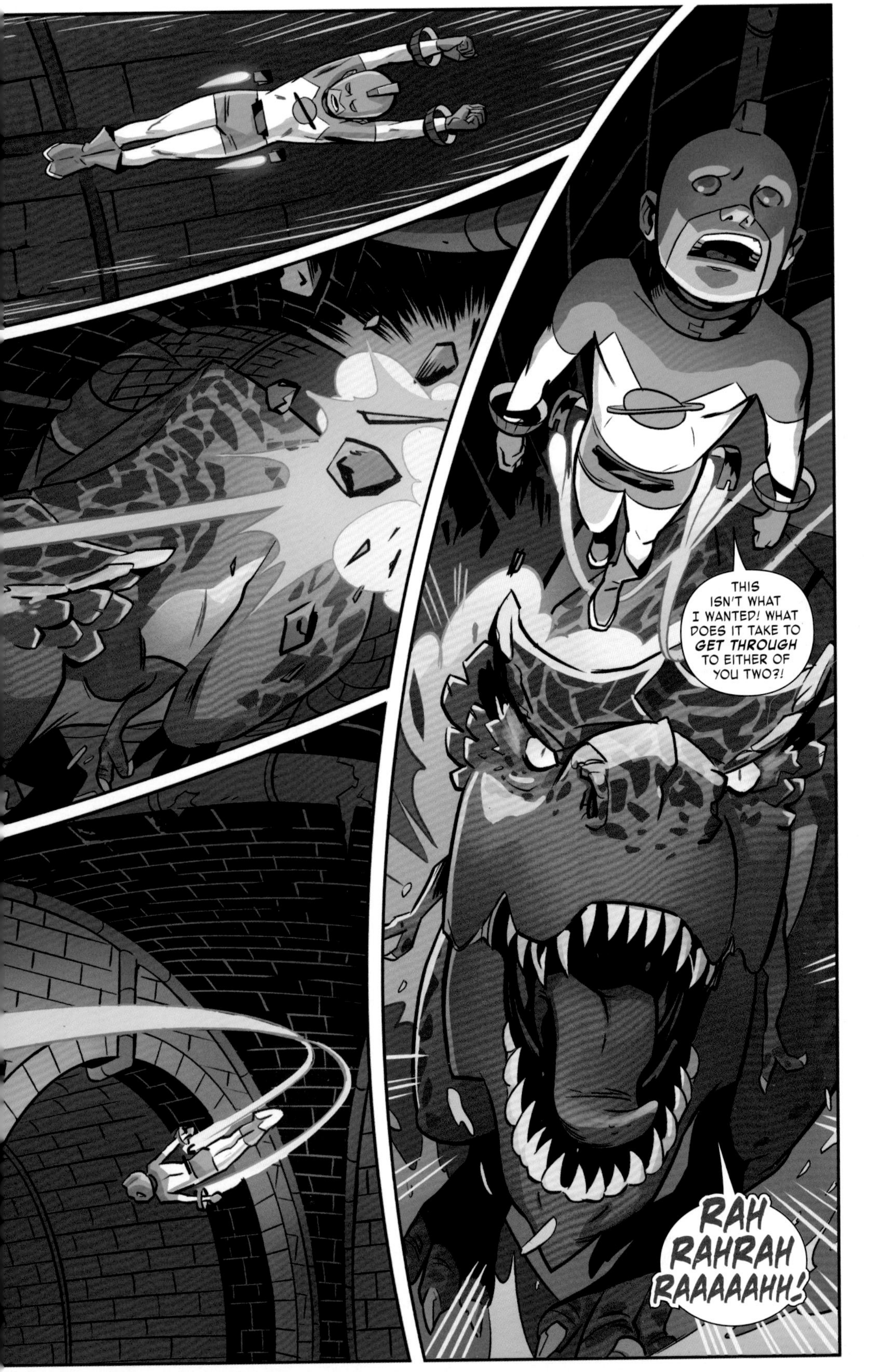
THIS ISN'T WHAT I WANTED! WHAT DOES IT TAKE TO GET THROUGH TO EITHER OF YOU TWO?!
RAH RAHRAH RAAAAAHH!

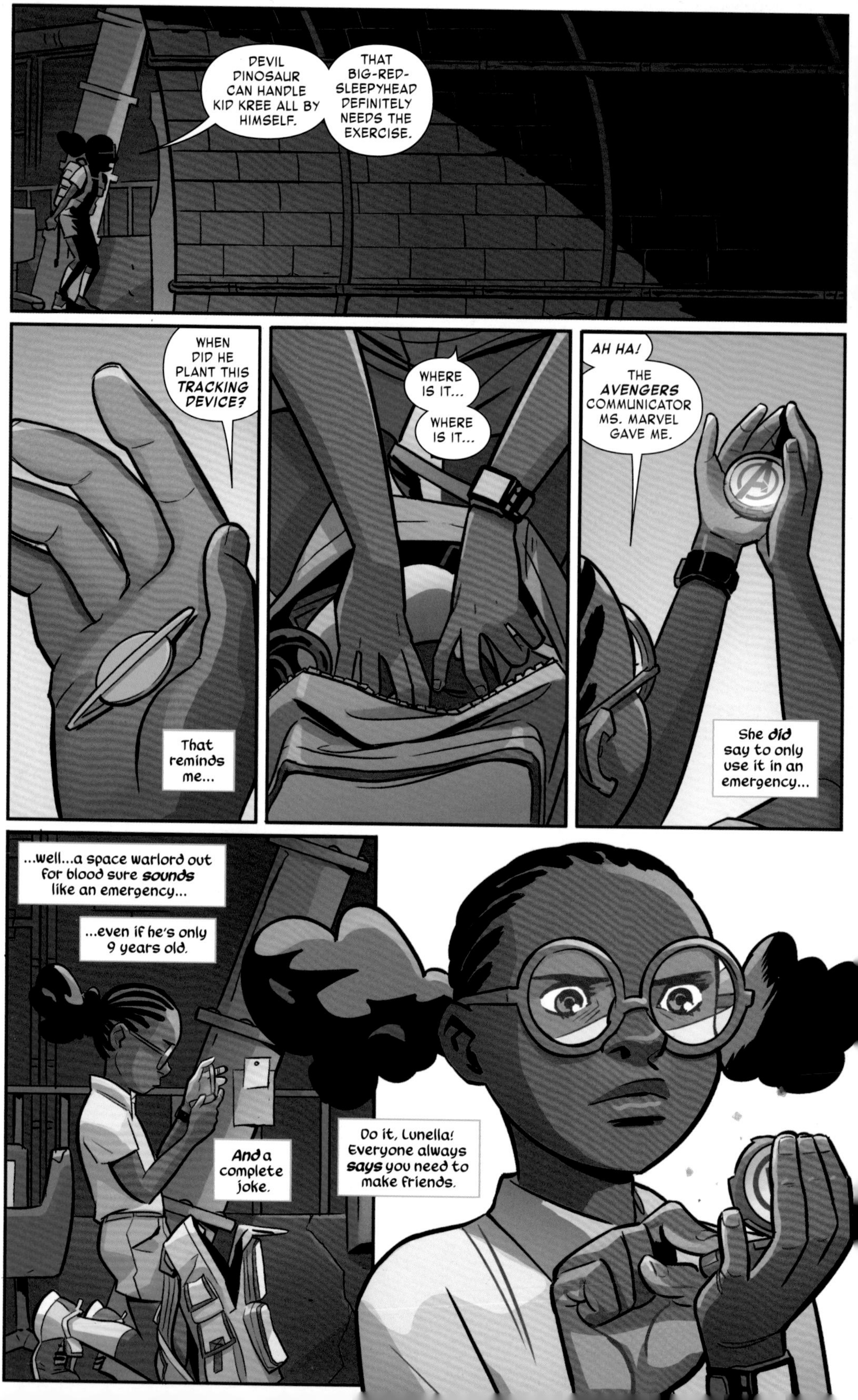
DEVIL DINOSAUR CAN HANDLE KID KREE ALL BY HIMSELF.
THAT BIG-RED-SLEEPYHEAD DEFINITELY NEEDS THE EXERCISE.
WHEN DID HE PLANT THIS TRACKING DEVICE?
That reminds me...
WHERE IS IT...
WHERE IS IT...
AH HA!
THE AVENGERS COMMUNICATOR MS. MARVEL GAVE ME.
She did say to only use it in an emergency...
...well...a space warlord out for blood sure sounds like an emergency...
...even if he's only 9 years old.
And a complete joke.
Do it, Lunella! Everyone always says you need to make friends.

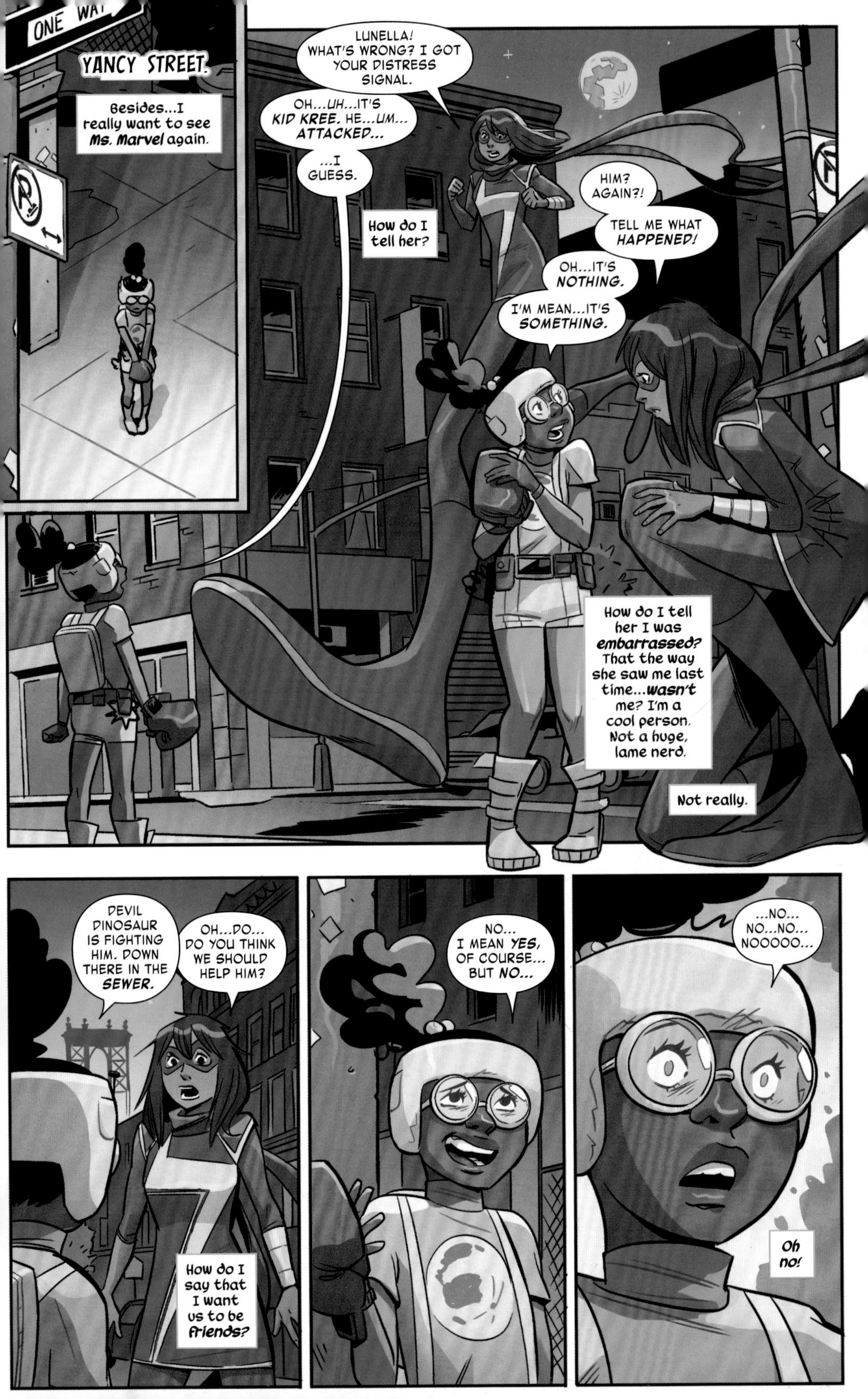
ONE WAY
YANCY STREET.
Besides...I really want to see Ms. Marvel again.
LUNELLA! WHAT'S WRONG? I GOT YOUR DISTRESS SIGNAL.
OH...UH...IT'S KID KREE. HE...UM... ATTACKED...
...I GUESS.
How do I tell her?
HIM? AGAIN?!
TELL ME WHAT HAPPENED!
OH...IT'S NOTHING.
I'M MEAN...IT'S SOMETHING.
How do I tell her I was embarrassed? That the way she saw me last time...wasn't me? I'm a cool person. Not a huge, lame nerd.
Not really.
DEVIL DINOSAUR IS FIGHTING HIM. DOWN THERE IN THE SEWER.
OH...DO... DO YOU THINK WE SHOULD HELP HIM?
How do I say that I want us to be friends?
NO... I MEAN YES, OF COURSE... BUT NO...
...NO... NO...NO... NOOOOO...
Oh no!

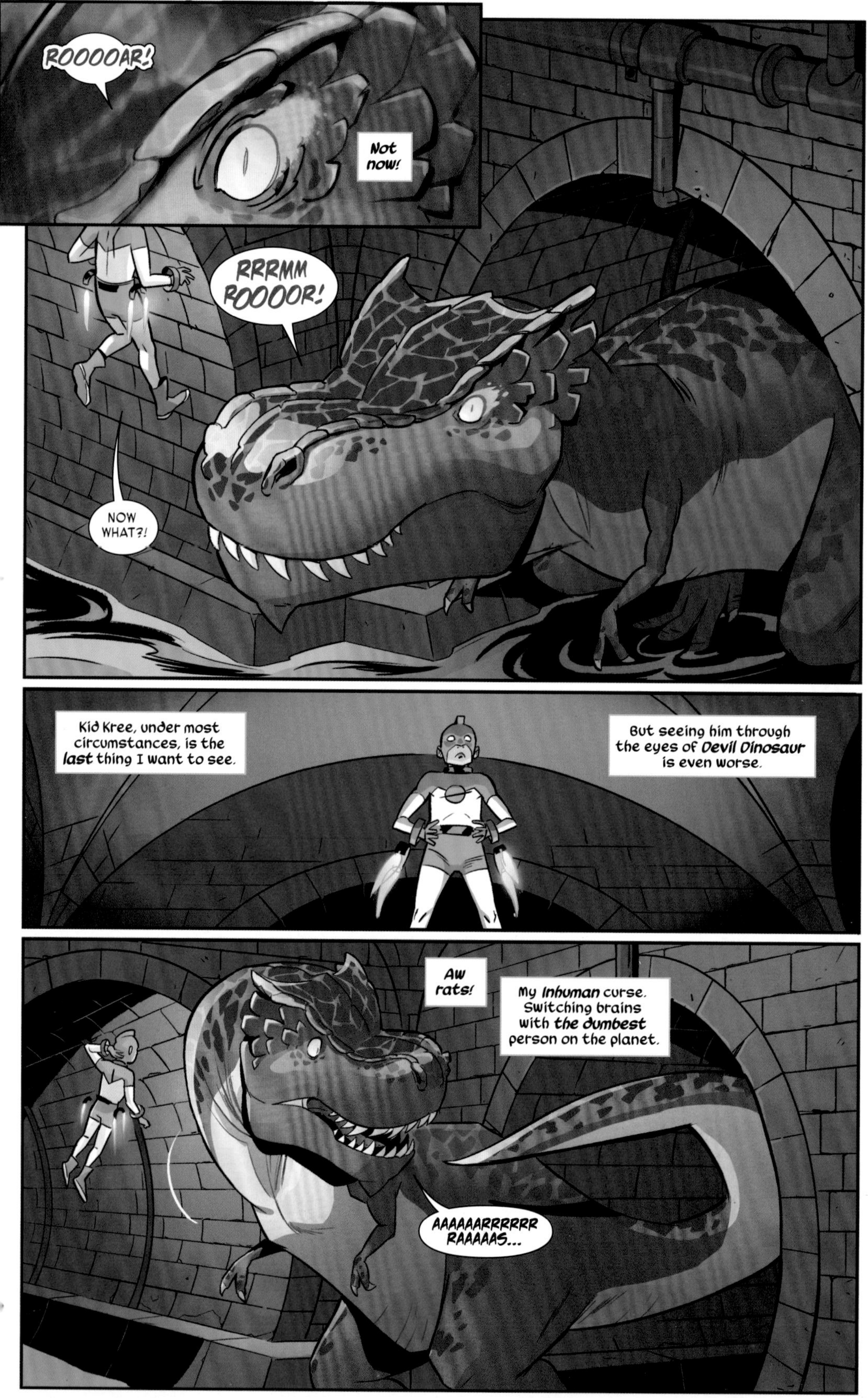
ROOOOAR!
Not now!
RRRMM ROOOOR!
NOW WHAT?!
Kid Kree, under most circumstances, is the last thing I want to see.
But seeing him through the eyes of Devil Dinosaur is even worse.
Aw rats!
My Inhuman curse. Switching brains with the dumbest person on the planet.
AAAAAARRRRR RAAAAAS...

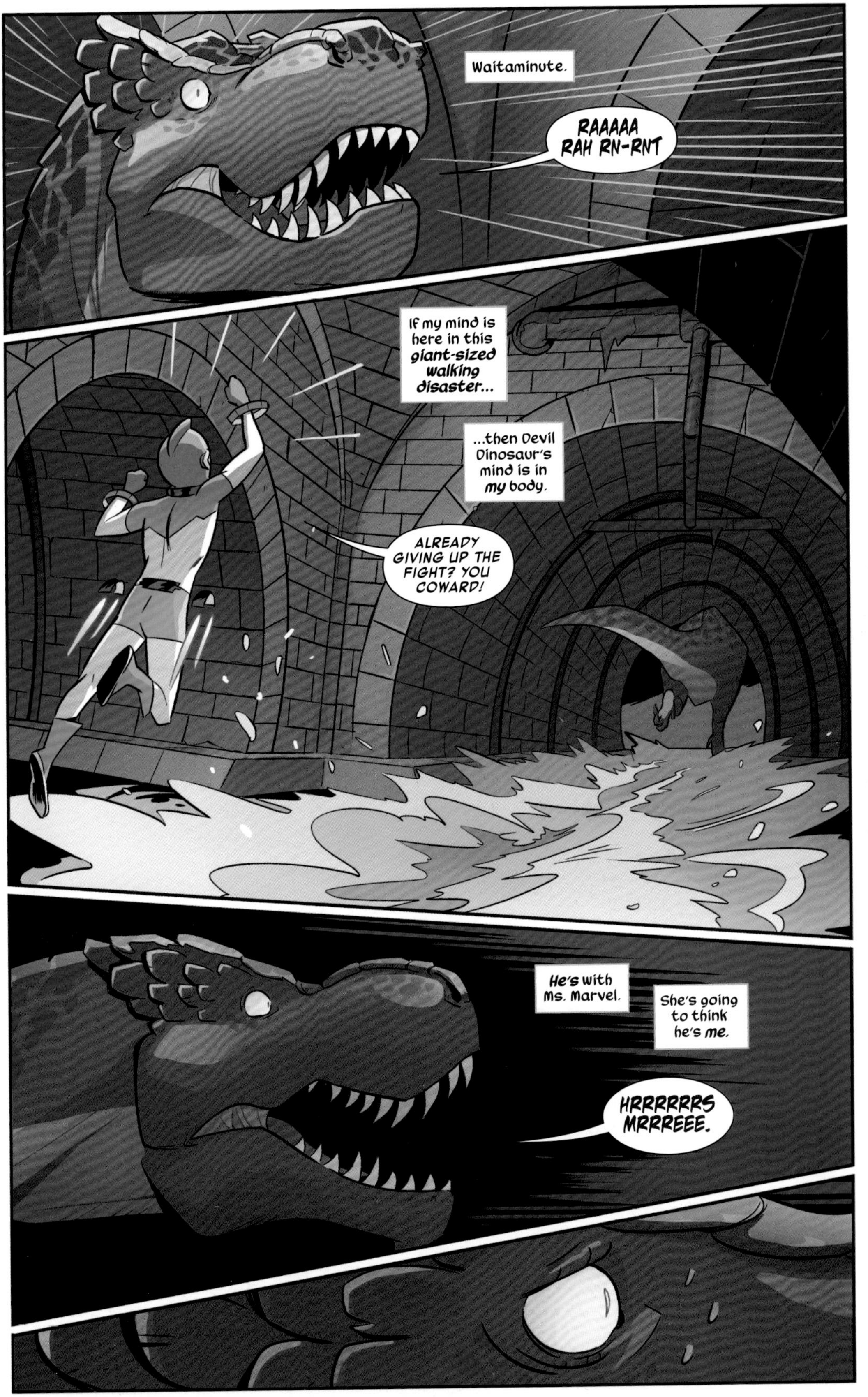
Waitaminute.
RAAAAA RAH RN-RNT
If my mind is here in this giant-sized walking disaster...
...then Devil Dinosaur's mind is in my body.
ALREADY GIVING UP THE FIGHT? YOU COWARD!
He's with Ms. Marvel.
She's going to think he's me.
HRRRRRRS MRRREEE.

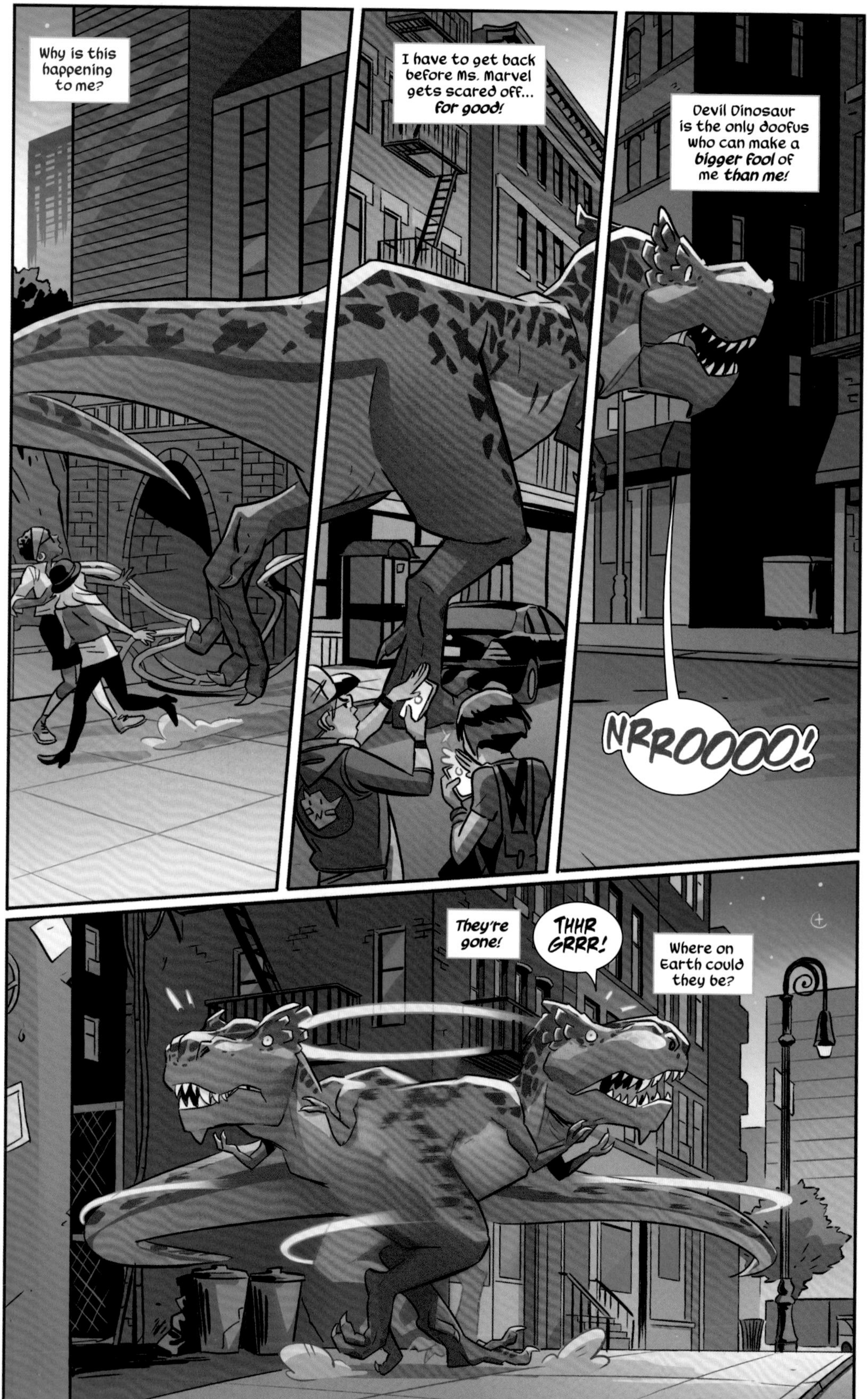
Why is this happening to me?
I have to get back before Ms. Marvel gets scared off... for good!
Devil Dinosaur is the only doofus who can make a bigger fool of me than me!
NRROOOO!
They're gone!
THHR GRRR!
Where on Earth could they be?

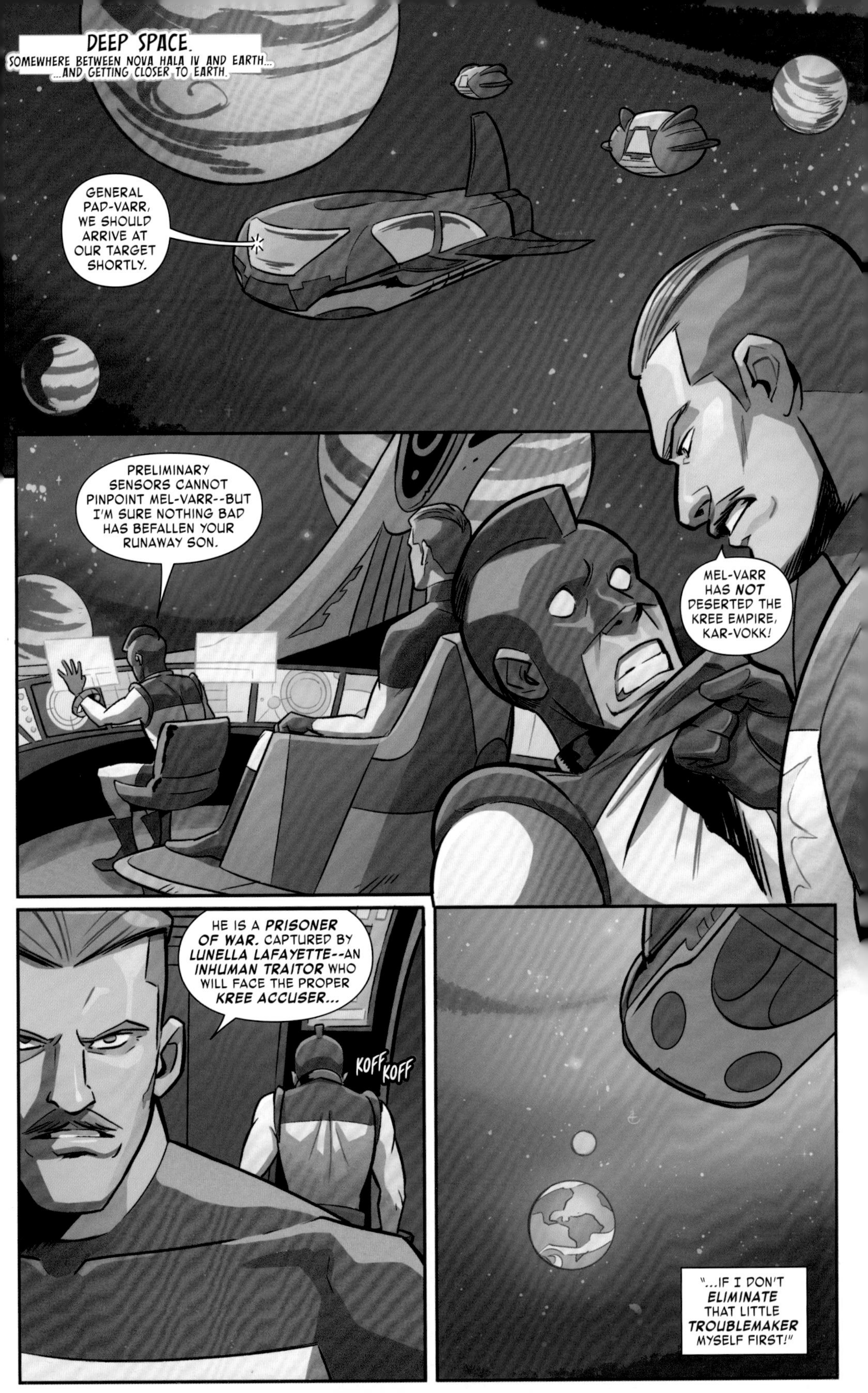
DEEP SPACE.
SOMEWHERE BETWEEN NOVA HALA IV AND EARTH...
...AND GETTING CLOSER TO EARTH.
GENERAL PAD-VARR, WE SHOULD ARRIVE AT OUR TARGET SHORTLY.
PRELIMINARY SENSORS CANNOT PINPOINT MEL-VARR--BUT I'M SURE NOTHING BAD HAS BEFALLEN YOUR RUNAWAY SON.
MEL-VARR HAS *NOT* DESERTED THE KREE EMPIRE, KAR-VOKK!
HE IS A *PRISONER OF WAR.* CAPTURED BY *LUNELLA LAFAYETTE*--AN *INHUMAN TRAITOR* WHO WILL FACE THE PROPER *KREE ACCUSER...*
KOFF KOFF
"...IF I DON'T *ELIMINATE* THAT LITTLE *TROUBLEMAKER* MYSELF FIRST!"

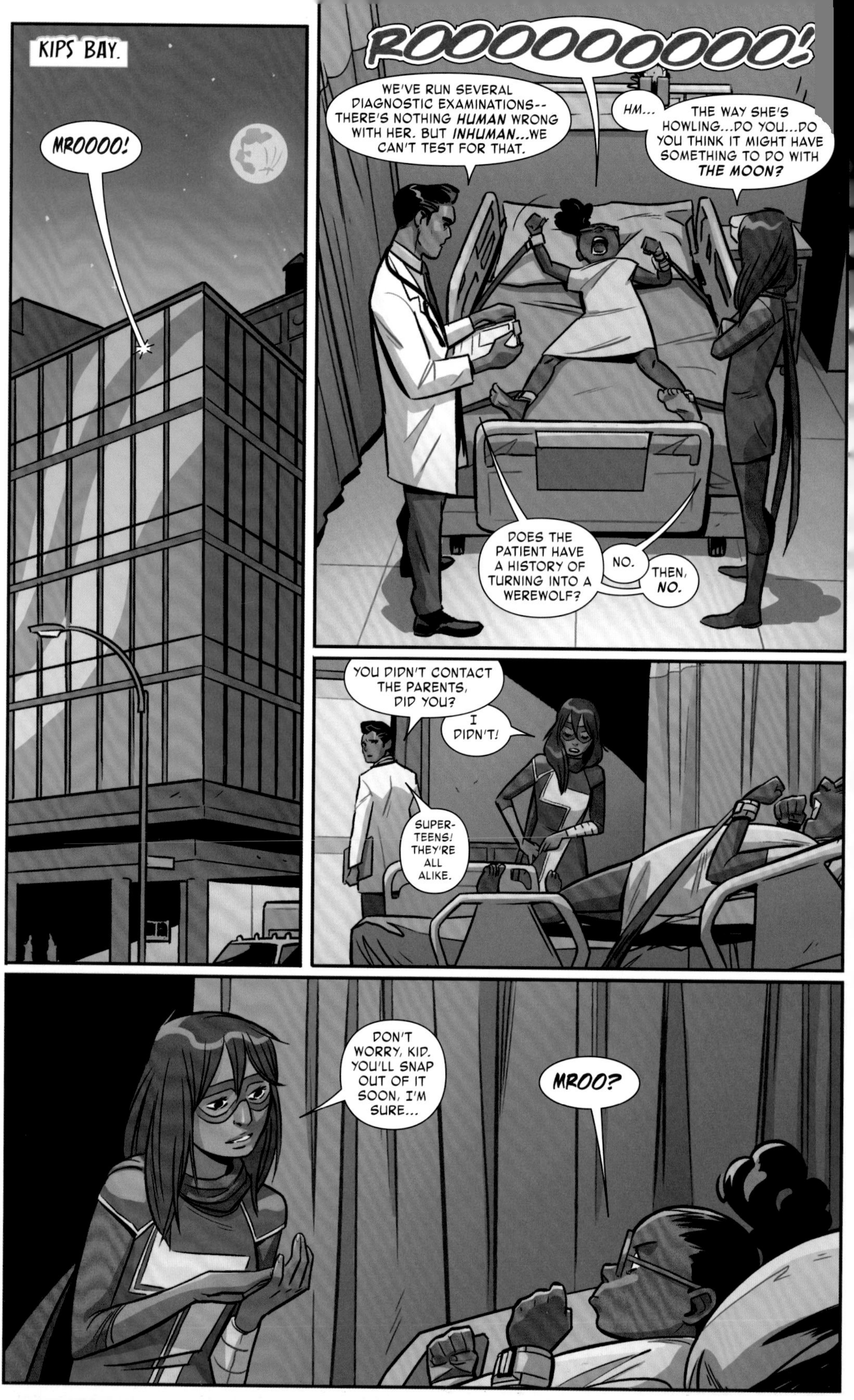
KIPS BAY.
MROOOO!
ROOOOOOOOOO!
WE'VE RUN SEVERAL DIAGNOSTIC EXAMINATIONS-- THERE'S NOTHING HUMAN WRONG WITH HER. BUT INHUMAN... WE CAN'T TEST FOR THAT.
HM...
THE WAY SHE'S HOWLING...DO YOU...DO YOU THINK IT MIGHT HAVE SOMETHING TO DO WITH THE MOON?
DOES THE PATIENT HAVE A HISTORY OF TURNING INTO A WEREWOLF?
NO.
THEN, NO.
YOU DIDN'T CONTACT THE PARENTS, DID YOU?
I DIDN'T!
SUPER-TEENS! THEY'RE ALL ALIKE.
DON'T WORRY, KID. YOU'LL SNAP OUT OF IT SOON, I'M SURE...
MROO?

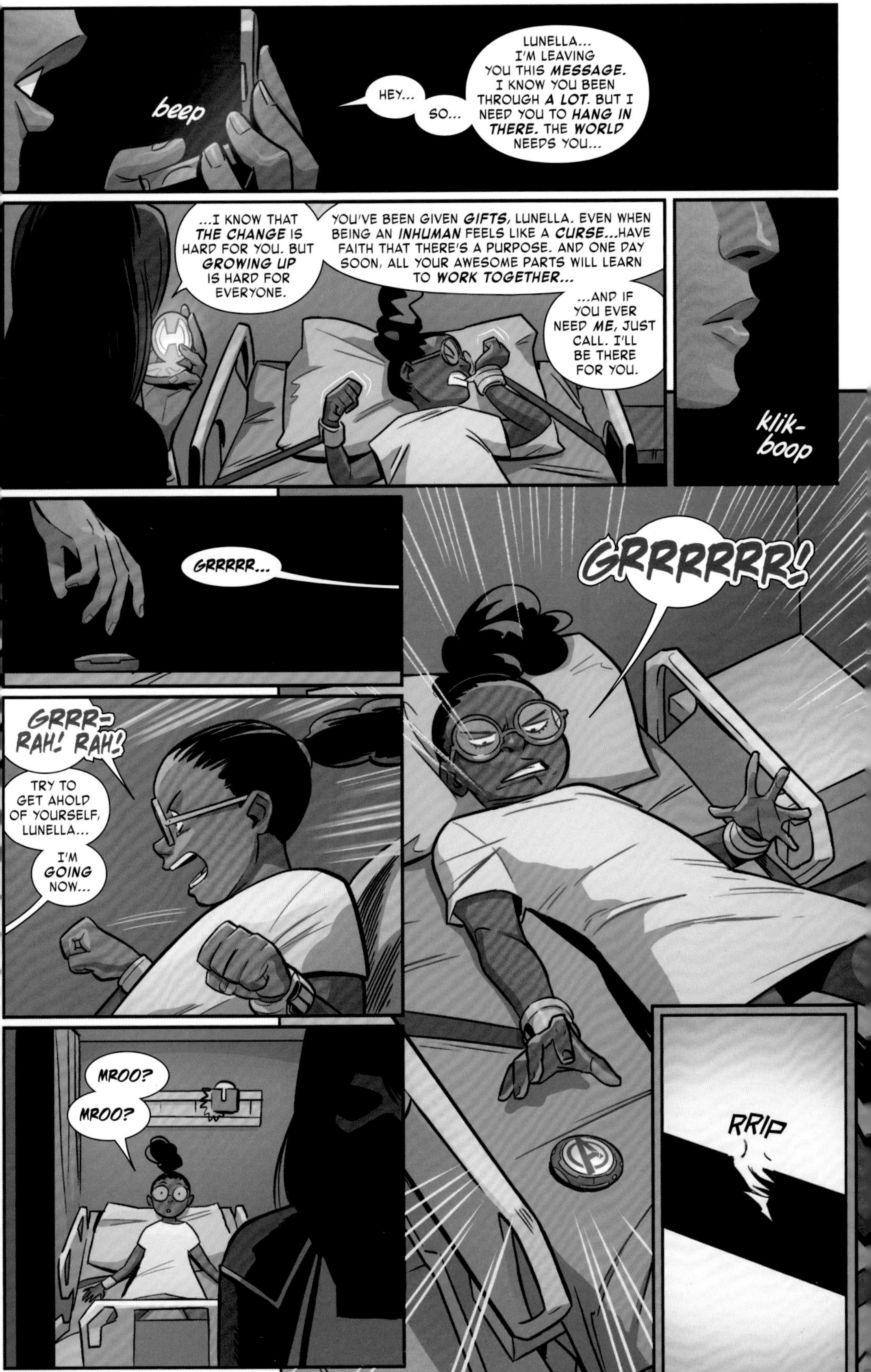
beep
HEY...
SO...
LUNELLA... I'M LEAVING YOU THIS MESSAGE. I KNOW YOU BEEN THROUGH A LOT. BUT I NEED YOU TO HANG IN THERE. THE WORLD NEEDS YOU...
...I KNOW THAT THE CHANGE IS HARD FOR YOU. BUT GROWING UP IS HARD FOR EVERYONE.
YOU'VE BEEN GIVEN GIFTS, LUNELLA. EVEN WHEN BEING AN INHUMAN FEELS LIKE A CURSE...HAVE FAITH THAT THERE'S A PURPOSE. AND ONE DAY SOON, ALL YOUR AWESOME PARTS WILL LEARN TO WORK TOGETHER...
...AND IF YOU EVER NEED ME, JUST CALL. I'LL BE THERE FOR YOU.
klik-boop
GRRRRR...
GRRRRRRR!
GRRR-RAH! RAH!
TRY TO GET AHOLD OF YOURSELF, LUNELLA...
I'M GOING NOW...
MROO?
MROO?
RRIP

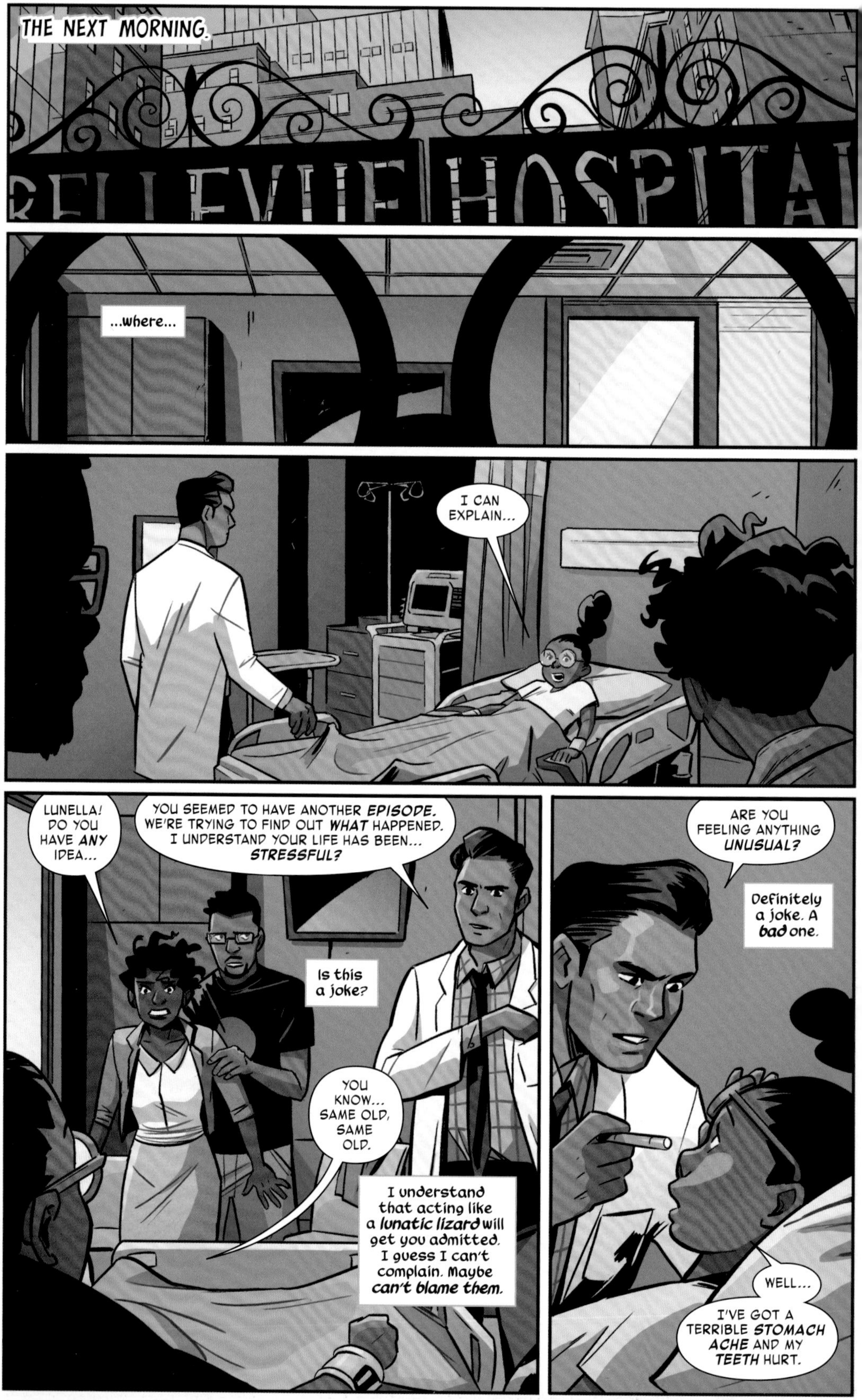
THE NEXT MORNING.
BELLEVUE HOSPITAL
...where...
I CAN EXPLAIN...
LUNELLA! DO YOU HAVE ANY IDEA...
YOU SEEMED TO HAVE ANOTHER EPISODE. WE'RE TRYING TO FIND OUT WHAT HAPPENED. I UNDERSTAND YOUR LIFE HAS BEEN... STRESSFUL?
Is this a joke?
YOU KNOW... SAME OLD, SAME OLD.
I understand that acting like a lunatic lizard will get you admitted. I guess I can't complain. Maybe can't blame them.
ARE YOU FEELING ANYTHING UNUSUAL?
Definitely a joke. A bad one.
WELL...
I'VE GOT A TERRIBLE STOMACH ACHE AND MY TEETH HURT.

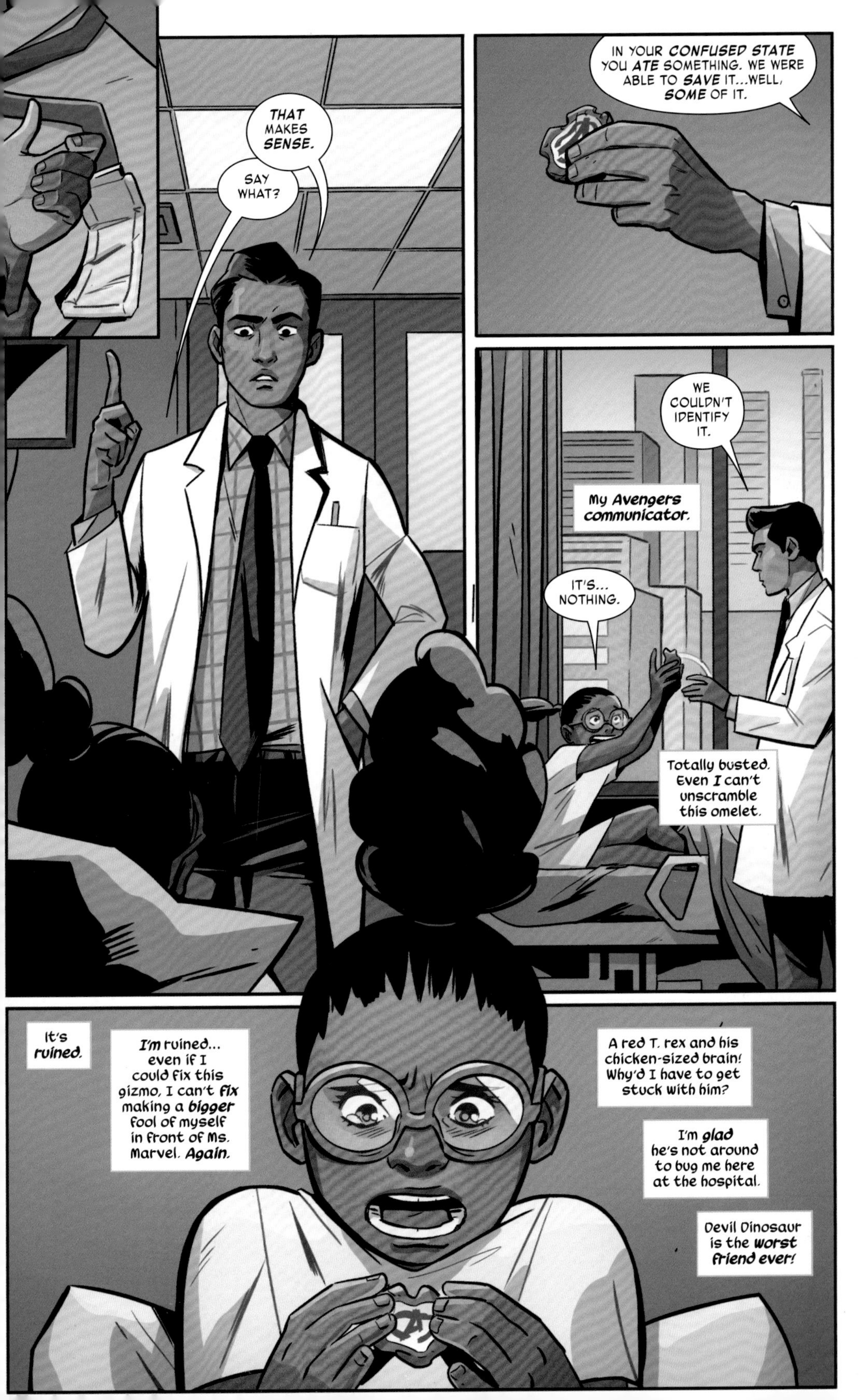
THAT MAKES SENSE.
SAY WHAT?
IN YOUR CONFUSED STATE YOU ATE SOMETHING. WE WERE ABLE TO SAVE IT...WELL, SOME OF IT.
WE COULDN'T IDENTIFY IT.
My Avengers communicator.
IT'S... NOTHING.
Totally busted. Even I can't unscramble this omelet.
It's ruined.
I'm ruined... even if I could fix this gizmo, I can't fix making a bigger fool of myself in front of Ms. Marvel. Again.
A red T. rex and his chicken-sized brain! Why'd I have to get stuck with him?
I'm glad he's not around to bug me here at the hospital.
Devil Dinosaur is the worst friend ever!

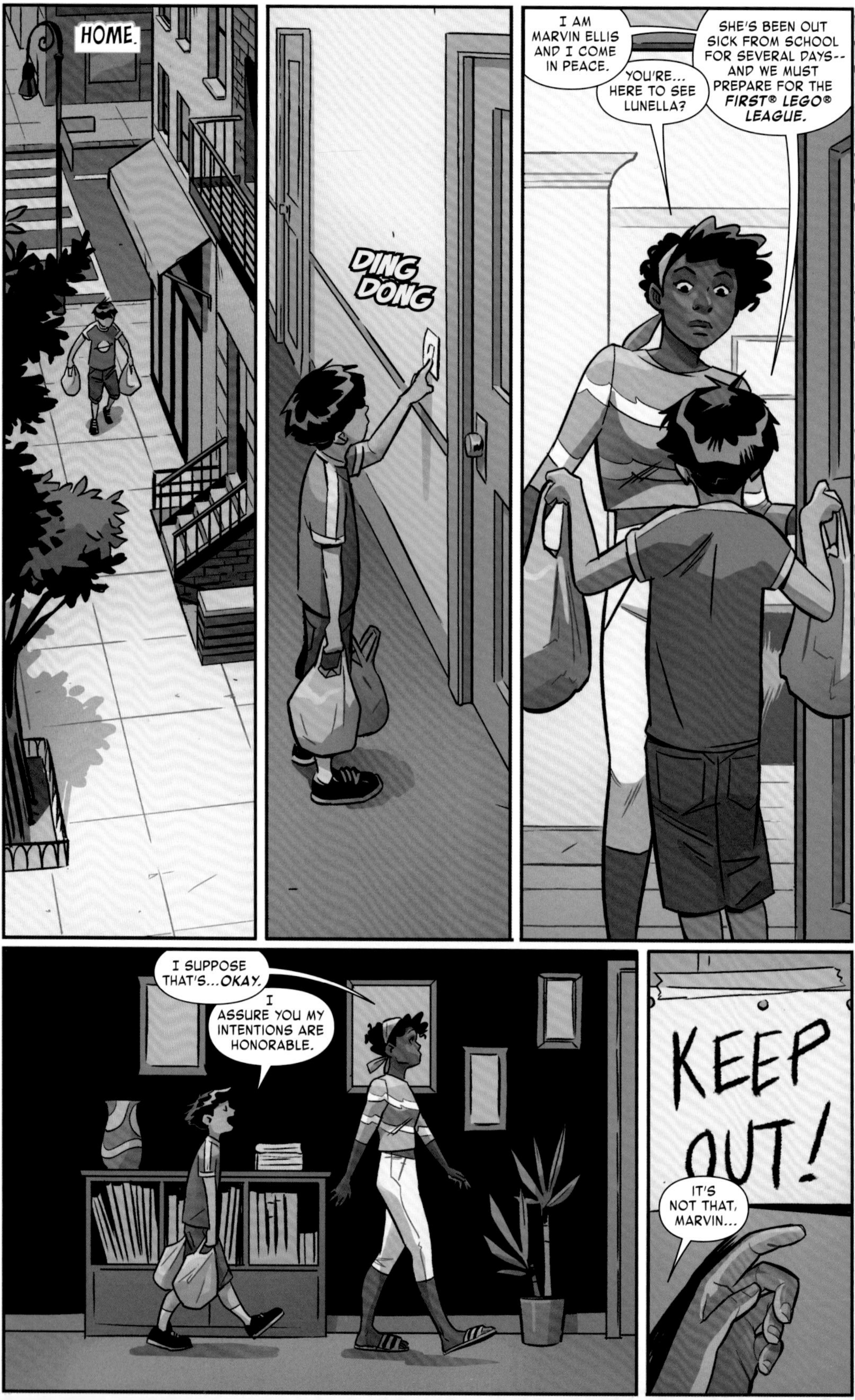
HOME.
DING DONG
I AM MARVIN ELLIS AND I COME IN PEACE.
YOU'RE... HERE TO SEE LUNELLA?
SHE'S BEEN OUT SICK FROM SCHOOL FOR SEVERAL DAYS-- AND WE MUST PREPARE FOR THE *FIRST® LEGO® LEAGUE.*
I SUPPOSE THAT'S...*OKAY.*
I ASSURE YOU MY INTENTIONS ARE HONORABLE.
KEEP OUT!
IT'S NOT THAT, MARVIN...

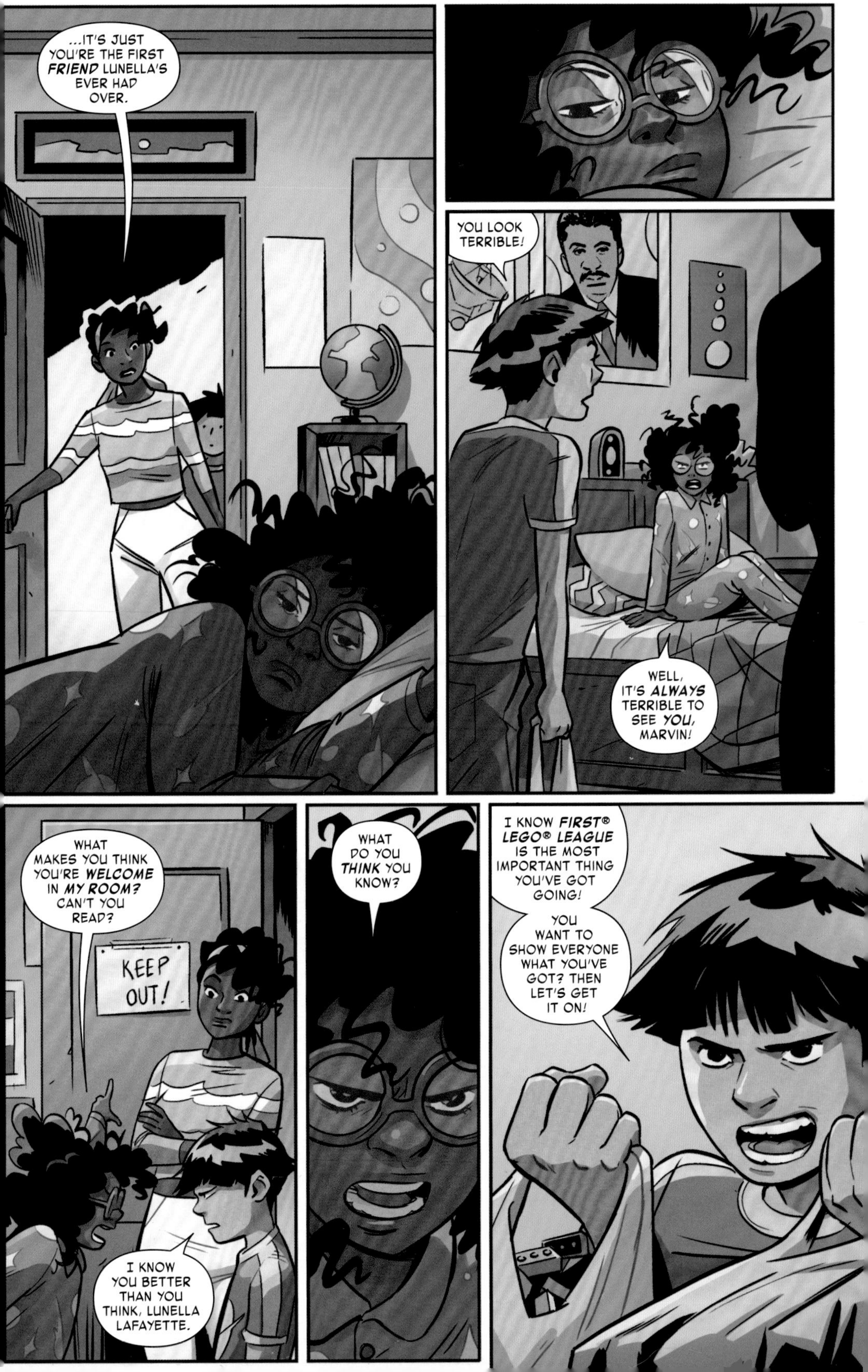

...IT'S JUST YOU'RE THE FIRST FRIEND LUNELLA'S EVER HAD OVER.
YOU LOOK TERRIBLE!
WELL, IT'S ALWAYS TERRIBLE TO SEE YOU, MARVIN!
WHAT MAKES YOU THINK YOU'RE WELCOME IN MY ROOM? CAN'T YOU READ?
KEEP OUT!
I KNOW YOU BETTER THAN YOU THINK, LUNELLA LAFAYETTE.
WHAT DO YOU THINK YOU KNOW?
I KNOW FIRST® LEGO® LEAGUE IS THE MOST IMPORTANT THING YOU'VE GOT GOING!
YOU WANT TO SHOW EVERYONE WHAT YOU'VE GOT? THEN LET'S GET IT ON!

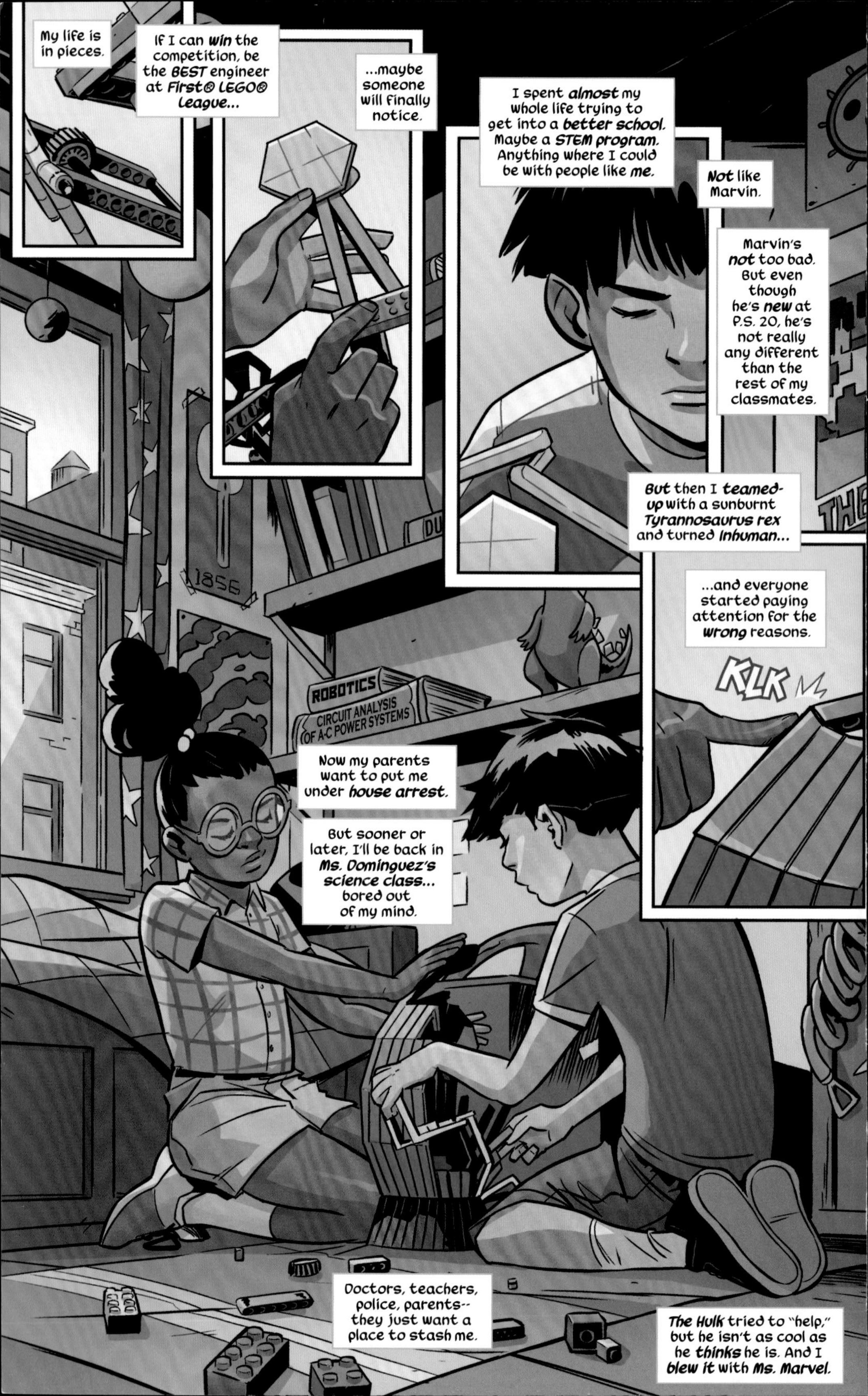

My life is in pieces.
If I can win the competition, be the BEST engineer at First® LEGO® League...
...maybe someone will finally notice.
I spent almost my whole life trying to get into a better school. Maybe a STEM program. Anything where I could be with people like me.
Not like Marvin.
Marvin's not too bad. But even though he's new at P.S. 20, he's not really any different than the rest of my classmates.
But then I teamed-up with a sunburnt Tyrannosaurus rex and turned Inhuman...
...and everyone started paying attention for the wrong reasons.
KLK
1856
ROBOTICS
CIRCUIT ANALYSIS OF A-C POWER SYSTEMS
Now my parents want to put me under house arrest.
But sooner or later, I'll be back in Ms. Dominguez's science class... bored out of my mind.
Doctors, teachers, police, parents-- they just want a place to stash me.
The Hulk tried to "help," but he isn't as cool as he thinks he is. And I blew it with Ms. Marvel.

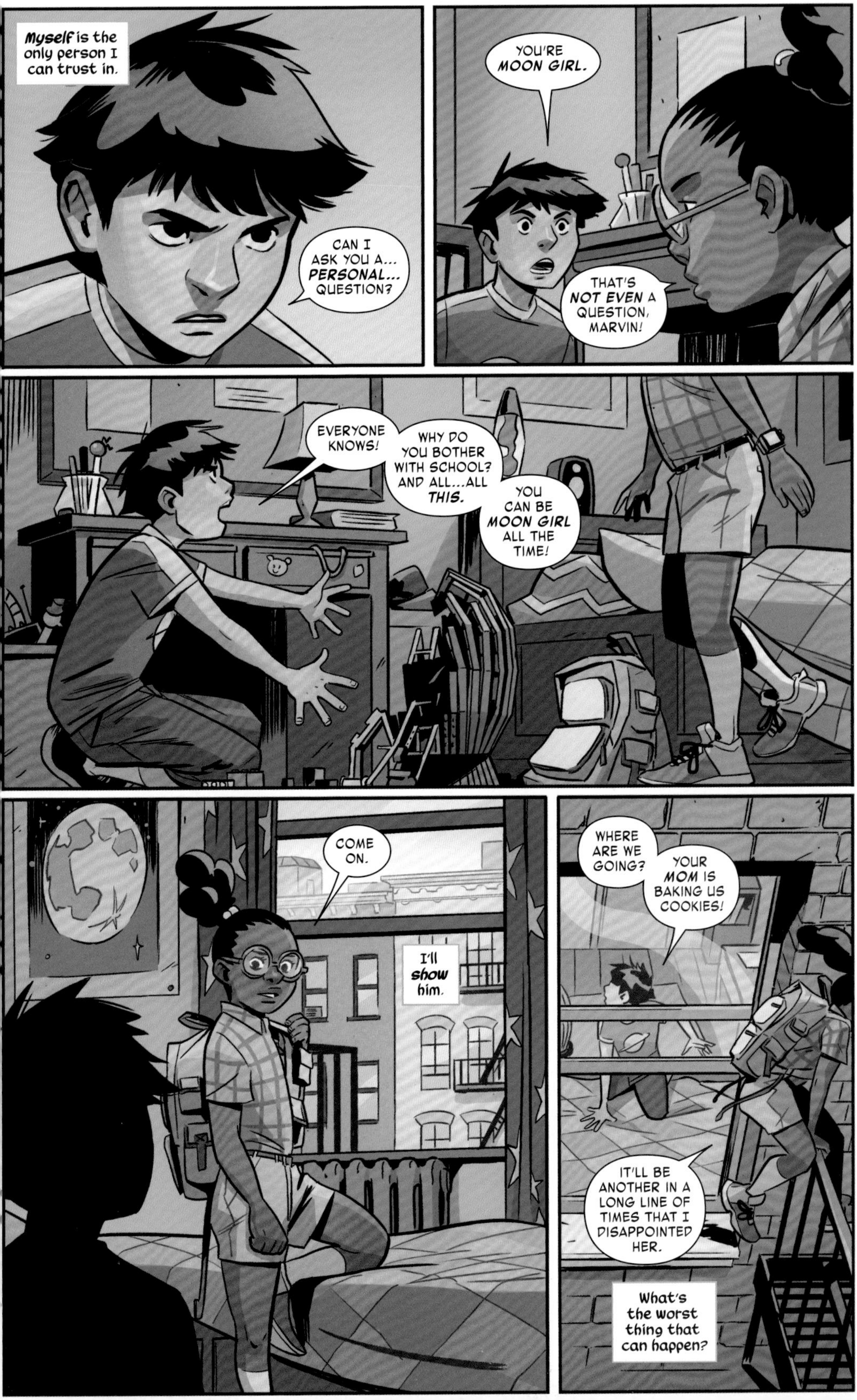
Myself is the only person I can trust in.
CAN I ASK YOU A... PERSONAL... QUESTION?
YOU'RE MOON GIRL.
THAT'S NOT EVEN A QUESTION, MARVIN!
EVERYONE KNOWS!
WHY DO YOU BOTHER WITH SCHOOL? AND ALL...ALL THIS.
YOU CAN BE MOON GIRL ALL THE TIME!
COME ON.
I'll show him.
WHERE ARE WE GOING?
YOUR MOM IS BAKING US COOKIES!
IT'LL BE ANOTHER IN A LONG LINE OF TIMES THAT I DISAPPOINTED HER.
What's the worst thing that can happen?

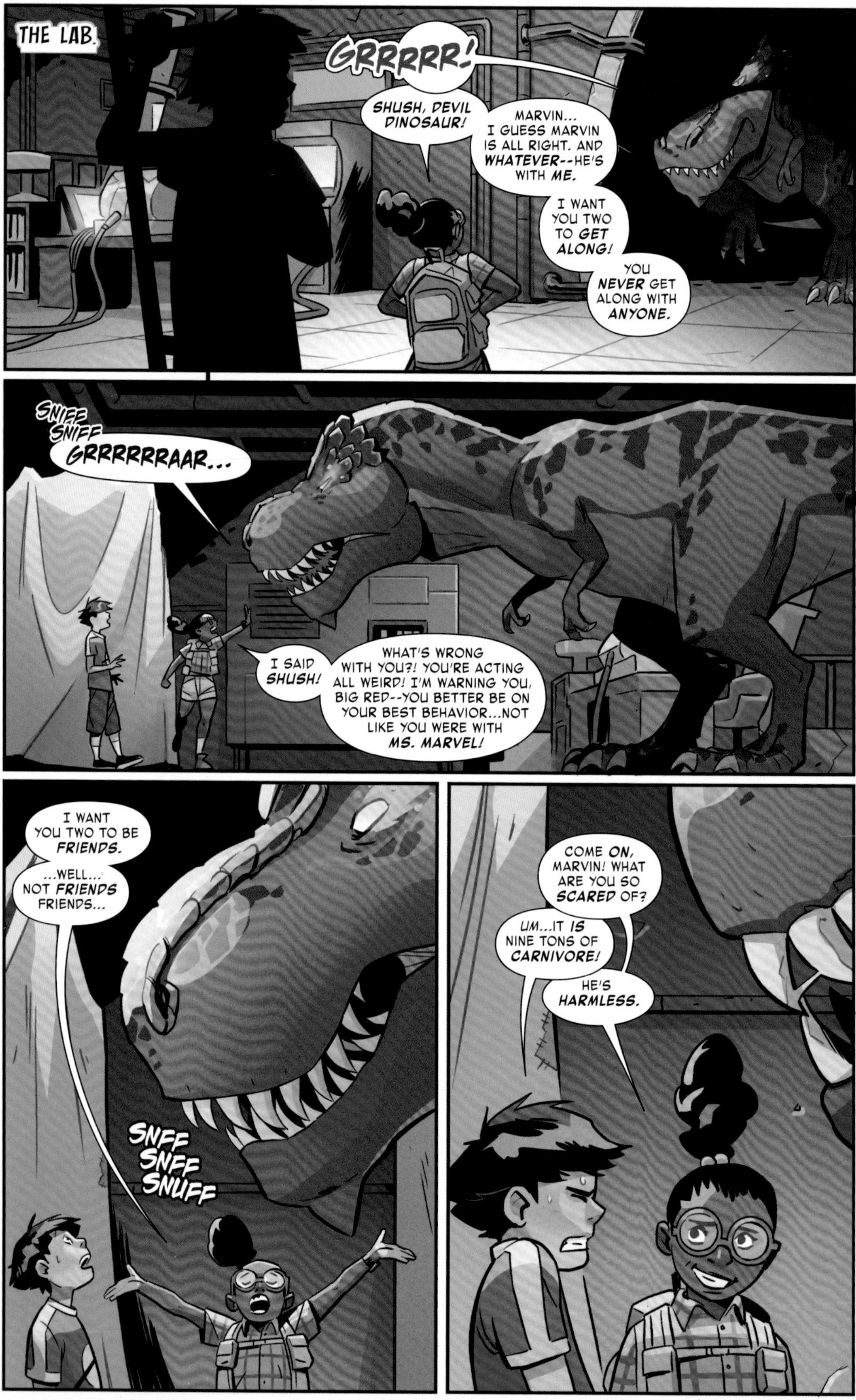
THE LAB.
GRRRRR!
SHUSH, DEVIL DINOSAUR!
MARVIN... I GUESS MARVIN IS ALL RIGHT. AND WHATEVER--HE'S WITH ME.
I WANT YOU TWO TO GET ALONG!
YOU NEVER GET ALONG WITH ANYONE.
SNIFF SNIFF
GRRRRRRAAR...
I SAID SHUSH!
WHAT'S WRONG WITH YOU?! YOU'RE ACTING ALL WEIRD! I'M WARNING YOU, BIG RED--YOU BETTER BE ON YOUR BEST BEHAVIOR...NOT LIKE YOU WERE WITH MS. MARVEL!
I WANT YOU TWO TO BE FRIENDS.
...WELL... NOT FRIENDS FRIENDS...
SNFF SNFF SNUFF
COME ON, MARVIN! WHAT ARE YOU SO SCARED OF?
UM...IT IS NINE TONS OF CARNIVORE!
HE'S HARMLESS.

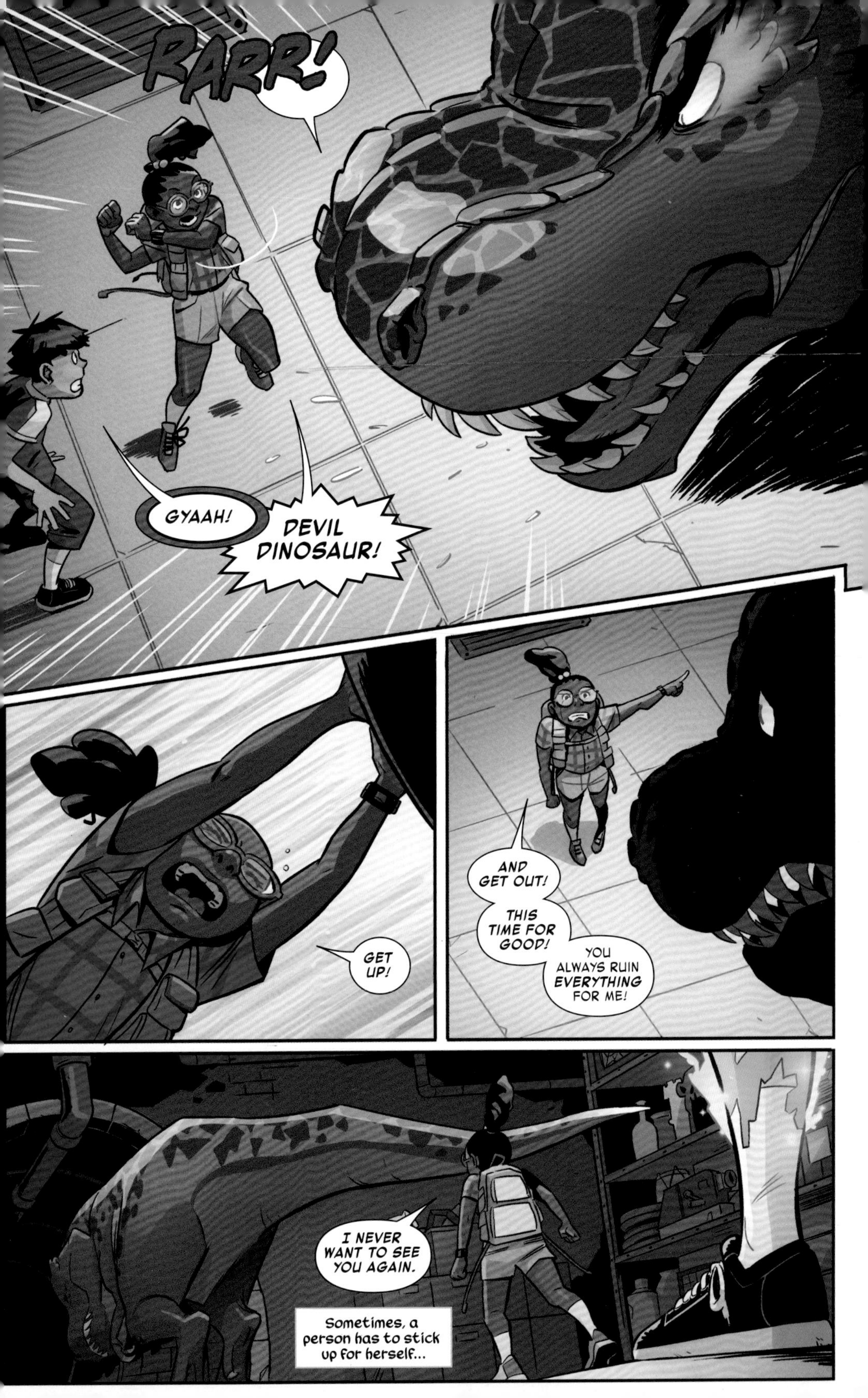
RARR!
GYAAH!
DEVIL DINOSAUR!
GET UP!
AND GET OUT!
THIS TIME FOR GOOD!
YOU ALWAYS RUIN EVERYTHING FOR ME!
I NEVER WANT TO SEE YOU AGAIN.
Sometimes, a person has to stick up for herself...

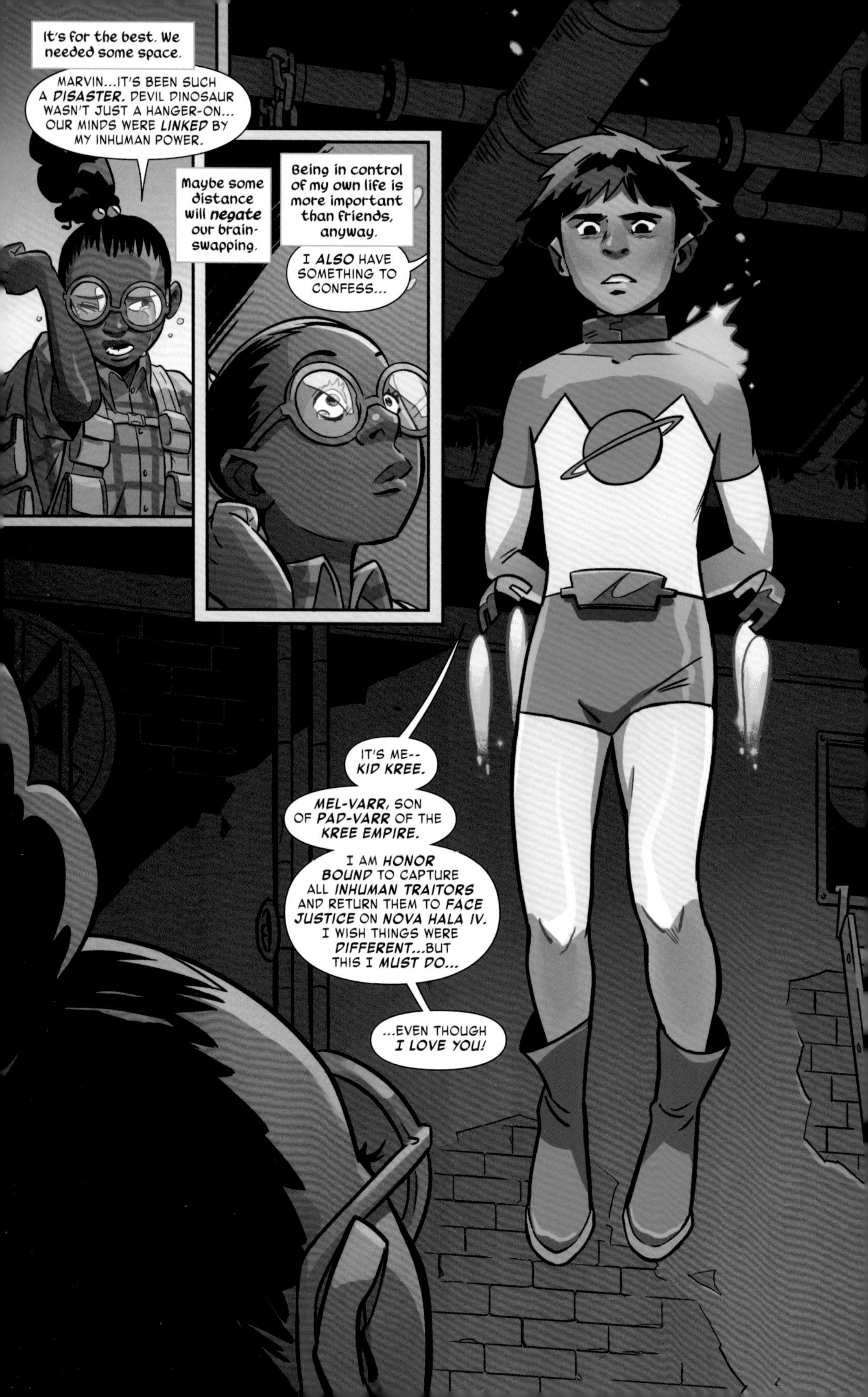
It's for the best. We needed some space.
MARVIN...IT'S BEEN SUCH A DISASTER. DEVIL DINOSAUR WASN'T JUST A HANGER-ON... OUR MINDS WERE LINKED BY MY INHUMAN POWER.
Maybe some distance will negate our brain-swapping.
Being in control of my own life is more important than friends, anyway.
I ALSO HAVE SOMETHING TO CONFESS...
IT'S ME-- KID KREE.
MEL-VARR, SON OF PAD-VARR OF THE KREE EMPIRE.
I AM HONOR BOUND TO CAPTURE ALL INHUMAN TRAITORS AND RETURN THEM TO FACE JUSTICE ON NOVA HALA IV. I WISH THINGS WERE DIFFERENT...BUT THIS I MUST DO...
...EVEN THOUGH I LOVE YOU!

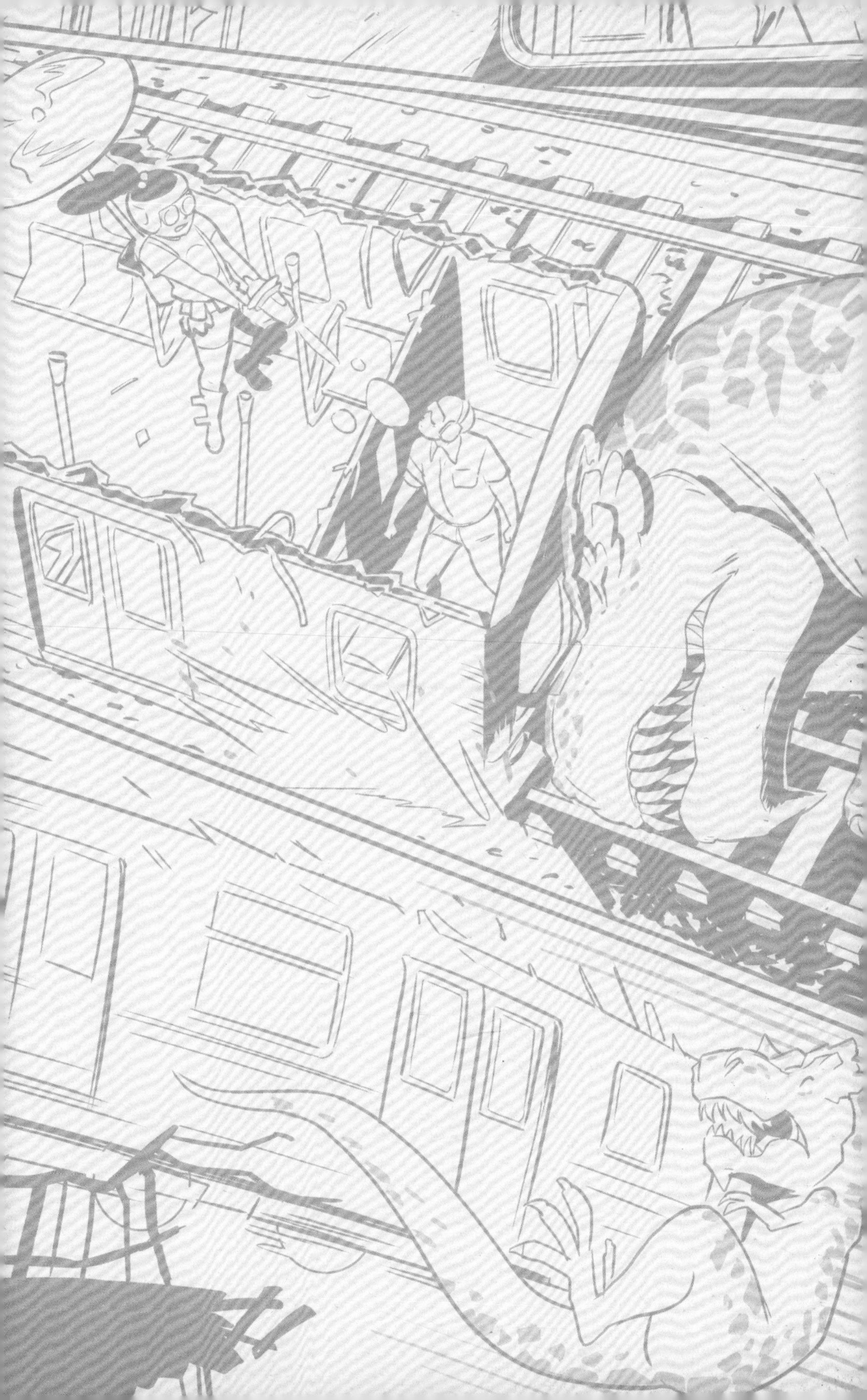

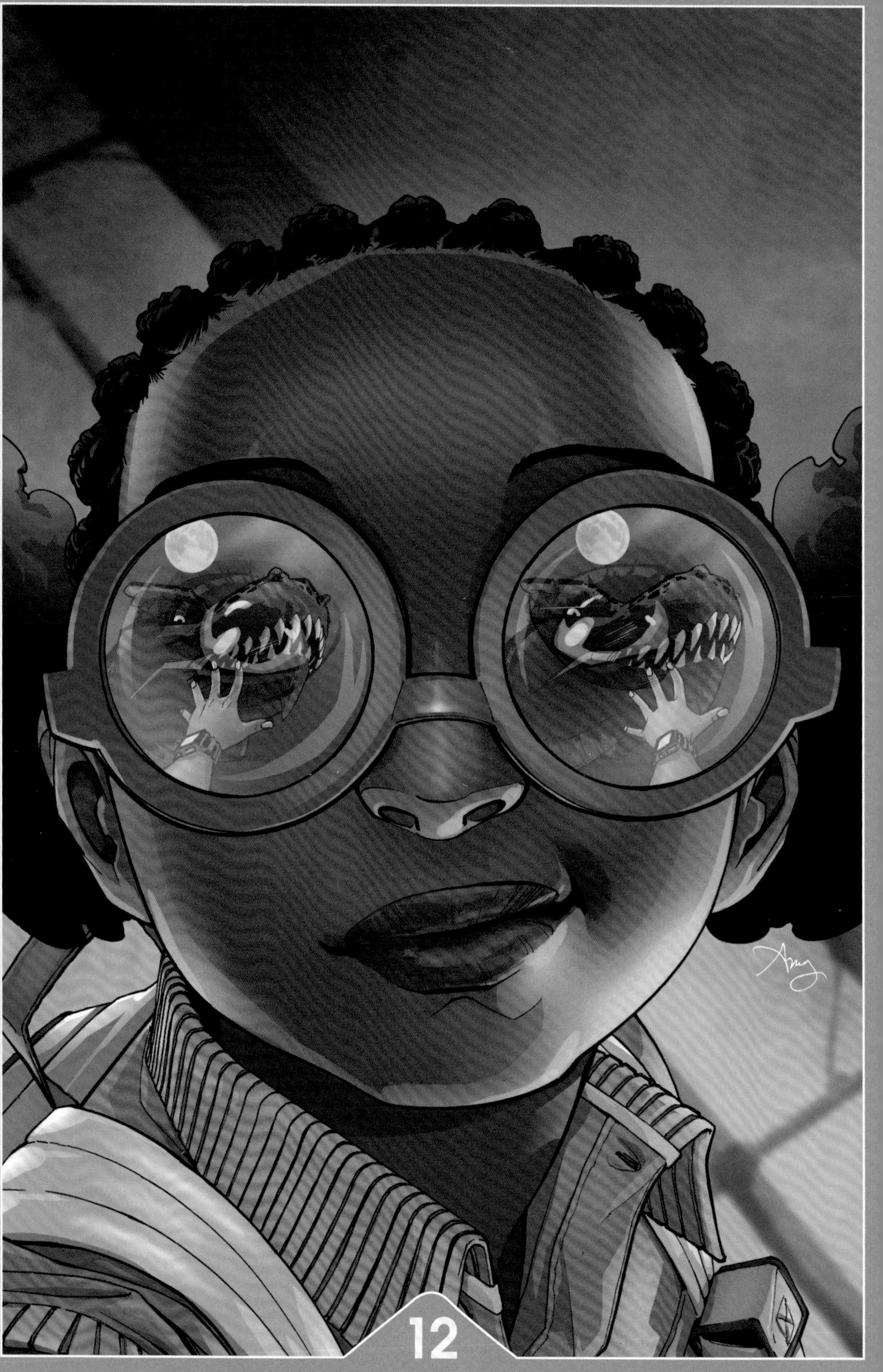

12

"UNREQUITED"

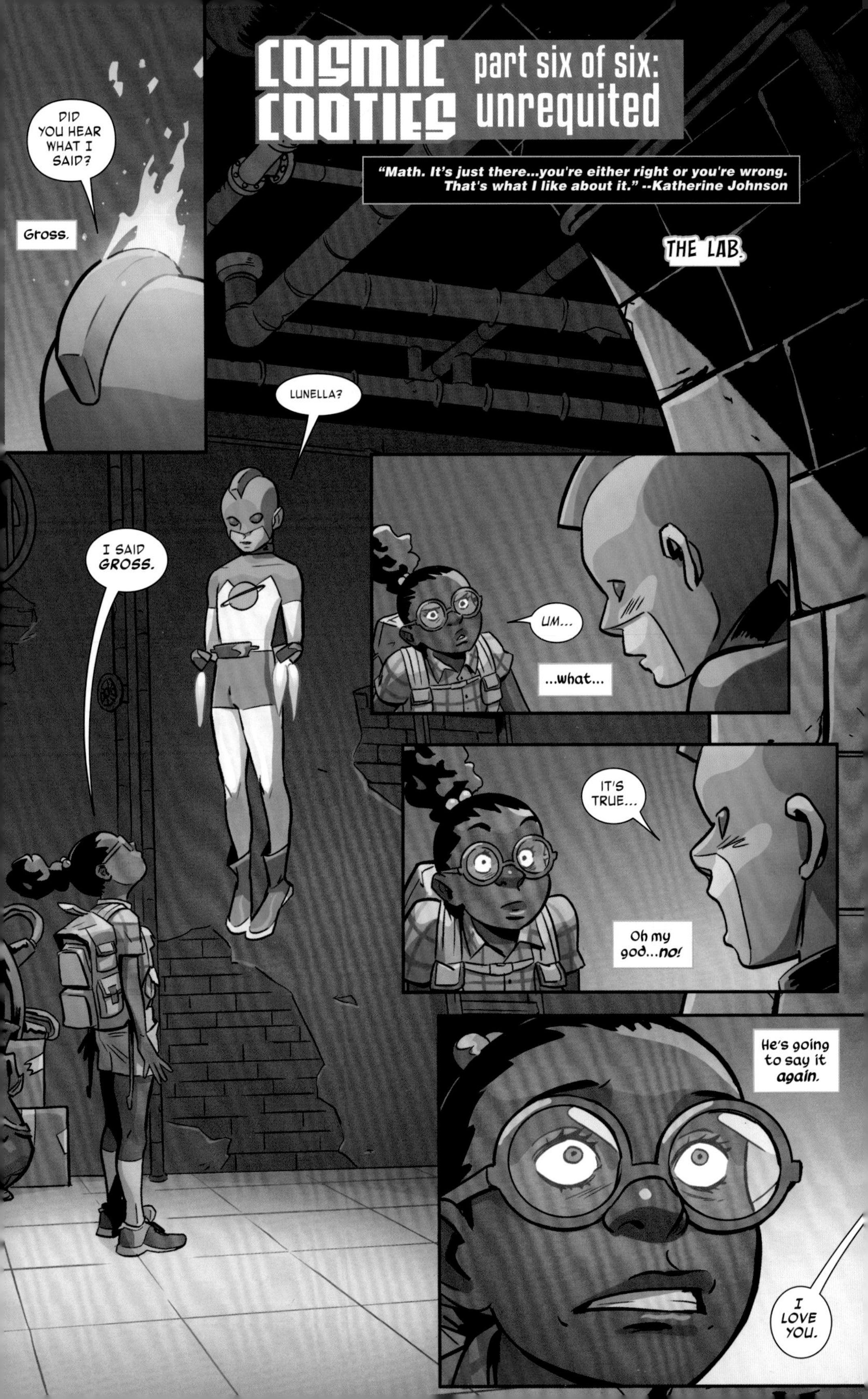
COSMIC COOTIES part six of six: unrequited
"Math. It's just there...you're either right or you're wrong. That's what I like about it." --Katherine Johnson
DID YOU HEAR WHAT I SAID?
Gross.
THE LAB.
LUNELLA?
I SAID GROSS.
UM...
...what...
IT'S TRUE...
Oh my god...no!
He's going to say it again.
I LOVE YOU.

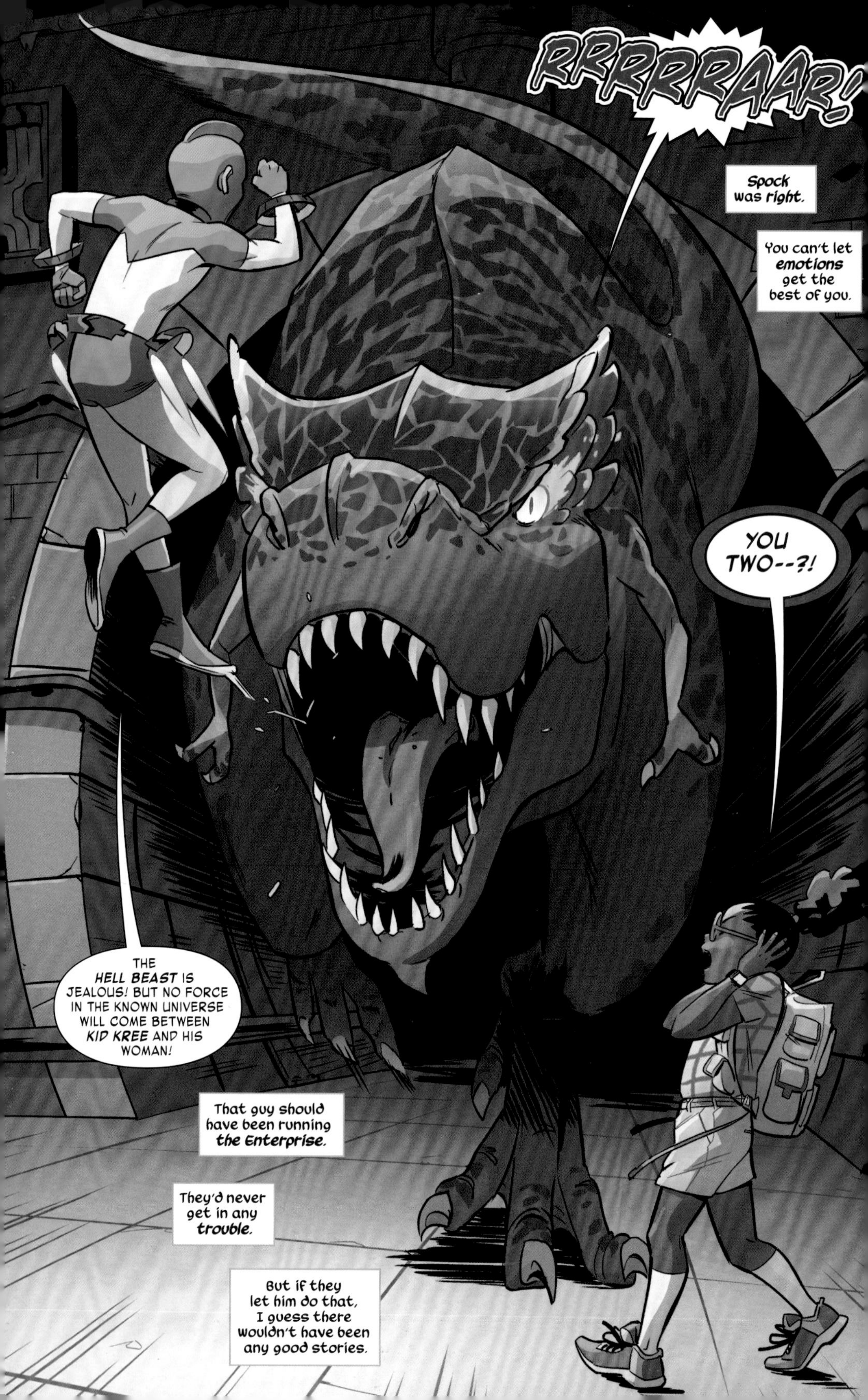
RRRRRAAR!
Spock was right.
You can't let emotions get the best of you.
YOU TWO--?!
THE HELL BEAST IS JEALOUS! BUT NO FORCE IN THE KNOWN UNIVERSE WILL COME BETWEEN KID KREE AND HIS WOMAN!
That guy should have been running the Enterprise.
They'd never get in any trouble.
But if they let him do that, I guess there wouldn't have been any good stories.

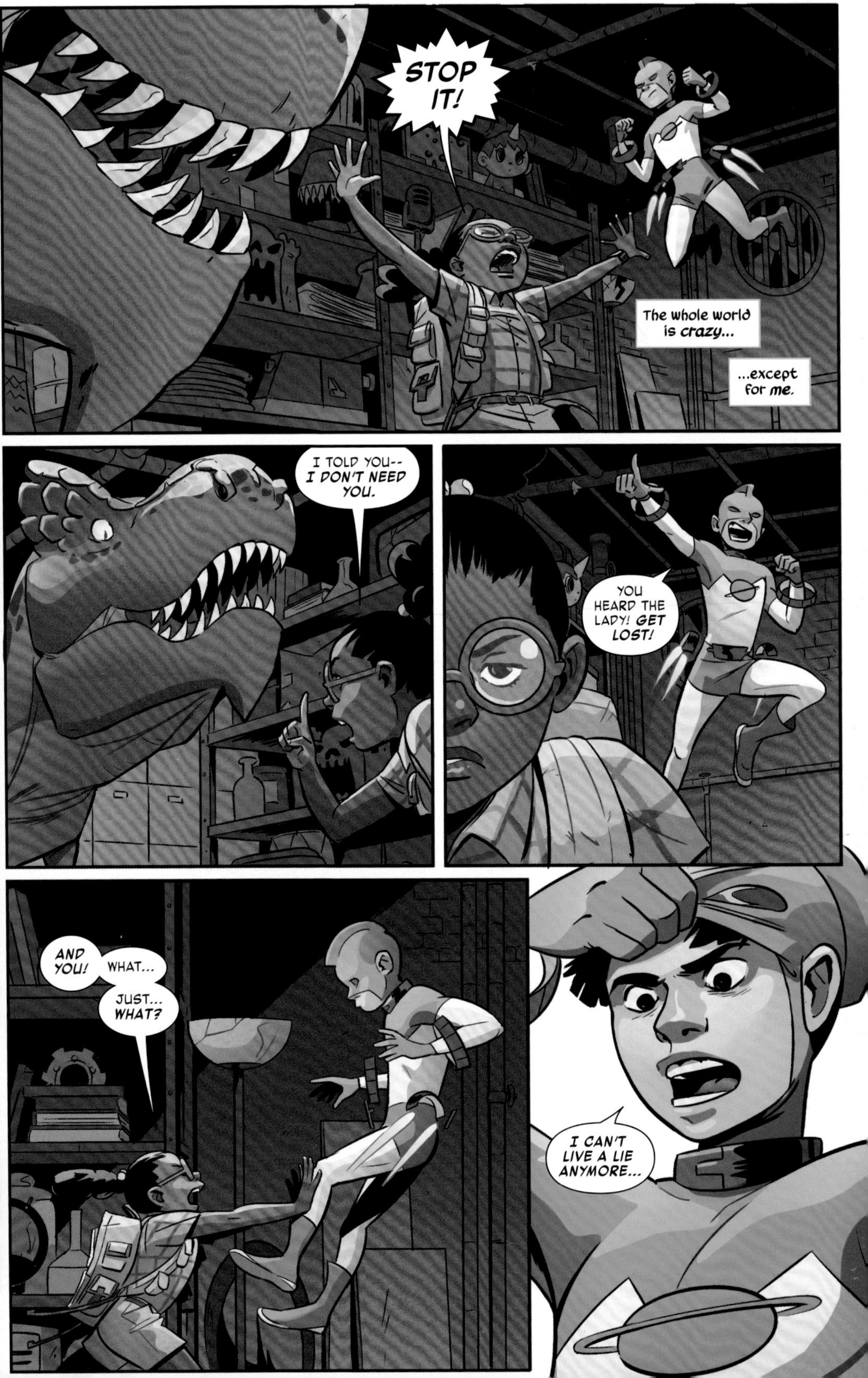
STOP IT!
The whole world is *crazy*...
...except for *me*.
I TOLD YOU-- *I DON'T NEED YOU.*
YOU HEARD THE LADY! *GET LOST!*
AND YOU!
WHAT...
JUST... *WHAT?*
I CAN'T LIVE A LIE ANYMORE...

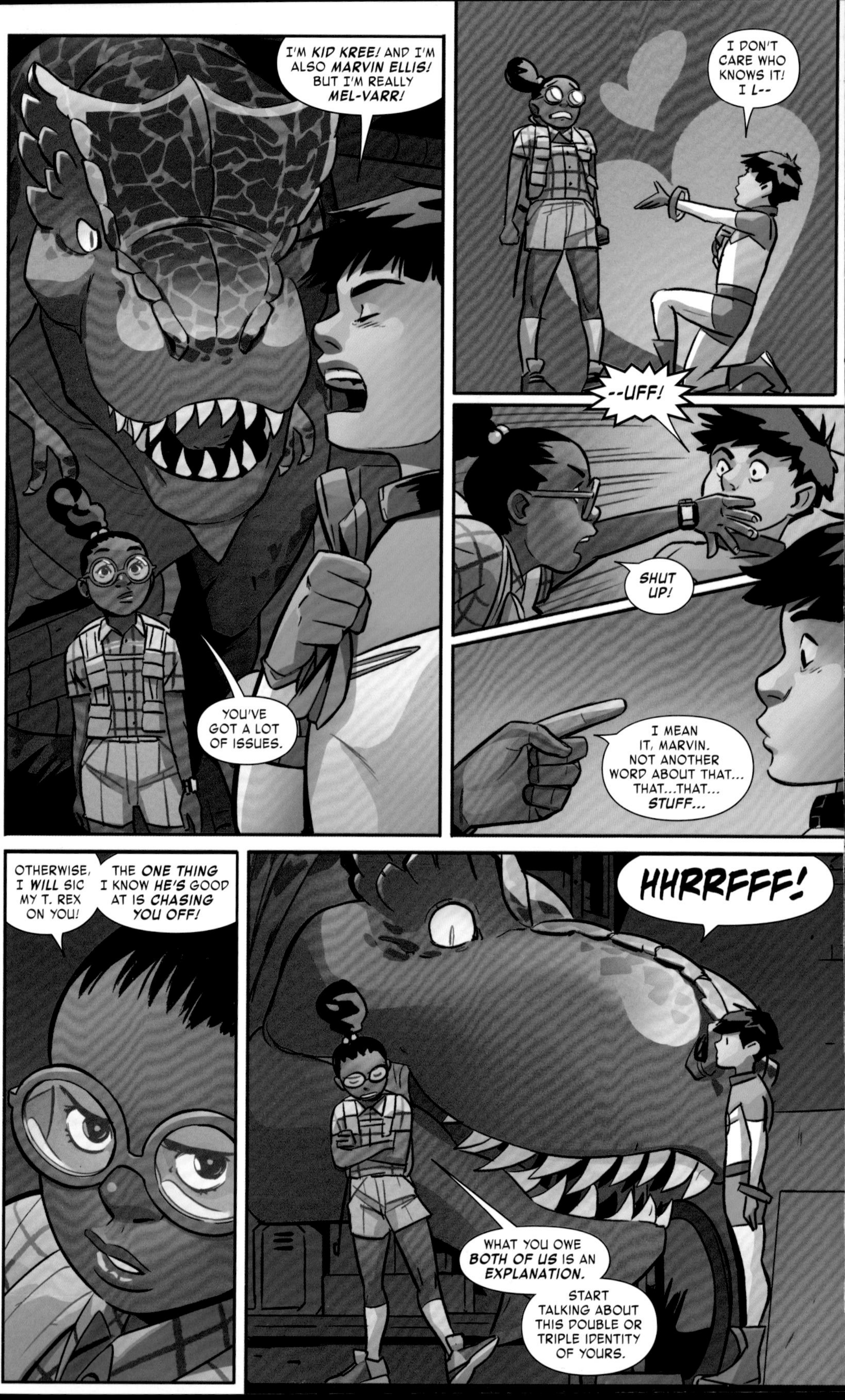
I'M KID KREE! AND I'M ALSO MARVIN ELLIS! BUT I'M REALLY MEL-VARR!
YOU'VE GOT A LOT OF ISSUES.
I DON'T CARE WHO KNOWS IT! I L--
--UFF!
SHUT UP!
I MEAN IT, MARVIN. NOT ANOTHER WORD ABOUT THAT... THAT...THAT... STUFF...
OTHERWISE, I WILL SIC MY T. REX ON YOU!
THE ONE THING I KNOW HE'S GOOD AT IS CHASING YOU OFF!
HHRRFFF!
WHAT YOU OWE BOTH OF US IS AN EXPLANATION.
START TALKING ABOUT THIS DOUBLE OR TRIPLE IDENTITY OF YOURS.

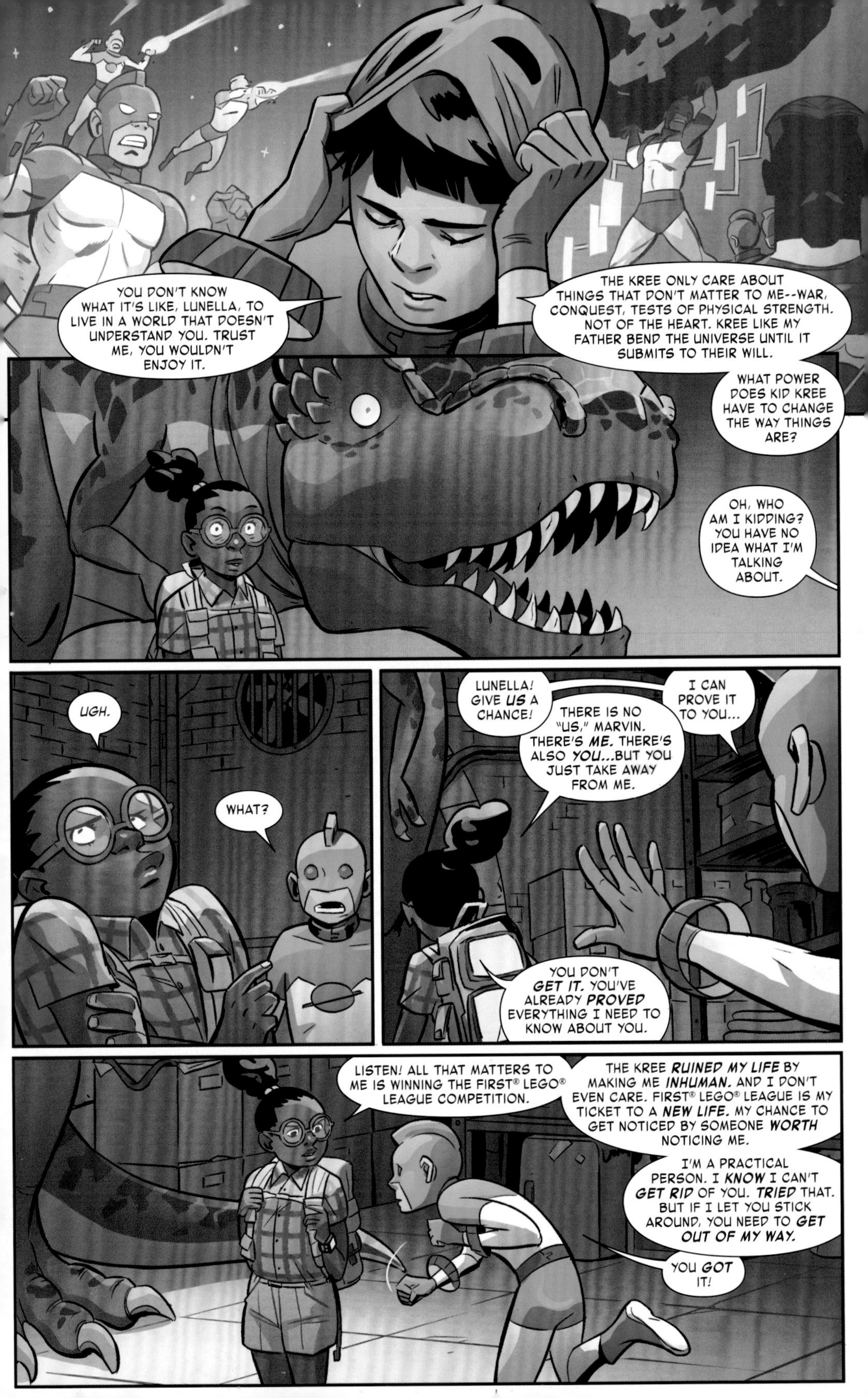
YOU DON'T KNOW WHAT IT'S LIKE, LUNELLA, TO LIVE IN A WORLD THAT DOESN'T UNDERSTAND YOU. TRUST ME, YOU WOULDN'T ENJOY IT.
THE KREE ONLY CARE ABOUT THINGS THAT DON'T MATTER TO ME--WAR, CONQUEST, TESTS OF PHYSICAL STRENGTH. NOT OF THE HEART. KREE LIKE MY FATHER BEND THE UNIVERSE UNTIL IT SUBMITS TO THEIR WILL.
WHAT POWER DOES KID KREE HAVE TO CHANGE THE WAY THINGS ARE?
OH, WHO AM I KIDDING? YOU HAVE NO IDEA WHAT I'M TALKING ABOUT.
UGH.
WHAT?
LUNELLA! GIVE US A CHANCE!
I CAN PROVE IT TO YOU...
THERE IS NO "US," MARVIN. THERE'S ME. THERE'S ALSO YOU...BUT YOU JUST TAKE AWAY FROM ME.
YOU DON'T GET IT. YOU'VE ALREADY PROVED EVERYTHING I NEED TO KNOW ABOUT YOU.
LISTEN! ALL THAT MATTERS TO ME IS WINNING THE FIRST® LEGO® LEAGUE COMPETITION.
THE KREE RUINED MY LIFE BY MAKING ME INHUMAN. AND I DON'T EVEN CARE. FIRST® LEGO® LEAGUE IS MY TICKET TO A NEW LIFE. MY CHANCE TO GET NOTICED BY SOMEONE WORTH NOTICING ME.
I'M A PRACTICAL PERSON. I KNOW I CAN'T GET RID OF YOU. TRIED THAT. BUT IF I LET YOU STICK AROUND, YOU NEED TO GET OUT OF MY WAY.
YOU GOT IT!

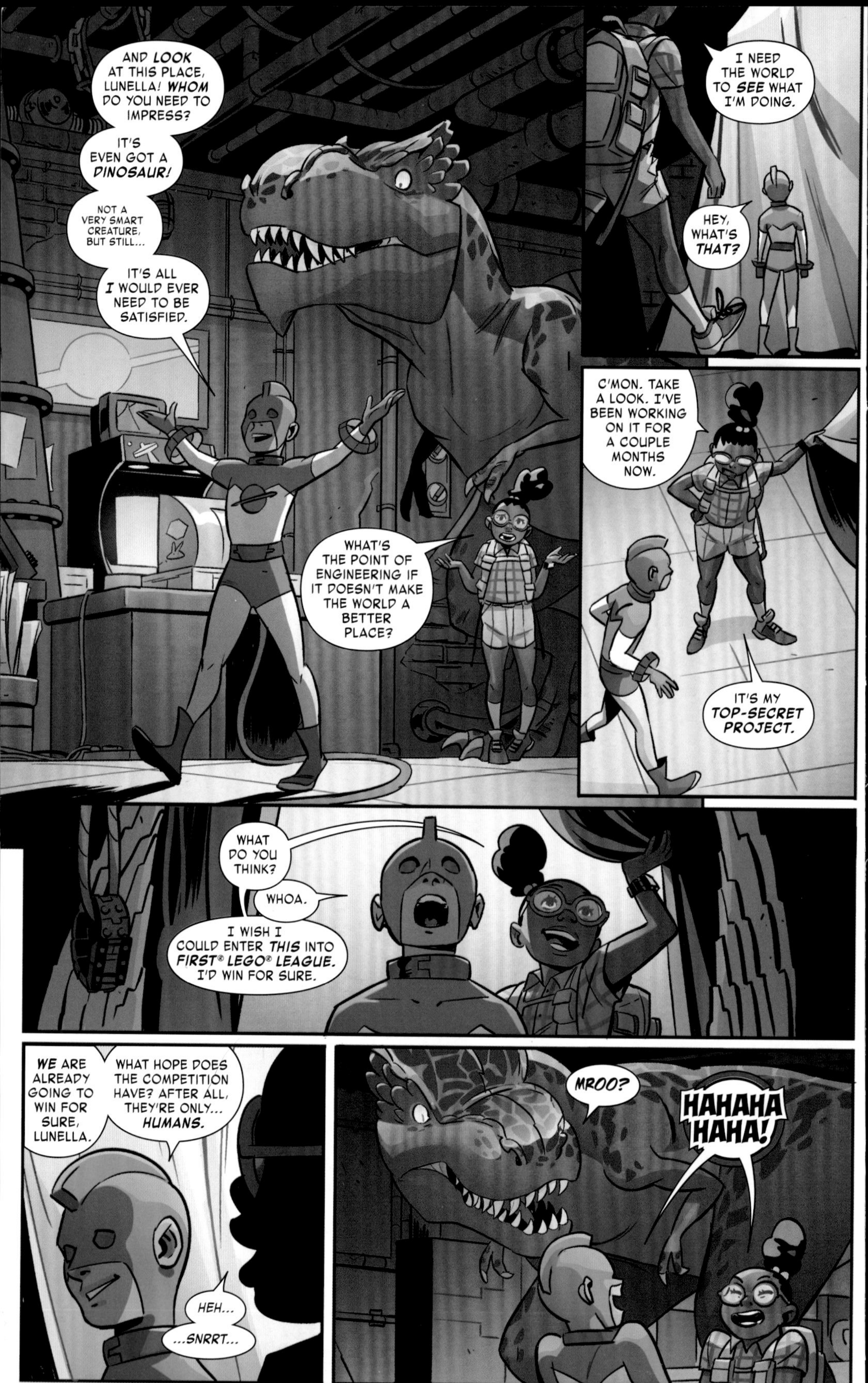
AND LOOK AT THIS PLACE, LUNELLA! WHOM DO YOU NEED TO IMPRESS?
IT'S EVEN GOT A DINOSAUR!
NOT A VERY SMART CREATURE, BUT STILL...
IT'S ALL I WOULD EVER NEED TO BE SATISFIED.
WHAT'S THE POINT OF ENGINEERING IF IT DOESN'T MAKE THE WORLD A BETTER PLACE?
I NEED THE WORLD TO SEE WHAT I'M DOING.
HEY, WHAT'S THAT?
C'MON. TAKE A LOOK. I'VE BEEN WORKING ON IT FOR A COUPLE MONTHS NOW.
IT'S MY TOP-SECRET PROJECT.
WHAT DO YOU THINK?
WHOA.
I WISH I COULD ENTER THIS INTO FIRST® LEGO® LEAGUE. I'D WIN FOR SURE.
WE ARE ALREADY GOING TO WIN FOR SURE, LUNELLA.
WHAT HOPE DOES THE COMPETITION HAVE? AFTER ALL, THEY'RE ONLY... HUMANS.
HEH...
...SNRRT...
MROO?
HAHAHA HAHA!

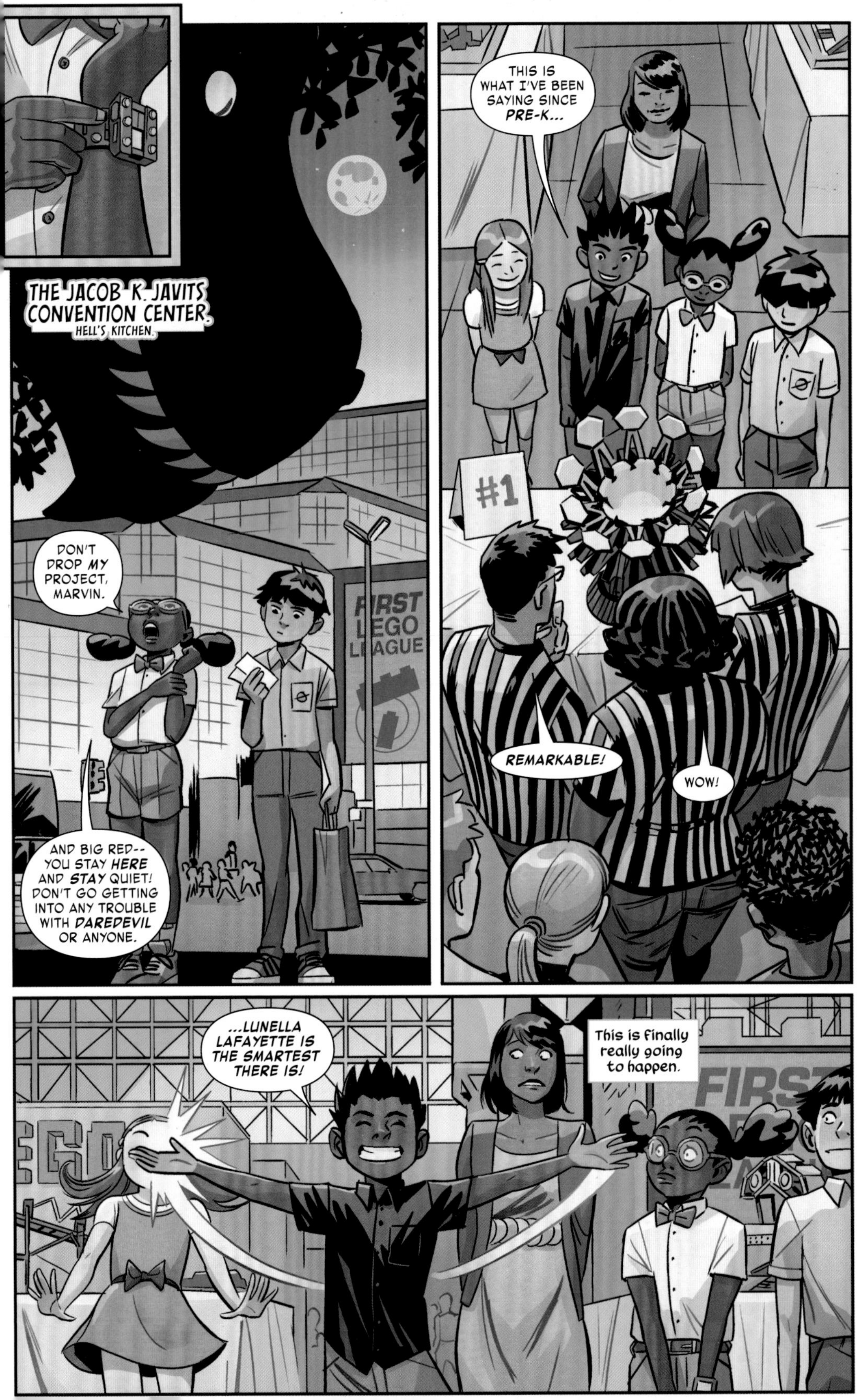

THE JACOB K. JAVITS CONVENTION CENTER.
HELL'S KITCHEN.
DON'T DROP MY PROJECT, MARVIN.
FIRST LEGO LEAGUE
AND BIG RED-- YOU STAY HERE AND STAY QUIET! DON'T GO GETTING INTO ANY TROUBLE WITH DAREDEVIL OR ANYONE.
THIS IS WHAT I'VE BEEN SAYING SINCE PRE-K...
#1
REMARKABLE!
WOW!
...LUNELLA LAFAYETTE IS THE SMARTEST THERE IS!
This is finally really going to happen.

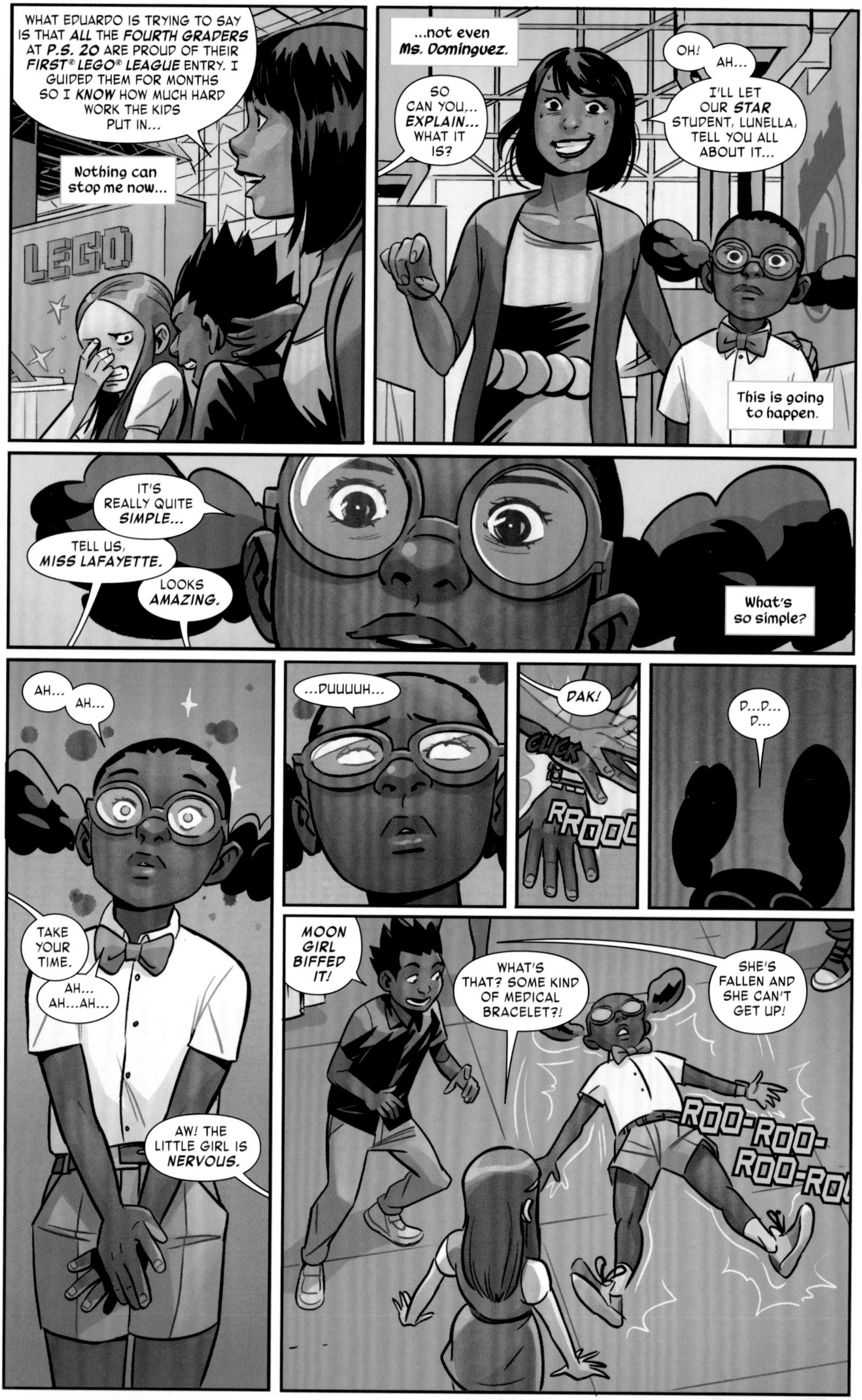
WHAT EDUARDO IS TRYING TO SAY IS THAT ALL THE FOURTH GRADERS AT P.S. 20 ARE PROUD OF THEIR FIRST® LEGO® LEAGUE ENTRY. I GUIDED THEM FOR MONTHS SO I KNOW HOW MUCH HARD WORK THE KIDS PUT IN...
Nothing can stop me now...
LEGO
...not even Ms. Dominguez.
SO CAN YOU... EXPLAIN... WHAT IT IS?
OH!
AH...
I'LL LET OUR STAR STUDENT, LUNELLA, TELL YOU ALL ABOUT IT...
This is going to happen.
IT'S REALLY QUITE SIMPLE...
TELL US, MISS LAFAYETTE.
LOOKS AMAZING.
What's so simple?
AH...
AH...
TAKE YOUR TIME.
AH... AH...AH...
AW! THE LITTLE GIRL IS NERVOUS.
...DUUUUH...
DAK!
CLICK
RROOO
D...D... D...
MOON GIRL BIFFED IT!
WHAT'S THAT? SOME KIND OF MEDICAL BRACELET?!
SHE'S FALLEN AND SHE CAN'T GET UP!
ROO-ROO-ROO-ROO

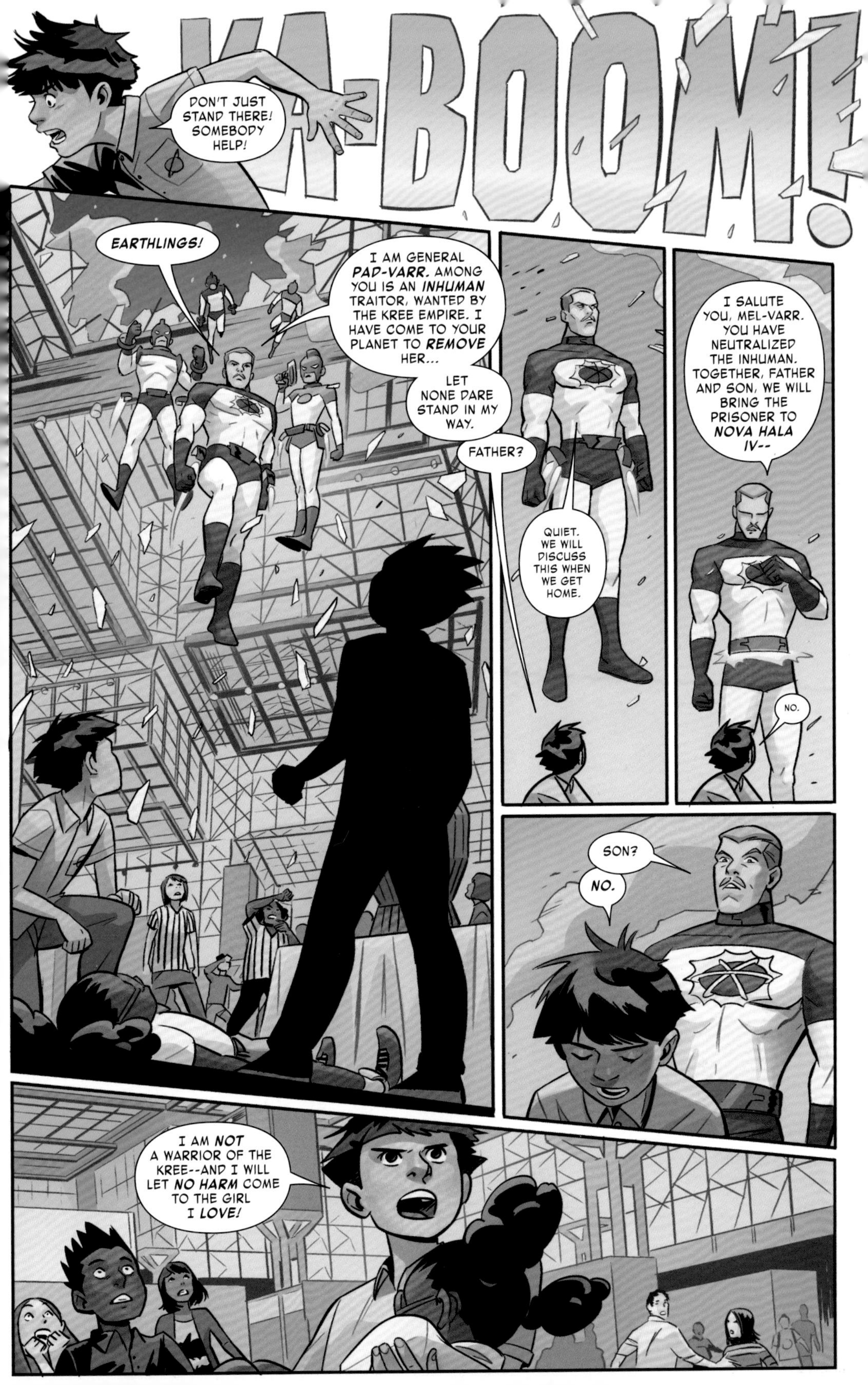
KA-BOOM!
DON'T JUST STAND THERE! SOMEBODY HELP!
EARTHLINGS!
I AM GENERAL PAD-VARR. AMONG YOU IS AN INHUMAN TRAITOR, WANTED BY THE KREE EMPIRE. I HAVE COME TO YOUR PLANET TO REMOVE HER...
LET NONE DARE STAND IN MY WAY.
FATHER?
QUIET. WE WILL DISCUSS THIS WHEN WE GET HOME.
I SALUTE YOU, MEL-VARR. YOU HAVE NEUTRALIZED THE INHUMAN. TOGETHER, FATHER AND SON, WE WILL BRING THE PRISONER TO NOVA HALA IV--
NO.
SON?
NO.
I AM NOT A WARRIOR OF THE KREE--AND I WILL LET NO HARM COME TO THE GIRL I LOVE!

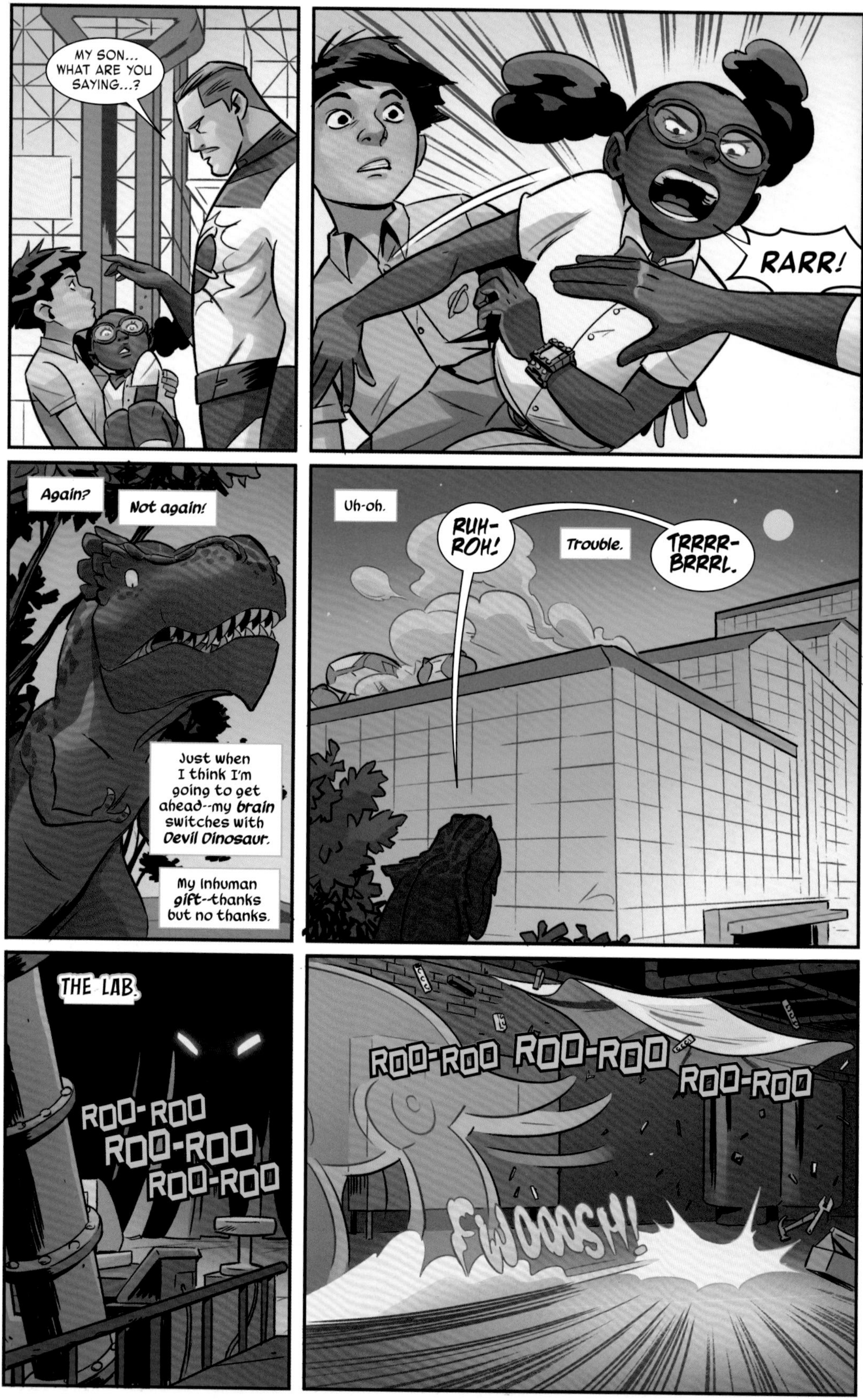
MY SON... WHAT ARE YOU SAYING...?
RARR!
Again?
Not again!
Just when I think I'm going to get ahead--my brain switches with Devil Dinosaur.
My Inhuman gift--thanks but no thanks.
Uh-oh.
RUH-ROH!
Trouble.
TRRRR-BRRRL.
THE LAB.
ROO-ROO
ROO-ROO
ROO-ROO
ROO-ROO ROO-ROO ROO-ROO
FWOOOSH!

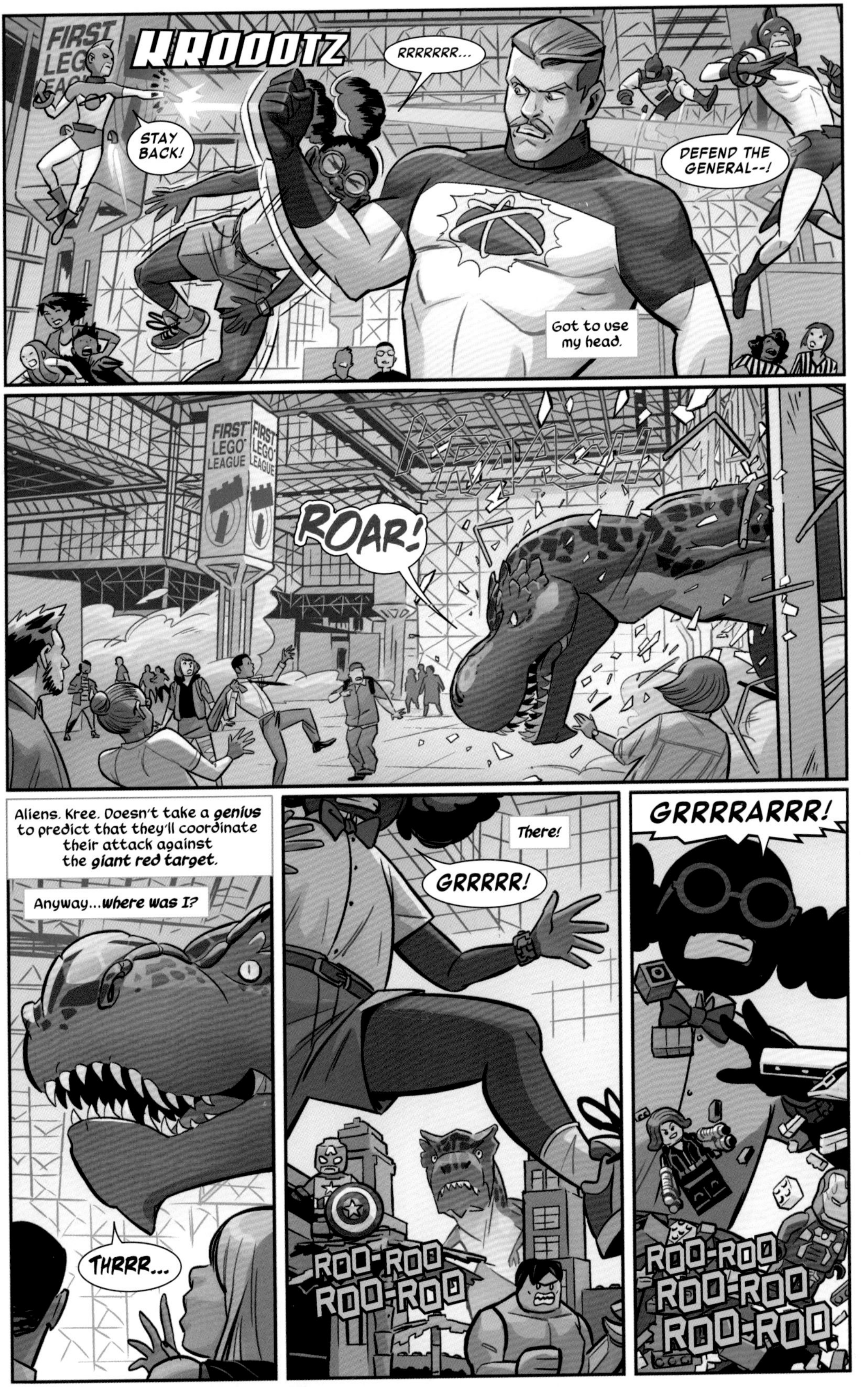

KROOOTZ
STAY BACK!
RRRRRRR...
DEFEND THE GENERAL--!
Got to use my head.
FIRST LEGO LEAGUE
KRAAACH
ROAR!
Aliens. Kree. Doesn't take a genius to predict that they'll coordinate their attack against the giant red target.
Anyway...where was I?
THRRR...
There!
GRRRRR!
ROO-ROO ROO-ROO
GRRRRARRR!
ROO-ROO ROO-ROO ROO-ROO

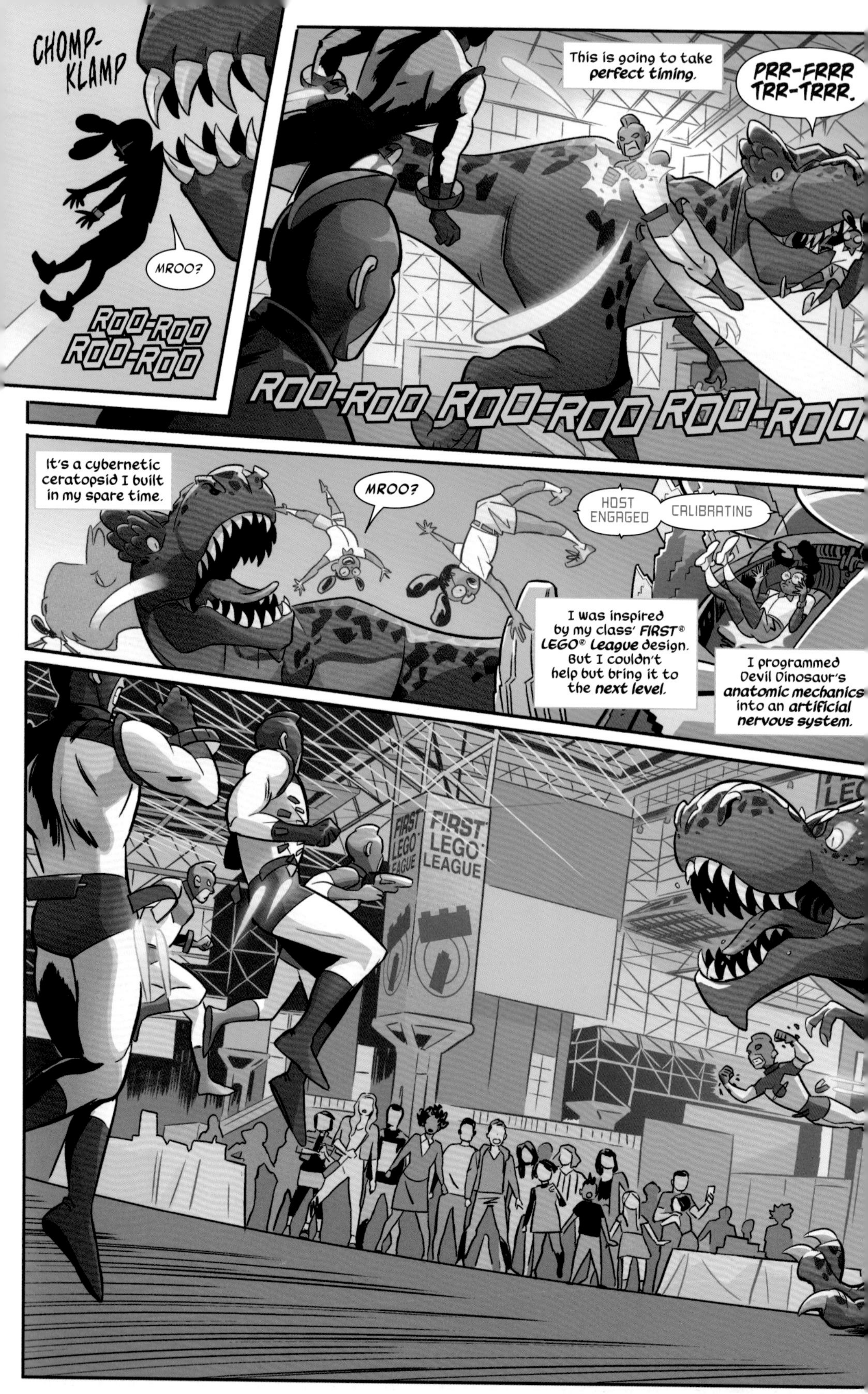

CHOMP-KLAMP
MROO?
ROO-ROO ROO-ROO
This is going to take perfect timing.
PRR-FRRR TRR-TRRR.
ROO-ROO ROO-ROO ROO-ROO
It's a cybernetic ceratopsid I built in my spare time.
MROO?
HOST ENGAGED
CALIBRATING
I was inspired by my class' FIRST® LEGO® League design. But I couldn't help but bring it to the next level.
I programmed Devil Dinosaur's anatomic mechanics into an artificial nervous system.
FIRST LEGO LEAGUE
FIRST LEGO LEAGUE

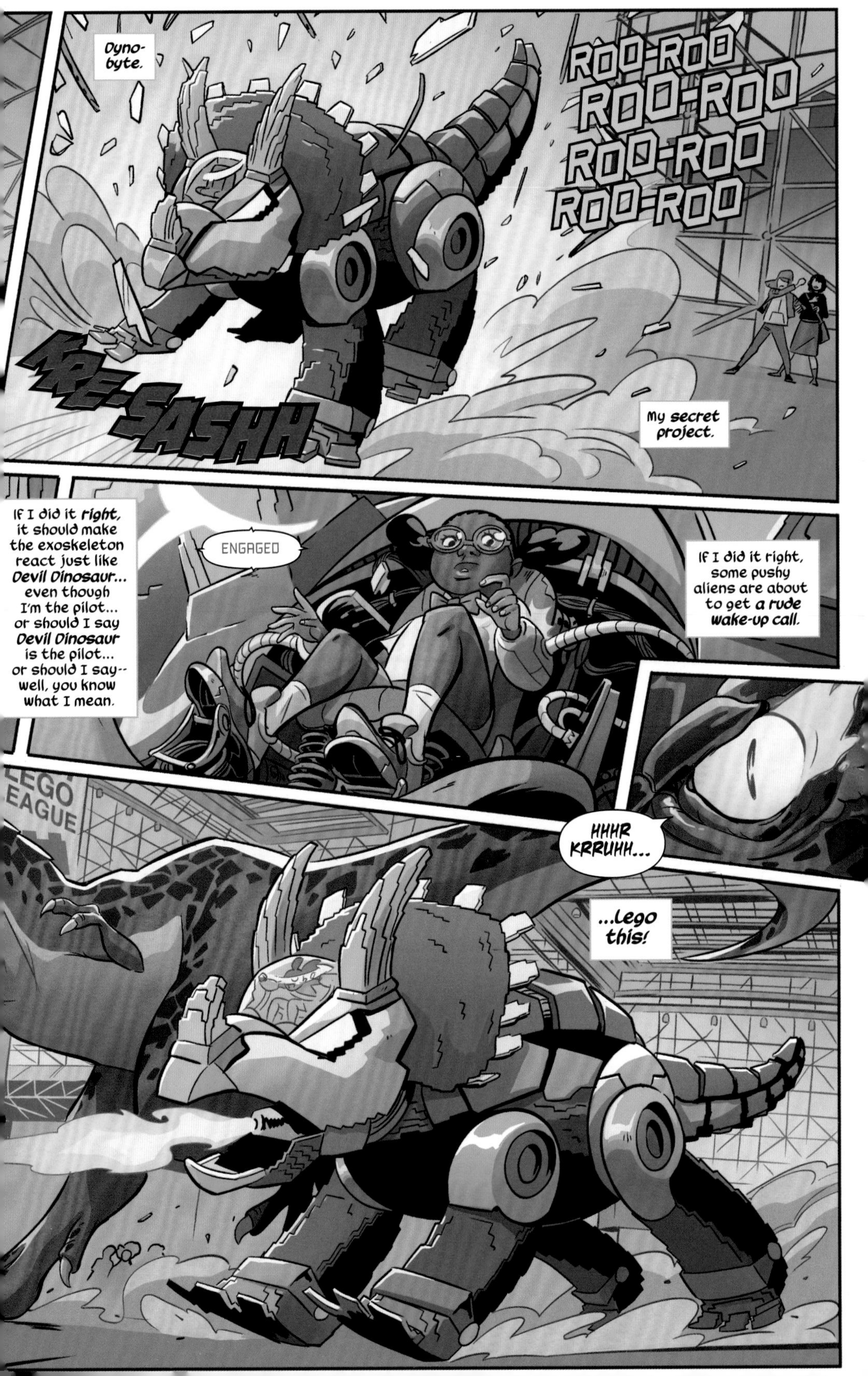
Dyno-byte.
ROO-ROO ROO-ROO ROO-ROO ROO-ROO
KRE-SASHH
My secret project.
If I did it right, it should make the exoskeleton react just like Devil Dinosaur... even though I'm the pilot... or should I say Devil Dinosaur is the pilot... or should I say-- well, you know what I mean.
ENGAGED
If I did it right, some pushy aliens are about to get a rude wake-up call.
LEGO LEAGUE
HHHR KRRUHH...
...lego this!

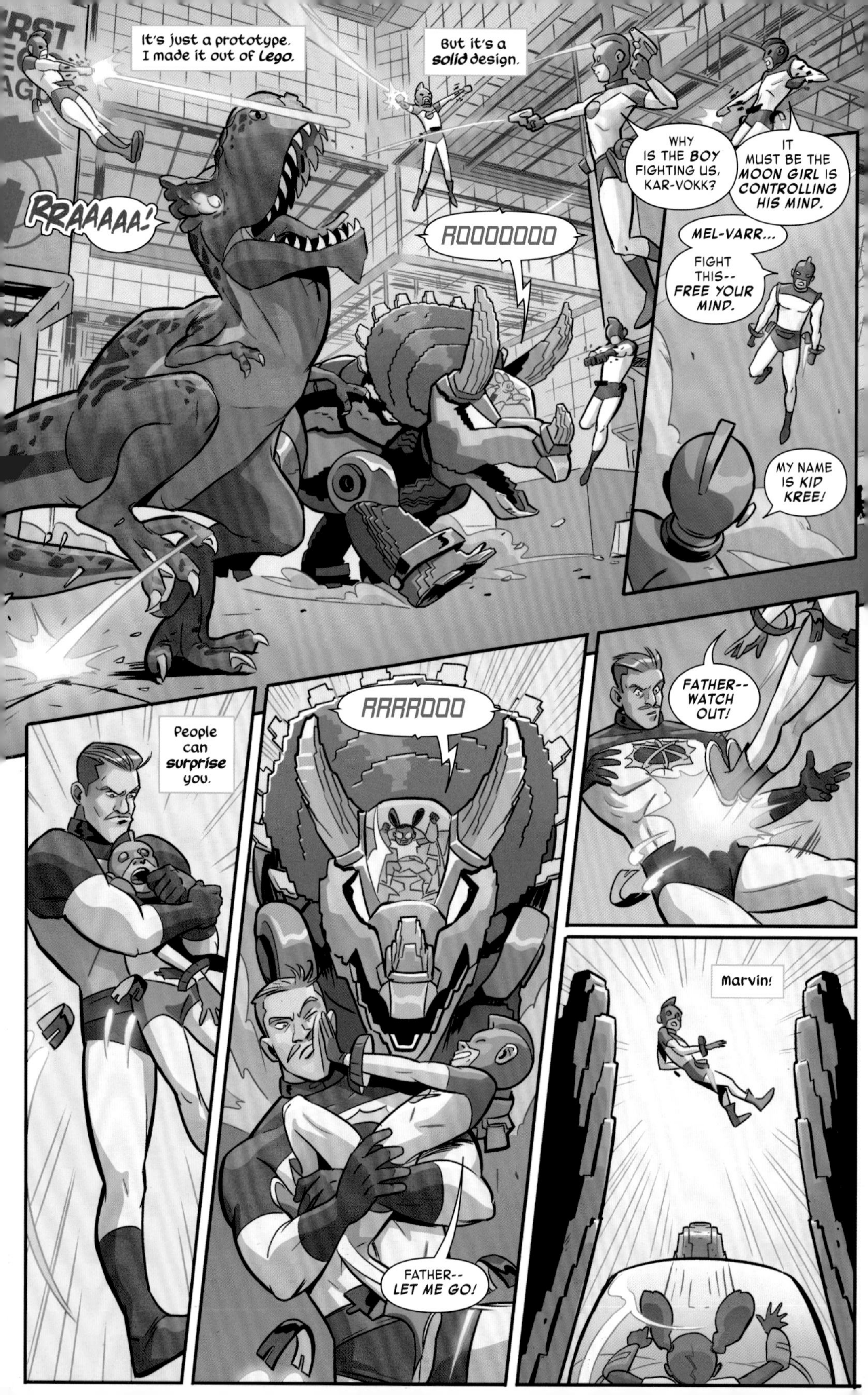

It's just a prototype. I made it out of *Lego*.
But it's a *solid* design.
RRAAAAA!
ROOOOOOO
WHY IS THE BOY FIGHTING US, KAR-VOKK?
IT MUST BE THE MOON GIRL IS CONTROLLING HIS MIND.
MEL-VARR...
FIGHT THIS-- FREE YOUR MIND.
MY NAME IS KID KREE!
People can surprise you.
RRRROOO
FATHER-- LET ME GO!
FATHER-- WATCH OUT!
Marvin!

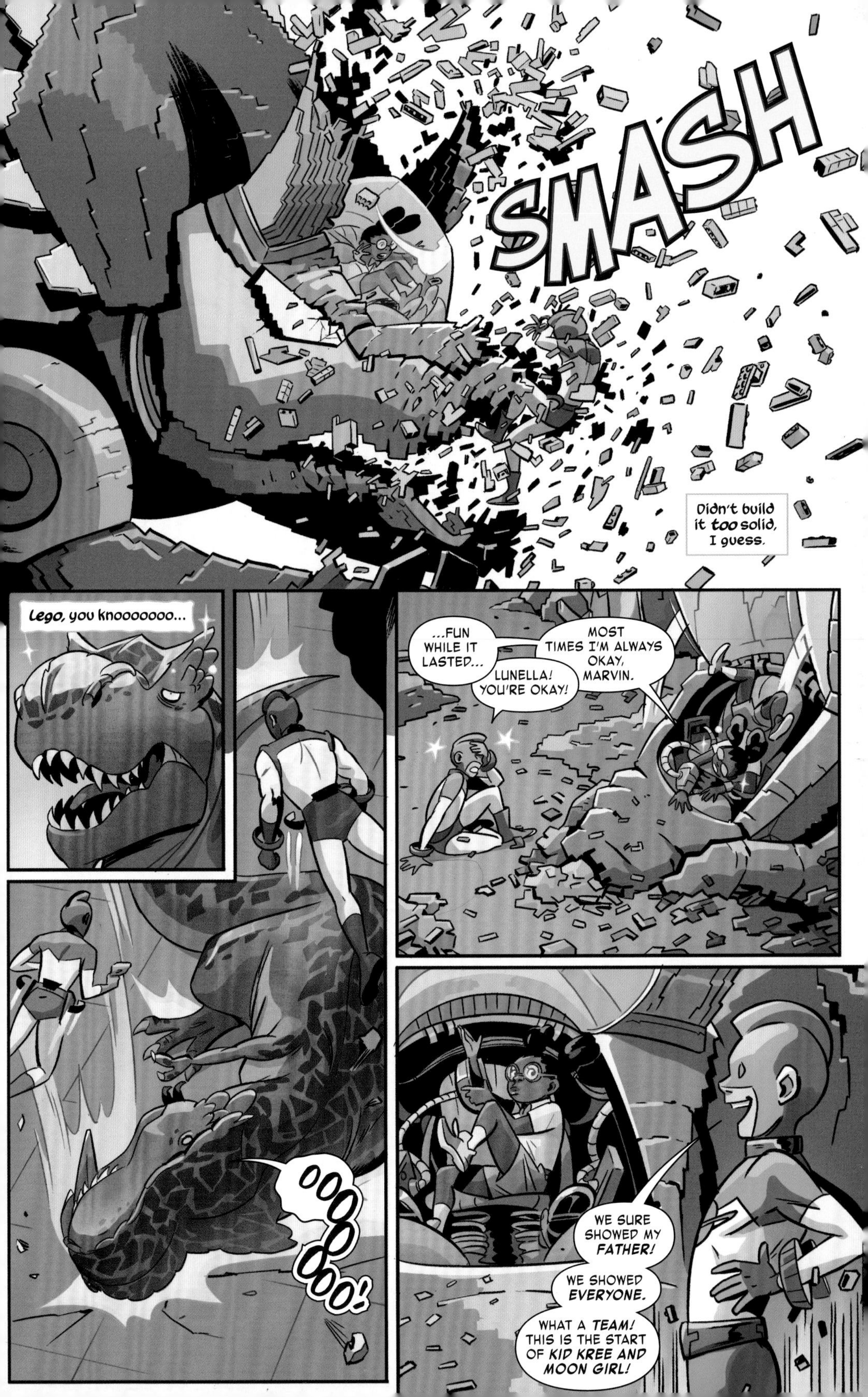
SMASH
Didn't build it *too* solid, I guess.
Lego, you knooooooo...
...FUN WHILE IT LASTED...
LUNELLA! YOU'RE OKAY!
MOST TIMES I'M ALWAYS OKAY, MARVIN.
OOOOOOO!
WE SURE SHOWED MY *FATHER!*
WE SHOWED *EVERYONE.*
WHAT A *TEAM!* THIS IS THE START OF *KID KREE AND MOON GIRL!*

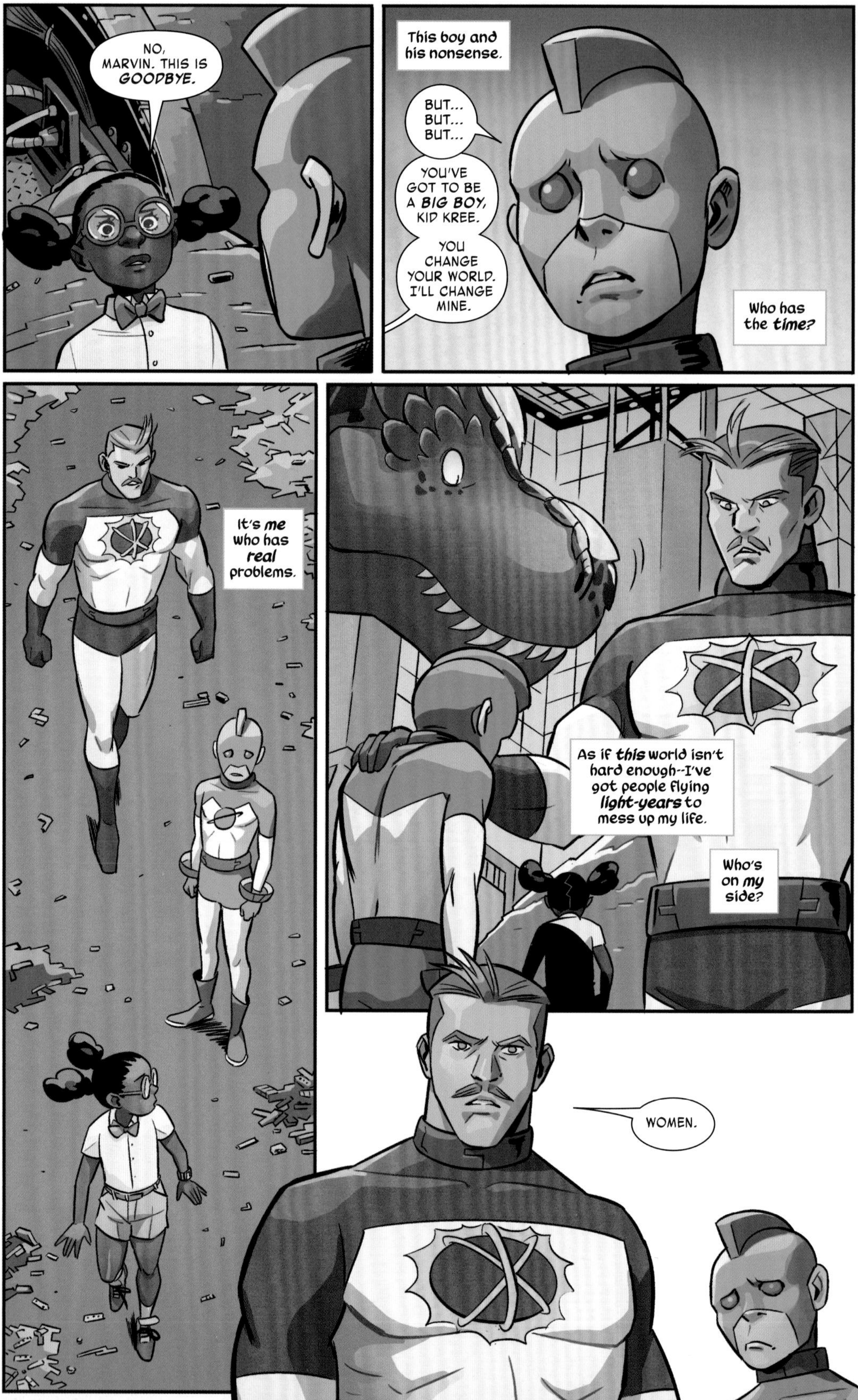

NO, MARVIN. THIS IS GOODBYE.
This boy and his nonsense.
BUT... BUT... BUT...
YOU'VE GOT TO BE A BIG BOY, KID KREE.
YOU CHANGE YOUR WORLD. I'LL CHANGE MINE.
Who has the time?
It's me who has real problems.
As if this world isn't hard enough--I've got people flying light-years to mess up my life.
Who's on my side?
WOMEN.

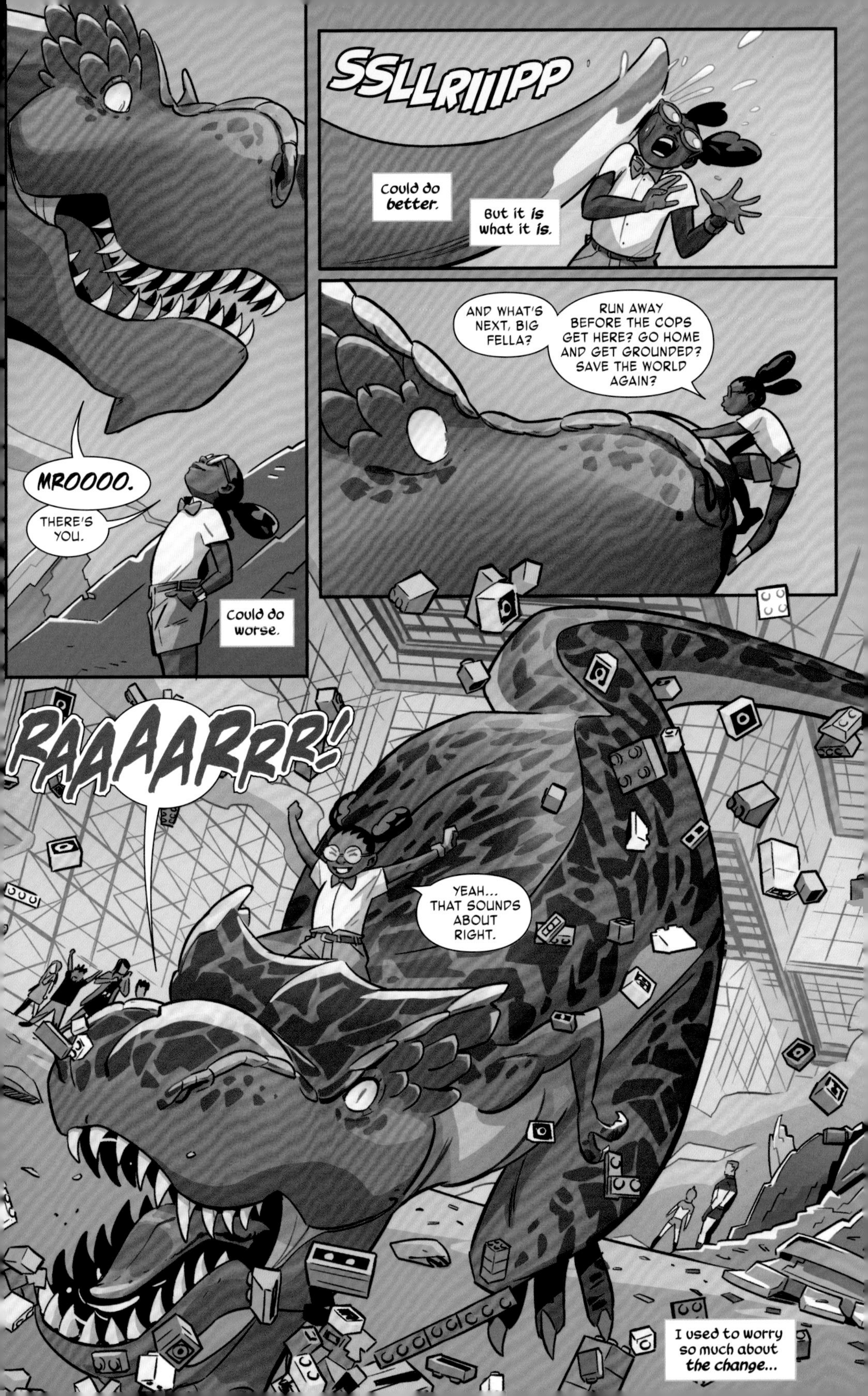

SSLLRIIIPP
Could do better.
But it is what it is.
MROOOO.
THERE'S YOU.
Could do worse.
AND WHAT'S NEXT, BIG FELLA?
RUN AWAY BEFORE THE COPS GET HERE? GO HOME AND GET GROUNDED? SAVE THE WORLD AGAIN?
RAAAARRRR!
YEAH... THAT SOUNDS ABOUT RIGHT.
I used to worry so much about the change...

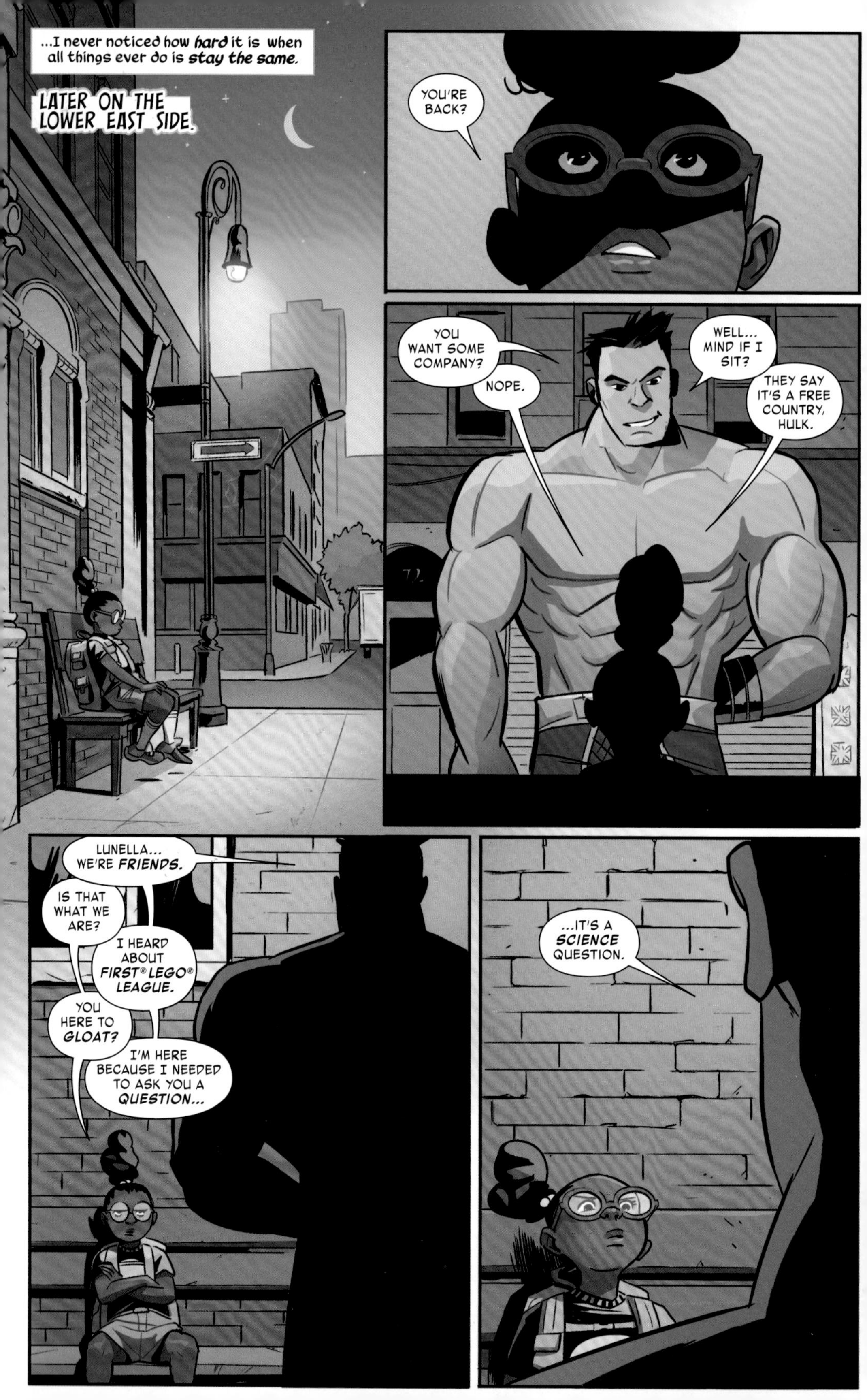

...I never noticed how hard it is when all things ever do is stay the same.
LATER ON THE LOWER EAST SIDE.
YOU'RE BACK?
YOU WANT SOME COMPANY?
NOPE.
WELL... MIND IF I SIT?
THEY SAY IT'S A FREE COUNTRY, HULK.
LUNELLA... WE'RE FRIENDS.
IS THAT WHAT WE ARE?
I HEARD ABOUT FIRST® LEGO® LEAGUE.
YOU HERE TO GLOAT?
I'M HERE BECAUSE I NEEDED TO ASK YOU A QUESTION...
...IT'S A SCIENCE QUESTION.

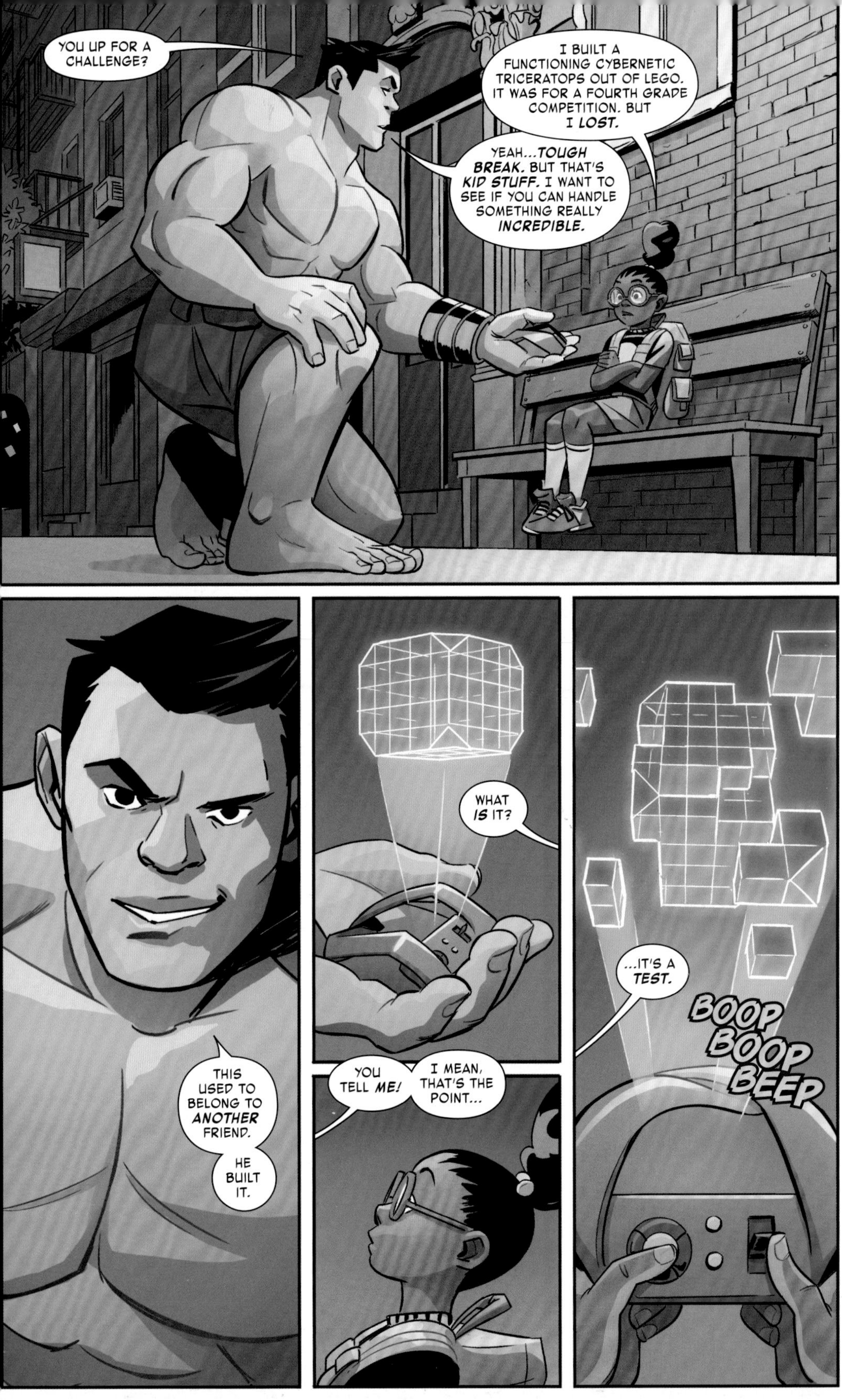
YOU UP FOR A CHALLENGE?
I BUILT A FUNCTIONING CYBERNETIC TRICERATOPS OUT OF LEGO. IT WAS FOR A FOURTH GRADE COMPETITION. BUT I LOST.
YEAH...TOUGH BREAK. BUT THAT'S KID STUFF. I WANT TO SEE IF YOU CAN HANDLE SOMETHING REALLY INCREDIBLE.
THIS USED TO BELONG TO ANOTHER FRIEND.
HE BUILT IT.
WHAT IS IT?
YOU TELL ME!
I MEAN, THAT'S THE POINT...
...IT'S A TEST.
BOOP BOOP BEEP

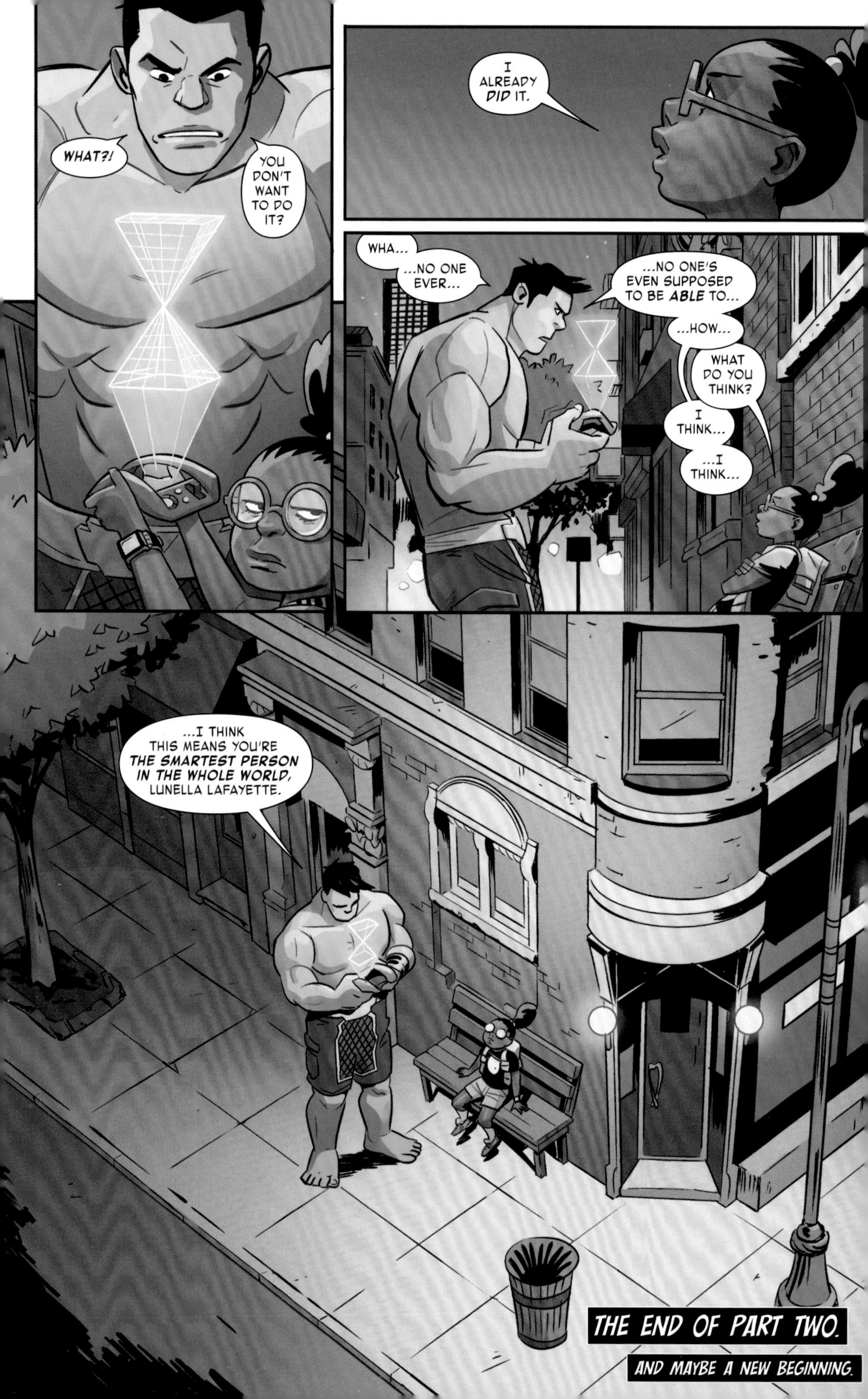
WHAT?!
YOU DON'T WANT TO DO IT?
I ALREADY *DID* IT.
WHA...
...NO ONE EVER...
...NO ONE'S EVEN SUPPOSED TO BE **ABLE** TO...
...HOW...
WHAT DO YOU THINK?
I THINK...
...I THINK...
...I THINK THIS MEANS YOU'RE ***THE SMARTEST PERSON IN THE WHOLE WORLD,*** LUNELLA LAFAYETTE.
THE END OF PART TWO.
AND MAYBE A NEW BEGINNING.

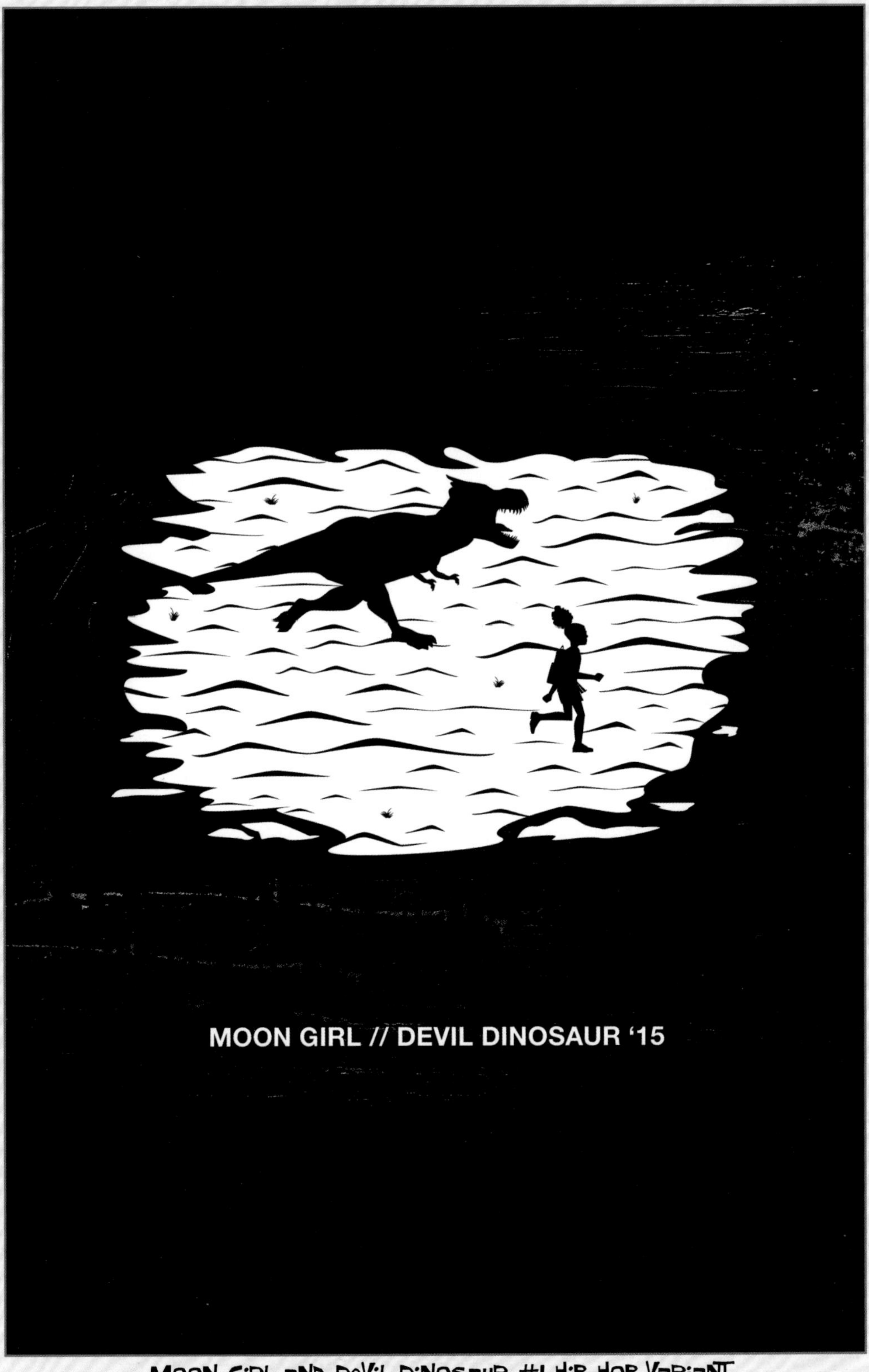
MOON GIRL // DEVIL DINOSAUR '15

MOON GIRL AND DEVIL DINOSAUR #1 HIP-HOP VARIANT
BY JEFFREY VEREGGE

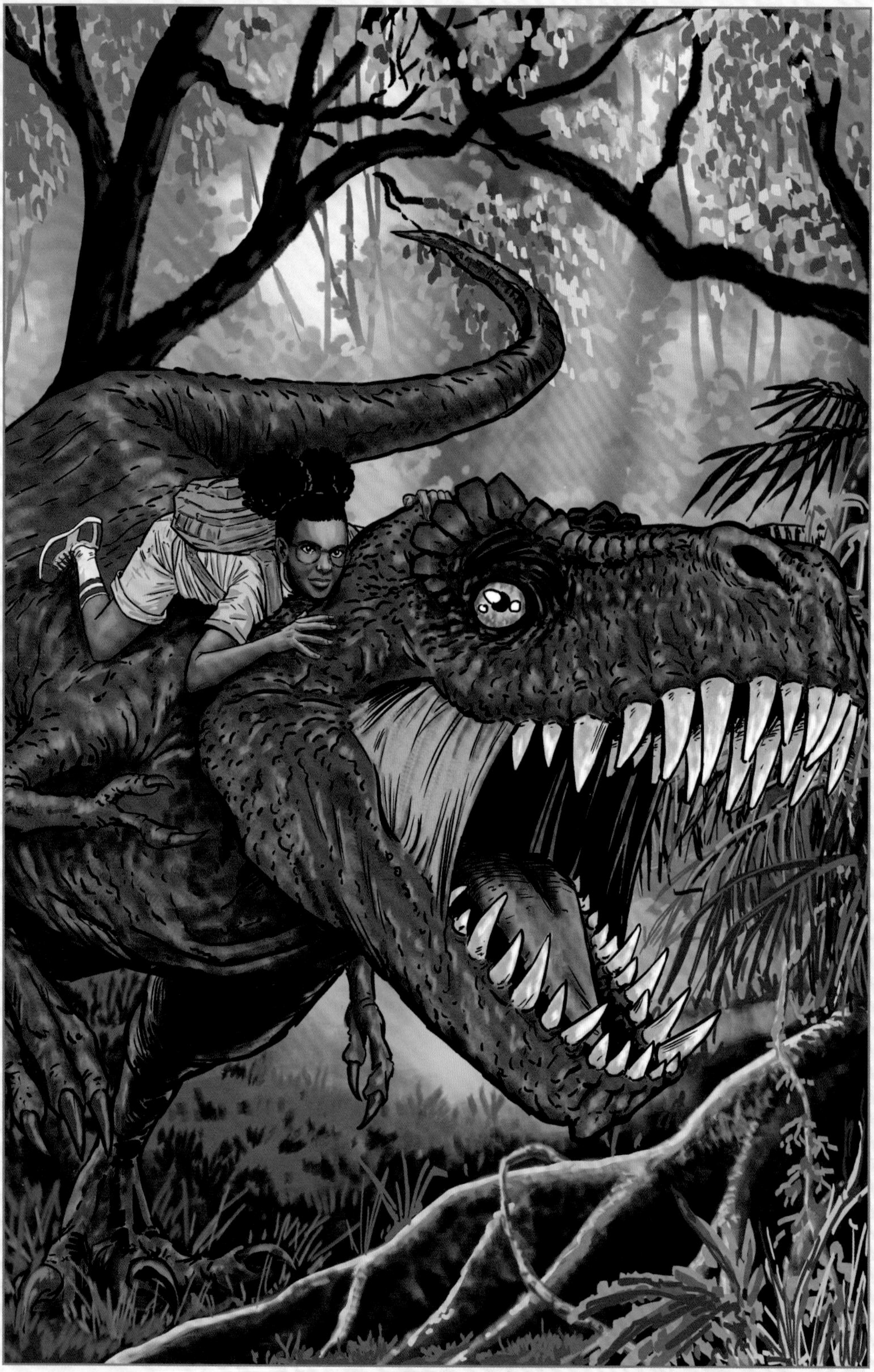

MOON GIRL AND DEVIL DINOSAUR #5 WOMEN OF POWER VARIANT
BY PIA GUERRA

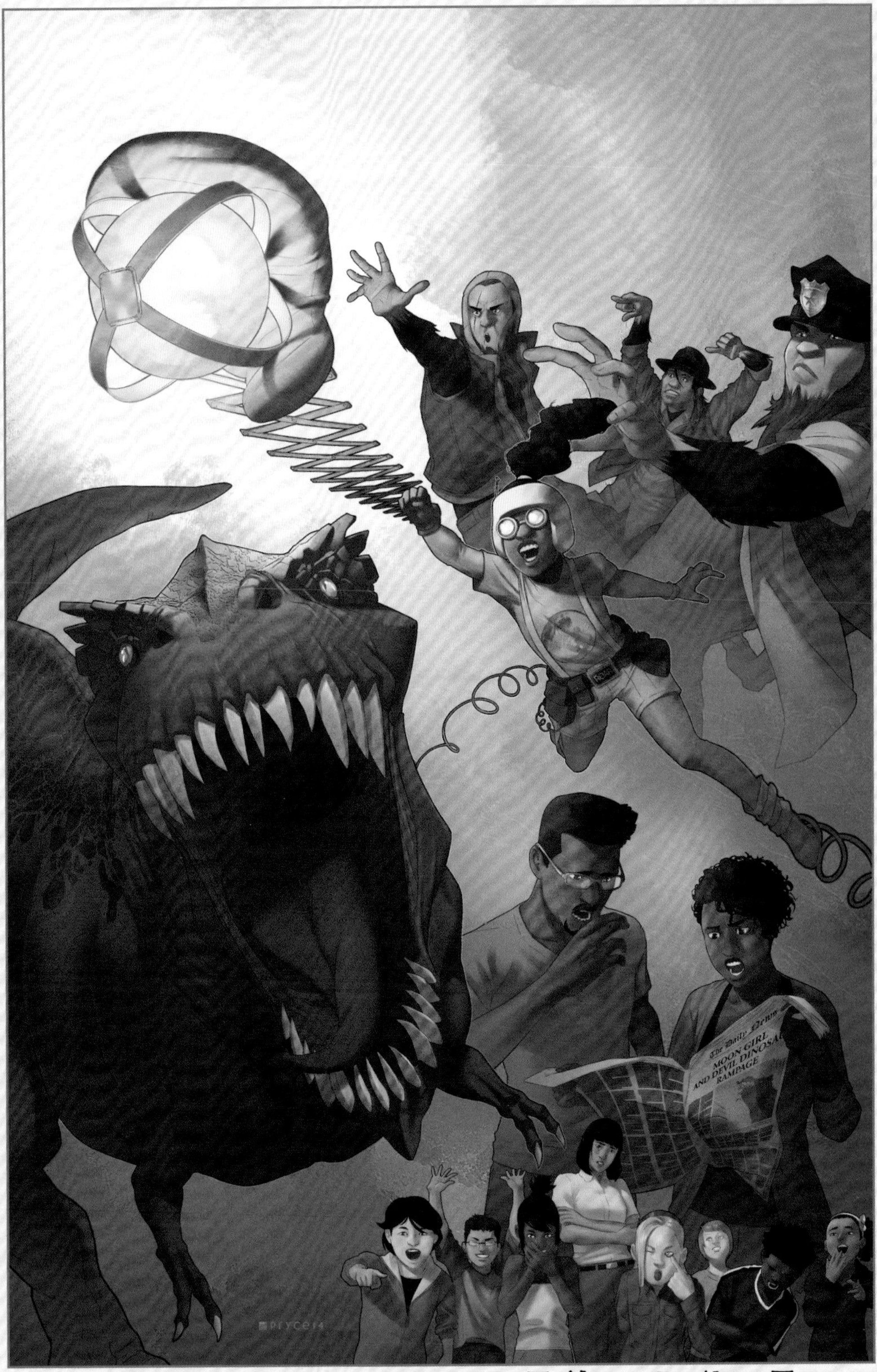
The Daily News
MOON GIRL
RAMPAGE

MOON GIRL AND DEVIL DINOSAUR #7 STORY THUS FAR VARIANT

BY PAUL POPE

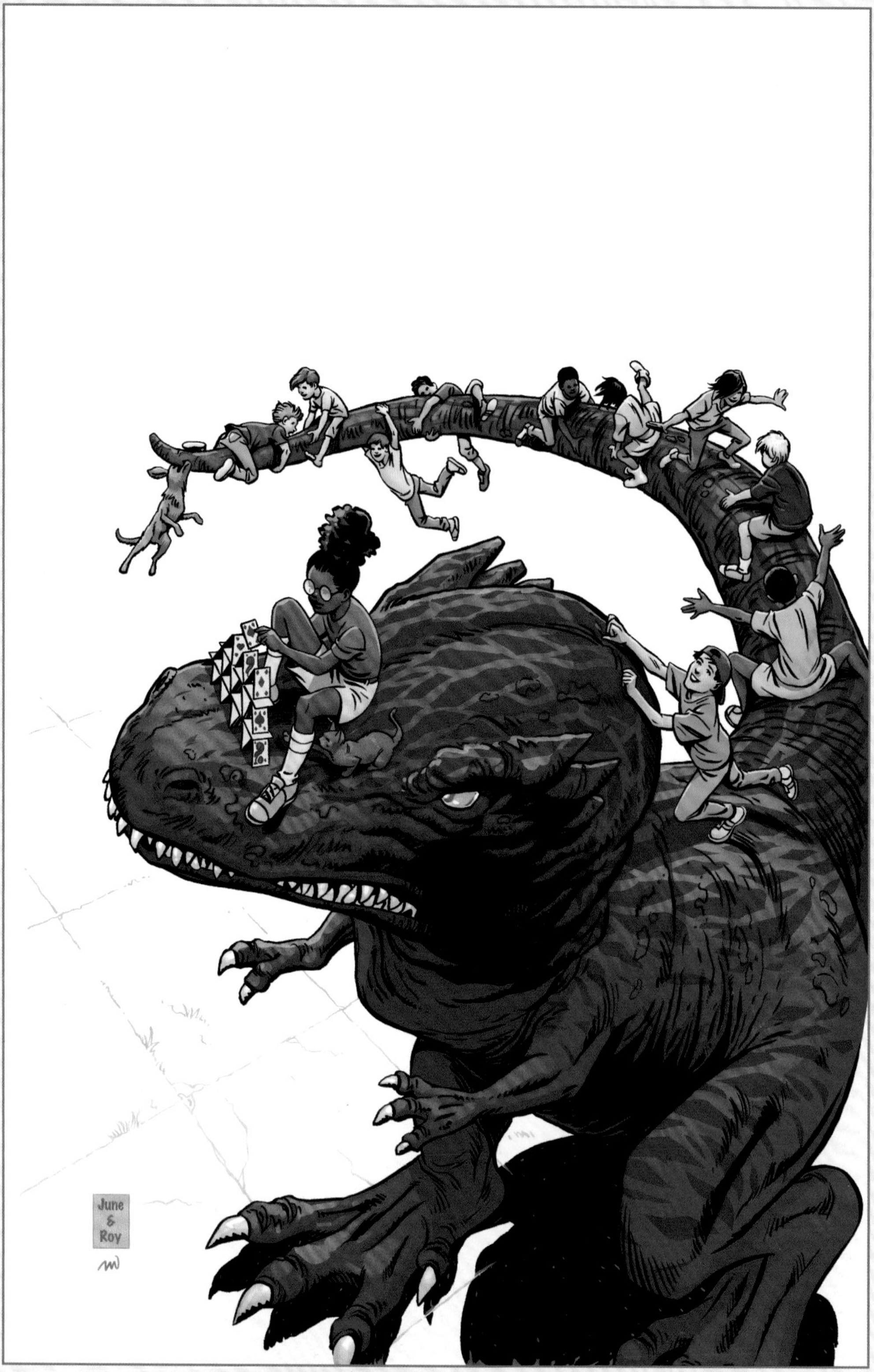
June & Roy

MOON GIRL AND DEVIL DINOSAUR #7 CLASSIC VARIANT

BY JUNE BRIGMAN & NOLAN WOODARD

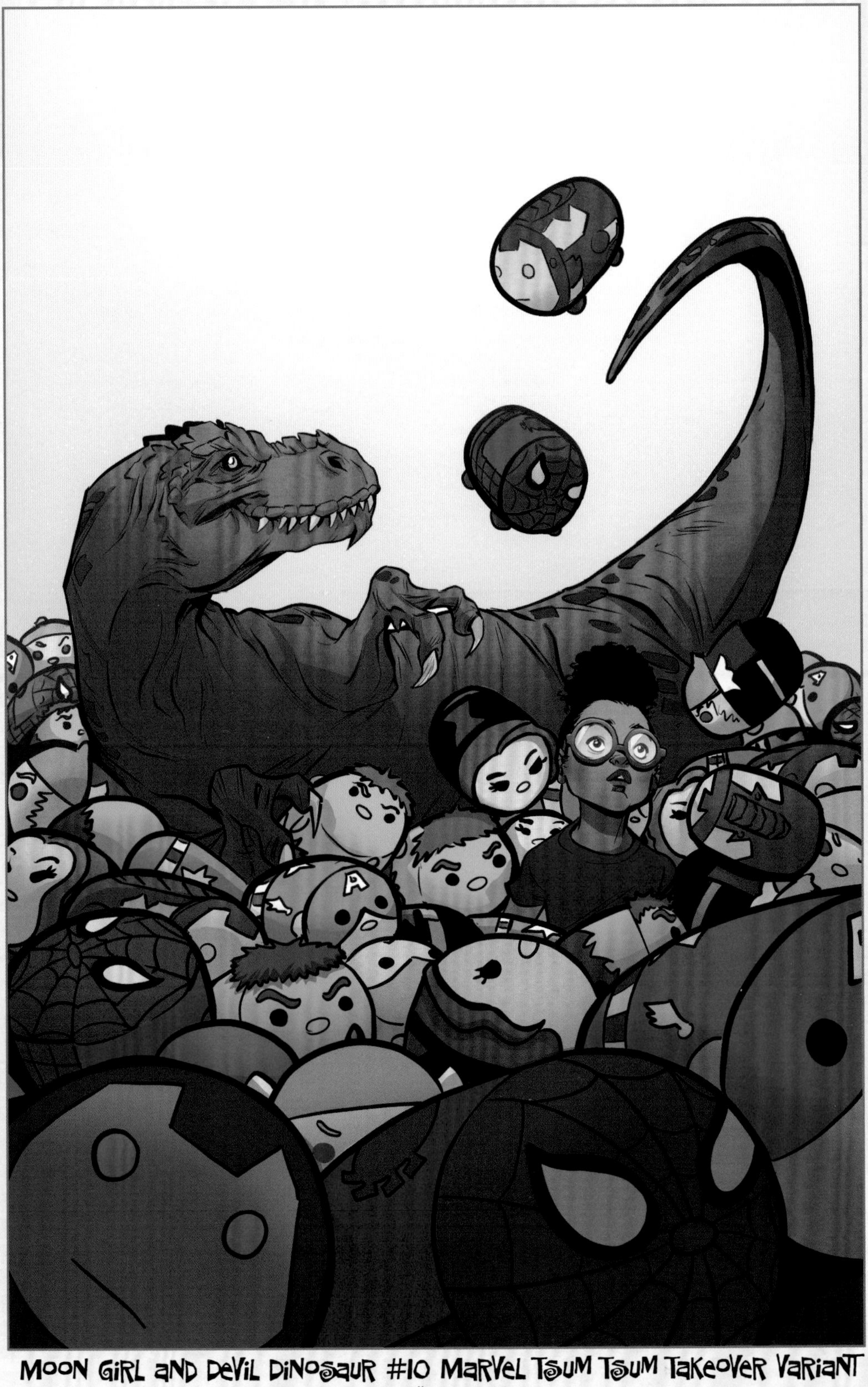

MOON GIRL AND DEVIL DINOSAUR #10 MARVEL TSUM TSUM TAKEOVER VARIANT
BY JOËLLE JONES

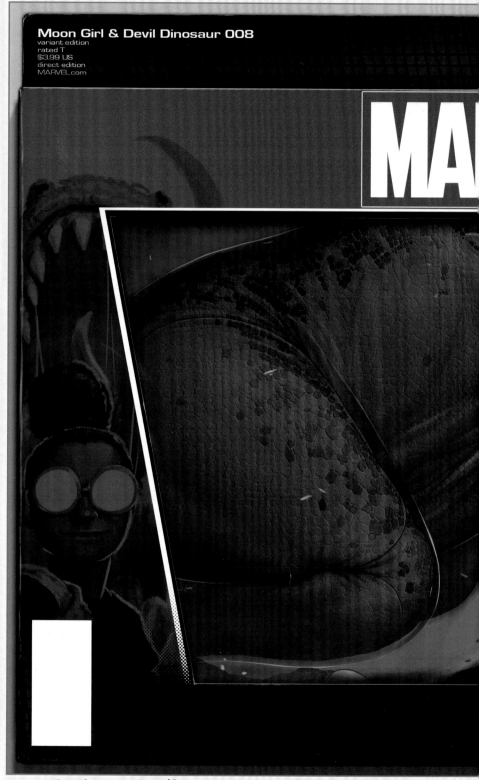

Moon Girl & Devil Dinosaur 008
variant edition
rated T
$3.99 US
direct edition
MARVEL.com

MOON GIRL AND DEVIL DINOSAUR #8 ACTION FIGURE VARIANT
BY JOHN TYLER CHRISTOPHER

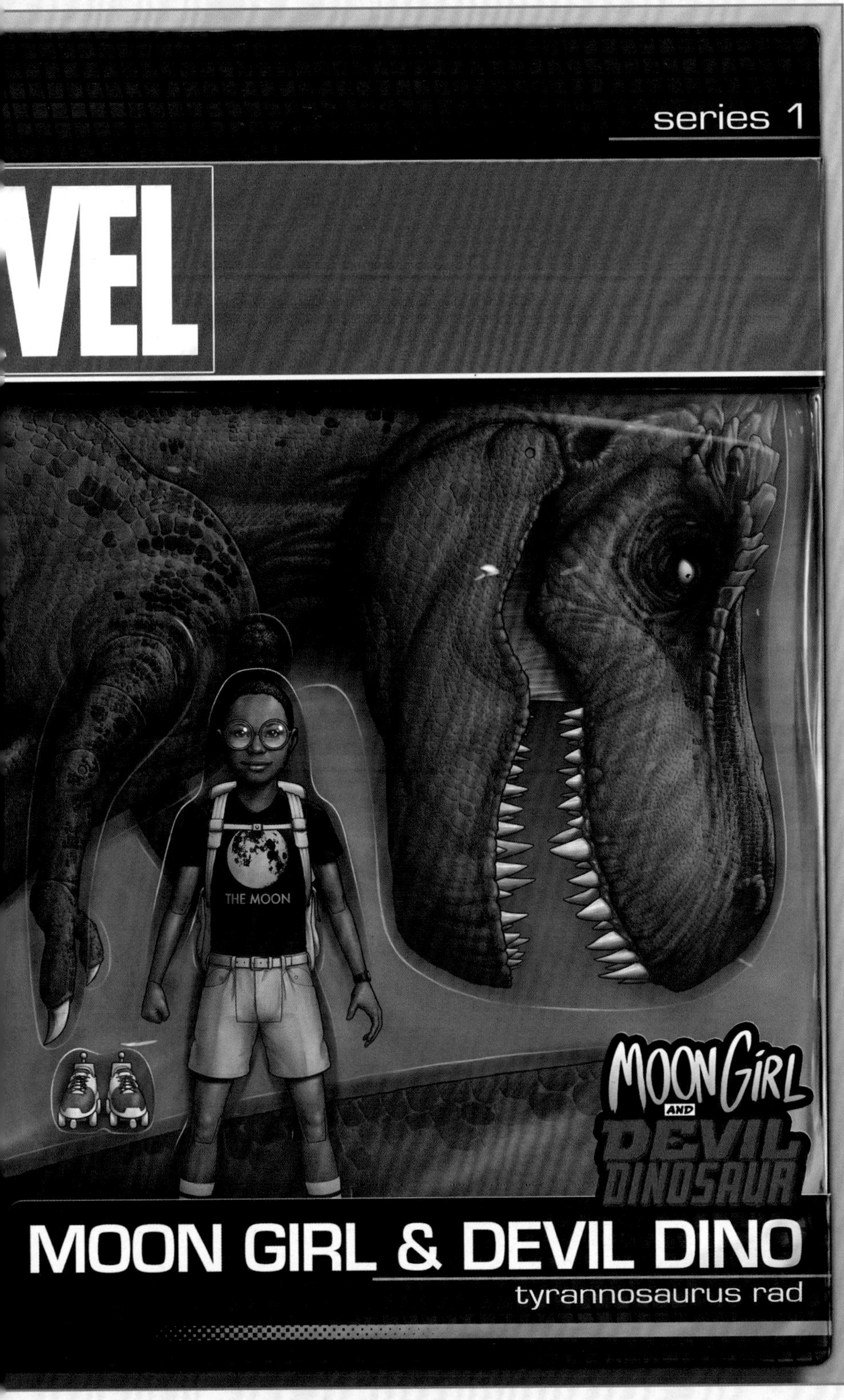
series 1
VEL
THE MOON
MOON GIRL
AND
DEVIL
DINOSAUR
MOON GIRL & DEVIL DINO
tyrannosaurus rad

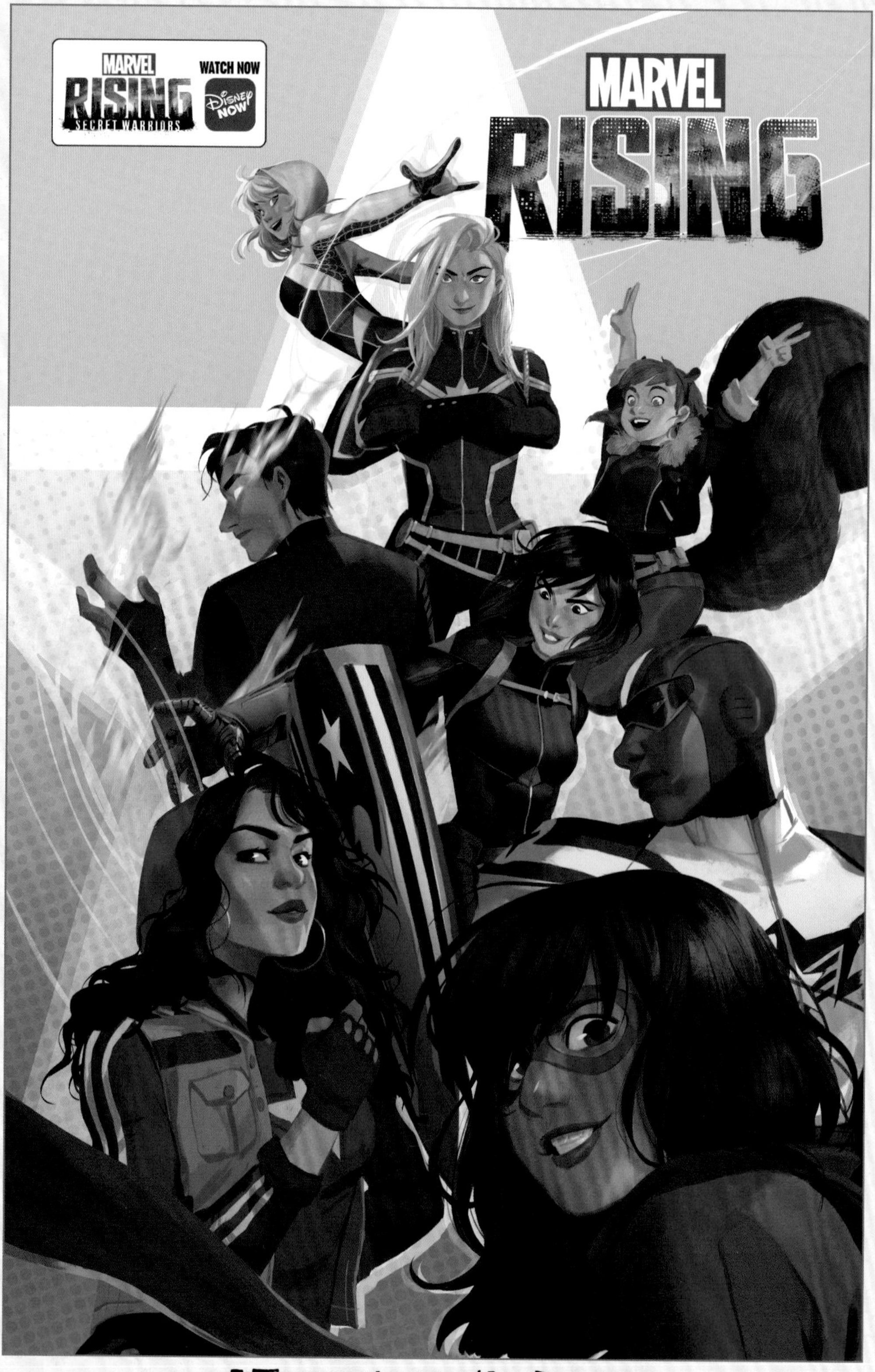
MARVEL
RISING
SECRET WARRIORS
WATCH NOW
DISNEY NOW
MARVEL
RISING

INTRODUCING MARVEL RISING!

MARVEL RISING

THE MARVEL UNIVERSE IS A RICH TREASURE CHEST OF CHARACTERS BORN ACROSS MARVEL'S INCREDIBLE 80-YEAR HISTORY. FROM CAPTAIN AMERICA TO CAPTAIN MARVEL, IRON MAN TO IRONHEART, THIS IS AN EVER-EXPANDING UNIVERSE FULL OF POWERFUL HEROES THAT ALSO REFLECTS THE WORLD WE LIVE IN.

YET DESPITE THAT EXPANSION, OUR STORIES REMAIN TIMELESS. THEY'VE BEEN SHARED ACROSS THE GLOBE AND ACROSS GENERATIONS, LINKING FANS WITH THE ENDURING IDEA THAT ORDINARY PEOPLE CAN DO EXTRAORDINARY THINGS. IT'S THAT SHARED EXPERIENCE OF THE MARVEL STORY THAT HAS ALLOWED US TO EXIST FOR THIS LONG. WHETHER YOUR FIRST MARVEL EXPERIENCE WAS THROUGH A COMIC BOOK, A BEDTIME STORY, A MOVIE OR A CARTOON, WE BELIEVE OUR STORIES STAY WITH AUDIENCES THROUGHOUT THEIR LIVES.

MARVEL RISING IS A CELEBRATION OF THIS TIMELESSNESS. AS OUR STORIES PASS FROM ONE GENERATION TO THE NEXT, SO DOES THE LOVE FOR OUR HEROES. FROM THE CLASSIC TO THE NEWLY IMAGINED, THE PASSION FOR ALL OF THEM IS THE SAME. IF YOU'VE BEEN READING COMICS OVER THE LAST FEW YEARS, YOU'LL KNOW CHARACTERS LIKE MS. MARVEL, SQUIRREL GIRL, AMERICA CHAVEZ, SPIDER-GWEN AND MORE HAVE ASSEMBLED A BEVY OF NEW FANS WHILE CAPTIVATING OUR PERENNIAL FANS. EACH OF THESE HEROES IS UNIQUE AND DISTINCT--JUST LIKE THE READERS THEY'VE BROUGHT IN--AND THEY REMIND US THAT NO MATTER WHAT YOU LOOK LIKE, YOU HAVE THE CAPABILITY TO BE POWERFUL, TOO. WE ARE TAKING THE HEROES FROM MARVEL RISING TO NEW HEIGHTS IN AN ANIMATED FEATURE LATER IN 2018, AS WELL AS A FULL PROGRAM OF CONTENT SWEEPING ACROSS THE COMPANY. BUT FIRST WE'RE GOING BACK TO OUR ROOTS AND TELLING A MARVEL RISING STORY IN COMICS: THE FIRST PLACE YOU MET THESE LOVABLE HEROES.

SO IN THE TRADITION OF EXPANDING THE MARVEL UNIVERSE, WE'RE EXCITED TO INTRODUCE MARVEL RISING--THE NEXT GENERATION OF MARVEL HEROES FOR THE NEXT GENERATION OF MARVEL FANS!

SANA AMANAT
VP, CONTENT & CHARACTER DEVELOPMENT

DOREEN GREEN IS A SECOND-YEAR COMPUTER SCIENCE STUDENT – AND THE CRIMINAL-REDEEMING HERO THE UNBEATABLE SQUIRREL GIRL! THE NAME SAYS IT ALL: AN UNBEATABLE GIRL WITH THE POWERS OF AN UNBEATABLE SQUIRREL, TAIL INCLUDED. AND ON TOP OF HER STUDYING, NUT-EATING AND BUTT-KICKING ACTIVITIES, SHE'S JUST TAKEN ON THE JOB OF VOLUNTEER TEACHER FOR AN EXTRA-CURRICULAR HIGH-SCHOOL CODING CAMP! AND WHO SHOULD END UP IN HER CLASS BUT...

KAMALA KHAN, A.K.A. JERSEY CITY HERO AND INHUMAN POLYMORPH MS. MARVEL! BUT BETWEEN SAVING THE WORLD WITH THE CHAMPIONS AND PROTECTING JERSEY CITY ON HER OWN, KAMALA'S GOT A LOT ON HER PLATE ALREADY. AND FIELD TRIP DAY MAY NOT BE THE BREAK SHE'S ANTICIPATING...

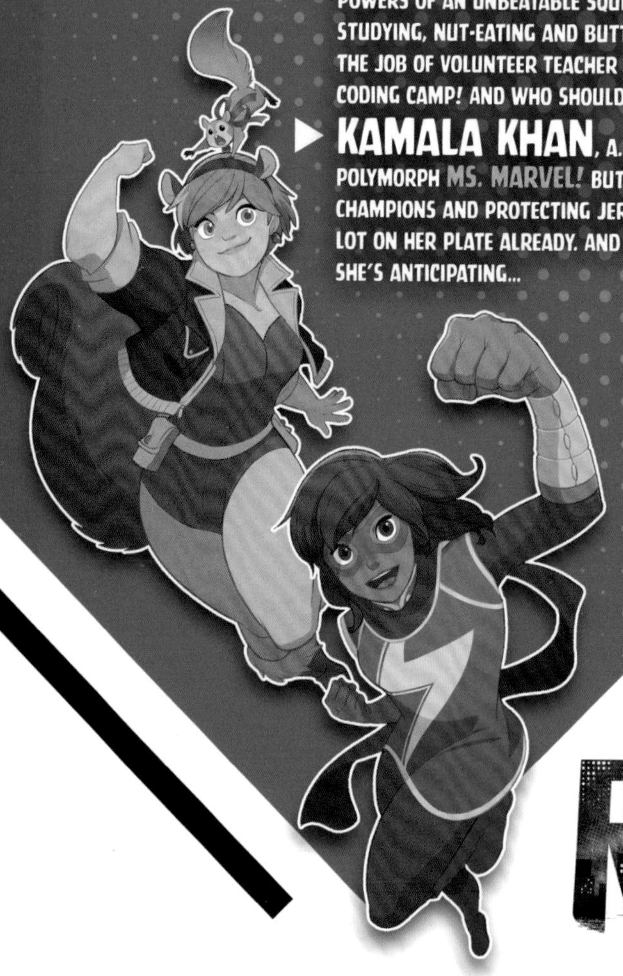

MARVEL RISING

PART 0

DEVIN GRAYSON
WRITER

MARCO FAILLA
ARTIST

RACHELLE ROSENBERG
COLOR ARTIST

VC's CLAYTON COWLES
LETTERER

HELEN CHEN
COVER

JAY BOWEN
DESIGN

HEATHER ANTOS AND SARAH BRUNSTAD
EDITORS

SANA AMANAT
CONSULTING EDITOR

C.B. CEBULSKI
EDITOR IN CHIEF

JOE QUESADA
CHIEF CREATIVE OFFICER

DAN BUCKLEY
PRESIDENT

ALAN FINE
EXECUTIVE PRODUCER

SPECIAL THANKS TO RYAN NORTH AND G. WILLOW WILSON

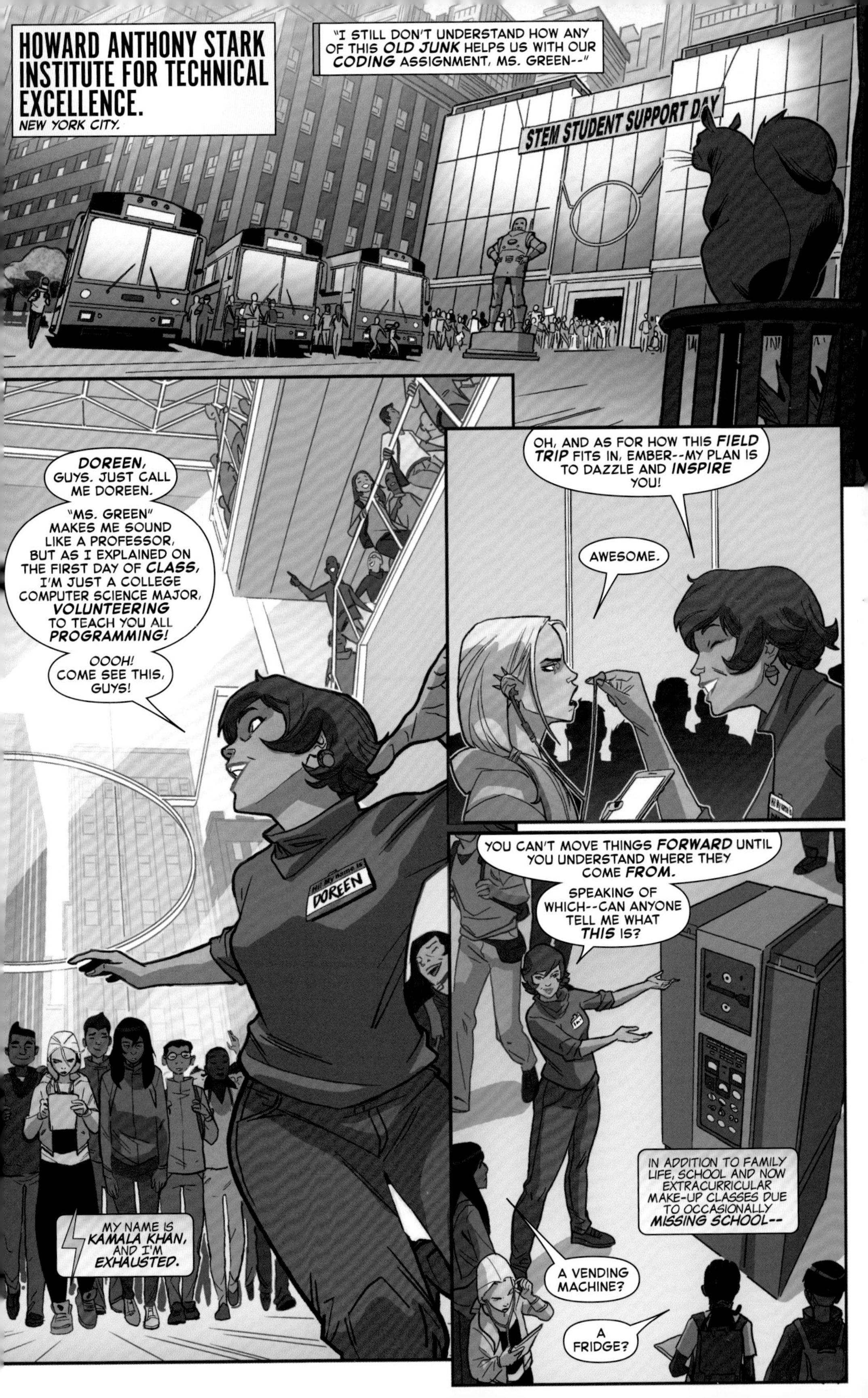
HOWARD ANTHONY STARK INSTITUTE FOR TECHNICAL EXCELLENCE.
NEW YORK CITY.
"I STILL DON'T UNDERSTAND HOW ANY OF THIS OLD JUNK HELPS US WITH OUR CODING ASSIGNMENT, MS. GREEN--"
STEM STUDENT SUPPORT DAY
DOREEN, GUYS. JUST CALL ME DOREEN.
"MS. GREEN" MAKES ME SOUND LIKE A PROFESSOR, BUT AS I EXPLAINED ON THE FIRST DAY OF CLASS, I'M JUST A COLLEGE COMPUTER SCIENCE MAJOR, VOLUNTEERING TO TEACH YOU ALL PROGRAMMING!
OOOH! COME SEE THIS, GUYS!
HI! MY NAME IS DOREEN
MY NAME IS KAMALA KHAN, AND I'M EXHAUSTED.
OH, AND AS FOR HOW THIS FIELD TRIP FITS IN, EMBER--MY PLAN IS TO DAZZLE AND INSPIRE YOU!
AWESOME.
YOU CAN'T MOVE THINGS FORWARD UNTIL YOU UNDERSTAND WHERE THEY COME FROM.
SPEAKING OF WHICH--CAN ANYONE TELL ME WHAT THIS IS?
IN ADDITION TO FAMILY LIFE, SCHOOL AND NOW EXTRACURRICULAR MAKE-UP CLASSES DUE TO OCCASIONALLY MISSING SCHOOL--
A VENDING MACHINE?
A FRIDGE?

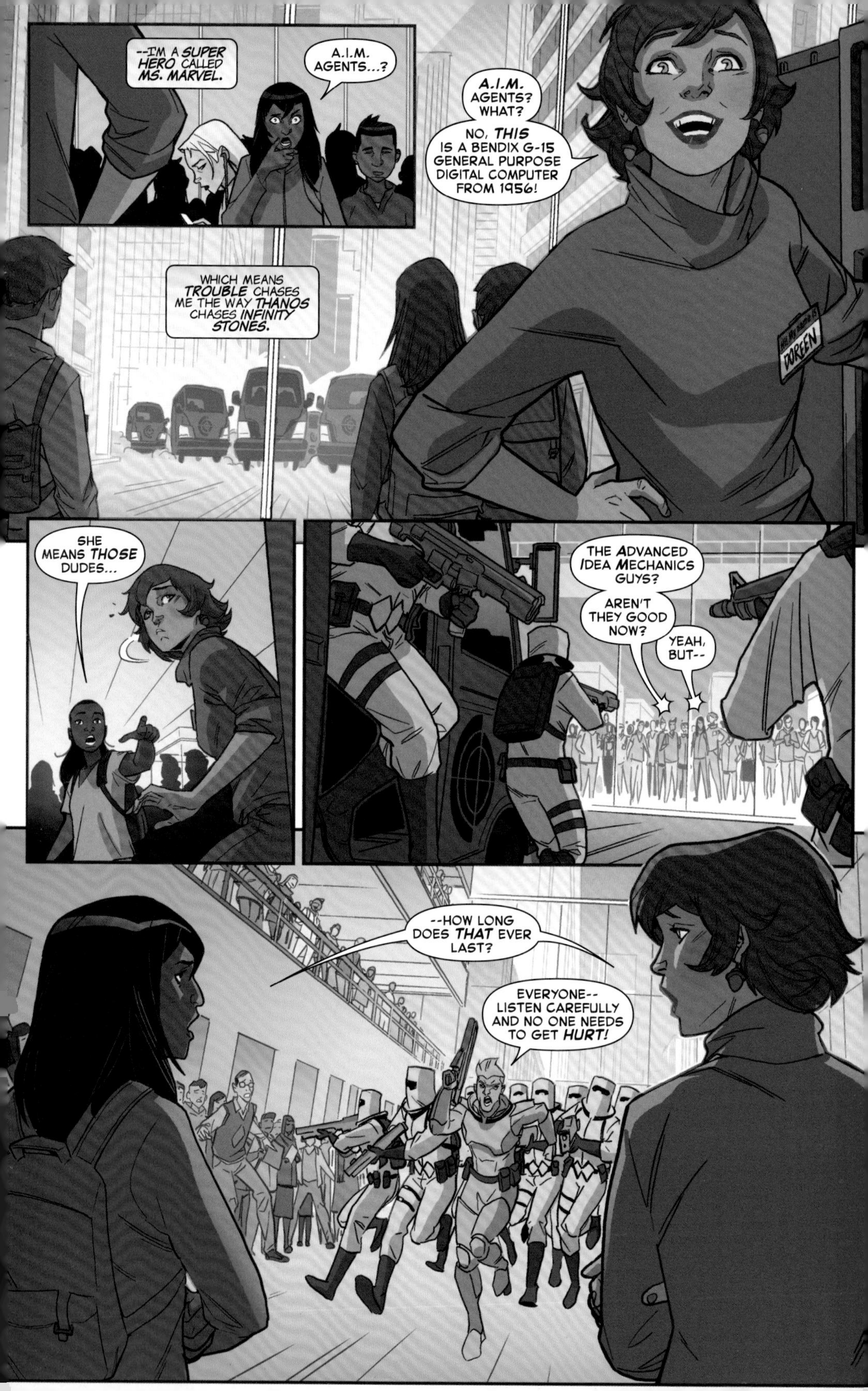
--I'M A SUPER HERO CALLED MS. MARVEL.
A.I.M. AGENTS...?
A.I.M. AGENTS? WHAT?
NO, THIS IS A BENDIX G-15 GENERAL PURPOSE DIGITAL COMPUTER FROM 1956!
WHICH MEANS TROUBLE CHASES ME THE WAY THANOS CHASES INFINITY STONES.
DOREEN
SHE MEANS THOSE DUDES...
THE ADVANCED IDEA MECHANICS GUYS?
AREN'T THEY GOOD NOW?
YEAH, BUT--
--HOW LONG DOES THAT EVER LAST?
EVERYONE-- LISTEN CAREFULLY AND NO ONE NEEDS TO GET HURT!

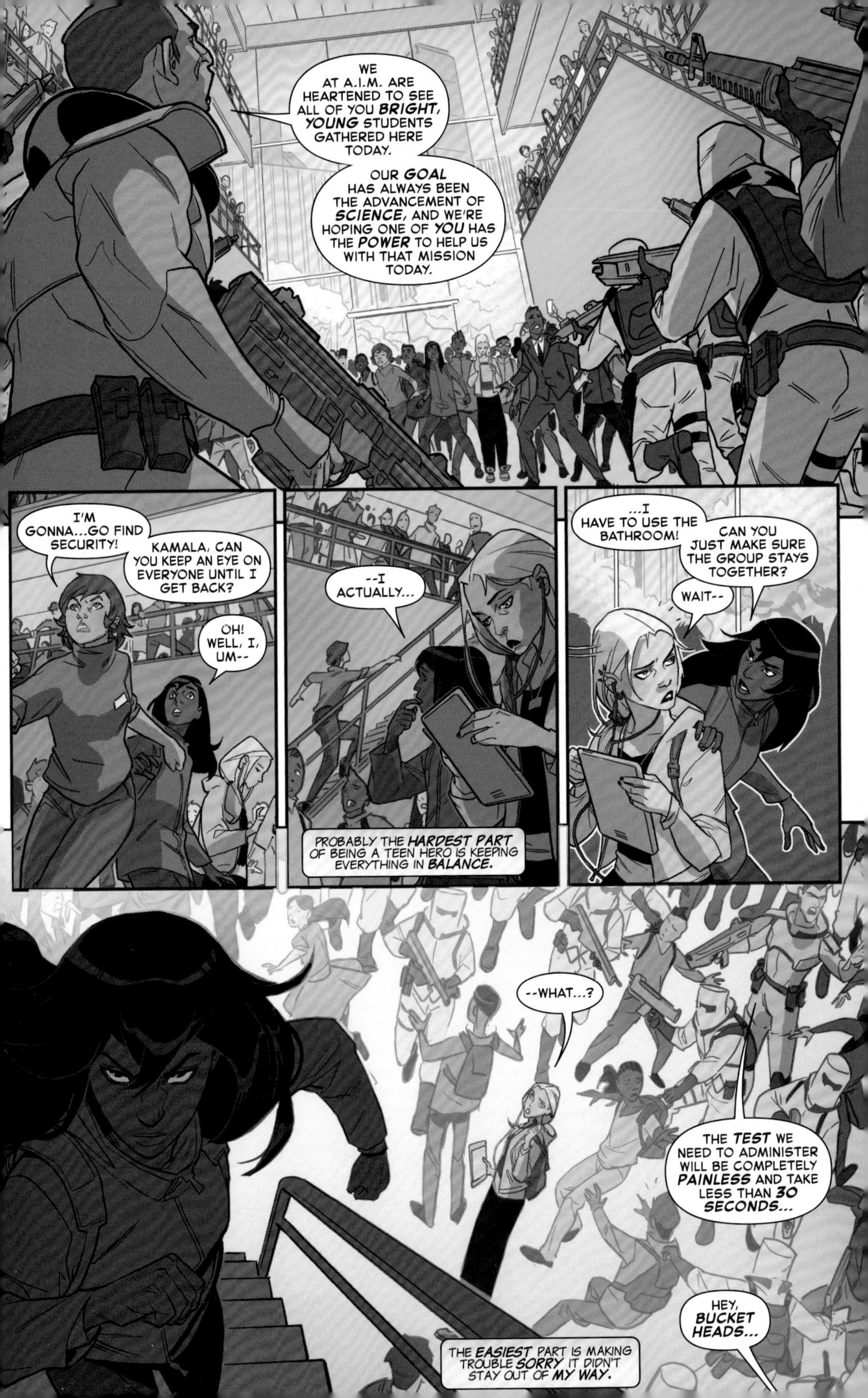
WE AT A.I.M. ARE HEARTENED TO SEE ALL OF YOU BRIGHT, YOUNG STUDENTS GATHERED HERE TODAY.
OUR GOAL HAS ALWAYS BEEN THE ADVANCEMENT OF SCIENCE, AND WE'RE HOPING ONE OF YOU HAS THE POWER TO HELP US WITH THAT MISSION TODAY.
I'M GONNA...GO FIND SECURITY!
KAMALA, CAN YOU KEEP AN EYE ON EVERYONE UNTIL I GET BACK?
OH! WELL, I, UM--
--I ACTUALLY...
PROBABLY THE HARDEST PART OF BEING A TEEN HERO IS KEEPING EVERYTHING IN BALANCE.
...I HAVE TO USE THE BATHROOM!
CAN YOU JUST MAKE SURE THE GROUP STAYS TOGETHER?
WAIT--
--WHAT...?
THE TEST WE NEED TO ADMINISTER WILL BE COMPLETELY PAINLESS AND TAKE LESS THAN 30 SECONDS...
HEY, BUCKET HEADS...
THE EASIEST PART IS MAKING TROUBLE SORRY IT DIDN'T STAY OUT OF MY WAY.

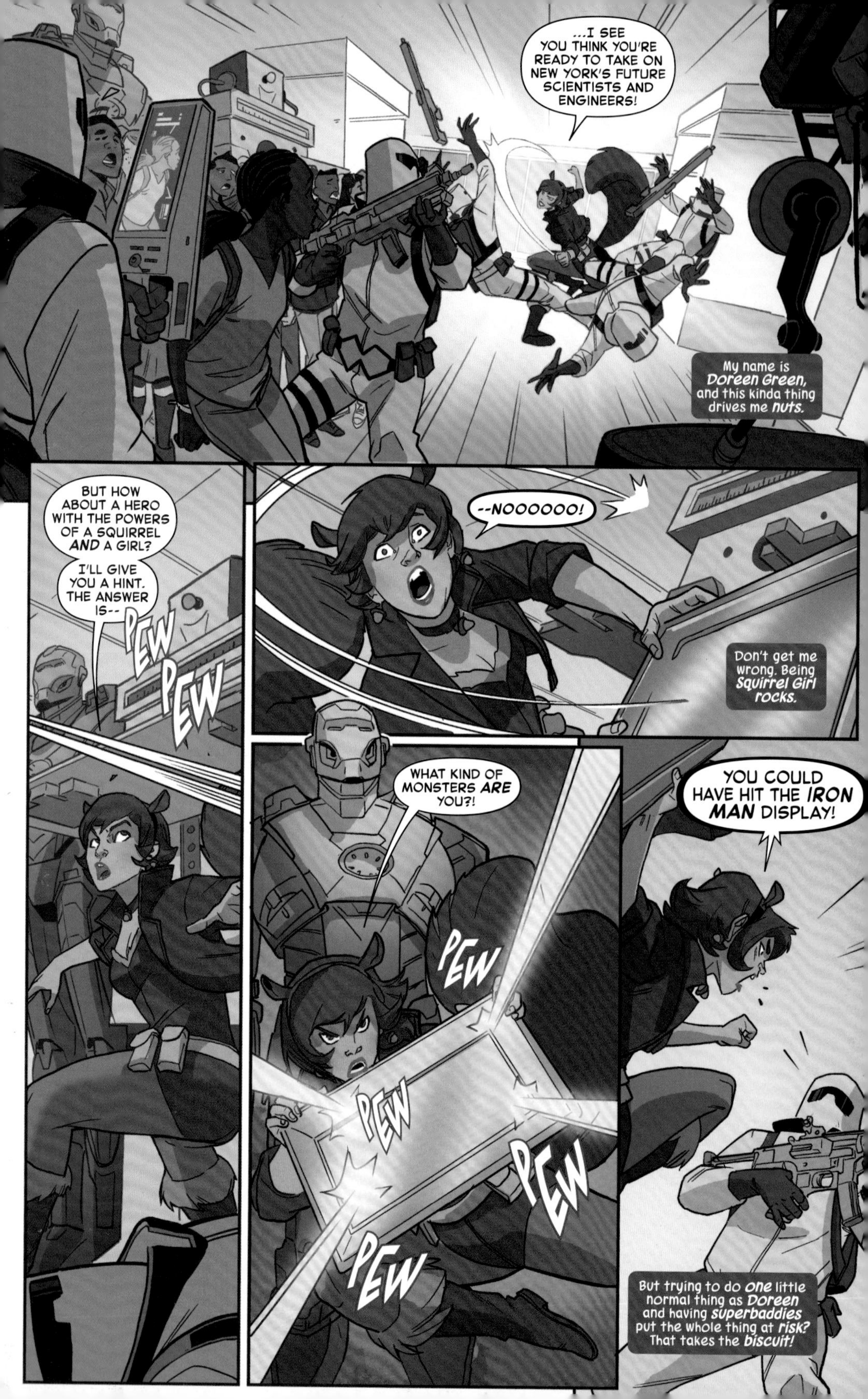
...I SEE YOU THINK YOU'RE READY TO TAKE ON NEW YORK'S FUTURE SCIENTISTS AND ENGINEERS!
My name is *Doreen Green,* and this kinda thing drives me *nuts.*
BUT HOW ABOUT A HERO WITH THE POWERS OF A SQUIRREL *AND* A GIRL?
I'LL GIVE YOU A HINT. THE ANSWER IS--
PEW PEW
--NOOOOOO!
Don't get me wrong. Being *Squirrel Girl* rocks.
WHAT KIND OF MONSTERS *ARE* YOU?!
PEW
PEW
PEW
PEW
YOU COULD HAVE HIT THE *IRON MAN* DISPLAY!
But trying to do *one* little normal thing as *Doreen* and having *superbaddies* put the whole thing at *risk?* That takes the *biscuit!*

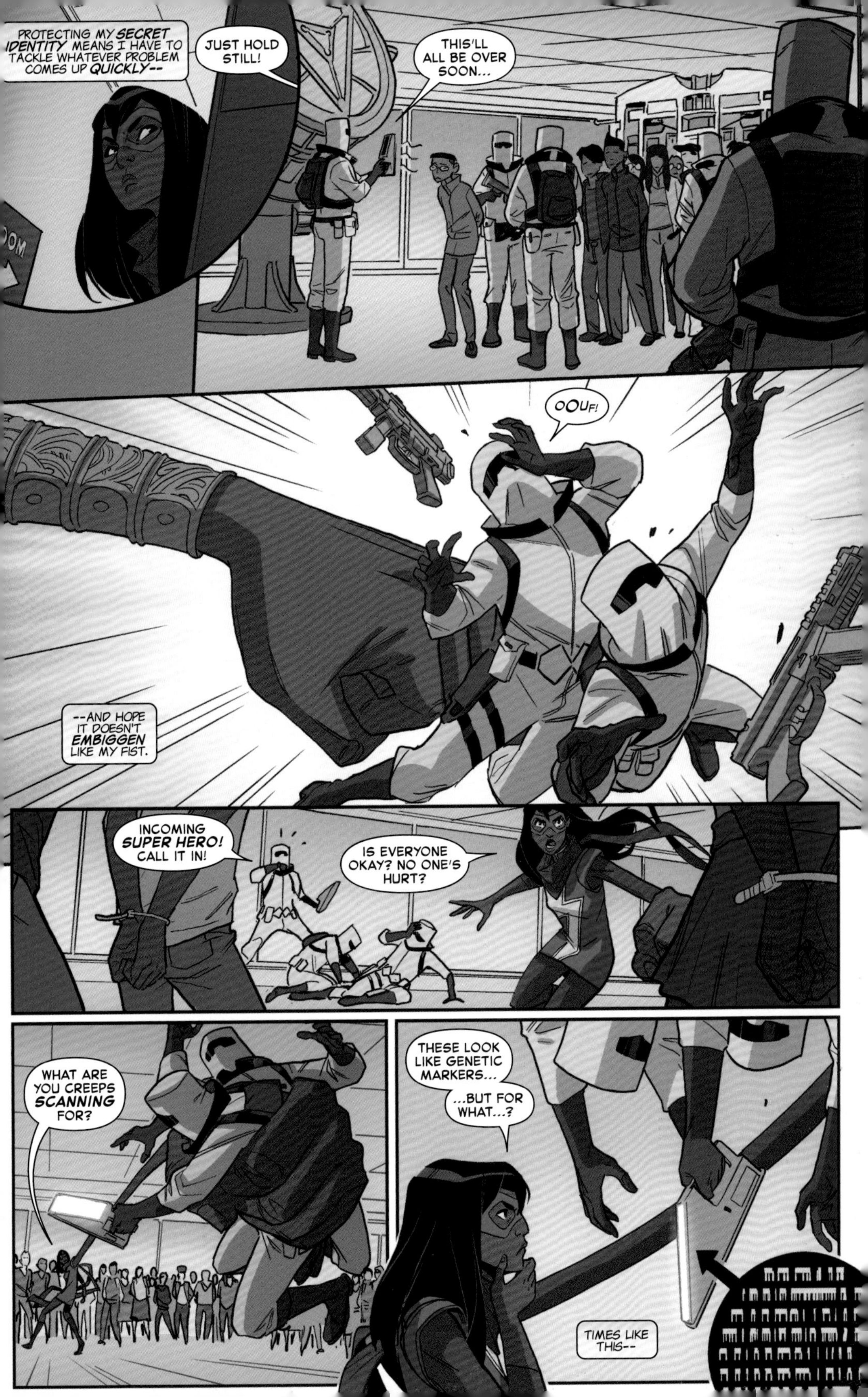
PROTECTING MY SECRET IDENTITY MEANS I HAVE TO TACKLE WHATEVER PROBLEM COMES UP QUICKLY--
JUST HOLD STILL!
THIS'LL ALL BE OVER SOON...
OOUF!
--AND HOPE IT DOESN'T EMBIGGEN LIKE MY FIST.
INCOMING SUPER HERO! CALL IT IN!
IS EVERYONE OKAY? NO ONE'S HURT?
WHAT ARE YOU CREEPS SCANNING FOR?
THESE LOOK LIKE GENETIC MARKERS...
...BUT FOR WHAT...?
TIMES LIKE THIS--

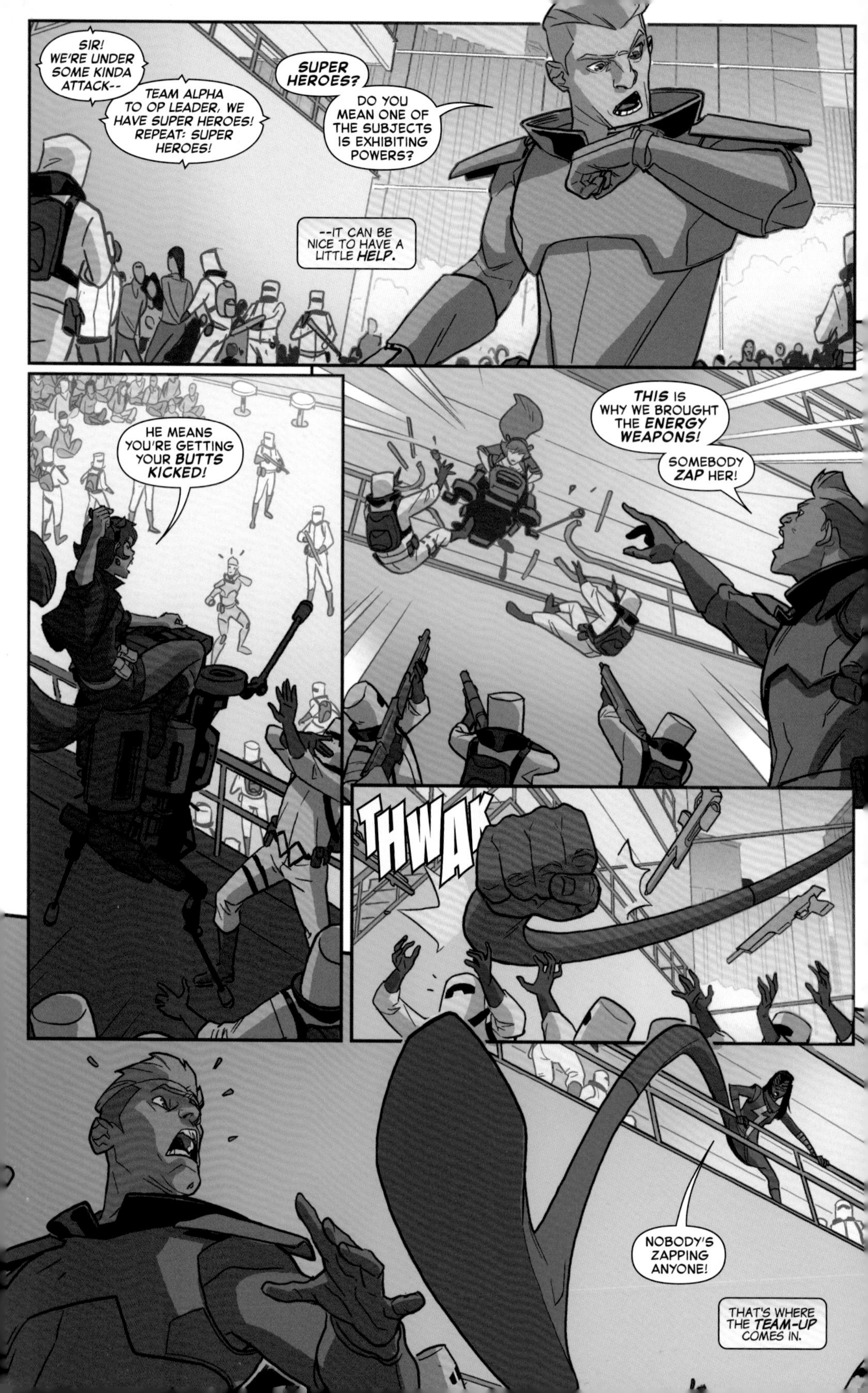
SIR! WE'RE UNDER SOME KINDA ATTACK--
TEAM ALPHA TO OP LEADER, WE HAVE SUPER HEROES! REPEAT: SUPER HEROES!
SUPER HEROES?
DO YOU MEAN ONE OF THE SUBJECTS IS EXHIBITING POWERS?
--IT CAN BE NICE TO HAVE A LITTLE HELP.
HE MEANS YOU'RE GETTING YOUR BUTTS KICKED!
THIS IS WHY WE BROUGHT THE ENERGY WEAPONS!
SOMEBODY ZAP HER!
THWAK
NOBODY'S ZAPPING ANYONE!
THAT'S WHERE THE TEAM-UP COMES IN.

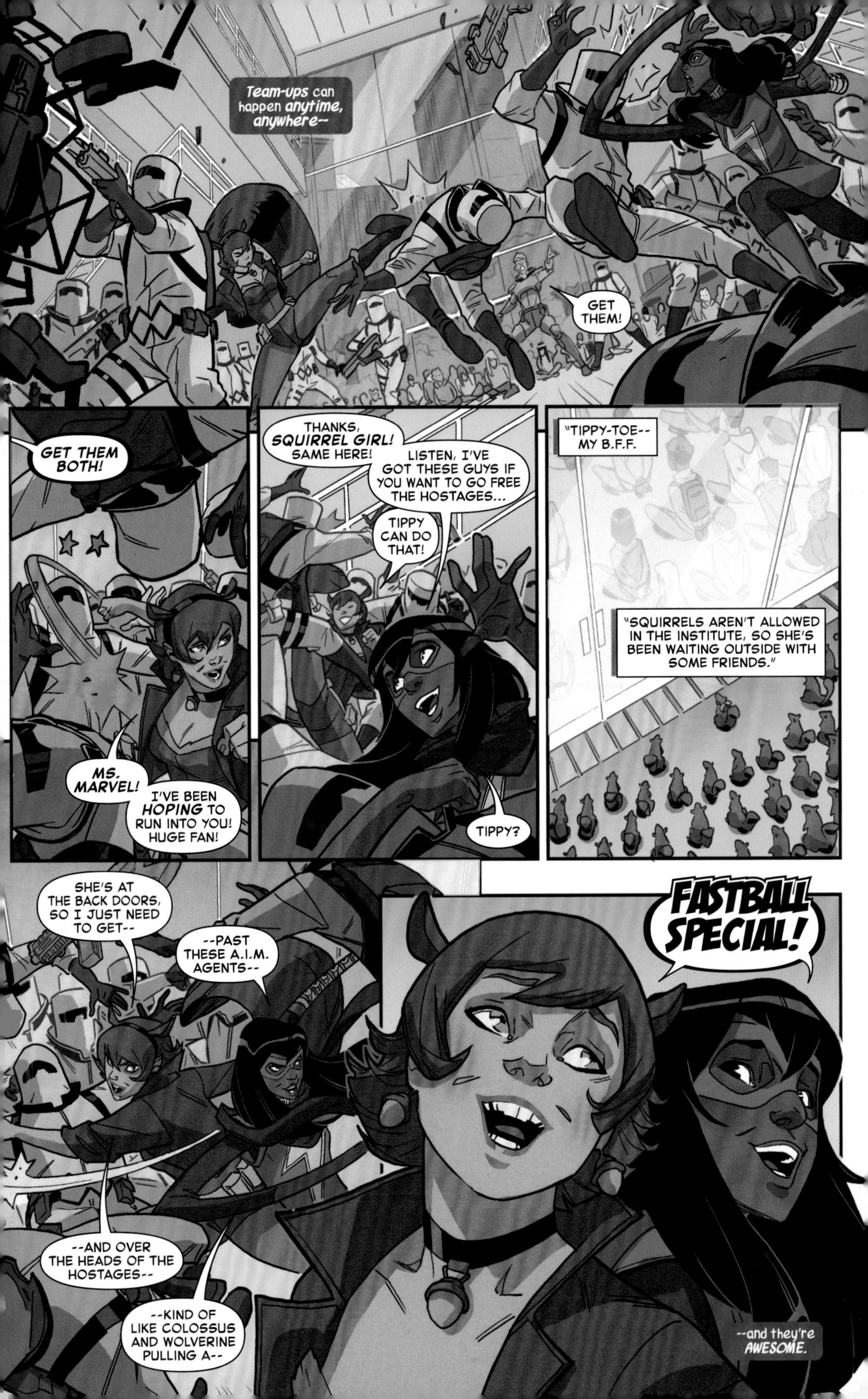
Team-ups can happen anytime, anywhere--
GET THEM!
GET THEM BOTH!
MS. MARVEL!
I'VE BEEN HOPING TO RUN INTO YOU! HUGE FAN!
THANKS, SQUIRREL GIRL! SAME HERE!
LISTEN, I'VE GOT THESE GUYS IF YOU WANT TO GO FREE THE HOSTAGES...
TIPPY CAN DO THAT!
TIPPY?
"TIPPY-TOE-- MY B.F.F.
"SQUIRRELS AREN'T ALLOWED IN THE INSTITUTE, SO SHE'S BEEN WAITING OUTSIDE WITH SOME FRIENDS."
SHE'S AT THE BACK DOORS, SO I JUST NEED TO GET--
--PAST THESE A.I.M. AGENTS--
--AND OVER THE HEADS OF THE HOSTAGES--
--KIND OF LIKE COLOSSUS AND WOLVERINE PULLING A--
FASTBALL SPECIAL!
--and they're AWESOME.

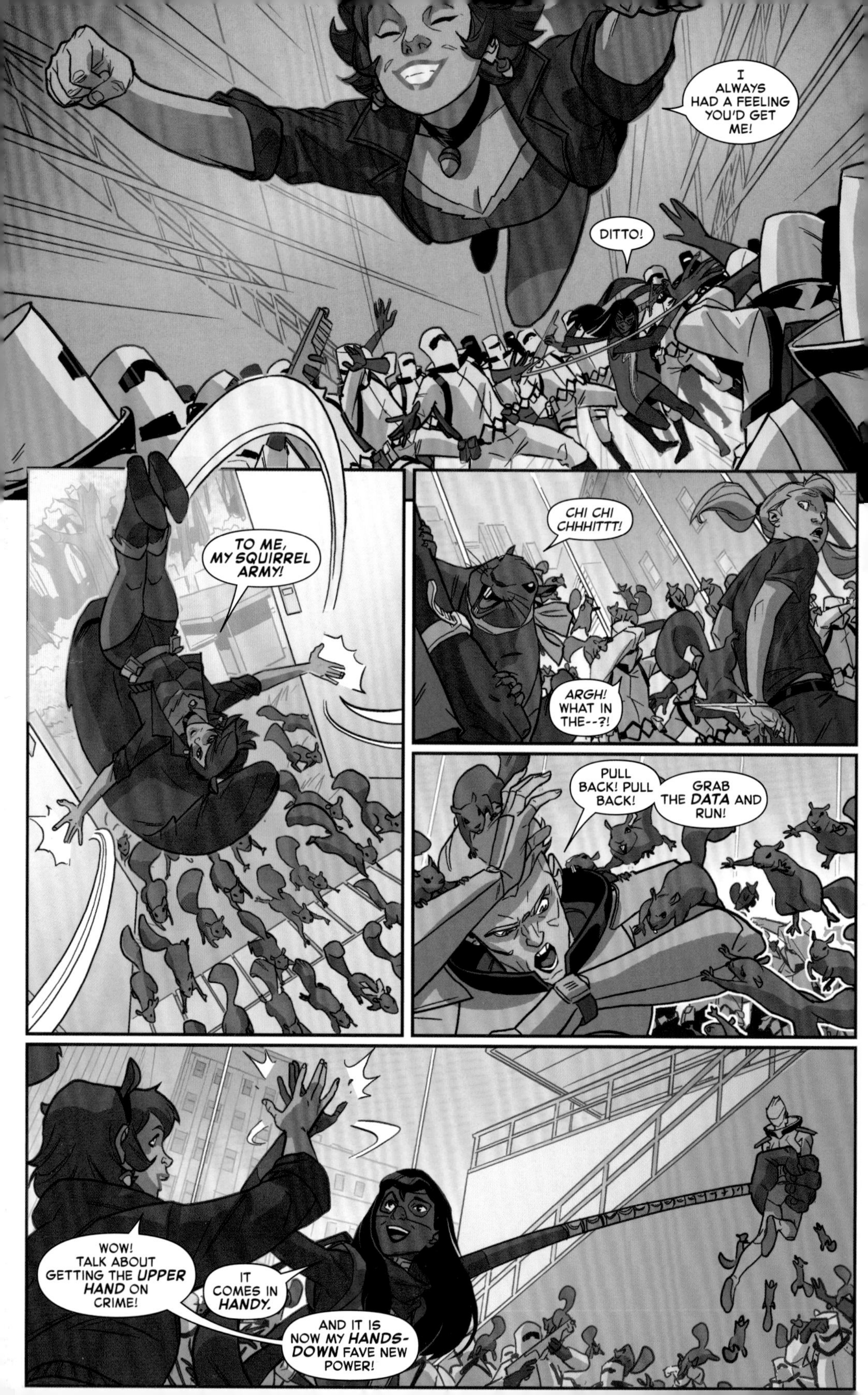
I ALWAYS HAD A FEELING YOU'D GET ME!
DITTO!
TO ME, MY SQUIRREL ARMY!
CHI CHI CHHHITTT!
ARGH! WHAT IN THE--?!
PULL BACK! PULL BACK!
GRAB THE DATA AND RUN!
WOW! TALK ABOUT GETTING THE UPPER HAND ON CRIME!
IT COMES IN HANDY.
AND IT IS NOW MY HANDS-DOWN FAVE NEW POWER!

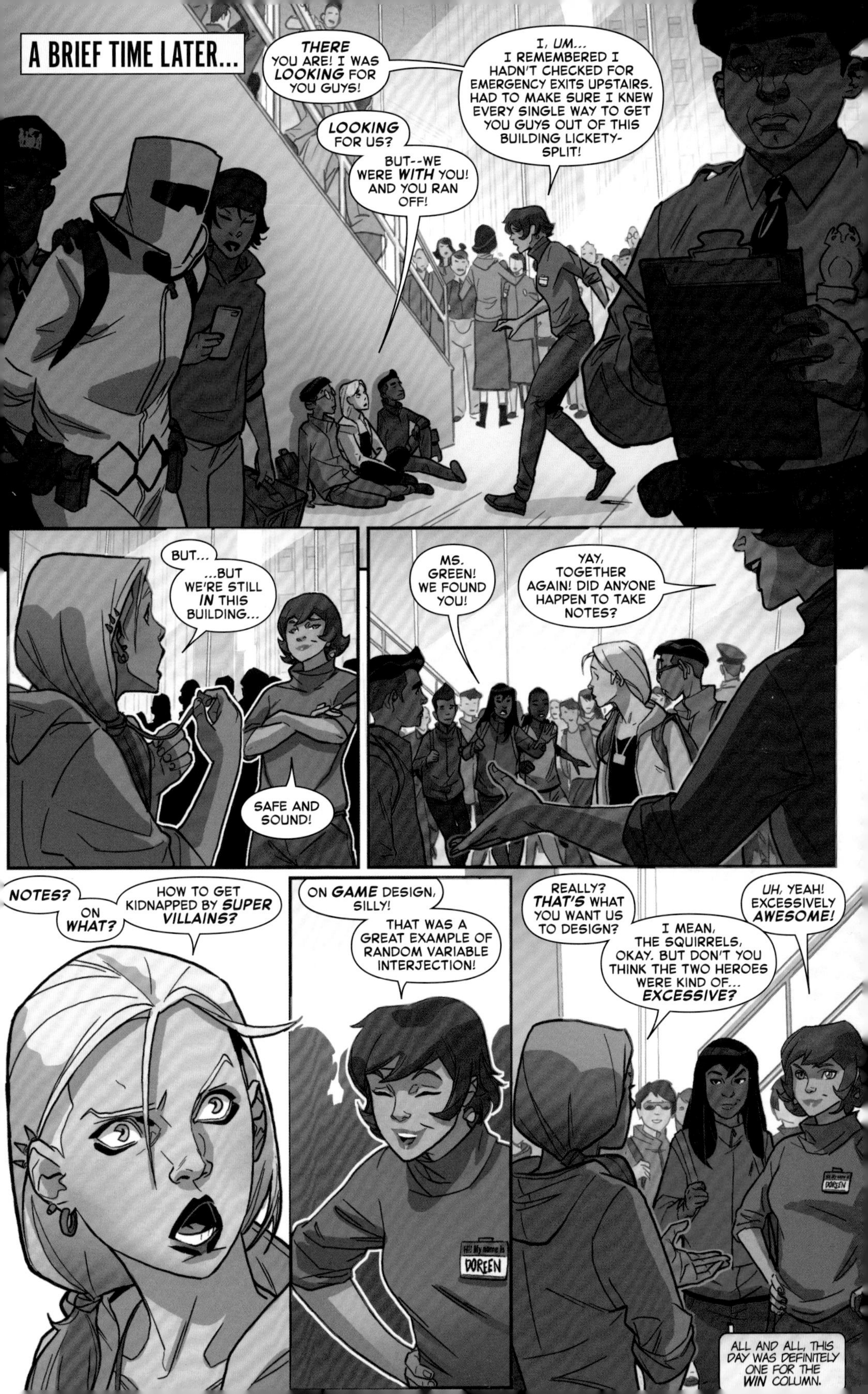

A BRIEF TIME LATER...
THERE YOU ARE! I WAS LOOKING FOR YOU GUYS!
LOOKING FOR US?
BUT--WE WERE WITH YOU! AND YOU RAN OFF!
I, UM... I REMEMBERED I HADN'T CHECKED FOR EMERGENCY EXITS UPSTAIRS. HAD TO MAKE SURE I KNEW EVERY SINGLE WAY TO GET YOU GUYS OUT OF THIS BUILDING LICKETY-SPLIT!
BUT...
...BUT WE'RE STILL IN THIS BUILDING...
SAFE AND SOUND!
MS. GREEN! WE FOUND YOU!
YAY, TOGETHER AGAIN! DID ANYONE HAPPEN TO TAKE NOTES?
NOTES?
ON WHAT?
HOW TO GET KIDNAPPED BY SUPER VILLAINS?
ON GAME DESIGN, SILLY!
THAT WAS A GREAT EXAMPLE OF RANDOM VARIABLE INTERJECTION!
HI! My name is DOREEN
REALLY? THAT'S WHAT YOU WANT US TO DESIGN?
I MEAN, THE SQUIRRELS, OKAY. BUT DON'T YOU THINK THE TWO HEROES WERE KIND OF... EXCESSIVE?
UH, YEAH! EXCESSIVELY AWESOME!
ALL AND ALL, THIS DAY WAS DEFINITELY ONE FOR THE WIN COLUMN.

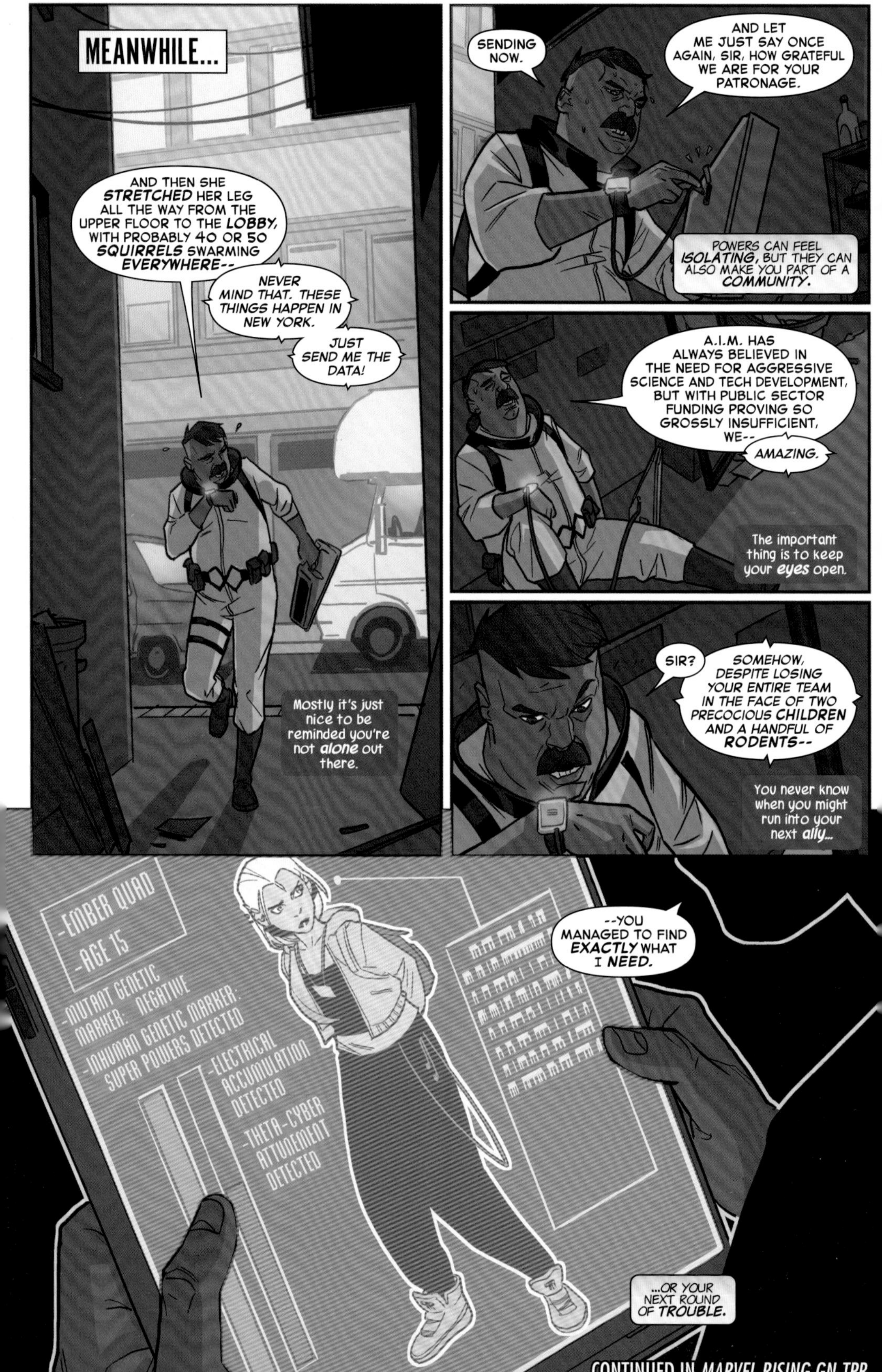
MEANWHILE...
AND THEN SHE STRETCHED HER LEG ALL THE WAY FROM THE UPPER FLOOR TO THE LOBBY, WITH PROBABLY 40 OR 50 SQUIRRELS SWARMING EVERYWHERE--
NEVER MIND THAT. THESE THINGS HAPPEN IN NEW YORK.
JUST SEND ME THE DATA!
Mostly it's just nice to be reminded you're not alone out there.
SENDING NOW.
AND LET ME JUST SAY ONCE AGAIN, SIR, HOW GRATEFUL WE ARE FOR YOUR PATRONAGE.
POWERS CAN FEEL ISOLATING, BUT THEY CAN ALSO MAKE YOU PART OF A COMMUNITY.
A.I.M. HAS ALWAYS BELIEVED IN THE NEED FOR AGGRESSIVE SCIENCE AND TECH DEVELOPMENT, BUT WITH PUBLIC SECTOR FUNDING PROVING SO GROSSLY INSUFFICIENT, WE--
AMAZING.
The important thing is to keep your eyes open.
SIR?
SOMEHOW, DESPITE LOSING YOUR ENTIRE TEAM IN THE FACE OF TWO PRECOCIOUS CHILDREN AND A HANDFUL OF RODENTS--
You never know when you might run into your next ally...
-EMBER QUAD
-AGE 15
-MUTANT GENETIC MARKER: NEGATIVE
-INHUMAN GENETIC MARKER: SUPER POWERS DETECTED
-ELECTRICAL ACCUMULATION DETECTED
-THETA-CYBER ATTUNEMENT DETECTED
--YOU MANAGED TO FIND EXACTLY WHAT I NEED.
...OR YOUR NEXT ROUND OF TROUBLE.

CONTINUED IN *MARVEL RISING GN-TPB*.

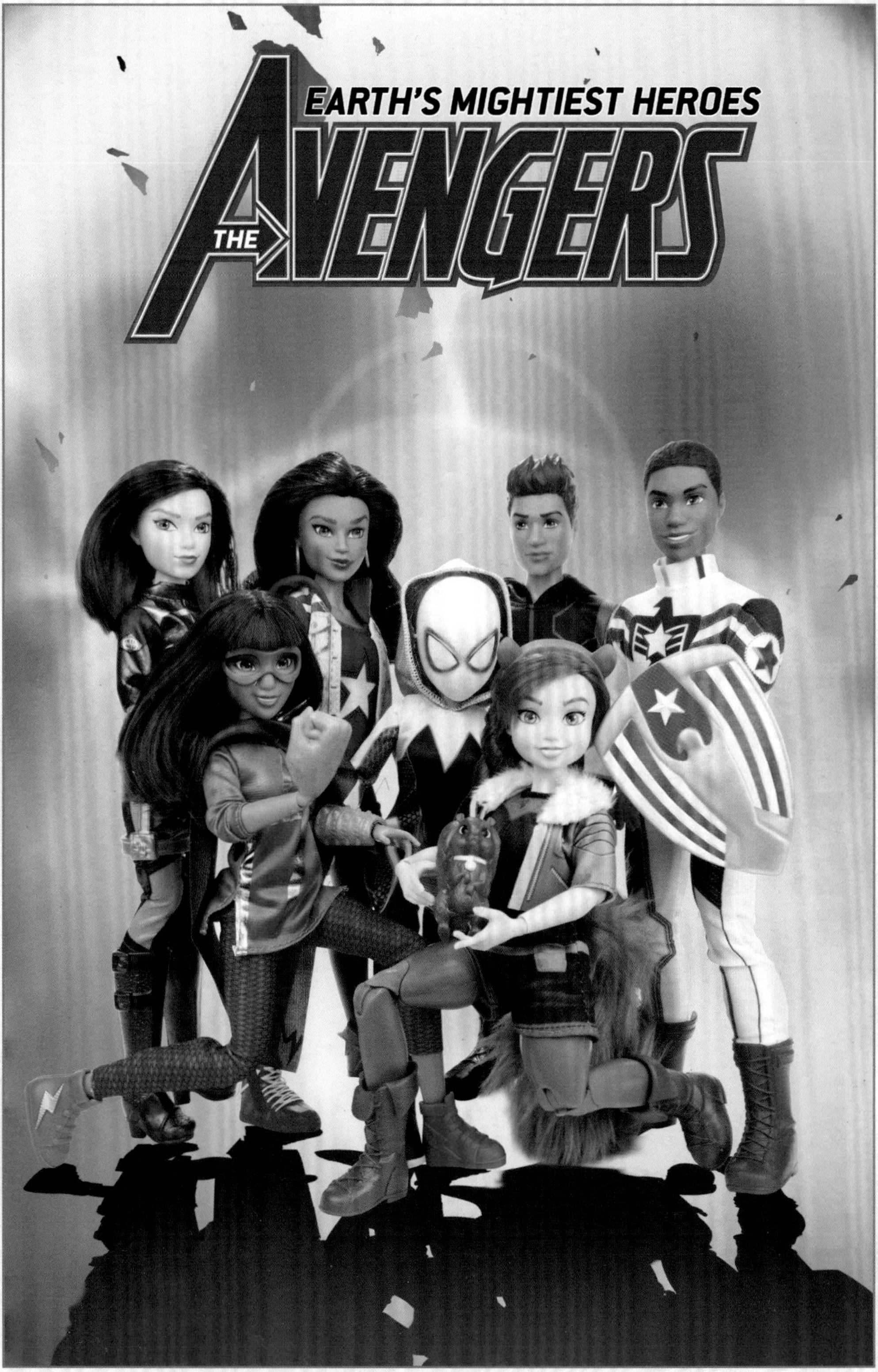
EARTH'S MIGHTIEST HEROES
THE AVENGERS

AVENGERS #12 MARVEL RISING ACTION DOLL VARIANT

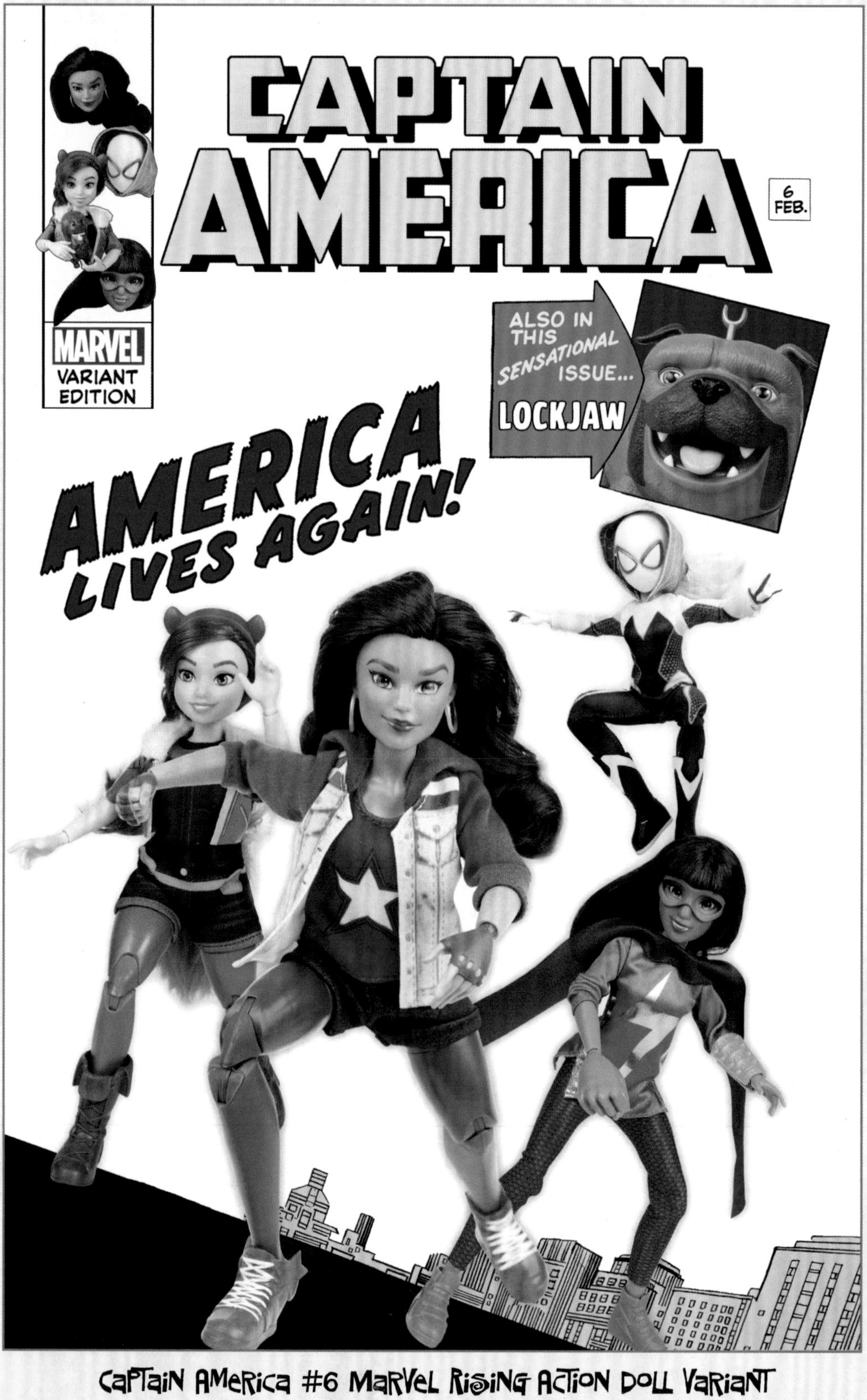
CAPTAIN AMERICA
6 FEB.
MARVEL
VARIANT EDITION
ALSO IN THIS SENSATIONAL ISSUE...
LOCKJAW
AMERICA LIVES AGAIN!

CAPTAIN AMERICA #6 MARVEL RISING ACTION DOLL VARIANT

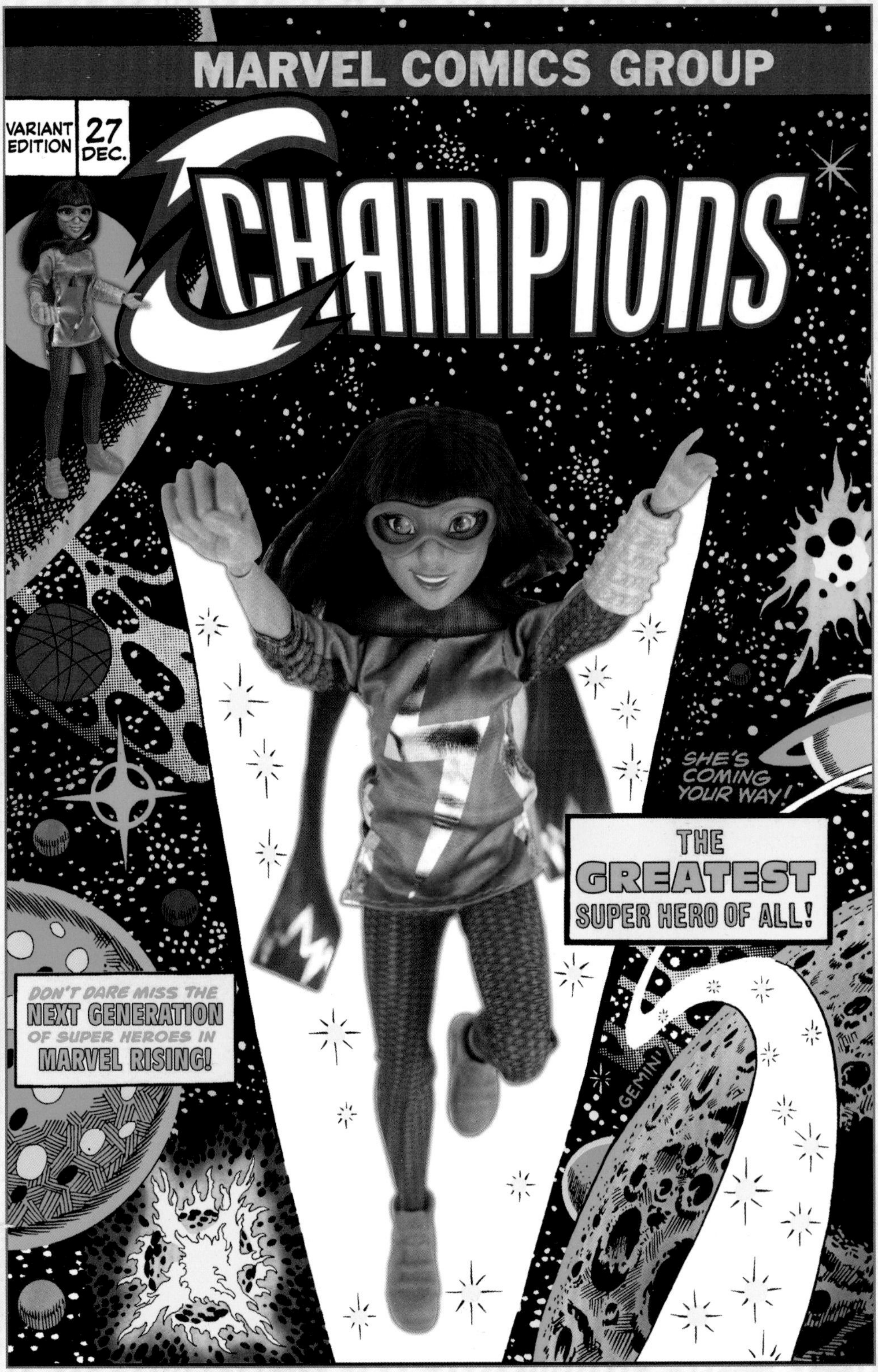
MARVEL COMICS GROUP
VARIANT EDITION
27
DEC.
CHAMPIONS
SHE'S COMING YOUR WAY!
THE GREATEST SUPER HERO OF ALL!
DON'T DARE MISS THE NEXT GENERATION OF SUPER HEROES IN MARVEL RISING!
GEMINI
CHAMPIONS #27 MARVEL RISING ACTION DOLL VARIANT

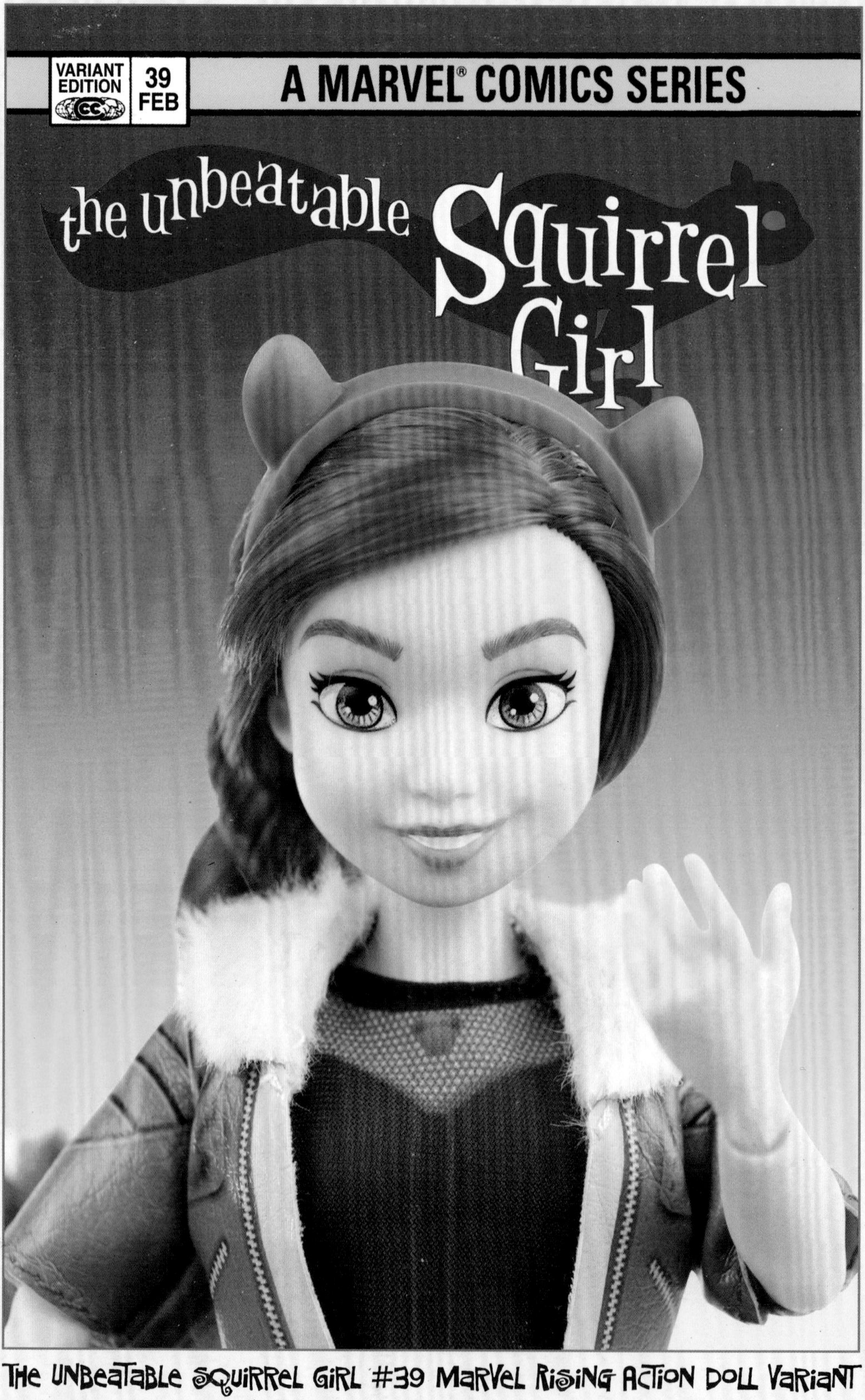
VARIANT EDITION
39
FEB
A MARVEL® COMICS SERIES
the unbeatable Squirrel Girl

THE UNBEATABLE SQUIRREL GIRL #39 MARVEL RISING ACTION DOLL VARIANT